BRIDGES:
A GLOBAL ANTHOLOGY OF SHORT STORIES

EDITED BY MAURICE A. LEE

ISBN 978-0-9846199-5-5

Cover by Mitchell Crisp

Te
me
nos
PUBLISHING COMPANY

Temenos Publishing
www.temenospublishing.com

To short story writers around the world: Thanks for your commitment to this complex, bewitching, and fulfilling literary genre. It doesn't get any better than this.

To Paulette
dear friend, long-
dear writer of stories
enjoy these latest
mercies
on p. 102. With love,
HB

CONTENTS

PREFACE

This astonishing collection of short stories is actually a "family affair." It began as an idea to support those writers attending the 12th International Conference on the Short Story in English, held in North Little Rock, Arkansas in June, 2012. By support is meant to publish their mostly new, and in some cases, previously published, short stories. When I began collecting them, however, I realized that I was amassing a collection which in part reflected the history of the conference and in other ways was predicting its future.

The conference began in Paris, France, in 1988, through the collaborative efforts of Dr. Claire Larrière and Dr. Mary Rohrberger. It came to the United States in 1992 and remained here for ten years before going abroad to Spain in 2004. This year, 2012, marks its first return to the States since the venue in Spain. Included in this volume is a short story by Claire Larrière, one of the conference founders. Attending that conference in 1988 was a young professor, Dr. Allan Weiss. He is now, in addition to being a professor at York University in Toronto, an emerging writer of short stories, and I am pleased to state that he has a story in this collection as well.

Likewise, when we first came to the States, two writers who participated for the first time were Clark Blaise and Bharati Mukherjee. They have attended every conference since 1992 and thus now extend the "family" tradition by each having a story in this volume. I wanted to honor their continued commitment and support, and accordingly, have used their wonderful stories to envelope this collection, with Clark's at the beginning and Bharati's at the end. This collection, therefore, is a reflection of the history of the devoted and committed writers who have continued to support our biennial conference. With a minimum of financial support, they have traveled to Spain, Portugal, Ireland, and Canada and have spent four to five days sharing their creative talents and their critical insights about this important literary genre.

The names of Minoli Salgado, Katie Singer, Vijay Lakshmi, Katherine Vaz, Jayne Anne Phillips, Moira Crone, Alecia McKenzie, Billie Travalini, Susan Rochette Crawley, Cyril Dabydeen, and Velma Pollard are among the names of those representing the early years of the conference. Those of Sylvia Petter, William Wall, Nuala Ní Chonchúir, Alice Clark, and Marion Bloem represent the middle years. Among the newest list are Alistair MacLeod, Licia Canton, Alison MacLeod, Tsai Suh-Fen, Su Wei-Chen, Michael Mirolla, Tzeng Ch'ing-Wen, Belinda Chang, Mary Morrissey, Xu Xi, and Paula Morell.

Paula helps to further enhance as well as complete the cycle of the family tradition. She was an MFA student of one of the founders, Dr. Mary Rohrberger, at the University of New Orleans, and began attending the conferences in 1996. She became interested in the short story genre, moved from New Orleans to Little Rock, Arkansas, and now hosts an international radio show which reads stories each Tuesday evening from her restaurant, The Starving Artist Café, which she manages with her husband. She has a story in this collection. She also owns a publishing company, and her company, Temenos Publishing Company, is the one which published this collection of short stories! So, in many ways, this collection was given birth in 1988 and comes to maturity in 2012. It does this, however, through the dedication and incredible commitment of the many writers who have given their time and effort to the short story genre and to this conference. In my own small way, I wanted to provide this incredible global anthology to honor them, to thank them for their hard work, and to praise their outstanding talent. This anthology, therefore, is dedicated to them, to the initial foresight of its founders, Claire Larrière and Mary Rohrberger, and in memory of Mary, now deceased.

Maurice A. Lee
April 2012

INTRODUCTION

Maurice A. Lee

There are forty-five stories in this collection, representing forty-four writers from more than fifteen different countries. It is common to have works from Canada, the United States, the West Indies, and Ireland, and those countries are aptly represented. However, this collection likewise has stories from writers whose cultures represent China, France, Hong Kong, Indonesia, Singapore, Sri Lanka, and Taiwan. The goal of this text is to publish stories of writers attending the 12th International Conference on the Short Story in English, held in North Little Rock in 2012. As such, this compilation is a reflection of the diversity and multi-cultural nature of the conference. More importantly, it is a testimony to the broad range of stories from different countries and how they have impacted on the history, culture, politics, and social fabric of these various countries.

One aspect that they all have in common is the oral tradition, and regardless of when the written form of the genre began in these countries, they all began with this common sense of storytelling. This commonality among them provided me with a temptation to organize these stories in similar fashion, or more precisely, to structure them around a common theme, a set of formal topics that could serve as an umbrella to a set number of stories organized topic by topic, until they were all neatly settled under this umbrella of sameness. Or I could easily list them by country or nationality, and therefore enable the forthcoming scholar to pick and choose among them as he or she saw fit. A time period approach would be simple enough since most of these stories were written within the past five years, and many within the past year specifically for this volume. None of these approaches seemed right for this particular collection, however, because I felt that if this was truly a global collection of stories, then the stories should be unified. I did not want readers to pick and choose among men, women, Asians, Irish, Canadians, or Americans. I wanted the reader to simply take up this volume and start reading from front to back, or in reverse if he chose. I felt more and more comfortable in using this approach, because after reading these stories, it is clear to me that there are excellent stories among them and that the range and diversity of them makes this particular text unique in that it does not matter which story is read first or which last.

Having said that, however, I did establish this structure: I intentionally used a short story by Clark Blaise to open the text, and one by Bharati Mukherjee to end it. The reason was personal, however, not structural. I did this to honor these two wonderful writers who have been loyal participants and supporters of the short story conference for more than twenty years, and their writing reflects the excellence of writers who have been nurtured by this conference, and whose works are now embedded within the pages of this volume. They have seen some of the writers begin as scholars or young writers, and then witnessed their growth into mature, patient, and skilled writers. Although they would not say so, I am sure they understand that they have served as mentors and inspiration to new writers. I am pleased that their stories envelope this volume.

There is one major gap and absence in this collection. There are no stories by African-Americans or Native Americans. This is not due to there not being excellent writers from these groups; it is a reflection of the fact that for the past several years, it has been difficult to attract them to the conference. In the early stages of the conference, names like Ray Young Bear, Simon Ortiz, Leslie Marmon Silko, and Diane Glancy were regular participants. Likewise, Ishmael Reed, Amiri Baraka, and Sonia Sanchez were constant attendees. Although the last three were more poets and novelists, their narrative poems and political satire informed and challenged us all in the outstanding readings they gave. Attempts to continue that presence from both spectrums have not been successful. In this regard, there are more concerted and aggressive efforts planned by the Board for the coming years. The oral tradition in both the African-American and the Native American community is a key factor in their development, and one of the reasons why their short stories are so reflective of their culture. Their absence in this collection is one which I, as editor, regret.

It is my hope that you enjoy reading this important collection of short stories as much as I enjoyed putting it together. Admittedly, the Table of Contents represents a forced pattern of selection for the reader, but the idea I worked from in choosing stories and writers is that each story tells its own history; each writer is a reflection of that history; and that they all are of equal importance. They tell a wonderful story of how we as individuals and separate countries have come to a point in life in which distance, space, and even time are irrelevant to one's ability to accept the concept of "others" in their growth and development. We are in a global society, and we now have to become global citizens. This text, I hope, will assist us in embracing that reality. Please enjoy this collection of wonderful stories.

SECTION I—THE BEGINNING

BREWING TEA IN THE DARK

Clark Blaise

My youngest uncle and I and a busload of other English-speakers were on a tour of Tuscany, leaving Florence at dawn, then on to Siena, followed by a mountain village, a farm lunch, another mountain village, the Leaning Tower of Pisa, and back to Florence after dark. I had planned to spread his ashes unobtrusively over a peaceful patch of sloping land, but each stop seemed more appealing than the one before, and so by lunchtime I was still holding on to the urn.

The mountain towns on our morning stops had been seductive. I could imagine myself living in any of them, walking the steep streets and taking my dinners in sidewalk cafés. I could learn Italian, which didn't seem too demanding. The fresh air and Mediterranean diet could add years to my life.

The countryside of Tuscany in no way resembles the red-soil greenery of Bengal. Florence does not bring Kolkata to mind, except in its jammed sidewalks. My uncle wanted to live his next life as an Italian or perhaps as some sort of creature in Italy, maybe just as a tall, straight cypress (this is a theological dispute; life might be eternal, but is a human life guaranteed every rebirth?). Each time that he and his lady friend, Devvie, a painter, returned from Italy to California, he pronounced himself more Italian than ever, a shrewd assessor of fine art and engineering, with a new hat, shoulder bag, jacket or scarf to prove it. He said Devvie was the prism through which the white light of his adoration was splintered into all the colors of the universe. (It sounds more natural in Bangla, our language.) If that is true, many men are daubed in her colors. She taught him the Tuscan palette, the umbers and siennas.

At the farm lunch a woman of my approximate age—whose gray curls were bound in a kind of ringletted ponytail—sat opposite me at one of the refectory tables. She was wearing a dark blue University of Firenze sweatshirt over faded blue jeans. In the lissome way she moved, and in the way she dressed, she seemed almost childlike. I am forty-five, but slow and heavy in spirit.

She dropped her voice to a whisper. "I can't help noticing that urn you're carrying. Is it what I . . . "

I had placed it unobtrusively, I'd thought, on the table between the wine glasses. It was stoppered and guaranteed airtight, a kind of Thermos bottle of ashes. I was afraid that if I put him on the floor an errant foot might touch him.

"Very perceptive," I said. "It's my uncle."

"Lovely to meet you, sir," she said to the urn. Then to me, "You can call me Rose." *Call me Rose?* I must have squinted, but she said, "You were talking to him back in Siena. You were sitting on a bench and holding it in your lap and I heard you. Of course, I couldn't understand what you were saying, but I'd never seen anything like it."

"Why the mystery about your name?" I asked.

"You'll find out," she said. Perhaps she changed her name every day, or on every trip, or for every man she met. I told her my name, Abhi, short for Abhishek.

The farm landscape reminded me of paintings on the walls of Italian restaurants: mounded vineyards framed by cypress trees, against a wall of purple hills sprinkled with distant, whitewashed villas. She moved like a dancer to the fence, then turned, and called to me.

"Why not right here?"

I walked over to the fence, but a goat wandered up to us, looking for food, and tried to butt me through the slats. Then he launched a flurry of shiny black pellets.

"Maybe not," she said.

When we remounted the tour bus, the aisle seat next to me turned up vacant. "May I?" she asked. She told me that my morning seatmate had also made a connection with the urn and a possible bomb, or shortwave radio. He too had seen me talking in a strange language in Siena, probably Arabic.

During the next leg of the trip, she opened up to me: "You came here on a mission. So did I, in a way. I read that an old friend of mine was going to be in Florence for a Renaissance music festival. He plays the mandolin. And suddenly I wanted to see him again. Not to be with him—goodness, he has a wife and family—but I thought how funny it would be if we just happened to run into each other."

I could not have imagined so much disclosure in a single outburst. I couldn't even understand her motivation. Funny? The impulsiveness of my fellow Americans is often mysterious to me, but I listened with admiration. We'd never met and we were on a bus in Tuscany, but she was spilling her secrets. Or did she consider me a harmless sounding post? Or did she have no secrets? And then I wondered had she—like me—been pried open by some recent experience? Perhaps our normal defenses had been weakened.

"Maybe you had a wake-up call," I said. The things we do that elude all reason, because suddenly, we have to do them.

She seemed to ponder the possibility, then consigned it to a secret space for future negotiation. After a few moments she asked, "Where are you from?"

Always an ambiguous question: where are you really from? India? Am I from Kolkata? California? Bay Area? She said, "I work in a library in a small town in Massachusetts, two blocks from Emily Dickinson's house."

She'd been married, but not to her mandolinist. She'd gone to New York to dance, she married, but she'd injured herself and turned to painting, and then she'd divorced and started writing. By her estimation she was a minor, but not a failed, writer. Like most Bangla-speakers of my generation, I've known a number of poets and writers, although most were employed in more mundane endeavors by day. I had never considered them minor, or failed.

And then her narrative, or her confessions, stopped and I felt strangely bereft. I sensed she was waiting for me to reciprocate. What did I have to match her?

"Are you married?" she asked.

I began to understand that something thicker was in the air. "Why do you ask?"

"You have an appealing air," she said.

It is my experience in the West that Indian men, afraid to press their opinions or exert their presence, are often perceived as soulful. Many's the time I've wanted to say, to very well-meaning ladies, just because I have long, delicate fingers and large, deep-brown eyes and a mop of black, unruly hair, do not ascribe to me greater sensitivity, sensuality, or innocence, or some kind of unthreatening, pre-feminist manliness. Our attempts to accommodate a new culture are often interpreted as clumsy, if forgivable. I think my uncle and his painter friend enjoyed such a relationship, based on mutual misreading, but in his case all of the clichés might have been true. He was, truly, an innocent. Unlike him, I have no trouble saying "fuck" in mixed company.

"Do you have children?" she persisted.

I have two boys, who stay with their mother and her parents in San Diego. In my world, the love of one's family is the only measure of success, and in that aspect, I have failed. I said only, "Yes."

"I'm sorry," she said. "It's none of my business."

My uncle was an afflicted man. He never married. His income paid for the education of all the boys in the family, and the dowries of all the girls. In a place where family means everything, and if part of the family is pure evil, even one's house can be a prison. Literally, a prison: he lived in a back bedroom, afraid even to be seen from the street. He was forced to pay his grandniece's husband ten thousand rupees a month, on the threat of his turning over certain documents to the CBI that would prove something. You ask why he didn't protect himself, why he didn't sue, why his passivity was allowed to confirm the most heinous charges? And I say, Indian "justice" is too slow and corrupt. Cases linger before judges awaiting their bribes. Cases go on as lawyers change sides, as they win stay after stay.

That grim prison was the house of my fondest memories, the big family compound on Rash Behari Avenue that our family began renting the moment of their arrival from the eastern provinces, now known as Bangladesh. Our neighborhood was an east Bengal enclave. We grew up still speaking the eastern dialect. We thought of ourselves as refugees, even the generation, like my grandparents', which had arrived before Partition. In soccer, we still supported East Bengal against the more-established Calcutta team, Mohun Bagan. It's the most spirited competition in all of sports, perhaps in the world.

Six years ago, I'd arrived for my annual visit, this time with a quarter-million dollars in year-end bonus money. It was the dot.com era nearing its end—although we thought it would go on forever—and I had been a partner in a start-up. When my uncle spilled out his story, and I could see the evidence all around me, I also had the solution in my pocket. I acted without thinking. No courts, no police, no unseemly newspaper coverage that would tarnish the family name. I simply bought the house and kicked the vermin out. But I had forgotten that my wife had a use for that money; a school she'd planned to start. I came back from Kolkata with my uncle in tow. She and the children left for San Diego a week later.

She slept on the long ride to Pisa. She slept like a child, no deep breathing, no snoring. I wished she'd turned her head towards me. I would have held her, even embraced her. It was the first time in years that I'd felt such a surge of protectiveness.

There is very little good I can say about Pisa. I'm of two minds about the Leaning Tower. It is iconic, but ugly. It's a monument to phenomenal incompetence, and now the world is invested in a medieval mistake. Actually, I'm not of two minds. It is an abomination. Preserving the mistake is a crime against the great Italian tradition of engineering. In the wide lawns around the Tower, various bands of young tourists, mostly Japanese, posed with their arms outstretched, aligning them for photos in a way to suggest they were holding up the crippled Tower.

We walked towards the Tower, past stalls of souvenir-sellers, most of them, if not all, Bangladeshi, hawking Leaning Tower T-shirts and kitchen towels. They called out to us in English, but I could hear them muttering among themselves in Bangla, "It's an older bunch. Put out the fancy stuff."

I stopped by, drawn in by the language. We may be one of the pioneering languages of Silicon Valley, but we are also the language of the night, the cooks and dishwashers and hole-in-the-wall restaurants and cheap clothing stalls around the world. Then they studied me a little closer. "Hey, brother!" This came in Bangla. "Something nice for your girlfriend?" They held up white T-shirts, stamped with the Leaning Tower.

"What kind of gift is that?" I answered back. "She'd have to lean like a cripple to make it straight."

They invited me behind the stalls. Rose came closer, but stayed on the edge of the sidewalk. I felt a little guilty—this was my call from the unconscious, the language-hook. I remembered my uncle, who had brought his devotional tapes to California, and many evenings I would return from work and the lights would be off, and he would be singing to his Hemanta Mukherjee tapes, and I would keep the lights off and brew tea in the dark.

Behind the display bins, the men had stored trunks and trunks of trinkets and T-shirts and towels and tunics, nearly all of them Pisa-related. On each trunk, in Bangla, they had chalked the names of cities: Pisa, Florence, Rome, Venice and Pompeii.

The three stall-owners were cousins. They introduced themselves: Wahid, Hesham and Ali, cousins from a village a kilometer from my grandparents' birthplace. They knew the town well, and the big house that had been ours, the zamindari house, the Hindu's house. Maybe their grandfathers, as small children, had worked there, or maybe they had just stolen bananas from the plantation.

"Then you are from the Ganguly family?" they asked me, and I nodded, bowing slightly, "Abhishek Ganguly." Hindu, even Brahmin: opposite sides of a one kilometer world.

The buried, collective memory forever astonishes. Nothing in the old country could have brought our families together, yet here we were in the shadow of the Leaning Tower of Pisa, remembering the lakes and rivers, the banana plantation, my great-grandfather's throwing open his house on every Hindu and Muslim feast-day. In the olden days, in the golden east of Bengal where all our poetry originated, the Hindus had the wealth, the Muslims had the numbers, and both were united against the British.

My ancestral residence (which I've never seen; after Partition, my parents even tore up the old photos they'd carried with them), I learned, is now a school. The banana plantation is now a soccer field and cricket pitch. Wahid, Hesham, and Ali, and three remoter cousins—what we call "cousin-brothers," which covers any degree of relatedness including husbands of cousins' sisters—have a lorry, and when the tourist season is over in Pisa they will strike their stalls and go to Florence and sell Statue of David kitsch, or to Venice and sell gondola kitsch. In the winter they will go to southern Spain and sell Alhambra kitsch.

But think of the distance these cheap but still over-priced T-shirts have traveled! Uzbek cotton, spun in Cambodia, stamped in China and sent to a middleman somewhere in the Emirates, to be distributed throughout Europe, matching the proper Western icon to the right city and the proper, pre-paid sellers. For one month they will return to Bangladesh, bringing gifts to their children and parents, and doubtless, enlarging their families.

The cousins had come to Italy four years ago, starting out by spreading blankets on the footpaths and selling China-made toys. Now they have transportable stalls and in a couple of years the six cousins will pool their money and buy a proper store, somewhere, and bring their wives and children over. Right now, they send half of their earnings back to their village, where the wives have built solid houses and the children are going to English-medium schools and want to become doctors and teachers. Their wives have opened up tea-stalls and stitching-shops. "We are Bengalis first, then Hindu or Muslim after," said Wahid, perhaps for my benefit. "If anyone says he is first a Muslim or a Hindu, I give him wide berth. He has a right to his beliefs, but I do not share them."

All of this I translated for my girlfriend, Rose. Then we sat at a sidewalk café and drank a glass of white wine, looking out on the Tower and the ant-sized climbers working their way up the sides, waving from the balconies. I was happy.

"I think you're a little too harsh on the Tower," she said.

We reached Florence in the dark. There seemed little question that we would spend the night together, in her hotel or mine. Outside the bus-park only one food stall was still open. I bought apples and a bottle of wine. The young man running it did all his calculations in Italian, until I stopped him, in Bangla. "That's a lot of taka, isn't it?" and the effect was of a puppet master jerking a doll's strings. He mentioned the name of his village, this one far, far in the east, near Chittagong, practically in Burma. His accent was difficult for me, as was mine to him. "Bangla is the international language of struggle," he said.

The unexpected immersion in Bengal had restored a certain confidence. It was the last thing, or the second-last thing, I'd expected from a trip into the wilds of Tuscany. I was swinging the plastic sack of wine and apples, with the urn tucked under my arm, and Rose said, "Let me take the urn." I lifted my arm slightly, and she reached in.

"Oops," she said.

My religion holds that the body is sheddable, but the soul is eternal. My uncle's soul still exists, despite the cremation. It has time to find a new home, entering through the soft spot in a newborn's skull. I felt he was still with me, there in Italy, but perhaps he'd remained back in California. The soul is in the ether, like a particle in the quanta; it can be in California one second, and Kolkata the next. But he'd wanted to find an Italian home, and now his matter lay in a dusty, somewhat oily mass on the cobblestones of Florence, amid shards of glass and ceramic. It will join some sort of Italian flux. It will be picked up on the soles of shoes, it will flow in the gutter, it will be devoured by flies and picked over by pigeons. If I am truly a believer in our ancient traditions, then it doesn't matter where he lies like a clot of mud while his soul still circles, awaiting its new house, wherever that house might be.

"It's all right," I said. In fact, a burden had been lifted.

Her hotel was near at hand. This was an event I had not planned. It had been three years since any sexual activity, and that had been brief and not consoling. In the slow-rising elevator, she squeezed my hand. Sex with a gray-haired lady, however slim and girlish, lay outside my fantasy. How to behave, what is the etiquette? She'd taken off her glasses, and she was humming something wordless. Under her University of Firenze sweatshirt, I could make out only the faintest mounds, the slightest crease. Even in the elevator's harsh fluorescent light, I saw no wrinkles in her face.

As we walked down the corridor, she slipped me her key-card. My fingers were trembling. It took three stabs to open the door. The moment the door was shut, and a light turned on, she walked to the foot of the bed, and turned to face me. The bedspread was a bright, passionate red. It was an eternal moment: the woman's smile, her hands closing around the ends of her sweatshirt, and then beginning to pull it up. I dropped the bag of wine and apples. So this is how it plays, this is how people like us do it. Her head disappeared briefly under the sweater, and then she tossed the University of Firenze aside on the red bedspread and she stood before me, a thin woman with small breasts, no bra, and what appeared to be a pink string looped against her side.

"Now you know," she said, and began kissing me madly. "Come to my bed of crimson joy."

What I knew was this: she was bald. Her wig had been caught in the sleeve of her sweater. The pink string was a fresh scar down her ribcage, then curling up between her breasts. But we were on the bed and my hands were over her scalp, then on her breasts and the buttons of her jeans, and her fingers were on my belt and pants.

There is much to respect in this surrender to passion. After sex, there is humor, and honesty. I poured the wine and she retired to the bathroom, only to reappear in her red "Shirley MacLaine" wig. With her obviously unnatural, burgundy-colored hair, there's a flash of sauciness atop her comely face and body. And so passion arose once again. "I've got more," she said. There was a black "Liza Minelli," and a blonde.

When we sipped the wine, she told me she'd been given a year, maybe two. But who knows, in this world miracles have been known to happen.

It is overwhelming, the first vision of *The David,* standing a ghostly white at the end of a long, sculpture-lined hall. An adoring crowd surrounds him, whatever the hour or the day. Viewed from afar, in profile, he is a haughty, even arrogant figure. His head is turned. He is staring at his immediate enemy, Goliath.

"That pose is called contrapposto," Rose whispered. She was wearing her red Shirley MacLaine wig, and she looked like a slightly wicked college woman. David's weight is supported on the right leg—the left leg is slightly raised—but the right arm is lank, and his curled hand cradles a smooth stone. The left arm is bent, and the biceps bunched. The leather sling lies on his shoulder and slithers down his back. Yet when I stood at his side, looking up directly into his eyes, the haughtiness disappeared. I read doubt, maybe fear. It's as though Michelangelo were looking into David's future, beyond the immediate victory. If I remember my Christian schooling, David would go on to become a great king and poet, the founder of a dynasty leading eventually to Jesus Christ, but he will lose his beloved son Absalom in a popular uprising against him and he will send a loyal general to his death in order to possess his wife. In the end, for all his heroism, he will grow corrupt in his pride and arrogance; his is a tattered regime. All of this I felt at that moment, and tried to communicate.

There is so much tragedy in his eyes. He knows he will accomplish this one great thing in the next few minutes, but regret will flow for the rest of his life. David is a monument to physical perfection, the antidote to the Leaning Tower.

And what about us? I wonder. She took my arm as we walked down the swarming sidewalk outside the Accademia. We passed through a great open square, near the Uffizi Palace. Crews were setting up folding chairs for an evening concert of Renaissance music.

"Will you come with me?" she asked.

Of course I would. I would see her mandolinist. We would get there early and sit in the front row. I would stand behind her after the concert, assuming she could make her way to the stage against the press of admirers, and she would ask him, “Remember me?”

Maybe she would wear her gray ponytail wig. He would be more comfortable with that, more likely to remember her. In some way, I would learn more about her. *“Oh, Rose!”* he might exclaim. Or he might dismiss her with a flick of his fingers.

“If I'm still above ground next year, and if I came to your house, would you welcome me in?”

And I can only say, “I will open the door.”

“Brewing Tea in the Dark” was first published in the 75th anniversary issue of *The Fiddlehead* (2011, Fredericton, NB University of New Brunswick, Canada).

SECTION II

THIS DIDN'T HAPPEN TO YOU

Molly McCloskey

He had met her for the second time in the back of a Land Cruiser, one sunny, spring-like morning in Addis, where neither of them was living at the time. It took him a moment to recognize her. It had been three years and another continent—the east coast of Sri Lanka, in a room decked out with artificial limbs. She was a protection officer working with Tamils and was at the medical centre having tea with a doctor friend of hers. Matt had only just arrived in Sri Lanka; Anna was leaving in two weeks. He had remembered her intensely for a few days, then forgotten her entirely.

Matt was based in Dadaab now, the sprawling refugee camp in the east of Kenya. He was an engineer, managing water and sanitation projects, and he'd flown into Addis the day before for meetings. But he had nothing on till the afternoon, and so that morning was going to the jobs fair for Ethiopians—partly because he thought an old colleague might be there, mostly to avoid paperwork that needed doing. The fair was at the hideously glitzy Sheraton—what a friend in Nairobi had described as Versailles overlooking the slums.

He had been to Addis once before and had found it instantly dispiriting. He had long since learned that every impoverished city is ground down in its own particular way, but where Nairobi (his point of reference, since he'd lived in or near it the longest) had a kind of pent-up energy, a charge to the air that felt unmistakeably sexual, Addis seemed diffuse, and a little lost. He could see out the window of the Land Cruiser figures squatting on the footpaths, so thin they looked folded in upon themselves. There were people missing legs or arms, and there were others who were physically intact but were clearly deranged. They wore layers of rags and raved, like mad truthtellers, as they wandered up and down the footpaths.

He turned to Anna. "So where are you these days?"

"Uganda," she said, "since July. Between Gulu and Kitgum." She was working as part of a team that was attempting to prepare for the return of the hoards who'd been displaced by the war. She too had come to Addis for meetings, but unlike Matt was actually interested in the jobs fair. This year, it was focusing on the disabled, and Anna wanted to see what was being done for them. Where she worked, there were a lot of maimed.

On the second floor of the Sheraton, there were people with white sticks and others in wheelchairs and a few sat on ornate sofas reading job descriptions in Braille. The doors to the patio were open and the morning sun fanned across the carpet. At one of the stalls, two people signed to each other, smiling. A dwarf led a blind man by the hand, and they too smiled. Everyone seemed to be smiling. All these people, all these unemployed, disabled people with their so-slim chances of a better life, smiled. An air of trust and quiet optimism ran through the rooms that Matt seldom experienced at such gatherings and it filled him with sadness. The man who was the official signer for the event wore a pin on his shirt that read, in sign language, *I love you.* Anna asked about the button, and the man taught her how to sign it. Matt got coffee and croissants for the two of them and they took a table out on the patio, where the opening speeches were going to take place. The sun was just warm enough to make sitting out pleasant; the coffee was perfect, the croissants light and flaky. The whole scene was idyllic and bizarre. As though they had chanced upon some enlightened and progressive land where jobs were plentiful and compassion commonplace, where strangers said *I love you* upon meeting, and all shapes and colors mingled freely in the palaces of Versailles.

All that was worlds away now, everything: the sun, Anna, their lives together in the cities of that continent, the tentative sense of optimism you wanted desperately to safeguard, because it was among the finer impulses on earth.

It was Christmas morning and Matt was in Dublin, in his brother's empty house. Kevin had decamped with his wife Biata and their two-year-old to some frozen village in the Polish interior to spend the holidays with his wife's people. That was how Kevin had put it, *my wife's people*, as though he were making good on some ancient promise. Matt pictured them in voluminous hooded robes, walking sticks of crooked branch, the child slack-jawed in a sling, as his parents trudged the snow-covered plain until a squat cabin hove into view.

He had flown into Dublin the night before. Nairobi-Amsterdam-London-Dublin. Bad planning but he'd hardly minded that it took forever. He had often felt in the no-place of airports—nexus of so many lives, actual and possible—moments of a reassuring weightlessness, when the world seemed vast enough to vanish into. From the back of the taxi, he'd looked out onto Drumcondra Road and then the north inner city. There were kids in hoodies, some moving with an edgy and purposeful air, others stumbling, in a murk of drink or drugs; there were people smoking outside the doors of pubs, huddled into themselves and fidgeting for warmth; there was a man weaving drunk on a corner and a cluster of plumpish young women in minis and heels who parted to avoid him, then tottered back into formation. The city looked hard and ramshackle, but there were colored lights everywhere and Christmas trees in windows, and in the tattiness was something wondrous, too.

No one but Kevin and Biata knew Matt was in Ireland—not his widowed father in Rathfarnham, not his sisters or their families, not the one friend from college with whom he'd maintained a very sporadic contact. There was no hurry, he was planning to stay for a while. He would go to his father in a few days.

He had left the tree lights on the night before, and when he came downstairs this morning—the sitting room empty, his stockinged feet soundless on the floorboards, the lights blinking incessant patterns through the gloom like some code he had to crack—he felt like the last man on earth. Before bed last night he'd unwrapped what Kevin and Biata had left for him: socks, a scarf, two vouchers, a hardback that told the inspirational story of someone, somewhere, who'd done something good. There was nothing under the tree now, and it looked denuded and somehow sad with itself.

He made coffee and stood at the front window, which overlooked the canal. Nothing moved. There was not a person on the street. A thin fog smudged the view. The willows looked stricken. Rising from the primordial ooze of the canal were two broken branches and the algaed half-trapezoid of a shopping trolley, all breaking the surface at skewed angles. The canal and its banks had the look of a misty bayou, a look of stunned aftermath, as though civilization had been here and gone.

***

He had fallen in love with Anna that night, in Addis, over dinner. He didn't believe in love at first sight, that was just chemistry, just nature taking an extreme shortcut. But he did believe in love after four hours' conversation. He believed that whatever happened after that, whatever they were to discover about one another and whether those things bound them or drove them apart, what he felt for her that first night was love.

Anna was in her early thirties, French Canadian, lithe and bird-like, visibly pained and unrelievedly wry, a little hardened by years in Chad and Sri Lanka and a devastating love affair with a war photographer named James who was as beautifully ethereal as she was. Four weeks after they'd split up, James had been killed in a horrific car accident while holidaying in Mozambique. He had survived the Balkans, Columbia, Afghanistan, a smattering of African conflicts, and then had died in peacetime in some terribly ordinary way. Matt knew a few stories like that, the irony so stark you thought surely it must mean something. It was a holiday Anna and James had been meant to take together, and if they had, James would still be alive; Anna didn't like Mozambique, she'd have insisted on somewhere else. And even if he'd convinced her to go there with him, her presence would've altered things. She'd have dallied over breakfast, they'd have driven the road an hour later, or been on a different road altogether. She wasn't blaming herself, she just found the fact of randomness overwhelming.

In the first months of Matt's getting to know her, Anna was still raw enough to cry about it—though she always insisted she wasn't crying over James, she was just crying, because, well, *look around,* there wasn't exactly a shortage of things to cry about. Whatever the reason, she cried when necessary and was lovely as she did, one delicate hand cupping her forehead. Then she would quickly regain her composure, as though the whole thing had been a coughing fit rather than an emotional disturbance.

What saved her from becoming tragic, or morbid, was her resilience and a silly streak. One day, she'd told Matt that she and a friend named Robin used to dance in their little office in Chad, shaking off the gloom of their jobs or their lives or the world outside—*look around*—by performing mock ballet for each other's amusement.

They were in a grocery store in Nairobi when she told him this.

"Well, go on, then," he'd said, "show me."

And to his surprise she had. Twirling down the aisle, all arabesque and pirouette and giggles, while the locals looked on, a few charmed enough to offer a wan smile, most too tired—of their own hardships and of the sight of overpaid, cavorting *wazungu*—to respond with anything but apathy.

A woman about Anna's age laughed and called out, "Lady, you are *verrrry* good!" Those r's that rolled on forever.

Anna took a low sweeping bow and said to Matt, "Robin was the real ballerina, I was just the understudy."

She had a hundred anecdotes in which Robin figured. Robin was from Trinidad. She was Anna's closest friend. They'd met on a training course in Copenhagen in 2001 and had hit it off immediately, beginning a correspondence that hardly wavered in its consistency, that was both intense and girlish, full of dark realities and office gossip. They'd overlapped in Chad, and had both wound up working in Juba, in South Sudan, though at different times. It was Robin who had introduced Anna to James, and it was Robin who had come to stay with Anna when James was killed.

***

Matt didn't sleep with her that first night in Addis, he was too . . . maybe the word was *astonished.* He felt astonished at having rediscovered her and yet the sense of freefall had none of that anxiety that the early phases of love and desire tend to engender. Instead, it was shot through with an unexpected calm.

The next morning he was looking at the news on the internet and read a blog entry about a Canadian nurse headlined: "Sex Nurse in Kenya Making a Difference One Banana at a Time." He forwarded the link to Anna, and when he saw her that evening at a dinner one of her colleagues had arranged, she caught his eye where he was standing with a cluster of other people, and said, "*That* made me laugh!" And the mood—that first flush of love that can so easily grow precious, enamoured of itself, as though falling in love were some totally unprecedented accomplishment—relaxed and expanded. For a moment they just smiled at one another until he detached himself from the conversation and came over to her and she leaned forward and kissed him on the cheek in greeting.

"Good day?" she asked.

"Stuck inside, mostly. Finishing a report on what happens when you have 200,000 people and twelve toilets." He had long ago begun to couch his work—the business of shit and piss—in tones of droll indifference.

She gave him a wincing smile. "Well, we're going out to talk to some people from the Tigray Disabled Veterans Association tomorrow. Why don't you come?"

He took a sip of his beer. "I wouldn't miss it for the world."

On the way back to the hotel the next afternoon, he couldn't get his bearings. Addis seemed all wide hilly boulevards that looked just like each other, behind which lay webs of shack-lined dirt roads. The baby blue Ladas, the city's taxis, chugged past like toy cars in varying states of disrepair. Anna was texting—the office, her mother, Robin—and Matt was thinking about his return to Dadaab in the morning, wondering if he would ever see Anna again.

They were stopped in traffic. The sound of chatter suddenly filled the back seat. He looked over and saw that she had lowered the window and was giving birr to a clutch of beggars, a couple of teenage boys and two women.

When the Land Cruiser moved off again, he said, "Do you often give to beggars?"

"Fairly often," she said, staring absently out the window.

He looked at her and couldn't tell if he was in the presence of goodness or naiveté. How many times had he seen children make a beeline the minute they spotted a foreigner? The reflex of expectation. He thought of a teenager he'd seen in Sri Lanka, some months after the tsunami, wearing an orange T-shirt on the back of which was printed, simply: *Tsunami.* He said, "If you give money on the street, doesn't it just reinforce the whole trap, the whole donor-beneficiary trap?" He knew there was an argument to be made, but he hated the sound of himself, of this desiccated language he had learned to speak.

Anna shrugged, turning to him. "If they have nothing," she said, "what does it matter?"

She was right, of course. When it came to it, survival trumped psychology. But then he said something that shamed him as soon as it left his mouth. "It depends what we mean by nothing. Are they starving? The people you gave money to weren't starving."

Anna was quiet. He didn't think she was judging him. She knew as well as he did that such calculations were written, implicitly, into every day of their lives. Otherwise, they would all go around giving their money away all the time. He turned back to the window. The vehicle sat high on its big tires, so that he was not so much looking out at the beggars as down on them, and he felt ugly, and not a little bit colonial, dispensing arbitrary favors, or not, while considering the distinction between *starving to death* and merely suffering from malnutrition. (Even the word *beggars* sounded crass.) It was mean of him to have tried to call her out on a simple, well-intentioned act; he knew enough about her by now to know that she had seen far worse than he had in the course of her work, and he had no right to interrogate her.

He thought then that his time in the field was over, in any meaningful way, because he could no longer distinguish between rational decision-making and a kind of burnt-out petulance. But he would hold on for another three years, because of her, and because he didn't know what else he'd do.

***

Matt had never in his life spent a Christmas day alone, and he hadn't spent a Christmas in Dublin for fifteen years. He had left the city soon after finishing his degree. His mother had died during his final year at university, at the age of fifty-three, five months and twenty-one days after her diagnosis. In her absence, the already strained relationship with his father grew quickly brittle. Matt was too young then, and too consumed with his own grief, to make allowances for his father's behavior, and had heard in the things his father said not the ravings of an agonized mind, but merely all the criticisms that had been kept in check while Matt's mother was alive. When Matt announced that he was leaving, his father accused him of desertion. As though he were a spouse, or a soldier.

After lunch, Matt walked towards the city, along the canal, down Grand Parade. Rust-colored reeds as tall as he was rose along the banks. The black water ran like a tunnel through the fog. He went as far as Percy Place, then crossed the humped bridge and skirted round the church that was planted in the middle of the street as though set down there from on high. The street bulged either side of it like a snake who'd just eaten.

The fog had thickened slightly; it was the color of ash and cold to the skin. He walked slowly, as though moving through a billowy afterlife. He imagined himself in the wake of a freak disaster, one that had left structures intact but swept living things from the earth. The traffic lights played sentinel to empty streets, something homely and proud about them, like lighthouses, safeguarding people against their own misjudgements.

He saw no one until he was on the far side of Merrion Square. Then, a couple, a young family, a middle-aged man walking a small white dog. He turned up Grafton Street, where perhaps a dozen people strolled like survivors in the quiet. Everyone walked slowly, and because there were so few of them about, they took note of each other, glances of shy curiosity, infinitely gentle, as though they could not quite believe this world they were living in. When he'd gone as far as the quays, he turned back towards home.

Passing through Merrion Square, he saw two feet sticking up the far side of a shrub. His throat tightened as he stepped closer, but the man was only sleeping. He might've been forty or he might've been twenty-five, there was no telling. He had the caved-in face of an addict. Matt thought of gathering him up and taking him home, and imagined the house swept clean of valuables by morning. His mother's eldest sister had met her future husband when he was sleeping rough under a bridge in Canada. It was 1957. They were both immigrants. She'd brought him home and propped him up in front of a fire and within months he'd passed his test to become a bus driver, and for the rest of his life was a devoted husband and an upstanding citizen. He had a beautiful singing voice and he used to sing while she played the piano, and they were ordinary, good people who loved each other through many a long winter.

Matt was worried the gates would close and the man would freeze. He had seen a patrol car parked outside the Square; it was still there when he went out, and he told one of the guards about the sleeping man.

The guard said he wasn't to worry. "We always do the rounds."

In the course of his life, Matt had walked past a hundred such men, men who by the next morning could be dead. He'd told the guards not because it was Christmas, not because he was home, but because there were so few people left, so few survivors, that each one of them seemed precious and necessary.

***

After Addis, it was two months before he saw Anna again. They'd kept in touch, a few weeks of emails and they'd agreed to meet on Lamu, off the coast of Kenya. It felt like a honeymoon, with its air of confirmation and beginnings. They lolled about in a seafood-and-sex stupor for four days, and decided they'd try to make it work. What followed was several months of back-and-forthing between Uganda and Kenya, then a year together in Juba, a brief stint for her back in Chad, and finally, the two of them in Nairobi.

Once, he had brought her to Ireland. It was the summer before she fell apart, or whatever it was she had done. She'd had the usual notions about his country. It never ceased to amaze him how no matter what happened here, no matter how much Big Pharma came to town, how many hi-tech companies the place played host to, how many drug seizures made the news and how conspicuous and sudden had come the consumption of everything, the nation was expected to remain innocent. All the world could change, but *here* was childhood, artless and wide-eyed.

The visit with Anna was the first time he'd been back since everything crashed. Immediately he'd felt it, the sense of held breath, everybody waiting for the axe to fall, and then the axe after that. But along with the anxiety and the anger and the talk of negative equity and denuded pension funds, there were traces of the queerest sort of pride, like the pride people take in monstrous hangovers. Also in evidence was a perverse curiosity. No one knew what the place would look like when it was finished imploding, and the spectacle appealed at some deep level to a people habituated to fatalism. They tried to picture the eighties, that grim era often referenced as a kind of bogeyman come back to punish them for their hubris, but now with spanking new motorways and repossessed McMansions.

He and Anna drove to the West, and all through the midlands she gawked at the abandoned, half-built houses and unoccupied estates. She took pictures on her phone and emailed them to Robin. She said they looked like the devastation after some natural disaster, and Matt said, "They look like last night's party." It was true, the houses managed to exude an air of shame, or to induce shame, like the detritus that greets you the morning after, the sordid evidence of your excesses strewn in calamitous accusation.

In Dublin they walked the streets, and in front of the Aran sweater shops, with their ton-weight cable knits and their prim woollen cardigans, passed gaggles of middle-class teenage girls dressed like hookers from some grim pocket of eastern Europe. (No, the country could not be flung back to the eighties. The habits of acquisition and display were now ingrained, and if they couldn't satisfy themselves with high-end goods, they would work themselves out on kitsch.) They took the DART to Howth—Anna was dying to ride the DART—and sat behind a guy of about seventeen with very badly composed bedhead. He was clearly stoned, his giggle sheepish and supercilious at the same time. He and his female companion were listening to a podcast, what was billed "the funniest call ever." It consisted of some American DJ discussing his cock with a woman who was not a native English speaker and who clearly had something other than a cock in mind.

"So you can fix my ten-inch cock?" the man said.

"Yes, certainly," the woman said, "I fix. I make perfect."

Every time the DJ said *cock*, the two stoners were in kinks of laughter.

Matt could feel Anna squirming beside him.

Howth was better. They ate oysters and sole in a restaurant overlooking the water and drank a bottle of white wine and afterwards brandy, which neither of them ever drank. By the time they tripped back out into the daylight, a slight breeze had picked up. Everything was sparkling. The boats bobbed cheerfully at the pier, and all the colors looked clear and true. Matt put his arm around Anna and pressed his face into the crook of her neck, into her hair, and in a muffled whisper said, "I want to marry you." She turned to him and looked straight into his eyes until tears formed in her own eyes and rolled down her cheeks. (She had the capacity to cry in complete silence, and it was so beautiful Matt sometimes wondered was it a thing she'd had to learn.) Then she drew him to her and held him tightly, and he had no idea what any of this meant in relation to the sentence he had just, to his surprise, uttered.

On the whole, Anna tried not to show any disappointment with his country, and he tried not to say, *Why did you expect us to be different?* He tried not to feel a satisfaction in disabusing her of her illusions. God knew she had few enough of them left. This was a woman who spent her days interviewing refugees, trying to sort the true stories from the concoctions, gauging whether the truth was bad enough to warrant furthering a person's resettlement application. It was a perverse kind of competition people were forced to engage in, and she had told him how almost immediately her idea of what was endurable became warped; so much got relativized, measured against what she'd heard already that day, that week, that year. This was a woman who, when he'd asked her one day how work was, had answered: "The new normal is having been raped only once. Having been raped just once, by a lone man, is now regarded as a narrow escape."

He knew what she was thinking, they had discussed it often enough. She was wondering which was the more shocking: the ease, the prevalence of brutality, or the way people survived it without losing their minds. Of course not everyone did survive, but enough did that Anna could spend whole days humbled by the fact, made quiet, in the grip of an awe so sincere it looked strangely like prayer.

Sometimes he felt like a child beside her.

***

By the time he'd reached the canal again, dusk was leaching into the fog, and the air had gone a steely grey. The streetlights were furry globes. He looked at the sheen on the water, the opaqueness overhead. He looked at the trees along the opposite bank, different kinds he couldn't name, all bare and black-branched, and he thought that he preferred them like this, stripped down to their own severe beauty.

He had slowed to the point where he was no longer walking. Movement seemed, he hardly knew to what, a disruption. It was dark now. Nightfall was time made visible. He thought again of his uncle, in the hour just before his future wife appeared under the bridge. If his uncle had been granted a wish, he would not have dared to think so big as what in fact was given him. The opposite, of course, might also be true. If we knew of the misfortunes to come, would we carry on at all? Or would we carry on better? Would we do justice to the present instead of enduring it? He wondered—and this was the question he asked himself more often than any other, more often even than why she left—whether he would have experienced any of it differently had he known they wouldn't last. But then he probably did know. There was always that slight hesitation, always the sense of her not being entirely present and with him. There was the day he'd told her he wanted to marry her and she had been moved to tears but she had not returned the promise. And there was her way of withdrawing into herself, like an injured animal, when she was pained or troubled, as though unwilling to entrust herself to him. It had been that way since the first—he remembered it even from the day in the Land Cruiser in Addis, the people begging, his stupidity, her way of going silent as a form of speech—so that when trouble hit, trouble closer to home than the horror stories she'd mostly learned to leave at work, it was hardly surprising that her reaction should've been to retreat from him.

Matt had met Robin only once, when she was passing through Nairobi and the three of them had had dinner. She was almost exactly what he'd expected, which was hardly ever the case with someone he'd heard a lot about. She was both sharp and warm, animated, he kept thinking the word *vivacious*, though it made her sound shallow and she wasn't that. He found her transfixing, actually, not in a romantic or erotic sense, but because she was so alive. He felt lifted by her presence and he could see that Anna did, too. Anna's intensity eased a few notches, and she felt lighter beside him, and happier. It was the kind of friendship Matt had never shared with anyone, but that he knew to see, the kind that makes the world a different and better place. When they dropped Robin at her hotel, he and Anna walked back to the car arm-in-arm, and Anna was very soft with him, playful and loving, as though she'd been in receipt of something nourishing and vital and wanted him to share in it.

The day Robin was kidnapped in an ambush outside Kinshasa, Matt was in Geneva conducting a seminar on Sanitation in Emergencies. Anna was alone in Nairobi. She phoned him at four a.m. Details were sketchy. They had been taken the previous evening—Robin, the driver, and a local woman who was traveling in the UN car with them, against regulations. By the time Matt returned to Nairobi three days later, the driver had been let go and the local woman, her name was Justine, had been killed.

It was sixteen days before Robin was released. There were rumors of a large sum having changed hands, and there was the horrible, inescapable irony that had Robin not bent the rules and tried to help Justine by giving her a lift, the woman would still be alive.

Robin didn't contact Anna following her release; it was said she had hardly spoken to anyone. She went home to Trinidad. The word going round was that she'd been raped.

It wasn't fear, exactly, that took hold of Anna in the weeks after that; it was more like an incapacitating shock. She was unreachable. She wouldn't allow Matt to console her.

In a moment of exasperation, he said, "This isn't about you."

She looked at him. Her expression puzzled and oddly blank.

More softly he said, "I mean, this didn't happen to you. It happened to Robin and to . . . to Justine." He felt foolish saying the woman's name, as though he'd known her. As though he knew anything at all about who she had been, or what her days had consisted of, or the people who grieved her.

Anna's contract was up for renewal in five weeks and she said to him, very by-the-way, as though they'd been mulling it over together, "I'm going home for a while."

It had all happened so fast, the kidnapping, the murder and Robin's release, the rumors that filtered out, Anna's decision to leave, and to leave him. Matt felt like he'd missed something, like he'd skipped some pages, and suddenly there she was, standing in the driveway outside his Jeep, her two huge duffels on the ground beside her.

It was one of those balmy, deceptively gentle Nairobi evenings. He drove her to Jomo Kenyatta out a choked Mombasa Road and watched her from outside the glass until she disappeared behind some checkpoint. From the parking lot, he sent her a text and she phoned him from departures to say goodbye, again. In the sound of her voice, he heard whole worlds, worlds she was taking with her and away from him. And then he drove home, feeling like a dream she'd had.

The day Anna got on the plane to go back to Montreal, Matt knew he would leave, too. He had just been offered a new post in Nairobi, as a water and sanitation policy analyst for all of East Africa. Everyone assumed he'd take it. In fact, he felt flat with apathy. He had, he knew, reached the point in his career where his dealings would be almost exclusively with other high-ranking bureaucrats. Soon, having done his time in the field, he would be given a post in Geneva or New York, and the circle would be complete.

When he turned it down, when he said he thought he might leave altogether, people said, "You mean *leave* leave? But what will you do?" However chaotic the worlds in which they moved, there was an apparent, counterbalancing order—the hierarchies strictly defined; the deprivations precise, the sites of indulgence clearly mapped, the faces recurring and familiar; each city, zone, autonomous region stamped with a number purporting to quantify its dangers—and they believed that beyond the borders of all these crises lay a world of vagueness and uncertainty in which he could only take his chances.

He had a few months left in Nairobi while he was finishing out his own contract, then he would go to Dublin to do he didn't know what. Just breathe, maybe. It would be Christmas, and the country would feel like it was under lockdown, and he was almost looking forward to it. The cold, the silence, the few hours of nothing at all happening.

Most days, he still believed in them, still believed that if he was steady enough, patient enough, he could ease Anna back. But in moments of slippage he doubted it all, perhaps because she wasn't there to fortify it. There were times he wondered was love anything more than a collusion of belief.

In the wake of her departure, familiarity fell away. Places they'd got to know together grew strange, so that his own life felt to him like an unfamiliar neighborhood he'd wandered into. There were days he looked around him and all he could see was need, pressing from all sides, each person transmitting to him an urgent message of need: a look, a word, an upturned palm. He felt a sense of depletion that was unambiguous and almost pleasant.

Each evening, on the way home from his office in the Parklands area of the city, he had to navigate the big roundabout near the mall. At rush hour, rank with fumes and in a lurching state of gridlock, the roundabout took on the air of a living thing, and he felt a kind of pleasure in witnessing it, sitting in one of the feeder lanes as the day cooled and the light went pale over the jacaranda. A throng of cars would work themselves into a complicated jam, and when the resolution came, in the form of a peristaltic spasm, and the cars burped off in their various directions, he could almost feel a collective cheer going up.

Nearly every evening as he waited he would see to his left a man on the ground with no legs, begging for change. Drained by the day, lost in his own thoughts, Matt would find himself staring, his gaze blank but intense, as though the man were a vision both banal and inscrutable. There were always kids, too, knocking on his window or weaving through the waiting cars and along the shattered footpaths, moving with that straight-backed strut the kids there had. There were hawkers selling puppies and pirated DVDs and dodgy Ray-Bans, and there were workers hanging out of stuffed matatus and others starting the endless trudge home. There were young men so skinny their torsos looked incapable of accommodating all their organs.

But while the Jeep idled, it was mostly the man with no legs Matt looked at. He wanted to feel something, something more than just this weariness. He wanted Anna in the passenger seat, her hand on his thigh, the ballast of her. He wanted to see himself get out of the car, day after day, and give the man money. Once he had, pulled the handbrake, stepped out and handed him two thousand shillings, an absurd sum that he hoped the man would not be robbed of. But most days he simply waited for the knots of traffic to admit him, then fought his own way around the circle and headed towards home.

NOCTURNE

S. K. Chang

translated by John Balcom

It was nearly nine o'clock when the dinner party ended. The guests were crowded at the doorway waiting for an opportunity to say good-bye to their hosts. When Pei Hua's turn came, the hostess intentionally raised her voice and said, "Miss Wang lives in Yonghe; it would be nice if someone going that way could see her home." As she spoke she threw a meaningful glance at Dr. Wu, a PhD who had just recently returned from abroad. As expected, Dr. Wu stepped forward and said, "It's on my way; I can see her home." Pei Hua knew that it was a trap that had been set for her: she was the only unmarried female guest that night. The hostess, who was a college classmate of Pei Hua's, had married happily right after graduation and all had gone well since then. Even when Pei Hua's mother had nearly lost all hope, her friend refused to give up and continued to introduce her to eligible men. Whenever Pei Hua thought about asking her not to bother, she would see how enthusiastically her friend arranged things and would hold her tongue. From the very first that evening, she knew that Dr. Wu was the prospective match that had been arranged for her. But after so many such meetings, she was able to decide very quickly whether or not she would like the guy or not. This aggravated her mother to no end and she would scold her daughter: "What's wrong with just making friends? How can you tell with just one look whether or not someone will be a good match? Do you still believe in love at first sight?" Pei Hua obeyed her mother's wishes in most things; marriage was the only exception. No matter how much her mother pressured her with cajoling and threats, she would not submit. There was no counting the number of men she had allowed to get away.

Pei Hua wore her hair up that evening. Her jacket, vest, and long skirt were all light gray. Dr. Wu glanced repeatedly at her thin, pretty face and her aloof smile. He wasn't really a bad looking guy; he had a baby face and was a little on the short side, but altogether not unpleasing. But Pei Hua had already decided not to give him a chance—he seemed like one of those guys who would be a real pest. Pei Hua waited for him to run down the lane to hail a cab. She got in first but didn't scoot over; instead she said to him, "I still have to go to the office—it's on Zhongshan North Road. Thanks, Mr. Wu." Taken aback and unable to squeeze into the cab, he protested, "Going to the office so late! My, you do work hard, don't you Miss Wang?" Smiling indifferently, Pei Hua slammed the door and said, "I have to go to the office to pick up something. Bye." It took a moment before he understood what was happening. "I'll take you," he said. "I can see you home, Miss Wang." But he was too late—the cab had already pulled away. Pei Hua looked back and saw Dr. Wu standing there, bending down as if he were going to get into the cab. He looked like some wax figurine; it was so comical. Suddenly she regretted what she had done; perhaps she shouldn't have been so abrupt and final. But her regrets were short-lived: she told herself she couldn't like a guy like that and so there was nothing to feel badly about.

"Do you still want to go to Zhongshan North Road, Miss?" asked the cab driver.

"No, take me to Yonghe, and use the Zhongzheng Bridge."

"Alrighty."

Pei Hua stared at the meter in the front of the cab; the red numbers had stopped at twenty-eight. Twenty-eight years old and still so stuck up! She could imagine what that baby-faced Dr. Wu would say behind her back. Actually he wasn't that bad, just a bit of a sissy. He was probably in his early thirties. He had come back to teach a year of school in order to find a wife, no doubt. Perhaps he would still call her. But it was more like a business transaction, and the very thought of selling herself made her shudder.

The red numbers had already flipped to thirty-one. So quickly! Pei Hua noticed the music playing in the cab—it was a piece she liked—Haydn's Symphony in D Major. It was rare that a cab driver enjoyed listening to classical music. Then she suddenly recalled that the driver had asked her if she still wanted to go to Zhongshan North Road. How did he know she was going to change her mind and not go to the office? He was strange and Pei Hua suddenly became nervous. Having heard so many bad stories about cab drivers, she regretted not letting Dr. Wu see her home. At that moment the cab driver spoke:

"Don't worry, I'm not a bad person."

Pei Hua blushed furiously in the dark back seat. How did he know what she was thinking? Sitting behind him, she couldn't see his face. He was broad-shouldered and much too well built to be a cab driver. Then he spoke again:

"Do you like Haydn?"

"How did you know that I like Haydn?"

"I didn't know you liked Haydn." He guffawed. "I asked you whether you do or not. But you've already answered my question."

"I also like the blues and soft rock."

"Songs with lyrics easily affect the emotions. If you are emotional by nature and you really listen to the words of every song, you'll be exhausted after ten songs. Classical music is better."

Pei Hua didn't know how best to respond. As the cab passed through a brighter, busier part of town, Pei Hua noticed a piece of paper that had been pasted up on the dashboard to the right of the driver:

A bit of time, a bit of gold
A bit of time for a bit of gold
Time bought and sold. Those interested please call
281-0142

Pei Hua had seen ads in taxicabs for purebred dogs before, but this was the first time she had ever seen an ad for time. "Time bought and sold..." she murmured. Suddenly the cab driver turned around.

"That's right: time bought and sold. Are you interested, Miss?"

His face was broad like his shoulders. His facial features were set far apart and his pupils seemed to glow with a strange purple light. Pei Hua had no idea how old he was, and momentarily forgot to answer him. The driver grinned and said:

"Passengers who like Haydn are most certainly good passengers. This is one of my marvelous ways of assessing my passengers. Watch this!"

He hit the accelerator and the car sped toward the intersection. Startled, Pei Hua shouted:

"It's a red light! Watch out!"

The driver casually waved his right hand and pressed a button at the side of the meter on the dashboard. It was then that Pei Hua noticed a small strange device next to the meter. It looked something like an alarm clock but with an extra row of buttons. She looked out the window again and saw that all the cars around them had stopped, yielding for the cab she was in to pass. But the driver insisted on braking. The cab came to a halt in the middle of the intersection. Pei Hua decided that the driver was clearly insane. Cautiously she spoke:

"Hurry up, they've all stopped for us. You shouldn't go through red lights and now why have you stopped in the middle of the intersection? You'd better be careful or a cop will get you."

"It doesn't matter. They can't see us clearly. And actually they haven't really stopped to let us pass. Do you see that motorcycle?"

Pei Hua looked in the direction the driver was pointing. A big fat guy was riding a Yamaha 50; he somehow strangely managed to keep his balance though the motorcycle wasn't moving. Pei Hua was amazed. She took a closer look and realized that the motorcycle wasn't entirely motionless; it was moving at an excruciatingly slow speed. She looked once more at the cars around them and saw that they too were moving extremely slowly.

"Five hundred to one," said the driver. "One second for them equals five hundred for us. You see, by setting the time scale at five hundred to one and the timer at one second on the Chronobot, one second of objective time becomes five hundred seconds of subjective time with the press of a button. So we have plenty of time to get through the intersection."

He eased off on the brake, slowly drove through the intersection, and went down a lane where he stopped. Seven or eight minutes later, the world returned to normal. Pei Hua heaved a sigh of relief. The driver said, "By using my Chronobot, you can change a short period of objective time into a long period of subjective time whenever you want to. A student who has to stay up all night to cram for an exam, lovers who have to part the next morning, and employees who have to prepare reports can all utilize my Chronobot to extend time. Neat, huh?"

The driver spoke with a child-like pride without pausing. Pei Hua didn't know what to do. Should she jump out of the car and run away from the nutcase? Or should she remain seated and listen to his nonsense? Before she could decide, the driver continued: "This is borrowing time. But what is borrowed must be returned. By returning what is borrowed, borrowing again is guaranteed. But how is it returned? It's very simple. You see, by setting the time scale at one to five hundred and the timer to ten seconds on the Chronobot, five thousand seconds of objective time become ten seconds of subjective time with the press of a button. Neat, huh?"

Pei Hua looked at her watch—unexpectedly, it was already ten thirty. Wouldn't her mother be worried about her being out so late? But the driver had no intention of letting her go. He took what appeared to be a Chronobot like the one in the cab from his pocket and handed it to Pei Hua in the back seat.

"That's the end of the demonstration, so now you know how to use it. A Chronobot will allow you to borrow time, and return time. You just saw me borrow 499 seconds by changing one second into five hundred; later you saw me return 4,990 seconds by changing 5,000 seconds into ten. On the right side of the Chronobot you will notice a timer, the numbers of which indicate the time you can borrow. The timer on the Chronobot I am giving to you is set at zero; it cannot go to a negative number, so you should practice saving time. When you're waiting for a train or in the doctor's office, for example, you can save time and not waste it! Neat, huh? If you're good at saving time, you'll have more than enough to borrow from in the future."

Pei Hua stared at the clock-like Chronobot, and couldn't hold back:

"Mr. Driver, I don't even know your name."

"My surname is Shi. But actually that's unimportant. I'm the only driver on earth who deals in Chronobots. Ha-ha."

"Mr. Shi, your invention is a great one. But why do you want me to have it? I can't afford it. Perhaps you don't know it, but I'm just a minor clerk in a trade company...."

"Who's asking you to buy it?" asked the driver with an impatient wave of his hand. "Even if you want to buy it, I'm not willing to sell! I can only loan a Chronobot to those who are destined to use them. People who like Haydn, for example. Ha-ha."

But Pei Hua didn't find it funny.

"Mr. Shi, I really don't have any money. Nor could I afford to rent it for that matter. I'm an utter klutz when it comes to machines. If something were to happen to it, I wouldn't be able to replace...."

"I don't want money. The Chronobot is a copy that I myself painstakingly assembled. There's no way you can break it. Even if an expert were to rip it open, they would not be able to discover the source of its wonders, that is unless they went to my factory and found the prototype of my Chronobot... so you have nothing to worry about. Like I said, I just loan Chronobots to those who are destined. I'm not really interested in money. My only condition is quite reasonable; you won't object."

"What condition?"

"I will loan the Chronobot to you, free of charge for one year. At the end of one year you will return it to me. At that time, all the time remaining on the counter—that is the time you save—regardless of how much, you will have to give to me to use and we'll call that your rental fee."

Pei Hua considered his proposition for a while; her curiosity finally got the better of her fear. The driver didn't look like a bad person; perhaps he was an amateur scientist in his spare time. She had heard that lots of unemployed mathematicians and physicists were now working as cab drivers. Who knew how many heroes, how many crouching tigers and hidden dragons there might be? Holding his Chronobot, she figured that at worst she wouldn't use it and wouldn't get into trouble and at the end of one year return it. The driver didn't wait for her to reply, but handed her a card.

"That's what we'll do. One year from today, on the evening of the fifteenth of February, you'll find me at this address. Don't forget."

He started the engine and headed for Yonghe. He didn't say a word the whole way. Pei Hua asked him to stop at the entrance to the Guohua

Theatre. He dropped her off and was gone in a flash. Only after he had left did Pei Hua realize that she had forgotten to pay him. Under the streetlight, she carefully examined the card he had given her. Only one line was printed on the card: "Qing Tian Street at Hoping East Road, Section One."

When Pei Hua awoke the next morning she had all but forgot her encounter of the night before. Only after she saw the Chronobot on her dresser did she recall that big, tall driver. Her curiosity piqued, she toyed with that most ingenious of devices and, following the directions the driver had given her the night before, set the time scale at one to one hundred and the timer at two seconds. The very moment she pressed the button, her mother was there before her in a temper.

"Stupid girl, what are you sitting there staring at the mirror for? How many times have I called you and got no answer? You have a phone call. Do you hear?"

Pei Hua was secretly surprised that the Chronobot really did work. She then thrust it into her bag. The caller was Dr. Wu; he wanted to invite her out that afternoon to see a movie. Pei Hua immediately declined and hung up without even giving him a chance to suggest another time. The moment she hung up, she knew she had made a mistake. Her mother sat on the sofa staring at her wide-eyed.

"If someone is nice enough to ask you out, why not go?"

"I don't feel like going out."

"Today is Sunday; wouldn't it be nice to go out and have a little fun? What's the point of staying at home alone looking at the mirror? This Wu Jinguo seems like a nice guy. He has a good education. What's wrong with being friends?"

"That's strange. I don't even know his name. How is it that you know so much about his character and his education?"

"Well, he called and you wouldn't come to the phone so I chatted with him a bit. He's very polite and even asked if he could pay us a call..."

"Who said he could pay us a call? Mom, I'm not a child. Can't you just stay out of my affairs?"

Pei Hua knew that this was all inevitable. Every time someone wanted to play matchmaker or introduce a prospective spouse, mother and daughter would quarrel. She knew her mother was anxious for her, but she couldn't tolerate her mother interfering in her emotional life. It had taken her no little effort to construct a fragile emotional bulwark, which she intended to defend to the end, but her mother was always the first spy to breach her defenses...

She spent the whole morning alone and depressed, locked in her room. Every time they argued, her mother would let it pass after venting her spleen. Pei Hua was the only one who really got hurt. As they ate lunch, her mother tried to make up by suggesting that they go together and get their hair done. Pei Hua declined, claiming a headache. With her mother gone, passing the time was even more difficult. She considered reading or listening to music, but lacked any real enthusiasm. She finally thought about the Chronobot in her bag. She set the time scale at one to one thousand and the timer at ten seconds. She pressed the button and slowly counted: one, two, three, four, five, six, seven, eight, nine, ten....and all at once it was five o'clock. When her mother returned, she greeted her with a smile. Mother and daughter talked and laughed; one washed the vegetables, the other sliced them. They were reconciled as before. Although Pei Hua didn't have much of an appetite, she forced herself to eat a bowl of rice. Life had to be lived and since there was only the two of them, mother and daughter, they had only each other to love and depend on.

But then there was that strange Chronobot.

Pei Hua gradually realized that she couldn't do without the Chronobot for a single day. On the bus, she would set the time scale at one to five and though her movements would slow down, people wouldn't notice. Normally she didn't use the Chronobot during work hours. Occasionally, her boss would ask her to write a letter. She would wait until after everyone else had left for lunch, then she would take ten seconds and set the time scale at five hundred to one and without anyone being aware of it, she would finish all of her work. No longer did she work overtime and was able to return home on time and have dinner with her mother. When she was in a bad mood, she'd shut herself up in her room and set the time scale at one to two thousand and she'd get through even a sizeable stretch of time in the blink of an eye.

It didn't take long for her to realize that what the driver had said was right: there was no way she could use all the time she saved. Perhaps for some people there was not enough time, but that was not the case with her. She was like an opium addict and found it harder and harder not to use the Chronobot. The hardest thing in life for a person was to be lonely, but with a Chronobot, she no longer feared being alone. Sometimes doubts arose and she wondered if the driver hadn't anticipated this. He had said that all the unused time would serve as the rental fee. What would he do with so much time? Would he sell it to other people? Or did the Chronobot have some military application she wasn't aware of? Perhaps he was adept at scheming and she, without being aware of it, had already become his slave, saving up for him a great deal of youth. But she was willing to do so, was she not?

Although she was highly proficient in the use of the Chronobot, she noticed that her mother frequently looked at her with concern. Once when she was in a particularly bad mood, she steeled her heart and skipped seven hours at one go. When she fled subjective time, she found her mother already was sitting at her side, staring at her, her face streaked with tears. Her mother didn't say anything, but shortly thereafter she would actively seek matchmakers for her. She herself knew that she couldn't go on this way. It was a good thing that the driver had stipulated that she had to return the Chronobot at the end of one year. Each time she thought about him she wondered what his real purpose was. Although she had only seen him once, she often recalled the scene that night. She could scarcely wait to see him again. She skipped nearly half of the last month by using the Chronobot.

At last February fifteenth arrived. Before six o'clock, Pei Hua already stood waiting at Qing Tian Street and Hoping East Road, but the driver didn't show up until eight. She didn't notice how he arrived; he seemed to appear beside her in the blink of an eye. He wasn't as tall and sturdy as she remembered; his large suit appeared loose. Under the streetlight, his pupils still shone with a strange purple light. She still couldn't tell how old he was. He wore an aloof smile not unlike hers; perhaps this was the one thing they had in common.

"Sorry I'm late." The driver looked exhausted, but he didn't beat around the bush: "Did you bring the Chronobot?"

Pei Hua felt insulted and, without so much as a word, took the Chronobot out of her bag. The driver examined the counter and appeared overjoyed.

"Not bad, there's more than two months of time....then as per our original agreement, it all becomes mine, right?"

She nodded, but added sarcastically: ""That's all you want? Are you satisfied?"

"Of course I'm satisfied. You saved too much. In most cases I'm satisfied with just one month or so."

"Most cases? So you're like a bee that collects time everywhere! So, how many people like me have fallen into your trap?"

Momentarily taken aback, he replied, "Don't put it that way. I have never forced anyone to save up time and give it to me—everyone did so willingly. Don't be angry; I know you're unhappy with me, but I haven't harmed anyone, have I?" He watched her expression, and then laughed. "Okay, anyway, you're the last one, so I'll explain everything to you. Do you have time? I'll buy you a coffee. There's a nice coffee house on Yongkang Road."

He didn't wait for Pei Hua to reply. Instead, he took out a Chronobot, pressed the button, and the world grew motionless.

"It doesn't matter if you don't have time, I can borrow some cause I've got plenty."

"Have you ever done anything by first asking for someone else's opinion?"

He looked at her somewhat confusedly. "Ask you for your opinion? It will only cost you a second. You certainly have that much time. I want to explain to you why I go all over buying time. Don't you want to know?"

"But you should at least wait for my reply."

"Okay." He shrugged his shoulders. "Women are always so illogical. But if you are unwilling, then there is no reason for me to waste my breath; but if you had already agreed, then there would be no need to wait for your answer, right? So, what's your answer?"

Pei Hua thought about it for a moment and then couldn't help laughing. The whole world was motionless, as if everyone were in some sort of living wax museum. The driver took a stick of sugarcoated haws from the hand of a street peddler and handed it to Pei Hua.

"That's what I like—nobody can bother me. I can do what I like without interference. I go everywhere, just looking. I'm an out-and-out spectator that no one notices. All they can see is a shadow that is faster than a plane." He looked her up and down and said, "Tonight, they will see two ghostly shadows. The greatest ratio on the Chronobot I loaned you is two thousand to one. But there is no limit on my personal Chronobot—ten thousand to one, one hundred thousand to one, a million to one...it's up to me. Shortly after I had invented the Chronobot, I made a vow. I wanted to save ten thousand years and then set the time scale at a million to one. In that way I could experience ten thousand years in less than four days!"

The driver escorted Pei Hua into the coffee house and moved aside a couple of customers, who looked like they were molded out of clay or carved out of wood. He then went to the counter and poured two cups of coffee and motioned for Pei Hua to have a seat.

"The only bad thing about this motionless world is that you have to do everything yourself. After we finish the coffee we have to wash the cups and put them back where they belong and put those two fools back in their seats, otherwise they will think they met a ghost. All the reported sightings of UFOs and ghosts this year from all over the world were my own masterworks or those of my customers."

"What do you want with ten thousand years of time?" asked Pei Hua.

"I swore I would visit every corner of the world, and read every book in the world." The driver spoke in all seriousness; Pei Hua knew that his boast was not an empty one. "I once calculated that ten thousand years would be sufficient. In that period of time—although it would only be four days of objective time—the world would be practically motionless and that would be sufficient for my travels. Neat, huh? And I could go any place. I could walk on water like Jesus."

"Ten thousand years. How could you save ten thousand years?"

"With the help of all of you." Grimacing, the driver continued, "I've been at it quietly for more than ten years now. I have a hundred thousand customers all over the world to whom I have loaned a Chronobot for one year. Each customer is normally able to save more than one month of time for me. I have to be selective when it comes to my customers—I never choose businessmen, politicians, or any other so-called busy person. At first I thought senior citizens would be the best, until I discovered that they are the stingiest when it comes to time. They were unwilling to give me even one second. Later I went to Africa where I located ten thousand starving people. I figured that my Chronobot would be of most use to them. They could go to bed on an empty stomach and with the push of a button skip a night tortured by hunger. That plan was pretty successful except for the time saved was entirely useless."

"Why is that?"

"Because...what I was able to do was to change the subjective time saved by others into my own subjective time. But basically it was still their time, otherwise how could I use ten thousand years of borrowed time and not grow old and die? Because I was using someone else's time, I was still affected by their state of mind. The minds of those hungry devils were focused on nothing but food. I couldn't read in the library disturbed as I was by the images of food in my brain. So my plan of borrowing time from the bodies of the starving was a failure. It was only then that I thought of..." The driver stopped and Pei Hua finished for him.

"Using people like me. Right? You finally found a hundred thousand lonely old maids in all parts of the world and cheated them into willingly sacrificing their youths. How marvelous."

"Don't make it sound so bad." The driver blushed furiously. "You're not old. What's more...I never loaned my Chronobot to anyone for more than a year because I didn't want to take too much of their time."

"You've been very thoughtful! But there is still one problem. You said that by using other people's time you are still affected by their state of mind. Is my state of mind of any use for you?"

The driver looked out the window and nodded his head slowly. Pei Hua suddenly understood that he, too, was a very unhappy person. Her initial hostility melted away immediately. So he was just as unhappy as she was. Even if he possessed all the time in the world, how would it benefit him? She felt like giving him a few words of encouragement, but after a moment of consideration said, "What good will it do you to read every book that there is and traveled to every corner of the world? What are you trying to find?"

"The final answer to the riddle of life." The driver gave a desolate smile.

Unfortunately, I hold only half the key to eternity; half is still missing. I'm prepared to spend ten thousand years to find it. If I can't find it, then no one can. Tonight, from you, I have retrieved the last Chronobot. Everything is set. As the last person to see me, you are very lucky—no one else knows so many of my secrets."

"Why don't I go with you?" Pei Hua hastened to add: "I could share your joys and sorrows. Let me go with you."

"Would that do?" said the driver, shaking his head. His self-conceit was evident on his forehead. "That would only leave me with five thousand years, and that's not enough to read all the books in the world. Your kindness is appreciated. I will be gone ten thousand years, but it will only be four days for you. In five days, let's meet at the old place in the evening, and I will tell you the conclusion I have reached."

So saying, the driver stood up. Pei Hua assisted him in moving the customers back to their seats and putting the coffee cups back on the counter. When she turned around, the driver was already gone. Startled, the customers in the coffee house all stared at her.

She waited four days and on the evening of the fifth day she painstakingly made herself up. Before five o'clock, she was standing at Qing Tian Street.

But the driver did not appear. She waited all night and she took off the following day and waited the whole day for him, but he never showed up.

Had he had an accident? She didn't think that anything in the motionless world was capable of harming him. He could walk on water like Jesus. Then why had he not returned? She was confident that he wouldn't lie to her—he wasn't the type. So what was it?

She searched high and low for him. Once, when she was crossing Nanking Road, she saw someone from behind who resembled him. She pursued, calling his name, Mr. Shi, but the man didn't turn around. Bravely, she reached out and grabbed him. The man turned around and she realized he was blind and carried a cane. Startled, she was sure it couldn't be him.

On another occasion she went to Bi Lake with a friend. From the suspension bridge, she saw someone far away walking on the shore of the lake and for a moment she swore she saw him walk on water. By the time she had got off the bridge, he had disappeared.

She frequently went to walk up and down Qing Tian Road, hoping that he would show up. Had he been unable to stand ten thousand years of loneliness and returned to the world of human beings early? Had he really discovered something and was now visiting all parts of the world to buy more time? But he ought still to remember her. She had given him some time, so how could he have forgotten her?

Every night, where Qing Tian Street meets Hoping East Road, a woman, filled with longing, can be seen waiting, waiting for a driver who loves Haydn to return exhausted from his journey.

Around the Curve

Alice Clark

As if by some instinct the wretch did know
His rider lov'd not speed, being made from thee
Shakespeare, *Sonnet L*

She took the note out of her drawer and read it again. A crumpled white sheet of paper, with his handwriting scribbled across the page. If she had only been more attentive, more affectionate, more available, more . . . the list was long, never ending. Just like the images, which rushed through her mind. She could see him all those years, trying, trying so hard, so hard to be like Charles; to be liked by Charles. If she could only go back, she would have said things differently. No, she wouldn't have said them at all. She should never have pushed him to become independent so quickly. But how could she have known? He could be a trickster: funny, serious, sinister, and so hard to understand: a harlequin, always changing. She thought she knew him so well. But she couldn't have, could she? Or she wouldn't be holding this letter in her hand. It was all because of that accident; that's when things took a fatal turn. If only he hadn't run up against the Camel's Back, and she had not forced him to try to get over it, by going back. She paused. Touched the paper softly. Traced a finger—ever so slowly—over the black cursive letters squirrcled across the page, hurriedly, impetuously: the pressure of the pen had left a small rip next to his name, half smudged in ink, but perfectly legible to her eyes: *Marty*. "*Marty*," she whispered, holding onto the labial sound for a moment, pressing her lips together as if to hold it there for eternity. *Marty*, the name of her only son.

***

Marty leaned in Mary Ann's direction, and with one fell swoop of his hand, grabbed her knife off the plate. His wide grin broke into a long smile where a set of fine white teeth locked delicately into each other, giving off a sense of radiant indulgence.

"Aren't you a quick draw!" Mary Ann laughed, grabbing at the knife that twirled in the air and finally disappeared, mysteriously. She went back to her plate, picked up her remaining utensil, speared an overcooked piece of pork chop onto the spiked edges of the fork, and running it through the ketchup sauce, said: "You are such a flirt. I adore you Marty, as brothers go. I mean you are my older brother. And you're different from most humanoids, that's why I'm not worried about my knife, you're just horsing around, as usual. I'm the only one who doesn't take you seriously. I know you don't mean any harm. Now, if Mom were sitting here, she'd wonder; you know how suspicious she gets . . . "

"I know what you meant to say, Mary Ann. It's not really Mom; she'd never call me 'Mad Marty.'" He winced slightly, and his lips sealed themselves now in thought. Caught in the evening light, they trembled slightly with dejection.

"I'm sorry, Marty." Mary Ann tried to catch her brother's gaze. "You know I didn't mean it that way."

Marty was bright. Even brighter than the others considering the number of hurdles he had gone through by the time he had reached eighteen. He had survived a near fatal car crash when the neighbor's daughter, Lilly Buckles, was coming back from the pool, doing seventy instead of thirty-five in a residential area. They say her windows were down and you could hear her singing "Life in the Fast Lane," her blonde hair spraying out of the convertible when it happened. She had arrived at the third highest hill, perched on a hairpin curve, which the youngsters in town had dubbed "the Camel's back." Marty clamped his head down between his knees and slammed on the breaks, but it was too late. A go-cart, especially the kind Marty was in, is difficult to discern, since it consists of a motor set on two crossed iron bars, mounted on a set of four wheels, with a small steering wheel in front, and all of that only a few inches off the ground. Marty had started building it when he was thirteen, knowing he would be allowed to drive it in the daytime when he turned fifteen. He had done a lot of enhancement work on the go-cart. The very fact that it did not melt down, or fall apart immediately, but was able to sustain the impact of Lilly Buckles' one ton Maverick showed how much punishment the go-cart could take, not to mention Marty, who was pinned down between the two vehicles. Lilly screamed once, when she felt the impact, but she did not seem to fully realize that she had run over a body which was slowing grilling away under the heat and steam of her motor vehicle. A few women came flying out onto the street, gesturing to each other. Some of their children followed close behind. One of the women sent a child back to get some water for Lilly who appeared to be in a state of post-traumatic shock. A few more people came out into the street. But Lilly just stood there, frozen, with her hand over her mouth, in her bikini and her dark sunglasses. There was an odd smell in the air. An odor like fresh pork rinds was oozing its way out from under the car's fender. This was a sign that someone had to do something. Humans, fortunately, maintain some of their primal instincts, and it was Marty's luck that he did not have to wait for the ambulance or firemen to pull him out. Marty's lower body was a scarred marshmallow when neighbor Jenkins came running out, elbowing his way through the crowd; and with his own two hands, and his tall scrawny body, he managed a superhuman venture. Jenkins picked up that Maverick and pushed it up in the air so that it was resting on two wheels, alternately balancing it on one shoulder then the other while a group of youngsters tugged at the go cart, so as to extricate it from under the car. Part of the drivers' wheel had gotten twisted into the iron fender of the Maverick, and it took some time to finally separate the two entirely.

When the ambulance arrived, Lilly was still standing with her hand on her mouth, looking from her new car to the stretcher, which the young boy was hoisted up onto. Marty had sustained multiple injuries, with severe third degree burns situated mainly on his lower extremities, but he was just fifteen, and at that age, humans are astoundingly resistant. Such was the case of Marty, who after six months in the hospital, would be discharged. The scars would still be there, but the worst could not be seen with the naked eye. His mother, Mrs. Bankroft, detected a slight, if not inveterate stutter, which Marty had acquired during his stay at the hospital. It had started in the intensive care ward. That would be another hurdle to overcome. She was sure Marty could get over it, unlike Dr. Bankroft. After all, Marty had kept fairly good pace with the other tenth graders due to the private tutors who came to the hospital. Mrs. Bankroft felt it was not advisable for Marty to be forced to do all his schoolwork, and she allotted him generous time for his entrepreneurial mind to take shape and flourish. Without his lab, Marty had become desperately itchy. At hospital he had been given a private room, due to the length of his stay, and Mary Ann would bring him a mass of electrical instruments: bulbs, motors, pistons, small electrical wires for new inventions. Marty simply could not do without Mary Ann's assistance after a while and so it was necessary for her to miss school at times. Mrs. Bankroft fully supported their venture. She objected to her husband's accusations. Mr. Bankroft kept repeating that Marty was "out there" and that Mary Ann ought to spend less time in the lab with him, lest she too go astray. Dr. Bankroft feared that his wife's leniency would eventually taint what he called their daughter's "development." Mrs. Bankroft would nod her head in recognition, and place her hands delicately on her lap. But Dr. Bankroft was too often off travelling to keep up with what was going on at home.

Two years later, Marty was barely making passing grades, and although he had the highest average in his senior mathematics class, he embarrassed Dr. Bankfroft who kept telling everyone that his son was "out there." He was so exacerbated that he actually tried to get Marty's homeroom teacher to curve his grade point average for the year, on the account of the effect of his accident. She refused adamantly: "Curving grades is not standard procedure at Arlingville High, sir, and arguing the case that your son's a strange fish will not make him grow gills any faster. He has to learn how to breathe using his own system."

What Dr. Bankroft failed to see was that Marty's idiosyncrasies were what made him *above average*. What's more, he was blind to the fact that Marty was striving to be like him. The mirror image that his eighteen-year-old was sending him registered as yet another sign of filial impertinence in Dr. Bankroft's eyes. As far as Mary Ann, and Mrs. Bankroft, it was obvious: Marty was yearning for his father's attention, and prepared to do almost anything in the world to get it. And they saw that the harder Marty tried, the less his father took interest in him. "Why do you even care about what Dad thinks?" Mary Ann would ask. "Does he seem to care about you—about us?" Mary Ann insisted, adding: "I don't know why he has a family anyway. The American Psychiatric Association, and his patients are his REAL family; we aren't! He considers us *normaloids*. We just aren't sick enough for him to love us deeply, that's all." She paused to glance over at Marty who was playing tug of war with Betina. The dog had her jaw clamped down on a piece of meat, which Marty refused to relinquish. "Marty, listen to me, and stop torturing Betina! Please listen!"

"I'm listening very carefully, Mary Ann. Now, the way I figure it, Dad already has to worry about all those fools around him: half mad, raving idiots, all of them stitching themselves into some blue funk, or wanting to put an end to it all. We shouldn't make it any harder on him." Marty would most often take his father's side, particularly when Mary Ann started provoking him: "Dad has a point there, doesn't he?" That was his favorite opening line. "What's important is helping others who need help. That's Dad's vocation. He's a psychiatrist. Look Mary Ann, I don't need his help; they do. I'm in perfectly good health." Mary Ann would look at him dubiously. "No kidding," he continued, puffing out his chest. "Look. Me walk with back straight. Shoulders high. Me Homo sapiens, with very big brain, too much weight in central cortex. Me have to hunch down."

And he would walk around with his back humped up, placing a hand over his forehead, frowning and grunting furiously until Mary Ann cut in.

"Stop your monkeying around, now do you hear?" Marty would flex a naked bicep, tuck in his stomach and flash his sister one of his enchanting smiles, so full of indulgence, that she nearly stopped arguing. His dauntless ease, smooth smile and soft touch of virility would have made Marty a perfect double for Brando in years to come. At the moment, he still had the cheekiness of fleshy innocence. "Well, maybe I'll start calling you Dr. Jekyll. You and your lab, that's all that matters to you, isn't it Marty? Admit it. Well, I'm not complaining, I get to spend more time than anyone else with you, being your *personal assistant.* Say, when do I get a raise?" she said laughing, "I can't keep on moonlighting like this! "

Ever since the day Marty was released from hospital three years ago, he had thrown himself headlong into his workshop, even more so than before the accident. He was always making new discoveries in his lab downstairs: last winter there was the snow machine; in the spring there was the infrared camera which set off an alarm, snapping your photo if you forgot to knock on Marty's bedroom door, (or his lab, as Marty called it). When Mary Ann turned sixteen, Dr. Bankroft decided that it was time for her to excel in something; so things took a different turn for a while. Suddenly her mother was bringing her to singing and dancing lessons regularly, for she had been enrolled in the Miss Arlingville beauty pageant. Her father was clearly relieved to see her relinquish her lab smock: "Why, sweetie, you look so much nicer when you're dressed like a young lady."

And her mother supported the beauty pageant decision, wholeheartedly: "Now darling, you can't spend your life down there in the half darkness, dissecting bull frogs and garden snakes. And don't you deny it, I saw the scalpel and those poor beasts pinned to the canvas board." Mrs. Bankroft averted her eyes momentarily and took a deep sigh.

"Come on Mom, you know that Betina and Pustel are always dragging in their prey to offer them up to us, as and they expect us to be proud of them. Well, it's true that Betina's just a dog, all she does is sniff at what the cat brings in. All the same, it's in Pustel's nature; it's in an animal's nature—to hunt and kill and be praised for it, if possible."

"Well, you certainly have some mighty fine reasoning for a sixteen-year-old girl, I don't know about all that animal pride you're referring to, but I sure hope you don't go out there stalking those animals with your brother. Now, that would get me downright worried, you hear, darling?"

In the end, Mary Ann got what is commonly called a "frog in her throat" right in the middle of the beauty pageant finals. It was when she was singing "My Country 'Tis of Thee" that she suddenly drew a blank. The words came out in a croak. When she finally summoned up "sweet land of liberty," each syllable belched across the room. She was even more surprised than the judges who watched as her face, white as a cream puff, transformed; her cheeks flushed crimson, and she darted off to the exit ramp. The Miss Arlingville beauty pageant was a fiasco for Mary Ann, but a relief at the same time because she no longer had to go to her ballet, voice or music lessons. If Mary Ann was pretty, she was not aware of it. If she was smart, her shyness masked any sense of self-certainty. And if she was talented, the false notes in her rendering of the national anthem had thrust serious doubt over her innate musical talents. What Mary Ann liked most was to assist Marty in his laboratory. She refused to take credit for her beauty, and she attributed her intelligence to the influence of her brother. As soon as she stepped out of her role as his "personal assistant," she may just as well have been any other average girl on the street. Except for the fact that she did not have anything to do with any of those other girls. In truth, Mary Ann was in a league apart, which one she did not know: winning or losing, champions, or losers, these were distinctions she could not yet define.

As Marty's personal assistant, she would help him with discovering the mechanical world, a world alien to her, a world of valves, siphons, wires and other apparatus. That winter, the night before Christmas, the snow engine was on its way to being discovered. It consisted of four aluminum sprinklers, which were placed at each corner of the Bankroft's sprawling lawn. A long plastic hose, with reinforced nylon lining to preserve heat and cold, was attached to each sprinkler. Marty had been working the weekend shift to put money aside for the sprinkling system. It had all been planned in advance. He and Mary Ann rose early at dawn that day to get things prepared. It was a bit of a tricky venture because Marty would have to reroute the hot water system from the basement to the hoses to clear out the frozen gel on the lining. This having been done, they proceeded to turn on the cold water system from the outside of the house which now flowed freely through the hose into the four sprinklers and then freely, into the air. Within an hour and a half the entire yard was white with snow. When the neighborhood woke up that Christmas morning, the Bankroft residence cut a striking picture next to the other brick houses. Theirs was the only, the unique, white mantle. It spread its wings across a good sixth of an acre of land. Amongst all that dullness it shone. The three story red brick stucco house had molted in the night: looking magical and alien as it stood there perched on a high white hill from which there descended a long veil of soft white snow ending abruptly on all sides where the neighbor's green lawns started.

Mary Ann and Marty waited impatiently for their parents to rise. Mary Ann was the first to spot them: "Merry Christmas, Mom and Dad! We ordered the winter wonderland especially from *Scientific Santa Incorporated.*" Marty stood pointing out the large French window at the snowy lawn. Dr. Bankroft looked outside and shrugged his shoulders. Mrs. Bankroft sighed, "My flowers, why they'll all be frozen." Then she smiled at her children, and said: "Well, I'm sure they'll grow back."

"Do you mind if we have some of the neighbors over? Just for a while?" they asked.

"Well, it's Christmas day, that's not a good idea, do you think?" Mrs. Bankroft protested.

"Oh come on, we'll be back in at noon. Dad didn't object," Mary Ann insisted. "He'll be in his study all day, anyway. Please, Mom."

So, Mel Pickens, Johhny Walker, Sally Strutters and many other neighbors who ordinarily never even set foot in the Bankroft's yard came over that day. At least a dozen kids, if not more, all equipped with sleds. Never had there been so much merriment, so much laughter at the Bankrofts. It was a magnificent Christmas, a truly magical day, but like most magic, it wears off. The snow melted, and the spell was gone; spring came, but no grass sprung up in the Bankroft's yard. It was a desolate wasteland, a dull brown camel's back—where not only flowers refused to grow, but not even one blade of green grass would shoot up for a long time. Mrs. Bankroft was devastated. Dr. Bankroft put Marty on temporary probation (forbidden to use his laboratory for three months). None of the neighborhood children came over to the Bankroft's after that episode. There were sinister rumors that circulated in the neighborhood about the Bankroft's house. It had become known as "the cemetery" with its dejected bits of brown soil and meager green sprouts of grass growing in patches; indeed, it had lost its former grandeur. Rumor had it that it was home to a wandering spirit who lived somewhere in the subterranean regions of the house.

The following summer came along bright and crisp. Marty and Mary Ann had defined their mission for the next three months: they were to create a new hybrid species of tropical fish. Marty would purchase a fifty-gallon salt water aquarium for breeding; a thirty gallon quarantine tank for spawning grounds, and another fifty gallon aquarium for the final hybrid adult species. When the problem of getting the fish and the equipment home arouse, he went to talk to his mother. "I've financed the whole thing," he said insistently, and added, blushing: "I just don't want to drive there."

This was a fact Mrs. Bankroft could not deny—that her son was still afraid to get behind a driver's wheel. She summoned up her courage and decided to make Marty face up to it: he could not continue being chauffeured around his entire life. "Darling, you know I only want what's best for you, and I want to help you deal with Camel's Back in a positive way. If you could just manage to drive over that hill—just once—I'm sure everything else would fall into place. Darling, you are the only one in your high-school class that doesn't drive yet. I'll tell you what, let's go pick up your tropical fish and the tanks, and on the way back you can try driving over Camel's Back. You've already had simulated driving classes at school. There's no reason to be worried; let's just try this once." She nudged him gently. "What do you say, dear, shall we try?"

Marty shrugged lamely. Mrs. Bankroft rounded up Mary Ann and they all drove off to *Tropical Universe* where they spent a couple hours carefully choosing different varieties of tropical fish, flora and cardinal and neon tetra for feeding. They loaded the tanks and the equipment into the car. Marty's hands were sweating so profusely that one of the tanks slipped onto the pavement while he was trying to load it. The plastic bags with the orange and neon tetras had been placed inside the thirty gallon tank, so they all went down at the same time, hitting the pavement with a series of jangled high notes. Jagged bits of glass slashed open the plastic, letting out a rush of water and the orange striped tetras flew out, landing on the ground with a delicate plop amidst the wreckage.

Marty stepped back, enraged and appalled. "No, Mom, I can't do it, I can't do it today. I don't want to drive."

His mother looked at the small fish on the hard concrete, their tiny bodies flapping about, and then back to her son. It all came back to her; her jaw tightened and she made an extraordinary effort not to let him know that his scars were her open wounds salted over a thousand times, and his pain was her darkest hour. She never wanted anything more than to spare him this. "Of course, of course, sweetie. It was a dreadfully silly idea in the first place. We have plenty of time, plenty."

So Marty finished loading the tanks into the Sedan and then went back to the store for the second round which consisted of three varieties of tropical fish, that would, after the breeding phase, produce a half a dozen new species. Mary Ann helped him get them back home. The fish arrived unscathed, though bristled by the car trip, in a state of anxious agitation. Mary Ann, whose job it was to provide daily nourishment, gave them all a sampling of dried algae composition, which seemed to have calmed the fish down slightly. The blowfish, of course, would demand meaty foods, like bloodworms and brine shrimp twice a week. Being of the family of Tetradontidae, their teeth grow throughout their lives, and they need to have hard foods (snails, shrimp with the shell), on a weekly basis. If their teeth overgrow they can stop feeding and die. Unlike Marty, Mary Ann had memorized the nicknames of each fish. Marty stuck to the Latinate names.

And Mary Ann could tell you just what personality type applied to each fish, particularly the puffers. "Pillbox is lazy, he won't make for the food until it comes in his direction, " she had noted. "And any fish that gets within a half a centimeter of Electroid, when he's feeding on his plankton, gets thrashed away with his orange tail." Marty nodded in consent. Although he found it intriguing that tropical fish could have such distinctive personalities, he did not dwell on the dynamics of what all that meant. But Mary Ann was particularly worried about Puffer who was not getting "enough to eat."

"Oh stop worrying about Puffer, he can fend for himself," Marty insisted.

"But have you seen the way Choppers goes at Pillbox—if he even makes a move for one of those brine shrimp. . . . He nearly ripped out Pillbox's left gill the other day."

They had put the Angelfish in one aquarium and the Blood Parrots in another until it was time for interbreeding. When the eggs were spawned, the fish grew and when they reached adolescence it became evident that these progenitors were for the most part feeble. They had developed multiple gills, which consumed too much oxygen, and soon they grew other strange abnormalities that were grotesque enough to the naked eye. Mary Ann could not bear to look at them, and when one would die, she buried it in the outside lot of the backyard. After a period of three months it transpired that the progenitors of their tropical fish experiment were as sickly as the Hapsburg Empire's royal descendants after centuries of inbreeding among first, second and third cousins. All of this had led to a school of monstrous abnormalities so offensive not even Marty could stomach a peep at the tanks much longer. The whole lot would have to be destroyed. He dumped the contents of the tanks, one by one, into the food grinder and the small tails disappeared into the black mouth of the sink, whirling into the mash of waste. After a few spins of the blade's long gurring—there remained nothing of the evidence of this last experiment. Marty could not allow his father any proof. He would remain beyond reproach this time.

Marty was approaching the end of his senior year at Arlingville High School. Graduation was a matter of jubilation for most of the students, either because they had been accepted into the university of their choice, or simply because they could now leave home. Neither case applied to Marty. His SAT scores did not reflect his vision of the world. He ranked very low in language scores, but math boosted the total average, paving his way to a Technical school located near the Range Rover Artillery Center, a half an hour from home. His mother decided to take the news in stride, and looking at the bright side of it, she tried to convince his father to see things the same way: "At least Marty will be close by. He won't have to forego his lab. He's invested so much in it, now, maybe he'll be the next Bill Gates, one never knows."

"A perfectly fine idea, the next Bill Gates! I suppose we should buy him a log cabin and set him up there where he can spend eighteen hours a day thinking about his next project, too," Dr. Bankroft said, snidely.

"Well, isn't that what Bill Gates did in his early days, when he was thinking about the internet?"

Marty pressed his ear harder against the oak wood door; voracious, he tried to seize each word. He was standing at the end of the hallway, his left shoulder pressed against his parents' bedroom door, all the while maintaining weight on his right foot if he needed to make a run for it. His father's voice continued, gruffly, but articulately: "Marty, the next Bill Gates!" A long laugh rolled out from the bedroom, and clamored down the hallway. Then a short, but distinct silence fell. Marty released the pressure of his ear on the door. He pulled away and turned on his heels, but then he heard his name again. He moved toward the door, pushing his shoulder and his ear up against the cold wood surface again. He held his breath, forcing himself to swallow every word: "Marty doesn't have a cold chance in hell to get a glimpse of anything remotely close to genius, or vision, for that matter. The strategic masterstrokes recorded in the internet tidal wave memo which shifted Microsoft's focus to the Web, are the fruit of a genius, but that genius is not in our family. Marty cannot even make it on to the most mediocre college. In his high school days he turned our house into a laughing stalk with his snow machine. It made our home look like a burnt mud hut, and then that torture chamber for tropical fish downstairs. You know, I've had enough of his showing off. A mad scientist he isn't: but mad and mediocre he is! He's plagued the Bankroft family's reputation: with only a technical school acceptance for all his genius! All we need is another fool like my brother; another pariah in the family."

"Please, Charles, don't be so cruel. Marty is only eighteen; he has unfettered ambition. You just refuse to see it. You could give him a little support, now and then; just one word from you means more than a million coming from me, or anyone else. Marty drinks you in. Why do you think he keeps coming up with all these newfangled discoveries if it's not to attract your attention? All you show him is antipathy! Wrath! Disdain! Can't you see that? He needs more support from you. This is an age when he needs to bond. Why, if you continue to reject him, he'll, he'll turn into a monster, I tell you. Open your eyes!"

"What do you think you're saying? You spend too much time at home. You've become too partial to the children over all these years."

"And you spend too much time traveling. And too much time being impartial to your own family. You only care about your crazy patients.

What's a family to you? Just a bunch of trophies: trophy wife, trophy children . . . Why, the real monster is you, not Marty." She paused—continued—punctuating every word: "And if you are so concerned about his tainting the Bankroft family's IVY LEAGUE SCHOOL reputation—why you have all the power in the world to pull some strings and get him into a higher ranking university. You know that only too well, Charles."

"Nobody ever pulled any strings for me. And I have no intention of doing it for Marty. It's against my principles."

She turned now, facing him head on, with his full height bearing down on her. She felt like a Lilliputian in his world of giants. She must cut the cords now. They had been keeping her chained down, orderly, civilized. Why, she could have claws too, a mind, a brain, a soul, and if she had relinquished her body, long ago, to god knows what principle, she could surely get it back again, but it would be a struggle. So, she forced herself to look him in the eyes. Pinning him down, eye to eye, in sickness or health, sanity or insanity, she shot at him: "And so what are your principles? I thought psychiatrists didn't have principles, aren't they above all that? And why would you need a god, since you have replaced him with your high and mighty discoveries about human nature. But Dr. Bankroft, what you don't understand . . . "

"I think this conversation has gone far enough," he said, reaching for the door, nudging her aside.

Mrs. Bankroft intercepted his hand. Surprised, he backed off slightly. She stepped forward, her chest grazing his torso. It felt strange. How long had it been since . . . And what had ever brought her to this man in the first place? Her thoughts were smoked over by the past. Suddenly the filmy membrane began to dissipate. The numbness cleared away; her voice palpable, thick and filled with heat, jerked her back into gear, began switching so fast she nearly lost pace. Memory restored, there was no going back. In a rush, she could see Charles's lips parted, the particular touch of his hand on the nape of her neck as she gave way. But now, she could resist. She knew nothing but resistance and straightened up, almost forgetting what she had decided to say. She looked over at him. He had placed his two hands behind his back. They were cupped together as he contemplated the wall solemnly. She could feel him slipping away, as he always had: through her fingers, out of her life, into another world, into his world, full of his desires. His life was an intricate maze. And he was a puzzle. He had been putting himself together, over the years, never asking her whether this piece fit, or what she thought about it. He remained an impenetrable Rorschach. It was now or never; she had to take a stand. "No," she said, "I won't let you leave this time, you won't just get up and walk away, not so easily." She backed up against the door, standing her ground. "Since we are finally talking about a real subject, our son, Marty, about us, about me, about women, well, I'm ready. I'm not the Dark Continent, you understand!"

"Our son Marty!" a long wave of laughter washed up against Marty's body, piercing his ear, sending a current of uneasiness through him. "Our son, Marty!" the voice rocked out another jet of laughter, culminating in a jagged gag: "Now, now Amanda, don't try to turn the tables on me. We decided a long time ago to let things rest. I know you were much younger then, and I know you were desperate. I was your psychiatrist and it was, I admit, my professional misconduct, but I loved you."

"You loved me." Her voice was dry. "Just like so many other things that were once a blazing passion and finally snuff out, that's what you mean, isn't it? Isn't it?" She could feel the heat in her cheeks, the ebbing and flowing of her heart and the shock of tears, which hinged on the dike of all these lost and pent up feelings. Her very being was submerged first in wrath, then desire, for the impossible desire to be desired, just once more. Her throat was dry, then wet: a tidal wave of deception, she was caught between the cross currents of an undertow that was pulling her out further, further.

"I didn't mean to make you . . . " He looked flustered. He reached out to her. She stepped back. "Look, Amanda, you were my patient." He took a step closer, and said firmly: "Look, Amanda, this won't get either of us anywhere. Our relationship started as a breach of ethics. Professionally, I take responsibility for that much. But, Amanda, when I saw you in that state . . . well, after all, I do have a moral responsibility toward my clients—particularly when they are in desperate circumstances. Look, Amanda, what's important is that I took the responsibility of getting you back onto your feet. When I found you there . . . obviously I knew it was an act of desperation . . . Look we've been through this already. "

She took another step backwards.

He continued speaking, more quietly this time: "Look you wanted to talk, I didn't. Now, don't keep blaming things on me. You forget the past too easily. We both know he wasn't planned. And I know his father was . . . well . . . it's better this way. Amanda, I've done my best to fill in. But he's deficient in many ways, he couldn't be my . . . "

"Stop it, just stop it. Stop there. It's monstrous, how can you speak that way? You and your Rorschach tests and language scores; you don't even know the meaning of flesh and blood."

"Well, he's not my flesh and blood. I've done my best, that's all I can say. If you hadn't pampered him so much, he would have grown up to be a real man, not this freak scientist, this childish adolescent who cannot even drive for fear of . . . "

"For fear of . . . Charles, you are merciless! The accident left a deep scar on Mart. You should know that in your profession. Patients need help to get over those shocks. How have you ever helped him?"

"I've tried to help him grow up, but your constant pampering has spoiled any chance to make Marty into an intelligent and mature man. His emotional growth has become severely stunted by this strange world he has created in his laboratory, cut off from everything of substance. He will grow up to be a freak, an absolute freak, rest assured."

"He has made laboratory discoveries. He has created a new breed of tropical fish. I suppose you didn't even know that, did you? You are so consumed by devotion to your patients, to those Borderlines and your research—I can tell you, I am not impressed by the international recognition you have gotten over the past few years in the *Journal of Family Psychiatry*, not at all. If people only knew that you have lost all contact with your family: that you forget your children's birthdays, your own wedding anniversaries . . . You have become a stranger to us. Your professional genius has made you into a domestic psychopath, with no emotions, no conscience whatsoever. You have no feelings, no empathy for our weaknesses, for Marty's weaknesses," she said as her heart pumped wildly in her chest.

"And your empathy has made Marty into a permanently handicapped adult. For god's sake, you have to drive him to the store to pick up all those aquariums, sprinklers and whatever else he needs for his brainless experiments. He can't even get behind a wheel and drive somewhere on his own. It's pathetic," Charles finished dryly.

"Why, that's cruel of you. Cruel, cruel—as if the accident never happened. As if Marty hasn't persisted relentlessly in trying to go back there to get over it. Maybe if you would help him. But of course that would be expecting too much, from you . . . "

Their voices went on lashing at each other behind the door.

Marty shoved his hand into his pocket. It was cold. The chaos of words, accusations, laughter had chilled him. He put his other hand in his pocket. Behind him the voices were veering off into the distance.

He turned his back to that oakwood door and walked down the hallway, heading for the veranda where the cicadas were buzzing wildly beneath the flecked moonlight. He went down to the lab, ripped out a piece of paper and jotted down a note to his mother. "I'm taking Dad's car out. I know I don't have my license, but I'll prove what I'm worth this time. I'm going to take that curve now, *Marty*." He went back upstairs to get the keys to his father's sedan hanging in the kitchen, and slipped the note under the door.

The darkness fell in on him, deeper than any he had ever known. He and the motor were one, his foot and the pedal were smoldered in unison, as a terrifying veil of curiosity closed in on him. How fast could he take the curve? He would slow down afterwards, but it had to be at least ninety he figured to get over the fear, once and for all. He could feel a warm vortex of adrenaline siphoning his insides, animating his body like an electric current. He rolled down the window. It was a thick, balmy evening, which helped him forget about his hands that kept sweating, sweating away on the steering wheel. As he reached ninety, he removed one hand briefly, wiping his palm against his jeans. There were so many things to be discovered, so many, he thought. He felt free, at last, after all these years. He pressed down on the accelerator a bit harder. And as it hit one hundred, he glimpsed a motorcycle jetting over the peak of the Camel's Back. Marty braked, veering to the right; the motorcyclist jammed into the dust, and the Sedan slammed into the ditch as the needle flapped back to zero.

***

When the doorbell rang, Mrs. Bankroft threw herself out onto the front porch. She came face to face with the officer standing quietly there in front of her. The sun was rising and Marty must have been gone since midnight. "Mrs. Bankroft?" She stepped back and nodded. "Mrs. Bankroft; it's your son, he almost had a head-on collision with a motorcyclist last night, head-on, at Camel's Back."

She flinched, clutching the wrinkled letter in her fingers. It was damp with the sweat of her hands. For the first time in hours, she managed to separate her flesh from the paper, like so many rosary beads that become part and parcel of the fingers that stroke them.

"Involuntary manslaughter," the officer said gently, "it was involuntary, Mrs. Bankroft. They'll take that into consideration."

LAST RITES

Vijay Lakshmi

The tar road burns under our feet. The wind blows hot dust into our faces as we trudge along to the cremation ground. Clearing his throat and spitting out grit, someone grumbles, "What a day! The sun burns your skin off. Were it not for Ram Pundit, I wouldn't have stirred out of the house."

"A good man he was," another one says. "So learned and kind. A real pundit."

"So he was. So he was." More join in.

"But unfortunate. Not to have a son was bad enough, but to be cremated by the daughter? What else is misfortune?"

"And she is so stubborn. I hear she came back from Amreeka a few days ago."

"That's why she can't understand our customs and traditions."

"Poor Ram Pundit!"

"The wife died long ago, no son and no one except a half-crazy sister and a daughter who's now Amreekan."

"Sh-h, she'll hear you. Don't forget she has a sharp tongue."

I keep walking. Without turning or lowering my head. I'm not surprised at their comments, not after this morning when, on hearing of my father's death, neighbors and acquaintances had gathered in the verandah. Their sympathy had soon turned into shock and resentment when I refused to let Keshav, a distant cousin of mine, perform Baba's last rites.

"He is the only male relative you have," the priest, a lean, sharp-eyed man in his fifties, said. "Who will perform your father's last rites?"

"I will."

"You?" His eyebrows shot up.

"I am his daughter."

There was a shocked silence. The wailing inside the house stopped. Men looked at me with amusement and pity as if they were dealing with a moron. As if I didn't know what I was saying.

"That's not possible. According to our dharma that's never done," the priest said. "It's grief that has so upset you, my daughter."

"I am not upset," I said, wiping my eyes with the back of my hand. "I'll do what a son would have done."

"But that's not allowed." An elderly man, dressed in white *kurta* and *dhoti*, went into a brief explanation of the Hindu *Shastras* which forbade women from participating in the death rites, which only a son, or, in his absence, a male relative, could perform. "Keshav will do what is necessary."

"No!"

The group broke into a buzz. Someone raised his voice above the noise. "We can't be a party to that which our dharma doesn't allow."

They were taking my resolve as a slight to Hindu traditions and social customs.

"Please let her do what she wants to do," Keshav pleaded. He looked embarrassed.

"In that case—" the priest began.

"All of us will have to leave."

"No, don't leave," Bua, my widowed aunt, who had been standing behind a door, listening, came out into the verandah.

"Don't pay her any attention. She's crazy."

"And so is the niece."

"Crazy, huh?" The wildness of a trapped animal leaped up in Bua's dark eyes. "Call me and my niece crazy, do you? What about you? Your mother? Your daughter? Your whole family? Go, drown yourself in a handful of water. Shameless bunch—"

A mousy man blew his nose loudly and piped in, "Let's go. Leave the old woman and her niece to do as they will."

"Yes, let's go." The gathering rose as a body.

"Do as you wish," I said.

"Don't go," Keshav stepped forward. "You see, I can't do it, because I have to leave on official duty within an hour."

I looked at Keshav gratefully, but Bua's face crumpled as men got ready to depart. "But what about the cremation? It's a sin to leave the dead without giving them a proper cremation."

Placing my arm around Bua's quivering shoulders, I said, "You mustn't think that if these people go away, we can't get others to carry my father's body to the cremation ground. I will hire people. I will pay them."

The man in *khadi kurta* turned to me. "Madam, why are you creating problems for us? Do the right thing."

Even in my grief, I knew that by being addressed as Madam, I had been distanced. Not Anjali, not daughter, not even Bai—a nametag for a woman—just Madam, to stress my extraneous position. A foreigner among my own people.

A short fat man with a twitching eye remarked, "You don't understand,

Madam. You will have to atone for this breach of code. You will have to pay a priest to atone for the sin you will be committing."

The threat and posturing infuriated me. They were mistaken if they thought I was a lamb at the mercy of a pack of wolves. "I'm not committing a sin. I'll take my father's body to the electric crematorium," I said.

"She's right," Bua cried out, forgetting her grief. "Wait till I inform the local newspapers that people in this neighborhood refused to carry the body to the cremation ground because his daughter was going to perform the rites. Wait till the story comes out and the women's organization gets on your back."

Those turning to leave, halted in their tracks, glanced at each other.

"Calm down, Sister," the man wearing *khadi kurta* said. "We didn't say we wouldn't carry the body to the cremation ground."

Silence. No one said a word. No one moved.

"Why bring personal matters into newspapers?" the man continued after a while. "We'll do our dharma. Right?" He turned to the mute gathering. "Speak up brothers. Am I right?"

Some nodded. Some sat down. Some mumbled. One spoke up, "We'll follow our dharma. Let those who don't believe in theirs bear the consequences."

"Let's do the needful," Keshav said. "It's getting very hot."

A little past noon, when the rituals of cleansing the dead body and preparing it for the final journey had been completed, we started out on foot for the cremation ground. The sun was at its zenith; the heat, at its peak. The journey seemed to grow longer; the road lonelier.

Getting off the tar road now, we walk the dirt path to the crematorium—a barren land with eight concrete platforms for the pyres, a row of water faucets to wash, and a few neem trees for shade. The pall bearers stop near a platform where a *dom,* an attendant upon the pyres, is waiting. They lower the bier onto the platform, heave a sigh, and step aside for the priest to take over.

The priest draws away the beige silk shawl covering the corpse and tosses it into the hands of the *dom.* I flinch. My eyes linger on Baba's face—a clay mask with hollowed cheeks, pointed chin, pinched mouth, thin nose, and sunken eyes—expecting it to come alive. The *dom* arranges the logs over, and around, the body. The priest pours ghee on the logs.

More firewood. More ghee. More firewood. And more ghee.

Finally, the body is covered with ghee-soaked logs. The priest, chanting *slokas* for the peaceful return of Baba's soul, empties the ghee pot on the pyre. The *dom* steps aside, wiping the sweat from his thick neck with a smudged towel.

The priest quietly hands me a long tuft of dry grass, lighted from the embers brought from home in a clay pot. He asks me to walk counter-clockwise around the pyre, then torch the ghee-soaked twigs. They catch fire. Tiny flames race along the logs, licking Baba's feet, sprinting over his body, hopping on his chest. The dance of fire. "Pull him out," a voice screams inside my head. "He's your father. Pull him out." I heave ahead, then draw back.

"So she's scared now!" A voice snorts behind my back.

"We knew this was going to happen." Comments fall around me like gravel tumbling out of a sack ripped open.

"Absolutely. Our ancestors weren't fools to assign this ritual to men alone."

"It's not a woman's job. She's the only woman here."

"What can you expect from a woman who lives in Amreeka? An Indian no more."

An Indian no more? Does an assertion of my belief and what I consider right entitle this crowd to strip me of my identity? To cast me out as a pariah?

"Poor Ram Pundit! His soul won't find *gati*—it will just roam forever."

I dig my heels into the burning ground and swallow angry tears. My father's soul not finding *gati,* no release from the mortal bondage, because of me? His daughter? The thought is ridiculous.

"You know why I did this, Baba," I address the flames silently. "You understand, don't you?"

As if in response, the flames leap higher. Burn brighter. Baba's face appears in the fire, shinning like red gold, then melts away. A pungent odor of scorched cloth and singed flesh blends with the smell of burning wood and ghee. The smoke stings my eyes, an acrid smell pushes the bile up my throat. The priest continues to chant *slokas,* as if running over a memorized rehearsal. I find the general indifference unbearable and want to run away, to race all the way home, where my aunt, surrounded by neighboring women, is sitting in an empty house mourning her brother.

"Anjali Bai," the priest now adds the customary tag to my name. "It's time to perform the *kapal kriya.*"

He holds out a bamboo stick with a coconut pushed into the other end. I look at him blankly. "His head—with this," he says, motioning me to strike a blow.

Crack my father's skull?

Cold rivulets stream down my spine. I cringe. It isn't that I don't follow what is being asked of me. I do. It isn't that I hadn't thought out thus far. I had. But the enormity, the finality, the brutal reality of the task sinks in only now. I must perform the ritual that will finally liberate Baba's soul from the body.

"If you can't do it, Bai," the priest's voice is flat. "I will ask someone else to do it."

"She can't do it." Voices whisper.

"—doesn't have the nerve—"

"We knew it all along."

"Our *Shastras* are not idle gossip!"

"To show off is one thing, to do the real job, another. A woman can't be more than a woman."

Their words stab me, wrenching me out of my torpor. I grab the bamboo stick, and thrust the coconut into the flames. The impact with my father's skull sends firecrackers exploding inside my own skull. The priest chants, "May there be Peace everywhere! Peace and Peace alone! And may that Supreme Peace reign in our hearts!"

"Om Shantih! Shantih! Shantih!"

Men take chips of wood, a handful of whole grain, and toss them into the flames. Then they head to the faucets installed in a neat row under the open sky to wash themselves before returning home. I, however, stand rooted to the ground. Since women are not supposed to intrude upon the cremation ground, there is no enclosed space for me. No door marked WOMEN.

Dragging my feet to a *neem* tree I sink under its scant shade. Spikes of scorched grass dig into my palms. Those who came with the bier begin to depart. The priest stands talking to the *dom.* A little way off, a mutt and a cow have found refuge from the heat under the spreading banyan tree. Three lean men, *aghoris* perhaps, are seated under its shade. Followers of Lord Shiva, the monks hover around cremation grounds to smear their bodies with ashes from the fresh pyres. People treat them as pariahs. I look at them. They are either high on *charas* and *ganja* or indifferent to the surroundings. They do not pay me any attention. I wish I could join them, smoke *ganja,* and forget everything. For I, a Brahmin's daughter, raised in a family anchored in Hindu myths and rituals, have become an outcast. I had come from America to visit my father, not to cremate him. Not to cross religious lines, break social codes, or flout tradition. If I hadn't been here when he died, obviously, Keshav would have performed the death rites. But being here, I did what an offspring—son or daughter—should do.

"It's all over," I hear the priest's voice. Having finished his business, he has walked over to me. "Everyone has left, Bai," he says. "You too should go home now."

I don't answer, nor do I make an effort to get up and leave. The priest regards me with pity. Let him think I have lost my mind. I don't really care. He wraps the scarf around his head and walks away. I close my eyes, letting a fit of fresh tears roll down. I continue sitting in the sun, letting it dry my tears.

"You should go home." The voice is mellow. Startled I look up into a finely wrinkled face, the color of burnt sienna; his eyes, the color of moonless night. He holds a bucket in a gnarled hand. "I have brought you water to wash your hands."

Without a word, I hold out my cupped hands to receive the lukewarm stream. The hot wind feels cool on my wet face and hands and forearms. He sloshes the water remaining in the bucket on the patch of dried up grass which soaks it up instantly.

"Who are you?" I ask, feebly.

"A traveler. And you?"

I don't have the strength to solve riddles or ask questions. I fix my gaze at the steadily burning fire.

"He's at peace," he says gently. "Go home, child."

Would my father have done the same? Gone home to his rituals and duties? He would. That's what he must have done after lighting up my mother's pyre. That's what braced his life. Slowly, the fire inside me begins to subside. With one last glance at the pyre, I get up.

BETRAYAL

Belinda Chang

Waiting in the airport lounge, President Hu took out his cell and made two calls. The first was to Mrs. Hu in Taipei. "Hi, it's me . . . I've made it to Macau . . . ah, alright." He kept it to the point. The second call was also brief. "Hey there, what's up? I'm in Macau. Take a shower and wait up for me."

Hu returned the cell to his briefcase. He was a man in his fifties, a man who used pomade on his thinning hair, a man with a comb over. He had a square face; with the exception of several deep wrinkles between the eyebrows, it had no distinguishing features at all. It was the face of a middle-aged man, a weary, suspicious, dissatisfied face. Several times while he was waiting, complete strangers gave him a warm greeting and offered to shake his hand. He just shook his head: no, I'm not Manager Qiu. I'm not Chairman Chen. And I sure ain't Jim, Mark, or Jonathan. China-based Taiwanese businessmen and their employees all had English names, even if their jobs required no English at all.

Hu was wearing a pair of gray slacks. He was on the last hole of the belt, the result of years of convivial banquets with the mainlanders. His polished calfskin loafers matched with gray socks had been prepared for him by Xiuying. He'd had to go back to Taipei for a whole week for his mother's eightieth birthday celebrations. Xiuying and the children had made a huge fuss about everything. In bed the night before he left, Xiuying was clinging to him and nagging for all she was worth. How much longer would she have to put up with this?

"I trust you won't abandon this family. You might not want your old lady, but you'll always want your kids, right?"

Jacob did well in school, always in the top three in his class. Jasmine was Hu's little princess. How he used to look forward to coming home at the end of the day and doting on his daughter! Seven years before, he had ventured west into mainland China, all for his family's sake. After getting knocked down a lot at first, he was finally able to get his footing, stand firm and taste the fruits of success; yet for seven years he'd lost the joy of spending time with his darling daughter. Sixteen years old now, Jasmine wore thick glasses and had her mother's serious expression.

"Three years, just bear with me for three more years and I'll be ready to shut down the operation."

He had a factory in Shanghai's Songjiang Industrial Zone making high-quality plastic containers for an endless stream of customers. In the past two years he had even secured orders from world-class manufacturers and improved packaging production considerably. All he needed was a chance to sell the plant and he would have enough for the rest of his life.

"The good things only come to those who wait . . . "a familiar pop song echoed in his ears, but as soon as he opened his mouth to sing along he'd lost the tune. He gave a big yawn. Nobody understood him. His mother, wife and the kids just demanded things from him, none of them offering him the slightest bit of comfort.

There were only a couple of duty-free shops in the airport lounge. He bought a bottle of Estée Lauder's newest lotion and a tube of lipstick, a purchase which would have cost the average mainland worker a month's salary. He felt like a coffee. Walking past a fashion accessories store, he saw some of those gorgeous silk scarves. He went in and picked out an emerald chiffon kerchief embroidered with a luscious red peony.

When Hu came out of the Pudong Airport in Shanghai, his driver, Zhao, was already waiting by the door. Zhao was scrawny, with a washboard chest. Hu's complete opposite, Zhao always had a smile on his face and an apology on the tip of his tongue. He ingratiatingly took Hu's luggage and led the way to the lower lot where he had parked the black BMW.

The sedan raced through the metropolis. An autumn drizzle, illuminated by the lamplights of the buildings and the billboards on the Bund, veiled the city that never slept in an alluring haze, like the plum blossom in the rain—like the ill-fated imperial concubine in the ancient song. Hu squinted out the window at the endless flow of traffic. Could you tell Taipei and Shanghai apart anymore? He didn't know. This, too, was a land of luxury, a realm of voluptuous pleasures, but one that was bigger, deeper, more affecting, or simply unfathomable.

"How's everything, Zhao?"

"Everything's fine. Miss Tangyan attended a ballroom dancing class and went to Xintendi. Her country cousin was here, too, but he didn't come to the house. She took him to Nanjing East Road and Pearl City to do some shopping, and he left the same day."

Tangyan had mentioned this cousin of hers before they moved in together. "I won't let you be jealous!" Tangyan said with her arms around his neck. "He's my eldest uncle's son. We grew up together." Every time the cousin came to visit, Tangyan would get him to take things home for her. He was the only one in the family who knew about Hu. Everyone else thought she was a pink-collar worker in a foreign company. A college grad who was fluent in English and chic, Tangyan looked like a pink collar worker. Better to say she used to *be* a pink-collar worker, until old Hu had "headhunted" her—brought her over to his company.

They'd met at the Christmas party for Taiwanese corporate executives and entrepreneurs last year in the Grand Ballroom at the Paramount. It was an occasion to schmooze and party. An old Taiwanese entrepreneur like Hu, a man who had made it on the mainland, would receive a stack of business cards from those fresh off the boat. With a glass of red wine in one hand, Hu was humoring some, sizing up others. Oh well done! Where'd they find such a beautiful woman? She was dressed princess-style in a white lace dress and a golden bodice that hugged her frame. The flaxen curls of her perm bobbed prettily as she danced. What he found most appealing were those slender legs with sexy, shapely calves, a pair of lovely legs one saw once in a blue moon. Her golden three-inch heels tapped in time with the swing of her hips as she danced the cha cha, cha cha cha—hot damn!

When she finally came off the dance floor for a rest, Hu rushed up to introduce himself. Up close, minus the provocative dance moves, she was a completely different person. Sitting demurely, oval-faced and almond-eyed, she looked studious, like a schoolgirl. When things got hot and heavy, Hu usually went for foxy ladies, preferring girls on the fleshy side, but for some reason this slim schoolgirl made him ache with desire. She met his eager gaze with a sweet smile and introduced herself as a PR rep for a well-known international cosmetics firm.

From then on, Hu took her out every day. They went to the Bund to watch the pleasure boats, and the reflections of the boat lamps on the water were like dancing moons that shook and shattered on the waves. They had coffee in the Jinmao Plaza with a view of the cityscape by night. Hu listened to her reminisce in a faraway voice about her bitterly poor childhood in the countryside. How she would count down the days to New Year, when she was allowed a few feet of cheap patterned cloth for a new dress! In college, she'd worked as a private tutor, scrimping and saving until she eventually had enough to buy herself a fancy fur coat. What she wore underneath did not matter so much. The main thing was to look presentable.

"I just love to look pretty!" she said, puckering her mouth up daintily.

He gave her designer clothes and purses. In return, Tangyan gave him sweet kisses, one after another. He felt as if he was reliving the days when he would pamper Jasmine. He did not want other men to pamper her.

"Stay with me, sweetie, and I'll treat you right."

For their love nest, he purchased a two bedroom luxury refurbished apartment on an upscale block. He did his best to gratify Tangyan's desires, while she played her part by making him feel like he was on cloud nine. This was actually so much better than the guerrilla warfare approach to finding women, always hit and miss. He needed a safe haven, with a gentle, understanding woman waiting ashore.

To expand his market share, Hu often traveled the length of the country from north to south, from Harbin to Shenzhen, rushing back and forth between the major cities in all the provinces. When he was away, he needed Zhao to keep an eye on his woman. A very clever fellow, Zhao was from Shanghai and had been with him for three years.

Before he could even ring the bell, the door swung open and Tangyan flew into his arms, her body warm and silky.

"Did you bathe?" he asked softly. Tangyan writhed in his arms and said nothing.

"Wear this tonight," he said as he pulled out the green silk kerchief from his briefcase and draped it over her pretty head.

As old Hu was taking a shower, Tangyan pulled out the lingerie drawer of her wardrobe, in which she had sensual undergarments of every color and texture. She combed through her collection like a student looking for references in the library, or perhaps like a Shanghai housewife picking out the finest fruits in the market. She finally uncovered a red silk thong with sewn-on sequins to go with the scarf. Too gaudy. A further search revealed a pair of sultry raspberry-colored low-rise panties. A peony floated tantalizingly over the chiffon crotch. She was satisfied. She opened her shoe cabinet and took out a pair of silver pointed-toe heels. The props were all in place.

This was the second man she'd gone with. He'd been good to her, willing to spend: he immediately bought her whatever she wanted without flinching. She kept some of the trophies and sold the rest, saving almost enough to buy a place of her own. Her family had torn down the old house and built a new one a while back. Her parents were happy and her little sister had married well. She'd put her cousins through school. Her uncles would never have been able to afford the tuition on the income from the farm.

She trusted her judgment. She would find a tycoon with a heart of gold, go with him for a few years, and never worry about money again. She was a creature of vanity but kept a clear head, unlike some other girls who blew it all and ended up with nothing. She knew that the capital of youth would soon be spent.

She had a professional attitude and served her man to the best of her ability. He was very affectionate towards her and let her do everything she wanted. The only time she had felt constrained was when Mrs. Hu came to visit for a month over the summer. Jumping at every sound, old Hu was on edge the entire time. Apparently, his wife, from a well-to-do family in Taiwan, was not to be taken lightly, and if old Hu was caught cheating he could forget about ever seeing his children again.

That was also the month she ran into her college classmate, Songjun, on the subway. She got on at Xujiahui and it was packed. It was always like sardines down there, and people could get quite fierce trying to find a seat. Even if your destination was only two or three stops away, you just had to take an empty seat or you'd feel taken advantage of. A seventh person would squeeze onto a bench seat that could comfortably sit six, every time without fail. Everyone, no matter who, would be squashed together, the well-dressed white-collar worker cheek by jowl with the sweaty laborer, but you were always better off sitting. That day, some big fellow got up for his stop and Tangyan nimbly took his place, hardly filling the vacancy he left behind. There was really only half a seat left, but this woman just had to take it, pressing Tangyan up against the man beside her. Both of them shrank back slightly. She glanced over and saw it was Songjun.

They'd dated for a while during college. He was young, hot-headed and did not know how to woo a girl, so they had broken up. Here they were a few years later in Shanghai and Songjun had grown up. Still tall and strong, he looked debonair in a black Gap tank top and Levi's. He worked in the fashion industry as a sales rep and told her she could model. Really, a couple of years go by and he's such a sweet-talker. She told him she was in the PR department of an international brand-name cosmetics firm. She once was a salesgirl at one of the counters in the company's outlet and often used the name of the company when introducing herself.

She knew what she was doing, investing long term, enjoying it as long as it lasted. She wouldn't be able to do this forever. She would save some money and make other plans. People say that the first "buckct of gold" is always filthy, but after that you can roll in the dough and clean up your act. Yet Mrs. Hu's arrival gave her some new ideas. Her spirits were low that day on the subway, and she went a bit overboard chatting with Songjun and even got off at his stop. You couldn't blame her; it was still early—only five o'clock, a few hours until dark. What else was she going to do?

Songjun still remembered her fondness for pretty things. Seeing that she was dressed head to toe in designer labels, he knew that she wanted nought, that there was nothing he could afford to give her. So he took her to Shaoxing Road. It was a short street, only a few hundred yards long, with art galleries and studios and a few long-established publishing houses, cafes and tea shops. Speckled with white paint, the parasol trees along the way were in full bloom, and the sun was pouring down radiance, the light shattering into brilliant splinters as it passed through the chinks in the leaves. Their leather shoes clacked lightly against the sidewalk and she felt like a college student again, promenading with her beau. She had been in Shanghai for three years and had been to many high tone places, but she never knew this place existed.

Merrily, the two of them went in to check out several studios. The owners greeted them, assuming they were a couple. They seemed a perfect match. This was so different from her outings with old Hu; her fluid, youthful beauty next to his tired, stagnant age always attracted some strange looks. She went up to an oil painting of autumn leaves and checked the price. Perhaps one day she would buy it. That is the beauty of money—it can buy beautiful things. Songjun lingered in an art publisher's over reprints of old illustrated stories—there was *Madame White Snake*, *The Three Kingdoms*, and *Journey to the West*. He plunked himself down in one of the old chairs and wasn't getting up, so she, too, found a story to read, *The White Bone Demon Attacks Thrice*. They'd been reading a while when the owner asked them if they wanted tea. Songjun said yes and two cups made with tea bags were soon served. They read until it started to get a bit dark out. When they were on the way out the door without buying anything the owner charged them ten yuan for the tea. That cracked them up. It was like being kids again.

A few steps further and an elegant long white wall appeared. What fine family's fenced floral bower was this? They looked in and discovered it was actually a park designed to look like a secluded private garden. It had a little pond at the entrance with a few koi in it. There was also a sign there that read Take Caution Walking by the Lake. The two of them had another good laugh. Winding paths traversed the tranquil garden, leading to a covered corridor at the back. Nobody was there, so they sat down on the bench inside. How did that line go? The breeze blows, a bird cries, each sees the other in smiling eyes. She remembered the first time Songjun kissed her, in a pavilion in a little park. Before she got carried away there was a sudden rustling in the thicket outside, made by a man with his back to them who was undoing his fly. The two hurriedly stood up and left.

She told Songjun that sometimes when she was walking alone somewhere quiet she would get the funny feeling there was someone watching her, but when she turned to look it was just some guy looking for a place to relieve himself. Songjun laughed and said, "Someone must be following you. What man would not want to follow you?"

They were almost at the end of the street when she pulled him into an essential oils shop. They filled up the tiny space inside. Songjun seemed to be everywhere: his ears, his arms, his legs. She smelled roses, tea tree, and lavender while Songjun looked on smiling. If she wanted, he would buy something for her so she could have something to remind her of this happy encounter and excursion. Citron, jasmine, or bergamot? Which fragrance would embalm this moment in memory? She would need this memento, because she could not see Songjun again. They had not spent much on their walk down the street, but it had brought her such happiness. She was afraid.

They walked out of the store empty-handed and stood at the entrance. Two girls of about ten years old passed by and one of them pulled the other's sleeve and said, "This shop owner is such a snob. Last time, he wouldn't let us in!" The girls soon turned down a narrow alley, where some elderly people in well-worn grey-blue clothes were ambling in the evening cool. There were a few bamboo poles across the alley to dry clothes from. A woman in her pajamas was retrieving her laundry—perhaps the mother of one of those girls. The alley seemed quite a bit darker than the street, and older too. The sun set earlier in there. Tangyan shivered.

Hu left for Beijing first thing the next morning and would be back in three days. Tangyan slept in until nearly noon. She took out her new pearl grey dress and purple angora single-button cape and laid them out on the bed. Then she sat down at the mirror and piled her hair up, leaving a few stray wisps and curls to flutter and dangle. Glossy foundation was in this fall, along with shiny eye shadow and sparkly lipstick. She spread and traced and witnessed an exquisite, glowing face appear in the mirror, a face that gave her a feeling of festive delight.

When Tangyan stepped out of the building in her ankle boots, the car was already waiting at the door. Zhao was whistling under his breath while maintaining a respectful demeanor. He asked, "Where will you be going today, Miss Tangyan?"

"Take me to pick up Miss Jiang."

Obediently turning the car around, Zhao drove towards the Hongqiao District. He asked, "Miss Tangyan, will you luncheon with Miss Jiang?" and observed Tangyan's expression in the mirror. She looked stunning today. Every few days, she would meet up with Miss Jiang for lunch in some quirky little eatery. Miss Jiang was also in a relationship with a Taiwanese entrepreneur, a man who ran a metal processing business and was always traveling abroad. She had recently gotten into ballroom dancing, hiring a retired national-class instructor to take her on a tour of Shanghai's grand ballrooms to refine her skill. She would often drag Tangyan along. The boss didn't like it. Another thing the boss didn't like was when they went clubbing. He'd heard all of this driving them around. Sometimes they'd lower their voices and whisper into each other's ears so he couldn't listen in on the conversation. They were on guard against him, he felt. The two little vixens. The first time he'd driven the boss to pick Tangyan up, he could already see that the sweet young thing was a seductress. With that body and that strut, she was born to entice men. You only needed to take one look at her to know that only a man of means like the boss had the cash flows to keep her in clothes, let alone victuals and accommodation.

As Zhao weaved through the city street, an indescribable fragrance filled the car. A beautiful woman in a perfumed sedan—too bad they belonged to someone else. He glanced in the rearview mirror again and saw Tangyan looking out the window, a smile playing on the corners of her mouth. He couldn't help smiling as well. Seemed like the weather today would be particularly fine!

Miss Jiang got in. Petite, she wore a short, red leather miniskirt and a black cardigan with spangles. Combed up, her hair was wrapped with several coils of tinted beads. Like Tangyan she was very stylish, but she did not have the same allure, the power to make a man gratefully kneel at her feet and satisfy her every whim.

They got off at Hengshan Road. Zhao found a parking space and opened a copy of the Shanghai News, but he couldn't concentrate. He was thirty years old already but didn't even have a girlfriend, while a beautiful girl like Tangyan went and became someone's mistress. The boss had told him to keep a close eye on her. The boss wasn't stingy, paying him twice what other drivers got. Zhao was no ingrate, and would hold up his end of the bargain. In truth, the boss didn't have to tell him to keep his eye on Tangyan; he was doing that already. He took careful note of where she went, who she hung out with, what she bought, and even her mood. This one time, he remembered very clearly, one day during the month the boss's wife was visiting, the boss asked him to drive her to that Cloud Mountain Café they frequented. She was ten minutes late coming down, wearing large-frame sunglasses under an overcast sky. She got in the car without a word.

The boss's wife was nobody's fool. The first time he drove her around, she wormed out of him his family background and the boss's daily routine, including where he went after work and who he saw. He began to worry: what if she found out about Tangyan? A momentary lapse of attention and he made a wrong turn. Thank god the boss's wife didn't know the way. He calmed down at the realization that a total outsider wouldn't be able to spot the holes in his explanations. Still, he remained on alert the few times the boss's wife talked to him in private after that. The day before she took the kids back to Taiwan, she had him stop in front of a park. "Zhao, you get out, too, I need to speak to you." In the rearview mirror her eyes flashed daggers.

His cell rang. Tangyan said they were done eating and wanted to go to

Changle Road to buy dance shoes. When they got to the shoe store, Tangyan told him he didn't need to wait for them; they would be taking a stroll in a bit. He started driving in circles and found a space the second time around. He hurried back and stood behind a parasol tree across the street. The storefront was narrow. Five minutes went by and nothing. Just as he thought he had lost them, he spotted them around the corner, standing in front of a food vendor, each with a shoebox in hand. The vendor was selling autumn crabs he'd placed in two bamboo baskets on the ground. Tangyan bent down to look at the crabs as a leaf floated down, brushed her shoulder and, as if finally satisfied, fell down to the ground.

They kept moving ahead, and appeared to be walking along the street—there were many boutiques along the way. He followed from a distance. They walked quite slowly, stopping in the stores that looked interesting. A grown up man, he tended to take big strides, so he had to keep starting and stopping so he wouldn't get too close. He didn't know what he was doing. Even though the boss told him to keep tabs on Tangyan, he did not really have to follow them like this. Talking and laughing, they went into a place selling leather bags. He saw a public washroom nearby and suddenly felt the need to go.

Coming out, he nearly bumped into Tangyan. "Hey!" they both cried. Miss Jiang gasped with surprise.

"What are you doing here?"

"I, I had to use the washroom. My stomach wasn't feeling well, so I parked the car and . . . "

"We're going to the washroom as well," said Tangyan. "What a coincidence."

"Well, I guess there's no need for me to stick around."

"Zhao," Tangyan stopped him, "I won't be needing a ride today."

"Alright." He waved and hurried off.

The next afternoon at three, Tangyan came downstairs right on time. She smiled amiably at Zhao, releasing a day and night of tightness in his chest.

"Where to?"

"Wukang Road."

"Wukang Road?"

"Don't you know where Wukang Road is?"

"Yes, yes, I know where it is." Zhao forced himself to start driving.

"I went dancing with Miss Jiang yesterday," volunteered Tangyan. "She dragged me along. I said I was wearing boots, and she insisted I buy a pair of dance shoes—they're made in the USA, really comfortable. We were back before midnight."

"Aye."

"Do you believe me?"

Zhao's heart almost burst from his chest. "Believe you? I mean, why wouldn't I believe you?"

"Whatever." Tangyan didn't say anything else.

They arrived at Wukang Road. It was an old street; under the deep blue sky, shaded by yellow leaves, the irregularly spaced old Western-style residences on both sides of the street were exotic, but the poles poking out of the buildings were Chinese-style. Somehow the clothes hanging out to dry on the poles seemed more worn than they would if people were wearing them. There were five or six families living in each building—behind each sumptuous façade, a shabby interior, the correspondence between form and content long lost.

During the day, Wukang Road looked like an ordinary residential street, while in the evening the moonlight and the leafy shade would lend an enchanting ambiance to the trendy little shops and cafes tucked in between the homes. Why would she come here in the middle of the day?

"Zhao, you get out, too. There's something I'd like to speak to you about." In the rearview mirror, Tangyan's cold eyes flashed daggers. Zhao really wanted to get out of there, but instead he compliantly found a place to park.

He got out of the car, as if disarmed. Standing in front of her, he was nothing. He was even a little bit shorter than her. Tangyan turned and started walking, with him following submissively. Those toned, irresistible legs, the wondrous coordination of waist and hips, that straight back, those captivating curls: her swaying silhouette was oh so familiar. How many times had he quietly followed her like this, enthralled?

Tangyan stopped in front of one of the houses, glanced at him, and went in. For several nights now, he had watched her walk in. If he told the boss, she would evaporate like a drop of water, disappear into some remote corner of Shanghai with a new name and a new identity. He would never see her again.

He plodded on, stepping from a sun-lit world into an abysmal realm. There was a spiral staircase in there with a decorated banister, the carving nearly worn away, and on the windowpane was a thick coating of grime. Rays of afternoon sun angled in on the motes of dust wafting in the air. Mop handles dangled down from the upper floors. There was one door per floor, probably one floor per family. Over the grey door on the first floor was an equally grey window, through which he could make out a stack of cardboard boxes and a bicycle. Tangyan had already gone up several stairs. The tap, tap, tapping of her leather shoes echoed loudly through the silent, seemingly deserted building, harrying him.

What was there upstairs? A love nest for her and that man. For sure there would be a bed in there, soft as quicksand. What was he doing here?

The tapping of her footsteps stopped. Now all that echoed through the air was the sound of his heavy breathing. The sound of footsteps started again, this time coming back down. Zhao turned and ran.

"Zhao!"

The urgency in her voice made him stop. He turned round and saw Tangyan leaning against the banister, looking at him beseechingly.

"Zhao . . . "

"Miss Tangyan."

"I know that old Hu told you to keep an eye on me," said Tangyan, dewy-eyed. "You are too devoted to him. What did he promise you? Be careful you don't get left drinking hollow dumpling soup."

(As long as there is evidence I can hold in my hands, the terms I am promising you will immediately be fulfilled . . .)

"The boss has been always good to you. If he ever found out, it'd break his heart." Oh what long nights! All those long nights he shadowed her.

"Zhao, listen to me . . . "

"You shouldn't . . . betray . . . "

A hint of scorn flashed over Tangyan's glossy face, arced across the abyss of space between them and, like a long, thin needle, pierced his tender heart. Icily, she asked, "Tell me, how much do you want?"

(This amount would be enough to cover a down payment for a house. You could think about getting married . . .)

"I don't want your money."

"You don't want money? What were you tailing me for if not money? Just name your price!"

"I said no," Zhao's face turned crimson, but he still seemed to be smiling. "No!"

He rushed out, got in the car, and locked the door. She did not chase after him. What a fool he was, what an idiot! How could he let her see through him like that? Why didn't he have the guts to go up with her? She'd assumed it would be just that easy to buy him off with her body and her money. For him she had nothing but contempt.

There was only one thing he could do. He had no other choice but to become a betrayer. That evening, Zhao finally dialled that overseas number. It was the first call he'd ever made to Taipei.

"Hello, Mrs. Hu, it's me, Zhao . . . "

In the Stacks

Licia Canton

Should I grab them all and have a seat at one of the tables? Rita wondered.

"Bagnell . . . Harney, Iacovetta . . . Ramirez . . . Scarpaci . . . " she whispered.

The books were all on the same shelf at eye level. What luck. I won't have to roam about, she thought. And she wouldn't have to get the footstool. She hated getting up on that thing. She didn't have very good balance. It would be good to sit on it, though. Rita looked up and down the aisle to see if the stool was within reach.

She just wanted to look through the books. She wasn't sure she wanted to lug them all on the subway. She should have taken the car. It would have been easier on her back. But parking near the library was hard even at the end of the day. She didn't think there would be so many books to look through. Who would have thought, in a French university library. This is probably the last time I'll be here for a while, she thought.

She picked up Bagnell's *A Portrait of the Italian Canadians* and leafed through it. Rita had begun reading the introduction when she heard someone coming towards her.

"Excuse-moi," a man was trying to get past her.

"OK." She didn't look up. She moved over a bit but the man couldn't get through. She realized now how tight the aisle was and how wide she had become. He wasn't moving so she turned sideways.

"Sorry," Rita said in French. "Go ahead."

He moved over to the other side and then took a few steps back.

Rita continued reading Bagnell's book. She had read it years ago. She remembered. She had taken notes, but she might check it out of the library, she thought. They could ask her some historical questions. Rita wanted to be as prepared as possible even though she did not have a date yet. She did not want to waste any time. She had already wasted too much.

She picked up Ramirez's *The Italians of Montreal.* It was a dated book but still useful. And Ramirez taught in the history department at the university. She had never met him. He probably did not know about her research.

A light cough brought her back to the stacks. The man was still standing there. Not moving. She moved over slightly so he could reach the other shelves. He did not move.

Rita was uncomfortable with a man so close to her in the deserted library stacks. She remembered the man who had purposely stood behind her at the pharmacy while she pondered which brand to purchase. She had become increasingly nervous. She had walked out of the store without buying anything.

She turned around.

"Am I in your way?" she asked boldly.

He stood there tall, satchel in hand, leaning slightly against the stacks.

"J'attends," he grinned. "It's OK. Take your time. I'll wait."

"You are waiting for . . . ?" She looked at him quizzically. "What?"

"I need those books." He indicated the shelf.

"Which ones?" she asked, hopeful that he wasn't referring to the ones she needed.

"All of them," he answered.

"Oh." She wasn't sure if he was serious or just toying with her. He wasn't making a pass at her, was he? That belly of hers was sure to keep men away for a while. But she was weary of French-speaking artsy types who smiled too easily.

"You're looking at the books on Italian immigration. Right?" he asked.

"Yes," she said firmly. "Do you need to take them out?"

"I'd like to. But first, I'd like to browse through them." He smiled again.

He will not get these books, she thought. He was too self-confident for her liking.

"You're Italian, aren't you?" He caught her off guard.

She didn't look Italian, she'd been told. Red hair and freckles. Maybe it was that maternal glow she had now which brought out her Italianness. Or maybe it was the protective way she held the books.

"You don't look Italian," he said, "but I can tell."

"Oh." Rita stared at his jean jacket.

"I can tell by your accent. You speak a polished, correct French with a very slight inflection. You're anglophone Italian. Am I right?" He was beaming. Waiting for confirmation.

Who is this québécois, she wondered, telling me I have an accent. She did have an accent, when she spoke French. And when she spoke English. And when she spoke Italian. She spoke properly, but in Québec, if you don't speak like a québécois, you have an accent.

"I'm a Montrealer. Born in Italy. Raised in an Italian family in the east end. Went to English school. Studied French at Marie Clarac. Spanish in college. German in Germany. I speak a Venetian dialect with my parents.

Yes, I have an accent. Everyone does."

"I didn't ask for your CV," he chuckled. Then in a serious, kind voice: "I didn't want to offend you."

"No, of course not." It's the hormones, Rita said to herself.

"So where did the red hair come from? It's natural, right?"

"Now I could be offended by that," she smiled. "Do you know that there are twenty different regions in Italy? Do you know that not every Italian has dark hair and an olive complexion? Some are blond and have blue eyes or green eyes, and some have red hair like me."

"Of course I know that," he smiled.

"Oh?" Rita was intrigued.

"I know quite a bit about Italians. I'm from the east end, too."

"Oh."

"And my father is Italian," he grinned.

"Oh!"

"My name is Massimiliano." His pronunciation was perfect, mahs-see-mee-lee-ah-no but he put the accent on the o, as a francophone would. He looked québécois, he sounded québécois, but his name—a very long Italian name—was not a common one. This man was not a Tony, Frank or Joe.

She stared at him. He was not a Réal or Jean-Guy either.

Rita hadn't realized that she was hugging the books by Bagnell and Ramirez.

He smiled. He could tell she was confused.

"Nice to meet you," Massimiliano said, putting out his hand.

"Nice to meet you, too," Rita shifted the books and shook his hand. It was a genuine, firm handshake.

"My mother is a québécoise so I was raised in both cultures. But my father was the dominant force, of course. You know what I'm talking about, right? Italian men. Always right," he said. "I'm not like that."

She was surprised by his candor.

Italian men are all the same, she thought, whether they are born in Italy or not. She had stopped trying to convince herself otherwise.

"So you speak Italian then?" Rita asked.

"No, not at all."

His Italian father was the dominant force but he does not speak Italian, she thought. In all of her years at this university, all the hours she'd spent at the library, she had never seen him before. Where had he been hiding? This very québécois-looking, non-Italian speaking man, who had a very long name.

"So what do your friends call you?" she asked.

"Massimiliano," he said again with the accent on the o.

"I mean your francophone friends."

"I only have francophone friends . . . that's the way it is since I work in a francophone milieu and I don't speak Italian and I am uncomfortable with English. They call me Massimiliano. Everyone does."

"Not Max or Maxime?" she insisted.

"No. Why?" he laughed. "Why would I change my name? My name is Massimiliano. I like it. It's not Guy or Jean."

"Interesting! How about your mom and your girlfriend? What do they call you?"

"Massimiliano, of course! I have a mom, but no girlfriend," he said smiling.

He's a funny guy, she thought.

"We can speak English. That way you can tell me if I have an accent," Rita suggested.

"But I said I don't speak English."

"You must speak a little," she was surprised.

"I understand, but I don't speak."

"Why not?"

"I don't like the language," he said bluntly.

"You're serious?"

"Yes. And I went to French school, raised in a French neighborhood, work in a French office. No need to speak English. We're in Québec, remember?" He smiled again.

Oh no, so he is a *real* québécois, she thought. She did not want to get into a political debate.

"Yes. We're also in Canada," she smiled.

"Yes, but *I* live in Québec. Have you noticed that the signs are all in French?"

She sensed trouble looming in the next few minutes. She should just smile and leave it . . .

"What are you doing waiting for these English books then?" She couldn't help herself.

"I said I don't speak English, but I can certainly read it." He wasn't smiling now.

She wasn't sure if he didn't speak or if he refused to speak.

"Books on the history of Italians . . . " he said.

"Italians in *Canada*," she stressed.

" . . . for my thesis," he sighed. "My thesis is in anthropology. On Italians in Montreal . . . Écoute," Massimiliano was not annoyed. "Listen. I don't want to put pressure on you so why don't we take all the books and sit at a table?"

Rita wasn't sure what to say.

"We can go through them and decide which we need," he said, looking at her belly. "Besides you must be getting tired, standing here."

"Yes, good idea. I *am* getting tired of standing," she said. "Thank you." She was glad the mood had changed.

He picked up all of the books on the shelf. "I'll carry these," he said.

She glared at him.

"Don't worry, I won't run off with them," he teased, as if he could hear her thoughts. "I'm a good québécois-Italian guy."

She followed him slowly down the aisle.

"When are you due?" he asked as they reached the tables. There were very few people around on a Thursday night.

"In about ten days."

"Wow, you must be quite the multi-tasker," he said amused. "One of those women who wants it all."

Rita wasn't sure what to say to that. Was he being complimentary or critical? Was he making fun of a pregnant graduate student?

"I want to get my thesis out of the way. Just polishing it up. Getting references, reading for the defense. I don't have a date yet but I want to read as much as possible before the baby comes."

"Is the father Italian too?"

"Yes. *He* is dark and olive-skinned. Born here of Italian parents and if anyone asks him where, he'll say he is from St. Leonard. Won't say he's Italian though. He's Montreal-born."

"Oh you are a St. Leo dame, too. Very, very Italian then."

"Well, I adopted St. Leonard. Don't get me confused with the stereotypes," she said. The words had slipped out too quickly.

"Stereotypes? My thesis is in anthropology, remember?"

They sat in front of each other for the next forty-five minutes. He picked up one book at a time and wrote in his notebook. She read sections of Ramirez rapidly, worried that she might lose the book to the québécois anthropologist. She looked up at him every so often, and he smiled promptly every time. She was self-conscious, still unsure what to make of him.

He put the last book onto the pile on the table and put his notebook in his satchel. He waited for her to look up at him.

"I would ask you to join me for a coffee or a glass of wine, but you probably don't drink coffee or wine. And as a good Italian wife you will say 'no' because hubby is waiting for you."

She smiled at the fact that this very un-Italian man had asked and answered for her. She looked at her watch.

"It's 7:30. I'd like to get home in time to put my twins to bed."

"Twins?"

"Yes, I have two little girls."

"Oh. This is your third child then?"

"Yes . . . " she hesitated.

"An education and lots of children. Wow. A good little Italian girl." He wasn't teasing. His voice was serious, almost caring.

"Well . . . "

"I was married once," his voice was sad. "Now at my age . . . I look young, jean jacket and all, but I'm not. And I died many years ago when I lost her. I fell apart. I was so in love with her. I've only picked up my thesis again this year. I started it years ago. The therapy, the job . . . "

She was touched by his openness. She did not want to interrupt him.

"Now I want to finish. Coming here brings me back. Meeting you, like this, unexpectedly . . . " he sighed. "Sorry. I feel like I know you. I didn't mean to spill my whole story on you."

"Oh it's fine . . . I . . . " she paused.

"You have quite a bit of your own weight to carry," he chuckled. He was trying to get back into the happy-go-lucky guy she'd met in the stacks.

"You can take the books. I've waited fifteen years to come back, I can wait a couple more weeks or months."

"Are you sure?" she was sincere. "I probably won't have time to read them all."

"You take them home," he insisted.

"Massimiliano," Rita said softly. "We all have our stories. It's not always as it seems. I fell in love with the wrong man . . . And yes, now I am in a good place. But I know about therapy." Until then she had only ever said this to women.

"Give me your phone number and I will let you know when I bring the books back," she said warmly.

"Wow, a very pregnant, good Italian girl asking for my number!"

They laughed.

"I'm so happy to have met you," Massimiliano said, as he wrote his number on a scrap of paper. "I came over after work to look for books . . . And it looks like I found a friend."

Rita reached over to take his number and smiled.

Calendar Calendar Hanging on the Wall

Su Wei-chen

Tearing off a calendar page, Grandma came back to her room to write in her diary. With black ink on the paper, she wrote "hwa-hwa-hwa," the echo of life. Even far away, it could be heard.

After a while, on the calendar paper, new messages about daily life were transcribed, readily transferred through the corners of the house, and finally returned to Grandma's desk. After all, she was a ninety-year-old Grandma!

Mon Bien Aime,
It is nice to write to you from this little room. It is 5 p.m., the sun shines very softly above the village and the green hills; my window is open and the table is against the window.[1]

Each of the Fong Women learned from Grandma to enjoy keeping a diary. (Birds of the same feather flock together.) Grandma, the one belonging to the early republic, wrote with a fountain pen. (What's more, she favored Parker Ink; the Fong family was exhausted to find refills when it was in short supply!) Her daughters-in-law, as modern adults, used ball-point pens; Granddaughter A-Tong, with a comic temperament, loved pencils for they were ever peelable. What pen one preferred was not the point. The problem was, whilst daily trivia occupied the contents of each diary, Grandma's diary was like a Code Book. (First message in Morse code sent by Samuel Morse: What hath God wrought?) Her diary, kept for half a century, showed that something was hidden.

Another point was the choice of paper. For some unfathomable reason, Grandma started a diary on octavo, which was also used for domestic calendar paper. Due to its lightness and absorbency, she used such paper exclusively. Not until the late nineties, the era of increasing environmental awareness, was paper production cut so that the Fong family had to rustle up actual calendars for Grandma to write on. As fellow diary-keepers, they finally had to surrender to Grandma's insistence on calendar paper. But they did decide to train up a successor for themselves. A-Tong, the one on whom the Fong family had experimented, was nicknamed Pavlov. Given that

"Pavlov" was the Russian psychologist who trained dogs to expect food whenever he rang the bell, the Fong Residence became the modern Pavlov's laboratory.

From the very beginning, *Border Town* tells the story of a Grandfather living with his Granddaughter . . . *to a little mountain town called Chadong. By a narrow stream on the way to town was a little white pagoda, below which once lived a solitary family: an old man, a girl, and a yellow dog . . .*

The girl's mother, the ferryman's only child, had some fifteen years earlier come to know a soldier from Chadong through the customary exchange of amorous verses, sung by each in turn across the mountain valley. And that had led to trysts carried on behind the honest ferryman's back . . . [2]

Just starting her literary initiative, A-Tong was so preoccupied with knowing each mundane domestic triviality that she competed in grabbing knowledge with her family. They told her that rather than mundane occurrences, it is content that one writes in a diary, including people, things, time and space. "If so, could I write in calendar pages as Grandma does and come up with a content-based diary then? But we only have one calendar!" she answered. All day long, the little girl had been expecting to see relatives visit the Fong residence, such as Aunt Ellen. ("Were you in elementary school, Aunt Ellen?" "You idiot! Who hasn't been in primary school?" "Then I guess that I can talk to you for a while. Have you read 'Calendar Calendar Hanging on the Wall, Page Page Torn out of Time, I am anxious about it'? 'You are a crazy kid; Why do you talk such nonsense!" "I knew you hadn't studied it in primary school! We can't talk anymore!" She did give herself airs!)

But if no one came for a visit, she called them in a rush, then waited at the door, and once they arrived hurriedly dragged every newcomer upstairs. "Hurry up! Let's read the diary!" Ellen Zhu, with her belligerent nature, quickly squabbled back with this little girl. "Read it? Don't brag! We both know quite a few words!" Miss Zhu, with an unpredictable temper, was nicknamed by Grandma "Miss Contradiction" since Grandpa was charmed by the articles of Shaoxing counselor Lu Xun in the twenties: "What an idea! What strength!" Continuing to read, Grandma found that Miss Zhu was not so progressive that she could not but feel ambivalent about the works of Mao Dun, the author who lived in the same time period as Lu Xun but wrote about a lot of contradictions in old-fashioned families. Just for fun, Grandma nicknamed this Miss Zhu after him because the name "Mao Dun" sounds like "contradiction" in Chinese.

The Fong residence was an early-era, two-story building with one room upstairs and one downstairs; the upstairs, a master room, was chosen by Grandpa from the beginning. What a long, long time ago. In order to spare himself noise from the children, he took the upstairs as the very place where he could occupy a commanding position and leave all sounds behind at the same time. As a consultant in the government on economic policies and lecturing at the university at times, Grandpa had enough prestige to rid himself of noise. "Shall only men be protected from noise? Since he is so out of sight, what if the children have an accident?" As long as one referred to the Grandpa in the Fong family, Miss Ellen Zhu was sure to blame such a chauvinistic man. With both western and traditional temperament, Miss Contradiction, born into a family of import and export business, knew nothing cultivated but bills with pictures. But invited to the Fong resident for the first time, she was enlightened as she found the wall-hung calligraphy paintings really fascinating. The solemn "Copy from the Inscription of Hotae Wangbi" was her favorite—*when one leaves, the divine follows and drives on the shoulder. . . .* Or, in Xin Jiaxuan's *Poems,* a book of calligraphic style slender gold, she read these lines—*Not leading to Road of Chang-an, in Mountain temple I rest and rust the day. Keeping a pleasure to taste the untasted, I am gifted with an ungifted life.* She thanked Xin Jiaxuan's talent for articulating whatever she liked.

Also, thanks to Grandma's diary-keeping this joke survived: "See what we could do without an account!" (This was Grandpa's frequent quip). At the invitation of the Fong family, Ellen was strongly suggested to skim through Grandma's diary, since she was fascinated by the calligraphy paintings. She was so lost in such a temptation that Fong Chao, the boy she liked, had nothing to do with her fascination. It was said that the Fong sons were named in the order of precedence—*Wei Jing Nan Bei Chao* (Wei Jing Southern and Northern Dynasties) for inheriting the line of ancestors. But an arrival in Taiwan messed up the spirit. For example, Fong Chao, a model gentleman of the Fong family, proved a polite and shy man but liked lively and handsome girls. We can imagine with what trepidation he pursued Miss Ellen Zhu and how out-of-tune was his courtship.

Nelson, My Love,
I don't know why I love you so much on this grey cold Sunday, but I do.

But what was curious in Miss Ellen Zhu we cannot judge by her western appearances; it was fortunate that she, with a pure energy and straightforward nature, dared to take chances. Only seeing how the unlikely duet met each other could Grandma, having known a lot of people, know well what story was going to be told.

Here comes a chance. A night-long grand masquerade was held before the removal of an American military presence from Taiwan. Young Taipei ladies of note were busy dressing up, hoping that they could win someone's heart and fly away from here. Picking ancestral clothes from a hidden treasure box, Grandma calmly helped Fong Chao get dressed. How marvelous Miss Ellen Zhu made a culturally glorified strike! Before preparing to call for her, Fong Chao listened to Grandma's careful reminder: "If Ellen loses her temper and becomes contradictory, remain steady; neither follow nor rebel—let her torment herself!"

Dearest,
You say first you were not aware of me. Neither was I aware of you, that is the strangest thing in our whole story. . . . You see, it has never been very easy for me to live, though I am always very happy—maybe because I want so much to be happy. I like so much to live and I hate the idea of dying one day.

When the night fell, this handsome couple, driving by the Chung Shan N. Road where the American military club was located, made a three-quarter turn by the Grand Hotel—a palace reflected in the Keelung River alongside the dignified Taiyuan Grave of five hundred heroes whose bodies could not be found. And then both turned to the Western-style building of the American military club, a little fairy tale heaven.

. . . Households near the water appeared among peach and apricot blossoms. Come spring, one had only to look: wherever there were peach blossoms there was sure to be a home, and wherever there were people, you could stop for a drink . . .

Fully dressed men and women put on airs, like a plain cake wrapped in elegant fondant. Then Ellen said with a burst of energy, "What a displeasing story Cinderella is!" Excited but downcast at the same time, she could not be herself in these circumstances. "Let it be," said Fong Chao patiently, passing the test after all. At the highest moment of the party, the couple left and returned along the same road. But the night went from deep to deeper or, more exactly, the day was almost dawning. "Let it be," muttered Ellen again. At this time, Fong Chao could not but lean in for a kiss. She was silent and gazed at him, as if saying, "Did your mother tell you to kiss me? Women cannot resist the temptation to imagine legends!" Before the end of an era, Ellen was pushing herself so far forward that she asked for nothing else. Their legend would be spread in the city of Taipei for at least ten years.

Ellen emphasized that, "I don't know how Mamma could make it right! I must learn from her!" Admitting her inferiority, she gleefully began following Grandma. Since then, Miss Contradiction humbled herself and joined the Fong family; people called her the last Fong daughter-in-law. What was so extraordinary about the Fong daughters-in-law was that none of them ever criticized Grandma.

The so-called return to a unit meant that Grandma led five daughters-in-law and A-Tong.

Grandsons, grandsons everywhere . . . Grandma, however, refused to be called a grandmother. Not until A-Tong came from the clouds could she allow herself to be upgraded; what a modern version of an old tale—a single mother's sons finally succeeding. "What a long time she waited, suppressing her sadness!" said the mother of Ellen Zhu. The point was "suppression"! Ellen's mom used to be a diary-keeper as well, with a sharp-tongue but a soft heart, who loved shouting that Grandma could never give birth to a daughter; as did her sons: "Who could be blamed for this inheritance?" Let us see how dispirited Ellen Zhu also gave birth to three sons in succession, "three returned decks" of *Majan*—three hands of bad cards. "Nightmares have occupied my sleep since bearing the third son; I dare not sleep in case I dream of having another son," sighed Ellen Zhu.

Nelson, My Love,
Well, after this storm I became quiet again . . . the only woman I really like and respect is the old lady I spoke to you about. For the other ones I am something like a mother, an elder sister, but I do not feel they are my daughters. I do not wish any daughter.

As soon as A-Tong fell from the sky, the Fong family launched into the first year of the A-Tong era. Grandma formally declared that she and Grandpa would live with Fong Bei the Fourth.

Dear Simone,
I will not get along with this woman anymore. But one thing would remain. That is, one day I want to possess everything she used to give me during these three to four weeks—my place where I could live with my woman and even all my children together.

All families listened and listened well, for Grandma had lived in the house from the beginning; it was Fong Bei the Fourth getting married and living at home. Tian Linlin, wife of Fong Bei, gave birth to four sons before finally giving up. Now A-Tong was counted as her daughter so that she could justly live in the Fong's house. Secondly, because Grandma was the boss, Tian Linlin was given the responsibility of guarding the Madam of light and leading. No more Grandpa, however. Eight hundred years ago he forsook the family, especially Grandma herself, for a mistress. As was the fashion in those days, madams had learned to pretend to be unaware of all ill affairs.

Nelson, My Love:
Why can't I stay in your bed? And why can you lie in my bed so often?

Intellectual as he was, Grandpa however proved quite spiritually unqualified. Who hadn't heard Committee Leader Fong's guarded words: "Men, in a whole life, ask for nothing but romances, given we know nothing about what we will become in the next life." As Ellen Zhu listened to this, she could not resist accusing Grandpa: "Nonsense! How boastful he is! He forgets that he has not yet finished this life! If he were reincarnated into other creatures, even pigs would shun him!"

Since Grandpa was going too far, his "whore," taking advantage of such an occasion, blackmailed him for a marriage proposal: "You need to pay the price for it, given that we all know what kind of officer you, Fong the Second, are! How could I not know all too well? Only romances? Stop boasting of your ignorance!" she said, and gave him a deadline for his response. After all, she degraded Grandpa by calling him "Fong the Second."

At this time, this man of books, afraid of such a woman with her weapons, could not help but feel degraded for protecting his fame. The collections and research in the house were all he felt reluctant to leave behind. Since Grandma did not leave home, Grandpa had no time to pack his belongings. Anxious about the approaching due date, he was too nervous to collect himself.

Nelson, My Babe:
Next time, if you want to sleep with another woman, just do it! You did not do so before this time, so I regard it as a gift of love. But such a gift does not equal alimony; you owe me nothing, after all. In this sense, this gift is extremely dear. Allow me to say it again: please, forever tell me only the truth.

Who could forget that day? Desperate to run away, Grandpa, by writing a catering menu to ask Grandma to buy food materials at downtown Bei-da Market in person, lured her away from the house. In the menu, he made such a fuss over a feast of fat things that Grandma would have to spend a whole morning shopping; moreover, the paper and ink that he frequently used were ordered as well, available in the downtown's west side.

Then Grandma returned to a home that seemed burgled. Tightly holding the best xuan paper, she, with conflicting expressions, stood silently for a long time until she could no longer contain her fury: "What a real show, even though he planned to leave. It proves how stupid and cowardly Grandpa is."

It was completely dark. Blue light shone from the tail of a big firefly that flew past Cuicui in a burst of speed. She thought, "Let's see how far you can fly!"

She then went downstairs, washed and chopped all of the ingredients, and cooked up the feast according to Grandpa's menu. After dining, she went upstairs to write a diary entry: "Let us say cooking is analogous to falling in love: appropriate heating control, cutting skill, food materials and the right guests are required. Those knowing love will make you feel something inside, understanding that before really tasting a dish, you've already started to miss its flavor. Our Grandpa is the one good at this." A creative vacuum opened up since then. In that very year, even Fong Chao got married.

Darling,
Something rather sad is happening to his quiet house: people begin to come here . . . and it is over with our peaceful life.

On octavo calendar paper Grandma kept a diary. Each and every day, she carefully tore one piece of paper and densely filled in the blanks, ridding herself of dating the diary. (We live a story on-stage, according to *the Scripture.*) Now here's the strange part: the calendars had their own solar terms:

At 17:03 on Nov. 7 is Beginning Winter: at 18:06 let's plant broad beans, three-colored amaranths, leaf mustards, garlic and pumpkins. At 12:00 on Aug 26 is Heat's End. At 22:14 on Sep. 7 is White Due: one grows spinaches, cauliflowers, chilies, carrots, garlic, lettuce, blue cauliflowers, Chinese broccoli, Chinese cabbages, perillas, and three-colored amaranths. At 9:48 on Jul 7 is Slight Heat: the moment of dawn is 5:18 and the sunset's moment is 18:52. At seven o'clock on Aug 5 is Beginning Autumn: the sunrise's time is three o'clock and the moment of sunset is 18:40. At 23:18 on Jun 4 is Grain in Ear: a typical summer day as it is, one cannot grow plants with beard. At 13:22 on Jan. 27 is Great Cold: one plants cilantros, spinaches, crown daisies, eggplants, paddy rice, lotus roots, and white mushrooms; big dipper perches, white porgies, silver pormfrets, and sharks are available at the time.

Grandma made no reference to weather. (John Cage: "Which is wrong? The weather or our calendars?") If wanting to know the sun and humidity on that day, it was the calendar that the Fong family resorted to; none of them wanted to check the weather. After the day of each lunar Eve, they would bind Grandma's diary pages altogether. The Fong's calendar, based on the solar calendar, started on lunar New Year's Day and ended with lunar eve. After it was tied up, here came another seemingly new calendar.

In her early years, Grandma was quick in movement: she was capable of putting down the pen, doing some housework, and then returning to write afterwards. After years of this habit, Grandma always stood while writing so she could be ready to take action whenever she felt the inspiration. "What I remember is always the sight of Mom's back: she forever stood alone and kept a diary." Fong Chao said that he could never understand Grandma's insistence: "People eat if they feel hungry, make money to earn a living, and fall in love due to hormone changes. But why do people keep a diary?"

Taking care of Grandpa and children occupied Grandma's everyday life; but at the core of her life was Grandpa. Five children altogether did not require much more attention and care than one Grandpa: Grandma practiced a monogamous lifestyle as if believing in the only god.

Dear Simone:
I must return here, back to my typewriter and my loneliness as well, feeling something that needs my closeness; it is because you are so far away.

Nelson, My Husband:
I can give up traveling, entertainments, friends and the sweetness of Paris, staying with you forever. But I cannot live only for happiness and love: I cannot give up the place which means so much to my writing and work. It is not easy, given that love and happiness are so real and sure.

After Grandpa left, Grandma still kept her diary but began wavering in her belief, but she kept this doubt from her sons. The only thing that remained was the Fong family's habit of reading together: they read the diary without feeling any difference, for people were free to be lost in abstraction. Even though staying with Grandma, they found her the same. The way she saw Grandpa was how owls gaze at night, allowing only her to see it and see it normally.

My Own Old Owl,
I work and work, living more like an owl, because I don't accept the faces of

people in cafés and restaurants. . . . When all that is over, maybe I'll go, maybe you'll come, maybe we'll see each other again.

But those reading the diary did not include Ellen Zhu anymore; she despised Grandpa so much that she rejected him totally, let alone reviewing his headnotes and scripts with family members—as if seeing him in person. Her "three negations" were not listening to, not asking about, and not reading of Grandpa, so she declared that she would withdraw from the diary's readership. Ten years passed this way.

Dearest Man with the Golden Arm,
How is it when you write such good books you like such bad ones? Maybe you'll answer: how is it when you write such bad books you are so critical about good ones?

So she knew nothing about how those visions, different from all that had happened before, came through Grandma's diary. Another journey was launched, reborn from the ashes.

What's more, Grandma's appetite changed and became hearty. She started to paint a lot, practicing as a self-taught artist capable of creating pictures with their natural qualities. Mountains and figures were her most grounded memories, vaguely and dimly emerging from her calendar paper like some life-like fountain pen sketches. Octavo black-and-white memories had migrated from the north, through the south-west, to the east; they came across the East Ocean and arrived in Taiwan. (In the small Finn town of Aurora North, the Lapps, with their snow-white fur coats, drive reindeer sledges to places in lower latitudes; people call them "the chase.") Flocks of geese migrated to the south, from solar terms to seasons, through Beijing, Gui Zhou, Guangxi, to Taipei; suspiciously, the very map's coordinates were wiped out so that all stories belonged to nowhere. But those visions were not the point but rather the background, whilst the diary proved the key to all mysteries. Why? (Said writes, "Exile is one of the saddest fates") Didn't you understand? "What she wrote about was nothing but exile," said Fong Chao.

And then Ellen Zhu, after years, found her seemingly pregnant again: "No way! What bad luck!" Anxiously crying out for immediate proof, she set aside her principles and turned to Grandma's diary for clues.

After quite a long time, Ellen selected some dates of relevance to quickly skim through in the diary; even so, some uncanny passages popped up from time to time that broke into and transgressed Grandma's narratives of memory. Another story plot was just forming:

At dawn I was woken up by the rich aroma of sweet olives in a dream; with the warm spring wind last night, Grandpa woke up with a comforted face and allowed our home to be filled with his breath. With those fragrant sweet olives this autumn—what a good omen—let's shake flowers from the tree, before the dusk dew falls, to make wine: it not only helps with our tastes but also counts as a serving in Grandpa's birthday feast.

In unfamiliar territory, Grandma narrated her diary somewhat like novel chapters or literary sketches. Continental drift took place, with the average annual sub-zero temperature and even reaching seventy degrees below zero.

Indulging in a life of frozen plains, she let her blood flow as the ice migrated. Obsessed with breathing cold air, she, since the Inuit People moved to Greenland about one thousand years before Christ, felt that it was cold and getting colder. The star Polaris could be located near the W-shaped constellation: just find an intersection, then five times away from the distance. This diary, such a land-bridge, led all of them to be lost in the subtropical zone and to know nothing about all the lost writing time.

. . . Cuicui acted happy, running around outside the house singing. When not on the move, she sat in front of the house on the high bluffs, in the shade, playing her little bamboo flute . . .

Open to the public, Grandma's diary was laid out to be read by everyone: in an encyclopediac manner, one could look in it to see how much the rock-bottom price of Lee's credit association was, how many presents they'd given to General Chang when he acquired a daughter-in-law, what clothes they'd worn in a midwinter visit to the Zhao residence, what affairs they'd met with by chance on a shopping day in April, and whether Fong Chao had measles. Given that they were used to cross-checking their lives in it, the diary, according to Ellen Zhu, was "the ultimate reference book that was impossible to use!" The diary would be more readable if Grandpa, with his red-ink brush, had written some headnotes. Of course Grandpa simply entertained himself, showing off his handwriting.

Bei the Fourth invited both Grandpa and me to dine in a restaurant today; I found Taipei changing a lot during these years. Walking in downtown streets, there are buildings over buildings as if we are walking in an underground passage. Shops along streets are elegantly designed without losing uniqueness. And there is also the dense shade of some street trees reflected in shop windows, as if I had just returned to the most magical but ever-lost dream of youthful days.

Ellen, with several emotions playing across her face, knew Grandma hadn't left home for years. But how did she explain these narratives in the diary? Ellen rushed downstairs to find Tian Linlin to ask: "Did the Old Man return the day before yesterday?" "Did you read the diary?" implicitly answered Tian Linlin. Grandpa did not return; neither did they dine in a restaurant. Those street visions in the diary were very possibly based on something like either television shows or *Taipei Pictorial*; as it turns out, they had no idea where Grandma got them.

My Beloved One,
Paris is more beautiful than ever. I sat in the gardens of Luxembourg and I looked a long time to the bare black trees against the pale pink sky. I have a big cold and some fever, and so the whole day long I swallowed hot grog and some kind of pills; that made me a little stranger to myself. I felt different for once and enjoyed it.

The sisters-in-law, with tightly-closed lips, wished that they could keep the secret; however, was it a secret unknown to everyone? With dim thoughts, they drifted off course and fell into unknown territorial airspaces. Stuck in this same place for a long time, they saw the world from a new perspective: Grandma sat in a foggy window where the shadows of trees were reflected. Looking further inside, they vaguely pieced together a happy picture of the whole family. The problem was, they were not really "in." Life and dreams require a clear boundary lest one cross the line unknowingly. But from then on that line between reality and fantasy had disappeared for Grandma. The saddest part was that they could not keep in contact with that unreal nation.

Grandma arranged a banquet to celebrate Grandpa's sixtieth birthday, even though he was fifty-eight. Even adding in the ten months in his mother's body, it wasn't quite the proper number. Grandma did not bother to send out invitation cards; instead, the family celebrated his birthday as they always had before, a moderate party among family. They tried to maintain a proper spirit of family, forming their own small, small world.

Dearest Nelson of My Own,
Well, you say it was hard to die; it was hard for me, too, and in a way, it will never fade away. Now I have made a new life, in a definite way. But my love for you is more than a memory.

As the day approached, Grandma, asking ahead of time that all family members come, set out herself quite a banquet with a lot of time- and effort-consuming dishes obviously favored by Grandpa, such as garlic yellow croaker, shark fin with ginseng, ten varieties vegetarian, stewed winter bamboo shoot, stir-fried shepherd's purse leaves, oven-roasted eggplant, and stir-fried prawns with ginger and green onions. The family, while taking their seats, found all those dishes still steaming hot. Just skipping along with those delicacies, Grandma showed her well-trained cookery and good temperature control. It goes without saying that at Grandpa's exclusive seat, his favorite ivory moon white bowl and a pair of pagoda chopsticks inlaid with golden thread were arranged as before. Everything was bright and clean.

. . . where Cuicui stood . . . on the hilltop and listened for the longest time, letting those entrancing drumbeats carry her away to a festival in the past.

They were dining uncomfortably for fear that one of them might accidentally lay bare the truth. In an unusually formal manner, Grandma conducted the party as a ceremonial event; however, she did this in a mood of enjoyment. First, she greeted all the family members and asked them to sit in the order of generation and—for the first time—solemnly drank a toast. After several rounds of drinks, Fong Han, the first son of Fong Wei the First, mischievously occupied Grandpa's seat, and no one could persuade him to leave. The third generation of the Fong family was named in the sequence of major nationalities—Han, Manchu, Mongols, Hui (Muslims) and Tibetans. "That's Grandpa's own seat; how dare you, a child, take that seat!" shouted Fong Wei. "I see no Grandpa! This is my seat!" said Fong Han, giggling. Having drunk a little too much, Fong Wei was irritated that Grandpa had left them all but now, as an invisible man, sat with them as if nothing had happened. In response to Fong Wei's preparing to strike his son, Grandma said casually: "The Fong families did not used to beat kids; moreover, it is Grandpa's birthday so that we shall ask for luck anyhow." Those sons of *Wei Jing Nan Bei Chao* could do nothing but look at each other, face-to-face; knowing that Grandma was the boss, especially to their wives, they understood as well that their position as "Wei Jing Nan Bei Chao" could not compete with their sons' position in the name of nationalities, "Han, Manchu, Mongols, Hui, and Tibetans." Not only for the Fong family, Grandma also stood for the complex of history. Given that Grandpa was absent, laying blame was unnecessary. Thus the show went on.

Dearest You,
I am too tired and I miss you too much. You know, it is very hard to come back. It is very difficult for me to go through this coming back. There is something so sad in France, yet I love this sadness.

After several rounds of yearly shows, what the sons and daughters-in-law worried about first and foremost was Grandma's mental status; afterward they began wondering why things went wrong. (Calendar Calendar Hanging on the Wall, Page Page Torn out of Time, I am anxious about it.) Although they got used to the traditions, still some incidents came as surprises to them. Not until Fong-Fong, a fictional daughter, appeared in Grandma's diary did they sense the precariousness of their own status: how could they casually wait until their whole world changed in Grandma's mind? That's it: they had to live in it or were stuck with whatever Grandma created in that diary.

At the same time, it was a game. It would be safe if they didn't take it too seriously. Since then, the journey was embarked on freely, from the subtropics to Greenland and the North Pole. Only in the diary did Grandma's daughter exist. It worked if you thought of her as a character in a tale. Grandma needed someone to keep her company. In the same unidentifiable time period Cuicui, the girl in Shen Congwen's *Border Town*, kept watching Grandpa and their ferryboat; Simone de Beauvoir kept writing to Nelson Algren, her American secret love, for seventeen years (1947-1964); naturally, Grandma kept writing the life of her Fong-Fong in her diary:

Today Fong-Fong went to elementary school; it marks a key moment in her life. From today on, she will walk far forward. Accompanying her to school, both Grandpa and I walked through tall coconut palms and found this September morning as lovely as the beginning of the most beautiful journey. I was glad that Grandpa and Fong-Fong stay with me.

Fong-Fong became a member of the Fong family, living with them; what's uncanny was that they all felt the house become more crowded than before. "We've more or less given up some of our space," they thought. The reason was that Grandma was spending time with Fong-Fong; inspired by Grandpa, she made up her mind to consciously create Fong-Fong's life.

As a whole girl, the dual Fong-Fong made up by Grandma was her delight, anger, sorrow, and happiness. She progressed through adolescence and fell in love for the first time, missing nothing from a normal life.

Come winter, the white pagoda that had collapsed was good as new. The young man who had sung under the moonlight, softly lifting up Cuicui's soul from her dreams, had not yet returned to Chadong.

Ten years passed but it proved the same as a day living in the mountains. Grandma now led a life that fled from calendar dates: in order to live with Fong-Fong, she forgot her age and became younger and younger. If she died, Fong-Fong would find no way out. Her life itself relied on Grandma's real story, and so Grandma stubbornly kept living in reverse.

It was not until Grandma was unexpectedly laid up in bed that Fong-Fong weakened too. Every day, Ellen came home to keep Grandma company. And then Fong-Fong, turning into a young girl herself, was so crossed in love so that she committed suicide by taking drugs. So Grandma lay in the same way as Fong-Fong did. No words were necessary between mother- and daughter-in-law; it was the diary that kept all their thoughts. In that diary Grandma kept watching her dying Fong-Fong.

Repeatedly rushing to the border of death, Fong-Fong was like an aircraft addicted to flying to new lands. She survived after all while Grandma was also exhausted. Arising from the totem of the diary, Grandma witnessed the life of day after day, or a life having transcended the symbol of death:

Fong-Fong's wish to die, like a meteorite hitting the earth, made an enormous hole. As I hug you, I do not want to ask why: why did someone decide to leave? Why did my little girl love him so much? Why weren't you the one who just walked away? Love without meaning deserved nothing; how couldn't you understand? Return—through all these pains, with your highest speed, back to my side.

Closing the diary, Ellen Zhu mourned the exile in Grandma's sketch of life, for it passed through the present and showed Grandpa's prehistory, a self-genesis of ancient remains. How would later generations read it? Neither a legendary Mausoleum of the first Qin Emperor nor the city of Pompeii, it was modern time that was very much alive. Grandma knew nothing about the nonexistent history she had created; as always, she was a person hating to leave a place. Leaning on the bedside, Ellen Zhu gently held Grandma's hand and found it as big as a man's: "Mamma, one day Fong-Fong will understand for sure. Let us find solutions."

With tears covering her face, Grandma looked steadily at the front: "How do I explain it after her father comes back?" Who was Fong-Fong's father? Ellen Zhu did not ask and knew that no one would know.

They did not keep Fong-Fong at the end. It seemed that Grandma came to understand she was a dream and allowed Fong-Fong to leave her, but more importantly real life intervened: A-Tong appeared.

As if facing ruins of the house, Ellen Zhu sank straight down; she found a folded page, a sign marked by Grandma. She opened that page and read that Grandpa had returned to his homeland. "Everything happens in the diary!" she exclaimed.

The return of Grandpa evidently foreshadowed the birth of "Granddaughter" A-Tong. What was clear was that, in the future, only one of the two could exist.

On the day when Fong-Fong disappeared, Grandpa went abroad in the diary:

During the Slight Cold period, with the Star Ghost and in Xin Si Year, one shall not go to the west. Grandpa went abroad for the first time so that I saw him off in the Sungshan Airport: on Tunhua N. Road I found the treetops whistling and the tree-shadow waving, as a backyard of rich people. On the way through Japan for about three days, he would keep launching on an eastward trajectory, come across the International Date Line, and see himself two nights in a day. Why does he, whilst going to the west, travel in an eastward direction?

All of them saw Grandpa leaving westward.

In another book, in the folded page of a passage, Cuicui had an eternal wish to wait:

He may never come back; or perhaps he will be back tomorrow!

Afterward, could Grandpa come home still? In what way could he come back?

My Precious, Beloved Chicago Man,
We had nearly no night since we went to the East.

How did Grandpa pass away? Of course he died of women. It happened ten years after his "runaway."

Dearest Nelson:
No matter goodbye or parting-for-good, what I want to say was that I would not forget you.

On the burial day of Grandpa, the sons wore mourning to take part in the funeral procession. Just as they hid Grandpa's affair, they kept the funeral a secret from Grandma as well. After the funeral, the sons came home and concealed a baby girl, just a few days old and as small as a dehydrated mouse.

Dearest Nelson,
It was nice to hear about you before you died. . . . I did not feel like writing a letter neither, as long as you did not. . . . It would be nice to see you. I am fifty-five.

Only when A-Tong had been nurtured and gained some weight was she brought to Grandma; both of them recognized each other and laughed heartily. Here came the letter that kept them waiting so long: "Whose kid is it? Is it the daughter of Bei the Fourth? A-Tong's face is like your Dad!" She called sons in this manner since childhood: Wei the First, Jing the Second, Nan the Third, Bei the Fourth, and Chao the Fifth. Now A-Tong had her legitimacy too. Let her be Bei the Fourth's kid! The way A-Tong recognized parents was such a smooth turn that all Sons, as elders notwithstanding, had no idea what to do after that. A-Tong, like the youngest sister of them, was such a latecomer, arriving after forty years. So far, so close.

A-Tong grew up almost entirely in Grandma's room; Grandma said that Grandpa would love her. The first word uttered by A-Tong was "Grandpa" as well. In addition, A-Tong had also called out to the void: "Grandpa! Grandpa!" as if someone really stood there.

. . . Dusk draped the river in a thin coat of mist. A terrible thought suddenly occurred to Cuicui as she surveyed this scene: "Could Grandpa be dead?"

Day after day proceeded, and A-Tong turned ten years old.

From the very beginning, the story of *Border Town* started:

. . . As if by a miracle, the orphan lived and matured. In the batting of an eye, she had grown to be thirteen. Because of the compelling deep, emerald green of bamboo stands covering the mountains on either side by the stream where they lived, the old ferryman, without a second thought, named the girl after what was close at hand: Cuicui, or "Jade Green."

Then our A-Tong grew into a defiant little girl: with her thin waist and full bottom, she kept wondering all day long. For six years she kept a diary.

And then Grandma's dairy, written for dozens of years, was not on display anymore; no exhibition could be held in such a long time. No need to wait five decades, the diary was a living fossil, something you could visit, like those prehistoric cave paintings in the Caucasus, men—with medieval lizards, herds of cattle, goats, and cuspirostrisornis—danced, swam, and went hunting. . . . To those who wanted to archaeologize the life of ancients, here it was.

The days kept going by; since there was nothing abnormal about them, some called it a peaceful time. But one day, something fearful occurred: "The more afraid we are, the more the thing feared reveals itself to us," said Tian Lin-lin, the legitimate Mamma of A-Tong.

Dearest and Not-So-Stomach-Turning You:
How would chipmunks and orchid crows react to an upcoming winter?

Finding her way to the Fong residence, the birth mother of A-Tong came and mentioned Grandma's name. Before that day, the entire family had regarded her as dead.

Dearest Nelson,
November was a long sad month for, indeed, my mother was dying, and at last she died. But, as you say, how these old women cling to life! . . . The last three days she felt good, and slept nearly all the time: "Today, I have not lived." . . . Next time no mother will die and I'll not wait so long before answering you.

A-Tong went to school and the gateway was wide open. Grandma happened to answer the door, for she loved to do such chores during those years. Tian Lin-lin came out as she heard it. Grandma laughed with joy to face A-Tong's birth mother, without knowing that it was this woman who had destroyed half of her life. But Tian Lin-lin remembered everything. With a cold shoulder, Tian Lin-lin, holding the wrist of the visitor, secretly used her strength so that Grandma would not suspect anything. A-Tong's birthmother threatened to take A-Tong back and gave the Fong family a deadline to respond.

That's it. What were the odds of the family being thrown into chaos twice by the same woman? They kept it secret still. But it didn't work with A-Tong; somehow she just knew the existence of "that woman." Unlike before, although "that woman" did not know her flaw—A-Tong did not need her birth mother evidently—her blood revealed the secret. That would be more fatal than any kind of weakness.

. . . By now her father, the ferryman, knew what was happening, but he said

nothing, as if still unaware. He let the days pass as placidly as always. The daughter, feeling shame but also compassion, stayed at her father's side until the child was born, whereupon she went to the stream and drowned herself in the cold waters.

"That woman" made an urgent appointment. Earlier that night, all of them surrounded the table like King Arthur and his Knights of the Central Asian Round Table, the "paganism" of the Fong family. Everyone treasured words like gold. As if still in Grandpa's era, they were so self-respecting that they were afraid of hurting A-Tong. Of course no one would say: "We should have known better than to take A-Tong back. See! Here comes trouble!"

For supper, Grandma was allowed to eat half of a hand-made steamed bun—which charmed her utterly—and she went to bed well satisfied. Then the occasion, exactly like a midnight coven meeting, gathered all the children upstairs as before, no one missing. (*I also experience the anxious moodiness of travel . . . for those stay behind, whom I see on my return, their faces un-shadowed by dislocation or what seems to be enforced mobility, happy with their families, draped in a comfortable suit and raincoat . . .* Edward Said, *Out of Place*)

In Fong's house A-Tong's birth mother wanted to make a bargain; as soon as she came, she asked to see her daughter: "Shao-mi—that's her name given by her father!" "Didn't you forget that it's already night and kids need to go to bed? Let's return to our question: what do you want after seeing her?" said Ellen Zhu coldly, cutting straight to the point of contention. A-Tong's birth mother, obviously aged after these years, proved much more confused than before: "It's up to you—elder brothers and wives!"

"Who cares about them? Look at me!" Everyone turned their heads, followed the voice, and found A-Tong standing on the threshold and sternly staring upward at her birth mother.

Cuicui grew up under the sun and the wind, which turned her skin black as could be. The azure mountains and green brooks that met her eyes turned them clear and bright as crystal. Nature had brought her up and educated her, making her innocent and spirited, in every way like a little wild animal.

The Fong families had imagined the coming of this day thousands of times, but they were so simple and honest that this had never occurred to them; what a surprise to see A-Tong's strength. Never had such a trait shown in the Fong lineage. So it had been the right decision to bring in new genes.

A-Tong's birth mother became wooden at seeing the cold, inscrutable face of her little daughter. Immediately she regretted coming so late that A-Tong had developed her own thoughts already. "You want me to be your hostage? No way. Now you've seen me so that you can leave. If not, I'll sue you for abandonment!" So there was never a scene of mother and daughter, with tears and memories, reuniting and recognizing each other.

Here came a "strong" second generation in the Fong family in Taiwan; the elder generation, dominated by Grandpa, was more like flat paper persons.

"Don't be fooled by them; remember that I am your birth mother!" "No one deceives me. You know yourself in heart." Concisely and pithily, A-Tong thus announced and simultaneously bared her sensitivity and sophistication among people. The family—father-, mother-, uncle- and aunt-in-law—felt shamed but had their eyes opened. At that time, they should have asked such a person to carry out the negotiations. Ellen Zhu was a defiant one, but she was a daughter-in-law still. If Grandpa had stayed, how could they have had A-Tong?

Cuicui sat by the stream bank, observing everything out on the creek, which was now enveloped by the dusk. She also looked at the crowd of passengers on the ferryboat, including one who knocked the ashes out of his long-stemmed tobacco pipe by striking it against the side of the boat before lighting it with a sickle-shaped striker. She suddenly began to cry.

"What do you say? Make up your mind as soon as possible!" said A-Tong compellingly. For the first time, the Fong family would not wait for things to get worse. Neither wanting to be sued nor wanting to take A-Tong back after all, the woman could do nothing but be honest: "No wonder I don't want you since you're so bad." "It doesn't matter; everyone has a different destiny." Calm and strong, A-Tong was not moved a bit and looked like an adult. Where did her honest, straightforward traits come from? Let's attribute it to either a divine gift or the training of keeping a diary. When A-Tong saw the visitor out, she was secretly told something. Being just a kid after all, she turned around with tears in her eyes.

On the next day, A-Tong did not come home after school. A child like her would leave clues for sure; all of them skimmed through her diary and found a message: she didn't want others to disturb Grandma. After solving all these problems, she would come back.

Dear,

Once more the cab drove away and I saw your face for the last time; a little later I heard your voice for the last time, and there was grief in my heart, but in my ears I felt love.

Nobody knew how to tell Grandma; neither did Grandma ask. After five days with no news about A-Tong, Grandma gave up tearing off calendar pages as well. Let the old dates hang on the wall; it was as if these days had not passed, as if A-Tong had never existed.

Also, nobody knew in detail how A-Tong got along with her birth mother. All the money she had deposited in her postal office account had been withdrawn by her birth mother; nevertheless, the only condition was that not until Grandma passed away could they discuss it again: "You can do anything but come here!" A-Tong's fierceness was rational and clean, without retort.

After A-Tong came home, Grandma began tearing calendar pages again. No more did she leave the house. The Fong family had believed that all things were possible and even the most absurd thing could occur. Naturally, they formed themselves a group, which was called family. (" . . . a sort of dirigible suspended above new strange places, making our way through foreign cities but remaining untouched by them," said Said.) Ellen Zhu said, "Isn't it so?" Anyone could have a five-minute romance: Ellen Zhu, A-Tong's birthmother, Grandpa. . . . But it was only Grandma's diary that was kept for life.

Dear Beauvoir:
I am stuck here in a way as what I told you, as you know, my work is to write this city. But such a life does not allow me to have someone to talk to. That is, I'm caught in my own trap.

Writing and writing continually, Grandma suddenly broke out of her amnesia as if she had chosen to. But she had a symptom remaining, nibbling up her sense of time. In a gradual, secret manner, Grandma was losing memories; however, when she was herself, she would say: "Things occur to us and then fade away, right?" Signs are like buoys, when you see them move, there is already a problem. She did not know her sons but kept her diary still, with every word clearly written. In addition, she knew only A-Tong so that she formally gave her an infant name: Fong-Fong. It was the very name of a forever protagonist in Grandma's diary.

Did Grandma know A-Tong was the daughter of Grandpa's affair? How could she not know? But it was an ever-secret not to be revealed.

In this way, Grandpa kept living in the diary; until the day of his formal death, Grandma kept her diary unwritten to mourn for Grandpa. So he died again.

. . . Cuicui thought to herself: "Can it be true? Is Grandfather really dead?"

Before long, Grandma chose one date on the calendar to "follow him," announcing her own disappearance from the world of mortals.

Dearest You:
When all that is over, maybe I'll go, maybe you'll come, maybe we'll see each other again. I should like to say "farewell Chicago" before dying.

But that did not mean her diary would end. Her past self was still alive. Facing the river of familiar memory, she saw herself leaving the family and moving closer to the diary.

Shen Congwen believed, even though their lives were isolated from common societies, they, with tears and joy, shared similarities with other young lives in another land; they experienced love, hate, gain and loss and allowed themselves to be permeated, feeling cold and warmth and forgetting everything.

Soon, Grandma could neither recognize anyone before her eyes nor those of the past. Families pointed at Bei the Fourth and asked her: "Mamma, who is he?" "He is Grandpa!" And she asked back, "Who is Mamma?"

Then she came into another level of selective amnesia; she no longer knew anything, as if she had assumed her own death. At first, those coming for a visit pretended that she was fine but before long revealed themselves. She was still alive. Her visitors spoke about her in the past tense and exaggerated her story in front of her, as if they were acting in a Chinese opera: "How interesting she used to be! During lunar New Year, she'd invite us to dine, to play Majan, and even to leave with some souvenirs. No more, no more!" "She lived her life sincerely, not that talkative but always considerate of everyone. How understanding and reasonable she was. Alas! A good woman's life cut way too short." Grandma came together to listen when they were talking; those repeated words declared that Grandma, breathing still, was a dead-alive person. Yet the Fong family did not take these rumors seriously, for Grandma was quite alive though she did not recognize anyone. That she remembered to tear the calendar sheet everyday was the most evident proof of her very being. (It seemed that time, in a way, made sense to her still: if people distinguished four seasons by wrapping up clothes, it was by tearing pages off the calendar that Grandma lived.) At other times, she was a spirit: wandering around the house, eating after forgetting that she'd eaten, grasping a pen and writing. "Who could decide how we live?" said Ellen Zhu.

Nelson:
Walking in the Greenwich Road, I, sitting on the bench in Washing Square, felt that that old, phantom self has a body already.

After a few months, Grandma came to the state of not feeling full or cold. She would eat all the time if the family was not paying enough attention; she kept swallowing food and might be unaware of being full until it killed her. Thus the Fong family began to hide edible things from her so that Grandma thought that they were playing hide-and-seek! (Was this the way Grandpa disappeared, in a game?) She would be so excited to find something to put into her mouth. "It would almost be a farce if Grandpa was found!"

The drumbeats from afar had already begun to sound. She knew that this must mark the dragon boats, painted with their vermilion stripes, going into the river. It was still drizzling endlessly and a layer of mist hung over the creek.

A-Tong had a mission now—to watch Grandma. Grandma and Granddaughter painted together, grew flowers, and planted trees; A-Tong was good at soothing Grandma when the latter said that she was hungry: "Let us eat less, and be healthy." A-Tong was also gifted with shifting Grandma's attention: "Come! Let's tear the calendar. You could tear off one more page today; aren't you happy?"

On this day, the mother of Ellen Zhu asked both Daughter and Tian Lin-lin to appreciate ancient Chinese jade with her. In these years, she was cultivated a little but gave up keeping a diary after all; she saw it as juvenile and unproductive. Given it required day-after-day effort, she regarded it as a proof of misbehavior— an accumulation of sins, a record of guilt.

As soon as Mrs. Zhu came into the living room, Grandma went downstairs. Seeing her, Mrs. Zhu kept screaming as if encountering a spirit. Following the sound, A-Tong came out and composed herself to comfort her: "Grandma Zhu, that's my grandmother! Don't be scared!" Mrs. Zhu was soothed, in a way. "What are you doing, Mom?" asked Ellen Zhu bafflingly. Mrs. Zhu hadn't come for a visit for years; she used to listen to those rumors, expelling Grandma from her life and subconsciously thinking her dead. No wonder she was frightened when she saw Grandma. As for Grandma, she looked like she was just seeing a woman screaming at her and did not react. In reality, she could no longer recognize anyone—including relatives-in-law, colleagues, or other relationships. Messages no longer reached her.

Dearest Nelson,
I work, work, work, and nothing really happens.

At night, after Grandma finished writing in her diary, Tian Lin-lin looked it over in the same way as she checked A-Tong's homework. After that, she made a phone call to Ellen Zhu and read aloud: "Today Ellen came for a visit and screamed when seeing me as if I were dead already. Yes, someone has to die so that the lives of others can be changed. It is said that everything changes with time, but I wonder why I don't believe in 'change.' The only thing that will not be changed is change, such as death." Tian Lin-lin felt puzzled: "Mamma thought your mom was you." "Perhaps she didn't! Don't forget, normal time-space is meaningless to her and A-Tong," said Ellen Zhu in a low voice. Tian Lin-lin could not help but sigh: "Everything makes sense, really. Do you know that? I'm not afraid of such a thing. Though A-Tong keeps her company, it is still strange." This was the world of the diary, without depth of field:

The dawn hasn't yet arrived. I woke up in a way as if emptied out. What a strangely flat body it is, lying on the bed. There was never a moment as empty as now.

It was in Lanyu that the dawn of Taiwan shone, welcoming a new century. The sun rose at 6:33 and the century sunset was dated for the last time.

Dearest You,
I work on the last book of my memoirs; it will be much longer than the other ones.

1. De Beauvoir, Simone . *A Transatlantic Love Affair: Letters to Nelson Algren.* Trans. Ellen G. Reeves. New York: New Press, 1998. Print.
2. Shen, Congwen. *Border Town.* Trans. Jeffrey C. Kinkley. New York: Harper Perennial, 2009. Print.

TELLING

William Wall

In the high cold room there were sixteen boys. Each boy had the space for one bed and a bedside locker. Under each bed was a suitcase containing clothes, comics, football boots. In there went wet gear after games because it was forbidden to hang wet clothes on the bed for health reasons. Generally there was nothing in the bedside locker. Nobody had a watch or a clock because all time was marked by bells. At half past six, for example, a bell rang. Between then and the next bell at quarter to seven the boys were expected to wash and dress. At quarter to seven they were to move out of the dormitory towards the chapel. At seven o'clock the Mass bell rang. During Mass a little altar bell rang to inform them of the necessity to stand, sit or kneel. After Mass they were released for ten or fifteen minutes. Then at eight o'clock the refectory bell rang and they went in to breakfast. Breakfast was lumpy porridge and sometimes bread. A bell informed them that father Tunny would say grace. They all stood, repeated the prayer and its following injunctions and sat down again. At that point, although no bell rang, they had permission to eat. Tunny was a bastard and everybody hated him. Sometimes he added a decade of the rosary to the grace so the porridge was stone cold when they sat down. The tea also was cooling.

Tunny was the Dean of Discipline.

He was the only teacher they had no nicknamc for. Othcrs were Cocky, Snit, Weasel, Mucker. He was always just Tunny. Once a first year had gone to the staffroom and asked for Father Mucker. There had been laughing. Perhaps the priests and teachers knew their nicknames though they were supposed to be almost a secret code. But you could go the staffroom and ask for Father Tunny and there would be no laughing.

First class on a Monday morning was math with Tunny. It spoiled the weekend.

Tunny says, Come up to me Billy boy.

You go up and he hands you the chalk. He wants you to prove the theorem. So you start to draw the triangle or the line or whatever it is you have to draw. You start to write down the letters, a, b, c, or A, B, C. Capitals and smalls are important. You have to get them right. You know if you get them wrong because you hear Tunny snickering behind your back. You rub them out and change them, small for capital or vice versa. Then you start to put up the writing. If you get the first line wrong, that's when you know you're alive.

Tunny says, Turn round. You turn round. Hold out your hand.

You hold out your hand. He has a cane in a special pocket of his soutane. He holds your hand in a special way, with his thumb crooked over your thumb. He has soft fat hands. Your father would say he had never done a day's work in his life, hands like that. Whing the cane comes down. It is a special cutting pain, not like a punch or a slap or like getting hit with a stick or a ruler. The pain is a straight line across your palm from a to b. If he gets angry it comes across your wrist which is too much altogether and will make you cry or even scream. Don't make him angry. You get one on each hand.

Now can you do it?

Or

That might help you concentrate.

So you turn back to the blackboard. But now all you can think about is getting the line wrong again or getting the next line wrong and that whing and the pain. What you don't understand is that this is a commonplace. All over the world people are getting it in the neck for fucking up the first line of Pythagoras. It is how the system works and it's for your own good.

Father Tunny prowls the dormitories at night. Sometimes he slips inside in the dark and waits at the door. After the bell for lights out there is meant to be silence. No talking between the beds. And no getting out of bed. If he's there and all. In the dark. You can't see the crows in the dark because of the black soutane. I think there's someone there. Sssh. Sixteen boys listen. I think he's there. The light comes on.

Tunny says, He is there. Who was talking.

Nobody owns up. If you own up you will be caned.

If the boy who was talking does not admit it everyone will be caned.

That is the way Tunny talks. He has grammar. Nobody owns up.

Right, everybody out.

You all get out and stand beside the beds. Tunny comes to the first bed. Right, he says, bend over.

The boy bends over and Tunny pushes him down on the bed. He grabs the string of his pyjamas and pulls it down. We all see his bare bottom. We are embarrassed. Boys do not like other boys to see their bottoms. Whing, whing, whing, whing. Four across the bum. We can see stripes. Then another four. Eight laces. Oh Jesus. The boy is crying. I didn't do it, I wasn't talking.

Tell me who was talking after lights out?

I don't know, I swear I don't know.

Do not swear child, God does not want you swearing.

Whing, whing, whing. Whing.

Twelve.

Next boy.

Oh Jesus Mary and Joseph.

The next boy is crying already. He bends. Tunny pulls his pants down. Four quick ones. The same thing. Tell me. I don't know. Four more. Tell me now. Please Father I don't know.

Twelve again.

Next boy.

Next boy.

The same for each boy except the cane is getting harder. The stripes are like lines in a diagram. Intersecting lines, radiating. How to prove the theorem. Twelve lines is too much. Nobody knows the theorem for twelve lines.

You're next. He knows your name. He laced you that very morning for Pythagoras.

Billy boy, he says. He smiles when he says it. Come here to me Billy boy.

You don't know if you can stick it. You know who was talking. You take your twelve. After each four the pain is unbearable. That's why he stops to ask you. He wants you to feel it and know there's four more coming. You feel the pain in your hole and in your bollox and round in your belly. He's hitting low so he's coming close to the bollox all the time. Fuck the fucker, fuck the fucker. You say it in your head over and over again. Hoping you don't say it out loud.

Twelve of the best.

Next.

Nobody squeals. He cuts the second last boy. He draws blood. That's not supposed to happen. Each of us thinks if there was only someone we could tell. There is no one we can tell. It's not so much a secret as a thing that never happened. Nobody would believe it.

It's a song: Where have you been Billy boy, Billy boy.

It's just mocking. If he was another boy you'd fight him for that.

If he keeps it up you'll kill him. In the dark you can cry. Sixteen boys crying without a sound. In the dark you can plan ways of killing him. You try to think of the worst ways. But none hurt as much because they end.

Come up to my room after ref Billy boy, he said. So at ref you couldn't eat a thing. You went into his room. There was a smell of polish. There was a fire burning in the grate. There was a comfortable chair. There was a desk and another chair. The Dean's room was in the same part of the building where the boys' dormitories were because he was the Dean of Discipline. The other priests lived in a different part through a big wooden door with Private written over it. Also in Irish *Príobháideach.*

Tunny was sitting in the armchair.

Come here to me Billy boy, he said.

You were to stand in front of him. He pointed at the spot on the carpet. You went and you stood where he said. He likes you, someone said. If he likes me. You don't know what's happening, standing there on the spot on the carpet. You start to cry.

Don't cry Billy boy, he says, I'm not going to hurt you.

And when you went home for Christmas your mother said, How are you getting on with your cousin Father Tunny?

He's not my cousin, you said.

You said it without thinking but then you knew it was true. Of course he was your cousin.

It was a boarding school. How else could they afford it? Now you remembered seeing him before. In your own house. He pinched your cheek one time. A long time ago.

I was always one of his favorites, your mother said, smiling like a baby. When I was a little girl.

And that was the end of something too. Not innocence, of course, because childhood is a myth. Not childhood either. And it was not the end of love. But something ended that day and nothing has ever taken its place.

You twisted your ankle, turning suddenly to catch the ball. They sent you to the infirmary and the sister gave you aspirin and a cold compress. So you were sitting on a chair there with your foot on another chair and she was talking about the big strong men that were there when she was a girl and how they could lift this much or that much and how they used to challenge each other outside the blacksmith forge and the blacksmith could lift the anvil and no one else could. How old was she anyway? In those days you thought she was a hundred or more and maybe she was. She was a little wizened woman with a twist in her spine. People said she couldn't lie down in a bed because of that twist. And then other people said that nuns never lay down in bed anyway because of the temptation. They had to sleep with their hands outside the blankets. But she kept putting cold compresses on your ankle and chattering like she never met people and you were quite happy for once, for one day in that place. And then there was a tap on the door and Tunny came in.

How's the patient, Sister Michael?

Oh he'll live father, Sister Michael said. Turned his ankle is all.

Will he be off games?

He will.

Well now, he said, I'll give him a note. We'll give him tomorrow off classes too.

Sister Michael beamed. Lucky boy, she said. Then she got up and went into the other room. And your gut twisted in the sack of your belly. Like an animal inside. You could think of nothing but fear blinded and deafened you.

He sat down where Sister Michael had been sitting.

How are we Billy, he said.

All right father.

That's my boy, he said.

He turned the compress. You should write a letter home, he said. How long is it now since you wrote to your poor mother? She must be thinking of you. I'll go and get pen and paper and you can write it while you're sitting here. It's better to have something to do.

All right father.

He came back in ten minutes with a letter pad, a pen and an envelope. He had a book too. It was *The Call of The Wild.* You read it afterwards. It was brilliant. He gave it into your hand. He didn't touch you. Then he took a bar of chocolate from his soutane.

He never said a word.

He looked around. The door to Sister Michael's dispensary room was closed. That was where she kept her pills. There were boys who were always talking about breaking in because there was good stuff in there. They never did.

He stood up. He kissed you softly on the forehead. Then he went out.

If ever you told anyone they would not have believed you. But you knew from the beginning that there was no telling.

Anna's Flags

Sylvia Petter

It was the little things, Anna thought. The ones you hardly noticed, like the single white hair that clings to your shoulder until someone like Mrs. Darton tweezes it off. Mrs. Darton was the middle-aged woman from the Catholic Fellowship who'd take Anna to Mass and check out her general well-being, like whether she'd been eating her greens, drinking enough, taking her medication.

Where were the keys, Anna thought. When they were on the sideboard, just beneath the hook labeled "keys," that was all right, but when three hours went by before they turned up in the butter, well, that was a waste of a perfectly good morning.

Recently, Anna Miller had been losing more and more perfectly good mornings, so that she even started to confuse the times she needed to take her medication. It didn't take long for Mrs. Darton to notice, and when she did she was quick to suggest that Anna move into a home.

Anna did not like the idea, although she knew deep down that Mrs. Darton was right; but she prayed that she might just not wake up one morning before Mrs. Darton came to take her to Mass.

Mass, or rather the Catholic Fellowship, had brought her Mrs. Darton, who one day stood on her doorstep. A cake sale was on over the road at the community hall to bring people together and incite them to help the needy. Christmas was just three months away.

"You don't have to be Catholic to buy a cake," Mrs. Darton had said. "And we even have Schwarzwälder Kirschtorte. Did you know that it doesn't come from the Black Forest? A baker in Bonn added the Kirschschnapps." She laughed.

Anna had stared at the small woman who seemed to be bouncing insider information as if hitting a tennis ball against a brick wall. "I am Catholic."

"All the better," she said.

"But I've lapsed, I'm afraid," Anna told her.

"No need to be."

Anna stroked one tip of her collar and Mrs. Darton leant forward and plucked a white hair from Anna's shoulder.

"Afraid? You can always pick up again. Do come on over and look at the cakes." And she turned and waved in the direction of the community hall and the people streaming towards it. "No doubt the Kirsch," Mrs. Darton said with a smirk.

Anna bought two slices of the Schwarzwälder Kirschtorte. One she ate at the coffee stand at the hall and the other she took home and put away in the freezer to have the next week after Mass. She glanced at the key rack and sighed. They were all there. But Mrs. Darton had said she'd have to be selective, only take special things, ones she couldn't bear to leave behind, like the photos of her husband and son.

All week Anna went through her cupboards and drawers. Every day she would place an item aside. The six-piece coffee set with the blue trim. The wine glasses. She wouldn't need all six anymore. Hadn't needed them in ages. Like the extra sheets and tablecloths in the dresser drawer. She would attend to those later. She had time.

The following Sunday, after she had thanked Mrs. Darton, Anna defrosted the Schwarzwälder Kirschtorte. She made herself a cup of tea, placed the cake on a plate and settled into the large armchair facing the front window. She began to eat. It was still very good although a bit soggy. She closed her eyes and savored the dark sweet chocolate cake with its slight tartness of spiked cherry. Suddenly she saw a jagged flash in a deep red sea of flags. She felt weak. Memories swam into each other. Red apples and bows on a small fir tree. The scent of mulled red wine and cinnamon. Christmas smells. And then flags, and farewells. She saw long-buried mind shots of Rothenburg ob der Tauber, the small town in Germany where she had been born. Bits and pieces. Snapshots and mind blasts. Are they all mine, Anna thought as she felt her pulse quicken.

Anna went to the dresser and opened the top drawer. She took out a ball of tissue paper the size of an orange and carefully unwrapped it. She gazed at the red glass bauble sprinkled with flecks of white and gold that she'd bought on a visit to Rothenburg a year after her son, Bill, had failed to come home. The medieval town now had a permanent Christmas shop just off the market square, which sold ornaments all year round. She remembered her awe. When was that now? She started counting. Over twenty years? Anna shook her head. There were too many memories.

Anna wrapped the bauble carefully. There was no going back there ever again. She would take the red bauble with her, she decided. Red was Christmas. Red was home. As she placed it back in the drawer her fingers touched material folded around two framed photos. Red. And blue. Yet red. Anna slipped the frames from the material and sat down in her rocker with the two flags. She stroked each one. One for Doug. Vietnam. The other for

Bill. She rocked gently.

Anna heard a tap at the window and then a voice. "Mrs. Miller?" Someone was watching her. Anna remembered her first days at high school. She couldn't speak English well then. She felt people staring at her. It eventually wore off the more her accent resembled their own. But her mother could never get used to the staring: "They will always see me as German," she said. "You will be lucky. You will become them."

Anna stood and moved to the window. There was nobody there. She looked over the road to the community hall and then gazed at Mary Callahan's front garden which was laced with the blue and mauve of freshly planted hydrangeas. Anna had seen Mary Callahan plant the row of potted plants. "It's the soil, the more alkaline, the bluer it gets. You can make it so," Mary had said. Anna didn't know which way the soil was, but the thought of changing its makeup just to get a different color of flower seemed somehow unnatural, if not plain wrong. She wondered if Mary Callahan was watching her now.

Then Anna heard the doorbell and a voice. "Are you ok, Mrs. Miller?" Anna opened the door.

Mary Callahan stood on the doorstep and smiled, buoyed by relief. "Get your flag. Come on over to community hall," she said and turned back over the road.

Anna stood in the doorway. People were congregating on the steps of community hall. They were dressed in long tunics with some sort of pajamas; the men had beards and flat sorts of hats, their fingers fiddled with beads as if counting a rosary; some of the women wore black veils, others colored ones. Lovely, Anna thought. The children had black hair; they were well behaved. No screeching and pulling. They seemed to be gentle folk, Anna thought, but she couldn't help feel a tinge of bitterness. They could have been the people who killed her son.

Anna looked for her keys. They were not on the sideboard. "Ah, on the rack where they belong," she said aloud. She dropped them into her pocket and pulled the door shut and crossed the street to where Mary Callahan was waiting.

"Didn't bring a flag Mrs. Miller?" Mary Callahan said with one eyebrow raised. "Doug and Bill would be right there with you." Her voice had a slight edge.

Anna stroked the side of her neck and slowly shook her head. Mary Callahan was too young to know.

"Take this one," Mary said and pushed a red-white-and-blue flag into her hand. "Hold it by the stick. Wave the flag."

She sounds a little like Mrs. Darton, Anna thought and smiled a thank you. Anna remembered the euphoria. She remembered standing with her mother, waving the flag to bid farewell to her father in uniform, a steel helmet almost covering his ears. Anna was five in 1939. Doug had been in uniform thirty years later and Bill had been only twenty-four when she waved the flag for what she thought was the last time. But now she was waving it again. Waving it for her husband and son.

"Go home," they shouted. Mary Callahan's voice rang through clearly. Then Anna heard another voice behind her. "Go home, it's Sunday." Mrs. Darton's hand was on Anna's shoulder, steering her towards the small group of strangers.

Then Anna saw the little girl. She was five or six. Her eyes were wide, almost frozen an instant before she turned her face into her mother's side. Moving away from Mrs. Darton, Anna let the flag glide from her hand and crossed back to her house. She trembled as she unlocked the door and her breathing became a little faster. She went to the dresser and wrapped the photo of each of her heroes in tissue paper, and moved them closer to the Christmas bauble. She closed her eyes and remembered a little girl in a crowd in a small town in Germany, waving a flag in a blur of red.

To Body To Chicken

Xu Xi

for Maggie H.

"*To chicken*, that should be a verb," Teresa said. The teacher asked if she was thinking of chickening out, or even funky-chickening. "The dance for losers," was what he said, cackling to himself. Teresa Teng Lai-sin shook her head, not comprehending either expression. What she was mulling over at English class that day was the Cantonese verb *jouh,* which the dictionary defined as *to do. To do chicken,* meaning *to be a prostitute,* sounded clumsy. *To chicken,* she decided. That made more sense. She explained as best she could in her halting English.

It was already 2007 when our story began, so this was not the famous Teresa Teng, romantic singer of yore, although our heroine's mother had been an ardent fan, and thus her daughter was named. *You're joking, right?* The manager at Big Boy Massage in Tsimshatsui laughed, the first day she came to work there, not believing it was really her name. Now, everyone at work called her Teng Lai-gwan, the singer's more familiar Chinese name.

But at English class that afternoon, in an airless office above a noodle shop near her job, Teresa didn't care what her name was.

The teacher was a young Norwegian who spoke with a clipped, exact accent. "No," he said. "*To chicken* is not a verb. What you mean is *to* be *a chicken.*" He paused, momentarily flummoxed, and added, "Although in English, that has a different meaning."

Teresa groaned. "So difficult. Need so many words to say one thing."

At work that evening, things were quiet for the first hour or so and she took the opportunity to review her lesson. If what the teacher said was true, then perhaps *to body* wasn't a verb either. *I body you,* she had wanted to say earlier, when asked to construct a sentence with a newly learned verb, but chose *chicken* instead because it was provocative, something the teacher seemed to like. *She chicken because she want to make a lot money.* The rest of the class had laughed in apparent comprehension; the teacher frowned.

"Twenty-five," the manager called Teresa's number. "Half part feet and one part body," he instructed in Cantonese. A *part,* as a session was called, fifty minutes being the unit, cost HK$225, the equivalent of US$29, a steal by many standards. The customer at the front counter was a thin blonde woman. Teresa brought her to the massage chair, where she prepared the water for a foot soak. "It's so peaceful in here," the woman said, as she leaned back into the undulating wooden rollers and dipped both feet into the basin below. "Such a nice way to end a long day of sightseeing." Teresa smiled. "I come back few minutes, okay?" "Okay," the customer said, closing her eyes.

Halfway through her full body massage, the customer raised her head. "Can I ask how you learned to do this? You're very good."

"Thank you very much," Teresa replied. Teresa knew Americans expected thanks for compliments, not that she minded since they tipped generously, but it was just odd. "I learn from Master Teacher."

"Here?"

"Yes. I am Hong Kong girl."

"You speak good English. Did you learn it at school?"

"I take English lessons now, because of job. Many foreign customers speak English."

"Mmmh," said the woman. She put her head back down and was silent for the rest of her seventy-five minutes, or one-and-a-half-part session.

In fact, Teresa had studied English at school, the way everyone else had, something she never admitted to tourists who wouldn't know anyway. Her school had been Chinese-medium, where the English teachers were not native speakers and some might even have considered *to body* quite an acceptable verb.

At each class, since she'd started these English lessons two months ago, her weekly assignment was to use a new word in a sentence. The first two weeks had been devoted to concrete nouns, and Teresa wondered whether *oil* could be considered concrete, given its liquid state. To describe what she did at work, she said *I help you push oil,* which was how the industry's language translated from Chinese, but the teacher suggested that *rub* might be a better verb to use for *oil.* After four lessons, Teresa concluded that English was nothing like in the dictionary.

But as she signed out of work that night, *I body you* echoed in her head. She had wanted to ask the teacher earlier whether or not this was correct, but he was generally so morose and stern that she felt questions were not very welcome.

Her father was up, unfortunately, when she arrived home.

"Late enough for you, hah? Young lady, one night you're going to be raped wandering around in the city like that."

"Please A-Ba. I'm tired."

"Of course you're tired! This 'night-style' work is always tiring. Lucky your mother's 'passed over life' so she doesn't have to cry in this life for you."

"Shut your mouth, can you? Just for one night? Besides, it's late. Come on, I'll take you to the bedroom."

She helped her half-blind father out of his chair and led him to his room. Her older brother was already asleep, but Teresa knew A-Ba sometimes suffered from insomnia and would stumble his way back into the living room just to annoy her. *I body you*—like the *om* of Zen—as she made sure her father was properly situated. *I body you.*

It was around five a.m. when a commotion woke her. Teresa peered out the window of their flat and saw the police leading away the woman who lived two doors down. Her brother joined her at the window. "So finally nabbed, huh? I figured they would."

"What're you on about?"

"Hey, don't you know anything? She's a chicken girl. Everybody knew. She as good as hung out a shingle."

Their father spoke from behind, making them both jump. "How dare she spoil our neighborhood!" He stumbled his way to the front door and opened it. "Chicken girl!" He yelled into the dark of the corridor. "Keep her away!" But the lift door had already closed on the arrested party.

Teresa followed her father out, and placed a hand on his shoulder to calm him. He shook it away. "Don't touch me! My own daughter is just as bad as a chicken girl!" He groped his way back into the flat, and shut the door in her face. Her brother opened it seconds later.

And what would she have done if her brother hadn't been home? On her way to work later that afternoon, Teresa pondered the question. There she had been, in just a thin nightgown out in public, and did her father even care? Her brother, her only sibling, was a security guard who worked varying shifts, often overnight. She dreaded being at home alone with A-Ba and sometimes stayed out after work at the open-all-nights until dawn, her excuse being that work ended late and she was too tired to travel the hour-long bus ride home. Her father believed she slept at quarters at work and she did not tell him otherwise. He wasn't all bad, really, but if only he weren't so unreasonably nasty when he got in his moods. He once told her that at *Dai Gor*, the Chinese name for *Big Boy* (literally, *older brother*), the *dai gors* she'd meet would all be no-good losers who would only be after her body.

I body you. I body you. The bus sped along the highway towards the terminus by the harbor.

The manager buzzed her in the back room. "Twenty-five, will you do a *gweilo?*"

"Feet or body?"

"Both."

"Do I have to? I'd really rather not."

"All the guys have customers. Look, I'll explain our rules and personally come by to check."

"Do I get extra?"

"Twenty."

One of the other girls said, "Go on, do it. If he likes you he'll leave a bigger tip. The guys always do, just like the women give the guys more also."

Teresa said okay, but when she saw the customer, she immediately regretted her decision. He was massive, like the Terminator or Hulk. Feet were fine and she had foot massaged many male customers of various nationalities, and even done a few full bodies for the Japanese and Korean men who found their way to Big Boy. This, however, was her first body for a white foreigner since she started here eight months ago.

On top of everything, he was the chatty type, and, she noticed, spoke English with a strange accent, stretching out sounds in a way she hadn't heard before, not like the English, American, or Australian customers she was now used to hearing. He didn't look European either, she didn't think.

The customer was saying. "I'm from Tennessee, do you know where that is?"

Teresa was leaning into his back, trying her best to manipulate his waist bone, which was difficult to locate. It wasn't fat, just muscle, way too much muscle. He probably worked out in the gym all the time, or took steroids, or both.

"No, I don't know where?"

"In the good ol' U.S. of A. You been there?"

"Not yet. One day I go. Your home, how to spell?"

He told her, then added. "They'd love you back home."

The manager called in English from outside the curtain. "No problem in there?"

"No problem," she replied.

"Miss," Tennessee asked. "Would you mind using a little oil?"

Dead, she thought, *I'm dead on fire.* And right after the manager had left as well, timing never being his strong suit. "Er, not allowed," she said.

The man lifted the back of the cover-up shirt all customers were required to wear for cross-gender massages. "My skin's awful dry, especially in the back." He pointed at the flaking skin around his waist. "Just a little, please."

Teresa hesitated. Normally, it was no problem if she pushed oil on a man's neck or shoulders when doing a head massage. For full body oil however, only male staff could do that for a man. He seemed decent enough, though, not a *haam saap lo,* "accidentally" trying to cop a feel. Saying "don't tell manager," she grabbed the bottle of oil and rubbed a little on his dry skin, and then quickly covered him up again. "Thank you, Miss," he said. "I'll take care of you later, promise."

He was good to his word too, she decided, when she emptied her tip box later. A crisp green fifty was in there, and she was sure it was from him. Yet on her way home aboard the bus that night, she couldn't help feeling bad. *I body. Om. I body. Om.* She did not chicken. No, she did not.

Teresa was off the next day and she took her father to *dim sum* brunch at their neighborhood tea house. An elderly couple and several women from their building were at the next table.

"Did you hear?" one of the women began. "Chicken girl made bail."

The man of the couple snorted. "Police are no good. They make the chickens themselves and let them out! Half her customers are cops, everyone knows that. The arrest was just for show."

His wife nudged his elbow. "*Wei,* shut up. No one wants to hear your dirty words."

"It doesn't matter," one of the women said. "Speaking 'white,' we all know she deserves our scorn. If she didn't own her place, a landlord would have thrown her out ages ago." Seeing Teresa and her father, the woman acknowledged them. "Uncle, I hope you weren't too disturbed the other night."

He squinted at the next table. "Ah, Mrs. Woo, isn't it? Kind of you to ask. No, my son and daughter closed the window and kept the noise out. They're good children, not like that one."

Teresa nodded and did not say anything.

The rest of the day, she took care of the laundry and grocery shopping for the week. Most days before heading out to work, she cooked dinner, which her father and brother could heat up in the microwave, but on her day off, she could eat with family. Lately, though, she found this a chore, wanting instead to study her English lessons, see friends, do anything rather than trap herself at home with him. She said so to her brother that night while the two of them cleaned up after dinner.

"I get tired, you know. Massage is hard work physically."

"Change jobs then, if it's too much."

"After all the time I spent learning the trade? No way. I like it most of the time, but I'd just like a little space for myself."

Her brother glanced at their father who was in front of the television. "He's nodded off already."

"Typical," she said.

"So go out. I'll stay with him." He handed her a bowl to dry. "You shouldn't let A-Ba get you, you know. He's just lonely. And cranky because he's arthritic," he added, grinning.

She dried the bowl and set it back in place on the kitchen shelf. "Where should I go at this hour?"

"That I can't tell you."

She took a walk in the park below their public housing estate. The evening was cool and winter was definitely in the air. Teresa liked the cold. It was less exhausting at work than in summer. Less disgusting too, what with some of the sweaty customers who came in when the weather was hot. Big Boy was a good place to work for now, better than the previous center, which had been one step up from a chicken farm. Her brother had warned her—*It'll be rough*—when she first said she wanted to learn massage. Then, she had dreams of working at one of the fancy hotel spas or ladies salons, where the rich *tai tais* went, but she soon discovered that the ladder was a long, slow climb.

I body you. English lessons were a step up to a better position.

When Tennessee showed up the next day, asking for number twenty-five, Teresa blanched. The manager accommodated his request without asking her. When she objected he said, "It's only foot today, and he behaved, didn't he?" She acquiesced, because business was slow and turning away a customer, no matter how good her reasons, was frowned upon.

"I looked for you yesterday," Tennessee said as he dipped his feet into the basin.

Teresa set the massage chair on high and pretended to busy herself. "Right temperature?" She asked, not looking up from the tap.

"Just perfect." He leaned back.

While his feet were soaking, her colleague who had seen the customer follow her, said. "Got yourself a boyfriend?"

"Shut your mouth. You know me better than that."

"*To body* is like that. Brings out the worst in you."

"Get lost."

But as she began on his left foot, after first wrapping the right in a warm towel, a deep unease cut through her. *I body you.* The words took on new meaning, and she didn't at all like what they implied.

Tennessee asked to raise the massage couch up from its prone position. "So's I can speak to you more easily," he explained.

She knelt beside his head and adjusted the lever. He turned to watch.

"Miss, you have a name?"

"Twenty-five."

"You're not just some number." Because she hesitated, he teased. "Come on, otherwise I'll call you Fairy Girl, 'cos you're as pretty as a fairy tale."

Against her better judgment, but because he hadn't tried to touch her, she told him: "Teresa."

"Like my mother."

She was back at the foot of the couch and had begun in on his left foot. "Really?"

"Yeah." He laughed quietly. "My sisters and I, we used to call her Mother Teresa."

That made her laugh too because she understood him. "Is your mother in," she stopped, trying to remember how to say where he came from. "Ten-Nussy?"

He shook his head. "No, she died last year."

The customer was quiet for several minutes after that and Teresa wished she knew what to say. She thought of appropriate Chinese expressions—*You have a hard time passing on*—but somehow, when she tried to frame the words in English they didn't come out right. How did you express sympathy to a stranger in a foreign tongue? Teresa concentrated on her work and remained silent as well.

Finally, she said. "My mother die . . . had died last year too. Cancer."

Tennessee stuck his head up and looked directly at her. "Oh honey, I'm sorry. You're much too young for that. My mother, she was just old and it was time. I'm very, very sorry for your loss."

She nodded, then looked up at him and smiled. "I sorry you too."

"Thank you, Teresa."

At the end of the session, Tennessee said he was leaving in the morning and discreetly handed her a folded hundred-dollar bill. She hesitated, because it was against the rules. "Go on," he said softly, flicking it towards her. "Take it. I won't tell." She did. Later, she saw that he'd also left her another fifty, one of the old violet banknotes that were gradually being phased out.

She was already on board the bus when her brother's text message bleeped. *Got to work tonight. Someone's out sick. Sorry I couldn't let you know earlier.* Teresa flipped her cell shut. *Dead.* Her father would be in a mean mood for sure.

A-Ba was dozing in front of the television when she returned, his dinner half eaten. Teresa wrapped up the remainder and put it into the fridge. She was about to wake him, but then decided to sit a moment first, before having to listen to him carp. She was thinking how wrong she'd been about Tennessee, who really was just a nice man making polite conversation, and a very generous customer. An extra hundred! And no cut to Big Boy. Nothing her father said tonight should matter.

She glanced at his sleeping form. He looked peaceful, the way he used to when Ma would massage his legs while he dozed. A-Ba's legs tended to cramp. The heavy work at construction sites didn't help although since the accident that nearly blinded him, he'd been on disability. And a royal pain.

A-Ba shifted. A faint smile lit his lips and it looked to Teresa as if he were holding a conversation, his lips moving, then stopped, and then moving again. She gazed at his legs: roughened skin, but muscular, lean, still strong. Then, she began to massage his knee joints, tentatively at first. When he didn't awaken, she pressed harder, working her fingers around the calf muscles, pulling at them, loosening the tightness, expertly feeling for the problem spots. *Lai-sin,* she thought she heard him murmur. Her mother's name, and hers. *Beautiful spirit* was how she explained her name to the teacher at the first English class, although later, when she looked up *sin* in the dictionary, she saw it also meant *fairy.*

After about ten minutes, her father opened his eyes. "You?"

"If not me then who?" She pressed his knee joints with both hands and tapped his legs as she would a customer. "There, you're done."

He nodded, groggy, then looked around. Teresa said, "I've put away your dinner already."

"Oh." He blinked. "I'll go to bed then."

"Okay." She helped him out of his chair and led him to safety.

Before she went to her room for the night, she dusted the altar where the death photo hung. The frame was slightly askew, angling her mother's face in such a way that made her look especially kind. For a moment, she wanted to play one of Ma's old Teresa Teng tapes, just like old times, when Ma would sing along. She didn't though, since it was too late and would disturb the neighborhood. Tomorrow, perhaps.

Tennessee, flying home in the morning. Teresa brought her English workbook into the bedroom to study before sleeping. Next lesson was to use a new place name in a sentence. She thought for a bit and then wrote: *The man from Tennessee said his mother had died last year, so I say I sorry him too.*

Section III

The Crying of Black-Browed Barbets

Tzeng Ch'ing-Wen

Translated by Angela Ku-Yuan Tzeng

It was midsummer in July and the mountain was full of the braying of black cicadas.

Shortly after ten in the morning, we climbed up to the hilltop of Elephant Mountain. Shadows of people moved here and there in the barbecue area under the shade of Formosa Acacias. We walked along the trail by the barbecue area and arrived at the Spring Life Garden, a small hilltop where two arbors were built and decorated with all kinds of sport equipment including horizontal bars, supporting frames for push-ups, and a walking trail made of black pebbles.

Some people were using the equipment, others were just stretching out. The long benches in the higher, larger arbor were almost entirely filled by visitors.

My wife put down her backpack, took off her shoes, and got on the walking trail. Some say this kind of exercise could facilitate a person's metabolism by stimulating the soles of the feet.

I didn't do the trail-walking, but walked to the long stone bench located in the lower, smaller arbor. I found myself a seat and put down my backpack and water bottle.

Right then I saw a couple in their seventies sitting on a stone bench across the arbor, having their breakfast. Was it breakfast? Or lunch?

The two of them sat on the same long stone bench, one at each end. On the top of the newspaper spread between them, there were an aluminum pot, a small liquor bottle, a small cup, and several side dishes, including bean curd and small dried fishes.

The woman poured a cup of liquor for the man, some kind of light yellow liquid. What would that be?

The man took the cup and had a sip.

"You shouldn't drink too much," the woman said as she took over the cup, finishing the drink in a single gulp.

After finishing the drink, the woman picked up something with chopsticks from the pot and put it in the man's mouth. It looked like a piece of pig liver cooked with sesame oil. Very few people ate pig liver nowadays, especially not cooked with sesame oil on this kind of hot day.

The woman watched the man finish the food and took out a towel to wipe his mouth for him, like an adult looking after a child or more like taking care of a patient.

From where I sat, the woman looked quite normal, but the whole face of the man had turned hot red, all the way to the ears, even to the top of his head. Of his hair, there was nothing left in the center part; there was only a little on the rim, more gray than black. It seemed that his hair had the tendency to be bold as well as turn gray.

At this moment, my wife had finished her trail-walking and came to the small arbor.

"Isn't that Mrs. Sun?"

Mrs. Sun was our neighbor twenty something years ago, when we lived in an alley on He-Ping East Road. In fact, our apartments were both on the third floor, back to back, with a very narrow, deep fire lane in between. Back then, my wife and Mrs. Sun often chatted across this narrow lane while they were cooking. Sometimes, when one of the two families had low water pressure for the faucet, the other would throw a hose over, as a private backup water supply.

My eyesight was not good; for the several years that we lived on He-Ping East Road I rarely came to our back balcony and I didn't have many chances to meet her on the street either, so I didn't recognize them. It didn't help that their appearances had changed so much.

"Uh, it's you."

"It has been so long."

"More than twenty years, isn't it?"

After a little calculation, we realized we had moved from He-Ping East Road over twenty-one years ago.

"Are you still living on He-Pint East Road?" My wife asked.

"Yes."

"With whom?"

"Just the two of us."

"All of your daughters are married?"

"Um."

I remembered they had four kids; the first two were girls, then a boy, and then one more girl. Their eldest daughter got married when we lived on He-Ping East Road. The second daughter was working, and the youngest was in senior high school.

Right before we left He-Ping East Road, something tragic happened to them. The only boy in the family died very suddenly during his military service.

Mr. Sun and the family never knew the real cause of death. The army said he died of heart disease. That was during a time you could only take their word for it. In fact, they didn't even see their son's body; all they had was the ashes. The army said it was not convenient to transport the body, so without any consent from the family they simply took the liberty of cremating his body. They had the death certificate signed by a medical officer: it said the COD was heart failure.

This was what appeared to happen, a story forced on the family. What really happened could be more complicated. Before and after we moved, there were many theories in our neighborhood. None of these included sickness and disease. It was said that he was beaten to death in the troop by three squad leaders.

The Suns' boy, quite rosy and plump, didn't really have any bad habits, but loved colorful clothes. He was very quiet. His actions were somewhat sluggish, which jeopardized the performance score of the squad. His senior officers had him sent for some reformation training, where he was accidentally beaten to death by squad leaders.

"How could this be possible?"

Others said that he was shot by a gun and because there were bullet holes on his body he was cremated. As for whether the gun accidentally went off, or he was shot to death, nobody knew.

There was no war in Taiwan; however, it was said that several accidents like this happened every year. As for the truth, nobody from the outside would ever know. Sometimes, when there were people returned from the troop, Sun's family went over to inquire. They all hemmed and hawed; nobody would tell the truth.

At that time, my wife had gone over to comfort them too. Mr. Sun didn't say a word. With bloodshot eyes, Mrs. Sun kept crying "My Darling Son, My Darling Son." She kept saying, "The one thing that we can never find peace with was we couldn't even see the body." It was said that Mr. Sun lost half of his hair in just one month, and the rest turned gray shortly after that.

"You are hiking too?" My wife asked because we have been hiking in the Elephant Mountain for more than ten years, but this was the first time we encountered them.

The Elephant Mountain was not high. The elevation was only a little more than one hundred and eighty meters; as a matter of fact, hiking here was more like going to a picnic. There was a huge barbecue area on the hill and the road went all the way to about tens meters from the barbecue area. This was a very popular route, actually.

Because of this popularity, there were arbors all over the mountain and were also many unlicensed constructions—some even looked like mansions. People came here to play ball, to drink tea, even to play Mahjong. However, very few people came up to drink wine, like the Suns.

"We are here to look for some kind of birds, Black-browed Barbets." said Mrs. Sun.

There were all kinds of birds on the Elephant Mountain. There were Chinese Bulbuls, Japanese White-eyes, sometimes there were also Chinese Hwameis, even Black-browed Barbets.

"Black-browed Barbets, we have seen them." My wife said.

Yet, we didn't know they would be particularly interested in Black-browed Barbets.

According to Mrs. Sun, their son Guang-Hsiung, the son who died in the army twenty-one years ago, had become a Black-browed Barbet through reincarnation.

"Reincarnation?"

"Please do not laugh, and do not take this as a superstition either. Guang-Hsiung had come back. One day, really late at night, I heard some cackle sound. I thought somebody was knocking at the door. That was not a dream, nor hallucination. We knew Guang-Hsiung had come back. If it had been a dream, or hallucination, we two wouldn't possibly both hear it. Isn't it, Mr. Sun?"

"Hmm."

"We went to ask the Gods, and the Gods said Guang-Hsiung has reincarnated as a bird, a very beautiful bird. Guang-Hsiung cared so much about how he looked when he was alive, so this fitted him too. In the past, Guang-Hsiung was too soft, and too naïve; otherwise, he probably would not be beaten to death. He should be tougher," Mrs. Sun said as she picked up some side dishes with chopsticks for Mr. Sun.

In fact, we only came to know about Black-browed Barbets in these one or two years. We recently learned that Black-browed Barbets had been printed on the stamps. We used those stamps before. This kind of bird, we saw them on the Yang Ming Mountain, as well as the Elephant Mountain. We heard that the habitat of this kind of Black-browed Barbet was in the mountain areas from two hundred to six or seven hundred meters high.

"The Elephant Mountain is not high. This is the most convenient place to see Black-browed Barbets."

Therefore, here they were, at the Elephant Mountain. They had been here more than ten times already. They had heard their chirping, only hadn't seen what they really looked like yet.

Black-browed Barbets were indeed very beautiful birds. They have green all over their bodies, with red, yellow, black and blue shades mixed on the head and the neck. This kind of bird was only a little bit larger than a Chinese Bulbul. It is said that they are very fierce.

In the Elephant Mountain, we sometimes heard their chirping too, only it was not easy to find them.

"Just now, before you came up, we heard them crying."

"Cheep, cheep, cheep," was a black cicada's chirping.

"Crack, crack, crack." It sounded more like knocking on the log, not like a bird chirping at all.

"Listen, here they come again. Their crying is just like somebody knocking at the door."

There were woods surrounded the two arbors including acacia, bamboo bushes, and various trees. Beneath these big trees, there were hibiscuses, lantanas, cannas and alpinias in the open areas, as well as ferns. The small arbor also served as a trellis with bougainvilleas spreading and winding all over it. Some of these plants grew on their own; others were planted. We also saw palm grass waving in the weeds. There was only one folding on the surface of a palm grass leaf this year, so people said there would only be one typhoon coming.

"Crack, crack, crack, crack."

The trees were too thick. We tried to follow the chirping, but couldn't see anything.

"There, look. Over there." My wife had good eyesight, she saw it first.

"Where?" the Suns stood up.

The leaves moved. Leaves were thicker at some places, but thinner in others.

"Nothing there."

"Yes, there is. Right there. On the small branch right above the split of the big branches."

"Not too loud," Mrs. Sun said.

"Sough." I was not sure if it was the sound of the bird flapping its wings, or of it flying through the leaves.

"Is it gone?"

"It's probably gone."

This time, all of us heard the crying, but, except for my wife, the other three didn't see the Black-browed Barbet.

The Suns sat back down on the stone bench.

"Would you like a drink?" Mrs. Sun asked us.

From end to end, it was Mrs. Sun in charge of everything. Again it was like she was taking care of a child. Was she like this when she took care of her child Guang-Hsiung? They said this child was too weak—was it because of over-protection?

"No." We didn't drink.

Mrs. Sun poured another cup and passed it to Mr. Sun.

"What are you drinking?"

"Whisky with soda." Mrs. Sun said.

Was this a way to drink? While I was wondering about this Mrs. Sun poured another cup of the drink and passed it to Mr. Sun. Mr. Sun still only drank half of the cup.

At this moment, not only his whole face but also Mr. Sun's neck and arms all turned thoroughly red.

"Alcohol is not healthy. Don't drink too much," My wife said as she picked up her backpack.

"We only brought this small bottle. Up here on the mountain, we would never over-drink. Besides, after adding the soda, it is not strong at all. I would never let him drink too much either."

Today, our schedule was delayed for about half an hour by this encounter. We took a look at the watch, said goodbye to them and headed down. And yet, while we were walking down from the mountain, I kept thinking of the scene up there, Mrs. Sun kept pouring drinks for Mr. Sun, but kept advising him not to over-drink at the same time, and the redness on the face of Mr. Sun, the same color as cooked crab.

The second time we ran into Mr. Sun in the Spring Life Garden at Elephant Mountain was more than two months later. At the time, the chirping of black cicadas was long gone. Autumn cicadas took their place instead. Autumn cicadas were much smaller than black cicadas, and the cheeping was not as busy either, yet it was much more ferocious.

This time, we only saw Mr. Sun by himself. He sat on the same stone bench, with the small wine bottle in hand. There was no small pot, no side dishes, not even the small cup. He drank from the bottle, took one gulp, then moved forward his hand a little bit, just like he was passing the bottle to another person. But that space where Mrs. Sun used to sit was empty now. His face, like before, was all a deep red.

"Where is Mrs. Sun?"

"Gone."

"She went down first?"

"No, she lives on the mountain. She will never leave again."

At first, we were a little bit confused. Mr. Sun told us that about one month ago Mrs. Sun suddenly had a stroke, went to the emergence room, and not even thirty-six hours she was gone.

More than two months ago, when we first met them on the mountain, Mr. Sun was the one we worried about, not Mrs. Sun. Who would think that it was Mrs. Sun who went first?

"It is fine, too, that she could leave without any worry." Mr. Sun's voice was all dried out.

Could she really leave without any worry? I thought of the way she took care of Mr. Sun.

"Cheep, cheep, cheep, cheep. Cheep, cheep, cheep, cheep," came another burst of the Autumn cicadas' crying.

"Today, have you heard any Black-browed Barbets crying?"

"Not anymore. Guang-Hsiung had come to pick up his mom. They left me here and would never come back again," he said, then put the bottle in his mouth and had another gulp.

"Black-browed Barbets must be still here somewhere," my wife said.

"You really don't believe what I say?"

"Now whom do you live with?"

"Me, alone."

Their apartment on He-Ping East Road was not big, only about one thousand square feet. But it must be too huge for only one person.

"How about your daughters?"

"They are all married, all belong to others."

Alone at home, what could he do? Sit? Walk around the house? Or keep drinking?

"Mr. Sun, don't drink too much." It seemed this was the only thing we could do.

"Drink too much? Actually, drink much, drink little, it all makes no difference now." Mr. Sun picked up the towel to wipe his mouth, and raised his head to glance at us.

At this moment, we found his eyes were wet and bloodshot, probably not merely from drinking.

We stood up. The weather was very dry and hot. It had not rained in Taiwan for a very long time. Several typhoons only swept by at a distance. Above the small arbor, bougainvilleas were still furiously blossoming. But, the lantanas had faded a bit and the palm grass had dried out too; the folds on the leaves meant to forecast the number of typhoons was no longer obvious. Did this mean the number of typhoons had changed?

We walked up and there were still many people by the big arbor Some were using the horizontal bar, some were doing push-ups, and others were walking on the pebble trail. People nowadays knew more and more about health, and took better and better care of themselves. Mr. Sun seemed to be an exception.

We turned to take another look at Mr. Sun then. We suddenly realized that at his back, several hundred meters away, there stood the Nan-Gang

Mountain, like a gigantic screen.

The Girl Next Door

Katie Singer

Here I am on this airplane, taking the same trip that Jaimee and her fellow passengers took that last day of her life. Only, as it turns out, I will probably manage to get to where I'm going with nothing worse than a headache. I am surrounded by grieving people—people who have lost children and spouses and parents, people whose lives are forever changed. We're all sitting on an airplane making a trip we never imagined we'd make.

To distract myself, I first focus on the flight attendant in front of me. Then I peer past her, into First Class and at the closed cockpit door—locked tight, I would imagine, against any possible terrorist threats as well as coffees served by flight attendants. I remember when we used to be able to get a good look at the control panel, the steering system . . . I would always scan the area just in case I could see the famous Black Box.

Of course the Black Box isn't even black— it wouldn't stand out in the midst of the gray fuselage at a crash site if it was. It's actually bright orange and usually kept in the back of the plane. Everyone who flies knows the back of the plane is the safest place to be. The few times Jaimee and I flew together I wanted to sit in one of the back rows. But she never liked being the last one to get off the plane.

The woman to my left is wearing a multi-color striped blouse; a bit festive for a somber occasion. I was mildly checking her out from the corner of my eye when she turned to me. Probably felt my stare. I gave her a gentle look, the one you give someone who is grieving; that kind of closed mouth, eyes down turned, slow nod look. Then I respectfully turned my head away.

I like the window seat; you just have to remember to go to the bathroom before boarding. I don't like being the one to initiate that flurry of unbuckling seat belts, replaced tray tables, etc. I like to just stay put if I can. I enjoy being in the air. It's anonymous. You rarely see anyone you know on an airplane. Now sometimes you meet an interesting stranger and then you get to enjoy that unique experience of anonymous intimacy. You know, it's not relevant up in the air whether you're a particular ethnic group, religion, a vegetarian, married . . . With the proximity of seating, and the sharing of a drink, an airplane cabin can feel like quite a friendly place.

Not that I think right now is a time to be friendly really—just pointing out the opportunities of air travel.

The woman in the striped shirt was the kind of mourner I respected; the quiet type. There were real sobbers a few rows up; loud, sniffling, moaning grievers sharing their emotions with everyone on board. It was embarrassing and a little annoying. Even after I put my headphones on, I could still hear weeping.

Unlike me, my ex-fiancée was not easily diverted. Jamiee probably could have read a novel written in Sanskrit through all the wailing on the plane today. Actually, she wasn't really a novel reader. She read trade journals mostly. And prospectuses, those thin sheeted over-sized pamphlets full of tight little words and numbers all squeezed together. She was smart, good with numbers. Could add anything up in her head in a minute. I really admired that about her.

I do believe that things like crying should be performed only in private, though. Inside a small, soundproofed room, if at all possible. I mean what is one supposed to do with a crying person? Have you ever tried calming a crying person? I did with Jamiee once. I thought that it was my duty to console her. I put my arm around her shoulder when she was crying, like they do on TV. I pulled her close. Her body went rigid. She stayed upright, resisting my pull, completely immobile. I tried to bring her near me a few more times until finally I just started laughing at the absurdity of this tug-of-war we were having. Jamiee did not find it funny. But she did stop crying. And of course now I can't even remember what would have made Jamiee cry in the first place. Something wasn't going her way and it was probably my fault. I guess I didn't always make it easy to be with me.

Jamiee is gone. And I am not devastated. I mean, even if she was still alive she wouldn't be my fiancée anymore. When her parents called to tell me the news, I got the impression that they thought the two of us were still engaged. If Jamiee was around I would ask her why in hell she never told her parents we broke up. Months ago! Instead, I am put in the awkward position of remains identifier, representative of a family that isn't even mine. Not that I resent an impromptu trip to Florida during an especially frigid New York winter. But it's still an awkward position to be in.

Mona, my seatmate—I glimpsed her name on the engraved gold plate of her leather daily planner—was doing pretty well. Just a little sniffling now and then. She thumbed through magazines and tried to sleep at one point. I watched her eyes close. She shut them with such a vengeance as if telling herself, "You will sleep, goddamit. And when you wake up this will all have been a dream." I wondered who she'd lost but it just doesn't seem right to go around asking people that question. How would I broach it? Well, of course I wasn't going to ask around; I wouldn't have known what to say in response to my own question. I mean at one time Jamiee and I were going to marry each other. That would have made her my fiancée. But everything got complicated.

I had a bad feeling on the phone that day her parents called me, beyond the obvious bad feeling that comes when a plane crashes with someone you know on it. I thought about it, but it seemed an inappropriate time to break the news to my ex-fiancee's parents that their daughter had died unengaged. Plus, I've never been to Fort Lauderdale before. Why her parents didn't make this trip themselves, though, still eludes me. Even if they *did* think I was their son-in-law to be. Maybe they were trying to give me space for my grief. I mean of course it would have been a horrible thing to have to do, to identify your daughter's body; I would have found someone else to do it if I were them, too. Perhaps they thought my youth would allow me the strength to handle things better. More probably, they figured it was my job. The Potters tended to respond to obstacles by paying someone else to overcome them.

Mona and I didn't speak; we just left each other alone. I admired her restraint and therefore decided I liked her. She was a good looking woman, somewhat older, but still had sexy legs. That was one of the upsides of sitting in the Exit rows, women had room to cross their legs. Of course it wasn't the time to make a move on her; I had some thinking to do. Like how was I going to get through these next few days? Was everybody else on this flight in mourning? Was there no one besides me making this pilgrimage simply because of a misunderstanding? Because they had to? Because they wanted to go to Florida? Across the aisle sat some real parents; the kind that actually came themselves instead of sending estranged fiancés. This couple held hands throughout the whole flight and barely spoke. They probably belonged to one of the college students who had been in the crash. They looked to be that age. Jamiee's plane was meant to land in Miami. Apparently a bunch of kids were headed to the beach for Presidents' Day weekend.

Besides the wailers up in the bulkhead, it's a fairly quiet flight. I can't tell what's happening in First Class, of course, because the flight attendants keep whipping that blue curtain closed every time they walk through it. I bet there are some people up there drowning their sorrows in free champagne. How did the airline even choose who got to sit up there? Or maybe those passengers are not even involved with the crash. Maybe those were just leftover seats on the flight. Maybe not every one of the victims had someone in their life willing to claim a body. That would mean that on this plane there were possibly some regular, airfare-paying clientele blithely on their way to surf and sun. They must wonder what kind of flight they've gotten onto. I mean, you can feel the depression in the air. No one would dare laugh or yell out in any way. I must say I am grateful for the mood. I mean no one feels encouraged to get up and socialize—that milling about by people as if they were at a cocktail party. Even the flight attendants are polite. Their demeanour is so reserved; speaking in soft tones, and only when necessary. My flight attendant didn't even flinch when I asked for the whole can of tonic he was pouring. He just handed it right over.

When I requested the extra bag of pretzels, however, Kenneth knew he was being tested, like a dog with a bone balanced on his nose. Kenneth was the flight attendant who made the announcements before we took off. As he introduced himself, I wondered if anyone named Jack or Nick ever signed up for that job. Perhaps names did predestine us at times. He elected to remain calm at my request, but I think he really wanted to gnaw at me. As flight attendants usually do. Why are they so mean? Really, it's a stereotype, but a fair one. They only seem to like a certain type of passenger. I haven't figured out what type exactly, but it's not my type. Maybe they like Jamiee's type. Jamiee never would have asked for the whole can of tonic (or *quinine* as she insisted on calling it) or request seconds on snacks. I wonder now if, all her life, Jamiee actually wanted seconds and full cans and that now, wherever she is, she wishes she had just asked for them. Life is short after all—finite anyway—and, well, I plan to ask for what I want.

With hindsight, I realize that soon after I learned about the crash would have been the perfect time to start things up with Jamiee's sister. I could have offered to call her for her parents, in case they just couldn't bring themselves to do it. Joanne is such a good person; of course she'd be heartbroken to lose her sister. But I know it would only be because she was a sister. The two had little in common. One was cold and critical and the other loving and encouraging. Why did I pick the former? Probably because I met her first, I didn't lay eyes on Joanne until the Fourth of July Party at the Potters' country club. She was wearing a red one-piece bathing suit, cut high at the legs. Her muscular thighs were long and lean. The top of the suit showed off her powerful, yet graceful shoulders—one of my weaknesses in a woman. It was a Speedo swimsuit. The insignia lay just above her left breast. I stared at that word, envying its position. I imagined how soft the Lycra would feel, how warm her skin probably was beneath the material. In my mind, my hand slipped underneath her strap and I could feel her breast.

When I was a kid, I knew a girl named Johanna. I admit that the similarity in names might have played some unconscious part in my attraction to Jaimee's sister. One day I was following Johanna home from school. Something I did quite often. She lived on Greenview where all the kids who were anybody lived. Johanna was walking home with her best friend, Karen. Karen was a classified loser at school. This made me admire Johanna all the more for hanging out with her. I shuffled behind, keeping at least seven squares of cement sidewalk between us. I was feeling desperate, as if I didn't talk to her that instant I would become invisible to her for the rest of my life. I finally quickened my pace until just before I reached her and then slowed to a casual walk as I passed the two girls.

"Hey," I said, "I'm going to McDonald's. Wanna come?" I was very pleased with the relaxed sound of my voice.

Johanna didn't say a word. She just looked over at Karen with an expression I couldn't quite place.

Finally Karen said, "Uh, no thanks, Marc. Johanna and I sorta had plans."

I slowed down my pace again. I accepted the rebuff without a fight. I had used all my strength in the asking. I decided to go on to McDonald's anyway. I ordered large fries and a strawberry milkshake. When it came time to pay, I fished around in my jeans for money and found nothing; I'd forgotten to put my small wad of bills back in my pants pocket. After apologizing to the cashier, I silently thanked fate. It would have been so much worse to have had the girls accept my offer only to discover that I had no money. This way there was still a chance, still a minute possibility that Johanna would say 'yes' next time. And next time I would have the money. At that moment, as I left the McDonald's, I decided I was a lucky guy and that the heavens were with me and that everything really did always happen for a reason.

I caught sight of something out the window of the plane, a particularly odd-shaped cloud. It seemed to stand vertically; it was tall instead of wide. It was as if the plane had turned itself all around and had me looking at things from the wrong perspective. This cloud was so unusual and I wondered if maybe Jamiee saw it right before she crashed. I realize that the particular cloud I was looking at could not have actually been there on the day of Jamiee's crash. But perhaps there was a similar one floating outside Jamiee's window at that time. And maybe she saw it as a sign, directing her to heaven. She didn't really believe in all that—heaven, signs, stuff like that. I'm not sure I do either. But when our life is clearly about to end, we people tend to start believing in a lot of things—real fast.

It's difficult for me to imagine Jamiee scared or ruffled. She probably didn't even notice that day if there was an initial drop in cabin pressure, or whether the wheels were disengaging for an emergency landing—all those sounds we listen for during take-offs and landings when most plane crashes occur. But Jamiee didn't consider those sorts of things. She was the kind who seated herself on an airplane and immediately flipped open her laptop—had to be reminded to turn it off for takeoff. No respect for the gravity of the situation, the laws of physics that are being challenged right and left. I always envied her that calm. She never needed three vodka and tonics to get her through a flight.

And it's not that I don't—didn't . . . Do you still love someone after they're dead? I mean of course you do. So it's not that I don't love Jamiee in some way. I mean, she was my fiancée at one point. I wanted to marry her, and spend the rest of my living days with her. She was very rich. I don't mean to say I loved her because she was rich. It just so happened that she was. It took me a while to declare my undying love to Jamiee. I am distrustful of those who would hurry such a thing. Feelings should be carefully doled out. Even in circumstances such as air crashes. Even when there are others in the seat next to you supposedly going through the same thing you are. That is still not enough in common for me. I believe a person's *environment* affects one's sensibilities—one's potential for bonding—much more than a single event ever could. An event is a one time deal, while environment wears away at a human being like waves over rocks. And that is how we are formed, just like the beach, by waves.

I will miss Jamiee. After the break-up we used to run into each other now and then in the hallway of our building. We lived on the same floor, it was inevitable. Neither one of us was willing to give up our own apartment after the split; we just returned to our original lives-down-the-hall-from-each-other as if nothing had ever happened. I watched her through the peephole now and then, and I must say she always looked good. A bag of groceries in one hand, briefcase in the other, she looked just like a shampoo commercial; successful, beautiful, extremely busy with very shiny hair. I loved her hair. I loved being seen with her. We looked good together. I really miss that.

The crash was not what caused the missing, of course. Things had fizzled out months before we even broke up and we both knew it. There wasn't any chance to get back to how we were. Just as I know now there wasn't any chance that Johanna would ever go to McDonald's with me. I have learned to accept things like that as I get older. And I know there will come a time when I will meet yet another woman and force myself to believe I'm in love. And I will put all sorts of effort into that relationship. And then there will come that moment, that moment where we look at each other and realize we're headed nowhere, that actually we've been losing altitude for quite some time. And hopefully I won't have said too much, won't be haunted by my words that should have gone down with the ship but instead might live on as a reminder of just how ridiculously optimistic a man can be. There's no such thing as a perfect relationship between a man and a woman. It's just about getting the best ingredients you can before it's too late and then seeing what you can make with what you've got.

Well, here we are. Fort Lauderdale, Florida. I just love the sight of palm trees. They're hopeful. I am actually feeling good about this trip. I mean not that it's a good trip to have to take but I plan to make the best of it. Sunny and eighty-six degrees won't hurt! Who is that woman standing in front of the cabin? Looks like she's going to make some sort of announcement. I love the color red on a blonde woman.

He Wasn't There Again Today

Kelly Cherry

At Burnham and Burnham the coffee cart made rounds at ten and three and there were doughnuts and bagels as well as coffee. Robert had a habit of skipping breakfast, because he knew the coffee cart would come around. On Tuesday the sixteenth, it didn't.

He griped about it, but only to himself, at his cubicle near the far wall of the long room. It was his personal policy never to appear other than agreeable, a team player, and optimistic. This had stood him in good stead, or so he thought. He had been with Burnham and Burnham for twenty-two years.

The long room was divided into numerous cubicles, the walls of which rose four-and-a-half feet, so one could stand and look out at others who were standing. Standing, one could see the afternoon sun spilling through aluminum louvers. The building faced west.

After twenty-two years he'd become buddies with quite a few of his coworkers, male and female, but he lived alone. He had not planned to live alone. In fact, he'd always assumed he would marry and have kids, own a home; there would be a family dog, and a stray cat that they took in. His wife would want to work, of course, but she'd put the children's interests above her own. That this had not happened surprised him a little. When he tried to understand why it had not happened, he could think only that he hadn't found the right woman. Yet his friends had found wives. Sometimes he wondered if there was something wrong with him, some defect he was blind to while others were not. He smelled his tee-shirt before he pulled it on, making sure no armpit odor adhered. He wore clean underwear every day and changed it if he went out at night. He had drinks with friends but never drank alone. He didn't pick his teeth or his nose. His favorite car sticker was "Random Acts of Kindness." Was that a portrait of an unmarriageable man?

Had the firm decided against the coffee cart? Were Burnham and Burnham taking a cost-cutting measure?

He strolled through the long room, looking into cubicles. Some people had doughnuts. Some had bagels. Maybe they had bought them at kiosks and brought them to work. Maybe they had received a memo that someone had forgotten to give him.

His stomach was growling. He went out to lunch.

In the afternoon, the long room grew hot and sticky and the blinds had to be turned against the sun. But then it was too dark to read small fonts and people turned on their cubicle lamps, which were shaped like smaller versions of the aliens in the old *War of the Worlds*: an aluminum hood over a bulb atop a beastly neck that swiveled from the base.

The time was approaching three.

Robert waited in his cubicle for the cart's arrival. No cart came.

As he was leaving for the day, Robert asked Don, "How come there was no coffee cart today? Has it been cut from the budget?"

Don said, "What are you talking about? Of course there was a coffee cart today. You must have been away from your desk when it came by."

***

Had he been away from his desk and not realized it? He's taken a stroll—everyone did that, they were encouraged to do that—in lieu of an actual gym—but not during coffee-cart time. But maybe he'd been on the phone or computer and hadn't looked up at the right moment. But you could always hear the cart coming, the little wheels squeaking on the vinyl linoleum floor.

***

Robert's apartment was sparely furnished but comfortable. He had a Lazy-Boy in the living room in front of the TV. He ate off a TV table. Sometimes he thought about getting a decorator in—it would have to be a decorator, he didn't trust himself—but in the end he always decided there was no point in doing that. It wasn't as if he were besieged by guests. And he liked having dinner in front of the nightly news.

His bedroom was more welcoming: a double bed with down comforter, willow oak on view out the window. The ceiling was light blue and the walls were an unworrisome beige. A restful room, and yet cheerful, too, because of the window and the willow oak.

***

The coffee cart failed to stop at his cubicle on Wednesday as well. If it had rolled by anybody's cubicle. He stepped outside to look and could spot no coffee cart.

But when he went for his stroll—which had practically been mandated by Burnham and Burnham—there were people holding Styrofoam cups and crumbs on desks. He made a detour to his supervisor but stopped outside the office. Did he want to sound like a spoiled child? Did he want his supervisor to think he had nothing better to do than complain? No. He turned back toward his cubicle. Don brushed by him without speaking. Robert turned around and saw that Don was moving swiftly down the hallway. No doubt he had something urgent on his mind, Robert thought. Or maybe he was in a hurry to the Men's Room. Maybe, he thought, someone had baked a laxative into the doughnuts and bagels and he should be grateful the coffee cart had not come by his cubicle. He smiled a grim smile.

Jody knocked on the frame of his cubicle to ask if he'd like to join a group going out for lunch. "Indian," she said. "A buffet. They have Tandoori."

Jody looked good posing in the doorless frame. She was married to a man named Burt who worked somewhere else. He glanced at her wedding band. "No thanks," he said. "I think I'd better work through lunch."

"Okay, then," she said. "We'll miss you." Her voice was slightly sandpapery. He liked it. After she left, he thought for a moment about how much he liked it. Then he turned to his work. There was never a day when there was no work to turn to.

He tried to catch Don's eye when the closing bell rang but somehow he couldn't. He'd thought he might casually mention Jody and see if Don said anything about her marriage. Don was walking out with someone else and rushed right by him again.

***

Robert hoped Jody would drop by again on Thursday but of course she didn't. People didn't eat Indian every day of the week. Well, in India they did, but not here. Which made him think of the coffee cart. Once again, he was left out. He decided he *would* complain to the supervisor. He could do it in a friendly way, maybe ask if someone new was pushing the cart and didn't realize there were cubicles in the back of the room. Though his cubicle was the only cubicle in the back.

He knocked on his supervisor's door and waited. And waited.

"I don't know, man," Ed said, from his cubicle next to the supervisor's office. "He was just there. I didn't see him go out."

As Robert moved away from the office he saw Jody walk up to it. Saw her knock, saw the door open, saw her go in. Was Jody having an affair with their supervisor? She wouldn't be complaining about the coffee cart. He'd seen the half-chewed bagel on her keyboard.

Pictures of Jody and the supervisor behind a closed door flickered in his mind, something like a poorly made porn video in which you could never really see the faces or the parts.

He walked back to the supervisor's office. If sex was going on in there, they would just have to stop. He knocked, then knocked again. Then he knocked some more. He looked over at Ed's cubicle but if Ed was in it, he wasn't coming out, any more than Jody or the supervisor. And even if they were in the throes, wouldn't the knocking make them stop? He stopped knocking and put his ear to the door. Nothing. He couldn't hear anything. Wait—that was a gasp, he was sure it was a gasp. Followed by a sandpapery giggle.

He went to the Men's Room and stayed a while for the quiet. When he came out it was so close to quitting time that instead of going back to his office he took an elevator to the lobby and left the building.

How could they not have heard him, he wondered. They must have heard his knocking. They must have thought as long as they didn't open the door, they wouldn't be found out. If he knew where Burt worked, he thought, he might have gone to tell him that his wife was cheating on him. No, he wouldn't, he thought. He'd never say anything like that to anyone.

He took off his clothes and crawled under the comforter, though the comforter was not really necessary this time of year. He didn't eat; he didn't feel like eating, or TV.

He wanted to fall asleep so the video in his head would stop playing and after awhile it did slow down and he dozed lightly. He dreamed the coffee cart stopped at his cubicle and that it held not only doughnuts and bagels but creampuffs and cupcakes. He hated cupcakes and couldn't account for their presence in his dream. There was latte along with the coffee. He tried to see who was pushing the cart but couldn't. He could smell the coffee, though. It was dark and aromatic, like chocolate. When he thought of chocolate in his dream, he saw the ice cream sandwiches of his youth, with their chocolate cookie coverings frontside and back. Then he was in a pool like the one at the YMCA where his parents had taken him after his bout with rheumatic fever. The doctor had advised them that walking in a pool would strengthen his muscles. The water had been so warm, warmer than it usually is in pools. He woke up and threw off the comforter, which had overheated him.

***

Friday he slung his jacket onto the coat stand before sitting down at his desk. He'd been reviewing spread sheets for an hour when he heard Ed and Don at the entrance to his cubicle, which was so far in the back that visitors were rare. That was one reason the coffee cart had been so meaningful to him: a visit from a human being twice a day.

But now Ed and Don, talking loudly, were entering his cubicle. Their arms were full of boxes; Don's chin rested on papers atop the top box. He set his boxes down in a corner and said, "I've been sent to Siberia. It's a demotion."

"Nonsense," Ed said. "Look how much bigger this cubicle is than either of ours. You're getting it because they think you need the space. It's a bonus."

From the first box Don removed framed photographs that he placed on Robert's desk. Don with his wife and daughter. His daughter when she was young, posing with two kittens. A close-up of his wife's face, smiling and with her hair blowing in the wind (also, Robert thought, taken long ago). Don next to his Nissan Sentra.

Robert couldn't help but notice that the photographs transformed the space. The cubicle looked cozier, friendlier. Ed pulled out from under his arm two large pictures and from his shirt pocket a small packet of stick-on hooks; he stuck a couple of the hooks on the short wall to accommodate the two large pictures, and now Robert's cubicle looked like a real room. One picture was an enlarged photo Don had taken in England, of the Thames in Cambridge, surrounded by autumn trees. Don had invited Robert into his former cubicle to view it. The other, new to Robert, was a charcoal portrait. "My wife," Don said to Ed, "by my daughter." Robert thought it was very good. He said so to Don, but Don ignored him.

Robert tugged at Don's sleeve but again, Don ignored him.

A thought occurred to Robert, but not like a light bulb turning on. It would be more accurate to say that it broke over Robert's head like dawn, a slow sunrise. As his thought became clear to Robert he began to sweat. His armpits, his hands. His face. He wondered if he smelled.

"She's talented," Ed said. "Of course I understand zilch about art."

Don leaned against the desk. "What do you suppose happened to Robert?"

"Who knows," Don said. "Maybe he just got tired of showing up."

"I worry about him. Poor bastard."

"Well, there's nothing anyone can do. Enjoy your new crib." Ed slapped Don on the back and left. Don, still standing, gazed at the pictures on the wall. They reassured him against the idea of demotion. Family pictures will do that, will establish a man's reality, for himself and for others. He did need more space. Brightening, he flung himself into the chair that Robert had thought he was occupying. But Robert was not in the chair, nor anywhere else. If I were in the chair, Robert said to himself, then Don would be elsewhere, and if Don is in the chair, I am not. Logic couldn't be any clearer than that. He tried to shout—to Don, to anybody—but although a page of one of the spread sheets stirred slightly, as if lifted by a breeze, there was no sound.

Homer and the Enso

Sara Shumaker

"Don't know how it was. I's gone for two, three hours and when I get back it was like this," grumbled the old man, Homer. He thrust his hands deeply into the pockets of his faded overalls.

"Well, I can't say I can help you," replied the second old man, George. "You can't tell me anything more?"

Neither man looked at the other as he spoke. Both had rough reddened faces and each stood with his feet set wide apart. They appeared to be rooted to the ground, like two weathered stones. Perhaps each one leaned a bit towards the other as he spoke, but it was not a discernible movement.

"Ain't got no more to say," said Homer digging his hands even deeper into the pockets of his overalls. "Don't know no more."

George sniffed in reply. It wasn't much to go on. "Vandals, maybe?" he offered.

"Who'd come way out here to vandal my barn?" Homer responded.

They were both silent. It wasn't a likely hypothesis, but nothing was making sense about the events anyway. A large circular shape was painted on Homer's barn. When George had first seen it he thought it was an enlarged bulls-eye, like those used for target practice, but as he got closer he saw it was the unmatched line of the unclosed "o" that made it look that way. The white paint stood out sharply against the faded red barn. It was peculiar.

"Let's not jump to any conclusions. I was just saying. I mean, it didn't appear without someone's help. It's no sign from God or anything like that." said George. He was silent a few moments then offered, "Could be kids."

"The road ain't exactly a busy one," Homer replied. He moved his right hand from his overall pocket and rubbed the oily folds of skin over his eyelids. "Wouldn't a kid want someone to see it after he done it? Nobody's gonna see this but me, and I ain't had any reason to get vandaled just living quietly out here, tending my cows and sich."

"Oh, probably so, but you never can tell with kids these days. Queer ideas they got about how to go about having fun. My Marge says that some of the seniors at her school shaved their hair into mohawks because they were bored, and they wanted to look fierce during tournament ball," George said shaking his head and crossing his arms over his chest. The great cracked putty-colored fingers on his right hand curled around his forearm, which bristled with a frothy patch of white hair. It looked as if even the backs of his hands were callused or covered in pale dried on clay.

"Huh," Homer grunted, his expression sour.

"Yeah. I know," replied George, shaking his head and looking gravely at the tops of his work boots.

"Well, what in the blind moon is it anyway?" said Homer, using the first two fingers of his right hand while keeping his thumb hooked into the pocket of his overalls, to make a flicking motion towards the barn.

"Can't say," replied George.

Homer made a little huffing sound again, expelling air from his nostrils with excessive force. "Well, I ain't got all day to admire it. I best be getting my cows out to pasture and seeing about going into town to get some paint. Can't leave it this way, might scare the girls and put 'em off their milkin' fer a day or two, whatever it is."

***

Homer drove into town and bought the paint. The trip to town made him tense and wooden, but as he turned into his driveway, he relaxed. His elbows sunk lower and one hand dropped off the steering wheel and onto his knee, as the barn came into view. Although everywhere he looked he thought of the work that needed to be done, he also felt with a lovely shiver how the quiet of the farm settled over him. The barn stood exactly where it always had, solid and still in the glare of the afternoon sun. Overgrown grass brushed against the cement casement of the smokey blue-gray door to the root cellar. His mother's rhubarb patch frothed great green leaves near the back steps. The only oddity was that strange symbol of an open-ended circle painted on the barn. A couple of cows milled near it tearing off clusters of sweet red clover and Homer thought they were looking at the peculiar symbol on the side of the barn, seeming almost mesmerized by it. He too puzzled over the sign, worried there might be some trouble with the girls if he didn't do something soon.

***

Homer thought all night about that odd shape on the barn, a swirl, a target, an open circle, a hypnotist's spinning coin on a string, but no matter how he thought about it his mind couldn't come to any conclusions. It didn't seem a hateful symbol, but it wasn't right either. That barn was never meant to have any such sign on it. No other barn in the state had such a strange decoration. That, indeed, seemed certain to the old man. When he came to that conclusion, he finally drifted off to sleep. George had talked about coming over to take pictures of the symbol for the sheriff's office, but Homer promised himself not to wait. He'd paint over that white circle in the morning and be done with it.

But the next day came and went, the sun set, and still the gallon can of red paint remained unopened.

The following morning Homer stood in his kitchen boiling water for coffee, which he liked to make in an old enamel kettle, even though he had a perfectly good percolator in the cupboard under the silverware drawer. He couldn't remember which great aunt he'd inherited the percolator from, or for that matter whose enamel kettle it was that he'd preferred to use these many years, but after so many decades of bachelorhood, he found he couldn't break his preference and mend his ways now. Besides that percolator was really best for when he had a group of folks over. Though he'd long ago stopped doing that, but he still kept the percolator, knowing full well that if he chose to get rid of it it wouldn't have a home anywhere since everyone was using Mister Coffee and other such drip coffee makers now.

For some reason inexplicable to the old man, he found these thoughts were making him also think of the symbol someone had vandaled on his barn. When his coffee was ready, he took a hunk of cold bread with a thick slab of butter on it and went out to his barn to look at it again. He stood there till his breakfast was eaten, and he was hankering for a bit more hot coffee. He went inside, poured himself a thermos full of coffee, and took his old enamel cup outside again to look at the barn.

When the morning milking time came, he called the girls and milked them one by one and found himself mumbling to one or more, "Well now, what do you think of it? Have you gotten over your scare? Lucky them vandals didn't paint nothin' on your side too, eh?"

After the milking was done, Homer walked outside the barn and found himself standing in front of that symbol just staring at it. There seemed to be some mystery there meant for him to unlock. He'd stopped thinking much about who painted it and kept returning to what in blazes it was. Why did he look at it so often?, he wondered. All day long this was his pattern. He'd do some part of his everyday chores and then find himself standing, once again, in front of the barn staring at that open circle and not really thinking about anything at all. He wasn't *doing* anything either, and that unnerved him.

Homer was accustomed to being outside, but not used to being so idle as to stand gazing at something. He was always moving—shuffling off to muck out a stall, take a bale or two of hay out to the metal feeder that stood in the middle of a grassy field where the girls spent most of each day—but all that second day in between his usual tasks he'd find himself just standing out by the side of the barn staring at that vandaled symbol. 'What was it? Who'd do such a thing? Why that particular symbol?' he thought to himself.

By the fourth day he stopped questioning why he was taking the time to stand in front of the barn and look at the open circle. It had simply become a part of his routine to stop for a few moments between tasks to stand quietly near the enso. He'd begun to wonder what harm there was in something as simple as an unending circle painted on a barn, and he wondered how it was painted without there being any drips to mar it. Strange thing was that as he stopped before the symbol those many times throughout the day, he started to notice little things he hadn't really paid much attention to before. The color of the barn, he noted, would have been a very beautiful color for the fabric of a dress. He could imagine his mother clothed in that red looking younger than he remembered her ever being and happy. He noticed that one of the pairs of barn swallows in the loft had a broken mud nest and they were feverishly rebuilding, but that two eggs had fallen from the broken nest—one breaking on the ground, the other egg lay whole but cold upon the straw bedding. And he noticed an intersection where tiny red ants and big black ants' paths crossed. Both kinds were trying to get the other to abandon their path by having small scuffles at the crossing. Finally the red ants swung their path out and around the black ants' path and both sides went on about their gathering pleased to not have to interact with each other directly.

Homer wasn't sure what to do with these new imaginings and observations, but he found he was rather moved by them—so moved as to not really want to remove that symbol just to keep having those few minutes.

***

When George drove over with Marge's Kodak, it had been five days since he'd talked with Homer. To George's great surprise, the symbol was still there, but Homer was nowhere to be seen so George tilted his head back against the seat, stretching out some and waiting for Homer to get back.

A quarter of an hour later, George's head snapped forward, and he opened his eyes. The purr of an engine and the crunch of gravel could be heard. The car was a fancy new Buick, and the man behind the wheel had on a starched white shirt and a striped blue and gold tie. Legs stiff and knees popping, George slowly got out of his truck, leaving the door open and standing with the open door between him and the man in the Buick. The pickup's window was rolled all the way down and George stuck his arms through it and, stooping some, leaned on the frame of the window.

The electric hum of the Buick's automatic window cut the air, as the driver leaned his head out saying loudly, "Homer Bledsoe? Are you Mister Homer Bledsoe?"

George shook his head.

"Well, do you know where I could find him?"

George shook his head again, then said, "He isn't here. Don't know where he is for sure."

The young man in the Buick cleared his throat loudly, began shuffling what appeared to be papers in a small briefcase open on the seat next to him until he found a large manila envelope with H. Bledsoe typed onto the top. He stuck his arm out of the car window and motioned for George to come closer. Skirting around the open door of his truck, George hopped a little on his stiff legs. He approached the car, stopping near the Buick's open window but a few feet back.

"Look, you seem to know Mr. Bledsoe. I'd like to leave some papers with you to give to him." The young man's voice sounded like the staccato clacking of the keys on an electronic typewriter. He held a packet of papers out of the car window and smiled, showing a mouth full of mostly straight, but nicotine-stained, teeth.

"His house is right up there." George replied quietly. "You could leave him your papers in the screen door, and he'll get them. He isn't here now, but he'll be back in time for milking, no doubt."

The man in the suit made a snorting noise that might have been laughter, and said, "Yes, well, cows and milking, that's none of my concern." His faced grew serious, but convivial. He wrinkled his forehead and stretched his neck out, leaning his head towards George. "Couldn't you take them?" he said. He fiddled with his tie and smiled at George. "I need to get back."

George took a step towards the car but then stopped and looked over his shoulder at the house. His right hand stroked the stubble of new whiskers growing on his neck.

"Listen, I'm not sure how the hell I got here, I'm not suitably attired for a farm visit, and I don't have time to wait around for Mr. Bledsoe's cows. So why don't you help me out here?" the man said. He kept his voice light and pleasant, but there was beginning to be an edge to it as well. He was bouncing one of his knees up and down in the car, in nervous agitation.

"I'd like to help ya, but . . . " George began.

The young man's neck and face turned scarlet, spreading from his tie up to his forehead. He looked at the barn. "You see that over there?" he said, cutting George off mid-sentence and pointing at the symbol on Homer's barn. "That is a mistake," he said, speaking quickly with an undertone of anger. "That's the beginning of a sign that was supposed to be painted on a barn facing Highway 218 almost sixty miles from here. The sign painter confused the addresses and arrived here. God only knows how. At least he wasn't incompetent enough to paint the whole advertisement. Nevertheless, he was wrong to have painted anything onto this barn. I'm here to let Mr. Bledsoe know Orion Wireless Telecommunications Network will compensate him for the damage caused to his property. These papers are for him to sign and mail back to us."

George said nothing, but shifted his weight.

"Look, it's been raining here hasn't it? I'm not prepared for the mud, you know."

George looked down at the ground. Other than one or two puddles in the truck ruts it wasn't muddy, but there was no polite way to say this.

"I just want you to take this envelope over to Mr. Bledsoe's door and place it there. I assure you there's nothing unseemly about it. Your friend will be compensated once he signs these papers, and I'd appreciate the help," the man coaxed.

After a moment, George took the envelope. He shook his head as he walked up to Homer's backdoor and placed the envelope in between the screen door and the storm door. When he turned around, he saw the Buick was already backing down the driveway. George got into his pick up and drove home. He'd talk with his friend another day.

***

Homer had cut up half a pick up load full of downed wood from the edge of the south pasture, before he went back to relieve the girls.

It wasn't until he finished with the milking and returned to the house that Homer saw the envelope in the door. He took it inside with him and laid it on the table, going about his regular routine before returning to the table with beef and barley soup, Monday's bread, and a hunk of cheese for his supper. After supper he took the envelope from the table and opened it. The contents were puzzling, legal jargon, a signature sheet in triplicate, and envelopes with pre-stamped return addresses and postage already paid. He read the cover letter twice before he began to understand that this was about the symbol on his barn. Seems there'd been a mistake and his barn was painted (or rather painting had begun) for a large advertisement. The company that hired the painter was contacting him to settle out of court about the mistake. They'd included the offer of three hundred dollars in settlement money if Homer would simply sign and return the paperwork.

The possibility that any one would think his barn might be in an advantageous spot to advertise for anything seemed far-fetched. If they'd have talked with him in person he'd have told them they only owed him the equivalent of one gallon of red paint, but instead the envelope had simply appeared at his door and he was left to sort it out alone, the same way the sign had appeared on the barn and no one came to talk with him about its meaning.

After all the times he'd looked at the open circle over the past week he couldn't imagine it was an advertisement from a telephone and wire company. He left the envelope and its contents on the table and went into his bedroom to change his clothes and find his slippers.

***

It wasn't that he refused the settlement money or that he was thinking it over or even that he decided to do nothing. Homer just forgot about it altogether. He went on with things—tending the stock, chopping wood, and stopping three or four times a day in front of the open circle where he let his mind wander unguided. A few weeks later, he put the envelope in the cupboard with the percolator, having forgotten what it contained.

He began to dream about his mother. Quite often she'd appear in his dreams clothed in crimson, maroon, or scarlet and usually she was strikingly young and vibrant. Many times he dreamt of her walking in the autumn leaf-litter wearing a dark red dress and with her arms cradling her bulging abdomen singing to it. Singing to him, he realized. He was born in the early winter and, though he never saw his mother at that age or pregnant, he felt sure the image was almost a memory of her—an image of her beauty and her joy—long before her body became twisted by rheumatoid arthritis and later eaten away with breast cancer. Between the days in the barn and pastures with the cows and the dreams of his mother, Homer's life was full.

***

Autumn came early that year, the first frosts turned the woods a glorious palate of reds and golds. The leaves of the big maple tree out beside the driveway turned vermillion red. George pulled into Homer's driveway and waited in his truck until Homer appeared, before he turned off his engine and got out.

The two men greeted each other without words: each nodded, glanced quickly at the other man, and then kept his eyes on the ground as he continued walking towards the other. When they neared each other they both stepped out and to the side before coming to a stop—standing rooted to the ground and side-by-side about three feet from each other.

After awhile Homer coughed softly, and George said, "You decided to keep it, huh?"

The lines on Homer's forehead and around his eyes got deeper. He turned and looked back at the barn. He nodded.

"Well, you're the only one in the county that has one," George said, softly chuckling.

"The girls seem to like it," replied Homer. His eyes glistened a bit as he spoke. Then he laughed with George. "Strangest thing. I just don't feel like gettin' rid of it, ya know?"

"Folks may think it's peculiar, but it's your barn, Homer," said George. "Marge says she'd like to come by and see it some time. Oh, and she sent you some homemade donuts. They're in the cab. I told her about your circle there."

Homer nodded his consent, studying George closely. "You ever think of your mother, George? I mean, you ever dream of her?"

George left cheek twitched involuntarily. "Not to my knowledge," he said. "Why?"

"Oh nothin'," Homer replied. He knew his next words were slow in coming, but he didn't press himself to form them faster. He waited until he could see the words in his mind, and then he simply let them tumble out. "It's just sometimes I think on her. That damned circle makes me think on her more than I ever used to. And other things too, it makes me think on other such things. Never you mind."

George was silent, as if he understood that it was more important to stand there by his friend and not ask to understand what he was talking about. It didn't matter what he was saying exactly.

Homer cleared his throat, "You ever see that maple so red?"

George turned and smiled, "No. I can't say that I have."

"I didn't think so either," Homer replied. "I didn't think so."

The two men stood admiring the tree.

"Well, how about some coffee?" Homer asked, and without waiting for reply turned and started walking towards the house.

George called to Homer, "You still making coffee in that old pan on the stove?"

“Yep. Nothin’s wrong with that pan yet.”
“Alright then,” George agreed. “I’ll get the donuts.”

The Secret War

Katharine Crawford Robey

Kate dreads dinners at Great Grandfather's farm. She wonders if he dreads them, too. This evening it's her turn to try to get him down to dinner. She climbs the creaky stairs slowly. Outside his room she stops. She hears taps and footsteps. He's up. He'll come right down and she'll be through.

She knocks on the door. No answer, but she can hear him moving. She turns the knob and goes in. He's back in bed, covers up to his chin. She frowns.

"Great Papa?"

"They send you up to make me come to dinner?"

He's cranky as the old pump handle by the gate. She hesitates.

"Go away," he says, looking at the window, not at her. "Whichever one you are."

"I'm Kate. My mother says you come down to dinner."

Great Papa snorts.

"You have a cold," Kate says.

"Cold back then. Fifty years ago today." He keeps watching out the window.

"What was fifty years ago?" she says.

"Snowing then, too. I fell through the sky in the snow." His voice trails off.

"What are you talking about, Great Papa?"

"What do you care?"

"How would you know what I care," says Kate. She follows his gaze. She sees snowflakes catch on the glass and slide down. The curtains billow. Cold air fills the room. "You let in a storm." She hurries to shut the window.

He begins telling the one thing that everyone already knows. "Northern Italy. World War II. When I enlisted the Army doctors said I was one in a million."

She finishes it for him. "Your eyes don't match. One is blue and the other's green." She's his oldest great grandchild, the only one with green eyes. Not that he's noticed. "Keep telling how you fell."

She sits down. He turns his head and his eyes snap at her.

Her eyes snap back.

He says, "Open the drawer to my bedside table and get me my handkerchief."

She pulls out a large white piece of cloth. "There're wavy lines on it," she says, "in red and black ink. You wouldn't blow your nose on that."

"Spread it over my chest," says Great Papa.

Kate stands up and lays the handkerchief over the quilt. "Is this some kind of map? It's soft. Where'd you get it?"

"Army map. Silk. Easy to fold up and hide," he says. "I tried to read it in the middle of the night, but I didn't know where I was. Go away and let me remember."

"I won't go without you," she says. "The turkey's out of the oven. Mom says it's resting."

"*I'm* resting," he says.

"Now you won't tell."

He shuts his eyes. His eyelids flutter. "No place for a nineteen-year-old kid. It was night and cold. Brave Italian farmers led me around back to a haystack. Underneath the hay there was a dark hole in the ground. The tunnel. They pushed me in there to hide me. It was black dark." Under the quilt she can see his hands grasp the side of the bed. "You still here, Kate?"

"I'm here." She takes the extra blanket at the foot of the bed and wraps it around herself. Then she sits back down. "Tell more."

"I stayed underground for three months."

"You lived in a tunnel that long?"

He almost smiles. "Underground is another word for resistance. I fought in secret with the Italian farmers against the Nazis."

The room is nearly dark. The lamp in the corner seems dim.

"Keep telling," says Kate.

"The rest don't pay me any mind. You're the only one with green eyes, too."

He knows. "Go on," says Kate.

"At night we rubbed soot from the fireplace on our faces, so the enemy couldn't see us. We blew up bridges so they couldn't get through. Stole their blankets so they couldn't sleep. If they'd caught us, they'd have shot ten Italians for each one of us, including mothers and children." He shakes his head. "No one is safe in war. Not even in their own homes."

"Tell how you fell through the sky."

He shuts his eyes again and is quiet.

Kate gets up. He's back to his old secret self again. "If you won't tell, I'm taking you down to dinner."

"I couldn't hide in the tunnel all the time," he says.

"But how did you fall?"

"I'm telling you this now. The Nazis were looking for me."

"Did they find you?"

"I was in the kitchen. I made it down to the cellar and hid behind wine casks. I can still hear the clatter of their feet on the stairs. I could have touched their boots."

Kate's heart beats fast. "What happened?"

Great Papa half chuckles. "They didn't bend down to look. Didn't want to wrinkle their uniforms."

"Great Papa! Kate!" Mom calls from downstairs.

"Quick, go back. Tell how you fell," Kate says.

Great Papa shuts his eyes. His fingers grip the quilt. "I was a gunner on a plane, an A-20 attack bomber, very fast, the Lucy Kay. We'd just finished our mission and were returning to base. But there was ice on our wings. The plane was in trouble. Suddenly we were hit by flak."

"What's that?"

"Pieces of bombs. The pilot couldn't control the plane anymore. 'Bail out!' he ordered. 'Bail out!' It was a yell. I opened the door. The wind was icy cold. It was snowing. I leapt into the night sky. The wind whistled around my ears. Counted to eight."

"Why?"

"To get clear of the plane. Pulled the rip-cord. The parachute wouldn't open. I fell faster than the snowflakes. I knew the ground must be close. Pulled at my chest pack any way I could. Finally the silk began billowing out and filling with air. There was no time to maneuver. I landed in a pine tree. As I hit the tree I saw the plane crash into a mountain and burst into flames. I knew then that the pilot, my friend Jake, hadn't made it.

"What did you do?"

"Slid down a snowy mountain and knocked at the first farmhouse. Didn't know whether they would be friends or the enemy."

Kate breathes in. "You're brave. Show me your medal."

"I don't have one. I didn't have a witness."

"I'll be your witness, " she says softly.

Downstairs in the dining room her family has started the hymn. "Come Ye thankful people come," floats up to them.

Great Papa peels off his quilt.

"You're dressed, Great Papa! In your Sunday clothes."

"I even have my shoes on," he says.

"You tricked me," Kate says. "You were ready to come down all along."

"You tricked me, too," he says. "You wouldn't leave."

He stands up, tucks the handkerchief into the pocket of his suit jacket, and reaches for his cane. "Now I'm dressed proper."

"Why do you need that cane?"

"Keeps me from falling, Kate. I'm old now. Afraid of my own stairs."

Kate takes his large rough hand and they walk together to the top of the stairs.

Through the hallway window the moon shines on falling snow. They stand there a moment.

"There's an Italian word for what we need to do," says Great Papa. "Avanti. Forward."

He falters at the first step. Kate grabs his arm. "I won't let you fall," she says.

He hooks his cane over his arm and balances on her.

"Avanti," they whisper together and go down to join the others.

TAKING A STITCH IN A DEAD MAN'S ARM

Katherine Vaz

I changed the bandage over my father's knee in the final month of his life. His wound was purple, and blood heaved through. I never looked away from it. I swallowed my vomit when it struck the back of my clenched teeth; I was ready to swallow my insides as often as necessary—it was important to gaze at his flesh exactly as it was because I would not have it with me for much longer. I wanted to learn matter-of-factness about being this close to someone. The yellow fluid on the gauze around the bloodstains, the cortisone spray that would have made Papa scream if he'd had the strength: I thought of them as my own—my stain, my shock and my scream.

A brain lesion gave him double vision. Everything wore a register of itself, a crown of haze. It amused him to watch people walking around with the ghosts of themselves stuck to their skins. Papa's knee had ripped open when he fell off a ladder while trying to repair a broken window sash. Frantic to protect us, to seal every entry, he had crawled from his sick bed while my mother was at work at the Sunshine Biscuit factory and I was at school. A killer who called himself the Zodiac was roaming the Bay Area. He was sending letters with obscene ciphers to the *San Francisco Chronicle.*

"Isabel," said my father, his fingers brushing first the specter of my face and then my face. The rind of the moon cut through the windowpane. The wallpaper was an old pattern of "The Strawberry Thief," with sharp birds poking through tall red grasses. Saint Anthony of love and lost things had an arm span covering the top of the bureau, and someone had sent over a plug-in picture, with a light bulb in the back, of Saint Lucy with her plate of eyeballs. Papa was forty-two; he would stay posed in time with black hair. He did not know how to guard me anymore. He could no longer hide the newspapers, as he did when Richard Speck murdered those nurses in Chicago. *Fear gives off a smell. That's how evil finds its victims, Isabel. If you don't give it off, you'll be safe, you won't get hurt in the dark.*

I told him he must stop worrying. The Zodiac would not bother coming to our town: What was here? Every morning I walked to the boulevard to catch the bus to Bishop Delancy High School in Oakland, and we passed the Adobe Feed Store, where my father had said that hiding in the sacks were eggs, smaller than the eye could see, waiting to hatch into vermin. And sometimes I had caught it, in the days of holding his hand when we went to buy chicken scratch. The sacks jumped, they stirred a bit, moth wings straining against the weight of the feed. Eggs and wings: I thought of death as white. Our morning bus passed the Miniature Golden-Tee, with its hydra-head of neon dragons guarding the windmills, clowns with big mouths waiting for a golf ball to gag them, and a little wild-west corral with a gate that gave out a horse whinny again and again as it swung open. What was in San Damiano? It sounds like a place with terra-cotta earth and a Spanish mission, but it was an ordinary suburb, house after house with those netless basketball hoops, and a gauntlet of stores on San Damiano Boulevard. People favored wind chimes in the shape of pagodas, which they bought in Chinatown in San Francisco, as if crossing the bridge was going from part A of the world to part B, and the winds blew in and tilted the pagodas and no one ever straightened them; there was always a faint music, a trickle, really, coming from these shattered columns of pagodas.

I was in love with someone who was leaving me his own lessons in being unafraid. James was a Filipino boy in my sophomore class who wore three-piece business suits on Free Dress Day and smoked cigars with the Asian kids in the parking lot, and once when Sonny Barger and some Hells Angels rode through, as they did now and then, James threw a flaming butt end at one of them and was rewarded with an obscene gesture. I understood that the motorcyclist admired James for a moment, and it thrilled me, to watch how someone could go straight toward points of fear.

Violet Wong, my best friend, would get onto the bus with me at the San Damiano stop, and she'd take out the green eye shadow that she'd stolen from her mother. We'd put it on with our fingers, and my lashes were so long that they stroked green dust onto the inside of my glasses. She wanted to help me be beautiful for James. I had written a speech for him, and he won the regional Lions Club contest with it and would go on to state finals. He had not told me that he won; one of his friends did, and when I went to him, he said, "I was going to tell you, Isabel." I wanted him to bury his face in my hair and wet my scalp with his mouth, to breathe my name back to me inside my ear.

How could I explain any of this to my father—the odd, awful timing of my love? "I'm not scared of anything, Papa." That was all I could manage. "That's good!" he whispered. "I don't want you taking a stitch in my arm."

"No, I won't, Papa," I said, and we laughed.

It was a joke between us. When he was a boy on the island of São Miguel in the Azores, he suffered a fear of the dark. His mother explained to him that the cure for that in her family, she was very sorry to say, was taking a stitch in a dead man's arm. The cure was horrible, but its strength lasted forever. "Forever" had sounded wonderful to my father, so he said yes, next time there was a dead man in the town of Sete Cidades, he would take a stitch in his arm. Nothing could be worse than the monsters roving in his bedroom at night.

My father was five years old. His mother stood outside the chapel, crying into a lace handkerchief. Fear of the dark is fear of aloneness; my father had to go by himself to the dead man in his casket. The thread in the needle was white. Papa thought the young man looked like marzipan, especially where a drip of pink paint stood out on his ear. He had died from falling off a stone wall, where he had been entwining hydrangeas through the gaps. Everyone agreed that the world fought back when you tried to make it beautiful.

My father pulled up the dead man's cuff and touched a waxy arm. His name was Jaime, and his mustache was trimmed neatly for the first time ever. My father stuck the needle into the wrist and pushed until it dipped through flesh and emerged from under the skin, and then he thought, all right, that's enough. Two drops of fluid seeped at the prick marks. My father's stomach shrank smaller than a fist. He left the thread in the man's skin and drew the sleeve down and ran back to his mother.

It was easy to give up fear of darkness rather than repeat such a cure. Maybe it was some old-world remnant, sticking a man with a needle to make certain that he was not merely in a coma. At one funeral in Sete Cidades, a man had bolted upright in his coffin while being borne to the cemetery and roared, "How will I breathe underground?" Maybe the idea was to stitch the body to earth, so that it would not cling with its worms to the spirit trying to fly to heaven.

Death sinks a person's eyes back until they become bright creatures in a tide pool. I got up to go to my room, but my father grabbed my arm and said, "Don't leave me, Isabel! Not yet," and I saw, on the gleam of fever, on the water on his eyes, a terrible fear, and I did not know if it might be from him, or if it were my own, reflecting back to me. Perhaps I was so far into fright that I'd touched clear round to the other side, where I could claim to be past it; perhaps I was a liar; I could stand that. But I could not bear to think that the fear might be coming from him.

For once I did not mind Mama's habit every night of getting out our glow-in-the-dark rosary set. The Holy Family statute had a hollow compartment to house the rosary. I held it under a lamp's light to turn the beads into glowworms. My mother snapped off the lights, and she, my father, and I handed the fluorescent beads from one grasp to another in the dark. Fingering this string of lights like the souls of infant stars, I finally knew what to pray: I'll give up love, if You'll save my father.

That was my bargain with God.

***

Our Alameda County transit bus, #80, went from San Damiano through San Leandro and then under the "Free Huey" banners along East 14th Street into Oakland. Near the General Motors plant, we picked up the riders going to Castlemont High, near Bishop Delancy. They had Afros with fro-piks stuck in them and wore Angela Davis glasses and hiphugger lace-up football pants, including the girls, with angel-flight hems. On their Pee-Chee folders, they had penciled dashikis and black-haloed hair over the Waspy white kids in tennis outfits. We lifted our schoolbooks onto our laps to free up seats for them.

One day Charles Mayer, a Castlemont Knight with his purple-and-white letterman's jacket, sat next to me. Everyone knew him from his picture in the newspaper. He was heading for the NBA. He ripped out a sheet of binder paper from a folder and began writing in pencil. Out of the corner of my eye I saw his writing, and I did not know what came over me when I leaned over and said, "No, 'receive' is 'e-i,' not 'i-e.'"

I cringed when he said, "What?" and looked right at me. I glanced near his eyes and told him about the spelling of 'receive.' He jotted it down and insisted it didn't look right, but I told him, "Believe me, I'm sorry for speaking to you, I didn't mean it, but I'm telling you the truth: *receive*."

Charles Mayer handed me his paper and said, "What else is wrong here. Tell me."

I got into the habit of moving my books for him to sit where I could help with his homework. Once when some Castlemont kids pried up a bus seat and crammed it out a window to protest the arrest of Eldridge Cleaver, and the Delancy kids were jostled around, Charles Mayer told them not to touch me. It had nothing to do with the usual sort of love; that was understood. He had a girlfriend and plenty of other girls after him. I was ugly, with my skinniness and battles against fright. We all rolled our blue herringbone tweed skirts at the waist in a crude attempt to have mini-skirts. He was taking a portion of my mind, but not as James had. Not long into knowing him, Charles handed me five pralines made by his grandmother, in a baggie secured with a psychedelic-streaked rubber band.

He said, "Thanks—tell me your name?"

"Isabel Dias."

"Isabel Dias," he said, as if pleased with locating an obscure country on a map. "I got a B on my essay about my future," he said.

My hand was moist around the bag of pralines.

"Thank you," I said.

"No problem, thank you," he said, and we each settled back into our books.

In that essay, he had written: *This is my world at this moment. Everyone I meet is my history. This is the year that Charles Mayer has stepped into his life.*

When we disembarked at Delancy, Violet said, "What's wrong, Isabel?" I ran to the rest room, willing to let the smokers beat me silly, and I locked myself into a stall and wept, I wept without making noise, I was good at that; imagine me counting just a tiny bit as someone's history. How uncanny, too, that my father should seep inside my lonely hours: With the raw instincts of a small animal, with the Zodiac on the loose, I found myself a protector on the bus, a guardian angel on his way to money and fame, far, far above anything I was, but I counted now in his tally of moments, owing to my lack of fear in spelling out *receive*.

An essay or two later, Charles Mayer stopped taking our bus. I never saw him in person again, though I continued to see his photo in the sports news. I heard that he had a car now. Rumor had it that it was a gift from a recruiter, because his future was so much on the rise.

***

I studied my mother the way I looked at the eyes and blood of my father, to preserve her as she was right then, down to the safflower oil with its faint scent that she rubbed into her skin. Already, young, her skin was overly set, like the film on a pudding, and her light brown hair was thinning, and her glance seemed not to be owning things but making blank spaces where she looked, and I forgave her. I never thought that not seeing me meant that she did not love me. She could hardly bear to look at my father. I would make watery soup but she refused it. Right through her skin it was poking out, the dryness in her bones. When she curled up next to my father on their bed, I took off her shoes and set them upright on the carpet, where they exhaled her entire day of standing and picking the pink marshmallow cookies off the conveyor belt and putting them bottom to bottom inside the compartments of a box. My father had moved in this rhythm alongside her for years. The Sunshine people let the workers eat all they wanted, but one week we had devoured four boxes of pink cookies and three boxes of Sunshine cheese crackers on purpose, to break the habit of wanting any more.

Mama, dozing next to my father, would give a startled shudder of remembering me, and with her eyes still shut, not looking at either of us for fear of dying of it, she let me crawl between her and Papa. Their silver carpet was bare, stripped to its gums. Somehow the roses on the carpet had worn themselves onto the bottoms of our shoes but since we saw no roses on our shoes I think they must have gone up into our feet, roses inside my mother's feet and climbing inside her sore calves as she stood at the factory.

When I roused myself to go off to my own bed, I could not sleep. Suddenly the dark drifted into a white blindness, like the belly of a night turned inside out. I got up in the white sac of night to clean the green leather couch, Comet on a rag that made the green pale. The majolica Christ child over the stove, inside His ring of majolica fruit, had collected streaks of grease, too far to reach.

I piled bedclothes on top of myself and put my arms and legs around them and thought of them as a man, and I thrust around like a stupid fish on land, and that made me feel worse, because a man would move in ways beyond predicting. Even then I suspected that when a woman got to be experienced in love, that was the point—for him to surprise you; the very touch of love was a plunging reminder of the unknown, the same unknown I carried with me now.

***

I heard that James came in third in the state finals of the speech contest held by the Lions Club. I was about to round the corner to find him at his locker, to tell him that he had gone quite far with my speech and should not think of it as failing. I decided this would not violate my vow to give him up. I stopped when I heard his voice say, "Deborah, I'm dying to fuck you." And thereafter I saw him with this girl, who had long blonde hair that she plaited and undid so that it held a ripple. Her rouge compact fell out in the bathroom and I kept it: Mauve Turbulence.

In religion class, Sister Miriam showed a filmstrip about sex, in which a priest's voice-over affixed every act of physical love onto a scale. "Looking at, talking to, walking with" was at the end marked "Early Stage of Arousal." "S.I."—for "sexual intercourse"—was at the far other end, in the Marriage part of the scale. The projector went "Ping!" whenever Sister Miriam had to move the filmstrip. The narrating priest said, cheerily, "I really don't know where to put the fondling of the breasts!" and the screen showed an "F" surrounded by question marks that ended up straddling the line between Engagement and Marriage.

So God was merely amused. I had not even been on the scale with James. I had not owned this love enough for me to offer it up. And the pain I was in meant I had not even truly surrendered the nothing I had. But what of any of it? My father might be saved now, but there comes a time when such a prayer is not answered.

My lungs flattened so that it was impossible to get air into the bellows. I took an early bus home and crawled onto the bed where my father lay with his pounding double vision. I did not speak; I tried to get some breath into me so I would not die. He put his hand on my hair—kindly, though I had failed him. My glasses fell off and the birds on the wall, the strawberry thieves, blurred into a red ironworks, becoming almost pretty. He said that he'd been wrong his whole life; taking a stitch in a dead man's arm hadn't been about fear of the dark.

Was I listening to him? Was I?

I moved a shoulder a bit to signal him yes.

It was about leaving behind the curse of waiting. "Waiting is the fear you have to get over, Isabel," said my father, so lightly I barely heard him. It frightened me that he could hear my heart battering its way onto the sheet. "Don't wait for anyone." Because waiting was darkness, having no imagination to see beyond the fallen curtain, where you were right then. But when you were young and looking at a dead man, and actually sticking it to him, you were saying that it wasn't your time to die, it was your time to enter your better and better future.

There were so many cracks in our house that I was sure that water ebbed in while we slept, filling every room to the ceiling. The Zodiac got in through one of the cracks, but we fought him, and his knife, instead of killing us, opened gills on our sides and we could breathe. The Zodiac had a fear of drowning and swam away. My mirrored vanity plate of gardenia soaps and vanilla cologne got swept up in a vortex of water. My father had been a champion ocean swimmer, and this, to him, was child's play. This was nothing, getting to dance underwater until morning, when the water receded and daylight began and a string of water was lying out of our mouths, connecting whatever had gone on in our heads in the night to our pillows.

My mother and I threw out the newspapers, though my father could no longer read. We had to protect him from the latest: The Zodiac had written a letter that said: *Ha! Ha! Ha! Your pigs can't catch me!! When a busload of Catholic kiddies step off in their uniforms I'll go pop! pop! and I am going to find me some niggers too.*

My #80 bus, with Delancy and Castlemont students, was a gift box, wrapped and delivered, for the Zodiac. Everyone thought this, but no one worried. The Zodiac would stay in San Francisco. Surely death would not trouble itself to stalk us on this one obscure line from San Damiano to Oakland.

Death was too busy, death was in my father's body. I stitched my gaze to my father's when he yelled, "Isabel!" He looked straight into me, and I looked back, into the iris and nerves.

When he died, my mother insisted on a simple, closed-coffin affair, no flinging ourselves at the dead, no kisses that drew back embalming paint. But at his wake, I almost fainted from the smell of the casseroles, the Chinese noodles baked over ground beef and peas, the lasagnas oozing like a cutaway of magnified muscle, the Boston pies leaking their middles—I stopped eating for days, and then, all at once, my bones shook as if my father were shaking me, I saw black puddles moving along the floor and sticking together to make odd black-water animals, and I could not wait to eat, I ate, my mother said, like someone who was going to be shot in the morning.

As a girl, I had attended a school run by Carmelite nuns from Spain who told us stories about their parents being killed in the Civil War. Once a year, we filed into the convent's chapel and the priest held out a black speck housed under a small glass dome. We had to kiss the glass over this black jot, which was a particle of bone from the founder of the order.

How had this bone chip been obtained? What part of the body was it from?

Why did we turn the color of night down to our bones when we died?

There is always some way in which we lend ourselves to taking a stitch in the body of the dead. Someone had taken not a needle but a knife and carved out of the bone. At school, Violet held out her biology book and said, "Isabel! Did you know that the skeletons in the wings of birds are the same shape as the inside of the human hand?"

That would be just like my father, to hide where he would not frighten the living. He and the other dead could sweep across the daytime sky, over my head, caressing the face of the air. The home he had made for us on the ground was continuing to grow in order to contain all light, and it contained bones so coated with light that he could touch us forever.

My mother would sit in dark rooms and not move. In the living room, the dotted Swiss curtains bulged with air blowing in through the screens. It was as if the air had shape, and the curtains were stretching themselves over it. "Shall we go for a walk, Mama?" I asked, and out we ventured under the birds in the sky, stunned and silent. At a distance I imagine we must have seemed to be striding quite fearlessly.

***

While walking down Redwood Road to the bus stop on San Damiano

Boulevard, I noticed a car—maybe a station wagon—going in one driveway, pulling out, going into the driveway of the next house, pulling out. Someone was following me, entering and idling for a moment in every driveway so that he could stay behind me. I walked a little faster and stepped closer to the curb. Hardly any other cars were out at that hour, still dark, before seven. I was wearing my trench coat over my uniform, with the fringe of my herringbone skirt showing, and blue knee socks and coffee-and-cream saddle shoes.

I passed the San Damiano Library, a low glass building across from Faith Lutheran Church; the car went into its parking lot. I thought that if I took care not to look at the car, it would leave me alone. I tried a fast walk, afraid to look over my shoulder until I told myself, Fear nothing, your father is with you: Don't give off the smell of fear; that's when the larger animal will catch the smaller one. I knew how to protect myself. The boulevard wasn't far, and men worked all hours at the Union 76 station near the bus stop. I wondered if I should get the license plate number, or look at the man behind the wheel, but I broke into a run when I saw the gas station.

The A.C. Transit driver, Owen Campbell, was getting coffee out of the vending machine. When I ran up to him, breathing hard, I said, "There's a car back there I don't like."

Mr. Campbell and two of the station attendants walked out with me and looked down the street, but the car had vanished.

"You get the number?" asked Mr. Campbell.

I shook my head. I told him what had happened, and he put his hand on my shoulder and said, "Maybe it's just one of those things."

"Maybe," I said.

"Because it's a strange world," he said.

"That's right."

He escorted me to the bus. I told Violet that someone had come after me in my Catholic uniform, and she stifled a yell and started a whisper in the bus about the Zodiac. By the time we stopped at the General Motors plant for the Castlemont students, the fear in the bus went into their skin too, and they picked up the murmur: Of course he'd find us. We're a two-for-one deluxe murderer's dream. A girl next to me opened her Bible to the twenty-third Psalm: *He leadeth me beside the still waters / Yea, though I walk through the valley of the shadow of death, I will fear no evil.*

She took hold of my sleeve. We did not speak, but she clutched these stitches all over my arm. I hope it made her less afraid. For me it was a sweetness out of nowhere. How close to dying it still arrives, the better and better surprise. We could be minutes from gunfire, and someone finds the time to take hold of me.

When the bus stopped at Delancy, Mr. Campbell opened the door and exited first. He turned around and walked a bit, and then I stepped off. If the car were lurking, I would be able to identify it. It was the most fearless moment of my life. When I was out in the open, and the other students poured out, Mr. Campbell said to me, "God bless you, sweetheart," a further gift in the middle of all that terror. No one had ever called me sweetheart before, not even my family.

There was no news that day, nor on any of the following days, about the Zodiac killer. He was never found, though it was guessed years later that he might have been apprehended for a different crime. Who knows? We refuse to believe in the persistence of the sinister. Perhaps he is a clerk or a dental technician or a professor, his skull's interior filled with webs that no one else can see.

Violet Wong drowned in the Bay during a marine biology trip in her freshman year at the University of California at Berkeley.

As far as I know, Charles Mayer never made it to the NBA; I hope life has not disappointed him. I hope he did not die in Vietnam. I wish him a good and cheerful family.

James came into my life twenty years after I last saw him, at a school reunion. He touched my elbow at the banquet table as a greeting, and we had a drink together. I told him that I lived in a flat on Fillmore Street in San Francisco, where I grew African violets under special lighting, and I mentioned working as a botanist and hybridizer of grains. I added that I was divorced, but not that I was madly, utterly, out-of-my-skin in love with a married man. James said he ran an Asian import/export business, and he appeared distant but fine, but he was no longer beautiful to me, because he reminded me of what I still was—someone perpetually learning not to wait forever. There are times that contain all we shall ever be; everything we learn can be traced back to that start of the shading in of all we more fully come to know. Back then in the year when I learned to step into my life, there lay the first threads: darkness, waiting, the dragon in the landscape, love running in blood and water through my grasp.

My mother still lives in our little house with the red wallpaper in San Damiano, the sort of artless place that no one wants to admit being from, the place where I thought, What was here?

With Andrew, my married man, I gave up many things, including my notion of "here." When he came to where I lived—here, there, it didn't matter at all—anywhere was everything. We'd kiss to swallow each other whole, and I wasn't afraid of my face going violent and heaving, but when I was by myself, when he ripped up the seam we formed skin to skin and went home to his wife, I was quite clear about one definite new fright. I had crested something and hit up against that farthest fear of the dark: Nothing would touch me more than this that I was about to lose. Soon he and I would end this passion simply because it refused to have an end of its own. You could take a stitch in a dead man's arm in order to defeat the night, because you wanted to live. But what if you hit up against a love that would cling to you, so that no one else would be able to touch you directly, not ever again, because that—him, it, the hours, this created thing between you—would stay adhered?

Oh, Papa. One lifetime is never enough to figure everything out, not the mystery you left off solving, the mystery that began when you were very young and took a stitch in the body of death and thought: *There it is, I've finished, I will never again be afraid of the dark.* What happens when it's you that's the body lying there alone?

"Taking a Stitch in a Dead Man's Arms" originally appeared in *BOMB Magazine*, Issue 77, Fall 2001.

The Thaw

Alison MacLeod

for Marjorie Genevieve

Wisdom after the event is a cheap enough commodity—but go back.

The smoky light of a March sunrise is seeping through the winter drapes. Outside, the world is glassy; the trees on Pleasant Street, glazed with winter. Every bare branch, every dead leaf is sheathed in ice, like a fossil from another age, an antediluvian dream of blossom and green canopies. Below her bedroom window, the drifts rise up in frozen waves of white—even the sudden gusts and eddies of wind cannot disturb those peaks—while overhead, the warmth of the sun is so reluctant in its offerings, so meagre, you'd not be alone if you failed to notice the coming of the first thaw.

Above her room, a sheet of ice on the eaves gives way, smashing like a minor glacier onto the porch roof, but everyone in the house sleeps on. Marjorie—or Marjorie Genevieve as her father always called her—sleeps in what the family still calls "Ethel's room", though it has been thirteen years since Ethel was taken from them by TB. Ethel, 1913. And Kathleen, just two years later. Marjorie still keeps one of Kathleen's Sunday handkerchiefs, spotted with her blood.

As for their mother, Cecelia Maud, it is true what people say. She has never recovered from the deaths of her three grown children: Ethel, Kathleen and, finally, senselessly, Murray, just two months after Kathleen. Before Christmas, Marjorie found her mother sitting in the ice-house with her coat unbuttoned and sawdust in her hair. Her lips were blue.

After seven daughters, Providence gave Cecelia Maud and James MacLeod a single son, a boy who would become the youngest lawyer ever admitted to the Bar in the province of Nova Scotia.

Some say the MacLeods hold themselves too high—which is perhaps why the fight broke out, behind Batterson's Dry Goods, which, everyone knew, doubled as a bootlegger's after dark on Saturdays.

No man that night would ever say who was involved or who threw the first punch. Only this was clear. Murray was laid out on a table in the store room. Concussed, they said, that was all. Come morning, he'd have a devil of a sore head, and a hard time defending himself to his mother and his wife, lawyer or no. Louis Clarke, the town's Inspector, gave them ten minutes while he turned a blind eye, stepped outside, and marveled, as he was known to do, at the plenitude of stars in the Cape Breton sky. Two men—suddenly stark sober—heaved Murray into their arms. They took the shortcut through Plant's Field; saw only the Portuguese fishermen who were camped, as ever, by the brook, their damp clothes hanging, pale as spectres, while their owners slept.

That August Sunday morning, Cecelia Maud woke early. She planned to pick a few gem lettuces from the garden before they wilted in the day's heat. But when she opened the inside door of the back porch, she found her only son slumped against the rocker, blood still seeping from his ear.

Her legs gave way. She could neither scream nor cry out.

Indeed, it was only after the clockwork of the day had begun—the stove swept (no char on a Sunday), the breakfast table laid—that Marjorie found her mother on the floor beside her brother, and for a moment she struggled to know the living from the dead.

But no charges were laid. No notice of the funeral was given in St. Joseph's weekly bulletin. It was an usually quiet gathering, family only. Murray MacLeod was the youngest lawyer ever to be called to the Bar—dead after a Saturday night at the bootlegger's—and the MacLeod's, Catholics, were not unaware: they were fortunate to reside on Pleasant Street, in the enviable, Protestant district of Ward One.

Again.

Wisdom after the event is a cheap enough commodity—but these words and the article in *The North Sydney Herald* are still unimaginable. As she wakes this Saturday morning in a frozen March, Marjorie Genevieve is enjoying the knowledge that her coat was anything but cheap.

She works Mondays and Wednesdays at the head office of Thompson's Foundry. Before her father died, he made it clear he would consent to a part-time position only. She did not *need* to work, he explained with a benign smile, and although James MacLeod is now eight years gone, no one, not even Marjorie's eldest sister May, with her fierce intelligence and heavy eyebrows, has the authority to overturn his decision.

Marjorie knew it had to be beaver, not muskrat, not even muskrat dyed to look like mink.

A three-quarter-length, wrap-round coat in unsheared beaver.

She saved for two years.

In the darkness of her room, she slides it on over her nightgown and rubs her palm against the nape of the fur. The shawl collar tickles her bare neck. The silk lining is cool against her chest. When she pulls back the drapes, she can see almost nothing of the day through the bedroom window. The pane is a palimpsest of frost; the world is white. But she is radiantly warm.

She is twenty-nine, and it is only right. There has been enough grief. Thirteen years of grief. Ethel. Kathleen. Murray. Her father. And now her mother, the husk of herself.

Wearing the fur over only her nightgown, Marjorie feels nearly naked.

The furrier at Vooght Brothers had the voice of an orator. "I do not need to persuade you of the elegance of this coat. But remember, while beaver is sometimes known for being heavy to wear, it offers *exceptional* protection against the excesses of a Cape Breton winter. Notice how the long guard hairs give this coat its lustrous sheen."

She noticed.

He took the liberty of easing the coat over her shoulders. The drape felt exquisite; the weight of the fur, a strange new gravity. A lining of gold dress-silk flashed within. She wrapped the coat around herself, and felt the dense animal softness mould itself to her form.

"You won't find a more fashionable cut this side of Montreal."

It was the coat of a mature, stylish woman, the coat of a woman of nearly thirty.

She deposited her payment in a small metal box and watched it whiz away on an electric wire. Within moments, the box came sailing back down the line, and revealed, as if by magic, her bill of sale.

Her account was settled.

The coat would be delivered.

The dance was Saturday night.

The penalties of past mistakes cannot be remitted, but at least the lessons so solemnly and dearly learned should be taken to heart.

But not yet. Wait—

Because Charlie Thompson is pulling up next to the hitching-rail outside Vooght's, where William Dooley, the Funeral Director, has stopped his team. Steam rises from the horses" dark flanks as a small group of men—from Dooley's, the Cable Office, the Vendome Hotel, and the Royal Albert—gather to offer, with low whistles and eagle-eyes, their unreserved admiration for Charlie Thompson's new 1926 Buick Roadster.

Marjorie sees him—Mr. Thompson, her employer—and nods briefly before turning right, when , in fact, she meant to turn left for home. But it's too late. Her pride in her new purchase has distracted her, and she doesn't want to walk past the group again straightaway, so she slips into The Royal Café and orders tea with a slice of Lady Baltimore cake.

Outside the gleaming window, a single, tusky icicle drips, one of a long row that hangs from the café's awning, but Marjorie is unaware.

She watches, vaguely, the gathering of men across the street. William Dooley, the funeral director, has eased himself into the driver's seat. Mr. Thompson is leaning on the door of the Buick, showing him the inner sanctum, but even so, he is taller than the others. She supposes he's handsome for a man of his age: dark-haired, grey only at the temples, an easy smile. Shame about the one short leg. A birth defect, she was told.

According to Eleanor in the office, he always walks fast, trying to disguise it, and his tailor "gets hell" if the hem of his trousers doesn't hide the top of his block of a shoe. "Maybe the bad leg's the reason he likes *speed*," Eleanor murmured, leaning forward. "Well, there's that new automobile, isn't there? Plus some fine breed of horse up at the race course." She lowered her chin and whispered into her bosom. "Apparently, he's a *gambler*."

Maybe, thought Marjorie. But married, fifty, sober, Protestant, well off, with three children. Respectable.

She leaves two bites of cake on her plate, as May taught her. She pushes in her chair, slips on her wool coat and pays the bill. Across the street, Charlie Thompson has resumed the ordinary shape of the man who lopes unevenly past her desk each morning while the secretaries, Marjorie included, lower their heads out of courtesy.

As she slips through the door of The Royal Café, there can be no way for Marjorie to know that the man she is about to pass for the second time that day—Charlie Thompson, married, fifty, Protestant, with three children—is her future.

On Route 28, the chains on the car's tires grip the snowy twists and bends. They hum, then clunk, with every rotation, a primitive rhythm that sends Marjorie into a world of her own. It's a sixteen-mile journey from North Sydney to Sydney, and, wrapped in her new coat, she enjoys every moment, staring through her window at the frozen expanse of Sydney Harbour, mesmerized by its white, elemental glow.

So she makes only the poorest of efforts to shout over the engine for chit-chat with Eleanor and Eleanor's brother Stan up front. The forty-minute journey passes in what seems like ten, and in no time, the flaming tower of Sydney's steel-works looms into view, spitting like a firework about to explode.

The Herald will assure us that, as she arrives at The Imperial Hotel on Sydney's Esplanade, Marjorie is *a young lady* whose thoughts are *centered on an evening's innocent recreation.* In the lobby, she passes her fur to the cloakroom attendant, wondering if the girl will be tempted to try it when no one's looking. *Go on,* she wants to say. *I don't mind*! But she doesn't want to presume.

"Don't forget your dance cards!" the girl calls after them, and Marjorie dashes back.

The names of the dances marked on the cards make her and Eleanor laugh: the Turkey Trot, the Wiggle-de-Wiggle, the Shorty George, the Fuzzy Wuzzy . . . Sixteen in all. "I hope I've got a little Negro in my blood," shouts Eleanor as they sashay into the ballroom. Marjorie can only force a smile, not knowing the polite reply. Besides, the twelve-man band is already bugling and strumming, swaying and tromboning, and Marjorie knows this one—"Everything's Gonna Be Alright."

"There must be more than five hundred people here," marvels Eleanor.

Marjorie is swapping her boots for her Mary-Janes. "And half from North Sydney!"

"I told you we wouldn't be stuck with Stan all night. Besides, there are enough men from the K.O.C. to mean that even the Pope himself would approve of our Turkey Trot. Look! Mr. Thompson's here too."

Marjorie spots him, smoking near the rear door. She shrugs.

But Eleanor is still squinting. "He's here with the race course set."

Marjorie turns to the band. Five of the twelve men are black. Two, the darkest black. She's heard there are Negro families in Sydney who have come all the way from the Deep South.

She's only ever seen a Negro once before, a stoker from the Foundry who came into the office because his wages were overdue. She liked the sound of his voice; the lazy music of his words.

Eleanor yells over the band. "He's come on his own."

"Who has?"

"Mrs. Thompson isn't here. She must be down with something again. Not that it matters! He never dances anyway with that short leg of his."

Marjorie can see Stan crossing the floor towards them, refreshments in hand. In a moment, thankfully, Eleanor will have another ear.

"Though you never know." She giggles and tugs at Marjorie's sleeve. "The Shorty George might be just the number for him!"

Marjorie knows she should, but she doesn't care enough about Mr. Thompson to protest on his behalf. Besides it's a new song now, one she's never heard—"If You Can't Land Her on the Ol" Verandah"—and beneath her satin dress, her hips are already swaying with a life of their own.

Dance after dance, time is shimmying and quick-stepping away, and

Marjorie has no notion of the hour. She's red-faced and giddy from laughing through all the new steps, but the room still heaves with dancers. Even Joe "Clunk" McEwan is stepdancing on a table-top to "The Alabama Stomp."

Someone has propped open the rear doors for a blast of cold winter air, and hip-flasks of bootlegged whisky are passing from man to man, across the dance floor. The M.C. is starting to slur, and the twelve-man band is three men down, but the music roars on.

She plucks her dress away from her to catch any breath of air.

"Excuse me, Miss. Is there room for one more on your dance card?"

Marjorie turns. One of the Negro men from the band—the double-bass player—is standing before her, his shoulders back, his tie loose at his neck.

Eleanor's hand flies to her chest. Stan takes a step forward.

Marjorie can see the man is not drunk. His eyes are clear; his gaze, steady. For a moment, she wishes he were. She might know what to do. She extends her hand. "I'm enjoying the music."

He nods, grinning at the parquet floor. "I'm Walter. Would you like to dance, Miss?"

"Marjorie." She clasps her palms. "But I have to confess, Walter. I'm done in for the night."

He clicks his tongue. "A fine dancer like you? Why, you just need your second wind."

She risks it. "I'm sure it's none of my business, Walter, but are you one of the steel-workers from down south?" *Are the nights sultry?* she wants to ask. *Do the women carry fans?*

He nods. "From Alabama, Miss."

She wishes he would call her Marjorie. "But Sydney's your home now?"

"Not Sydney proper, Miss."

"No?"

"No." He runs a hand across his chin and searches her face. "Me and my family, we live in Cokeville."

She smiles politely. Then it comes to her: Cokeville. The area by Whitney Pier, where the filthy run-off from the coke ovens pours into the estuary.

The band strikes up a waltz, "Wistful and Blue." Walter offers her his hand. She is surprised by the pale flash of his palms.

She can feel the eyes of many more than Stan and Eleanor now. But his hand still waits, and the truth is, she *would* like to dance.

As she takes his hand, she can feel the calluses on his fingertips. She has never met a double-bass player before. Up close, he smells of lye, like the bar her mother keeps by the set-tub.

From the seating area there arises a low drone of disapproval. Couple after couple leave the dance floor.

She reaches after conversation, speaking into his ear. "So you brought your family with you to Sydney?"

He leads well. "Yes, that's right. My mamma and my sisters."

She dreads the eye of the roaming spotlight. "That must be difficult—with just you to look after them, I mean."

She can see his eyes assessing the risk: is it better to lead her into the shadows of the ballroom or to keep to the bright center? "Yes, Miss, I do my best. But it's been especially hard since my brother was killed."

"Killed?" She stops dancing.

"'Fraid so. Just before we left Alabama. At a speak-easy in our town. Leonard was hired to wash glasses. But a fight broke out over something or another that had gone missing. The manager was drunk. Went mad as a hornet. Broke a glass—on purpose like—and cut Leonard's throat."

The shape of her brother Murray rises in Marjorie's mind's eye. Blood still seeps from his ear.

"Did they get the man, Walter, or did he get away?"

"Neither, Miss." He swallows hard. "They didn't get the man— and he didn't get away. That laid us low, my mamma especially."

Marjorie nods. *Her mother. In the ice house. Her lips blue.*

Out of the corner of her eye, she notices that several of the men from the K.O.C. have risen from their chairs and stand watching, their arms folded across their chests. They're wondering if Walter has offended her; if that's why she's having words. So she smiles at her partner, to say she is ready to dance again, and Walter waltzes her back to the center of the floor.

On stage, the M.C. is fiddling anxiously with his cuffs and trying, without success, to catch the eye of the conductor. But "Blue and Wistful" floats on into the wintery night—*one,* two, three—while the ballroom of The Imperial Hotel empties. The K.O.C. men, Marjorie notices, still haven't sat back down in their chairs, and Walter's hand has gone cold in hers.

A voice sounds at the dark edge of the spotlight: "Excuse me."

Walter stops short. Marjorie squeezes her eyes shut. She can feel the air around her about to break.

"May I?"

She opens her eyes. Charlie Thompson is standing before them. He has tapped Walter's shoulder.

Walter nods, then smiles, blinking too much, before he thanks Marjorie for the dance. Marjorie presses his forearm. "Thank you for asking." He makes for the safety of the stage as Charlie Thompson takes her hand in his. She feels his other hand, light on the small of her back. His face tenses as he strains to pick out the beat. Then they step into the mercy of darkness, his bad leg stammering.

***

When he returns her to her table, Eleanor is talking to Jimmy Monaghan. She doesn't turn to acknowledge Marjorie.

Charlie Thompson hovers, his head bowed. "Thank you for the dance, Marjorie. It was kind of you to put up with my two left feet."

"Thank *you*, Mr. Thompson!" She has to look away so the tears don't come.

He glances sternly at the backs of Eleanor and Jimmy Monaghan. "I'm driving back to North Sydney now, in case you need a lift."

She turns to the table and tries again. "Eleanor?"

But Eleanor pretends not to hear. So Marjorie finds her clutch on the floor and tries to smile. "Thank you. It *is* very late."

Outside, the snow that was falling earlier has turned to sleet. As she waits on the sidewalk for Mr. Thompson in his Buick, she watches two men approach, their unbuttoned coats flapping. Even in the wind, she can smell the liquor on them as they pass. When one slips on a patch of ice and almost hits the ground, she turns her face away. She pretends not to hear his friend mutter that the roads everywhere are "as slick as a buttered-up bride." But everything's fine because Mr. Thompson's pulling up to the curb now. He's stepping outside to open her door, and as she bundles herself and her coat into the passenger seat, she hardly knows what possesses her. "Cokeville." She stares into her lap. "Before we go back, Mr. Thompson, would you show me Cokeville?"

His hand hovers over the gearbox. He has to clear his throat. "Sure. It's not so far out of our way."

She smells it before she sees it: a stink of slag and human sewage. Under the angry candle of the steel-works' tower, rows of dark bunkhouses and shacks appear in the night.

Charlie Thompson turns off the engine, and she stumbles into speech. "But Bill at the Foundry said these men are skilled laborers. I thought that's why they were asked to come all this way."

"Yes."

"I thought all the steel-workers and their families lived in the Ashby area."

"Not all—sadly."

Marjorie pulls her coat tight. Charlie lights a cigarette for her, but she suspects her hand will shake if she tries to hold it.

He rubs the windshield clear of the mist of their breath. "It's after midnight, Marjorie."

"Of course. I'm keeping you, and my mother will be waiting up."

"Not to mention the fact that you'll get an earful from your big sister when she hears." In the narrow space of the two-door Buick, he turns to her for the first time—and winks. "I see her very . . . patient husband up at the track."

She lets herself laugh.

"We'll take the harbor, shall we?" he says. "Make up a bit of lost time?"

She sits up in her seat, surfacing from the depths of her coat. "Stan, Eleanor's brother, said the harbor is risky now."

Charlie casts his cigarette into the night. "I came that way. The ice was rock solid." He smiles. "You don't think I'd play fast and loose with this baby, do you?" He thumps the steering wheel, then releases the clutch.

A *gambler*, said Eleanor. "Apparently, he's a *gambler*." Of course, he'd have to be to offer her—a young, unmarried woman—a late-night lift home in the first place. Not that she had to accept. Maybe that makes them two of a kind, her and Charlie Thompson. She only knows that it's past midnight, the roads are bad—it will be a slow crawl back to North Sydney—and May will shame her come tomorrow morning. She has no idea how she'll explain: about Walter, the lateness of the hour, about Mr. Thompson, married and Protestant.

At Muggah's Creek, the new 1926 Buick Roadster glides onto the ice.

But even now, there's time. Will she say it?

Shall we turn back? Everyone says you shouldn't cross after the first of March.

No.

Because what's five days to twenty inches of ice, and hasn't it been snowing most of the night? Besides, it's just eight miles across. In a quarter of an hour, they'll be landing on the sandbar at Indian Beach.

She has never crossed by night before. The swollen sky bears down on them. In the wide, dark limbo of Sydney Harbour, the Buick's headlamps seem no brighter than a pair of jack-o-lanterns.

Every year the Council says it will provide range-lights and a few bush-marked courses, but the owners of the ice-breakers protest. How will they clear the harbor's shipping lane with lights, markers and more traffic to circumnavigate?

As the car moves out across the frozen estuary, Charlie Thompson's hands are rigid on the wheel. Now and again, the car fan-tails, but he pulls it back into line and on they go.

She'll laugh on the other side. Perhaps she'll even have one of Mr.

Thompson's cigarettes or a swig from his flask to steady her nerves.

She would lay her head back and close her eyes—she's so tired now—but cold air blasts through the windows. Mr. Thompson says they have to stay open so the windshield doesn't fog up.

And suddenly, for no reason, she remembers the old Mic Mac woman who came to the door selling colored baskets. "I'm sorry," the woman said, taking Marjorie's mother's thin hand in her own. "I am sorry about your three daughters."

How did she know?

But "No," said Marjorie, going to her mother's aid. "My mother has lost two daughters and the son of the house. *Two* daughters. Three children. But thank you for your condolences." And the woman looked at her—looked right *through* her.

She shakes herself. They are almost clear of the estuary. Another ten minutes and they'll be on *terra firma.* She tries to brighten. "All things considered," she says, turning to Charlie Thompson, "I enjoyed myself tonight."

He laughs, relieved to have conversation. "I haven't danced so much in years!"

"You danced half of one dance!"

"Exactly. My wife will never believe it."

She doesn't look at him as she says it. "You'll tell your wife then."

He leans forward, mopping the windshield with his sleeve. "Haven't decided yet. I have a policy, you might say. I try my damnedest to live in the moment."

She nods, as if his reply were neither here nor there.

"Which means," he says, winking again, "I'll think about it tomorrow when I'm sitting in church."

"Where you can calmly resolve to think about it later!"

"Bull's-eye."

She settles back into her seat, laughing. She recalls again the easy sway of her hips as she danced, and Walter's firm arm leading, and Mr. Thompson bending over her, tall, close, protective. There's a tune stuck in her head, one of the big jazz numbers of the night. What was it called? The windshield wipers are going, they're lulling her to sleep, and it's only when Charlie Thompson looks over and catches her eye that she realizes she's been humming the tune aloud. Her throat and cheeks go hot, but there's no need. He's not signaling for her to stop. He's *singing.* Eleanor wouldn't believe it. He's stringing together one line after the other, and it's all coming back: the deep, in-your-belly rhythm, the spell of the words, the stream in the moonlight, the honey who'll be gone by dawn. "Tonight You Belong to

Me." That's the one. Charlie Thompson has a fine voice, she thinks to herself—

when the car goes through the ice.

Her stomach drops; her spine stiffens. The hole opens like a black mouth. The Buick tips—her hands can't find the handle—and suddenly, unfathomably, the car is locked in jaws of ice.

The headlamps are out, and she can't tell if the space above her is the window that faces up or down. His or hers. There's no top, no bottom, no floor, no roof, no ocean bed, no blind hole. *Mr. Thompson?* Through the open window, water and ice are rushing across her lap—*my coat, my new coat*— and her mind can't catch up.

I tell myself this.

She feels his hand grabbing at her shoulder—*thank God,* she thinks, *thank God.* He's hauling her up by the collar of her coat. She's pushing off from the passenger door with her feet, gulping air. Is that his voice calling or the groaning of steel against ice?

But the car shifts again, a wave churns through, and—

No.

The car is falling, juddering, through the ice. *Mr. Thompson!*

But he's nowhere.

Such darkness. Such cold. Like she has never known.

Her coat clings, sodden. Heavy.

Unimaginably heavy.

A dead animal weight.

And the Mic Mac woman is beside her in the footwell—*sssh now, quiet*— as the car sinks to the bottom of the estuary.

In the article in *The Herald* entitled "Saturday Night's Tragedy," she will remain unnamed. A kindness perhaps.

There will be no obituary. No public wake. No crowd of mourners, warm and close in the kitchen.

Only talk.

Her funeral will be attended by just four, her sisters May, Laura, Alice and Ignace. As the mass is said, her mother will close herself in "Ethel's room" and draw the drapes. There will be only two words etched in stone: "Deeply regretted."

As for Charlie Thompson, he will never be able to get a song out of his head. In the black water of the night, it will slow into a dirge and boom between his ears. *Tonight you belong to me.*

Sometimes, I tell people about my great aunt who went under the ice.

When the Hearse Goes By

Nuala Ní Chonchúir

My brother's widow, Ivy, lived in Paris. I went there to sympathize with her, though I liked neither her nor him. Bernard was buried in Père Lachaise before I left Cork. I planned to visit his grave, to stand and look at it, to see where he was deposited and, maybe, say a prayer. Mostly to honor our dead mother's rampant religiosity.

I arrived airplane-weary at Ivy's door and, when she opened it, the first thing I noticed was her skin, puce from sunburn. On her chest, tattooed in white, were the letters of her name; strangely, the shape of the word sitting under her clavicle was like an ivy leaf. She was a stumpy woman with a man's haircut and downturned lips that made her look dissatisfied; Ivy didn't ask for that mouth, I knew, but it added to her uncharm.

Her greeting hug was warm. "*Bienvenue,* Fergus. How was your flight?"

"You got burnt," I said.

"I fell asleep by the river." She patted her chest. "Bernard would kill me if he saw it."

"Bernard so conscientious. Really?"

Ivy snorted. "Bernard was fussier than an old sow." She laughed. "A sow in an apron."

"Oh," I said. I presumed the faux hippy persona my brother cultivated meant he had relaxed into middle age. "Maybe France changed him," I said.

"Not at all. You Irish are so uptight; all that soggy guilt you carry around." Ivy pushed me through the hall of the apartment, which was lush with pot plants. "This is the salon."

I wanted to make some retort about the English—Ivy was a Londoner—but the room was lovely and I was jealous; it was like a scene from another age with its long windows that filtered light. I took in the picture rails and the crisp antique furniture. It confirmed what I had always thought: everyone else's home was better than mine. Even my dead brother's.

"What a smashing room," I said, though I hadn't intended to be pleasant.

"Bernard loved the salon. He used to sit with the windows open, smoking and looking out. It's a pity you never saw him here, Fergus."

"Smoking?" I said.

Ivy mentioned that my nephew—Nicholas—would be coming to stay while I was there. "He lives in Lyons now," she said. "He's been travelling to Paris once a fortnight since Bernard died. Checking up on me."

"Nick was so young the last time I saw him. Twelve years old, maybe."

I didn't say I thought Nicholas was wasted on Bernard, or that my envy of their relationship was one of the things that kept me away. My marriage was never blessed with children.

Since Bernard died I had been dreaming about insects: earwigs in my bath and shitty woodlice on my pillow, that sort of thing. The dreams disturbed my sleep and I had been awake early every day for six weeks. Then the morning chorus would start up. In Ivy's spare bedroom, I dreamt there were moths landing on my face. The birds in Paris were even more vigorous than the ones at home; they whirred on the balcony outside my window, hour after hour. I opened it, flapped my hands and shooed, but they ignored me.

"What are those awful birds?" I asked Ivy at breakfast.

"Sparrows—they go a bit batty at this time of year; they drove Bernard mad." She poured my tea.

"They're infuriating," I said. I told her about my dreams: about the creepy-crawlies, the wakefulness, the whole lot. "The dreams started after I'd heard Bernard was dead. And it's not just insects either. All my dreams are crazy since he died. I dreamt that jam was evil; there were health warnings about it." I sipped my tea and looked at Ivy; she had a collectedness that I would have liked for myself, her face was always set and calm. I wanted to stop blabbing, but I went on: "I wouldn't mind: only apart from one recurring dream I've been having for years, I don't normally remember anything."

"Funny, me neither," Ivy said. "But I dreamt last night that Bernard was in the chair beside our bed. He never sat there. It felt very real and I wanted him to go away."

"Oh," I said. Her dream had trumped mine.

"Are you afraid of burial, Fergus?"

"I don't know. What do you mean?"

"Well, maybe the insects in your dreams have something to do with that," she said. "You know, *"The worms crawl in, the worms crawl out; the worms play pinochle on your snout"*," she chanted. I was baffled. "It's a song, Fergus."

"So it appears. Well, I've never heard it." I drank my tea and examined her; what an odd woman, I thought.

She waved her napkin in my face. "Oh, cheer up, Fergus. Why don't we go out for a walk? Clear the clouds."

We took a Métro to the eighth arrondissement and emerged above ground near the Champs. I was familiar enough with Paris not to be enthralled or smothered by it, but I was happy to be there breathing its strange, pure air that endured even in summer. I've always liked that as a city it's both familiar and unknowable: the Eiffel tower pokes like the folly that it is from the quai; the Tour Montparnasse stretches blank and ugly over Saint Germain; the people are singular and entrenched in their lives—almost perfect. Paris is a city, I've often thought, that can provoke both lust and revolt in the dullest of hearts. I had always been fond of the place and it galled me that my brother made it his own because I had not.

For a small woman, Ivy walked surprisingly fast. We passed café after café where the people inside mouthed to each other across tables like fish in aquariums; they drank coffee and water, ate croissants and omelettes. Smokers cuddled outside under awnings, ignoring one another as they aimed blue jets into the street. Ivy marched on, pointing out shops that, by their scant window displays, seemed to sell nothing at all. She brought me to the place du Carrousel, where the guillotine had fallen on thousands of necks.

"Imagine the blood that flowed here once," she said, with a kind of manic glee.

"Just imagine," I said. I was overheated and, because I was wearing my stupidest shoes, my feet hurt.

Ivy waved a hand at the Seine and said she loved the river. "And the bridges, Fergus. My God, the bridges. The French know how to look after their city—they pour millions into its upkeep. Billions!"

"Can we stop for a cup of tea; something to eat?" I asked meekly, when she seemed determined to walk as far as the Marais without stopping.

"Of course, Fergus. You have to try the croque monsieur in a place I know off the rue du Rivoli. They do the best ones."

The bistro we entered had a weird smell—something foreign lurked behind the normal coffee-and-bread scent; it bothered me but I couldn't get to what it was. We took a seat by the window and Ivy chattered in French to the waiter. Two women sat across from us, stroking their lapdogs and talking quietly. Ivy pushed her arms over her head and grunted.

"Ah," she said, "that feels good."

"Will you stay here, now that Bernard is gone?" I asked.

"Where would I go? This is home."

"I thought you might go back to London."

"There's nothing for me in England."

I was glad to be sitting down and I stretched my legs under the small table. Ivy looked like she might jump up any second; there was a giddiness about her that didn't suit a mourning widow, I thought.

"You miss him, I suppose," I said.

"Like air," Ivy answered.

The waiter slipped my croque monsieur in front of me; I poked approvingly at the gruyère that lapped from the sides of the bread. He set down a pichet of white wine and I poured for both of us. Ivy urged me to eat, saying her dish would take a little while. I attacked the croque with my knife and fork but abandoned them in favor of my hands. It was delicious—the bread high and light, the ham salty. The waiter came towards us again—swerving his tray over the heads of other customers—and served Ivy with a huge fish. Its teeth protruded in gnashing spikes and the gelatinous marble of its eye glared at me. I couldn't believe that I hadn't realized the disconcerting smell in the bistro was the smell of fish.

"I'm an icthyophobe," I squeaked, fanning my face with my napkin.

Ivy was already filleting the fish's skin; she lifted her eyes to look at me. "What did you say, Fergus?"

"I said I am an *icthyophobe*; I can't let you eat that fish at this table."

Ivy clattered her cutlery onto her plate. "And what the hell is an icthyophobe?"

"I'm allergic to fish, you stupid woman!" I pushed back my chair and hurried from the bistro, gulping in the air on the street as soon as I got outside. I was nearly flattened by a man on roller-blades and immediately I had that why-did-I-leave-my-house distress that I always get when I'm away. I kneaded my eyes with my knuckles.

"First insects, then birds, now fish. What next?" I heard Ivy say. I turned to see her at my side. I was still trying to breathe after the shock of the fish's horrible face and bulging scales; after its stink. Ivy put her hand on my arm. "Do you want to see Bernard's resting place, Fergus?" she said, and I nodded.

Bernard and I were close as young boys, the way brothers near in age often are; we shared a grudging camaraderie and spent a lot of time in each other's company—hurling, roaming the fields, lighting fires. But we also never missed a chance to puck the head off each other, or rat to our mother about some small crime. We walked to school and tormented cats together; we slept in the same room at night. He was a year older than me and started young into girls—around eleven—so our drift started then.

I thought about Bernard and our wasted friendship as Ivy and I stood in front of the memorial wall in the cemetery; the foxy smell of yew trees filled my nose.

"You cremated him," I said.

"At his request."

"God, our mother would have hated this." I looked around. "So, his ashes are in there?" I pointed to the wall.

Ivy fidgeted with the strap of her handbag; she lifted her face to the sky and puffed out a breath. I watched her and waited for an answer.

"You know, Fergus, I was going to tell you his ashes were in that wall, but I don't feel right doing it now," she said. "You remind me so much of him sometimes it's like you *are* him." She looked up at me. "I took him home to the apartment. He's at home."

"Well, if that was what you wanted," I said.

Ivy grinned at me, looking a little guilty, and I smiled. I looked back at Bernard's name and dates on the memorial wall. I wanted to feel worse standing there, for my lost brother and for our mother who believed that cremation meant no chance of an afterlife, but I didn't. I couldn't muster any of the sadness that had been dogging me for weeks.

"He's safe from the insects at least," Ivy said. "No worms will play pinochle on *his* snout."

I sniggered and Ivy burst into chuckles; she wriggled the laugh through her whole body and stamped her feet. The two of us fell into tear-spilling convulsions, holding each other up and shaking off spasms of laughter. Some teenagers, who were making a pilgrimage to a rock star's grave, studied us and smiled. One boy did an impression of Ivy's foot-stamping and that made us both hoot loudly.

"We're turning this cemetery into a pantomime," I said. "Let's go."

Ivy linked my arm; we waved to the teenagers and strolled through the graveyard, admiring the plots and the jungle of headstones. Ivy was not really like an English person, I thought, she didn't look at you as if from a great height. She was unpredictable, outspoken—rude, even—but warm. Yes, warm.

Ivy had used Bernard's ashes to fertilize the pot-plants in the apartment's hallway. His empty urn sat in the armoire in the room where I slept. I thought about it each night before putting my head down, after a day spent with Ivy. We walked the places she and Bernard had walked: the Bois and the Jardin du Luxembourg; the open-air food markets and the riverbank. We ate in the bistros they had loved to go to together and we talked and talked.

We sat in her salon in deep sunlight one evening, after hours of walking, and drank wine. Nicholas, my nephew, was due from Lyons but he was late, so we had eaten dinner without him.

"Bernard was mad for girls," I said, wanting to talk about my brother; I felt we had been neglecting him.

"Oh, always," Ivy said.

"Was he faithful do you think?"

"What does it matter, Fergus? I loved him."

"I spied on him with a girl called Caroline Clear once, when we were kids. They were in the woods, against a tree, and he had his hand under her skirt, moving it fast. I could see her knickers and I was shocked because they were navy blue—a little girl's underwear." I sipped my wine and Ivy looked at me, her expression bemused. "Caroline became well known in the media and I could never watch her TV show, remembering Bernard's furious groping. It made me hate both of them. He found out I'd been eyeballing and hit me a few digs in the face; I had bruises on my cheeks. There was never a thimbleful of trust between us after that."

"Such a pity you two didn't stay close," Ivy said. "You're so very alike."

I looked out the window. The starlings were pegged onto the balcony grilles like ornaments, not making a sound; a leaden moon skulked over the rooftops even as the sun went down.

"Will Nicholas make it from Lyons tonight?" I asked.

"It's a bit late now."

"I'll sleep well," I said, waving my full wine glass at Ivy.

"No bad dreams for either of us, hopefully."

I told Ivy my worst dream, the one that nagged at me. "It's always the same: I've killed someone, an old neighbor from Watergrasshill. Years later his dismembered body is discovered and I realize I'm about to be exposed as the murderer. It catches me around the neck that dream; I'm so afraid that it's true. That I'm a killer. Thanks be to God I always wake up, but it takes a while to get over it."

"I hate those ones that linger. That dream is probably about guilt, Fergus. You know, about unfinished business." She sipped her wine. "I had a funny one this morning, actually; I've just remembered it. There were two smart-mouthed kids, yapping all this clever stuff at each other. It felt like the kids were me and Bernard. Or me and you." She frowned.

"I was in your dream?" I said. "Well, I'm honored. Mine seem to have dried up—no more spiders, etcetera."

I liked our small ritual of dream dissection; I enjoyed Ivy's insights and her reports on what she dreamt about. I stretched my arm and clinked my glass off hers. Her face was gilded by the setting sun; she looked radiant—beatific, almost—and it felt natural to lean forward and put my lips to hers. Her mouth was soft, which surprised me, and I kissed deeper, slipping my tongue against Ivy's, testing. She kissed me back and pulled away only to put down her glass. I placed mine beside hers on the coffee table and we fell on each other. Her body yielded under me but the sofa was tiny and we were soon sliding onto the floor.

"Fergus. Bedroom," Ivy said, her breath clashing off mine and her hands ruffling madly inside my shirt.

We jumped up and went to her and Bernard's room. Ivy pulled her jersey dress over her head in one swift yank. I noticed that her knickers were too big—they sagged over her belly. I was about to remark on it but I said nothing. Maybe I was growing kinder; maybe Ivy was having an influence.

We leapt into her bed and stared at each other. We made love furiously and I felt like the most able lover in the world; all our movements seemed to glide and meld. Her skin was butter soft, her thrusting strong and rhythmic; I welcomed the velvet pulse of her. I had to hold myself back and I stopped more than once to caress and look at her, to slow myself down. I traced my fingers over her sunburnt skin, over the ivy leaf on her chest. She wrapped her legs around my waist and urged me on. I couldn't believe this was Ivy; I couldn't believe it was me.

Ivy retrieved our wine glasses from the salon. We sat up in her bed, my arm around her shoulder, and drank. Though we were naked, we both acted like nothing out of the ordinary was happening. I kissed the top of her head.

"You know, you can't be that much of an icthyophobe," she said.

"Why's that?"

"I'm a Pisces."

We both laughed; I pulled her closer to me and fingered her chest.

"Don't get sunburnt again," I said, "it's irresponsible. Keep yourself safe."

"Oh, stop it, you sound like Bernard."

"Well," I said.

The bedroom was dim, lit only by the moonlight that scattered across the floor from the window. I heard the door-handle click before Ivy did. I clenched my body and watched the door open wider and wider.

"Maman?" a voice said. And then, in a higher pitch, "Papa?" Nicholas stood in the doorway, staring at me, his face confused. "Papa?" he said again and moved towards us.

"It's me, Nicholas. Uncle Fergus."

He lunged forward. "What the fuck?" he shouted.

Nicholas turned and left the room quickly. Ivy climbed from the bed, breasts swinging and wine slopping from her glass onto the eiderdown.

"Nicholas," she called. "Nick!" She followed him out to the salon and I slowly got up and pulled on my clothes.

I hung my outfit for the morning on the armoire. It kept me awake half the night, looming like a lurker in the room. I got up and opened the armoire to look for Bernard's urn. It stood on a shelf with his folded T-shirts and jeans: it was a black porcelain pot and it reminded me of a biscuit barrel. I took it out and snapped off the lid; the inside was ashy. I slid one finger over the inner wall of the urn and looked at the white residue it left on my skin.

"Goodbye, Bernard," I said, and instantly felt maudlin and foolish. I put the urn back.

The next morning Nicholas didn't come out of his room and I woke Ivy to tell her I was leaving.

"Good morning, you," she said and patted the edge of her bed, so I sat.

"Tell Nicholas I'm sorry," I said.

"There's no need, Fergus. I'm not sorry. Last night you were my 'péché mignon'—one adorable little weakness. I'm allowed that."

"I upset Nicholas."

She took my hand and kissed it. "He'll get over it."

"Thanks for everything, Ivy. You've helped me."

"And you me, Fergus," she said.

We kissed and I agreed I would come back to Paris before Christmas and stay for a fortnight. I left for the airport—half-bereft, half-ecstatic—and made my way home to Watergrasshill.

I never saw Ivy again. That November, in her Paris apartment, she took her own life. She sent me a long, rambling letter but she was already gone by the time I read her words. She said she couldn't go on without Bernard. She missed him far too much; she missed her life as it used to be and, she said, the present was no good to her.

"The past, for me," she wrote, "is a picture etched on glass, almost visible but not quite."

And it was safely in the past that Ivy most wanted to be.

The Lost and Found

Claire Larrière

Translated by Claire Larrière and Shirley Abott

"Listen, Arthur. Aunt Line's lost her ring. Arthur! You haven't seen her ring?"

Line has come back in through the garden door; her nephew and niece do not hear her. Loren looks up from her book and calls her brother, glued to his computer and annoyed.

"Which one of her rings? Do I know which one?"

"The one she often wears. Silver with a small cube set up on top and a pearl inlay in the middle. Looks like a poison ring."

"You don't say! Aunt Line, a spy hunted by bandits. Carries a powerful poison on her finger, in case of torture. Yes, I know that ring. When did she lose it? Did she look in her gardening gloves? A ring can easily slip off into a glove finger. A ring.

Arthur . . .

Yes, she looked in her gloves. And her ring is not in the grass under the clothesline, or mixed up with the first chestnuts under the chestnut trees, and not in the house in the Limoges porcelain bowls or in grandmother's pillboxes. Lost! Lost!

Outside the wind swirls and rustles the maple and chestnut leaves. It's cozy inside by the fire.

"How long since she lost it?" Arthur asks once more.

Sometimes Line wears no jewelery for days on end. Sometimes she wears whatever she's come across in her jewelery boxes, where the cheap and the precious are jumbled together, and sometimes she selects a favorite, like that ring, and wears it a week or longer. But she hasn't worn it lately.

Arthur has again dived into the Internet, Loren into her book, but surely halfway, with the ring still on her mind.

Line is their confidante, their shield between themselves and parental severity. As they are her shield against all kinds of misunderstandings.

"Mummy wonders will you ever find yourself a husband . . . "

"So you can have kids before it's too late . . ."

"In short you will soon be too old . . . "

"And miss the purpose of life, which is to get married, have kids . . . "

"The Middle Ages in the twenty-first century, interpreted by the same idiots . . . "

"All the same," Line retorts, "you have been allowed to spend your Halloween vacation here with me."

Jacotte, Line's older sister, regrets having inherited their grandmother's Paris apartment rather than the house in Brittany that went to Line. This is no secret for the children but they never mention it. It is not with their mother that they take long walks on the shore, interspersed with laughter and philosophizing.

The tide is strong. The sea comes far up, leaving seaweed and driftwood on the narrow strip of sand. Sometimes the rising tide brings back some object forgotten on the shore at low tide. The other day a mother and her little boy spied an unusual little wreck: a small green sandal that they had heedlessly left behind the day before.

"Look, Thibaud! The sea has brought back your sandal. Just where we were sitting. But don't forget anything again, the sea might not return it . . ."

Did the ring slip off her finger when she swam here last time? She was with Arthur; they had jumped up and down in the water, pumping their arms to keep warm, Loren watching them from dry ground, a bit envious, a bit nervous. But was Line wearing her ring that day?

Now they walk on, the three of them, very slowly, eyeing the ground, spotting glitters in the lovely deceptive sunset glow.

In the garden she discovers, emerging unexpectedly from the earth where they'd lain buried for years, horseshoes, bits of rusted metal and innumerable pieces of broken bottles, witnesses of the past inmates' lives.

"Perhaps," says Loren, "our descendants will see the ring coming out of the earth one day. Intact. One by one, the ladies of the house will try to slip it on their finger, like others on their foot Cinderella's vair slipper . . . "

"Nothing doing," Arthur retorts, "Aunt Line's fingers are as slim as a fairy's wand."

A precise vision: that ring is everywhere. There it is, in the gutter. There it is, among the supermarket supplies, among the stacks of papers on her desk, on the finger of a woman in the street or in an elevator. Line's eyes inspect the hands of other women. Could it be that thinking so hard about the ring will make it appear? The life of objects . . .

"You haven't found your ring?" Jacotte asks. "Have you thought of inquiring at town hall? They have an agency for that."

"Should we call at the Office of the Lost? Or of the Found?"

"That depends. If you come looking for something, it is the Lost Objects Office. If they tell you to come claim something, it's the Found Objects Office."

Jacotte . . .

Lost, lost. Not for everyone. The woman who finds it will lift her hand to admire it and feel thankful for her luck. A short-lived luck it will be. Poison ring.

"Funny word, 'Lost,'" says Arthur.

Dinner is over. They linger dreamily at the table.

"Yes," says Line, "and it is odd. You say 'lose your head,' but not 'a lost head.'"

"And the French call french bread 'pain perdu,' lost bread," says Loren, "but it is not lost since it is used again."

Loren . . .

"But sometimes all is lost, says Arthur. If you lose a battle, it really is lost."

"And when we say we've lost a dear person," Loren adds, "that really means the dear person is lost."

Arthur frowns at Loren insistently. She understands: a gaffe.

"Be nice to Aunt Line, their mother had told them. She is very sad now."

"Why?"

"Because she lost somebody she loved."

"Somebody who died?"

"No, but might as well have."

That could only be François, the only one she loved besides them.

Of course they had known it. It was Line herself who told them:

"François and I no longer see each other."

"One lost makes ten found," quips Arthur to cover up Loren's gaffe, but that only makes matters worse.

Line will be the closer to them and they will go out walking as a threesome more often than ever.

Line is editing recipes for herbs. She has a contract with a publisher. She grows herbs in a corner of her garden, makes them taste a few shoots, which they immediately spit out:

"Are you sure they are edible?"

But the dishes she cooks with them are delicious.

Loren, on a garden bench, is reading *Bérénice.* She underlines the words of love that make her French teacher swoon.

Line, working at her plants, feels Arthur looking at her; he is sitting in the sun on another bench, with his hands behind his head. She is wearing horrid old blue gardening gloves, which hide her fairy fingers. Her ample posterior makes the seat of her jeans bulge. In contrast with her sister, who is bony but has big thick fingers, red and a bit flabby.

"You're still hunting for your ring?"

"No, but I often think of it."

"Was it François who gave it to you?"

"No," she lies, without knowing why.

Would the wound always be so raw? Could she cure it by treating it with coldness?

"Surely your mother didn't tell you he left me for another woman."

"I didn't have to be told. He found some bird who's not worth your little finger and he'll live to regret it, the poor sod."

She hadn't thought he would use such terms: he used to be very fond of François. You never know.

"Aunt Line, how do you know you're really in love?"

Arthur has a girlfriend, Élodie. Maybe she wonders herself if she is in love.

"It's absence that tells you. If you aren't sure you love someone but you miss that person terribly, that's it. The missing, you see, the missing. That's how you know it's love. Radiance. Fireworks. You become someone else, you glow. You lose the wrinkles on your skin and in your mind. You grow beautiful, intelligent, tolerant. People you meet sense that you are in love and that you are loved. Absence reveals all this. It makes us unhappy beyond belief."

Arthur studies her. She looks just the same, however.

She sees François everywhere. A man in the street turns toward her . . . no, not him. Another at an outdoor café, talking to a young woman at his side. Line comes closer . . . how could she ever! In the evening mist, a couple on the path to the sea. Come now! François is much taller. Each illusion makes her heart flutter.

She thinks she'll never see him again. Maybe he is living far away with his new girl. It's not François she has a grudge against. If the lost ring were full of poison, she would give it to that woman.

"He's so charming, your publisher," says Jacotte. "I met him at a signing. He couldn't say enough about you."

Jacotte . . .

That's not all.

"You remember my friend Reine? I hadn't seen her in a bit. She asked after you. Of course I said nothing about your private life but she told me she had seen François with a young woman in his arms. You can well imagine I made no comment."

Reine . . .

This spring is as warm as summer. Line puts away her winter clothes, gets out her blouses, her shorts, which she holds in front of her. She's gained weight. Desertion, absence, solitude: those three clawing monstresses have carved wrinkles on her face. But she manages to get into her shorts. She strokes her hips, feels something hard in her pocket. The lost ring.

She stows it in one of her jewel boxes, where it mingles with the precious and the less so, the neglected and the temporarily loved, and she shuffles them with her two hands like dominoes before a game.

She has not seen her niece and nephew for a long time. They've grown up and changed unbelievably. Arthur is head over heels in love with Élodie. Loren dresses in the latest punk fashion but her boyfriend, whom she introduces to Line, talks like Titus in *Bérénice*. Loren makes brilliant grades in literature.

Hesitantly Arthur tells Line that he has seen François. François admitted that he arranged the meeting so he could ask Arthur to intercede with Line for him. He wants to see her again. He loves her more than ever. Arthur's face is expressionless. He looks at his shoes.

"Are you going to see him?"

"No," she says, truthfully.

If she runs across François, she will tell him that she looked carefully at the Lost and Found to see if he was there. They repeatedly told her that they did not have what she wanted. They clearly understood what it was, her description was very precise. But no, he had not turned up here. In the end they said:

"You know, if somebody locates him and brings him in after all this time, it's better for you not to claim him. He would never be the same. If you take our advice, you'll give up."

The Sandman

Sandra Jensen

They come in the night. In my half-sleep, diving deep but not deep enough. The corridor light is on, my door is open. It's always open. I want to hear the music. I want to know I'm not alone. But still they come. I can't stop them. I try, but I flop about in a soupy place. I can still hear the music but I can't move. I'm pressed down into my body, drowning in my own breath. They always come together. Not one, but two. I smell them first. It starts as a tingle in my mouth, climbs up the back of my nose, a smell like no other. I try to describe it to Mummy but I can't.

I'm slipping, grabbing hold of the sheet but it can't hold me up. I turn my head but I know they're here and if they're here I have to look. I shut my eyes but they are already shut. It makes no difference, I see through my eyelids so I might as well open them. Maybe this time looking will scare them away. It works with the living-room monster when I'm alone in the house. Open the door quick, turn on the light, look everywhere possible before the monster gets me. It never does. But not Stringman. Not Paperman. They force me to look and that's when they take me.

They come in the night, driving up and down Parkhurst Avenue until they find Elsie. She's hot after all her cooking. She's going for a walk to cool off. The Black Maria pulls up on the pavement, almost knocking her over. Three men get out.

"Passbook," one shouts, even though Elsie is two feet in front of him. The other two men lean against the side of the van.

"Passbook at home Baas," she says, looking at her shoes as she backs up onto the Anderson's lawn.

"You know you can't go out without your passbook."

"Yes, Baas. Sorry Baas."

"Wat doen jy uit so laat meise?" says one of the men by the van, his stompie sticking to his bottom lip. He sucks on it but it's dead.

Paperman flattens out like he always does, pouring himself across my bed, my floor, my ceiling, taking me with him. I flatten out, I become so thin

I'm see-through. My body stretches across my bedroom and my bedroom stretches across the house and the house stretches out over Parkhurst Avenue and Parkhust Avenue melts into Johannesburg and Johannesburg is nothing but a flat city, tracing-paper thin and I'm no different, we are sprawled across the land, we are the land, my body saucering, my arms reaching out, fingers splayed, and all there is is Paperman and nothing else.

"You know we must take you in, don't you?"

"Yes, Baas. No, Baas."

"What's that, you poes disagreeing with me?"

"Please Baas, my passbook is over there."

Elsie points to our house. The man with the dead stompie takes her by the arm, squeezing hard. He doesn't like to touch black flesh but he likes to make them squeal. That's what Barry told me. The stop light goes on. Elsie lets out her breath.

"Please, Baas."

My mother opens the front door.

"Elsie?" Is that you?

"Madam," Elsie says. She's trying to shout but it sounds like Marmalade, my cat who tore off half her tongue licking the edge of a sardine tin. My mother's walking hard across the lawn. She's got that look on her face.

Stringman pulls at me. He wants his turn. I can't now. It's too late. I looked at Paperman first. I couldn't help it. He was where my eyes went all by themselves. Maybe because Paperman is wider. They both stood there at the foot of my bed and before I knew it I was Paperman, floating across the universe. Before I knew it I was the universe, flat as a pancake. Then I hear Elsie scream and then I'm awake with a rush, my heart a thumpy ball in my mouth. My stomach's like sour milk. I can still smell the smell. They are still here and I want to get out. I want Mummy.

There's noise in the kitchen. Voices. Crying. Shouting. I stand in the narrow corridor. I don't want to go back into my room and I don't want to go into the kitchen. I'm frozen solid with fright, my bare feet turning to stone on the brown tiles. I look down. My feet melt. All I can see is brown.

I once held a black man's hand. I turned it over, showed the palm to Barry Anderson. Barry lives next door. He has hair like Daddy's shaving brush. Snot is always crusted on his top lip.

"Look," I said, "it's as white as mine." I pressed my hand next to the black man's hand. He's Samson the nice gardener from the other side of the road. He's leaning against the telephone pole, eating his polony sandwiches. "And my palms are not even white. Sort of pink. And blue, just like his." I traced the colors of our hands with my finger.

Barry snorted. "He's just a kaffir," he said and walked away.

The crying in the kitchen is louder. Men's voices. Mummy's voice. Daddy's voice. I'm not allowed to call him that. But I do in my head. Daddy.

I walk backwards, my legs dragging like sacks of concrete. I want to see, I don't want to see. I turn around, and walk past my door quickly. Not going in there. I can still smell Paperman. Going to Davie's room. The door is closed. Maybe he's not there. I don't know what to do. I knock. Nothing. Louder.

"Is that you, darling?" Mummy asks, and then the corridor is stuffed with people. Big people. I don't know them. I want to get away, they smell bad, worse than Paperman. Mummy pulls me close.

"It's all right, they are going now, aren't you?"

I don't understand. Where am I going?

Stringman's next. It happens that way. One and then the other. Whichever one is first, the other one gets his turn. I'm resigned now. I know it will happen. There is no point in fighting but I do. I think of putting toothpicks between my eyelids to hold them up but I fall into almost-sleep before I know it and then there's their special smell. It's filling me from my toes upward through legs and knees and belly and chest up to my throat until it finds my nose and now I know it's time. I don't fight anymore. I just look. There he is. Stringman. He doesn't really have a face. How could he, being so long and thin, stretching down through the floor up through the ceiling, I don't know where he stops and where he begins, and now I'm stretching too. I'm him, I'm so long I can't see my feet, I'm reaching upward, pulling like toffee into evermore.

I drag my blanket with me, my pink flowery one with the satin ribbon around the edge and it stretches up into Stringman, pulling my bed with it, my slip-slops, my Barbie doll, my room and all my toys and now everything is thin and long turning like a string merry-go-round pulling in our bungalow, the green lawn Sunday Times just mowed, the big cactus by the gate, pulling everything and everyone inwards and upwards. We are nothing but a strand. Even the stars are pulled in, even the dark plate of night is sucked into length. And then, suddenly, it's over. I'm dipping down, I'm falling into the crack of dreams where neither Stringman nor Paperman go.

He comes in the night. I'm in my room, playing with Ken by the yellow light from the corridor. I'm supposed to be asleep. But I can play awhile, no one notices. I don't want to meet Stringman or Paperman again. I know I have to, if not this night another night. I don't like Ken's plastic brown hair but what can I do about that. He looks a bit like Daddy who I'm not allowed to call Daddy. I have to call him by his name, Terence. I end up hardly calling him at all.

Mummy's screaming. I drop Ken on the floor. He bounces once and then lies face down on one of my slip-slops. I sit very still, holding my breath. Then Mummy stops screaming and there's nothing but silence. I'm still holding my breath.

My chest hurts. I have to let my breath out. I let it out in little bits, hoping it doesn't make any noise. Then I hear low sounds, man sounds. Mummy's voice again. A shadow passes my door, running. I know it's Davie because of the sound. He never wears shoes or sandals. Ever. I push Ken aside with my toes and wiggle my feet into my slip-slops. My slip-slops have got yellow daisies stuck to the V on top. I pick Ken up and walk with him to the door. I stop to listen, it sounds okay. No more screaming. Just talking. I walk out the door, as quiet as I can. Hard with slip-slops. They slop. Maybe I should just go barefoot but Mummy says I shouldn't because of splinters.

Sunday Times is sitting at the kitchen table with an axe in his head. It's not a very big axe. The handle has little colored beads like the bracelet Elsie wears. His face is nothing but two big eyes and blood. He's smiling, so there's teeth as well. Mummy's picked up her handbag and got her car keys in her fingers.

"No, Madam," says Sunday Times, "it's nothing."

"It's not nothing, Sunday," Mummy says.

Daddy, I mean Terence is nodding his head. He's leaning against the big white fridge, his arms crossed. He sees me.

"What are you doing up, Miss Muffet?"

"I heard a noise," I say, clutching Ken to my chest. It hurts because Ken's feet are sticking into me.

"You should go back to bed, darling," Mummy says, but she's not looking at me so I pretend not to hear. Davie's talking to Sunday Times and I want to hear what he's saying, I don't want to go back to bed. Sunday Times is laughing, his mouth a big wide hole, dark red like his face.

"What happened?" I whisper to Davie.

"He's got an axe in his head," he answers.

I glare at him. "I know! Who did it?"

Elsie.

Elsie? Sunday reaches out for me but I step back into Mummy.

"Is okay, is okay," he says, "Elsie shouts at me and I shout at her and she shouts back and I hit her and then she put the axe in my head." He laughs again. "She a good woman," he adds.

No one says anything for a bit and then Daddy says, "At least let them examine you. You might need stitches."

I stare at Daddy and then back at Sunday Times. He won't want stitches. They hurt. I had nine. Mummy gives Daddy a look. "He's not got papers, you know that."

Daddy, I mean Terence, says, "Christ."

"No worry, Massa."

"It's Terence, Sunday, Terence."

"I'll go to the sangoma, Massa. He always fixes me good," Sunday Times beams at Daddy. Daddy throws his hands up in the air and Mummy puts her keys in her handbag and puts her handbag on the table.

"At least let me take a look then."

Sunday Times's white shirt is polka dot red. He looks up at Mummy. His eyes are like Jackson's, Barry's cocker spaniel. I wanted a dog but we only have Marmalade.

"Go back to bed, darling," Mummy says.

"What about Davie?"

"He'll go too."

I know Davie won't go to bed but I leave anyway. I don't want to stay here. Daddy pats me on the shoulder.

"Here you go, Miss Muffet."

I hate that. I don't know what it means. What is a Muffet? And I don't like spiders. We have a huge black one in the bath and I hate to go in there and I hate to see it go down the plug when Mummy turns on the tap. I don't want it dead but I don't want it in my bath.

I don't sleep. I'm not going to sleep. I don't want them to take me. I sit up in bed and hold Ken and Barbie close. It doesn't help so I put them in their shoebox house and pick up Flopsy. She's a stuffed poodle dog and I love her very much. I hear Sunday Times and Mummy talking and then Sunday Times shouts something in Zulu. I know it's Zulu because he told me and he told me never to say what he said to another black man. I'm not sure if I like Sunday Times. He smokes a lot, nearly as much as Mummy and he never changes his shirt. He lives with Elsie in a tin room in the back yard. The room smells of sweat and kaffir beer. He came with the house. Mummy didn't want him but he made a fuss. Elsie arrived later. Mummy wasn't happy at all but when Elsie said she had her passbook Mummy said okay.

"I don't want servants," Mummy said to Daddy when they thought I wasn't listening but I was.

"Well, if you don't take them someone else will. At least we can make sure they are alright."

"Alright?" Mummy said. That sound in her voice. They were going to start shouting so I climbed back onto my chair and asked for a glass of milk.

"They're not alright! It's not alright. You know that. If I have them here what will the others think? I can't go to the meetings and say I have servants!"

"Don't go to the meetings then."

Daddy, I mean Terence, was really angry. I could tell because his face went blotchy even though his voice didn't change. He got up from the table and poured me a glass of milk. He pulled his chair out to sit down again and it made a scraping sound so bad I had to cover my ears quickly and on the way up my elbow knocked my glass of milk over.

"Jesus Christ," Daddy said, and walked out.

They come in the night. Sometimes they come in the day. I can tell because of their smell. They can't come all at once. It's not allowed. I don't know why but that's what Mummy told me. I've woken up between Paperman and Stringman and I hear their voices from the kitchen and I want Mummy. I walk to the kitchen door. I don't go in. The tall man talks at me and then laughs over my head like I'm the funny one. He winks but I'm not sure it's for me or for Mummy. Mike I really like a lot. He smokes fat cigarettes. He has a beard like Father Christmas and he's very nice. The beard tickles and smells like a bonfire. The tall man has a strange name, Geert, which Mummy says is German. I don't know where that is but it's not here. Somewhere where there's snow and snowmen and gingerbread houses. Geert has his shirt off, his back twisted round so everyone could see.

"Bloody hell," says Daddy.

No one notices me so I just keep standing there.

"You have got to be careful man."

"Did you get a tetanus shot?"

"Where am I going to get that without some fucker informing?"

"You don't have to tell them how you got it."

"They'll ask."

"Just say you were protecting your wall from the blacks with barbed wire."

"Yeah right. No one's going to believe that. I'm listed. They know what I do. They just can't prove it."

Mummy sits down and lights a cigarette. They are all sitting in the dark now. Why don't they put the lights on? I see little red dots like fireflies making zigzag lines in the air. I don't want to go in, I don't want to go back to my room. My feet are stuck again so I crouch down. I like to hear the voices. I feel safe.

And then Geert shoots up, yelling, "What the?"

They all turn around at once, sucking air in like a Hoover. And then they laugh.

"Come here, sweetheart," Mike says.

I do, but I can't, I'm stuck there on the floor. Geert's staring at me and Daddy turns on the corridor light.

"Hey man, be careful," Geert says and then looks at me again.

"Do you know what happens to little girls who don't go to sleep?"

I shake my head. Something tells me I should have nodded, but it's too late now.

"The Sandman comes. Do you know who he is?"

I shake my head again.

"He throws sand in your eyes and you know what happens then?"

Mummy's looking at him, smiling. Daddy, I mean Terence, is picking his fingernails with a fork.

"Well?"

I shake my head again.

"Hey, don't give the girl a hard time," Mike says, but Geert doesn't listen to him.

"The sand makes your head bleed and then your eyes fall out and the Sandman gathers up all the eyes of the children who don't go to sleep and takes them to his iron house on the moon."

"Geert!" Mummy says and Daddy laughs.

Mike walks to me and holds my face in his hands.

"Don't listen to him, he's just playing. There's no such thing as a Sandman," he says. I don't believe him.

He comes in the night. He lives on the moon. He knows I don't want to sleep. He knows I don't want to meet Paperman or Stringman. I think about the Sandman's iron home. I think perhaps he collects up all Mummy's knives and forks and makes a nest out of them. I think about my eyes. Davie once asked me if I'd like to go blind or deaf and when I said I don't want to go either he said I had to choose so I chose deaf. Maybe blind wouldn't be so bad, I'd not be able to see Stringman or Paperman but this doesn't feel comforting right now. I try to sleep and then I try to stay awake but my eyes hurt. They feel scratchy and I wonder if he is here already. The music is on. It's the one Mummy calls Lady Day. I can hear Mummy banging on her typewriter. I sit up, Ken and Barbie on my lap, poodle dog

Flopsy in my arms. I can't stand waiting anymore. I have to do something. Mummy won't listen to me while she's writing, and Daddy's away in Pretoria for an important meeting. I put Ken and Barbie on my pillow and keep hold of Flopsy. I put my slip-slops on and go to Davie's room. The door is open, his light is on.

"I can't sleep," I say.

He's on the floor playing Cowboys and Indians. He doesn't look up but he doesn't tell me to go away.

"Can I play too?"

"Okay. You be the Indian," he says, handing me the little man.

I like the Indian. He looks like the gardener across the road only with long hair in a plait down his back.

"He's called Samson," I say.

"That's not an Indian name. He has to have an Indian name and I'm going to shoot him."

I start to cry but hold it back.

"Can we play a bit before you shoot him?"

"Okay."

I curl up on my side, holding Samson and Flopsy.

"Do you know about the Sandman?" I whisper.

Davie looks at me. "That's just silly."

"Do you know what he looks like?"

Davie gets up and opens the tin trunk by his bed. He scrabbles around a bit and then pulls out a book. He opens it, and then hands it to me, pointing at a page.

"Here."

I don't want to look but I do.

They stop coming in the night. Mummy's crying. She's been crying since yesterday. I'm playing Cowboys and Indians with Davie on the stoep. He hasn't shot Samson yet. Sunday Times is digging a pond for goldfish, his head all wrapped up in a bandage. A Black Maria drives past, stops, and reverses and parks outside our gate. Two policemen get out, push the gate open without looking at Davie or me. They grab Sunday Times by the collar of his grubby white shirt and drag him across the grass to the van. There are no windows in the van, only at the front. Sunday is screaming, Mummy comes running out.

"You wouldn't do this if my husband were here!"

The men ignore her and shove Sunday Times inside the van and close the doors. Elsie is kneeling on the front lawn holding her stomach, leaning backwards and forwards, her face all scrunched up like a walnut.

"Don't look," Davie says, but it's too late. I've already seen. He takes me by the hand and we go around back where the swings are.

Mummy's been at the police station and then on the telephone all day. Something bad has happened. Worse than what happened to Sunday Times. She won't tell me but she doesn't know I'm listening. I'm supposed to be asleep but I don't do that anymore. I think the Sandman won't come if I'm near Mummy. I'm sitting in the corridor, by the kitchen door, Flopsy in my arms.

"They've taken Geert," she whispers into the telephone. "No, he's not gone on holiday, you idiot," she starts to shout. And then she says, "Oh," and quickly hangs up the telephone.

She sits there for a while, smoking in the dark.

He comes in the night. I'm lying in bed. Waiting. I think it's better to be Paperman or Stringman than have Sandman come and take my eyes out so I try to go to sleep. Perhaps it's good to be Paperman. After the first bit I quite like floating across Johannesburg. I like stretching out across the countryside, everything gathered up into one everwide circling sheet, spinning round and round, stretching out and out, my edges curling in the wind, the wind spreading into me until all I am is flat air and I can stretch no more, I am forever and then it goes dark, all dark, and then the dreams come and I'm lying in my bed again, my face pressed into my pillow.

He comes down through the ceiling. He turns my head with his fingers. His long, curling fingernails tangle in my hair and he looks at me. His pointed hat is askew; he has sticky-out ears and a big nose like Geert. He leans close and I can feel his hot breath, it smells like cheese and I wish I could smell Stringman but I don't. It's too late for that. I'm wide-awake now and the Sandman is sitting on my bed sprinkling sand into my eyes. It stings but not as bad as I thought it would. I wait for him to dig out my eyes. I wonder if he does it with those fingernails. I wonder if it will hurt, I wonder if I will look like Sunday Times with the axe in his head. I wonder where Geert is. Maybe he's up there in the Sandman's iron nest in the moon, waiting for me. I wonder if Davie will shoot Samson when I'm gone. There's a lot of things I wonder about but then it's all black and I know the Sandman has taken out my eyes so I just lie there in the dark, wondering what's going to happen next.

Section IV

For Work, Yes

Tania Hershman

When she gets to the front she is not sure what to say. She doesn't speak their language, they don't speak hers; her English is filled with polite yesses and little else.

"For work," she says.

"Visa," says the voice, the one that has no head, the one coming from the machine.

She pushes the electronic card they gave her into the mouth of the machine with the voice. A whir, another whir. She looks around, and as far as she can see, stretching away across the long long hall, machines whirring and issuing commands at other small women, small men, who don't speak their language, whose English is filled with polite yesses and little else.

"Nine," commands the voice. She stares at the machine.

"Nine?"

An arm shoots out of the side of the machine, unfurls into an arrow, and where it points she sees doors, numbers. The electronic card has been ejected. She takes it and walks slowly towards the 9.

Another machine, a table, a chair.

"Sit," and where the first voice was her schoolteacher, this voice is more like her grandfather's. She sits. She smiles. She looks around. Did anyone see her smile? Can this machine see her?

"Why have you come here?" says the grandfather-machine.

"Yes," she says, and swallows. A tissue, wiping her forehead. She is from a place of great heat, but this is not the same. The room is chilled, but she sweats.

"Why have you come here?" Grandfather-machine is measured, patient. It has all day.

"Yes," she says. She recognizes the "why," the "come." She tries: "I come, to work. I come, I help."

"Your visa is for a family. What will you do for this family?"

"I clean," she says. "Yes. Old person. Grand. Mother. Help."

The grandfather-machine makes a new sound, a series of buzzing clicks. Then: a piece of paper.

"One year," says grandfather-machine. "Goodbye."

She takes the paper, which is covered in words. She stares. One year? Twelve months? But she needs more, much more than that. A daughter going to university, a son in school. Years, it will take.

"But . . . " she says. There is no sound. Grandfather-machine is asleep. Is no longer interested. The door swings open. She understands.

The family is kind. Little children who speak too fast, much too fast, leaving her nodding, yessing, smiling, yessing, nodding. Cleaning is something she understands and she can do well, without instruction. They have a machine for this, too, but it stands in a corner and she has pressed some buttons but it seems to have broken. Every day she wants to ask why, every day she begins, in the morning, as the family has breakfast, but every day what comes out of her mouth is not that, is wrong.

The children chatter to each other, the mother and father mumble, and the grandmother doesn't speak at all. The grandmother needs cleaning, needs to be lifted, washed, dressed, and all the while the grandmother stares at something across the room. The grandmother's eyes do not move.

"It's very beautiful," she tells her daughter when they speak through the screen that is fixed to the wall in her cool room in the basement. She can see her daughter's hair, her daughter's eyes, and she has to make herself not cry. "It's like a palace, so large!" She forces her voice into excitement, forces it to rise at the end as if this was the adventure she always dreamed of, away from her children, her familiars.

A year later, and the mother takes her to an office in the center of the city. The mother's auto is voice-controlled, something she has never seen. Her command of the language is improving, but here is a vehicle that speaks better than she does. She looks out of the window. She still has not discovered why the cleaning machine sits in a corner, silent; why she is needed. She still cannot ask.

In the office in the center of the city, she nods, she says yes, yes, she smiles and smiles. Across the long long hall, she sees many machines ask questions of many small women and men. "For work," she says. "Yes, yes," she says.

A new piece of paper.

"We are so lucky!" says the mother, and she sees she has one more year.

"Yes!" she smiles, nods. Only one more year? Her daughter has two more years of university, her son five more years of school, and then.

The grandmother has not changed. She has not begun dribbling, ranting or waving her arms around. The grandmother hasn't even varied the spot on the wall at which she stares when she is lifted, washed and dressed. It is almost as if the grandmother is not getting any older, just staying very, very old.

The children, shoving each other, run past the open door. She has never seen them come in. She has never seen the mother or the father tell the children to do so. But she has seen the father sometimes sit in the chair in the corner. It is his mother, she thinks. He sits, with his hands on his knees, his earcam still in place in case someone should need him. Often, he says things, but so quietly that she, watching from the hallway, can't hear. He stays maybe for an hour, and then he gets up and leaves, closing the door.

No one touches the grandmother. Only she touches the grandmother.

She is renewed again, and then again. She speaks to her son and daughter through the screen fixed to the wall. Her son is so tall now. His voice is deep; she almost doesn't understand him and she tries so hard, tries so hard not to cry when she sees him. They used to cry when they saw her, they used to ask why she couldn't just come back, why they couldn't find another way, why did she, why was she, didn't she . . . ? Now they just chatter and laugh and talk about friends she has never met, new places built since she left where they go to do things, things that she doesn't know but doesn't want to ask. "They will understand," her mother had said to her when she told her what she had to do, where she had to go. "They will understand."

She does not go out very much. She lifts and washes and cleans the grandmother, cleaning the sores from the sitting, the leakings from the old, old body. She washes and cleans the grandmother carefully, thoroughly, and then she washes and cleans the house. She picks up an object, wipes underneath, and then sometimes she stands for a few moments with it in her hand, looking. Sometimes: a remote control. Sometimes: a discarded earcam. Sometimes: an animatoy. Then she puts it down and goes back to work.

While she works, she hums, melodies without words. She hums to the grandmother too, as she carefully and thoroughly washes and cleans, to make sure the grandmother knows someone is there, to keep the grandmother, to keep her from changing. She does not want anything to change. Not until her years are enough.

But soon, too soon, the grandmother is dying. It seems as though she will not be very, very old for much longer. When the grandmother tries to breathe there is a dark deep knocking from inside as if something wants to leave. Doctors come, scanning with their tools, but still, there is no stopping death. The mother is looking at the father. The father is looking at the doctor. The children are not home much anymore. Finally, the father nods, the doctor nods, and they go into the grandmother's room.

She is not needed. She stands in the hall outside, and then she stands back when they come to take away the grandmother, the grandmother's eyes closed now, no more knocking inside her chest. She reaches out a hand towards the grandmother. "Yes," she says. "Yes."

The mother is very sorry. The mother says something fast, and then she says it slower, about "carer allowance," about "not being able to," about "so sorry." Then there is a new machine in the middle of the room, a new cleaning machine, and they are saying, "Take a few days," and she is packing up, telling her children through the screen fixed to the wall in her cool room in the basement that she will let them know when, let them know where.

The mother's auto drops her off in the center of the city. She stands outside the doors to the building which gave her a piece of paper every year, just one more year. She reaches out her hand and the doors slide open towards the long, long hall with the machines and the small women and small men, but her legs take her backwards and she turns and walks away. Walks away with her small bag with nothing in it and her small purse with the electronic card, enough for a few meals, a few days.

She walks down the bright street, and she turns a corner and another corner and she finds herself walking and walking. She walks until there are no more walls and no more screens and no more autos and no more sliding doors or machines with pieces of paper.

She hopes for something like a tree. She hopes for some animals. She hopes for someone to talk to. In her head she speaks to herself in her own language, but after so long, after so many years, it is mixed up. It is filled with yesses and bits that have stuck to her from conversations: "detergent," "allowance," "earcam," "my turn," "bedsores," "homework." Her head is full of these sticky words, and what use is she now?

She stops walking. The road is everywhere, stretching on both sides. There is no grass. There are no animals. She has her small bag with nothing in it and her small purse with the electronic card and her head full of things that aren't hers, and she has no future and her past is dissolving. She sits down, just sits, right there on the road, and waits for someone to come and tell her what to do next.

SHRIVELED NIGHT

Hao Yu-siang

Translated by Howard Goldblatt

You fell apart right in front of me.

That's right, my father, that's how it happened. Your back bent gradually, you began to shrivel up, your mouth collapsed in on itself and your legs, once sturdy and powerful, turned so spindly they could barely hold you up. Just shuffling into your room and sitting on the edge of the bed had you gasping for breath. I went in to see you, and the suffocating smell of medicine that simmered there the year round attached itself to my nostrils and stuck to the membranes. Forcing back a cough, I helped you lie down and said I'd take you to see a doctor. But you shook your head weakly, gasping all the while, and said it was nothing new, that you only needed some rest.

It was late by then, one in the morning, so I went back to my room, where I listened to the sounds of your labored breathing, like waves beating against the shore. The stillness of the night was broken by the sounds of your struggle to keep living. I rolled over and heard the roar of a motorbike speeding down the street, loudly proclaiming how much faster and younger than us it was. The arrogant howl struck fear in my heart. How long had it been since I'd tasted the thrill of racing with the wind? For years I'd been imprisoned with you in this small apartment, where we spent our time looking at each other, until, over time, we turned into a pair of immobile, mute plants, existing behind a steel-reinforced cement wall that blocked the sunlight from the Tropic of Cancer, slowly becoming almost transparently pale. Sometimes you spent the whole afternoon on the sofa reading a newspaper, which fluttered in the occasional breeze, while my gaze passed through your body and out the window into a dazzling blue sky in stark contrast to the dark gloom of the apartment. I felt suspended in iced coffee searching for distant rays of sunlight.

But at that moment, brightness wasn't what I wanted. Accompanied by your struggle to breathe, the dark night seemed especially deep and scary, and that actually calmed me, since at last I could turn my gaze back to my own body. I pinched the sagging flesh of my upper arm, as chilled and slippery as a snakeskin hanging in a stall at the Huaxi Street night market. Slapping it back and forth created the fantasy that I was slowly, casually stripping away the loose outer skin, like a snake butcher. Then I lay alongside my pillow, naked and bloody, tiny capillaries buried in the exposed scarlet flesh still throbbing rhythmically. The look in those bulging eyes at the top of the head, was it agony, fear or arousal? All of a sudden I laughed through parted lips, like one of those mutating aliens in Hollywood movies. My cheeks split open, my teeth fell out, my intestines came spewing forth. I couldn't keep thinking those thoughts. If I had, I'd have climbed out of bed, gone into the kitchen, picked up the carving knife and turned those thoughts into action, like my mother had. Self-mutilation is the inescapable heritage of our family.

(Amid the chirping of cicadas at dusk. Mother sat on the floor in front of a tea table and lowered the blade of the carving knife toward her wrist. Frowning deeply, she laid the cutting edge against the artery and pressed down, never dreaming that this life conduit could be so tough, so tenacious. She kept trying, until she was bathed in sweat, but all she could manage was a tiny cut in the skin, releasing a trickle of blood that snaked down her wrist and into her palm, where it followed the ridges a short way before stopping. I threw open the screen, my school bag flung over my shoulder. Mother looked up with panic in her eyes.

"Home already? . . . " She rose quickly and wiped her sweaty forehead, then carried the knife into the kitchen, where she busily and noisily started dinner. I sat down at the tea table, the seat cushion still warm from her body. Turning around, I saw Mother's back as she stood at the stove. This time she raised the knife high in the air and chopped down . . .)

Startled out of my dream, I saw it was nearly daybreak. The smell of dew-covered grass seeped in through the window screen. I stretched, then got out of bed, as if a thought had just occurred to me, and went into your room. Apparently, you hadn't moved all night. Your hands were still clasped over your belly, your feet were together, and for a moment I thought you had died. But when I walked gingerly up to the bed, I saw your chest rise and fall weakly. Your eyes were shut, a trickle of dried blood like a centipede stuck to the corner of your mouth.

"Father! Father!" I fell to my knees by your bed and shook you. Your body was rigid and burning hot, like a suit of armor left in the sun too long. You no longer saw or spoke to me. What did that signify? My obligatory duties would soon be fulfilled, so after calling the hospital, I breathed a sigh of relief. Twenty-four hours later, in an intensive care ward, you opened your eyes again, an IV stuck in your arm. But that meant nothing. For by then you had become a different person, someone I didn't know. Your eyes may have been open, but you couldn't see me. No longer did you possess any memories of the daughter you'd pampered, scolded, even held a grudge against at one time or another, the person you'd lived with longer than anyone else. I leaned across the bed, putting my face up so close I could smell your putrid breath as you lay with your mouth open. Your unknowing, infantile eyes were cast down at the bedsheet, which had been used by countless patients before you, sweat oozing from your pores. Once you'd been stripped naked, there was hardly anything to distinguish you from a pathetic, bald, red-haired chimp. And this was my father.

(Was that you, Father? I hadn't seen you looking so young in a long time. I loved seeing you in that neatly pressed light blue uniform. Under orders of the Imperial Army, one kamikaze suicide airplane after another was created by your welding torch. Did you know, Father, that from the roof of the Gangshan Airport workers' dormitory, I could see you wiping away the sweat and working out there on the airfield? Sparks from your welding torch danced past your cheeks, so worrying me that I fidgeted nervously with my hair. And when airplanes flew overhead, you stopped what you were doing and looked up to silently commit their design to memory. I knew you'd come home after work, sketch what you'd seen, then point out for me the tails, the wings and the engines.

Of course you wouldn't forget to tell me all about the young beings who flew the planes. They'd left their parents and wives back home to take the controls of airplanes you had welded, soaring up into the blue sky for a brief moment before settling into the beautiful waters of the Pacific. Pearl Harbor, what a lovely name. You were young then, and your eyes were half closed as you talked, filled with pride over your involvement in such magnificent deaths. That always brought tears to my eyes.)

Could you sense that there were tears in my eyes? Is that why you rolled over, to turn away from me? Was I really crying? If so, it was for myself. When you rolled over, you lost control of your bowels and soiled the sheet. I took out a disposable diaper, rolled you back toward me and raised your hips; your eyes were fixed blankly on the head of the bed as you passively let me tend to you. When I removed your stinking diaper, your penis lay limply between your legs, now little more than a dark little piece of meat, so shriveled it shocked me; it was no bigger than that of a boy of five or six. I reached out to touch it; as I anticipated, there was no change, and I had to stifle a giggle. It had once proudly entered my mother's body, slipping mightily in and out between the warm lips of her opening, slow at first then fast, gently at first then forcefully, scraping roughly with no concern for the grimacing pain it caused. She was thinking at that time about how you'd lain atop the bodies of cheap whores performing the same mighty act. A rotating electric fan tried vainly to stir up the dead summer air, but only accelerated the breeding of sickness in the hot fluids of your copulation. Cheap perfume mingled with the sour smell of steamy sweat in the whore's armpits, as her pendulous breasts jiggled right under your nose. Your lips parted, releasing a long moan from deep in your throat as sticky sperm shot into the depths of her womb. You collapsed on top of her, spent. She pushed your sweaty body off, jumped out of bed and squatted over a bedside basin to give herself a rigorous douche. With rapt concentration, she inserted a finger between the labia and gently stroked herself, as if pouring out her heart to a lover's tender mouth. While you snored the night away, this silent conversation progressed in secret.

But now your penis hung there limply, as if contrite over all that had happened in the past. We know it had brought Mother pain and suffering, but had it ever brought her joy as well? I truly doubt it. (What a peaceful summer afternoon it was. The Japanese had withdrawn from our land, and were replaced by a new set of rulers. But for the man on the street, life hardly changed at all. They still walked along with their heads bowed, their backs bent. The change had cost Father his cushy airport job, and he had to open a rope-selling business. He was away that day buying from wholesalers; he had no sooner stepped out the door than Mother, who'd spent a listless morning, went to her room, got down on her haunches, opened a drawer and removed a cloth bundle. Sitting at the table, she opened the bundle and took out a little metal box filled with face powder. The cover was decorated with a painting of a beautiful woman in a cheongsam. Mother then took out our only mirror, a small, yellow one, and began powdering her face as she hummed a Japanese tune. She kept applying the powder, one layer on top of another, until her face was shockingly white. But she seemed pleased with what she saw, as she showed me the powder-coated tip of her finger. After a while, she sighed, then rewrapped the box in its cloth cover, stood up and put it back in the drawer.

She then walked over to the sink to wash her face, seemingly on tiptoes, her body swaying like a seductive breeze. I'd never seen her walk like that, and could hardly believe my eyes. I was reminded of legends of women possessed by fox spirits. But once her face was washed clean, she looked up and was once again the mother I knew: a tight-lipped, swarthy, expressionless face.

Mother took me to bed for a nap, where she fanned me with a cattail fan. But just as I was falling asleep, I sensed waves of heat coming from close by. The fan had stopped moving. I opened my eyes sleepily, aware that the bed was being crushed by a powerful force, pitching back and forth. It was Mother. Her right hand was buried between her legs, moving so fast it rocked the bed, tossing her from side to side. Her hand moved faster and faster, as she began to moan, a sound so prodigious I could feign ignorance no longer.

"Mother!" I screamed in spite of myself. As long as I live, I'll never forget the look on Mother's face when she turned to me. The light of ecstasy radiated from her eyes; her forehead still reeked faintly of face powder. Flinging open her arms with a joyful outcry, she hugged me tightly, something she'd never done before.

That was the day the incident born of deep resentment occurred. They say lines of men were kneeling in front of the tram station waiting to be executed, as underground passages filled up with corpses. There was no news of Father, who was out there somewhere. Mother hardly made a sound for two days as she moved about the house, sweeping, dusting, mopping. The neurotic aversion to dirt she exhibited later on probably had its beginnings then. Then, on the morning of the third day, Father appeared in the doorway, his clothes so grimy you couldn't tell what color they were; his blood-soaked shoes left red prints on the floor. Since transportation had come to a complete halt, he'd walked all the way from Jiayi along the railroad tracks.

The corpses piled up, their blood spilling onto the street. Saying it was as if he'd made it home by stepping on dead bodies, Father pointed to his shoes as proof. He could not suppress a look of joy in the aftermath of the massacre. While he animatedly related his harrowing experience in getting home, Mother was on her hands and knees scrubbing bloody footprints off the floor. From time to time she looked up and smiled to show she was listening, but the smile seemed ephemeral, as if viewed through a gauze veil. The sight of her gaunt back reminded me of how she'd looked on that afternoon three days earlier, light and airy, in an aura of floating face powder, a radiant glow in her eyes. I never saw her like that again.)

My father, on that afternoon, whose secret you never knew, I began to realize that Mother didn't need you to fill the gaps in her life. Your existence served only to suffuse her body with dirt and filth, which ultimately led to my birth. I emerged as a child of sin. That's why Mother spent the rest of her life cleaning everything in the house, everything but you.

The question then is, should I be grateful to you for favoring me with Original Sin? The year I reached the age of twenty, shortly after my graduation from the junior teachers' college, you and Mother had me marry an expatriate Mainlander. After removing my wedding veil, my husband mounted me, and I relinquished my purity and wholeness for all time. Did you give a single thought to how scared I would be? When it happened, your face and his merged together, as I shut my eyes, tensed my body and squeezed my lips together, not daring to make a sound, even though the image swirling around in my head was of Mother and her prodigious moans on that spring afternoon. My husband, meanwhile, was humping like a wild bull, breathing heavily and saturating my hair, stiff with spray for my wedding, with the pungent odors of garlic and soy sauce from the wedding banquet. Pale lamplight undulated above my head; my husband had left the lamp on that first night because he wanted to fill his senses with me as he cleaved me in two. Even with my eyes closed I could sense the painfully blinding light of the lamp. And at that moment, I recalled that once before I had seen a sliver of dawning love, but you two had joined hands to rip it away from me.

"Hi!" I called to the man and smiled as I walked by.

He returned my smile and stood there holding on to his bicycle handlebars all the time I was walking. Finally I faintly heard him say "Congratulations." I kept walking, each step more difficult than the one before. He was like an enormous magnetic field, drawing every cell in my body toward him. But I refused to turn back to look. By then tears were running down my cheeks.

What a lily-livered man. He knew I was getting married in a month, so why didn't he have the guts to ask me if I wanted to go away with him? Two months earlier, he'd found the nerve to write a love letter and stuff it into my hand as I left school; but then he'd jumped on his bicycle and ridden off. A thick bundle of his letters, which I'd saved all this time, still lay beneath my pillow. But the most moving words in the world could not turn things around now. In fact, that outpouring of heartfelt verbiage couldn't begin to compare with a single solid action. It was my first year teaching grammar school after graduating from the women's junior teaching college. He sat across and at an angle from my desk. A small man, he couldn't hold a candle to any of those high-octane, lively gym teachers. But from the moment he stuffed that first letter into my hand, in my eyes, he acquired an unusual aura of tranquility. While other men shouted coarsely and reeked of sweat and grime, he alone remained mild-mannered and refined. He had a fair, satiny complexion and coal-black sideburns; he always covered his mouth when he laughed and never left a single grain of rice in his metal rice box at lunch time. He'd carry the box over to the sink, unhurriedly roll up his sleeves and wash it. A man like that, who was always so proper, had actually written a shockingly bold and unrestrained letter, abandoning his natural temperance and drenching the pages with passion. With mounting interest, I gazed at this man, a mass of contradictions.

But the changes in my psychological state did not escape Mother's keen eye. When she took out the letters I'd hidden under my pillow and laid them on the dining table, I knew that it was all over for me. She glared at me sternly, banged the table with her hand, and said, "Forget about falling in love with anyone you please, like other people!" Father was sitting at the table the whole time, slurping his soupy rice and clicking his chopsticks against the rice bowl. He didn't even look up until the bowl was empty. "You should be getting married, so no funny business." They then began discussing the wedding arrangements.

Since I was their only daughter, Father was insistent that the groom take our family name. "A few days ago," he said after a thoughtful pause, "the matchmaker said there's a Mainlander in the next village who runs a clinic. She says he's a decent fellow, with no living parents. And even though he's sort of old, he'd be interested in finding a wife." In less time than it took to finish a meal, my future was decided.

What disgusted me was, when the other man heard the news, he smiled warmly, as if none of this surprised him, and with not so much as a word of congratulations. Not until school was out did he station himself by the school gate that I passed through every day and allow the word "Congratulations," nothing more, to form on his thin lips. I couldn't bring myself to look into his eyes, and all I saw was a loose black thread on the cuff of his dark green pant leg.

But he just stood there without moving as an early evening breeze passed between us. I kept walking; my tears dripped onto the asphalt, but immediately dried up.

***

Before I'd been married two years, my modesty and reserved nature had lost their appeal to my husband, and he abandoned me and our year-old daughter for a Hunanese woman, with whom he went to Gaoxiong. Reacting angrily to the news, my mother took to bed and never got up again. The woman spoke the same dialect as my husband and was keenly aware of his homesickness, which is why we became little more than a temporary rest stop for him. Who should I have blamed for that? You, of course, my father. If it were not for your whoring around, where you contracted syphilis and passed it on to Mother, making her infertile, while you insisted on a son to carry on your line, I wouldn't have had to marry a man just to take our name. I'd never have considered marrying a Mainlander I'd never met if you hadn't thought about the matchmaker while we were sitting around the dining table, would I? Besides, if I'd had brothers, I wouldn't have had to spend my whole life carrying you on my back. If your memory had been up to the challenge, you'd have been able to recall that I did have a chance to remarry. Back when I was still young and attractive, a fellow teacher was willing to put aside the fact that I'd had one failed marriage and accept my daughter as his own. But you stood in the way, saying I'd ruin the family's good name and the memory of my deceased mother, and that if any man dared step foot in this house, you'd show me up by killing yourself. You were so angry the veins on your forehead popped out, and you threatened to walk out on me. Even my daughter, who had just started school and picked up a sense of moral outrage somewhere, stood there staring daggers at me. You cornered me, the two of you together, so I got down on my knees to ask for forgiveness before you were appeased. So I lit joss sticks in front of Mother's memorial tablet and swore to look after my father for the rest of his life and to raise my daughter, vowing never to remarry. ("You've read lots of books, but what every woman needs to know are the three obediences and four virtues," Mother murmured. Illiterate herself, she was pleased I did so well at my studies, yet fearful at the same time, for reasons she didn't know. Having spoken her piece, she lowered her head and continued ironing my school uniform. Every crease in my blue pleated skirt had to be just right. My uniforms were always crisper and neater than those of any of my classmates. "I know," I said as I put down my school book and gazed out the window into the vast darkness of night. A tiny, pale light off in the distance flickered against the non-stop background chirping of insects. It was so dark out there I couldn't distinguish near from far. It seemed to me that Mother and I were encased in a black cocoon, tightly wrapped in fine silken threads, tighter and tighter, denser and denser.

All of a sudden I had trouble breathing.)

You won again, I had to admit it. And yet, I sometimes couldn't escape the feeling that you had another daughter, maybe more than one. When I was still in grammar school, you found an excuse to take a job out of town. For the next five years you came home infrequently, bringing with you a small portion of your wages. So every morning Mother and I went into the garden to glean vegetable leaves, then at night she'd do needlework for people, until she couldn't see straight. Given her deepening aversion to dirt and mess, on those rare occasions when you were home, she'd insist on taking your clothes down to the river to wash and scrub, over and over, dragging herself back home only after nightfall to prepare dinner. At bedtime, the three of us would crowd into the single bed, where Mother would wrap herself up like a mummy in the quilt to keep you from getting what you wanted. And so, the next morning, you'd gather up your clean clothes, and by the time I returned home from school, you'd be long gone.

Never once did you tell us anything about your life out there, but our gossipy neighbors never missed an opportunity to run over with spicy rumors about your life with that other woman. According to them, she was a widow with a milky complexion and a smile that seemed never to disappear. She already had an eight-year-old by her first husband, and had recently given birth to another: ours, I assume. With feigned looks of bewilderment, they peppered us with questions, until Mother, who tried never to show any weakness, finally closed our door and refused to have anything more to do with the neighbors.

During those five years, as Mother turned silent, scars began to appear on her wrists. I wonder if you ever noticed them after breaking it off with that other woman and coming home to us. Mother would wake up in the middle of the night sometimes, crying; she'd grab me and say she lived just for me, that I was the only thing that kept her from taking the easy way out. With her hair a fright, she looked like a mournful demon. Decades later, I grabbed the arms of my own daughter, shook her and told her that she was the only reason I endured the pain of living. The instant those words left my mouth, I realized that this was the nightmarish comment that had echoed in my ears since childhood, and had now exited from my own mouth, word for word. I ran into the bathroom, turned on the tap and frantically splashed water on my face. Then I looked into the mirror, only to face a woman whose hair was a fright, just like my mother's, another mournful night demon.

You must be shocked to learn how much I remember. You probably assume I was too young to form such memories. But you're sadly mistaken. Some things only require a tiny thread to take root in the limitless breeding ground of memory, then sprout and send out tendrils in later years. It's a lot like that daughter you had out there, my stepsister. I don't know a thing about her, but after years of fanciful imaginings, in my mind she grew from an adored little girl in pigtails into an enchanting middle-aged woman. That's because she and her lovely mother lived in a world of men, and without being aware of it, she acquired all the necessary seductive tricks and knew how to use them. As her full, scarlet lips part slightly, she removes her chubby fingers from the shoulders of one man and places them on the shoulders of the next. The thought that she has a father somewhere never occurs to her; only the soul of a fair-skinned, smiling mother remains with her. Eventually my sister turns into the image staring back at me from the mirror, and is the me I will never become. Except for one time, when, I recall, the images of my sister and me merged and folded into one. It happened on the afternoon when Mother was fluttering about like a butterfly, and her normally sallow face suddenly turned fair and silky, a smiling face; she lay gently in bed caressing herself and breathing heavily.

Then she rolled over and hugged me with her sweaty arms. My dear father, I've often thought about what might have happened if you'd been one of those innocent victims of the incident and could never have returned home. Would I have wound up like my own daughter, fatherless and brotherless from childhood, never really knowing if I was male or female? (On the same sort of spring afternoon, my eight-year-old daughter and I were stretched out lazily in bed, taking a nap. Just as I was falling asleep, I was startled awake by waves of strange dry heat coming from beside me. When I opened my eyes, I saw that the bed was rocking violently. It was my daughter. Her hand was moving quickly up and down between her legs. "What are you doing?" I was nearly shouting, shocked that an eight-year-old girl could have so much strength.

My daughter quickly covered herself with the quilt then turned to look at me. Her eyes were clear and innocent. "Who showed you how to do that?" I demanded. She just shook her head.

"Don't ever do that again," I said in the same demanding tone.

She nodded. But she couldn't hide the look of contentment and ecstasy in her eyes, just like the gentle Mother all those years ago. It was both pathetic and scary.

A few days later, my daughter's home-room teacher came by to tell me she sometimes absently played with herself even during class. I immediately called her away from the group of kids she was playing with and chewed her out in the hallway. She wore a contemptuous sneer the whole time, turning to watch her schoolmates running around chasing a ball on the playground. Sunlight fell on her face, with her tightly closed lips, turning it into a gilded mask. She looked just like my mother. There was, after all, something in our blood, regularly reappearing, unannounced, like an annual holiday, even now.) If this, if that, I was always thinking like that, while I waited for you to grow old. I know how heartless that sounds, but isn't that the way you treated me? Because of you, I was old the day I was born, canceling out any possibility of enjoying the springtime of youth. The shame of it all was, you were so full of life, fit and muscular; even at the age of seventy, that you could still dig a white shirt out of your trunk, put on a blood red tie and take a bus to Huaxi Street, all by yourself, not returning home until after dark. It was as if you'd been reborn. You dyed your gray hair black, your cheeks were ruddy, and whenever you walked past me, you reeked of cologne and semen. You had a zest for life, while the flower of my youth was nothing but a distant memory. It was so unfair. And still there was nothing I could do but wait. Ten years ago, at last, your sex drive began to wane. Except for your trips to the market for Chinese herbs to bring home and prepare over the stove, you hardly ever stepped outside the apartment. Then your eyesight began to fail, and it took the better part of the day to get through the newspaper. Five years ago, when your hearing began to deteriorate, I had to shout to make myself heard. Then three years ago, your teeth began to fall out, and after your dentures were in place, your diet was limited to soupy rice with sweet potatoes and fish meat and no green vegetables. Slowly but surely, your taste buds turned numb. A couple of years ago, you began to forget things like turning off the tap, and you never heard the sound of water running all night long. You couldn't even remember things that happened the day before. When your mind started to go, you stopped talking and never looked at me again. Then you could no longer keep your heavy lids from closing over your eyes.

Now, whenever I try to conjure up what you looked like, the only image that comes to mind is the black-and-white photo on the funerary urn. You are looking into the camera with a blank expression, your mouth opened slightly, with no indication of what you might be thinking. That's something I've never been able to understand, that and your attitude toward me. So I looked at you, filling up that urn, and was choked with tears, my chest heaving uncontrollably, until my eyes were red and puffy. I turned and walked out of the sapphire blue shrine of the public crematorium, wailing loudly. An attendant ran up to hand me the document and praised me as a profoundly filial daughter. I just shook my head as I walked past seemingly endless shelves of urns. All those blank faces and women, young and old, flew out of their urns and hung in the air in front of me to just stare.

Your room was empty when I arrived back home. During the week you slipped into a coma, I cleaned your room from top to bottom. Rusty nails, mildewed wood, medical books with anatomical drawings of blood vessels and acupuncture points, calendars with missing pages, and sheets of yellowed toilet paper with billions of dead sperm that were tucked into the folds of the bed gathered them all up, dumped them into plastic bags and put them out for the garbage trucks to take away. After one last inspection of your room, I went into my daughter's room. Now in her early twenties, she had long since spread her wings and left the nest, flying all the way to America. She left behind untouched books, a closetful of clothes, and a wall covered with large drawings of people embracing or kissing or dancing or lying lazily on a grassy lawn, every one of them a voluptuous woman and every one of them stark naked. Since I was alone in the room, I lay down on her bed and gazed for a long time at the serene women in the drawings, unaware even that the sun had set. The fragrance of my daughter's youth still clung to the soft yellow quilt on her bed. Slowly I reached down between my legs with my right hand. My thick pubic hair tickled the tips of my fingers, the pungent odor of my sex wafted up past my belly and inundated my nostrils. The motion of my fingers grew faster and faster, my entire body seemed energized and my mouth parted slightly, as if words were building up deep down inside me, ready to erupt thunderously. I squeezed my eyes shut and listened to the moan emerging from deep in my belly. It began as a faint unbroken sound, but kept getting louder, its surging echo seemingly on the verge of bursting through the concrete wall of the gloomy apartment.

I sat up abruptly and stumbled into the bathroom to look into the mirror. My cheeks were flushed; it was as if I were looking back through the years at the face of my mother. Gripping the sides of the sink, I bent over and stared at my reflection in the water, a smile frozen on my face. The mirror misted up from my steamy breath. Before long, the cold night air crept into the room from all directions and settled on my cheeks. Wrinkles chapped by a layer of frost cracked open in the corners of my eyes, on my lips, my cheeks, even the palms of my hands. My face, made stiff by the cold, looked exactly like yours as you lay in the mortuary cooler. Unable to bear the sight any longer, I walked out of the bathroom, steadying myself with a hand on the wall. As I looked down, I spotted a thick build-up of dried paint that had accumulated in the corner. When I looked up, I saw that the walls and ceiling of the apartment were covered with billowing mildew, something I hadn't noticed before; it seemed to be spreading like tenacious cancer cells. I ran into the kitchen for the broom, then went back and began sweeping the walls and ceiling. Flakes of paint settled around me like a sudden snowfall. They turned my hair white, much like the white mourning cap I'd been forced to wear when your body was turning to ashes in the crematorium. I brushed them off ferociously, both hands dancing frantically amid the snowflakes. At that moment, I was reminded of the sight of silkworms excreting silken threads to weave a cocoon. (With her head bent low, Mother was sewing someone's bright green cheongsam. Her reputation as a seamstress was well established in town. When she was nearly finished, she called me over. "Come try this on." I was in my fourth year at the teachers' college at the time. I put down my school book and went over sheepishly. I blushed as I took off my clothes in front of Mother, who helped me put on the dress. As I stood in front of the mirror, she zipped me up from behind, then ran her hands down my sides, stopping at my waist. "All I need to do is take in the waist a little and it'll be just right," she murmured. "Your waist is much thinner than Miss Chen's." Then she leaned her head over my shoulder to fix my hair as she took a satisfying look at herself in the mirror, as if she were the one wearing the dress.

But in less than a minute, her voice turned harsh and reproachful as she ordered me to take off the dress. "Be careful you don't ruin this dress. The customer wants it ready by tomorrow morning."

Not daring to show even a hint of reluctance, I took it off and handed it back to Mother, who sat down at the dining table, picked up her needle and thread and went back to work. I sat back down by the lamp and picked up my book, but my eyes were fixed on the wall and the shadow of Mother's hand rising and falling as it worked the long thread, like a silkworm spinning its cocoon. In my dream that night, the green cheongsam turned into a cocoon encasing me past the moment that I could break out, so all I could do was sit there with my arms wrapped around my knees and stare at the intermittent glimmers of sunlight that filtered through the tiny spaces between the silk threads. As the sun moved across the sky, my body began to shrivel, the muscles just beneath the puckered skin slowly wasting away. Once my eyes had grown accustomed to the dim light inside my cocoon, to my surprise, I saw Father and Mother resting on their haunches in distant corners, each of them reduced to less than half their original size. My mouth fell open in terror, but I didn't dare call out, afraid that their fragile bodies might crumble under the onslaught of the slightest sound. And so we all stayed just as we were, curled up in silence.

Because of that, my cocoon appeared incredibly spacious and incredibly empty.)

BLACK BOOK

Allan Weiss

It was only natural for Glenn to notice the little amber booklet; he usually walked with his head bowed, watching the sidewalk roll by beneath him like landscape seen from the air. The booklet caught a sharp gleam of streetlight as it lay in the grass half-shadowed by the bushes framing the front lawn of a semi-detached. From its bottom corner, a burgundy satin ribbon curled along the sidewalk like entrails.

He hooked the shimmering ribbon first with his forefinger, then picked up the chilled booklet and turned it over. On the front were the words "Address Book" in a shadowed serif font. Wavy maroon lines and matching spine added ornamentation to the laminated hard cover. A little black book, but not black. As he turned it sideways the thin ribbon draped itself gently over the back of his hand, tickling his hairs. The pages were edged in gold like some nineteenth-century novel. He slid his finger along the gold, which was so smooth he barely felt it.

He slid the address book into his square jacket pocket. He couldn't very well just leave the thing there, to be scooped up by a street cleaner. Maybe the owner would try retracing his or her steps, but there was no guarantee they'd find it, especially in the dark. He'd do a good deed, and it shouldn't be too hard to trace whoever had dropped it. Normally, he avoided things like this; he always pleaded ignorance when people asked him for directions, not because he didn't want to help but because he was always afraid he'd make a mistake and send someone the wrong way. But this time he'd do the right thing, at very little cost or risk. The cool, smooth coating on the cover warmed under his palm. He traced the bent-in corners with his forefinger. The ribbon hung outside his pocket, and jumped as he walked, fluttered as the wind caught the frayed end and made it dance.

***

He found two messages on his machine at home. He hated cell phones, refused to use one, and getting messages was almost as good as receiving letters or e-mails. As he expected, both were from Kristin, the first cryptic and the second an elaboration of the first:

"Glenn! Me. Wondering where thc lic-ons are."

"Me again. I'm back to hating Siobhan. She must have decided it was her time of the month or something so she's being bitchy again. I can't take her. Can I come over? I'm still at work."

Glenn hung his coat up and extracted the address book from the pocket. He dropped down onto the couch in front of the phone, which sat on the coffee table in black, angular, postmodern-design splendor. Before dialing Kristin, he opened the cover of the book and saw blank lines on the first page, where the owner's name, address, and phone number were supposed to be entered. More blankness on the inside of the back cover. Great. But the rest of the book was pretty full. Most of the names and details of contact information were written in uniform size and color ink; the owner probably entered those when she first got the book. And the hand was clearly that of a woman: broad curves, delicate curls on the Fs and Gs, tiny dots over the small Is and Js. A minority of entries appeared in the same hand but in a variety of pen-inks and pencil-sharpnesses, while two were written by others, presumably the contacts themselves.

He slapped the book against his left palm, establishing a rhythm as he thought this through. There was only one way to proceed—all that remained was to decide whom to call first.

First, though, he phoned Kristin, hoping she wasn't home. After two rings (always two rings—she never picked up on the first), he heard the distinct click of the receiver being lifted.

"Hello, Glenn!" Her call-display: it was nearly impossible to surprise her.

"Hi, how are you?"

"Good! You got my message? Can I come over?"

"Sure. But give me about a half-hour to get settled, okay?"

"Rough day?" she asked, as if there were any other kind. His father took a hands-off approach to Glenn's work, meaning there were always moments when he wasn't sure whether he was doing anything right. He'd had all the requisite design-school training, but that didn't mean his signs were what the customers actually wanted or needed.

"Same as always," Glenn said, shrugging unnecessarily.

"Sorry to hear that. I'll be over at eight o'clock, 'kay?"

"Yeah, okay."

Kristin hung up abruptly, as she liked to do.

Glenn settled back into the couch, the address book still in his hand. He leaned its cool top edge against his lower lip. Should he start alphabetically? Or find some other, deeper pattern that would be more efficient in the end? How would you determine which were the most commonly used numbers, in other words the people he or she would tell about the lost book? He wanted Kristin's company, but he wanted time even more—time to solve this puzzle.

Of all the names and addresses and numbers, the only set that counted was missing. It struck him that that's how it was with address books: everyone's information but your own. Like a hole, a black hole, a blank in the middle of the thing.

No time to start now, though—he'd have to give the problem a deep think instead, and proceed later.

Kristen buzzed exactly a half-hour later, and later entered his apartment carrying the night chill around her like an aura. He didn't tell her about the address book, for some reason. She flopped down on the couch after giving him his greeting kiss, then proceeded to outline her day as she drank her beer. Glenn gave her empty replies in return, trying to stuff his own day into a hidden place where it would no longer bother either of them. Meanwhile, he managed to stuff the address book under the seat cushion. All he told her was, "Just a pest of a client."

"That's it?" she asked.

"What?"

"I thought it was something more. Bigger."

"Isn't it big enough for you?" he said, with his dumbest smile. She rolled her eyes and cuddled against him. "No," he continued, "that's it. Maybe I should have been a real artist."

"You keep saying that."

"Got to make a living, though."

"You keep saying that, too."

He had no reply. Yes, he kept saying it; they were his father's words as much as his own. He felt sometimes as if his life's goal was to keep his parents from worrying about him. He hadn't hesitated to take the job at Dad's shop, earning a solid salary for churning out effective (he hoped) signs for stores, restaurants, and office plazas.

"Come on." She took his hand and led him into the bedroom, bumping him off his stride every few steps with her hip.

***

Kristin had to get up early, so she left around 10:30 p.m. It was almost too late to make any phone calls, but he decided to risk at least one. He chose to let the book open on its own, on the theory that where it splayed naturally would signify something. But the spine was equally tight everywhere. Little letter tabs were exposed by gnomen cut out of the bottom corners of the pages, and all the tabs were curled up to some extent. He stuck his thumb along the M divider and spread the pages to reveal a healthy number of Martins and McLeishes and Murrays. He selected the first original entry on the first M page.

After three rings a female voice answered sleepily, "Hello?"

"Hi. Is this Amy McLeish."

"Yes." Suspiciously.

"Hi. I found a little address book with your name and number in it but I don't know who it belongs to. Do you know anyone who's lost one?"

"Who is this?"

"My name is Glenn Eliot. I just found this address book so I'm trying to find whose it is."

"Right." *Click.*

"Okay," he said to the dial tone. Should he avoid the women? They'd think he was some kind of nut stalking them. He'd go down the list of originals first; taking a systematic approach would lessen the chance of missing someone.

The next answered after two rings. "Yes?" in a chirpy baritone, if that was possible.

"Hi, my name is Glenn Eliot and I'd—"

"Are you selling something?"

"What?"

"Are you selling something?"

"No." At this hour? Telemarketers only phoned at suppertime. "I found an address book that had your name and phone number in it and I'm trying to track down the owner."

"Doesn't it have the owner's number written in it?"

"No." He rolled his eyes, suppressing the urge to be sarcastic. "That's why I'm phoning around."

"What's it look like?" Glenn described it, although he couldn't see what good that would do. "Doesn't sound familiar. Why don't you just give it to the cops?" As if anyone would report a missing address book to the police.

"I'm trying to do a good deed here."

"Listen, I know a lot of people and it could be anybody."

"Do you know an Amy McLeish?"

"No. Who's she?"

"Someone else in the book."

"No. Look, why don't you just keep the fucking thing? Anyways, can't help you."

"Thanks anyway."

"Goodbye."

It was nearly eleven o'clock now, and Glenn threw the book onto the coffee table with a smack. Okay, so it was going to be a challenge. He'd meet it.

***

Glenn had one major project at work, a storefront sign for a manicure place: Nail Beautik. The shopowner wanted a giant, shovel-shaped red nail to the right of the cursive lettering. The image was supposed to complement the shop's name, but the Filipina owner kept returning the proofs complaining that it was too small.

"I want it to stand out!" Mrs. Pagao said. "So you can see it, you know?"

Her shop was in a bland, colorless strip mall on Wilson Avenue just west of Bathurst. Anything would make it stand out.

"I really think it'll be okay the way I faxed you."

His father, sitting across from him at the drafting table, looked up from his own work and flashed a look through his gold-rimmed glasses. Glenn read it easily: don't waste your time.

"But I want people to notice, to know it's my place. You have to see it from the road."

Yet most of her business wouldn't come from drop-ins. He knew that much about her business, but there was no point trying to explain it to her; it would take too long and just make him sound uncooperative. And his father would have a fit.

"Okay," Glenn said, keeping the impatience out of his voice. "I'll send something over right away."

As soon as the phone was safely down, Glenn's father said, "She's a real pain in the ass." His silver beard covered the sardonic twist of the mouth that Glenn knew was there.

"Yeah." Glenn ran his cursor over the fire-engine red fingernail on his computer screen. The arrow flickered as he raced it across the fiery background. "She's crazy if she wants it bigger."

"Give 'em what they want." His father reminded him of that simple rule every time he wanted to make some actual use of his art-school training. "There's no point arguing."

"Yeah, I know." And there'd been no point, really, in going to OCAD, really, if this was what he ended up doing. He was doing very little Art and not much Design here.

"Be careful what you ask for, eh?" Then, after a few minutes, "You and Kristin coming over for dinner some time?"

"Sure. Whenever." He dreaded those family dinners. They sometimes turned into subtle interrogation sessions about their relationship. He didn't need the pressure.

"I'll speak to your mother."

With luck, he and Kristin would be able to come up with some way to be busy that night, no matter what night his parents decided on. His mother wanted a wedding—as she did with every girlfriend he introduced to them. *Is this girl right for my son or would she make him miserable?*

"Anyway, give the crazy lady her big nail."

Glenn highlighted and enlarged the image. The nail seemed to be hovering over the shop's name, drawing the eye almost completely away from it, threatening to shovel it into complete obscurity. *Serves you right.*

***

"Hello?"

"Hi, my name is Glenn Eliot. Is this Marian Bruneau?"

"Yes." With anticipation more than fear, or so he imagined.

"I found an address book on the street and your name was in it. I wonder if you can help me find the owner."

"Seriously?" Amused. He heard the "waw" sound of the receiver being cupped. "Okay. But I know a lot of people."

"Well, did anyone report losing their book?"

"No."

"If I read off the names of some of the people in it, could that narrow it down for you?"

She snorted, gently. Then she replied with a drawn-out "Oh-kaay," as if humoring him. He read out a few of the originals' names that he'd separated out. There was silence at the other end of the line. "Nobody sounds familiar," she said, interrupting the flow. He went through the list alphabetically, keeping to a strict pattern to make the task more controlled, more scientific. "Sorry, but I don't recognize anyone."

"How about a few more? Sorry to take your time," he added quickly, when he heard a bit of a sigh through the pale static.

"Okay, sure. But I really have to get going."

He tried some from the secondaries—those added by the owner after the originals were entered—and finally what he called the selfers. Nothing.

"Listen, I really think what you're doing is cool. But is it really worth it?"

"Why not?" He couldn't imagine simply tossing the book out. He'd hate it if someone did that to a piece of his own valued lost property. He'd also hate to give up, and so soon.

"Well, look, good luck—Glenn, right?"

"Yeah. Thanks a lot for your time."

"No problem."

He looked at the VCR clock as he put the receiver down: seven minutes. He had to find a way to reduce it, or this would take forever. He pushed the Bs open more widely and proceeded to the next name, punching in the digits with his middle finger.

After his standard explanation to Ken Bacque—out of alphabetical order because he was a secondary—he asked if he could read out some names.

"How long is this going to take?" Ken sounded like the kind of person who insulted telemarketers. Glenn could picture him sitting there hunched forward, ready to slam the phone down.

"Not long. Just a few names, if that's okay."

"Yeah, fine, whatever."

It didn't take long before Ken stopped the list with a firm, "Look, this is a waste of time, right?"

"Just a few—"

"No, fuck it. Goodbye."

"Thanks anyway." He only managed to get half of that out before the click. Well, at least those sorts of responses would shorten the time. He'd never fully considered the possibility of failure before; it hit him that most people would probably decline to help, and he sank back into the couch and closed his eyes. He wasn't asking much of them—just a few minutes, long enough to hear about a friend or maybe relative of theirs whose property was in a stranger's hands, a stranger who wanted to direct it back to its rightful owner. Were people this selfish?

Idiot. *Shit!*

He flipped through till he found a selfer, then frantically dialed the number, his excitement causing him to misdial twice. He got Dale Stortroen's voicemail.

"Hi, my name is Glenn Eliot and I found an address book with your name in it, and I'm trying to find its owner. Do you remember writing your name and number in a book?" Glenn described it in as much detail as he could, and left his number twice, articulating the digits slowly to ensure that Dale could write them down.

As soon as he hung up, he searched for the other selfer and tried that number. It was out of service.

***

"I swear I'm going to kill her!"

Glenn held the receiver loosely in his hand, risking a drop and mad scramble to retrieve it. He didn't have the patience for Kristin's complaints right now, especially when he was getting so close. If Dale Stortroen called, the mystery would probably be solved, the whole thing resolved, and that wonderful feeling you got from completed puzzles would be his.

"Are you listening?"

"Sure. What's up now?"

"Christ, she starts getting on my case for how I arrange my icons. You believe that? My frigging *icons*!" And so she detailed the dispute, her tone a constant question: do you believe that? At the end, "You want to come over?"

He did: he wanted to see her, hold her. But not now. "I can't."

"Why not?"

"I'm expecting a call."

"A call? What do you mean? From who?"

"It's a long story." He still didn't want to tell her. It was his own concern, a private quest, and anyway it would sound too crazy as a reason to turn her down.

"Come on." But he refused to bite. "Seriously, what's going on?"

"Nothing. It's—"

"Do you want me to come over?" But there was something in her voice that seemed to say, *You don't, really, do you?*

"Yeah . . . "

"Fuck it." And she hung up. He cringed as he put the phone down, and crossed his arms over his chest. *Shitshitshit.* He'd have to phone back, apologize or something—if she would still listen. The address book lay conspicuously on the coffee table before him. How serious was this? When should he call her? Right away, or when he came up with something he could tell her? As he was trying to decide, he picked up the book and tapped its spine on the edge of the table. A couple of calls, then he'd know what to do.

"Hello, is this Noreen DiGennaro?"

"Yeah." Sounds of family in the background: kids, the TV on, a male voice raised to one of the kids: *Put that down! Now!*

"My name is Glenn Eliot and I found an address book with your name in it. I wonder—"

"Eh?"

He tried to explain, but Noreen proved hopeless; she didn't understand him, couldn't grasp what he wanted.

"I know many people," she said in a heavy accent. "In my club."

"What club?"

"Eh?"

He had to repeat every question, explain every nuance. She belonged to some sort of community organization. A crisis erupted behind her, and she shouted back and hung up.

Glenn put the phone down quickly, in case Dale was trying to get through. Dale—he or she—had actually seen the book, knew what it looked like and could identify the owner, because Dale had held it and written in it.

He waited, but the phone remained dead silent. So Glenn tried another number. No answer.

He hit 2 on the speed-dial. "Kristin?"

"Hi." It was a good sign that she'd actually picked up the phone at all. Her "Hi" was clipped, anticipatory.

"Listen, I'm really sorry. Please come over; I want to see you. Okay?"

"Right."

"Please?"

She breathed right into the phone, the sigh becoming an electric crackle, like crumpled cellophane unfolding. "Okay." He let out his own breath, away from the phone. If she got seriously mad, even dumped him, that would be too much.

It would take her twenty minutes to get to his place. He had time for two more calls. Just as he reached for the receiver, the phone rang. "Hello?"

"Hello. Is this Glenn Eliot? You phoned me, something about an address book?" A female voice, gruff and low, like someone who'd been through it.

"Yes! Is this Dale Stortroen?" He pronounced it as Europeanly as he could.

"Yes. Look, what's this all about?"

"Well, it's as I explained in my message. I found this address book, and you'd written your name in it, I think, so I wonder if you can help me track down the owner. I want to return it to her, and I was hoping you could help."

"Maybe. I don't know." She didn't sound positive or trusting—defensive or just plain puzzled instead.

"Well, do you remember writing your name in someone's book?"

"I always write my name in people's books. They can never spell my name right." And she was obviously sick of doing it, too.

"Look, if I show you the book do you think you—?"

"I don't want to get mixed up in this, whatever it is."

"If you could just look at the book. And if you don't recognize it, fine."

"I don't have time to meet you about this." Then she hung up. Glenn shook his head. Dale had seemed to be waiting for something—maybe something to convince her it was okay to meet him, okay to care. But he'd had nothing to offer her, just the same old request, the same empty message.

With no hope at all, he tried phoning Marge Johansen. He explained things to her according to his mental script, and she listened sympathetically.

"That's a really nice thing you're doing," she said.

"Thanks. So is it okay if I show it to you or something?"

"I doubt it would mean anything to me."

"What if I read off some names? Maybe you could tell me whether you know any of them. Then I can narrow her down."

"You keep saying `she' and `her.' How do you know it's a woman?"

"The writing. It's—"

"Oh, wow, you've really thought about this, haven't you? Sure, read off some names."

With renewed hope, he rhymed off a bunch of names. "Oh, Carol! Yeah, I know her. She does lots of volunteer work. So do I. I do coordinating, you know, with the Council."

"The what?"

"The Ontario Non-Profit Council. We coordinate for different groups, organizations, you know."

"Oh, so she's a volunteer, then."

"Who? Carol? Yeah, for different groups. Maybe your mystery lady, too. Give me more names."

He did.

"Yeah, Noreen! I've had dealings with her. Not much, though. Her English is none too good."

"I know."

"You spoke to her? Keep going!"

By now he roiled with a mixture of feelings: hope and frustration, and fatigue. He kept going as requested, and Marge would stop him. Why couldn't she just give him a name, the missing piece, once and for all? Or tell him whom to call to get a definitive answer? Instead, she teased him. "Phyllis!" "Oh, yeah, Ginette—don't talk to her, she's crazy." "Derek—must be the guy I met, though I don't remember if that's his last name."

"So, do you have any ideas about whose this might be?"

"No, it could be anyone's. I mean, I meet lots of people. But you might—" His buzzer went, blotting out her words.

"Could you hold on?"

"Of course."

He pressed the button under the intercom to let Kristin in, then went back to the phone. "If I showed it to you, do you think you could identify the handwriting?"

"Well, I mostly deal with people by e-mail. I never see their handwriting, I don't think. What about—?"

Kristin would arrive any second. "Listen, I want to thank you for all your help."

"Well, what you're doing is very sweet. Listen, if there's a Patricia Solon, try her. She's everybody's friend. Do phone me back and let me know if you're successful, okay?"

"I will—"

"Because now I'm also kind of curious—"

Kristin's door-knock came: low, double. "Hold on. No, listen, I've really got to go. But thanks again."

"My pleasure. And like I said—"

"Thanks. Really."

"Okay. Bye-bye."

He banged the phone down and rushed to let Kristin in. She wouldn't meet his eyes, just walked deliberately by him into the apartment, and dropped onto the couch without taking off her leather jacket.

"Kristin, look, I'm really sorry for how I acted. It was rotten, rude."

"Who were you talking to?"

"Nobody."

Now she looked at him, firing bolts. "Fuck, Glenn, I could *hear* you."

"I'm just trying to get some information." He squeezed by her, putting his body between her and the address book that lay on the table. He scooped it up and tossed it in the pile of old newspapers underneath. Fortunately, she paid no attention to what looked like a last-minute attempt to straighten up. "I'm dealing with some stuff, nothing serious."

"You've been more distracted than usual, and that's saying something."

"I know." He put his arm around her, and was relieved when she didn't flinch away. He pulled her close. "And I'm sorry that bitch has been hounding you." Then he knew what to say. "Your *icons*?"

"Yeah!" And she was off again with the story of her desktop. He nodded and made sympathetic grunts where necessary, then, when she was a bit calmer, got them beers from the fridge.

"So what's been going on with you, really?" she asked again when he returned. "Something at work, or what?"

"Well, yeah, things at work . . . there's this client who's a real pain in the ass."

"The nail lady?"

"Yeah." Now he was getting close to outright lying to her. He didn't want to go that far.

"Shit, Glenn, you're the artist. You should tell her that."

"Yeah." *Christ.* But if he changed the subject, as he so desperately wanted to do, she might get onto her own work again, and he didn't want to hear the same story again. There had to be more. *Artist*—some artist. There were people back at the college who'd had something—an energy, a sense of ambition and focus—he'd never seemed to be able to muster. He'd watch them obsess over what they were going to do, wishing he knew where they found the drive, and the guts.

"Come on," Kristin said, "let's forget about work."

He nodded, and drank his beer.

***

The following day he had to deal with more of Mrs. Pagao's bitching. This time, she was unhappy with the background color of the sign: maybe silver would stand out more brightly than white. He had visions of a glaring swath of aluminum blinding passers-by. And his father, half-seriously, recommended he simply give her what she wanted. "Would serve her right," he told Glenn.

But there were limits even his father wouldn't cross to satisfy a customer. And he was more flexible than Glenn sometimes gave him credit for—Dad had even agreed to buy a new latex-ink printer because Glenn thought it would be better for their lungs. But it was Dad's shop and usually Glenn kept his mouth shut because he didn't want to sound like he was trying to take over.

"Mrs. Pagao," Glenn said to her over the phone, "trust me. You'll be happy with what we showed you." And if not . . . he watched Dad, who shook his head while staring at his computer screen. Glenn felt like passing Mrs. Pagao on to him, washing his hands of the crazy lady. "Trust me," Glenn repeated, and got off the line with her.

At home, he heated up some canned ravioli and watched *Wheel of Fortune*. There were two kinds of contestants on TV game shows: the ones who passed the *Jeopardy* test, and the ones who failed and ended up on *Wheel of Fortune*.

"Hi, is this Patricia Solon? My name is Glenn Eliot. I found an address book and I'm trying to locate the owner—"

"You fucking *found it*?" she cried in an accent. "I don't believe it!"

Glenn's heart raced. "You know the owner?"

"Yeah! She's, like, my best friend. Caitlin. Shit, she was so upset! Like, she was using it to call someone when she was using her cell, and she shoved it back, like, really loose in her pocket? And then it was, like, *gone*!"

"This is great!" Amazed, he stared at the book. "So, how do I reach her?"

"Oh, I could bring it to her. That—"

"No!" He had to give it to her himself, present it to her personally. "No, I think it's best if I give it to her myself. Just to be sure, you know?" Finalize it. Complete it. Fill in the blanks . . .

"Um, okay. But I'm not giving you her address, like."

"All right. Could you arrange for her to meet me? In a public place?"

A pause; he could hear sounds like those of a person settling into a vinyl chair. He pictured her living in Parkdale, surrounded by creeps ready to attack. People in Toronto, the safest city in North America, were so paranoid. "Listen," she said at last, "what if you meet her at the Eaton Centre? Tomorrow?"

"Sure." He thought frantically. He could get out of the shop at six o'clock. And then he'd have to figure out something to tell Kristin, if she asked. By now, he was so far into it the truth would seem utterly lame. "I'll give you my number and you can phone me back, okay? When you have a time for me to be there?"

"Okay. Shit, that's great. She'll be so happy. She's lost without that thing."

"Great. I'll wait to hear from you."

And with that it was done, or almost done. As he exchanged goodbyes with Patricia Solon he felt a rush, a glowing wave, of satisfaction, like the moment when enough *Wheel Of Fortune* squares were filled in so that you could practically see the missing letters, read the full answer.

***

He spent the day half-working, half-phoning his answering machine to see if Patricia Solon had called. Ms. Pagao's nail looked done and ready to print. He turned to a couple of poster designs for a condo project. "Elegant Living in the Heart of North Toronto"—the usual shit to make people feel better about living in an apartment instead of a house.

When he checked at noon there were two messages, both from Kristin. "Want to hear about my layabout plan?" He skipped her next one and worked through the lunch hour to keep himself away from the phone, and prevent his father from asking questions. Around 3:30, at last, his machine announced that there was a new message awaiting him. He punched in the code to retrieve it. "Hi, Glenn? This is Patricia, you know, from last night? I spoke to Caitlin, and she's like, very grateful you found her book. She'll meet you at seven o'clock at the fountain, you know? Watch for a girl in a black coat?" *Yes!*

"What's going on?" his father asked from his desk, looking at Glenn over the top of his glasses.

"Nothing. Just checking my messages."

"You got a date? Does Kristin know?"

"Funny." Glenn returned to the posters, trying to steer the conversation away toward—silence, blankness.

"Seriously, you're not concentrating at all today." Dad pushed his glasses back up his nose with the heel of his hand.

"Sorry. Did you see the Pagao sign?" Glenn asked to stop the questioning.

"Yeah. Close enough to what she wanted." Not that it was good or anything; all that mattered was that the customer was satisfied. Or at least wouldn't complain.

Glenn called up the image of the sign on his screen. Too late to make any changes now. The giant nail glared at him. He measured its color balance again: it was the reddest red he could make it without setting fire to the sign.

"Keep 'em happy," his father said, for the thousandth time. "Keep 'em paying." Dad didn't bother to add the third part of the formula, because Glenn knew it too well: *Keep in business.*

Glenn arrived at the old, no longer functioning fountain on the bottom floor of the Eaton Centre a little before seven o'clock. He sat on the circular bench and took the address book out of his inside jacket pocket. He began to feel that moronic sentimentalism that he was prone to sometimes, still, over inanimate objects. He'd miss the thing.

He held it so that anybody passing by could see it, and briefly flipped through it absently, then realized Caitlin wouldn't appreciate such unnecessary prying. So he just slapped it rhythmically against his palm again.

"Oh my God! Oh my God!"

A short, dark-complexioned young woman in a black leather coat bore down on him, not looking at him—only the book. Her lips were thickly coated with 'stick. A black purse slapped her side, and as she turned her head to avoid a collision a ponytail briefly curled over her shoulder.

"Where did you *find* it? Oh my God!"

"Caitlin?" he asked, pointlessly. He stood up and held the book out. She took it gingerly from his fingers.

"Yeah! Oh my God!" She flicked through its pages, as if he might have stolen some. "Thank you so much!" She finally looked up at him. "You must have had such a hassle finding me! Pat told me all about you calling her."

"No big deal."

She opened her black purse and waved the book briskly. "I am putting it in *here* and I'm *keeping* it in *here*!"

"Wait!" He couldn't just see it disappear into the bag. He held out his hand. "Here."

She flashed a suspicious look at him. "What?" But then she handed it over, slowly.

He turned to the front page, where her name and address and phone number ought to be. The lines were still blank. "You're supposed to fill these in, just in case. You should do that." He stared at the page, the black hole, the blank underlined spaces.

With a slap he shut the cover and gave the book back to her.

"Anyway," she said, dropping the book into her purse and yanking the zipper shut. "Thank you so *much*. Seriously. Can I get you something? A reward coffee or something?"

He couldn't take his eyes off the purse. "No, jeez, forget it." Now, when he looked at her, he saw the mild agony in her expression: she felt she had to do something. She'd put him to all that trouble and he had to set her free of that. "It was kind of fun, actually," he said, almost finishing the sentence with "tracking you down." "Solving the mystery, I mean. You know."

"Thanks again!" she said, and squeezed his arm. Then she turned, waved goodbye over her shoulder, and walked away toward the subway, pinching her purse closed despite the zipper.

He watched her disappear through the glass doors, and sat down on the bench. In a moment he'd head home. There were those messages from Kristin; he should phone her. He'd be less distracted now, he'd hear her better. He'd know better what she was saying, and what she wanted him to do.

Nice Dress

Marion Bloem

"Nice dress," he said.

He guessed that in a moment like this, a compliment for the dress might have a better effect on me than a compliment for my looks. He knew how weak I was, even though I seemed happy in that particular moment, with the dress lying on my lap and the late sun shining on my brown Asian face. For several months I had been hiding myself under blankets in our large king size bed, worrying if the strange symptoms I had were fiction or signs of a serious disease. Though my recently published novel had excellent reviews and apparently my marriage had never known such harmony, I was close to a trendy burnout because my body was letting me down.

The red dress with purple and pink fragile flowers wrapped in elegant jade green leaves was bought on an impulse, just before closing time, that late afternoon. The strong autumn sunbeams made the day look like late summer. On my bike, heading for the village to buy bread, I passed the store. The dress in the window brought spring to the ivory white mannequin with her bold head, dead eyes and massive long lashes. And I was still in love with the man who stayed home writing his masterpiece about happiness and health or the link between those two undefined states of human beings.

I typed the code of my card to pay for the *autumn sales* dress about two hours before my beloved one made his unexpected reckless confession. The dress, carefully wrapped in soft white paper, was handed to me in a brown paper bag with red ribbons about twelve hours before I wrote that hatred poem, which was meant to stir up the peace in my family. That cruel verse was a scream for empathy from my friends, written to be printed for anyone who was convinced, just like me, and due to me, that my husband was a saint.

Of course the choice of language reveals that in my act of literary revenge there was just one thing I wanted to spare: him. Not myself, not my own silly stories of admiration.

I made him a saint. There is no one to blame other than myself for this marriage tragedy in which an admired worshipped man falls down from the pedestal that his wife created.

So much shame in so little rhyme. The rhythm was despair. Self-pity in every single line. Yet it helped me get over the pain. Not before I had kicked his ass literally though, directing my feet at his balls. He was always fast enough to protect those vulnerable things which he actually did not have. Not even literally. That, by the way, was the most revealing aspect of his confession: the lack of balls.

Any other language than my own would do in the saddest moment of my marriage, but I picked English, because that was the language I spoke with all the lovers I managed to hide from my husband for almost forty years. After having written the vindictive poem, I decided to never ever write a novel in my mother tongue again.

I sent the pathetic poem to all my friends abroad. By e-mail. I could not think of a faster way to express my anger and shame to the ones that mattered.

I also decided never ever to wear that dress, which was still in the paper bag, pale in the white wrapping, as ashamed as I was, longing to go back to the bold-headed, dead-eyed mannequin and the massive lashes in the window of hope for spring when winter arrived too early and seemed to promise to never leave again.

I rang him from the fitting cubicle. Mobile phones are invented by genius human beings who never had their hearts broken, otherwise they would have thought twice before giving birth to this tool which supports men and women all over the world screwing around like mice and rats, ignoring the promises they once made to the ones they're sharing the sheets with as automatically as they wipe off their asses a few times a day.

"This might be the very last sunshine before frost falls in," I said.

"You want me to jump on my bike and meet you?"

"Only if you feel like it," was my lie.

Of course I wanted him to feel those tickling rays on his face, to be reminded too of us undressing each other on the carpet of our living room in spite of our ages. Doors and windows wide open. Birds the only witness. We used to celebrate spring instantly when clouds for once forgot to turn the naked sky into the usual grey. But back then the wrinkles around his mouth were still just emphasizing his beautiful smile and did not yet look like traces of pain, disease and sadness.

"Why don't you come home, so we can sit in the garden. I'll make us some tilleul."

Since he appeared to have caught the disease only men could get, he limited his daily amount of alcohol to one glass sipping while cooking and one glass sipping at dinner. His delicious vegetarian meals, or butter free fish dishes with seven kinds of vegetables were my daily treat, though he hated anything green when he was a teenager. His mother could stuff him with meatballs but all the rest was left cold on his plate in spite of her punishments. Living with me he gradually began to like spinach and lettuce, but with all other vegetables he would happily fatten our neighbor's goats. The harsh diagnosis by his colleagues though, led to a fundamental change in his food pattern. His deceased mother, if not having been cremated, would crawl from her grave to watch his daily consumption of sprouts, cabbage, broccoli and his intake of all kinds of herbal tea having the reputation to reduce the chance to get the disease which he actually already got. Lemon grass infusion became his favorite afternoon drink. Proposing tilleul was a gesture of kindness to me.

I should have recognized his tilleul proposal as a warning. But of course I didn't. I begged him: "Please come, let's bike in the forest till sunset."

While I tried on three different sizes, starting off with ES, ending up with L, wondering why pins were needed to make the S fit the baldheaded bloodless lady in the window, my sixty years old husband raced against the wind on the bike which I gave him for his birthday twenty years ago. He stood next to me when I punched the four digits. The mirror had told me that this dress looked better on my brown body than it did on the white mannequin, even though I had grown chubby over the years. Only forty nine dollars to make myself feel young, beautiful and irresistible.

The dress was mine.

I noticed that he was hiding worries behind a shy almost artificial smile. But I ignored that signal too, assuming he considered one more dress on top of so many piled up in my cupboard was one too many.

Blind for the silence around him, I said: "I am so happy with our life."

No reply. I suspected him to consider if he'd be cynical by saying: "It would have been fair if you had used the word 'life.' Not 'dress.'"

I knew that the dress was bought to celebrate the deep happiness I felt since I left the house, feeling the heat of the golden sun on my face. Nevertheless I liked to believe it was our tool to awaken the sleeping desire for each other's tongues to explore the softness of each other's skin like the very first time, though in less hurry than we did back then, discovering places where we had not yet been, which I knew there would be.

He sighed. That sigh was ignored after it had been registered somewhere on my cortex making sense a few hours later, in my garden, just before I smashed the teapot against our wall, and the fragments landed in our blooming rosary. He took the paper bag from me, as if its weight were too heavy for the woman he had married almost forty years ago.

"Let's go home straightaway," he said, "then you can put on that dress for me. We'll have tea on our favorite wooden bench, and pretend it's still summer."

He seduced me using the word summer. I followed him. He took the narrow unpaved path through the woods to our house. As always since the day we met he biked faster, though the path allows a couple in heat to bike kind of cheek to cheek.

His bended back was my view.

Umbrella, cushions, pillows on a bench were waiting for us in our garden, but after our shortcut through the park, crossing just two streets, one traffic light and one railway, I was pushed back into the period before his prostate appeared to have betrayed him, when treatments had not silenced his manhood yet, and our love was still a continuous passionate battle.

When we were both students he'd bike with me sitting sideways on his uncomfortable back carrier, like he intended to win the yellow jersey. He hated wasting time as much as waiting. Lights were always green, gates open or avoided, bridges never too high. He would push us in between truck and tram without any fear, forgetting that my legs were sticking out at one side and my feet might hit one or the other.

I had just one wish when I moved in with him: to buy my own bicycle. I ate less, I wore my winter coat in summer to save money, and happily bought my own bike after having been living together for exactly one year.

He didn't understand. It was a waste, he said, we could have used the money for a holiday instead. He felt in heaven biking around with my hands around his waist. And I did not lie when I said that my skinny behind would not survive road bumps any longer, though I suppressed admitting that I could live with the idea of us growing old together only on one condition: if I could stir my own wheel.

There we were. Our bikes embraced each other against our little brick stone barn. While I sat in the sun and took the package out of the plastic bag, unwrapping the dress, he left for the kitchen to boil water. I smelled the lemon grass before I could see him coming out of the door with the teapot and cups on a too large tray. The teapot slid dangerously over the wooden tray. Nothing could change my great mood. I was accustomed to him being a man of habits. The dress was lying on my lap. I waited for his encouragement to put it on.

While putting the tray next to me, spilling tea when pouring it into our cups, he said those important two words: "Nice dress."

"Lemon grass is okay too," I replied, smiling at him.

"Sorry," he said, "you are right, you asked for tilleul."

"No, you proposed tilleul, but lemon grass is fine."

"I'm so sorry, I'll boil some more water and . . . "

Then I almost screamed my interruption: "No! Please sit down! Let's enjoy this hour before the sun is gone again."

Suddenly my crotch hurt as if long narrow pointy knives entered me between my legs. This pain had been ruining my days for some months already and I had taken antibiotics on his prescriptions thinking it was my bladder. But that cure had had no effect, and more complaints had followed. He probably suspected Menopause to be responsible for the theft of the cheerful side of my character or at least he pretended to. The sun, the bike ride, the dress had taken my mind off my worries but buried trouble showed up again with the lemon grass and turned me into that bitchy wife which I am ashamed to admit that I am so often nowadays.

"You biked too fast and now my bladder is eating me. My sore cunt feels fucked, like you've given me some venereal disease or so."

While I heard myself saying those nasty words, blaming him for my stupid physical complaints, I felt ashamed that I wanted him to feel guilty for my weak bladder as much as for the lemon grass that was not the promised tilleul. The lemon grass infusion was still too hot to drink, but I picked up the cup and started sipping, burning my tongue.

Then I looked up at him, piercing his blue eyes with sincere surprise, I heard him saying without a stutter: "Yes, you are right, I think I have."

I stared at him. His face looked weird. I had never seen it grey like this. His mouth seemed not to be able to decide if it was going to smile or cry. The irises of his eyes were as if there were no pupils. Colorless, like frozen water.

"What do you mean?"

He gave no reply. And I still did not believe him. It was as if we were reading some screenplay together, checking out if the dialogue might work. I was waiting for reality to come back. There was no cloud in front of the sun, the temperature was still great for this time of year. And it was no problem that he made lemon grass and not tilleul. So why was he talking all this nonsense?

"I think we've got syphilis."

Then I understood that he was suggesting that I had been with someone else, so I said: "Impossible! I haven't been with anyone but you . . . "

I looked him in the eyes and I saw shame. I could not believe what I read from his cold blue eyes and asked: "Or . . . have you . . . ?"

He nodded slowly, like an old man he whispered: "I've been with someone . . . "

I needed to believe that he was joking. I searched to find proof in his face that he was making fun of me, that he was trying to cheer me up with a tasteless crack, though that was not him. But it was not him to ever kiss another woman, so how could he have been with someone else without me knowing this? He had hardly been out of my sight for many years. I had to teach him how to make love again with so much patience since medication took all his testosterone away.

People who survived severe accidents often tell how they saw their lives passing by in a split second. I always wondered what that would be like, if it was just a saying or if it was truly like watching a movie with oneself as the main character, and if it were fun or scary to relive so many details of the past in such short time. And now I knew.

It was my sexual past that passed by. I saw myself, eighteen years old, still a virgin. Three boyfriends had colored my long time puberty. From the first one I had learned to kiss. He woke me up, he changed a too shy Asian girl into a too proud Western lady. The second one taught me to like to be undressed. So far I had only been nude in the shower. We spent many hours naked in bed holding each other tight. We caressed each other endlessly and somehow he must have felt that he could not touch me there where my senses preferred to stay asleep. The third one prepared my body to feel the wish to be deflowered, but just not by him. We broke up when I realized that he was not a man to live with, though our bodies spoke the same perfect language from the start.

A couple of months later I met him at a bar. He did not try to flatter me, like other men would do. He gave no compliments, but spoke about his political ideas, about his wish to travel around the world, and most of all about his wish to make a career as a medical scientist, and not as a general practitioner.

I saw him touching my knee, moving too rapidly, talking too much while I desperately waited for his very first kiss. His mouth felt familiar, though impatient, as if he was afraid that the green traffic lights might turn red. Some hours later, he parked his old car on a sideway of the main road near the woods, where my parents with the whole extended family used to go for picnics and where I, as a kid, played hide-and-seek with my nieces and nephews until sunset sent us home. He kissed me longer than before, with far more passion. The kiss I urged for, though in haste. And while actually still kissing, he unfolded something from a tiny package, which he had taken out of his pocket. I wondered why he needed chewing gum in the middle of our first time making out. But he did not put it in his mouth, he kept it in his hand, while his other restless hand rushed from my breasts to my vagina, rubbing my labia as if his nervous fingers were searching something he had lost. He gave up on that before I could wonder what he was looking for. He slid the tight rubber sock that I had taken for chewing gum, quickly around that hurtful body piece which I had never caressed, licked or kissed, even hardly seen. I felt a sharp pain. Nothing else.

Once he had arranged to borrow a friend's room for some hours in a student house. We had gone dancing first. At eleven he showed me his watch and told me to get my coat. I didn't know where we were going. The house was not far away, a short ride through narrow alleys without lanterns and it surprised me that he did not stop to press me against the wall and kiss me on the mouth. When we arrived at a large grey building where loud music came from an open door, he was in too much of a hurry to lock his bike.

Students, all men, were playing billiards in the living room. The place smelled like a pub. The furniture was a ragbag of times and tastes. Their eyes on me felt uncomfortable. They were all older than me, all white, and probably all of them future doctors or dentists. He pushed me more or less, though it might have looked different, as he had his arm around my shoulder. I felt pushed and pulled when he crossed the room, straight to one of the closed doors with a large poster of the Beach Boys on it. A large tear in the right lower corner of the poster was fixed with an overdose of sell tape, some yellowish one of the cheapest kind.

Once inside he looked for a key to lock the door, and when he did not find one, he shoved a chair against it. The noise from the living room, even the music, was not heard in this room. It was awkwardly silent compared to the rest of the house.

He took off his shoes and his jacket. Not the rest of his clothes. I observed the room. Golf sticks were lying in a corner on top of three different kinds of hockey sticks. Skies were leaning against the wall. It did not look like a bedroom though there was a bed. It was going to be the first time to share a bed with him, and I was wondering if he expected us to be totally naked.

Of course, right now, I had my menstruation. I did not feel so well, cramps had been bothering me already the whole evening. Dancing was the best cure, so I had almost forgotten about it at the club, but in that room of an unknown person it hit me worse. Anyway I would rather be with him than with the same cramps alone in my bed at home. As usual the blood was streaming like the Niagara waterfall though. I feared that I would be leaking soon and I was sure that in this student house there would be no one to borrow sanitary towels from.

I took off my coat, but that was all. He pulled me on the bed. His hands went straight to my skirt and he tried to pull down my underwear. Then I warned him, with some guilt and shame as if I my bloody period was arranged to pester him: "I'm bleeding heavily."

He cursed. Not just once. Many times. And after some angry grumble he opened his gush and pushed my head brusquely above his huge proud pride, pulled my long black hair together in a ponytail and demanded: "Put me in your mouth!"

It tasted like bad fish. It felt too big between my lips. I hated the feeling of this huge thing deep in my throat. I wanted to cry, wanted to push him away, but then I thought: Maybe this is what love is like. You do something for him that you don't like and next time he'll do something for you which he's not crazy about.

He pulled my hair back and forth. It was too fast for me. My belly hurt. The cramps got worse. I was afraid to vomit.

He mumbled: "Yes, yes, this is good, this is so good, this is perfect . . . Go on, don't stop, yes, good girl . . . "

I tried to stop thinking of the cramps and the urge to throw up. I tried to not be there, to let go and to just be that robot which he wanted me to be. His groans of pleasure were a relief. I did not know if I was allowed to spit the proof of his excitement out or if I had to swallow it all to show my love for him. I hoped he did not see my tears when he came. His eyes were still closed. I spit the sperm secretly in my hand and smeared it on the sheets.

We left that room without having showered and there was no wash-basin or anything like that. I wondered why we had not kissed. It was as if he avoided looking at my face. Did he hate the taste of his sperm as much as I did?

His bike was gone, but he did not seem to care. We walked to the station. He had his arm loose around my neck. We did not talk. He whistled, which I had never heard or seen him do before. I was happy when I got on the bus home, to be alone again. He kissed me goodbye on my right cheek and whispered in my ear: "You were great today."

There weren't any other opportunities to just be by ourselves, undisturbed in one room, one bed. He had his examinations and I had mine. Our moments together were in his car, and he was always in a hurry. Things changed when I left home to move in with him. Only then his kisses became less restless and he wanted me to enjoy those fifteen minutes before bedtime as much as he did. He effortlessly tried to make me come, still skipping the stuff that I had liked so much with the few men before him, guys my age which I had not loved like him. He was driven by an endless need to give me pleasure after his own rapid ejaculations. Spooning, with his lips resting in my neck near my ear, he had almost always already fallen asleep when I finally tended to vaguely feel some kind of titillation that reminded me of the excitement I used to feel when being kissed and caressed by my former boyfriends. In these moments it seemed to make sense what he was doing with his right middle finger. His sleepiness made his touch evolve into the needed softness. The unpredictable rubbing, due to him falling asleep from time to time, helped to awaken my arousal. I was quietly waiting for it to come, I hardly dared to breath. We were fork and spoon. Then, after hours, I was finally wet and he was snoring.

He gave me *Human Sexual Response* as a present for my nineteenth birthday, the first birthday since we met, which we celebrated at some Spanish beach with two of his friends and his parents. He showed me the graphics of male and female orgasms when we were still between the sticky sweaty white sheets in a hot room in a cheap Spanish hotel where he had also booked his parents and his two best friends. Even then we had to hurry because all of them were waiting for breakfast. I missed my family heavily while they were telling lousy jokes hanging in those beach chairs in the shade. I was hopelessly in love with him. I adored his broad-shouldered body, his strong legs, his muscled arms, the big hands, the few hairs on his flat chest, his prominent nose, the high cheekbones, the blond hair on his tanned skin, his talent to remember all he has read, and his quality to tell what he has read better than how the text had been on paper. I knew that I wasn't able to love anyone else the way I loved him, that I could never listen to someone else like I was hanging on his lips. I knew what was lacking in our relationship and I knew that he had no clue of what he did not give. Maybe this awareness made me love him even more, as I might have been fond of him because of all his talents, but I was madly in love with his incapacity to let go.

While he made everybody roar, I longed to kiss his ugly toes which were playing with the grains of sand as restless as his fingers when caressing my nipples. On my nineteenth birthday there was no time left to make love. He got drunk and we went back to our room late after midnight. He vomited, hanging over the closet for twenty minutes, immediately when we got back to the hotel. The bathrooms were shared with other guests. I sat next to him, massaging his neck while he was puking. He was mumbling all kinds of compliments and expressing his love for me for the very first time when we stumbled to the room. I was totally sober, I never drank, and I did not understand why others found so much pleasure in drinking if the result was not to be able to stand on your feet just by yourself. I kind of dragged him to the room, helped him taking off his shoes and clothes. And while he appeared to be in some comatose sleep I studied the curves in *Human Sexual Response* and read about my own sexuality, longing for his hands to discover my hidden erotic zones.

Actually I did not wonder why I had always felt lust when I embraced my former boyfriends and never yet when I was being kissed by the man I wanted to grow old with. I accepted the fact that in true love sexual desire seemed to disappear. I thought harmony and the lack of secrecy caused the lack of excitement. I assumed that our liberty to spend as much time together as we liked ruined it all.

But one day I found out how I could reach the state of lecherousness without any foreplay, independent from him. It was mere coincidence. I was not searching. It happened after a cold shower, when I was putting on my first brand new black lace pre-formed padded bra in front of a too small heavily damaged mirror in the evening darkness of some public Ladies at a camping ground in Bois de Boulogne in Paris. He had bought this expensive fancy lingerie for me, though he actually preferred me to wear no bra at all.

I always obeyed him if it came to clothes because I feared to see his face of disgust when I was wearing some piece of cloth that he detested or, as I realized only later, which did not turn him on at first sight. I would change pants if he preferred a miniskirt and throw a long dress in the garbage if he thought it made me look like a fifty-year-old. I ignored blisters and pain if I could work a miraculous smile on his serious face by wearing high heels.

Somehow, due to my inexperience with such a bra, the thing was twirled and upside down, and I tried to fix it fast. To check myself in the mirror, I had to bend over. My head was cut off. I could not see anything else but my torso. My breasts, already kind of twisted in the straps, were reflected esthetically deformed by the broken mirror. And the created image made me return into the moist shower room, lock the door carefully, run the water, and touch myself. For the first time in my life I made myself come, screaming out loud, not aware of others walking in and out, and if there were, I did not care.

Happy to have found the key, since then, I closed my eyes as soon as his hands touched my nipples and focused on that image that happened to drive me there where orgasms seemed to be waiting. I became more active in our lovemaking thanks to that present from the Ladies in Bois de Boulogne. I even managed to have my climax before him and he did not show any surprise to have this horny woman in bed, all of a sudden. I never told him my secret and I discovered more ways to be rank, randy or rich in bed.

I saw us in that single bed. Our happy embrace, and how we fell asleep at the same time and woke up in the same position the next morning. I saw how it lasted until he decided that he needed to travel. He frequently left me behind for weeks, and without any mercy for months. His ambition was to help the poor. He was born to solve the problem of poverty. While I was going to concerts, spending time being with friends, he visited refugee camps at the other side of the world. When I wrote my first novel, he took part in prevention programs concerning venereal diseases and gave workshops to hookers, which he called sex workers. I wrote poetry while he went to congresses, symposia and had meetings with government officials in countries like Thailand, Malaysia, Indonesia, China, Philippines, Vietnam. When he came home, whatever time of the day, he pulled me into the bed and we had sex like true lovers.

I missed him though, when he was on his trips. I missed being hugged. I missed our conversations, our togetherness, but he did not like to hear any critiques about his frequent travels. When I complained about being alone so often, threatening that I did not like a life like this, warning him that there were many other men out here who liked to give me pleasure while he was far away, he encouraged me to do whatever it took for me to feel satisfied. If that was to go traveling too, alright, make trips on your own. If I needed to have lovers, I should go for it. He assured me that he was never going to give up his first joy in life: saving the world.

The only promise he needed, he said, was to grow old together. We had fights, long conversations, and sadness crept into our daily life. In every day we spent together I already felt the loneliness of him being away hanging above us. And he was continuously bothered by the knowledge that the days before his departure flight would be ruined by arguing in my efforts to make him stay.

I actually got much more writing done when he was not at home. I made my own living. I did not need him. I did not have to find lovers, they appeared to me, they showed up in every corner, in any moment. The only thing I needed to do to meet potential lovers was to leave my writing desk. It was harder to avoid them than to let them make me come.

Of course I told him honestly about those men in my life, who gave me comfort when he wasn't there. He said: "If that's what you need, I want you to have it. You're different from me, I'm not like that, you're the love of my life, and I don't need anyone else. But you, just go ahead, spare me the details, just have your fun. The only thing I demand from you is to let me know in time when there is any kind of danger for me of losing you."

I folded the new dress slowly, and put it carefully back in the soft white paper, as if wrapping up this brand new dress was the only thing that mattered. I did not look at him. I did not any longer want to watch the film that we both were in. Nevertheless I went back into our desperate past, or rather into our euphoria a few weeks before that, when we were traveling together in Japan, exactly eight years ago.

They had put us in the best hotels, always a luxurious suite with marvelous views, kimono's and slippers sealed in plastic on the king size beds, a big private whirlpool and an oriental, continental, American or Japanese breakfast after our own choice served in the room. We made love a few times a day.

He was invited to inspire scholars to teach illegal migrant sex workers about the importance of safe sex. While he was doing his workshops and giving speeches, I was visiting temples and writing my travel story on a bench in a park, or having a tea ceremony with Japanese friends. He was in some kind of ecstasy at the end of his working day. He was beaming, energetic, and looked ten years younger than at home, though the first thing he said was: "I'm exhausted!"

It wasn't my habit to accompany him on those trips and this time I came along because I liked going to Japan and he more or less begged me to accept his invitation to pay for my ticket. I looked at my exhausted but nevertheless vital fifty two years old husband with a mixture of curiosity and admiration. Often I waited at the entrance of the building where his provoking speech was held and observed him, being surrounded by Japanese students who were still hanging on his lips and who obviously hated to let him go.

We always made long walks before having dinner in some traditional restaurant to experience unknown Japanese dishes. And after one of those successful presentations he quickly headed for me, embraced me in front of those young Japanese, and took me by the hand. We left the big university building holding hands, when he said: "I have never felt so great like this before. The way we live . . . Our perfect lives . . . I'm afraid that this will be taken away from us. It's scary. I fear to lose it all."

Seventeen days later, back home, his friend and colleague called him. He had to go for a second blood test, since he had been tested there earlier for some minor problem. He said it was nothing serious, more some routine to exclude severe diseases.

His visits to the clinic did not differ from the way he left to go shopping for shampoo or orangcs. I was ncvcr surc if hc was giving blood, buying bread or both. But all of a sudden, after an early call from his friend, he sneaked out of bed and I heard him whisper in the hallway, downstairs, being too silent, asking questions with too many pauses. Some minutes later he stood next to my bed and said that he had a kind of cancer. The urologist, a friend from when they were students, had told him it was too late. He should have come one year earlier. The tumor was growing fast, and if his body didn't respond to the medication—hormone treatment that was the same like chemical castration—there would be no cure to stop the malicious growth.

From the day he got the news he stopped traveling, he stopped going to the university, he stopped teaching, he stopped having meetings, he stopped looking at me, he stopped touching me, he stopped caressing me, he stopped embracing me. Not even kisses on the cheeks. He stopped having sex. He hardly talked with me, only the most necessary sentences that had to do with the primary needs in life. And when they injected his pale belly, things got worse. He changed in character as much as his body changed. I could not share my worries, and I hid my sadness for him. He never cried. He never complained. He acted like a reptile, sitting motionless for hours or quickly getting away when he thought he smelled a threat. He avoided my look at all times. He always went to bed before me. Even when I tried to go ahead of him he managed to creep under the blankets before I had undressed by skipping brushing his teeth. He always slept with his back towards me, on the edge of the bed. When I crawled up to him, even in his sleep, he'd push me away growling: "Why are you waking me up?"

After one year the doctors said that the chemical castration had helped the prostate shrink enough to start with radio therapy. He expressed his happiness embracing me for the first time since the diagnosis. A new period started. He allowed me to massage his feet when we were sitting on our sofa and he was too tired to watch TV or to read any book but far too awake to go to bed. I directed my passion for him on his feet. His toes had not changed like all the rest of him. I caressed his ankles for hours because I had heard from a Japanese friend who was into finger pressing that this part of the male body was connected with the sexual organs.

In this period of deep loneliness I tried to make love with one of my lovers from the past, like mice eat paper when they cannot find wheat. I knew it was better than taking sedatives, and I did not feel guilty yet. Maybe that was wrong. But there was no right or wrong inside of me concerning my need for affection. We spent six hours in a hotel room and he came seven, I came five times. We had neither drinks nor food. I insisted on paying for the room and asked him to leave the room at least twenty minutes later. In the lobby someone recognized me. I felt miserable, in spite of the sexual satisfaction. Full of guilt that I had picked the wrong hotel, in shame that I had not been discrete enough by having chosen this place, I walked to my car in the cellar garage. On top of that the lover was hooked again while he actually had recently finally fallen in love with somebody else. He kept sending me text messages, starting with four before I had taken my car key from my handbag. Steamy messages with the hope for another date soon, while he was taking a shower, risking his mobile phone getting wet. I promised myself to never ever have a lover again and to take care of my husband only, even though he did not seem to appreciate my devotion to him.

At home I found him standing in the kitchen baking an egg. I begged him to hold me tight, but he replied in his indifferent way:" No. That may hurt my back."

I bought red high heels and the kind of dresses he always liked me to wear but which I found too uncomfortable. And I put on some lipstick to draw his attention. I went into his study, where he always was if he was not going to the clinic, staring at the screen. When I gently tried to sit on his lap, he said: "Please go, I can't see my keyboard this way."

After two years of treatments the doctor said that we should keep on trying to have sex or the muscles would never work again. The same urologist had never warned us about the side effects of the treatments he had prescribed. "Use it or lose it," was his remark when we were about to close the door of the doctor's office room.

The same evening, sitting on our bed, he told me that he was open to find out if there would be any life in his sleeping prick. I saw a glimpse of the man I used to know. His hurry returned. The eagerness to stimulate his tool that had had its pension for some years, had nothing to do with being aroused. He wanted me to rub his little thing to make it grow. His fragile cock however, did not want to grow, whatever we tried. All of a sudden he pushed me away and said angrily: "Sex is an overrated concept."

I did not want to give up. I took his shrunken prick in my mouth, sucking soft and slowly, with all the love I felt since we first met, with a devotion that I did not yet have when I was young. His prick wasn't any larger than my own thumb and I was moved by its clumsiness. I loved playing with it, even though it did not at all respond to my acts of love. And then he grabbed my arm, hit me hard on my head, and screamed with deep disgust: "Stop! I've always hated this."

Nevertheless, when he stopped the chemical castrations, advised by some colleagues who had once been his friends, he gradually became the man I knew physically and with the same speed his old personality returned as well. After just a few months it was on his initiativc that wc tricd to havc sex again, and this time his drive was sexual, not scientificaly. His cock did grow, but not for long, and it was never hard enough to penetrate. We practiced. We both knew there would never be any sperm anymore, and we were aware of the damage all the different treatments had caused. But I wanted to do all I could to make him have some kind of climax that would be as profound as when he was a healthy young man. He tended to give up easily, would abruptly turn away from me saying that he just wanted to sleep. I kept encouraging him to keep on trying.

It did not happen overnight. There were many unsuccessful efforts. Making love, to him, seemed to be a nasty task like peeling raw potatoes in a dark room without any knives or other tools, not even being hungry, and not knowing if there would be any chance to bake or boil the potatoes once peeled. I had to convince him to try again, not every day, but frequently enough to maintain the little progress we actually did make. I knew better than him how to rub his prick to prevent it from a premature failure. My own orgasm was still like another book that might never be opened by him again.

After an enormous amount of disappointments he finally did get his orgasm by letting me play with it as long as I liked. He thanked me for my persistence to help him regain his self-confidence. It had an immediate effect on his self-esteem. He proposed to make me come and did not understand why I cried when he asked.

Four years after the diagnosis, he was able to have the so-called normal sex again, and in the four years after that, our lovemaking got only better. I came easily and he as well. We kissed and caressed each other for hours at any time of the day or night. He never got tired of eating me, and there was a growing understanding of each other's speed and rhythm. The penetration was never easy, but the little physical struggles, due to his medical history and my age resulted in more intimacy. We had to be more creative and we needed lubricant, even when we were smoking hot.

To my great surprise he forgot that there had been times that sex did not exist for him. He did not like to be reminded of those four years in which his only goal was to survive the deadly disease. When his close friend once asked how it was to be castrated by medication, he replied without blinking that it didn't have any physical effects, and that only the lust had more or less been gone, but technically nothing had ever changed.

The tumor was still there; his enemy was temporarily asleep. We were aware that every year was a gift and that no doctor could reassure us that he would have more than five years to go. In spite of the lack of time given to him, he had no more hurries. And I never needed images or flashes from the past to be in sexual heat. Just being with him, feeling his fingers on my skin was enough to feel a burning longing for him and only him.

A few times, in moments of peace and rest, when we were in complete harmony with each other, I proposed to him to become open about our infidelity, as there must have been quite some secrets to reveal to each other from over the years. I explained to him that I needed a clean and pure last period. Nothing should be on our chests. I pleaded for more frankness to achieve more integrity. But he claimed that he had nothing to confess. He had never ever been with another woman. There had always been just one, and that was me. He had never loved anyone else, never touched anyone else, never wanted anybody else. Just the thought of it made him sick, and since we met he had devoted his life happily to me.

With the dress like a treasure pressed against my belly, my voice stayed calm as if we were talking about milk he claimed to have bought and put in the fridge but which was nowhere to be seen. I asked him: "When?"

I don't know why I asked "when" while I actually wanted to know "why?" I don't know why I did not start screaming or weeping, I don't know how I could act this detached, while actually he had turned our house, our romantic garden, the wooden bench that we were sitting on upside down. He had destroyed and humiliated our forty years together, and I was just sitting there with the new dress re-wrapped in soft white paper on my lap, waiting for him to say: "Sorry, I only wanted to see your response. Don't worry, nothing ever happened."

He seemed as calm as I seemed when he replied: "In the Philippines."

I had forgotten about those days, actually five days in and out. Almost four months earlier he had to go on a trip again, his first journey abroad on his own since his disease. It was the final part of a project that he had put aside when cancer rooted through our lives. He had told me about it, mentioned that he was going to send someone else to finish that project instead, but I had encouraged him to go there himself. I told him:" I know how much you always liked it. You always returned home beaming from such work trip. Please go yourself, and enjoy yourself."

From the moment that I dropped him at the airport, we had an almost continuous contact by text messages, e-mail, phone and on Skype, those days. Modern technology helped us through those first days apart since eight heavy years. Before he left, standing in our hallway with his bags in his hands, hesitating if he should bring a raincoat or not, he said that he was a little scared to go, because he wasn't the same man anymore and he was disgusted by the idea of being alone in his hotel room. He had asked me to come along when he booked the ticket. He offered to pay for the expensive ticket from his pocket money so that we could stay a little longer and have a short holiday at some Philippine beach. But I preferred to be at home in summertime and I thought it was weird to spend so much money on a ticket while I wasn't crazy about Manila and needed to check the proof prints of my novel.

One evening, reading the last chapter of my manuscript, I reminded myself of the past, when I almost always felt the urge to call any of my lovers when he was abroad. I was happy that the usual longing for other men, like in the past, was over. I felt content about our present relationship. I thought that all we had to go through had made sense, as we had not been this close ever before. I felt proud that I no longer begged him to stay, but that I had encouraged him to go.

On his fourth day away he had sent me the shortest message by phone, just three words which he hardly ever said when we were young: "I love you."

I replied to that in three ways, by e-mail, by text message and by phone on his voice mail to contact me through Skype. I did not get any response. About four hours later he send me the following message by phone: "I will try to call you tomorrow after my last meeting, before I catch my flight. I am going to sleep now, I am very tired like in the past."

"You mean . . . last July?"

He nodded.

"Who was she?"

"A stewardess," he mumbled.

"A stewardess?"

Until now I somehow thought of someone he worked with, someone he knew for years. Someone he had always loved but never admitted to himself. Someone he just had to make love to because he did not want to die thinking, "Why did I not try for just once to make love to that terrific woman from work?" Some inevitable passionate farewell.

I was astonished and did not hide that when I screamed: "Why? You picked up a stewardess on the flight to avoid being alone in bed?"

I articulated the word "stewardess." I did not try the least to hide my condemnation.

He quickly replied: "No, no, not from the flight. We met in the lobby of the hotel. Just once, on my last night."

The way he said that was as if he thought that picking up a stewardess in the lobby would be less humiliating for me. I stuttered when I asked: "Have you ever done stuff like this before?"

He replied hastily, again as if he hoped that his answer would reduce my pain:

"Never in the past eight years."

And then I yelled at him, louder than the toughest fishwife on the market: "You mean: never since you got the god damned cancer!"

He kept silent. I continued screaming: "You mean you regularly screwed a stewardess when you were away for work?"

I did not like to find myself screaming in the garden on this sunny late afternoon before sunset. But I did not like either to hear from my husband that he had been screwing around in those forty years, pretending he was the pope himself.

"It didn't happen that frequently, love, it wasn't the way you think," he said with his warmest voice ever.

"Don't say love!" I cried my lungs out, "just tell me who that woman was! Why did you pick her of all the women in the world?"

"As I said, just some stewardess from Asian airlines. She was twenty-six, living in Singapore, and she stayed in the same hotel with the rest of her crew. They were all at the bar where I was drinking a glass of whiskey before going to bed. She smiled at me a few times and we started to talk together."

I did not scream for a moment, I tried to lower my voice when I said, "And that's how you met the other women in the past as well? In the hotel bar? With a whisky in your one hand and the other hand touching her knee?"

He nodded: "Yes, that's how things go."

I pressed my both hands against my stomach to extinguish a burning flame that went up to my throat and down to my ovaries, but that I could not quench. I did not want to feel this pain. He did not have the right to do this to me. Not now, after those eight difficult years. I realized that I had asked him, when he returned from Manila, if he had been with someone else. I was astonished myself how this question fled from my mouth without having been on my mind for a tenth of a second while he was away. It was only based on the smell around him. Something I sensed, when he came home and immediately undressed himself, pulling me into the bed, had made me ask that. And his surprised response had been fast, while shaking his head: "Please, don't be ridiculous."

I screamed the burning pain away: "And the medical scientist who made his goal in life to teach about safe sex did not know he had to use a condom?"

He looked at me and whispered: "Please calm down, the neighbors . . . "

That remark made me lose my mind. I smashed the teapot with the hot lemon grass against our brick-stone wall. I threw the full cups as well, the tray, and anything I could find near me, except for the dress. The dress calmed me down. It was still wrapped in the soft white paper. I shoved it back in the bag that I got from the store and walked inside the house, where I put the bag on the kitchen table. I was like in a trance. I wanted to hurt him, hit him, kick him, and probably kill him as well and I knew that wasn't the right thing to do. I walked through the house, not knowing where to go or what to do if not kill the man who betrayed me and had thrown forty years of marriage away. Even my own workroom wasn't inviting. Nevertheless I sat down in front of my computer and started typing, not exactly knowing what. Then the poem wrote itself.

While I was writing he stood in front of me. He said: "Don't think I didn't use a rubber. But you know how it is with me now, the whole thing was a big joke, of course I could not have anything done, it slid off before . . . I mean . . . It was no fun . . . I was totally embarrassed."

I stood up from my chair screaming: "So now I should feel sorry for you that you did not have any fun screwing some Asian stewardess?"

"No, no, please . . . I am only trying to tell you that probably I was infected by her even though I had safe sex."

"Don't talk to me," I cried out trembling, with a broken voice.

"Can we please hug?" he asked.

I did not know if it was anger or pain that made me scream: "Can't you see I am writing? Don't you have any respect?"

I thought: either he or me, one has to die. All of a sudden I understood the women who wanted to cut off their husband's prick though I had never ever thought I would be able to empathize with any kind of violence. I had never felt this destructive power before. I started hitting him, and kicking him. I picked up a wooden chair to hit him on the head. He defended himself as much as he could and we fought. He hurt me as well. I asked him to leave and I told him to stay. I screamed, I spoke, I whispered, I cried. I kept yelling at him: "Why? Tell me why? I just don't understand why. Why? Why now?"

He repeatedly replied with: "I don't know."

From the conversation in which I mostly screamed and cried and he hardly spoke, I understood that he could not count the amount of women he had slept with, but they had all been Asian. They were doctors, nurses, stewardesses, waitresses, hotel maids, students, even police officers, and all of them had just one thing in common: they were wearing some kind of uniform. Somehow the uniform made it seem unreal. He had never made love twice to the same woman, he never spent the night with any of them, and he never felt that he had been unfaithful to me having been with any of them because he never ever remembered their names.

My anger came out in eruptions. I could not stop myself, kicked him again where I could, broke the chair in three pieces though it was the heaviest chair we had in the house. I kept repeating my question: "Why?"

And then, when the early birds started singing, some roosters crowed, and in the far distance a peacock screamed like a crying baby, he honestly replied. "Lust."

I tried to not care anymore, I only wanted to know why he had done this now, why he had not been honest when I asked him right after he returned from Asia if he had been with someone else. Why he never told me the truth when I was strong enough to hear it all. Why after those years of struggling, did he do this with a woman that age? And why did it always have to be some Asian girl? What did that tell about his love for me? Could I be any Asian woman? Did I not matter? Was it just my brown skin, the form of my eyes, and should I have bought myself some uniform instead of a new ordinary flower dress to turn him on?

We sat together on the wooden floor of my workroom. My head on his lap. My voice had left me and I was too tired to kick or punch him more than I had already. We had been in my workroom for I don't know how long, as the sun had been rising till it was high up in the sky again. Soon after that it was covered by heavens, lightning had come, and thunder had tried to drown my voice a couple of times, when I said to him: "Leave me alone!"

He left the room and I completed the poem. I typed myself into sweat, undressed myself in between the lines, threw my clothes on the floor, and continued writing naked. The new dress, that somehow had survived the battle and still not lost the paper wrapping, was lying on the carpet, covered by pieces of the broken wooden chair.

"Disenchanted" was the title. I did not read it before I sent it at once to all my friends abroad and to some close family members who had always considered him to be a hero. Then I wept in silence on the floor, next to the door, blocking him from entering my workroom with my naked, curled-up body.

Snowfall

Susan Rochette Crawley

Today he has someone he calls Dad, but he doesn't know his father. Chances are, his mother doesn't either.

He never knew her: so he can't ask. All he knows are a string of other people's houses, other people's children, people whose children call them Mom, Dad, Pa, Gran. Paps.

He always calls them Yessir and Nomam.

He's special; different.

A state-case, a foster kid, a meal ticket; he made the Yessir's and Nomam's rent, paid the heat and water, the lender, the dealer, the taxes—whatever. The grocery list, the electric, the gas for the car.

All he knows about anything before he was told he was five is what he's been told, as a taunt, cajole, in a drunken outrage or as the moral to his story: He is lucky to be alive. Lucky to have a roof over his head, clothes on his back, food on his plate and a place to call home.

Lucky, and he knows it.

He remembers being told, more likely by a Nomam than a Yessir, that his mother never held him. And his feet never touched the ground until he was two. Kept in a crib, a highchair, a jumping jack, a playpen, the backseat of a car: He was a late walker.

Of all the things he knows about himself, this is the only one he swears, always, is true.

At twenty, with a daughter—state-case—of his own, his gait is still uneasy, awkward. And his feet are very big. Big like canoes, hydrofoils, kayaks, snowshoes, waddings. Big like things that keep him from ever really touching the ground, things that big he knows are in complete sympathy with him and ache for all the ground he will never cover.

He runs, but only because he knows exactly how to fall. The grass whispers in his ear, tells him to stand tall. He listens.

After all, he's a man of mystery.

That's okay.

He's okay.

Just don't, he tells himself, get angry. That scares people.

He knocks at the door, setting off the dog, the bark of an alarm and she almost doesn't answer.

He stands at her door, asking to shovel her walk for money; and, he tries to tell her all these things. But not like he just said them to himself.

Instead, he uses his eyes.

"His eyes are homemade." That's her first thought when she sees him. She's very tired. It's almost 7 p.m. on an early December night after her over-time hours, "put-in" time she has heard it is reported to Internal Revenue.

Already there has been a record amount of snowfall for this time of year in Northeast Iowa.

He can see she is working to be friendly. And his feet so big and he from such a bad, bad family.

At least, that's what he thinks.

"Well, if you shovel this long walk," she says, "how much will I owe you?"

"Whatever you think a job like this is worth."

"It's a very long sidewalk. It's a corner lot of the city."

She must know how silly that sounds, since he must have sized the job up even before he knocked.

But she's distracted. He thinks she wants to say something like, "How did you know to stop here, at this house, at this time in this day in my life? How did you know how tired I am and how hard it would be for me to do this by myself? How did you know I didn't have a man here already who'd take care of it himself?"

But to say anything like that, especially to a stranger with a shovel who confesses that he frightens his Dad when he gets angry, does not seem like a good idea even in her tired state of mind.

"Fifteen dollars?"

A pause.

"How does that sound, good?"

He nods assent.

As he heads back down the walk, she brings the dog in, even though the dog seems half-interested in staying outside. Something familiar and almost safe is triggered in her memory. But it is time after this long day to refill her bowl.

She knows the man shoveling her walk, working so silently, needs to be paid. She will pay him in cash because it is that sort of arrangement. He has been out for the day working with a shovel and the cash will feel good in his pocket when he finishes. Although he probably could change the twenty she was thinking of when she offered him fifteen, she feels the need to search for actual change, to expiate some sense of personal obligation, reenact some memory from her past, her childhood. The days when it was not unusual for strong men to appear as if by chance and offer their labor up and down the street. A past beyond the recent one, further back. A past no less painful than the present one, but nostalgia, and a hope that in it lies a turn toward something she overlooked, a thing more bearable, strengthened, not as all-consuming as these thoughts she must push behind her, shovel to the side, and clear a way past.

The change is in the bottom drawer of her mother's dressing table. To open the drawers of all the furniture belonging to her parents hurts her ears, abrades her mind, etches again a mark on all their souls. But, like everything exquisite, it bears the sting of beauty and so she takes a deep breath and dives under, into the gunnysack of pennies, dimes, nickels, quarters and buttons she has been collecting, apparently for a moment just like this.

As she does, her thoughts go back to those intimate parts of her childhood she shared with him, the man who after twenty-five years has just left her to be with another woman.

The dimes make a small sound as they drop upon the pillow. The nickels tell her they are hollow. The pennies, sharp. The quarters are heavy and tell her not to believe that they are worth anymore than the others.

She is caught between every past moment and his absolute refusal to take her forward with him into his future. Between his refusal to let her lead him into one of their own and her realization that all these thoughts are only, and always were, elegy.

This is what he had wanted all those years, she thinks. All those years, he probably thought: how wasted, delayed, diverted his life had become along this wayside, beneath this underbrush. This horrible mistake called "their marriage."

She stops herself at that thought and listens to the coins as they speak to each other.

"We have let ourselves be slipped into the pockets of each other's memory," they say, "And now we hope that as we draw each other out, our value has increased."

She meets the shoveler at the back door. She has a gift box full of fifteen dollars, fifteen hundred pennies in all their copper silvered glory, and she hands them to him. She apologizes, since it so heavy. Never mind how strange and anonymous. Something you might give a child, or the wild geese, at this time of the year.

He is sweating. He has shoveled in a heavy coat, with a cap on his head. She wonders at all this work. She would have undone the coat, taken off the cap were she him.

"I suppose I can take the change to the corner and have it made into bills."

He is disappointed. It disappoints her to see him like that. She was hoping he'd see how much work she had done to count it out like that and even think of the box.

He must think I'm cheating him.

"Keep it all in the box," she says. That's what she thinks she says, at least. The words thumping in her head say, "I know you believe me because you knew before you came to the door that I would give you exactly what I promised, even if you thought it would take a different form." The thumping thumps again, big footfalls of "Take this, it's yours. I stole it from myself so you could have it!"

"I'm going to buy my daughter a present with this," he tells her.

Yes, yes. Of course you are, she says to herself.

She isn't looking when he leaves.

But later, when she looks out at the corner to be certain the streetlight is lit, she sees the empty shape of a hollowed figure in the snow. Something a kid or the shoulder of a woman, an angel, might lightly press upon a winter blanket, not wanting answers and not offering more than that.

Look Who's Coming

Cyril Dabydeen

Her *special* party, she called it; but she started becoming less enthusiastic about it, though she believed the two Russians would make a difference: she'd invited them on a whim, didn't she? Anne-Marie nodded, as if she knew I would understand her motives. *Really*? She was going through an inner turmoil; she wanted a change in her life, I figured. The way I too also seemed to want change. Not the Russians too? Ah, Sergei, morose-looking, as he came towards me. Mikhail, well, he was indifferent.

Anne-Marie nodded to me; as Sergei mumbled to me something or the other; Mikhail, on the other hand, went straight to the piano, like the most natural thing in the world for him to do . . . and started playing. Oh, how he played. The women quickly came around him. Anne-Marie whirred to herself. She really did, and glanced at me again.

Would I do something? I simply waved. And it would be Anne-Marie's first and last party, I figured, shy as she often was; but she'd thought about a party to "celebrate" what she hoped would be a new life.

How new really? Her being alone . . . and someone to distract her? Mikhail's curly blonde hair spread over a broad forehead was all as he banged away at the piano, becoming the party's live-wire.

Sergei let out a lugubrious moan.

Applause again from the women surrounding the handsome Mikhail looking like a Cossack. Didn't he? Anne-Marie curled in her lips. I simply thought of political change in the former Soviet Union; and were the Russians with us exiles? Indeed Sergei wanted to know what I thought about exiles, as he drew closer. I simply kept an eye on Mikhail with his mixed Mongolian and Cossack features; he intrigued me, and the women. Anne-Marie's lips twitched. And Mikhail wanted to be called Mickey, he declared: it sounded North American; and he waved to all. But Sergei seemed rueful, muttering that being in Canada was a far cry from being in the Gulag. *Oh?*

Yes, in Canada there was so much freedom; and one could drink all the vodka he wanted.

I laughed at that. Yes, look at Mikhail: how free he was at the piano, making up for all the years he'd been denied freedom in the Soviet Union. But Sergei merely saw himself as an exile, maybe what he figured he and I had in common. Again I glanced at Anne-Marie moving from one group to another, as the party went on; and did she think Mikhail might have been with the Bolshoi the way he kept entertaining an entire roomful.

One attractive female redhead bawled out, "Gosh, he's so handsome!" Mikhail, indeed.

Sergei merely growled something or the other: now about Pushkin; he loved Pushkin's poetry. "But Anna Akhmatova's poetry is best," he added. He wanted me to pronounce the latter's name the correct Russian way, as I seemed to struggle with it. Sergei went on about being forced to study Engineering in Leningrad, not poetry. Then, "It's a nice city . . . Leningrad."

I waited to hear more about the city renamed as St Petersburg. "I loved it there, zee education," Sergei crinkled his eyes; and he'd written stories at the University of Leningrad. Now he wanted to have his stories published in Canada, he said, and looked fiercely at me.

Anne-Marie flitted from one group to another, seeming out of sorts, I noted; as more women whooped it up around Mickey.

Julie, a brunette, declared, "Yeah, the Russians are coming!"

Laughter.

A tallish blonde with distinct freckles wanted all of Ottawa to know this now, she hissed. *Really coming?* Maybe right then Anne-Marie regretted inviting the two Russians; and, did I have my own secret aspirations with Anne-Marie? But Sergei now insisted on asking about the names of Canadian literary magazines, so he could get his stories published.

I mentioned *Descant, Grain, Exile.* He liked the latter name, then mulled over the fact that I too was a writer, a poet.

"A real poet?"

I nodded.

I added something about some people who always saw themselves as "outsiders," like the poet's fate. Sergei was fascinated. Next I mentioned something about exiled Chilean artists living in the city, who'd escaped General Pinochet. *Did they want to be known as exiles?*

Then Sergei started telling me about his best friend back in Leningrad: Boris Lichstenfeldt, a poet since his student days. "Boris shovels coals to make a living in Leningrad, and he's still there, a real poet, writing at night only."

"Oh?"

"Boris Lichstenfeldt thinks all writers should be like that. All should be like Hemingway, who was an exile wherever he went. Yes, Hemingway isn't like other American writers, you know," Sergei grated.

I tried to sustain the image of Sergei's friend in Leningrad still shoveling coals. Far unlike Canadian poets? Anne-Marie moving closer to Mikhail I looked at, even as the other women flirted with Mickey, his exotic appeal and all. "Mickey, play some more," one party-goer cried, flaunting her braceleted arm. More boisterous it kept becoming. "I am zee best," Mickey sang, unstoppable at the piano.

Anne-Marie's lips tightened.

Sergei murmured, "As a poet laureate you could have lots of women around you, no? In the Soviet Union, you would have girlfriends everywhere." Did he still have his friend Boris Lichstenfeldt in mind? And see, I wasn't accustomed thinking of myself as a *poet laureate*, the title given to me; and when Andrei Voznezensky, the famed Russian poet, had come to town I'd been invited to meet him, I told Sergei.

Sergei brightened; I must know that Voznezensky and Yevtuskeno were like rock stars when they performed their poetry in the Soviet Union. Ah, tell Sergei that Voznezensky only wanted to know about Margaret Trudeau—wife of the former Canadian Prime Minister—when he visited here. What was Margaret Trudeau really like? Did she actually meet Mick Jagger and the Rolling Stones? Yes, Voznezensky had kept asking me; indeed, Ottawa was now no longer a staid town, I figured.

Mickey at the piano again waved, to Anne-Marie now . . . as she desultorily waved back. Sergei simply asked if I ever wanted to be a bureaucrat like so many others in the city. Did I? Odd, Sergei was now making me see things in a different way, as I also kept thinking about poetry, if Anna Akhmatova's only. Then I asked Sergei why he and Mikhail left the Soviet Union.

He smiled a wan smile. An exile he was, I must know.

Then he started telling me about Jewish persecution, and how those like Andrei Sakharov had suffered; indeed, Sakharov was a real hero. But Sergei never wore a helmukah-he didn't know much about Jewry, or about the Talmud; in the Soviet Union he was simply described as a Jew, as stated on his passport. When Mickey's voice rose again, I vaguely wondered of his being Jewish too, and if he might have been persecuted, though happy he now looked . . . as more party women shrieked around him. Not Anne-Marie?

Sergei frowned. He murmured that in Russia being labeled a Jew was an expression of one's nationality, not one's religious affiliation. I must know this because of the poet in me, he said. Then again it was about his friend Boris Lichstenfeldt shoveling coals in Leningrad . . . and writing poems late at night, like Dr Zhivago did: that image in the novel by Boris Pasternak, and yes, the famous movie by that name.

Sergei hummed on about there being so much freedom in Canada, and why didn't people go on a drinking spree—drink all the vodka they wanted because of freedom. *There's no one to stop you in Canada.*

I laughed.

But he kept me contemplating life in the Soviet Union, and about the poets, artists, all being depressed, and then their drinking vodka.

No, no. And were the train stations named after writers like Pushkin and Mayakovsky in the former Soviet Union? Odd, instinctively I wanted to visit Russia right then. But Sergei was the closest I was to getting there; as he also seemed bent on getting his stories published in Canada. Indeed, I must tell him how to submit his stories to the magazines because, well, I was a celebrity.

Was I?

Anne-Marie forced a smile, as she flitted by us.

I told Sergei to write his impressions about Russia while everything was still fresh in his mind, as a way to let Canadians know about it, and who he was; and, he could change people's views about stereotypes of Russians; it'd no longer be what they saw in movies like *The Russians Are Coming.*

He almost beamed. And had I really seen that movie?

There were tears in people's eyes in Moscow when they first saw it, he wanted me to know. He and Mikhail had also cried.

Immediately I turned around, to see Mickey still being boisterous at the piano. Sergei continued on, about how he and Mikhail really liked Canada; they also had friends in Boston and in Brooklyn . . . who were also exiles? Next he talked about his parents back in Leningrad living in a small apartment; but his mother didn't want to leave to start a new life in the West. *Not as exiles.*

Sergei talked about his roundabout route to Canada next. First he'd traveled to Athens, where he lived in the back of a beat-up Chevy for a while; and he did many crappy jobs, but kept learning English from the Greeks. *What's lost in translation?*

"Were you an exile there too?" I asked.

He continued on about the Mediterranean and Europe; it was where he first met Mikhail, and Mikhail persuaded him to come with him to Canada. Did he not know Mikhail in Russia? The Bolshoi, remember? Sergei grew more introspective.

Anne-Marie flitted by again, looking almost worried.

"You're really an exile," Sergei muttered to me.

"Am I?"

Then he insisted that I must teach him *good* English, so he could get his stories published in the literary magazines . . . as an exiled writer.

He might become like Yevtushenko too, who was now living in Boston.

And Sergei continued on about his roundabout trip . . . to Canada. First, he worked on the beaches on the island of Scorpios; and in Athens, after a while, life started becoming difficult. "The Greeks are a strange people; the men chase after the women all the time." He again glanced at Mikhail with the Canadian women round him.

I allowed my gaze to fall on Anne-Marie being by herself in a corner. And Sergei liked the Greeks alright; they were true democrats. Then on a whim he said that he and Mikhail decided to come to Canada, not go to Israel where they would have had the best chance . . . as Jews?

My thoughts wandered: what if Anne-Marie, when she heard about them, invited them to her party because she wanted them to experience freedom, odd as it sounded? With our plates of food, we moved to where Mickey was playing at the piano. Anne-Marie kept being anxious. Did she want me to do something . . . about Mickey's "revelry?" *But . . . what?*

Sergei moaned as he watched Mickey drinking more vodka.

Freedom, remember?

Then, Sergei, wanted to know about what kind of poet I was.

What kind?

Indeed, Ottawa wasn't the place where one shoveled coals, as Sergei's friend Boris Lichstenfeldt did in Leningrad. The poet laureate in me I vaguely thought about, then remembered what a civil-servant friend had told me he was starting to do because of his dream of levitating . . . because the Conservatives were now in power. *Really levitating*? I shifted attention back to Sergei, who talked about Ottawa as a high-tech city: where he could fit in—he'd been trained as a software engineer at the University of Leningrad.

Not as an exile?

"Lots of high-tech people come here to live and work," I emphasized. But Sergei was still preoccupied being an exile.

"Ottawa now has people here from many parts of the world living here," I countered. Sergei wasn't impressed. Anne-Marie looked at me questioningly; it wasn't about Sergei, was it? Yes, Mikhail urging everyone to sing along with him. *Sing . . . everyone.* But Sergei looked pained. Anne Marie twisted her lips again.

Mickey waved to Anne-Marie, as if she was miles away, and he wanted her close by as he raised his voice, singing heartily. He swept his hair across his broad, round forehead. Just for her? The other women, coquettes all, grinned. I merely swallowed vodka, not rum-punch.

Sergei looked at his own glass. "Mikhail, you know, he not always been like that. In Moscow when I met him, he said all zee time how much he wants to come to America. He was depressed about not able to leave quickly." Sergei heaved in. "I am an artist," he grated; then again it was about Boris Lichstenfeldt shoveling coals in Leningrad.

Anne-Marie was now accepting her fate, it seemed: how things were turning out, as Mikhail kept being unstoppable.

Truly.

***

I was determined not to work in the bureaucracy, my being a poet laureate and all: as I resumed my teaching career, to be in line with living an artist's life, I contemplated. And my English class in the new semester attracted a variety of students, though mostly immigrant types: all who liked having me as their instructor, I sensed. A commonality . . . but because I was an exile? Indeed, the campus was a genuine meeting place; new students milled around at the coffee machine.

"Ah, Sergei," I let out when I saw him.

He nodded.

"What are you doing here?" I drilled.

"I'm studying English."

"Oh?"

"To become writer."

"Who's your instructor?"

"*You.*" He stabbed at my stomach. "I hope to learn from you."

"But . . . ?"

"You are an exile."

Our "friendship" at the party, I recalled; and where was Mickey now? I feared Mikhail might have already gone to Boston or Brooklyn to live the fast life. Never mind Anne-Marie, as I dwelled on it.

Sergei nodded again, as if to pre-empt me from thinking about that.

In class Sergei kept up a staid manner, not unlike how the former Russian Premier Brezhnev looked, I thought. He sat right in the front row. Would he bring up the story of Boris shoveling coals? His eyes moved left and right; and vaguely I wondered how everyone was taking him. *Not taking me?*

We discussed writing strategy, and I solicited easy responses, my teaching style. And did anyone think Sergei was an exile? During the break we sipped coffee in the main lounge; and Sergei, I sensed, once more wanted to talk about Boris Lichstenfeldt.

"What about Mikhail?" I tried; I almost called him Mickey.

"He's . . . somewhere."

"What d'you mean?"

"He's thinking about America."

"Not Montreal then?"

Back in class Sergei struggled with his words; but he was determined. I urged him to write stories about his past, and to keep a journal; and to write about what he thought of Canadians, maybe. He could tell us more about the Soviet Union too, as a bona fide exile? Imagine Sergei conjuring up Yevtushenko, Voznezensky, Akhmatova and Pasternak all in one breath; then it'd indeed be stories of his Leningrad days, if about his parents still living in a cramped apartment, yet who didn't want to leave there.

Sergei looked at me blankly.

One story he handed to me, written in longhand, the words almost in Cyrillic alphabet: it was about his returning to Leningrad and going to the familiar old house, and to his room, which was as just as he'd left it: his parents hadn't moved his clothes, pictures—nothing. Odd, this story sounded like a fable.

Sergei handed me more text: two long, handwritten pages.

I made suggestions to improve the stilted English. Yes, the exile that he persisted being; his story had a haunting quality. I struggled to imagine seeing it in print in a Canadian magazine.

"I am an exile," Sergei said.

I asked about Mikhail (Mickey) again—I kept seeing him still at the piano.

Another class, and Sergei handed me more hand-written pages.

The other students became curious about him. A few, though, giggled because of something or the other he said. About Boris Lichstenfeldt? Oh, they weren't exiles.

Sergei's next story: one he'd seriously been writing for a long time, he said. But my interest was really on Mikhail only, I knew; and when last did he talk to him? Odd, I grew instinctively curious about details of Mikhail's life, if about his "Bolshoi" career, and whatever else.

"Mikhail's getting married," Sergei announced.

"Married?"

"To . . . Anne-Marie."

The party came back to me, and Anne-Marie walking around looking concerned, maybe because of the women around Mickey. Sergei added that Mickey was thinking of becoming a real estate agent, same as Anne Marie, all in the new Ottawa. Yes, here where Mickey would plant his roots, but not as an exile. Was Sergei somehow disappointed in his friend? I imagined Mikhail and Anne-Marie living comfortably, in a new home, in a ritzy part of town. Then he and Anne-Marie holding one party after the other, as Mickey kept playing the piano to his heart's content; yes, the freedom he enjoyed.

And Anne-Marie would be transformed, in a manner of speaking, though from time to time her lips twitched.

All the while Sergei kept being an exile; and the next poem I wrote would be about where I came from, too . . . as Sergei kept me thinking about origins, with the image of Boris Lichstenfeldt shoveling coals in Leningrad. Yes, each new poem would somehow have a metaphor suggesting coals, like a time-worn symbol, I construed. Then, it was about Anne-Marie and Mikhail leaving for America to go and live in Brooklyn or Boston—as Mikhail wanted.

Ah, America. Sergei sighed; and would he mention Hemingway?

I sighed with him.

Anne-Marie's lips twitching, I evoked, as Mikhail kept banging away at the piano. Freedom only. Yes. Being an exile.

Marrow

Darcie Friesen Hossack

Frieda steps from the bottom stair onto the creakiest board of the old wood floor. She knows how to reach the kitchen without making sound, but these days her mother startles easily. It's better when she knows what's coming.

The first creak is a warm-up. The next floorboard groans out Middle C, and from there she stretches to stand on each note in the broken chord.

Over the years, the notes have changed from sharp to flat as the nails loosened, though never deviated far enough to change keys.

"We should have that floor tuned," says Frieda's mother, who's struggling with the weight of a teapot. She allows Frieda to take the handle and pour.

For a time, since the last round of chemo, things seemed to be going well. Marie's platelet count had climbed, color returned to her skin. Now, though, Marie has shrunk back down to her bones, thin as the bone china that cups her morning chamomile.

At three o'clock this afternoon, they're meant to visit Creekside and make the final payment on the Marie Reimer Package. "A light embalming," as Marie calls it. A simple birch casket, wallpapered inside using leftover rolls of tangerine damask. A ticked cushion, which Frieda sewed from an old farm quilt.

On top of the casket will be roses, not because they're anyone's favorite, but are in season.

Once Marie's been prepared, there will be a trip in the hearse, from the funeral home to Bridgeway Church, where the Evangelical Mennonites have agreed to stand in the gap between the Old Colony folks who will come in from the country, and those from the Catholic Church, to which Marie lately converted.

"We have time for another practice run before we leave, don't you think?" Marie says.

Suddenly Frieda regrets coming downstairs.

"I thought you were happy with what we did yesterday."

"Happy, yes. But practice makes perfect. Not so much mousse this time." Marie sits down at the kitchen table with her back to Frieda.

Almost the minute Frieda arrived home last month, her mother announced that Ms. Dyck, who had been Creekside's beautician for decades, had retired. Marie didn't trust the new hair and makeup girl to get things right.

"We'll just have to do it ourselves," Marie had said.

And then they fought.

"I don't want my hands to remember you cold. I'm sure if I talk to the girl, tell her exactly what you want, she'll do just fine. They wouldn't have hired her otherwise."

Marie has never stopped being disappointed that Frieda dropped out of the beauty college in town to go to music school out east. Halfway through learning about how to position rollers so the curls fell in the right directions, Frieda'd announced she couldn't stand the feel of other people's scalps. Either thick and spongy as fried pork rinds, or thin and tight as though already in rigor.

Frieda had won that argument by leaving home.

They both knew she wasn't going anywhere this time.

"They poached the new girl from North End," Marie had said simply.

The fight ended there.

Now, Frieda goes into the living room and opens the piano bench. Inside are her hair scissors and other tools, where she'd put them three years ago, after emptying out her music and theory books.

Back when Frieda was in grade school, she and Marie used to eat breakfast together at the kitchen table where Marie now sits. Rice Krispies popped softly in matching cereal bowls as they passed the newspaper back and forth.

"Here's one," Frieda said, snapping the freshly-delivered Prairie Post to keep it from slumping. "Meeks, Dorothy. Born February 27, 1939 in Kyle, Saskatchewan, passed away September 22, 1984. Arrangements in care of Creekside Memorial Home."

It was the holy grail. A forty-five-year-old woman. For a minute, Frieda thought her mother wasn't going to make her go to school that day. But then, Marie stood and took their bowls to the kitchen, rinsed the cereal down the sink. "Best hurry," Marie said. "Can't be late for Homeroom."

When the three o'clock bell rang that afternoon, Frieda was first out the door, the zipper on her knapsack not quite closed, a crumpled bouquet of homework photocopies bunched into the front pocket.

Creekside, which was not actually beside the creek, but several blocks from it, sat directly across the street from her school, Mable Brown Junior High, where Frieda had just gone into the eighth grade. From her side of the crosswalk, Frieda could already see Marie waiting for her at the bottom of the front steps that led up to the funeral home.

Inside, a cozy gloom enveloped Frieda, blocking out the September afternoon just on the other side of the front doors. Frieda stood a moment, to let her vision adjust, even though she could have made her way through the uncomplicated warren of viewing rooms with her eyes closed.

When she could see again, she realized that Marie had gone ahead.

"Is that her?" Frieda asked when she caught up.

"Just look," Marie said, as much to herself as Frieda. "This is why it pays to go to a place that does good work."

Dorothy Meeks looked restful. Her face was relaxed, only lightly manipulated into an almost smile. Soft chestnut curls framed her face, but were cropped neatly at the nape of her neck. She wore a mauve pantsuit, the kind that could be worn either to the mall or an evening event at church without looking either too dressy or plain.

Frieda didn't need to ask whether to get out the camera. She reached into Marie's purse for their Instamatic, advanced the film, stood back, stood a little taller, and snapped. The flash bulb blinded them both.

"Why don't you let me cut it for you instead of doing a perm? Something short and stylish," Frieda says, standing behind her mother and looking into their reflection in a round mirror set on the table. It's flipped to the magnifying side and the two of them are distorted as if seen through a watery window.

"We did a trim when you came home," Marie says.

Frieda knows her mother doesn't want to do something now that she'll regret. Marie intends to go into the ground with a good perm and the nut-brown rinse Frieda gets from her friends at the salon in the mall. The ones who finished school.

Frieda gathers what's left of her mother's hair into her hands. There's more of it than there was a month ago. Still, it's uneven and brittle and Frieda worries it won't survive the rollers and chemicals.

"Maybe I should just curl it with the iron when it's time," Frieda says.

"If we do that, the curls will be out before they cover me over. A perm will last forever. But I think we can wait another week," Marie says. "Remember to ask Dr. Minhas what he thinks when we see him tomorrow. He might say we have a little time yet."

Frieda plugs in her most slender curling iron, which she uses to simulate the fresh chemical curls her mother loves so much. It's pointless to suggest something more modern. Since Dorothy Meeks, Marie has known how she wants to look when she takes her place in her family album, next to her own mother and older sister, both of whom died of leukemia at the same age.

Reimer women live for forty-five years.

It used to be Frieda's job to take pictures of all the women who died at the right age. Over time, though, Marie had become more particular. They had to be just right. No big hair, false lashes or blue shadow. Blonde and red haired women were also omitted. Those with premature wrinkles, with rosacea or a sheen of relaxed palsy, or if they were more than ordinarily well-looking or wasted away.

Some of those things couldn't be helped. But blue eye shadow alone had been enough to make them stop visiting the North End Funeral Home. At North End, everyone from ancient men who'd stroked in the night, to toddlers who slipped under the creek ice in winter and were dredged up days later, were given the same treatment: pinkish primer, chalky powder, whorls of rouge. Cheap hairspray that lay over their heads like halos of spider mite silk.

At Creekside, women were styled with dignity. Men never looked like women. Babies had a bit of apple brushed onto their cheeks, that's all. And if a girl was the right age and her parents requested it, they'd pierce her ears with little studs. Hearts or stars or plain gold balls.

Pierced ears was one of two birthday presents Frieda received when she turned thirteen.

"Doesn't hurt at all," said Ms. Dyck as she held a potato behind Frieda's earlobe: a pincushion to catch the sewing needle used to make the holes.

It hurt plenty.

"Well, dear," said the woman, who patted Frieda on the knee and smiled. "You're the first one who's complained."

Over the years, Frieda had learned a lot of ways a person could die. Not just middle aged women, like Dorothy Meeks, who mixed ammonia and bleach while cleaning.

Young people, too.

A high school boy died at the annual Sidewalk Jamboree when he inhaled compressed helium directly from the canister, and his lungs burst in his chest. A girl was shipped home in a crate after her missionary parents took her to Africa and she was bitten by a cottonmouth. Twins boys killed separately, but on the same day. The first laying pennies on railroad tracks. The other quietly playing fort in his grandfather's silo when loaded grain trucks returned from the fields.

Old men died from heart attacks. Even older women just reached the end of long lives and died of death. Like Old Maid Goosen, who Frieda discovered when she left her mother alone with Dorothy Meeks.

Old Maid Goosen looked better in her casket than the last ten times Frieda had seen her at church, or even last Saturday at the Mennonite Village's Rollkuchen and Watermelon Festival, where she'd been propped up in a row of other slumped, wheel-chaired ancients. Her teeth were in today, which was the biggest improvement. A woman simply can't look her best with sunken cheeks.

Frieda reached over the edge of the casket and patted the woman's hand, congratulated her on her dress, black with flowery trim at the wrists and neck. Well chosen.

The last dress Marie will wear is pale, cornflower blue. It has been dry cleaned and hangs, still draped in plastic film, in Frieda's closet. Frieda hasn't been able to make herself hang any of her own clothes on the same rod. She keeps the closet door closed and her suitcase in front of it. Her shirts, jeans, skirts and a single dress hang in front of the window, instead, darkening the room. If she could, she would cover the walls and every last inch of wallpaper with her clothes.

Frieda pushes aside her suitcase, takes her mother's dress out of the closet and holds it against the tangerine damask walls.

Frieda chose the pattern for her room when she was thirteen. She hadn't known her mother kept two extra rolls for herself.

There were three viewing rooms at Creekside.

After visiting Dorothy Meeks and Old Maid Goosen, Frieda went into the third room. In an impossibly small casket, a baby girl was laid out. Skim milk skin revealed a web of blue veins. Rosebud lips. Lashes curled onto plump cheeks, like butterfly legs. She'd been dressed in white eyelet cotton and hand knit booties tied with perfect satin bows. Much better than the little sailor suits or satin gowns mothers often chose for big occasions.

There was no mother in sight today, though, besides Frieda's. So when air conditioning began to pour in from a vent overhead, making Frieda shiver, she looked over her shoulder to make sure no one was watching, and tucked the baby girl under a chenille blanket that had been left folded over the side of her casket.

Although she knew her mother would tell her to stop wasting film, Frieda snapped a picture of the baby girl, then went back to take one of Old Maid Goosen.

Afterwards, Frieda and Marie went to Pickadilly's on Central Avenue and Frieda ordered her usual: A scoop of Black Forest and one of Double Fudge.

In a cup not a cone, with a cherry on top. For supper Marie roasted marrow bones, the familiar smell of scorched minerals giving way to a meaty aroma as the pink pulp of fat and blood turned to tunnels of beige, animal jelly.

If the bones cooked too long, the marrow would liquify, leaving the bones empty, with nothing to scoop out onto toast.

The trick was to know when it was time.

Four days later, when Hegg's Drugstore called to say the pictures were ready, Frieda slipped the baby and Old Maid Goosen from the envelope and brought her mother the rest. Usually Marie taped the women into a scrapbook, but Dorothy Meeks was different. Instead of becoming part of a catalogue, Marie daubed the back of the photograph with a bit of Frieda's school gluestick and lightly fastened it inside the family photo album, next to Frieda's grandmother and aunt.

Fourteen years later, Dorothy Meeks is still filling in. Frieda wonders what the woman's family would think.

Later that night, Marie lies in bed. Her fingers alternately reach up to touch her perfectly curled hair and move over the string of rosary beads she carries with her everywhere.

She'd grown up Mennonite, of course. Spent most of her life wishing for a few beads of comfort, and on Sundays, a church with some stained glass to dress up an otherwise plain wood box.

The day Marie had her first nosebleed, two years ago now, she had walked to the clinic and waited her turn. Listened to the on-call doctor tell her to be optimistic. As she walked home, she turned down a different street than she usually took. Without meaning to, she followed a group of women up the stairs to Christ The Redeemer Church on Circle Avenue and sat through her first Mass. She found a string of rosary beads abandoned on the pew and took them home with her. Six months later she converted, so she could both confess to their theft and carry them without feeling like a fraud.

The last thing Marie remembers of her own mother, already forty years old when Marie was born, is being lifted up by a family member to see inside her casket. A moment later Marie was set back down and didn't move from that spot. She stood facing the planed and plumb wooden sides of the box, as those gathered recited hymns in German. She stood while an uncle with an AutoMagic camera snapped a picture to go next to Marie's mother's wedding photograph. In both, her hair is scraped over her head into a bun, and around her waist is tied the same white apron over the same black dress.

Marie didn't leave her mother's side, even when everyone went to the front of the house for buns and cold pork. Even after the horse-drawn hearse arrived in front of their door and took her mother, Marie stood, until she fell asleep on her feet and someone carried her away, too.

Over the next years, Marie often returned to the place where she'd stood.

"Something should be done about that one," her father remarked to Marie's older sister, until she gave Marie the photo album that contained their mother's last picture. After that, Marie never went into the room again.

Not until she stood over her sister who, in death, wore the same grey bun as their mother.

When Marie and Frieda return home from their appointment at Creekside, Frieda helps her mother upstairs and into bed, covers her body with a quilt that suddenly feels too heavy. She closes the door softly as she retreats into the hallway.

A few steps away is the bathroom. Frieda goes in and locks the door before turning on the tub and sink faucets as hot as they will go. She sits on the toilet lid, hugs her knees to her chest and rests her head. She always forgets how dry it is in Saskatchewan, having grown accustomed to Ontario's brothy air. Every day since coming home, Frieda has had to hide at least one nosebleed from her mother. Marie would never believe a bit of dry wind could be all that was the matter.

With her head on her pillow, Marie listens to water rushing through the pipes of her hundred-year-old home. Half asleep, the sound becomes water filling the sink in her mother's summer kitchen on the farm. Marie stands on a milking stool, five feet back from the stove, and watches her mother tip a spoonful of water into a pot of hot lard to see whether it's ready for frying.

The fat spits and screams like a living thing.

In Sunday School the next day, when Mrs. Rosenthal reads to them of Jesus casting a legion of demons into a herd of swine, Marie's hand pops up. She says she knows exactly what those demons sounded like when they entered the pigs.

After being called down to the Sunday School basement, Marie's mother asked where she got such an idea.

"From your cooking," Marie said. "The water was the demons and the lard was the pigs.

That night, her mother's nose began to bleed and hardly stopped until she died two weeks later. The next time Marie went to Sunday School, she sat quietly and didn't say a word.

Frieda combs and twists her hair into a ponytail. The steam has flattened it, the way skinny hair always falls down at the least disturbance.

Her nosebleed has stopped and she dabs at a crust of blood with a wad of wet toilet paper before going to check on her mother.

Until Marie's diagnosis, Frieda didn't believe in fate, or that God measured the length of people's lives like a cook snipping noodles into a pot.

"We should put out our bulbs before it's too late," Marie says the next morning. Her color is a little better, and without meaning to, Frieda allows a bubble of hope to rise into her chest.

"It's too late in the season, Mom. People will stare. Besides, you have to see Dr. Minhas this afternoon."

Ten minutes later, the two of them are on their knees before the front flower bed, hand-troweling the soil, careful to leave the headstones of hamster and guinea pig graves undisturbed, before pressing conical-shaped holes a few inches apart with a tool.

"Do more of the purple tulips. And daffodils. They go well together," says Marie.

Frieda reaches for the cardboard box she'd carried from the basement and set on the lawn behind them.

They hadn't always planted plastic flowers. When Frieda was younger, she and Marie used to put out bulbs in the fall for tulips and daffodils, crocus and hyacinth. And they'd come up in the spring, in the order God intended. Now Frieda tries to remember how long it's been since Marie changed to plastic. She doesn't ask, instead takes a few stems of the purple tulips, plunges them into the holes. Packs enough dirt around them so that they, rootless, won't fall over in the wind.

Later, Frieda knows, couples out for their evening strolls will stop and nod towards the flower bed. They'll squint, trying to figure it out.

If she's strong enough, Marie will watch them from the window in the dining room, pleased with herself and her little purple and yellow lies.

For now, once Frieda and Marie are finished, the two of them return inside with the box and a few leftover blooms. In the kitchen, they begin to rinse dirt from their hands down different sides of the double sink, until Marie reaches over and rubs granules of powdered soap into her daughter's palms, gently washing away the soil between her fingers, carving it from beneath Frieda's fingernails with her own. After, Frieda helps Marie back to bed, and returns to the kitchen. Days ago, she'd noticed a puddle of spilt cream in the fridge. Since then it had dried and crackled into flakes.

Frieda opens the fridge to see what else needs wiping. She finds crumbs on the bread shelf. Yolk seeping through a cardboard carton. And an apple, shrunk into its skin. The vegetable drawer is littered with sloughed-off onion skins and potato eyes. The fridge has been possessed by an untidiness she knows must upset her mother. Untidiness out in the open is one thing. Another thing entirely when pushed under beds and closed behind doors.

Taking an ice cream bucket from the Tupperware drawer—which contains no Tupperware, but an assortment of margarine and sour cream containers, washed so many times their labels have faded—she fills it with warm, soapy water and begins to empty the fridge. Frieda works, one shelf at a time, top to bottom, removing items she shopped for by herself, using a list her mother gave her: Cottage cheese, mushroom soup, iceberg lettuce, white bread and eggs. A package of marrow bones from the butcher shop, wrapped in meat-colored paper. For as long as Frieda can remember, Marie has believed marrow might ward off blood cancer. Even now, Frieda can taste the salt bones used to make blood cells, and the way hot gelatin mixes with her saliva and spreads over her tongue, leaking down her throat.

When she was little, Frieda had always eaten the marrow with ketchup. But no longer.

So when she lifts a mostly-full bottle from the trough inside the refrigerator door, she wipes and sets it aside.

There's mustard, too. Relish. Soy sauce, pickles, gherkins and olives. Thousand Island dressing, and Lea & Perrins. She wipes each container and sets them next to the ketchup, then faces the assembly of partially-filled bottles and jars.

Frieda picks up the mustard and turns the bottle over. Seven months until it will expire.

The Thousand Island will last another year. Soy sauce, as far as Frieda knows, keeps forever.

Frieda opens the pickles, forks one and then another into her mouth until nothing is left but green-grey water, floating spindly branches of dill and blanched cloves of garlic. She pours the liquid into a glass and drinks it before moving on to the gherkins and gherkin water. By the last olive and last swallow of brine, her stomach is cramped with regret.

She empties and rinses the three jars, leaving them upside down in the sink, then takes a plate from the cupboard and pours out the ketchup. She eats it with a soup spoon, mouthful after mouthful. By the time she blades up the last smears with the edge of her finger, her tongue is raw from so much vinegar.

Relish. Sweet and sickening. Then mustard, its spicy sulphur catching in the back of her throat. Miracle Whip, found hiding behind the cream. Frieda scrapes the insides of the jar onto the plate with a rubber spatula, flavoring it with Thousand Island and soy sauce. And the Lea & Perrins.

With the spatula, Frieda swirls the mixture until only the relish can still be identified with its bits of sweet pickles speckling the brown slurry.

Now none of it will keep longer than the shortest date. Still, that is months longer than Marie has.

Frieda lifts the spatula to her mouth, then dips it back into the plate for another, then another, mouthful. Afterwards, she throws up in the sink, rinses it down with a steady stream of water and lots of soap, before washing the plate, spoon and spatula, which she dries and puts away. The bottles and jars she pushes into a garbage bag and takes outside to the trash can in the alley.

Dr. Minhas has nothing new to offer except a sympathetic sigh. When they get home, Frieda unwraps the marrow bones, sets them on a tray and into the oven.

After supper, Marie sits at the kitchen table with a cushion behind her back and another on her lap. Frieda tents her under a black salon cape and gently rolls her mother's hair into grey and white rods from the piano bench. She would use the pink and blue, but Marie's hair might not have time to relax.

Two hours later, dizzy from fumes, mother and daughter lean over the bathtub and, with cupfuls of warm water, Frieda rinses out the neutralizer, unclasping and dropping rods and perm papers into the tub. Marie's hair is as straight as when they began.

"We'll use the curling iron when it's time." Frieda says. "I'll make sure it holds."

That evening, Marie sits quietly at the table, turning the pages of the family album. Dorothy Meeks has fallen onto the floor.

Occasionally, Marie reaches up to touch her ruined hair, the ends of which break off into her hand. Her mouth feels too dry to speak, but after a little while she unsticks her tongue from the roof of her mouth and says, "No. We'll leave it straight."

"Mom?" says Frieda.

"And no color," Marie adds.

Frieda stops what she's doing and comes to kneel in front of her mother.

"I just have to be careful, is all," Frieda says. "I can still do this for you."

Marie lets hair sift from her hand, like dust, onto the floor, then looks into her daughter's face.

"Short and stylish," she says. "Let's give that a try."

BECKER, MY BROTHER

Michael Mirolla

The Portraits

Quick now. No time to waste. If I had to make up a brother . . . to conjure one up on the spot . . . what kind of sibling would I invent? Someone who flies an F-161 fighter jet to drop bombs on universities/hospitals in Gaza? No, that might be me. Not my brother. The high-soaring mode. The vertigo of power. Of the word gone berserk and no longer under control. The full-blown paranoia that our god must be bigger, stronger, more atomic than yours. That would definitely be me. But not any brother that I would materialize out of thin air. Thin words?

My brother (let us call him Becker as I've always found that name appealing, especially when combined as "Becker, My Brother") would be idealistic and filled with the spirit of peace, the milk of human kindness, the joie de vivre. He might not like me saying so but he would also come across as a bit naïve, the type of person who takes everyone at their word and at face value. You know what I mean, right? He believes the sob story from the drug addict on the corner who begs a fiver with the claim it's for a cuppa java; he allows little old ladies and teenaged single moms at the poor people's "Anything-For-A-Buck" supermarket to go ahead of him when at the checkout, despite the stream of swear words and other crudities that often flows from their well-painted, cigarette-staining lips; and he picks recycling material out of the garbage to place it in its proper container, even after he has witnessed the recycling collection boys and girls scatter that very same container, still half-filled, across the neighbor's lawn in their rush.

Should I make him inordinately tall, awkward, gangly, unwieldy? Like one of those big-boned, lantern-jawed creatures who look out at the world with impenetrably sad eyes from behind a fortress of cheekbones and lank hair? Who are never quite in phase with the rest of the Big Bang universe? Or dwarfish, quicksilver-like, slithering into whatever crack makes itself available? A bargain-basement kind of guy always looking for middleman deals for leveraging? Venting fury against his creator for not allowing him any further expansion? Against the cruelty of genetics?

No. I think he'll be within the normal statistical range for this day and age. Neither too high nor too low. Neither too tight nor Toulouse, as the old joke goes. No outliers allowed, thank you very much. Only one quirk: I think I'll make him born without tear ducts. Thus, he cries all the time, unable to drain those tears away. Yes, I like that. But I do reserve the right to suddenly provide him with those ducts if it suits me. Crying all the time could get awkward.

You might recognize my brother by the cheerful if somewhat a-tonal tune always on his lips, that happy-go-lucky "keep on the sunny side of the street" type of humming that irritates the shit out of those around him. And the way he stops to smell the roses, even when there are no roses to be smelled. I was going to have my brother write poetry, the kind of socially-enlightening yet introspective and earthbound poetics practiced by many Palestinian intellectuals, for instance. But I decided against that. That would be a bit much, I felt. Best to stop at the scent of imagined roses. No sense stretching an already tenuous metaphor. After all, one hopes the age of *Hymn to Intellectual Beauty* is long past.

At this point, it is customary to provide a bit of background. A back story, as it is usually called in those instructional writing booklets with a great deal of bold-faced material. At first, I wanted to go the conventional route. A set of parents ranking right up there in terms of education, a colonial-style home with winding staircase and four bedrooms, enlightened attitudes and a loving and caring approach toward the children they raised. Solid, upper middle-class folks with a touch of music about them, some earnestness, a Masters Degree or two (even if on the qualitative side of the ledger), green consciousness, and a definite tendency to go a bit overboard in terms of parenting by the book. You know, the meta-psychology of increasing childhood para-stimulation levels beyond the point of no return? The ocnophilic versus philobatic attachment styles in skewed parental caregiving or some such? But, after reflecting for a while, I decided to muddy the waters somewhat lest readers were tempted to attribute my brother's special qualities to a genetic endowment alone. Or to the results of an environmental advantage over others. Or even, as seems to be in vogue today, a combination of the two. I wanted my brother to remain inexplicable, unique, *sui generis*.

Thus, I made our parents neutral at best. Not vicious but not gentle either. Neither dumb nor especially capable of learning. Neither super-intelligent nor utter buffoons. Neither bitter nor all that sanguine about their own childhoods. The idea being that whatever traits my brother has could not be laid at their feet in any straightforward way. Like all good back stories, they fade into the ambience without having much effect on what is going to take place. I simply wanted to make you aware that I can do that sort of thing if called upon. And oh, one last thing, I've made sure my brother was born in 1982. Why? No reason, really. Just one of my little jokes. A numerical lark. A playful doubling of previous numbers.

The Introductory Ceremony

It is on the verge of summer. A mid-morning in mid-June when early-rising poets flit from one inspiration to another in the hope of pollinating the sensible world and teasing the essential animating force out of things, during one of those all-too-brief moments when such things are possible. Or even thought to be possible. Anyway, I'm in my camouflage Hummer (the original military Humvee, by the way, minus weapons platform naturally, and not some pussy H3), about halfway there on a journey to visit the aforementioned Becker, My Brother. Without telling anyone, Becker has up and flown the big city. Headed for the hills, as it were. Well, actually, I think he did try to tell me but I just didn't take him seriously enough at the time.

One of these days, he was fond of saying whenever I visited him (hospital, hospice, halfway house, safe house, whatever) and he was clear-headed enough to be able to string sentences together, *I'm going to find my very own Main Street to live on. You bet your bottom dollar I will. And . . . and . . . you can come and live with me, too. We'll experience the re-birth of the spirits together. The brotherly thing.*

Yes, of course, I would answer before seeking out the nearest doctor to find out (a) if he had been given the proper meds; and (b) when it would again be safe to take my brother home.

I should explain: thanks to one of his encounters with a street-corner medicine man who told him he'd materialized out of another dimension, my brother had come to believe that he too was a shaman. Or could become one with a little work. A harmless pre-occupation most of the time. Unless he happened to score some peyote. *Buttons,* he called them. *To hold the strands of reality together. The multi-dimensional strings where the real lurked.* He went on to read everything by some French guy named Artaud and the connection between so-called spiritual practices and drugs. You can *Google* him and get stuff like: "Are there still forests which speak and where the sorcerer with burnt fibers of Peyote and Marijuana still finds the terrible old man who teaches him the secrets of divination?" And: "In consciousness dwells the wondrous, with it man attains the realm beyond the material, and the Peyote tells us, where to find it." Wow! Heavy shit, man, as the flower children used to say.

I also found a book in his house titled *Religion and Psychoactive Sacraments: An Entheogen Chrestomathy.* Pardon me? How the hell am I supposed to know what it means? Besides, last time I looked, it was doing a very poor imitation of a phoenix in the fireplace. Oops, did I just say that?

In any case, Becker was giving me all kinds of hints all along and now he's gone and done it. He's fulfilled the dream of living on his very own Main Street. And not any Main Street either but one situated in a town with a name befitting my brother's own sensibility, if the one and only text message he's ever sent me is anything to go by: "c u on de mt. U no?"

I think I know which "mount" he's referring to. We used to drive through it as children on the way to the cottage our parents rented each summer. From the time we were old enough to understand double entendres and nod nod wink wink jokes, my brother and I would always go into a giggle fit when we read the inscription, written in massive black letters, on the water tower at the town's entrance: "Welcome To Mount Pleasant. Happy And High." No matter what we were doing in the back seat of the car at the time, we made sure to stop and look up when our dad announced we were coming to the town, located midway between the city and the cottage. And my brother and I would make puffing noises and pretend to sway around all light-headed, crashing into each other before crumpling into that fit of giggles.

But, as I still have an hour or so before my arrival and have nothing more to add at this time in terms of moving the story forward, I'll switch point of view (indicated by *italicized* writing that isn't part of a character's direct quote) and let the reader get an enriched experience.

Road to Main Street

Several weeks after the bus first deposited him here, Becker stands on the balcony of the second-floor flat and looks out at a passing parade of small-town summertime traffic. Combines and convertibles; tractor-trailers and two-ton pick ups; horse-drawn carriages and soft-tailed Harleys. He breathes in deeply, the kind of breath he'd never have dared take back in the city. It smells of newly-mown lawns and fresh manure, of lilac bushes and lacquer. The lawns, manure and lilac bushes are obvious; the lacquer comes from the casket factory tucked away in a corner of the town, wafted on the winds that swirl constantly, that make the giant maples and oaks creak and sigh. He looks up at the sky, the pure sunlight shimmering down on his face. He beats his chest, Tarzan-like. Just for fun. Just because he feels like it. He whistles a tune, quick and shrill. A blue jay, pecking neurotically at the birdfeeder, responds. Mount Pleasant. Mount Pleasant. Mount Pleasant. Becker repeats it like a mantra. Like a good luck charm. The very sound of it fills him with a sense of calm and well-being. Of the present with no thought of past or future.

If he cares to, Becker can walk the entire length of Main Street in less than an hour—forty-five minutes if he's brisk about it. He can say hello to every single person passing by without fear of being reported to the police. He can sit in the playground all day long, watching the mothers with their tots—some of them (the mothers, that is), pony-tailed and chain-smoking, admittedly less excited than they should be about the bounty of procreation. He can follow the nearby river into the surrounding hills and valleys, fields and forests. Follow it to its source, if he wishes. Or to where it loses itself in the waters of an icy bay, choked with salmon in a rush (and no, they do not recite any verses, satanic or otherwise). Not that Becker has done any of these things as yet. But he can if he wants to. Anytime he wants to. And that's the important thing. That's what counts. He can when he wants to . . . if he wants to . . . anytime he wants to.

As for this particular morning, Becker hasn't quite decided yet what he'll do. He's never been very good at making decisions. Especially in the morning. Sometimes, he thinks that all his past troubles have stemmed from that simple fact. Make simple decisions first, one therapist had told him. That's always good practice. Plunge right in, another had said. Make it a habit to decide one tough thing per day, a third had opined. Now, he realizes his first decision—simple or tough—was deciding to stay away from therapists. Maybe he'll just go down to the donut shop and hang out, hands wrapped around a warm coffee cup. Maybe he'll do that—for a start. That would be very convenient indeed as the donut shop happens to be right beneath his flat and permeates the rooms with its sometimes overpowering odors of fried fat and roasting coffee beans. They seep up through the cracked linoleum and serve as a wake-up call. Yes, a visit to Aileen in her beige uniform, but not for a donut and coffee. Becker is a multi-grain bagel and Japanese green tea (Sencha leaves with roasted rice, thank you very much) type of guy. Even if he does have to have it ordered special . . . from the less than admired city.

Before anything else, however, Becker carries out his morning toilet: the brushing of teeth; the disentangling of shoulder-length hair; the splashing of water on face. Then, he glances up at the mirror. Is it just his imagination or is he starting to fill out a bit? Is he starting to lose that cadaverous look that, towards the end, had him avoiding mirrors and reflective store windows when he still lived in the city? No, it's not his imagination. The shadows under his eyes are definitely fading and his cheeks are rounding into shape. Macintosh apple shape. Why, he's even developing something of a pot, something that will no longer allow him to vanish when he stands sideways in an effort to escape his enemies. Not that he had any. Only wishful thinking.

He grins and winks at himself. At the last minute, almost as he's going out the door, Becker decides a pony-tail would look good this morning. A tribute to the recalcitrant mothers perhaps. He searches around for a rubber band, making a mental note to buy a proper beret the next time he's in the Big V personal hygiene section. He remembers having dozens of them in the city—but they must have got lost or been stolen. He was always losing things or having them stolen. Family photo albums. Galoshes. An automatic can opener. Books. Oh well, Becker says to himself. Nothing you can do about that. Becker's favorite expression. Actually, it's not really Becker's favorite expression. He's "borrowed" it from a local character who uses it to terminate all his conversations.

After much searching, he finally finds a rubber band in the fridge—holding together an ancient stalk of celery. Becker slides it off and the celery wilts, slithering into a pool of its own lack of backbone. Oh well, time to chuck it out anyway. He holds his hair tight with one hand and eases the band into it with the other. He knows this is a delicate operation, requiring all of his attention. If he slips up and only captures a portion of the hair, he can end up in an intertwined mess—and not knowing which way to turn, how to undo the whole thing. Once, he remembers screwing up so badly he had to cut a bunch of his hair just above the band to free himself.

That was when I really didn't know what I was doing, *he tells himself. Those were the days when he dreamt of monstrous insectoids trumpeting their way through the city, crushing all in their path and replacing it with secretions of reinforced concrete. More and more steel-reinforced concrete. Those were the days when the light felt trapped—inside his head, inside the city, inside the universe. Nowhere to go. Bouncing from one synapse to the next, from one skyscraper to the other until it was too intense to look at directly. Or fractured beyond recognition by the acid-rain-fog-mist that burned through his very core, touching it with slimy fingers that caused him to shudder all over in revulsion.*

That was before the light finally escaped and Becker opened his eyes again and, one-way ticket in hand, he looked out at a long ribbon of road surrounded by broken topsoil and there was chlorophyll working its magic as far as he could see. Green shoots forcing their way towards the sunlight that was suddenly life-giving.

Carefully, with no intention of bringing any of the nightmares back, Becker pulls the hair through the loop, missing only one or two strands. Then, just as carefully, undoes it, letting the hair cascade back to its original position. In case he decides to visit the playground and the mothers don't appreciate the gesture of solidarity.

Sadly, despite re-applying the rubber band, he can't seem to prop up the stalk of celery. Can't get it back to its previous state. Can't rejuvenate it. And it lies there on its side, bent almost double. Soggy and wimpish in its misery. One more lesson in decision-making. Becker sighs—and steps out, following the scent of the coffee. Of frying dough.

On The Via Sacra

I didn't really burn Becker's book. That was a little white lie. I wouldn't do that. In fact, I have it here beside me on the car seat. Right beside another little package I'm bringing up for Becker, my brother. *Religion and Psychoactive Sacraments: An Entheogen Chrestomathy.* I thought it might be a good excuse for coming up to visit him. A conversation piece, as it were. An ice-breaker to fill in the gaps between those awkward pauses. *Here, Becker, my brother. I know how much you've missed this . . . probably has left a huge hole in your psyche.* And he will be so pleased and very grateful and gleeful and hug me tight and call me the best brother ever. The only person who truly understands him. Unless, of course, he has taken one of those buttons of his. In which case, he'll be in a trance or trying to tell me how miraculously the grain of sand reflects the captured starlight in the palm of his hand. Or that the same starlight is trying to crucify him, trying to nail him to the ceiling. Or that he needs to fly, to test his wings. To roar like a fighter jet deep in enemy territory. To tell the truth, not sure which condition is preferable but in the end it really doesn't matter. It's really all the same condition, isn't it?

Hey, I've even gone to the trouble of finding out what the fuck the book is about. I think, anyway. I now know, thanks to *Wikipedia,* that an "entheogen" is some type of stuff used to discover the "god within." Or something of the sort. Psychoactive, you know. Which I think simply means that it gets you high. And peyote is one of those drugs. And *Chrestomathy*? Surprise, surprise. It has nothing to do with drugs. Or Christ. Or religion of any sort. Instead, it refers to, and I quote, "a collection of selected literary passages, often by one author and esp. from a foreign language." Hmm. So here's a sample of the type of writing in the book; this from the introduction by one of the authors, Thomas B. Roberts:

Unlike most research databases which store empirical observations (usually as numbers and statistics), Religion and Psychoactive Sacraments *is a reservoir of ideas—a concept base. By collecting samples of entheogenology under one roof, I hope this chrestomathy will vitalize additional study that may someday grow into new scholarly and scientific specialties.*

And let me read you another by the other author/compiler, Paula Jo Hruby:

This Guide *illustrates that what is outside is also within. The two, although they may seem separate, are part and parcel of the same Oneness. A wise teacher, Betty Bosdell, once counseled me that there are no secrets in life; everything which is in the other is also in me and all that is within me is also in the other. Once one realizes this basic truth, fear loses its grip. And I ask you, if hate is based on fear,* **What would this world be like without fear***?*

Wow. Crazy shit, eh? What's within me is also within you, it says. Jeez, I hope not because there is some stuff in me that you probably wouldn't want within you. Wouldn't want within a hundred miles of you. Like the fact I like to scare other people, to stir up the fear in them, to keep them looking over their shoulder. A world without fear would be a pretty boring place. And scary in its own way. Like, I mean, if there were no nuke weapon alarms, mass starvations, genocides, greed-driven wars, climate change scares, then what would distract us from our own mortality, eh? What would keep us from constantly dwelling on the fact we're going to slip, slide into de cold cold ground one of dese days? And the realization there ain't nothin', sweet fuck all, we can do about it? Just as Mr. Shelley.

Naw, man. The trick is to keep busy. Keep on truckin'. Keep on trackin'. Think of ways to torture that inconsiderate neighbor when the S.O.B. goes out and buys the same car as you. (I keep a funnel and some sugar ready for just such an eventuality). Make plans to cheat on your lover just to see what his/her reaction will be. Starve a cold and feed a fever. Never do the expected until you're expected to do the unexpected . . . and then . . .

Cult Cull Skulduggery

Becker steps out onto Main Street. He holds a white cardboard box in his hands. It is one of those take-out boxes from a fast-food place. Or a coffee shop, maybe. You know the ones? Slotted on the outside for easy folding and with moulded cardboard inside for holding beverage containers. He stops for a moment to stare at the horse and buggy tied in front of the hardware store. The old-fashioned, pre-Home Depot Main Street hardware with a front entrance featuring braces of broom handles in round containers, buckets filled with nails and used appliances for sale ("200 bucks. As is. Call Becky").

The buggy is an enclosed wooden affair, painted black with a tiny rectangular window on either side. Through the sidewalk window, Becker can see a small child in the buggy, seated on a wood bench. The child is also dressed in black and wearing a large wide-brimmed circular hat that seems much too large for him. Becker smiles and waves at the child; the child waves back timidly, an abrupt movement of the hand that a blink would have missed. Better than nothing, he thinks.

Becker had never even seen a real live Mennonite before his journey to Mt. Pleasant. But here they are everywhere. He has tried to talk to them ("engage them in conversation") but, despite being polite and gracious and religiously returning greetings and nods, they keep mostly to themselves. In fact, this is one case where "holding things close to one's vest" is very a propos, given that they can often be seen wearing just such vests beneath their dark, sweat-stained jackets. As for the women in their flowery bonnets and collared shirts, Becker has quickly learned that the best thing to do is to ignore them.

At the tavern where Becker occasionally drops in for a game of pool or to talk to one of the men who rent rooms above it, he was once told the Mennonites are "some kind of cult." And that their women were absolutely off limits to anyone who was not a member of the "cult." Becker had nodded as if he had understood. And perhaps he had. For he himself claims to have once been under the spell of a cult. And not any cult but perhaps The Mother of All Cults: the Children of God. In fact, he still has some of the writings of the cult founder, David Brandt Berg, somewhere: Why Does God Allow Sin And Suffering? *Becker remembers the start of the tract:* "I was talking to a pretty young travel agent the other day, and during the course of our conversation we began to talk about God." *And he likes to remind people that Fleetwood Mac guitarist Jeremy Spencer was and still is a member. Only now, last he's heard, it is called The Family International.*

Strangely, when Becker thinks of the Mennonites, he can't help but make some sort of weird connection with the other well-organized, highly-structured and uniformly-dressed groups that often come rumbling through the town: the Outlaws, the Bandidos, the Vagabonds, the Hells. Becker thrills to the roar of the motorcycles as they circle and loop to park in symmetrical ranks in front of the tavern. He loves the trembling, earthquake-y feeling that starts beneath his feet and travels up through his spine, that causes the hairs on his neck to rise. He loves the smell of the exhaust and the backfiring black smoke. In fact, he loves everything about the honking big motorcycles except their riders.

But, as it is a Monday mid-morning and there are no motorcyclists in sight, only a small black-clad Mennonite boy sitting shyly on an enclosed buggy bench and awaiting the return of his father from the innards of the hardware store, Becker turns and continues down the street. Besides, he wants to make sure the coffee is still warm when he delivers it.

Dancing The Betrayal; Skirting The Progeny

Fuck it! I tell myself. Why should I go out of my way to bring this stuff to somebody who won't even appreciate it? Even better: why should I bring it to someone that I invented in the first place? What is he going to do with it? What is Becker, my brother, going to do with all this *Lophophora williamsii*? Knowing him, probably some spiritual initiation ritual or some shit like that. Or maybe his version of a Ghost Dance, ha ha. You know . . . dancing naked under the moon-star light with Chief Shitting Bull as his astral guide in the ways of how to keep a winter tipi warm with only three wives.

No way, man. I've made up my mind, This stuff goes no further. Not one inch closer. It's not going to be squandered by some lost soul who thinks this is the route to salvation. Who thinks that he can follow the path of the shamans and travel into the shadowlands between worlds. No way. That is pure bull. Offence to the chief intended. Journeys to find yourself, indeed. I dumped that crap along with my kindergarten catechism. And all that stuff about the ecstatic experience. Give me a break. My ecstatic experience journal begins and ends with that precise, specific and indelible moment when Bobbie (name changed to protect the easily shocked and more importantly to indicate the androgynous nature of the ecstasy, so eat your heart out, goddess and spirit leader) . . . when a certain Bobbie reached into my stiffly starched blue jeans with the coolest of fingers. Ah, to be eighteen again.

Anyway, that stuff on the seat beside me . . . laying there oh so innocent (who me? I'm just a cute little blue-brown-grey cactus) beside the *Chrestomathy,* rest assured that it is going to be put to good use right here, right now. Hmm, I wonder where I can get some hot water. I said "get some," not "get into." Why, good old Tim's, naturally. Not so tiny Tim. You know the Tim of which I speak? Of whom? Once trying to convince the Inuit on the merits of caffeine, Tim. Now urging soldiers to fight on in Afghanistan, Tim. The Canadian icon who drove a car almost as well as he played hockey. Isn't it strange how you never see an image of the guy in any of the outlets? Almost like they're embarrassed. Almost like he's too much of a hick to merit the honor of being equated with a multi-billion-dollar fast-food chain bearing his name. Give us the name, we'll remake the image. Anyway, none of my beeswax, really. All I want is some hot water. Plenty of hot water.

A Visit To The Underground

Becker stands in front of a half-burnt-out building that, at first glance, seems to be on the verge of reparation. On the verge of having its charcoal-toothed studs and fire-whittled joists replaced. There are piles of bricks, bags of cement, two by fours, roof shingles, door and window frames, buckets of nails and screws, beams, those hard cardboard tubes used to pour concrete for posts and pillars . . . that sort of thing. Stacks of such materials surrounding the dark skeleton. However, on closer inspection, it is easy to note that the grass has grown through and over the bricks and wood, the nails and screws are tawny with rust, and the cardboard tubes have collapsed onto themselves, losing all resiliency in the absorption of water.

He places the takeout box on one of the two-by-four wood stacks heaped next to the remnants of a stairs that at one time must have led into the basement. He sits down beside it, elbows on knees, hands on chin. He sits that way for several minutes, watching the blue jays flitting angrily about in a neighbor's tree from which a colorful bird feeder dangles. The blue jays are angry because a squirrel, a black one, has managed to dangle itself from a branch and thus clutch onto the supposedly rodent-proof feeder. Now it is busy gorging itself, scooping handfuls of seeds with its utile paws. Unable to let a wrong pass, Becker allows the squirrel to stuff its cheeks with seeds and them claps his hands to scare it off. Of course, the clapping also frightens off the blue jays.

But he has little time to ponder on the nature of good deeds and how they can easily go astray. A head pops up from the stairs, looks around nervously.

Hey, *Becker says,* how you doing? *He points to the box.* Coffee and donuts, man. Cinnamon and raisin. Your favorite. Aileen even put some double glazing on them.

The man, who is wizened and weather-beaten but doesn't seem to be all that old, looks first at the box, and then at Becker. He tips his baseball cap, which is startlingly new in contrast with the rest of his clothing, and then flips open the box.

So, how's it goin' this mornin'? *Becker asks.* Nice sunshine, ain't it?

The man nods and sits down, making sure, however, that he is between Becker and the stairs. He reaches in and pulls out the coffee, taking careful sips while holding it with both hands.

Came down pretty good last night, though. Hope you didn't get too soaked.

The man shrugs and then smiles. He has no front teeth. Just a dark cavernous gap where shades of white should be.

Oh well. Wasn't too cold though. A good bath once in a while, right?

The man nods and grins again before reaching for a donut. He eats it daintily, pinkie held up, as if in remembrance of some more elegant time. He licks his lips to absorb any icing sugar lingering there.

Well, *says Becker, standing up and stretching,* time to head on down the road. Things to do; places to see; promises to keep.

The man holds up his finger, then turns and heads down the stairs. Becker waits patiently. The man re-emerges a moment later. He is holding a cup in his hand, in the palm of his hand. It is a delicate, painted cup, with tiny branches and birds on it.

Hey man, *Becker says,* that's a beauty.

The man brings the cup out towards him.

No, *Becker says, shaking his head,* I couldn't take that.

The man nods his head vigorously and thrusts the cup forward.

No, really. That cup must have belonged to your mother. Or your grandmother. I wouldn't feel right taking it.

Becker places his hands around the man's, as if to push the cup back towards him. But the man suddenly tips his hand and the cup flies out. Becker just barely grabs it before it hits the ground.

The Tripping

I vomit. Again. And again. I can't help myself. It erupts out of me as I sit half-in half-out of the Hummer. Flies out to be sucked up by the dust. I'm parked on the edge of town, in one of those roadside picnic areas with the chained table and garbage cans rigged against the wiles of raccoons. There are no other cars this morning. Everyone else is too busy working, I guess. Or in line for their welfare checks. I look up. Way up. From here, I can see the water tower sign that announces this place of happiness and highness. Behind it, the orange ball of the sun. It is pulsing. I shut my eyes. The sun grows larger. It continues to pulse. I shut my eyes more tightly. Squeezing them fiercely now against the ever-pulsing, ever-growing light. But it doesn't help. The light continues to pound against me. Beats me to the ground and pins me there. I start to panic. The light feels like a set of fingers, of very agile very strong fingers, gripping my lungs and squeezing, preventing me from breathing. Or with each breath, I find myself unable to expel, unable to complete the cycle. I struggle, thrash about, attempt to cry out. I'm on the point of blacking out. I can feel my mind going, my consciousness fading away. *No!* I scream. *I'm too young—.*

My eyes fly open. I take a deep gulp of air. The light fails all around me. Bursts away as if retreating into itself. Patches of it vanishing pieces at a time. And then it is dark. Dark without end. I am walking but I don't know where. Branches slap me in the face and chest. A forest. It must be a forest of some kind. I'm walking along a path in a forest somewhere and it is dark. Oh so dark. No stars, no moon. For a moment a faint glow on the horizon as if to designate the edge of something. And then that too is gone. The wind tingles on my skin and I can tell I'm unclothed. The soles of my feet slap against the packed earth as I pick up my pace, walking more and more swiftly. I am gripping something in my left hand, something with a handle. Something with what feels like raised lettering along the side of the handle. Like Braille. I slide along the shaft with the fingers of my right hand. A blade. A sharp blade that comes to a tip. A knife of some kind. A whopping big knife with a thick curved blade. What am I doing with a knife in my hand walking naked in a forest in the dark? I try to stop. To pull up. But I can't. My legs keep on propelling me forward. Faster and faster. *This is déjà vu,* I tell myself, whisper to myself. *I've seen this before. But where?* And then it strikes me: I haven't *seen* this before; I've *read* it before. I laugh without mirth. Christ! I'm inside one of my own fictions:

"The conclusion of the story goes something like this, if not precisely: 'Someone, perhaps naked but certainly not well-clothed, is running down a thin trail that leads deeper and deeper into the forest. Only his breathing can be heard. Only his breathing. The branches of giant trees curl and twist overhead, shutting out more sunlight at every step forward. Sharp twigs whip at his face and stones cut his feet as he runs by. Now, there is someone else behind him and perhaps another in front. And still another in front and behind those. And they are all running. And the echo of their breathing, now in unison, now overlapping, now one at a time, is all that can be heard. Their feet are soundless. They are running quickly. No, they are running in slow motion. They are running in slow motion past the limbs of others who were running just a moment ago. And these limbs are running: arms, legs, torsos. They are running in slow motion past those who were running past them a moment ago. And then they all turn in slow motion and run in the other direction, also deeper and deeper into the forest. Or are they standing still? And the trail itself moves in slow motion like a conveyor belt, and the sunlight gleams reflections from polished machinery barely visible behind the giant trees that curl and twist overhead.' On the other hand, it may perhaps be only the start of the story, with the conclusion a foregone one."

No! I try to scream but the sound thuds dead before me. Falls at my feet. I must stop. It is imperative that I stop. I try even harder to put on the brakes, trying to skid backwards on my heels. I try to throw myself forward so that I stumble and fall. I try to swerve and run into a tree. I try to wrap my arms around a tree. Nothing works. I'm torn away. The movement is relentless, unaltered. Unstoppable. There is no other path. No other way. What have I done to myself? What have I done? Suddenly, I am crying, weeping for no reason. Suddenly, it all seems so beautiful to me. All seems so real. All seems in hyper focus.

At last, I simply let go. Simply allow myself to be pulled forward. Without spirit. Without soul. Without the least resistance. I want to feel free. Everything within me screams at me to feel free. But it isn't possible. I know it isn't possible. For there are voices coming from the dark, from the trees. Strange how I can recognize them as the voices of priests, the bringers of rules: *Have you eaten the flesh of man? Do you suck the blood of others? Do you roam around at night, calling on demons to help you?* And then there are other voices, not familiar voices: *One day all will be as you have seen it there, in Wirikuta. The First People will come back. The fields will be pure and crystalline, all this is not clear to me, but in five more years I will know it . . . The world will end, and the unity will be here again.*

The voices continue to battle. It is a battle inside my head. I know that. They push me to and fro, first one way and then the other, using my body as a toy thing. They laugh at me; they cry mysteriously. They run me ragged. My lungs grow, threatening to burst within my chest.

What have I done?

Approaching The Path

As much as he enjoys walking the streets of Mount Pleasant, greeting and chatting with the various inhabitants who call the town their home, including banter with the always jovial old lady who stands on the corner with a sandwich sign that reads: Won't Someone Give Me A Fucking Job, Please?, *Becker sometimes feels the urge to be alone. This is especially true after he has paid a visit to the Main Street Tavern with its back-slapping camaraderie punctuated by the occasional fist, boot and flying chair. Don't get him wrong. He loves going in and hearing his name being called out, having people ask him to join them, being clapped around the shoulders like a good old boy. He loves having the waitress smile at him and bring him his order without even the need to ask (plain cheeseburger, fries and bottle of Molson Export, eh?). He loves when some of the regulars (especially the ones at the top end tipping point of their lives who reside upstairs) drop by his table and chat for a bit: about the weather, about the latest old timer to bite the dust, about the new superstore they're talking about putting up, about the young daughter who suffocated inside a discarded refrigerator. He especially loves the impromptu games of pool that don't seem to take themselves too seriously and that go on endlessly into the evening as more and more players take turns.*

But then, surfeited, he craves some peace and quiet. Like Greta Garbo, he "vants" to be alone. The best places he's found for that, much better than his cramped rooms above the coffee shop, are the areas on the outskirts of the town. This consists of a mixture of farmland, walking paths and trails, and woods. Old maple groves and oak trees mostly. Verdant and idyllic, in other words, with a river meandering through it all and giving it that final Norman Rockwell touch. It is under an oak tree that Becker normally squats when he takes his walks into the woods. Becker has read somewhere that the oak tree is supposedly a door or gateway to other worlds. Even while he lived in the big city, Becker would often search out oak trees under which to sit.

Of course, back in the city, some folks were none too happy when he chose the tree in their front yard. Or other enclosed private space. But here he doesn't have to worry about being chased away or threatened with a call to the police. Here, he can sit under any oak tree he pleases, including those in front yards. Even the dogs have become accustomed to him. Today, he decides he needs to sit beneath an oak tree in the woods. He turns off Main Street and heads down the Queen's Highway. He nods at the old man with the bright-red suspenders working in his flowerbed, on his knees in the flowerbed. The old man waves an earthworm-y trowel at him and then returns to his weeding. When the old man isn't working in his flowerbed, he sits smoking a pipe on an old stone that resembles nothing so much as a Leprechan's chair. Becker has heard he has emphysema or lung cancer or some other terminal illness. He reflects on the fact that one day the old man won't be there—and the weeds will overrun the garden. This leads to the further reflection that one day he too won't be there. And the weeds will overrun the garden.

Appropriately, it seems, as Becker continues walking, he catches the scent of lacquer. It grows stronger and stronger. They are piling a pallet of caskets onto a trailer-tractor, another example of just-in-time delivery. The workers are all wearing white masks and Becker wonders if those who make the caskets die younger than those for whom the caskets are made. And whether those who make the caskets get an employee discount. This makes him laugh out loud.

He continues out into the more sparsely populated areas. Not yet the countryside but with homes sitting amid large expanses of lawn. He passes a park onto which a class of young children has just been spilled from the nearby grade school. They run madly back and forth, tripping, falling, leaping back up. They swing from the monkey bars, chase one another, pick fights, kick soccer balls aimlessly. Becker is so jealous he could cry. He doesn't know how to treat children; he just wants to be like them; he doesn't remember ever being like that; he doesn't remember his own childhood. He's often asked himself: Shouldn't I remember my own childhood? After all, I'm not that old. It wasn't all that long ago. Why don't I remember my own childhood? Maybe I just didn't have one. Nah, that's stupid. Of course, I had one. One way or another. How could one not have a childhood? We all have childhoods, whether we like it or not.

More oddly still, Becker doesn't remember his parents. Or whether he had (has) any siblings. He believes he has been brainwashed. He believes that his time with the Children of God was used to wash away his memories, to cleanse him and prepare him to be filled like some newly-minted vessel. But then he escaped their clutches and thus only one-half of the process was completed. And perhaps that explained why he likes to get away from people once in a while and sit under oak trees. They threaten to fill him up and he needs to empty himself.

Blind Exposure

What have I done?

The dark is complete now. Total. A bucket of black ink tossed over the pristine canvas. I stumble and trip over snake-like roots. I bounce from tree to tree. The knife slashes before me. Sings in the air. It leads me forward. I breathe deeply, try to recollect myself and follow.

Sooner or later, a voice tells me, *you will see the deer tracks. Sooner or later, you must pierce that veil. Sooner or later, the ceremony commences. Sooner or later, you must wield the knife.*

Sober. Shivering. With a skin that no longer keeps the external world out. With a complete understanding that rises from the very muscles of my chest. I stumble forward.

Good, the voice says, but without any pleasure in the statement, *you at last know what it is you must do.*

Without warning, almost without knowing it myself, I twist the blade towards my own chest and deliberately fall onto it. I gasp as it pierces my flesh, as the blade nicks one of my ribs, slips slightly, and comes out the other side. I twist and lie on my back, both hands pushed against the knife handle. And I await the next level of blackness, that which I've tried to imagine all my life. But I know something isn't right: I feel no pain. There should be excruciating pain. And heaps of blood. A vast spillage, no? Knife wounds have a tendency to create such flows.

Nice try, the voice says. *But your timing is all wrong. The sequence of events can't be upset. Even by someone who claims to have created that sequence of events in the first place.*

I push harder against the knife handle, push against it with both hands. But it isn't enough. The knife flies out again, slides to its former position pointing outwards. I shrug. *Oh well. Can't say I didn't try.* The wound heals. I feel the wound healing. Closing up behind itself. Leaving but a tiny pinprick of a scar. *So wound-healing reversals of time's arrow are okay then?* I am lifted off the ground. Literally. Several feet off the ground. And then slammed back down, dust flying in all directions. I grip the knife even more tightly. Thick and so very real. I stumble forward.

Enjoying The Path-ology

Deep within the woods, Becker stands precariously on the edge of the riverbank, brushing mosquitoes gently from his face and neck. The water flows quickly at this point, constricted as it is by the jutting out of land on both sides. But it is eating away at the earth and sand, undermining its solidity. Perhaps in a hundred years, it will have removed the constriction. He looks up. A slight wind stirs the higher branches of the trees, a mixture of old and new growth. Further down, a beaver works tirelessly to slacken the flow of the river. It is cool this far into the woods, the canopy keeping out most of the sunlight. The mosquitoes buzz their enjoyment. Becker breathes deeply, holds the air in as long as possible, and then exhales with a satisfied grin on his face. On the spur of the moment, he decides again to beat his chest, Tarzan-like, to let out a shout. It reverberates for a moment before being swallowed by the surrounding silence.

That's twice, *he says in a whisper.* I need to do it a third time for symmetry. Can't let the "twice" be the end of it.

Becker climbs up from the riverbank, pulling himself branch by branch, and steps onto the path, a two-meter or so wide clearing that here runs alongside the river. He strides forward, whistling. He feels carefree this morning, with no other decision to make save for which tree to choose as the site of his daily meditation. But even that isn't much of a decision. In true egalitarian style, Becker rotates the meditation trees so that none of them can complain about being left out. So he knows perfectly well which tree it will be this particular morning: a favorite of his, located near the midway point of his walk and barely a few meters from where he just recently emerged.

Hello, old friend, *he says, bowing to the massive, misshapen oak that carries with it the memory of a burnt streak of lightning.* Isn't it a beautiful morning? Stunning. I trust all is well in your neck of the woods.

He walks up to the tree and touches it, softly, with the whorls of his fingertips, feeling the full effect of the rough grey bark. Then he backs up a meter or so and squats down facing it, crossing one leg over the other yoga-style.

Ouch, *he says, laughing gently as he rubs his legs.* Don't know how much longer I'll be able to do that particular maneuvre. Hope you won't mind some standing-up meditation in the near future. Or lying down. *He laughs again.* Oh, I'm sure you won't, eh? You're too greedy for contact to care how I plant myself.

With a slow incline of the head, Becker works to clear his mind of all thoughts and then of the thought used to clear all thoughts. Of course, being human, a complete clearing is impossible, especially the one used to clear out the others, but close is good enough. No one asks for miracles. In appreciation, or so Becker wishes to believe, the tree shimmers, its leaves turning and flashing in the breeze. Like countless tiny mirrors. Or semaphores sending greetings. Warnings. Messages of fellowship.

The breeze dies down; the leaves settle; the mosquitoes sing.

We were created for this, *the tree sighs.*

Becker can only be grateful for having been included.

Gateway To The Clouds

My knife twangs like a tuning fork, looking for something to pierce. Hums before me, an instrument that knows its purpose.

Chew good, chew good. Then you'll see your life. Chew good, chew good.

Prepare for the sacrifice. Chew good, chew good. Then open your eyes.

I open my eyes.

For a moment, it seems as if nothing has changed. As if I'm still blind. But slowly glimmers of light appear. The absolute darkness is gone. There is moonlight. Starlight. Objects glowing as if radioactive. I marvel. I'm amazed. I have to keep reminding myself of my role in all this. And not to be so in awe. To keep my amazement at a controllable level. But it is difficult . . . it is terribly difficult.

Nothing is familiar. I had entered a wood, thick with trees and vegetal growth. In the early morning. I now walk on sand. Sand that glitters in the moonlight like an infinity of minuscule diamonds. There are cliffs on the horizon, rising perpendicular against the sky. Before me, a set of tracks. Ungulate. Even-toed. Artiodactylous. Sharp and clear in the sand. Almost as if frozen.

With no other signposts, I follow the tracks. Perhaps I can walk it off. Get back to normal. Find some water to splash on my face. To shock myself back to the real. To where a black Hummer awaits in a sylvan parking lot.

And then I see it, as if suddenly springing up out of the sand: a grey-limbed, gnarled, twisted, malformed, contorted, ill-proportioned tree that for some reason wants the adjective "socratic" attached to it. Nay, demands it. Socratic? I laugh. Not on your life. I barely have time to dismiss the thought when yet another object bursts out of the sand. Not a few meters from the tree. A stone. A pedestal. Something hunched over. Something grey and somewhat brown. Or blue. Several smooth round stones layered one on top of the other. Rocking slightly but maintaining their balance. Vibrating. Silhouetted before the tree.

I move closer, hoping to make it out more clearly. Instead, the opposite happens. The tree and the stones blur. I squeeze my eyes shut, rub the eyelids before opening them again. The grey, utterly ungreen tree sways as if leaning forward. The knife quivers in my hand. Tugs me towards it. The pile of stones, grey with a brown one on top, rises on its haunches and turns towards me.

I shudder violently. It is no longer a pile of stones. It is a long-legged, long-necked, long-beaked bird. Half-snake; half-bird. It spreads its wings for a moment, its iridescent blue wings. It opens its beak for a moment and words fly out, one at a time: "Is," "this," "real," "this," "life," "I," "am," "living." The words fly up, only to be lost in the tree. Only to tumble to the sand again. All in a jumble. No, not all in a jumble. Exactly backwards. Precisely in reverse. The bird settles back, wings spread over its head, head against its chest.

I don't understand any of this. I don't know what any of it means. I'm not a shaman. I'm not a medicine man. Only a thief of words. A creator of lies. Of untruths as the only possibility. The knife quivers. The letters rub against the palm of my hand. I hold it before my eyes, trying to read what it says. But it is too dark to make it out. The knife quivers again, as if impatient. I raise it high in the air, point down, and move stealthily forward.

Where Our Mothers Live

Becker stirs from his meditation which, as always, has been about sunny days and the light that flits from one creature to another with dance-like synchronicity. About matter and the spaces between matter. Through his meditation, he examines all the people he knows in Mount Pleasant. He goes over them, one by one: the progressive farmer who believes in far-left socialist causes; the octogenarian lawyer who continues to dress in a three-piece suit and sits on his wraparound Victorian porch sipping Earl Grey tea and arguing long-settled cases; the high school teacher who has offered to help Becker write down the story of his life; the housewife who leaves a pie on the back step; the coke addict who dreams of running an ice cream parlor. The list goes on and on, grows larger by the day.

Shaking the bloated mosquitoes from his face and neck, Becker stands and stretches, making sure he doesn't cramp up. He raises his arms over his head. He turns to the left and right. He looks up at the sun as it glints occasionally through the branches of the tree. He feels a sudden gust of wind rush up towards him. Fill his mouth like some type of inspiration.

Showing The Way

The bird is a pile of rocks again. Of smooth, round rocks. Large at the bottom and diminishing in size as it rises. With a fleshy brown button at its top. A glowing, pulsing fleshy brown button. I find myself thinking: *How perfectly balanced it seems.* I find myself thinking: *I need to kill the hallucination. I need to do away with what I've brought into being. You do understand, don't you?*

I bring the knife down into the heart of the flesh. Straight down. With one sharp blow. Without hesitation. And my scream is muffled by the gurgle of blood. Like a blossoming flower of crimson that bursts from within. That explodes into the sky, a gusher of raw nerves and sliced tendons. Staggering I continue forward. Out into the sand dunes. Through ghost fences and the promise of fertile ground. Eons. Moments. Lapses. Staggering I fall on my back . . . twitch . . . the moonlight . . . the smiling face . . . the shock of the blade still imbedded . . . twitch . . . my fingers desperate to read the words etched along its side . . . the semaphores . . . the smiling face . . . an understanding . . . at last . . . an understanding . . .

Ceremonial Beginnings

Becker breathes out, air gushing. Bows once more to the tree and continues his walk. Soon, he comes to the edge of the woods where he emerges from the towering oaks, elms and maples into sunlight, the bright sparkle of another day. There, he leaves the mosquitoes behind. He whistles, anxious to get back into the rhythm of his various relationships and connections. Some separate; some overlapping; some of the verge of becoming separate or overlapping.

The path he takes runs alongside one of the few remaining farmers' fields that lie close by the town. That has not yet met the fate of subdivision. On this particular June morning, the field is being plowed. Becker leans on the fence and watches as crows and gulls lift off the ground before the plow, then settle back down behind it. Squawking and fussing at being disturbed. Fighting among themselves for the grubs and other insects brought to the surface in the sliced open earth.

As the tiller comes through for its final passes, Becker notices something else that catches the sunlight amid the furrows. White. Ribbed. The farmer's tractor turns away, having finished, and heads for an adjacent field. Becker also turns to continue walking—and then changes his mind. Instead, he slips carefully between the barbed wire sections of the fence, using the thinness of his frame to his advantage. The sunlight is in his eyes, causing him to squint. He shields them with his hand.

The whiteness gleams in the dark brown earth. Points to itself. But Becker can't make it out until he is almost over it. Thus, only then does he see the half-buried skeleton with only the rib cage exposed. The polished tooth-like rib cage. Still proud. Still puffed. And a knife. A knife no longer attached to it but rather leaning jauntily against one of the ribs. A nicked-edge rib. It is a large hunting knife, the type with a groove down the thick side of the blade for easier draining of blood during the cutting up of the carcass. Becker notices some writing along one face of the handle. He tilts his head sideways to read it: "Meet Thy Maker."

Meet Thy Maker, *he says aloud, scratching his head.* What's that all about?

As he waits for the farmer to come back to see what is going on and most likely to call the police, Becker sits on one of the plowed mounds of earth. He is sad that this is one person with whom he won't be sharing a relationship. Either separate or overlapping. Nevertheless, he would like to beat his chest, to complete the symmetry. He knows it's inappropriate but he can't help himself. He can't help a quiet thumping, three times, like a tom-tom, to declare his presence in a world composed too much of those who don't exist.

One Good Day

Paula Martin Morell

The Little Rock Airport is just southeast of town, the slope of the state where the earth plunges from the rolling hills and crashes into the flat, dry Delta. It's been six years since Kate's been back to Arkansas, and she takes a deep breath as she weaves the rental car out of the airport exit and heads south toward Boggins Branch, the road flattening and the trees closing in around the highway like sentries. Two days ago she was on call at San Francisco General, *The New York Times* spread out on her bed, when the phone rang. She glanced at the caller ID over her glasses and saw it was her sister Carolyn. She almost didn't answer. Carolyn found their father face-down in his backyard—a heart attack and he was gone. As Carolyn sobbed, all Kate could think about was all the years her father had given, and how that giving had defeated him in the end.

The trees give way to dusty farmland. Kate turns up the radio and stares at the blacktop. Boggins Branch is a dying town of four hundred in the heart of the Delta. As children Kate and Carolyn would spend hours riding their bikes down Main Street and around the old courthouse in the middle of the square, then back to the edge of town. They weren't allowed to go any further, but they would sit on their bikes on the side of the highway and count the cars racing by. Carolyn is two years younger than Kate, and she would crawl into her bed late at night and run her fingernails down Kate's back and talk about running away. Carolyn had grandiose plans, a pilot flying around the world, going to exotic-sounding places like Borneo and Katmandu. Kate would listen to Carolyn's plans, goosebumps running up and down her back. "Come with me, Kate. We can fly together." "Only if I get to be the co-pilot," Kate would say. They would giggle and turn onto their backs and close their eyes and fly all over the world. "Kate, look! There's Hawaii!" She would steer them down over the tops of steaming volcanoes. "Hey! Over there! I see Hong Kong!" She glided their plane over red-tiled roofs and watery gardens.

Kate knows the exact date they stopped taking their nightly flights. It was December 24, 1985. They had been sitting at their dining room table eating dinner before midnight mass at St. Paul's. It had been raining all day, that cold, wet rain that is common in southeast Arkansas in December. There had been a chance for snow, but it had only snowed once in the past several years, and a white Christmas was all but unheard of in Boggins Branch. But the temperature was dropping, and the news had said the roads were getting slick.

Kate could hear the ice tinkling in her mother's vodka tonic as she downed one after the other. Even at twelve, she knew that her mother was drowning in the bottles behind the trashcan in the carport, in her drawer beside her bed, under the seat of her car.

"Katybelle," her mother slurred as she leaned against the swinging door that separated the kitchen from the dining room, drink in one hand, cigarette smoldering in the other, "you know that I love you, don't you babydoll? Please tell me you know I love you."

Her mother's wavy black hair covered one eye, and Kate could see a tear fall out of the other and roll down her soft, olive cheek. Her mother had been crying a lot lately, and it always scared Kate when she cried. Still, Kate thought her mother was beautiful.

Kate looked over at her father, but he kept his eyes on his plate. He never said, but she knew it must have been like dying a little each time.

Kate watched her mother brush the hair from her eye with a trembling hand and take a long sip. "Yes, Mama, I know you love me," she stammered.

"I love you, too, Mama," Carolyn cried as she pushed her chair back and encircled her mother's waist with her arms. Carolyn was only ten, but she was already as beautiful as their mother with her thick black hair and olive skin. Their father would put Kate and Carolyn to bed at night in the room they shared, but Carolyn would always get up before sunrise and find their mother, sometimes in her and their father's bed, sometimes on the couch, sometimes on the floor, and curl into her and go back to sleep.

Their father gently placed his napkin on his plate and slowly stood up. "Lynn, why don't you go sit down in the den and I'll make some coffee. The girls will help me clean up so we can make it to church."

Ten minutes later they all three stood in the open doorway as their mother stumbled down the slick driveway to her red 1985 Mustang. The previous Christmas morning that car sat in the driveway with a huge white bow on the top of it, and their mother had run out the front door in her baby blue silk pajamas, jumped on the hood, and kissed the windshield. Her face had lit up in the way that the moon lights up an inky black lake, reflecting back and illuminating everything around it. Kate figured her father spent their entire twelve years of marriage trying to find ways to make her face light up like that.

Her mother's black high heels slipped on the driveway as she pulled open the shiny red car door. And that's when Kate realized the rain had turned to a light snow.

Then her mother stopped and looked over the top of the car. They all three stood in the open doorway of the house, holding their breath. Kate will never forget the look on her mother's face as her eyes locked on hers, and then Carolyn's.

"I love you girls," she said again, her words slipping and sliding across the lawn to them. Kate watched as fragile snowflakes touched the top of the car and then disappeared.

"I love you too, Winston. With all my heart."

With that she slumped into the seat, slammed the door shut, and fired up the engine. Their father said, "Wait here, girls," but it was too late. The headlights lit up the house as their mother punched it out of the driveway, put it in drive, and then sped down the road. Her taillights shone red in the darkness until they turned toward the highway and were gone.

The official word was that she was driving too fast, the road was slick, and she lost control. She hit the cypress head-on. She was killed instantly.

From that Christmas Eve until she left when she was eighteen, Kate wore the rumors like a wet blanket: that her mother was driving 80mph and never hit the brakes. That she had left a note for their father in his Christmas stocking. That she had a lover in Gillett and a baby on the way. The rumors grew over the years like small town rumors do, rolling like muddy floodwater down the street and taking over the neighborhoods, smothering and suffocating everything and everyone in its path.

Kate still doesn't know what the truth is. What she remembers is her father's sister, Aunt Rose, nervously but quietly hovering around the house over the next six years. She remembers Carolyn and their father spending hours tinkering with his old radio or singing Paul Simon songs as he played his ukulele. She remembers staring at the TV or her plate as they laughed at each other's jokes, and them eventually giving up trying to get her to play along. Once when she was fifteen Kate caught Carolyn taking a twenty out of their father's wallet. When Kate confronted her about it, Carolyn cried and begged her not to tell. She promised she would never do it again. That same year Kate got a job at the Tastee Freeze and spent all her time off studying. All she could think about was getting out of Boggins Branch. Her father made her take Carolyn along with her when she got her driver's license, but after a while Carolyn finally got the hint and found her own friends.

But Carolyn did not choose good friends. By the time Kate left to go to undergraduate in Colorado on a scholarship, what started out with Carolyn just smoking joints quickly escalated. Apparently there was nothing Carolyn wouldn't try. Even some of Carolyn's old friends were tracking Kate down across the country to tell her how Carolyn had gone off the deep end, was sleeping with anybody and everybody, was hanging out with lowlifes and was going to end up in prison. Instead, Carolyn ended up knocked up by Jesse, the local Meth dealer, at the beginning of her senior year of high school. She dropped out and worked at the EZ Mart while Jesse stayed up all night partying.

Carolyn had the baby. Predictably, Jesse fell off the face of the earth, and their father basically raised Carolyn's son Casey from the moment he came home from the hospital. Kate is surprised Casey doesn't have any kind of mental disabilities, at least none she's aware of. She doesn't know for sure, but she suspects Carolyn continued to do drugs while she was pregnant. Casey is now ten years old. And Carolyn chooses to smoke Meth instead of take care of him. She has destroyed her life and everyone's life around her.

Kate turns off the highway and onto Main Street. The square looms ahead at the end of the road. Boards cover most of the shop windows, and an old man with faded jeans held up by red suspenders dozes on the bench in front of the courthouse. A woman in a flower-print dress leans under the hood of a rusty car.

She takes a left onto her old street and takes a deep breath. Her father wrote her a few months back that Carolyn had moved into the old Johnson house. As she drives by, she turns and looks. Carolyn's yard is overgrown and weeded, a broken bicycle dangling off the front porch.

She pulls in the driveway of her childhood home behind her father's blue Ford pickup, a puddle of oil glistening underneath. He had that truck since she was in junior high, replacing parts as they wore out. He bought Carolyn a car a year ago so she could get to work at Winn Dixie. Kate wonders if she even still has it.

The last time she was here she sat in her and her sister's old bedroom and watched Carolyn and her father plant flowers in the backyard. Casey was four and running behind them, his pudgy hands full of moist, brown soil. Carolyn had just gotten out of rehab for the third time, and her father was once again letting her and Casey stay with them until she got back on her feet. Kate remembers her father's laughter as Carolyn chased him around the yard with a tulip bulb.

Later that evening after dinner Kate had walked down the hall to see if Carolyn was still up. She doesn't know why she was looking for her—after her father's letters detailing Carolyn's arrest for shoplifting, two DUI's, and possession of Crystal Meth, the few times she spoke to Carolyn on the phone she felt like she was lying, no matter what they talked about. Through the cracked bedroom door she saw Carolyn bent over her old twin bed, snorting a line off her compact. Kate turned and walked away.

Sitting on the backporch, she had pulled out her cellphone and changed her flight back to California. She left the next morning without saying goodbye. As she pulled out of the driveway at sunrise, she saw her father open the curtains of his bedroom window.

When she got back to med school she wrote her father a long letter. She wrote how she was the successful one. How she had never asked him for anything. She didn't tell him what she saw that night, but she wanted him to think about how much he had given Carolyn, and how much Carolyn had taken. Though they talked on the phone several times over the next year, he never mentioned the letter. She wondered for a long time if he ever got it.

The day before her graduation from med school, her father called from the San Francisco airport. He had flown out to see her graduate. That night her father sat across from her at a two-top at Costello's, his tie crooked and his sleeves hanging out of the bottom of his dinner jacket.

"Your sister really wanted to come out and see you," he said, his fork spinning around and around in his fettuccini, "but she couldn't get off work. She's so proud of you."

Kate took a sip of her wine and stared at the basket of bread. She should have known that the conversation would end up on Carolyn.

"She's doing much better," her father continued. She could feel him staring at her, but she kept her eyes down. "She and Casey have their own house now, and she's got a steady job. I have them over for dinner every Sunday, and I pull out the old ukulele and we'll sing all night. Remember when we used to do that?" The weight of her father's denial made her shoulders sink.

"She really needs your support right now, Kate," her father said.

Suddenly she couldn't keep her mouth shut any longer. "Maybe that's what Carolyn's problem is, Daddy. Support." Her jaw ground. She set her wine glass on the table and looked at her father. "All these years you've given Carolyn everything—she's never had to make it on her own. I've done everything by myself, and I'm doing great."

Her father set his fork down on his plate, the lines on his face like a roadmap. He wiped his mouth with his napkin. "Some people need more than others, Kate. You are the strong one—always have been. You've been able to do what you wanted to in life. Not everyone is so fortunate."

"I don't want to talk about this anymore, Daddy," she said as the waiter leaned over and took her plate. All this bullshit about how she was the fortunate one was making her stomach hurt. She got where she was in life because she worked for it, not because her father kept bailing her out. Carolyn was destroying herself and him in the process.

"I just want to say one more thing, Kate. I know it's hard for you to understand, but one good day with Carolyn is worth all the bad. Sometimes we have to take whatever people are able to give us. I just hope someday you'll find a way back to your sister."

Kate shook her head and looked towards the door.

Carolyn's name wasn't mentioned the rest of the trip, but she hovered around them like a cloud. Two days later, her father stood in line to get on his plane back to Arkansas. Kate hugged him and told him she loved him. That was the last time she saw him alive.

Kate steps out of the rental car and the thick Arkansas heat wraps around her. Out of the corner of her eye she sees a tan, blond boy strolling down the sidewalk, and realizes that it's Casey. Even at ten he's tall and fluid like his mother.

Casey walks up to the car as she pulls her bag out of the trunk. "You probably don't even remember me," she says. Casey looks down at his tennis shoes. "I'm your Aunt Kate."

Casey looks up at her and she sees her father's eyes. "Nope, I don't remember you. But Mom talks about you all the time, so I figured it was you when you pulled up."

Great. Carolyn's been talking about her. She wonders what kind of lies she's told him. A line of sweat runs down her back.

"Well, don't believe everything you hear," she says. She shoves her purse in her bag and zips it up. She looks at Casey, and he stares at his shoes. She ruffles his hair and then shuts the trunk. The screen door opens as they walk up the porch stairs.

At first Kate doesn't recognize the woman standing in the doorway. Then she realizes it's Carolyn. Her eyes are sunken, her hair long and dyed platinum, and her scalp shows in places. Her once long, slender hands are blotchy and Kate can see the bones trembling underneath the skin as they reach for her. The screen door slams behind her as Carolyn throws her arms around her. Kate's bag drops with a thud.

"Let's get out of this heat," Kate says. Carolyn smells like burnt yellow tobacco.

Carolyn grabs her bag, pulls open the screen door, and leads her and Casey into the house. As Carolyn walks back toward their old room, Kate stops, trying to adjust to the dimly-lit room.

Several women are scattered around the room, iced tea sweating rings on the mahogany coffee table. Aunt Rose is sitting in the middle of the faded flowered couch. Kate leans down and hugs her. The house smells like freshly-baked pies.

"Kate, honey, it's so good to see you," Aunt Rose says. Her legs are trembling as she stands up. She looks old and wrinkled as she blows her nose.

Someone hands her a cold glass of sweet tea, and Kate sits down on the couch with Aunt Rose and takes a sip. She listens to Aunt Rose talk about how everyone has been so nice and brought over food and helped her make the arrangements. Her voice cracks when she gets to the wake this afternoon and the funeral tomorrow. Kate reaches down to pull out the bottle of Xanax she brought for her. And with a start she realizes that Carolyn has her bag.

She glances quickly around the room. Casey is sitting on the edge of her father's chair, his long legs kicking the ottoman. Aunt Rose has stood up and is brushing the wrinkles from her skirt. Kate's head jerks toward the hallway, and she sees that their old bedroom door is shut.

Her glass tumbles onto the floor as she jumps up from the couch. Brown liquid seeps into the carpet.

She hears Aunt Rose behind her, "Don't worry, don't worry, I'll get that," as Kate walks briskly down the hall and throws open the bedroom door.

Carolyn is sitting cross-legged on Kate's old bed with her back to the door. The contents of Kate's bag are spread out on the pink comforter. Kate steps inside the door and slams it behind her.

"What the hell do you think you're doing?" she says to the back of Carolyn's head. Carolyn doesn't move.

"You have some nerve," Kate says. She snatches her bag off of the bed and starts shoving her things back in. Carolyn just sits there. Kate can't even look at her. "You're nothing but a thief—always have been and always will be. Daddy gave you everything, and all you did was lie and steal from him." Kate's hands tremble as she shoves the bottle of Xanax back into the bag. "When you called to tell me Daddy died, the first thing I thought of was how you drove him to a heart attack. That's what you do to people, Carolyn. You take and take and don't give anything back." She finally looks at her.

Strands of brittle bleached hair hang in Carolyn's face, and Kate can see mascara running down her cheeks. Then she realizes Carolyn's holding her wallet.

"Not even one picture," Carolyn whispers. She wipes her nose with the back of her hand.

Kate leans forward and snatches her wallet out of Carolyn's hand. "What the hell are you mumbling about?" She takes a step back and shoves her wallet in her bag.

"I tell Casey about you all the time," Carolyn says, staring at her empty hands. "You should see my house. It's full of pictures of when we were kids. Daddy had the picture from your med school graduation blown up and I have it on the wall beside my bed. I even took a picture of you from high school and put a doctor's coat on you so I could see what you look like now. It's really not even close, but it's all I have." She pulls a ragged wallet out of her back pocket and holds it out to Kate.

Kate stares at Carolyn's wallet for a moment and finally takes it. She puts her bag on her shoulder and opens the rusted clasp.

Staring back at her are Kodachrome pictures of their childhood. Her and Carolyn jumping through a stream of water as their mother laughed and sprayed the hose. The day their father took Carolyn's training wheels off of her bright orange bike and Kate grinning and peddling beside her. The two of them in matching bunny costumes for Easter. Kate's first day to drive without her father, and Carolyn smiling and waving in the front seat of the truck.

The next to the last picture is from Kate's senior year in high school when she was giving her graduation speech. Carolyn had Photoshopped a lab coat on top of her. She had written *Dr. Kate Bridges* at the bottom of the picture.

Kate turns to the last photo. Carolyn is sitting on the tailgate of their father's truck, her father on her left and Casey on her right. Though the picture must have been taken only a few months ago, the way the light shines on her father's face he looks like a young man. Kate stares at her father's face, the blood rushing to her head.

After a moment she shuts Carolyn's wallet. "I don't know what to say, Carolyn. I thought you were looking for money or drugs."

Carolyn lies back on the bed and smiles. "I don't blame you. Once a junkie, always a junkie." Her bottom lip trembles.

Kate feels like the bedroom walls are caving in around her as she stares at her sister. She may pass out if she doesn't get out of here. "I'm sorry, Carolyn," she says, but she doesn't recognize her own voice. She sets Carolyn's wallet on the bed beside her and walks out of the room, down the hall, and into the stifling heat.

***

Kate feels like she's underwater as she follows Aunt Rose, Carolyn and Casey down the hallway of Gaston Funeral Home to her father's casket. It has only been two hours since she walked out of the house and got in her rental car, but it feels like a lifetime. She doesn't remember even starting the car, much less driving out of the driveway. Before she knew it she was making her second lap around the square. She got on the highway and drove south, only to turn around at DeWitt and go back to her father's house. She has no idea where she thought she was going.

The funeral director's soft, gentle voice lulls her towards a red velvet curtain, the words *Family Only* waving before her. She steps into the candlelit room.

The open casket stands dark and shiny at the end of the room. Aunt Rose stumbles up to it and cries out softly. Carolyn takes Casey's hand and leads him to a white folding chair. Kate stands in the back of the room.

Kate watches as Carolyn walks over to a white table beside the casket. Suddenly she realizes that the table is covered with her father's things. His ukulele is propped up against the wall, and there's his old train set that sat dormant in the attic for years. Pictures of him are scattered around the table, and with sudden clarity she recognizes the picture from Carolyn's wallet of her father, Carolyn and Casey. For the first time since her sister's phone call, she feels the ache of grief of her father's death. She clumsily sits down on the edge of a chair.

After a moment the funeral director puts his arm on Aunt Rose's elbow and leads her through a wooden door. In a haze, Kate stands up and walks to the casket. Her father looks pale and lifeless, not like himself at all. She reaches down and straightens his tie.

Suddenly Carolyn picks up her father's ukulele and starts singing "St. Judy's Comet." At first the off-key singing hurts Kate's ears, but as Carolyn gets louder and louder, it starts to become soothing, until it fills her so completely that she thinks she may burst. And she understands, at last, that Carolyn didn't kill their father. She kept him alive.

The sobs come fierce and uncontrollably as the years race by. She vaguely senses that the music has stopped, but she isn't sure of anything anymore. Suddenly she is eight years old again and her sister is beside her.

"Don't cry, Kate." Carolyn takes her hand and squeezes it.

Kate looks over at Carolyn, and she's a child again, too. She looks around the room and sees that Casey is gone. Kate closes her eyes and feels the warmth of her sister's hand.

"Come fly with me," Carolyn says. "I'll be the pilot and you can be the copilot."

Kate can't find any words to say, and just nods her head.

At first there is nothing but silence and darkness. But then the air begins to whirl around them. Kate takes Carolyn's other hand and they take off from the ground and circle above the funeral parlor. They soar out of Boggins Branch and over the land until there is nothing but wide, blue ocean beneath them.

The Hurricane

Hope Coulter

It began as a "disturbance," a white blur off the coast of Africa, which the man on the Weather Channel said was becoming organized. "I'm not," said George, in a cheerful way that Jill, his wife, ignored. She stood watching the TV in boxers and a tank top, and her frown suggested that she was organizing her own system of turbulence.

She was a neurosurgeon, veteran of years of training more grueling than a fighter pilot's. She could guide a buzz saw through a skull or a scalpel along a spinal cord. One scornful glance from her gray eyes could wither an errant resident or nurse. George admired her strength and steeliness and loved the girlish guise in which they were packaged: she stood five-four in her loafers—notched like a piecrust, the shoes of a third-grade teacher—and chewed the ends of her hair when she was stressed.

"We can't go," she said.

"What do you mean?" He knelt by his suitcase, thumbing a stack of his favorite, softest T-shirts. They and some swim trunks were all he'd need for a week at the Gulf Coast beach where he and Jill were headed in the morning.

"We can't go driving into a hurricane."

He rocked back onto the heels of his flip-flops and looked up at her face. Set. Frowning.

"That thing is a thousand miles away," he said. He stood up. Together they watched the royal-blue map of the Caribbean. A pale, fuzzy mass whirred toward the Florida panhandle again and again as the Weather Channel projected the course of the storm.

"See?" said Jill.

"They always turn," said George. "They always veer away."

"We'll drive five hundred miles and have to turn around and come right back."

Over the course of their marriage she had predicted that loose parts would fall off, that noises in the car would turn into major system shutdowns, that uninvited people would hear about their parties, and—George hated to admit it—she was usually right.

She too had been packing when the news of the storm interrupted. Now he saw that she was holding tampons. Two light-blue boxes. His heart constricted. "Aw, sweetheart, you won't be needing those."

Her voice was stern, but his ear picked up its strain, the effort it took to make it so. "This is the type of stuff that sells out in a hurricane. I may start any day now," she said. "If I don't bring tampons on the trip, that'll jinx it."

This was their third in vitro try, and it would be their last. After this—what? He pictured placing ads in newspapers around the region:

Rocking chairs and birthday parties! Jolly executive dad and loving, cookie-baking mom want to give your baby a beautiful childhood and a life full of the best opportunities. Call toll-free . . .

Only in their case it would have to say: *Successful brain surgeon mom and lackadaisical dad want to raise the kind of child who gets their sarcastic jokes and likes old Tarzan movies.* He could add: *We do have a golden retriever.* Sometimes their dog seemed like their only real qualification for parenthood. Nonetheless, George, a percussionist who had failed to get tenure at the local college, hoped that this next gig would be his last—that of stay-at home dad.

By bedtime the white blot had the beginnings of arms, like an octopus. A man with bouffant gray hair pointed out the eye. "Landfall by eleven p.m. Monday," he said. "Of course, these storms often turn from the projected path. That's why we're going to stay with Tropical Storm Hattie through the night, and that's why *you* need to stay with the Weath—"

George went downstairs to let Tess out. While she ran around in the back yard he stood on the kitchen stoop, smelling the summer dew and mimosa blossoms, watching fireflies wink in the bushes.

He wanted this vacation so much—wanted to be at the seaside with Jill, away from her beeper and call list, away from this house where he made his own lonely rounds. Why was she never so thrilled by the beach as he was? Because he liked to rendezvous with his brother in Mobile, his brother who was a wide-load escort driver? Jill and Floyd didn't have much in common. Or was it that George always arranged to spend a day with Jill's sister in Pensacola and her four kids? He adored them. Blond hair and big brown eyes. Wide, thin-lipped faces. Their father a school principal, their mother an aerobics teacher, their house overflowing with toys, but maybe that whole scene was painful for Jill.

A few days into the vacation, though, Jill always seemed to like the beach. It took a while for the awful tensions of her work to relax their hold and slide off her shoulders. Eventually she'd loosen up, happy and excited to spot dolphins from their deck, go for a sno-cone, and snort about

George's made-up Scrabble words. It would happen this time too. It had to.

Early the next morning Jill turned on the television. "Great," she called. "It's been upgraded to a hurricane. Two hundred miles southeast of the Keys. Is it too late to back out?"

George came out of the bathroom zipping up his shaving kit. "Come on. So we have a little rain while we're there. It'll still be a change from routine, and in two or three days the sun'll come out again." He slipped an arm around her and tried to kiss behind her ear the way she liked.

"You need to call that rental place and find out their policy for cancellations due to a hurricane."

"The office won't even be open for four more hours. By that time we could be halfway there."

She closed her eyes briefly and shook her head. "You're always so fucking *optimistic.*"

She hadn't always been this profane—not back when they first met, she a shy flutist and George the funny guy behind the glockenspiel in their college orchestra. But a salty mouth, apparently, was basic equipment for a neurosurgeon. Now Jill could cuss, all right.

It was Tess who settled the argument; she jumped in the car when George wasn't looking, sat on the back seat with her ears pricked and tongue lolling, and refused to get out. Soon after, they were on the road, angling down through the delta on a two-lane highway, bean fields stretched out on either side.

Jill started out driving. She was telling a long story about one of her patients, Mr. Carmichael, who had a rare brain tumor that was benign but recurred in unfortunate parts of his head. This time he had lost his ability to see color. Last time it was his short-term memory. So far Jill had successfully removed each tumor. But if one ever popped up too deep in his brain, where motor function is housed, surgery would have a low chance of success.

"I ran into his wife the other day in ICU, and she—Hang on." Jill twisted up the volume on the radio.

"—in a moment, with the latest on Hurricane Hattie." They waited through the newscast—new Middle East peace negotiations and the dying of Mickey Mantle—to learn, at last, that Hattie was still rated category one, the lowest strength, as she rumbled through the Caribbean.

"So your patient's wife?" said George. "In ICU?"

"She thanked me. She was crying."

A crop-duster buzzed the road, its shadow engulfing the car. Tess startled to her feet and barked.

Jill watched the white mists that trailed the low-flying plane. "Is the air-conditioning on re-circ? I'm probably inhaling all kinds of pesticides."

"They don't allow farmers to use harmful pesticides," said George. "Do they?"

Jill rolled her eyes.

During lunch, at a Wendy's outside Jackson, she poked at her salad. "If my period starts," she said, "I'm going to have a cheeseburger and a large order of fries."

"If that happens, it's not a disaster. We go to Plan B."

One corner of her mouth shrugged down. "More like Plan E, at this point. At my age, right, adoption agencies are going to love me." She gathered their trash and got up to throw it away. "I'm going to hit the bathroom before we leave."

He nodded, and once she vanished into the bathroom got back into the food line. He'd buy her a milk shake as a surprise. If she learned bad news, a milk shake would be of no comfort, but if all was well, the calcium and calories would be a little boost to . . . to their optimism. Their fucking optimism.

For years now, starting even before their marriage, they had talked about how med school, then the long residency of Jill's chosen specialty, would occupy her prime childbearing years. But the path through neurosurgery was rocky and sheer, even without a baby in the picture, and they decided to put off having children. Finally, when Jill had moved into the relatively calmer routine of a fellowship, they'd quit using contraceptives. They waited in happy trepidation for the first sign of pregnancy—and waited, and waited. That was four years and a lot of tears, tests, and treatments ago. Not to mention much grimly calendared sex.

Jill came out of the women's room, her chin lifted in the expression of angry hope that had been stamped on her face for so long. But when she thanked him for the milk shake she gave a trembly smile.

At four o'clock, an FM station out of Ocean Springs sang out, "They're battening the hatches in the Florida Keys, where—" George scooted a Beach Boys CD into the audio player. Surf and fun and Californ-i-ay bounced around the car until Jill, down the road, punched the player off, swearing. "*Enough* already, George."

She was right. He should have picked soothing James Taylor . . . or Jimmy Buffett . . . with his shrimp and flip-flops, a beach boy all grown up. *Neurosurgeon mom with good taste and stay-at-home dad with questionable judgment want to parent your child . . .*

They exited onto a state highway that wound through pine and hackberry woods. Jill pulled a medical journal from her satchel and put on her reading glasses, which gave her an air of sweet gravity that George found fetching. But at the same time they reminded him of her age—thirty-seven—and what she called her Ticking Clock. He tried not to dwell on the ominous side of this clock, focusing rather on its sexy overtones. "Baby, I want to climb right into your Ticking Clock," he growled sometimes, in bed. "I wanna put my pendulum right into your"—he lost the metaphor—"your housing."

"What?" Jill would say, giggling and shifting under him. "My *what?*"

He loved making her laugh; that was what he needed to recover, must recover, at the beach—the giggling Jill.

His hopes rose as they reached the high, slender-spanned bridge and crossed the bay to the island. In the rental agency office where they picked up their keys, George said, "Any word from Hattie?"

"She's giving Cuba a good whaling," said the gray-blond woman, sliding a contract toward him. George remembered her from other years, her twangy Northern accent and sun-fissured skin. "But that's a long way from here."

George agreed. As he went back out to the car, he saw that the sky was a regal, studio-backdrop blue. No hint of anything bad in the offing.

The rental was a stained-cedar A-frame, raised on pilings. Sliding glass doors along its ocean side showcased the Gulf and a swath of pale sand. Jill turned on the Weather Channel in the midst of their unloading, but left it readily enough when George suggested they change and head right out to the beach.

Oh, it was what he'd dreamed. She looked so . . . available . . . her skin pale and lustrous against the black sheen of her halter suit—and was there, maybe, a slight swell in her lower belly? He rubbed sunblock down the sweep of her back and kissed her freckled shoulder right through the coconut coating. They walked along the surf hand-in-hand like a couple in a resort vacation ad. Brown pelicans labored overhead, seagulls shrieked. Tess chased sandpipers and sneezed at the salt spray, wheeling around now and then to bay at the breakers.

A couple of houses down, a toddler with big cheeks squatted near her father's lounge chair, patting a mound of wet sand. She looked up at them as they passed, lost her balance, and plopped back onto her bottom, her round eyes widening with surprise. Jill's fingers squeezed George's. Next year that'll be us! he thought, in a blitz of happiness.

Sun and waves gave him an almost uncontainable sense of well-being. It was like what he used to feel playing in the symphony. Something about the bombast of, say, Berlioz, or Tchaikovsky, exhilarated him the way the ocean did.

He used to love being in the middle of the dense, rich orchestral sound. He'd lay an ear close to his tympani, adjusting the tuning, then straighten up in the gathering silence and raise his mallets. He always smiled at the conductor in the moments before the downbeat, even though conductors never smiled back, in fact at that moment were rarely looking his way.

A percussionist's biggest challenge was not intricate rhythms; it was counting dead time, the silent bars when the rest of the orchestra didn't need him. But George had a high tolerance for tedium, and enjoyed the challenge of rallying his wandering mind for one great fortissimo boom.

It was the rest of life that confounded him—the murkiness of departmental politics; Jill, and her moods, and her overweening career; the dynamics of their extended families, their household, and the bafflement at the heart of marriage itself.

That night he grilled snapper for supper, Jill roasted vegetables, and they ate on the deck. George had two beers, one for himself plus the one that Jill wouldn't take—just in case. The moon came up, a yellow dime, and they went for another walk, watching the waves break white in the moonlight. After washing off their sandy feet—and Tess's—George toppled Jill onto the king-sized bed and enveloped himself in her. He finished quickly, and sleep felled them as they moved apart.

He woke with a start, his head full of a bad dream and his heart pounding. There were lights on the walls—wavery, elongated ovals, growing and fading. He was sweaty, itchy with alarm. Every few seconds the watery light hit him full in the eyes like the headlight on a locomotive, headed straight for him.

He eased out of bed and into the living room, slid the glass door open, and peered out to sea.

A cone of light moved westward along the surf, bobbing as if hand-held. The water it touched became amber, three-dimensional, rather than the black nothingness of the rest of the Gulf. A second figure in red shorts held a net. When the light-holder turned a certain way the powerful beam blazed right in George's eyes. He guessed the pair was fishing for flounder, though nothing they turned up in their illuminated cubit of sea—starfish, mermaids, sting rays—would have surprised him, he felt so other-worldly.

Back in bed Jill had rolled in his direction. The bluish light from the windows, even and still now, bathed her face, her worried forehead had relaxed, and her cheeks looked plump and smooth as a girl's. Her nose was a little bit snub, as if snipped in a childhood accident—another one of those innocent features that belied the high-powered nature of her work.

Maybe a tiny child-seed was snagged somewhere deep inside her—their own little zygote, fertilized in its Petri dish cradle, then tucked back into its mother, implanted and beginning to grow.

Yet how unconnected they seemed, for two people who might have made a baby. He would have said, about his marriage, "We get along okay"; yet there was unease behind the okay-ness. They talked about their house, they compared notes on their separate days, they had sex when they were supposed to—lately, only when they were supposed to, now that their bedroom was populated by the ghosts of Dr. Jenkins, the fertility specialist, and his technicians and nurses. But they also bickered. Behind their banter was a rancor George couldn't account for. There were hours of loneliness, punctuated more and more now by a searing sadness, which in the busy light of day would seem silly to describe aloud. Often, now that George was unemployed, these spells came in the middle of the day, in a blank morning or afternoon. When Jill got home, preoccupied, her patients' urgencies and emergencies trailed her like a cape. She was remote as a queen—a queen obsessed with kingdoms, armies, bloodshed—while he was her jester, a goofy page. He knew he should take a back seat to her patients. They were in comas, in ICU, the victims of tumors and wrecks and oxygen deprivation, more important devastations than his ordinary angst, his everyday emotional code blue. Yet, to his shame, he resented them. Yes, he was *jealous* of the mortally ill, the anesthetized, the brain-dead who took up Jill's attention, obsessed her day and night, got her out of bed, took her away from home, and kept her on the phone when she was at home. How mature was that?

How would he care for their baby, hour after hour, while Jill was off in her grueling consults and surgeries? What if something went wrong with it, and all he could do was stare helplessly, having no idea what to do? What if one of these terrible heartaches came over him when he was supposed to be feeding it or pushing it in a swing, and he just stood there, checked out?

The next morning he slept hard and late. Jill was sitting out on the bright deck, looking through her binoculars at a boat about thirty yards out. "Take a look at this guy," she said. "He must be checking crab traps."

George set down his coffee mug and took the glasses. A young man with a ponytail stood at the wheel of the idling boat, bracing his legs as it rocked against the swells. He was sorting his catch with a big pair of tongs. George watched the surety of the man's movements, the bulk of his shoulders under his T-shirt, the muscular forearms decisively moving to flip undesired creatures overboard, and the unstudied way he balanced, firmly planted, as the boat rose up and smacked down. He looked the way George used to feel above his tympani.

He handed Jill back the binoculars.

"Cool, huh?" she said.

He changed into his running clothes although he felt lethargic from his broken sleep. The day's rhythms were somehow out of sync. The world seemed populated by people who moved with easy purpose, in concert with its movements and currents—sexy people who pulled things from its depths—while he was an edgy outsider. A fish out of water.

Yet at her post in the deck chair Jill looked secretive, placid—dare he think maternal?—stitching at a needlepoint sampler. She waved as he headed down the beach.

The sky that morning was clear, pale, piped around the edges with lemony heat. As the hours passed it got moodier, and the color of the ocean changed too, to an intense blue-green tinting even the foam on the breakers. The waves rose, and the southeast horizon grew cloudy.

A little after one, George was rinsing the lunch plates when he saw, through the window over the sink, a police car turning onto the lane to their cottage. It nosed into their driveway, and a few seconds later a stout officer came up the stairs, tugging at his belt. "Uh-oh." George dried his hands as he went to the back door. Policemen made him self-conscious—nervous, as if he'd done something wrong. He greeted the officer with a furrowed brow: Citizen Concerned about Impending Weather.

"Hate to tell you folks." The officer took off his hat, directed a "ma'am" past George to Jill. "She's been upgraded. We got orders to evacuate the island."

George nodded gravely. "How long do we have?"

"We're asking that ever'one be over the bridge by four o'clock."

"All righty. I guess we can handle that." He knew he was nodding too much. Jill was afraid he would be like this in the adoption agency interviews.

They packed haphazardly, not sure what to leave or bring with them. Maybe the hurricane would turn and they could come back the next day; or maybe the whole island would be blown away, this house scattered, its ceiling fans and mini-blinds strewn up and down the beach. In the end they took everything. When George went out to load the car, he heard the tapping of many hammers. Neighbors on either side were pounding plywood sheets over the windows.

"What about ours?" said Jill. "Should we be nailing up plywood as well?"

George reread the rental agency's instruction sheet. "I think we just close up these fancy shutters."

At three forty-five he locked the door behind them, feeling a little silly—

what was a deadbolt to Hattie? Tess jumped into the back seat, and George and Jill joined the procession of cars moving bridgeward on the island's main road. "At least it's an adventure," said George.

They drove inland a hundred miles, stopping at motels in vain to find a room. Finally, once they left the interstate and the older four-lane, a crumbling two-lane highway led them to a "VACANCY" sign at a motor court. There was an oystershell driveway overhung with Spanish moss and small, mildew-stained units once painted pink and green.

"We'll be lucky not to be stabbed in the shower," said Jill.

The room smelled like roach spray, and the bed was swaybacked. George was tapping a dead fly out of the water cup in the bathroom when Jill called, "No cable."

"No cable?"

"We managed to find the only room in the entire Southeast with no Weather Channel."

"We did?" He came out of the bathroom and squatted to offer Tess the water.

"God," said Jill, "my head hurts." Her face was pale, twisted.

"Let's drive to dinner," said George, "and listen to the radio on the way. Come on, Tess, get your leash. It'll be fine, sweetie."

"Have you noticed how often things are fucking *not fine?*"

Once again they were in the car, George backing out of their parking spot, eyeing a giant palmetto in the rearview as he cut the wheel. "I think there's an Applebee's back at the interstate."

Jill jabbed the radio search button. "Nothing but AM stations! Nothing but country music!"

A DJ talked about evacuation routes and stores that had sold out of batteries. "And now, back to your requests. Kickin' K-hits, more back-to-back songs for *you.*"

"Oh, God."

"Really," said George, pulling onto the highway, "it's gonna be—" He stopped himself. There was one long slit in the western clouds, where a virulent-looking orange-green light shone through. Sunset.

Shortly after dawn Tess flung herself up on the bed and hunkered between them, trembling. The clock radio beside the bed was dark. A high, continuous wail came from outside. Jill rushed to the window and gasped. George peered over her shoulder.

The trees around the motor court were bent as if a giant's hand was pushing them, bowing the trunks and bending the smaller limbs over to the ground. The highway was a cable of taillights. Across the road a No U-Turn sign flapped, tore from its pole, and went whipping through the air, a two-foot piece of metal cartwheeling among the cars.

George pushed at the television's buttons and shoved the rabbit-ears antennae this way and that.

"Who cares what they're saying?" Jill pulled her nightgown over her head and grabbed shorts and panties from her suitcase. "Can't you tell we just need to *leave?*"

"It may be too late," said George. "By now we might be safer inside."

The picture was fuzz, but the sound worked: "—bile Bay Tunnel is now, as of six a.m., closed; Interstate ten, from Pascagoula to Bay Saint Louis, closed; Highway 367 from Bel Crain to LaSalle Bay, closed—"

He flipped channels and heard, "The eye of Hurricane Hattie is now seventy miles southeast of Mobile, and again, the storm has been upgraded as of five a.m. to a Category Three hurricane. A hurricane warning has been declared along the Gulf Coast from Pass Christian to Destin. Residents are advised to move inside all unsecured large objects—"

"What *is* an unsecured large object?" said George. "Like, a house?"

"Let's just *go.*"

They had barely entered the river of crawling traffic when he said, "Hell, we need gas."

They passed a convenience store on their left with lines of vehicles snaking from every pump, but George was afraid turning left back into the traffic would be impossible.

Jill fiddled with the radio.

"Many routes are already underwater. Residents fleeing the area are advised to use the approved Hurricane Evacuation Routes and not to delay their egress from the area."

"Egress." George shook his head.

"And now back to Bob, on Caraway Island. Bob has made the decision not to evacuate. Bob, can you describe the scene where you are?"

"Well, Mickey, there's a lotta water—lotta wind blowing lotta stuff around—"

"Tell us what the authorities told you. For our listeners just now tuning in."

"They came by and they were like, 'If you decide to try to ride out the storm, will you go ahead and put a toe tag on? Like, write your name and your next of kin on it.'"

"And have you done that yet?"

Bob laughed. "Lotta time for that later."

"Listener Bob there on Caraway Island, riding out the storm! We wish you well. Now let's go to the latest from Pensacola—"

George crooked his own big toe. How sweaty and tense it was—how *alive*—pressing his flip-flop against the accelerator. How would it be to tie a morgue tag to his toe, and pad around the house in it, riding out the storm?

A few miles later, they saw a truck stop with cars queued at many gas pumps, and George turned in. The pumps were roofed, at least; he wouldn't have to stand in the rain.

"What line are we in?" said Jill. "That jackass! He's trying to cut you off."

"Go on and go to the bathroom."

He pumped gas in a wind full of salt, blown rain, and fumes that made his face and unbrushed teeth feel even gummier. A woman standing beside a gold Chrysler was shouting back and forth to a heavy red-haired man in mechanic's coveralls.

"Not gonna ride it out?"

"Unh-*unh!*" she said. "I rode out Alistair in '83 and I said, I'm not ever gonna do that again!"

"Well, my stepfather's in the hospital. I've got to run down to the coast and help my mother get his boat in."

"God bless you, sugar," the woman answered.

"Triple bypass."

"He don't ever give us more than we can bear, do He?"

"I hear you, I hear you."

Was there something about the emergency that made strangers open up to one another? Hollering confidences. George became aware of a blur at his elbow. Jill rushed past, hands over her face, jumped in the car, and slammed the door. "What?" He tried to open her door but she had locked it. He went around to the driver's side and slid in, out of the wind. "What's wrong?"

"I've started my period." She moved her hands apart. "I'm not pregnant, ohhhh."

Behind them people started to honk.

She flung her hand toward the road. "Just *go.*" Sobs started wreathing out of her, rising, disemboweled cries, like the keening of Arab women he had once seen in the news.

Well, George thought, hunched behind the wheel—well, things have got to go uphill from here. If he said that aloud Jill would scratch his face. Even though her fingernails were short he could picture deep gouges down his cheek. He had never seen her like this, not in her worst exhaustion and despair about work, her worst rants about chauvinistic superiors. She was wild, irrational.

"I didn't even want to vacation at the beach! The *mountains* were where I wanted to go. Cool, crisp air. Sweaters at night—"

"Mosquitoes can be really bad in the mountains this time of year," he said.

"Who says? Who says?" She was practically yelling.

"It was the Porters. Yeah, Lyle Porter told me that! They went to Montana, and even in Montana the mosquitoes were bad!"

"They didn't go to Montana, they went to *Maine!"*

"Well, the mosquitoes in Maine were fucking awful."

"Ohhh—" Her anger trembled and deflated, and she burst into fresh sobs.

Mean-spirited, foul-mouthed baby boomers want to give your infant a fighting chance. Call 1-800 . . .

Mosquitoes were not the point. The vacation was not even the point. The baby was the point, the lost baby, the un-baby, the lost potential of a new person, the road untraveled, the DNA sequence that didn't align.

Or maybe the point was just her and him, the venom between them laid bare.

Did he dare to reach for her hand? Did he want to? They would definitely never conceive if they couldn't bring themselves to hold hands any more.

Jill took a deep sniff, tucked her hands under her chin, and set it on her drawn-up knees. "I don't want to be a famous neurosurgeon." She raised her face, placed it down the other way, away from him, and cried. "I just want to be a, a, a *mom."*

"Oh, honey," he said. Brake lights flared ahead, and he skidded as he hit his own brakes.

"I don't want to be in the goddamn Head and Neck Society!"

"Of course you don't!"

"I just want to be in the PTA—" and the "A" trailed off again into hiccuping sobs.

Traffic had picked up and he was able to hit forty now, though he could hardly see through the rain.

The radio yammered on. A pair of announcers this time. "Yes, Debbie, things are bad in Pensacola. As you know, one of the dangers of a situation like this is not the gale-force winds and torrential rains of the hurricane itself—"

"—but the storm surge?"

"Actually I mean the tornadoes that spin off in the wake of the hurricane. Even one tornado can be devastating, and in a hurricane system dozens of tornadoes can be generated. Part of our precautionary measures are related to the tornado threat rather than directly to the hurricane threat."

"Robin?—I hate to interrupt you, but we're hearing from our on-site reporter in Pensacola that a state of emergency has been declared there. A state of emergency in Pensacola, where the eye of Hurricane Hattie will be passing in the next hour—"

"Turn it up."

"Seven confirmed dead, and dozens of injuries, from a tornado that struck a shopping center. Most of the dead were in the parking lot of a Wal-Mart in the Chestnut View suburb northwest of Pensacola."

Jill sniffed and turned up the volume.

"You know it's not them, sweetie—they wouldn't go to Wal-Mart in the middle of a hurricane." As soon as he said it, he knew that her sister and brother-in-law were the very people who would go to Wal-Mart in the middle of a hurricane.

George glanced at Jill. Framed by her matted hair, her face was pale, her eyes pink-rimmed.

He reached for her hand and she let him take it as if she didn't even feel it. "Why don't you find a phone and call your brother?" she said. "He could drive to their house and check on them. He's got that emergency vehicle."

"Not exactly," said George.

"You know what I mean. It has lights on top."

"We won't get through," said George.

"Just try," said Jill.

"'Hey Floyd,'" said George, releasing Jill's hand and splaying his thumb and pinkie into an imaginary receiver at his ear, "'you know Jill? Who's always been so crazy about you? She wants you to drive over to Pensacola and check on her sister and her husband and kids. Then run back and let us know how they are. We'll be somewhere along the hurricane evacuation route.'"

He dropped his hand to the steering wheel. Jill had turned her head away and was crying again.

Miles went by. The windshield wipers thunked a dull four-four.

George sighed. "I'm sorry," he said. "You want to try to find some coffee?"

Jill looked at him sharply. "No. Find me a working phone."

It took almost two hours to find a pay phone that worked. Finally they located one outside a Kentucky Fried Chicken deep in the interior of Alabama. George led Tess to a tiny patch of grass rimmed with orange marigolds, while Jill talked on the phone across the parking lot.

George watched her in the open door of the phone booth. She waved a fly away with one hand—or maybe she was gesturing—her hips in cuffed denim shorts cocked sideways, one shoulder hitched up to squeeze the phone and the other supporting her big purse. He swallowed the last melting ice from a fountain Coke and felt beads of sweat roll down his ribs. Tess ate a french fry she found in the grass, then stood panting affably, her tongue drooping.

In a minute Jill would hang up and come this way. Maybe she was about to say that her sister and brother-in-law were dead, and that the will would name her and George as custodians of the four children. He was fated, then, to accumulate kiddie tapes in his car and Lucky Charms in his cupboard, to spend weekends at soccer fields and pizza arcades, and to watch over and over again with hammering heart while slight, short figures who were dear to him climbed into cars and rode away.

Or maybe, as Jill crossed the parking lot, he would realize that he had known for a long time, deep inside, that the marriage was over. The chain of consequences unspooled: After divorce, hibernation, and drift he would start dating the twenty-three-year-old English lit grad student who worked part-time at the bookstore. He would be startled to discover that not only her earlobes and one eyebrow but one of her labia was pierced. He would marry her, but not before he impregnated her, quite without planning. One night as he leaned over the back of her desk chair to nuzzle her nape, he would read this sentence, highlighted in her Shakespeare: *Thou mettest with things dying, I with things new-born.* George, who in other years had felt himself to be one large unsecured object, would start to feel solid again. He would land a modest job in arts administration, and wheeling his daughter to day care one morning, would hear her chuckle at the pigeons that flew up in a cloud before the stroller, and would find himself a happy man.

Jill gave several big nods and hung up. Instead of coming back to the car she stuck her arm out of the phone booth and raised her hand, a palm-shaking, finger-wiggling salute, then edged deeper into the shadow of the phone booth and picked up the receiver again. Was that a wave? Did it mean "They're okay" or "Sorry I'm taking so long"? Now she must be phoning the hospital to tell them she'd be home five days early, to put her back in the call rotation. Or checking on Mr. Carmichael, or Mrs. Silva—a woman who had had a heart attack when tending her garden, striking her head on a concrete bench when she collapsed, then lying oxygen-deprived for hours before her husband found her.

God, it was hot. The car would be unbearable. If he'd known Jill was going to take so long he would have tried to find shade. He and Tess could squeeze under the awning of the KFC, panting together in the prickly shrubbery.

Finally Jill emerged into the sun shimmers of the asphalt. George's sight was shot through with hot blue lines like the cracking in cement. He shook his head, but that only intensified the radiance around his wife. He had another vision, that she was standing by the hospital elevator, absorbed in a chart in her hands. She wasn't wearing her operating scrubs but her light-blue physician's smock, and her hair was short and floured with gray. There was no ring on her slender, strong left hand. The elevator dinged and she glanced up, walked through its opening doors, then turned and looked straight at George as the elevator doors closed over her.

Now she approached him, squinting. She cleared her throat. George felt his shoulders starting to shake and heard a cry rising from inside him, a cry he hadn't given permission to come out.

"Oh, Jill," he said. "I can't bear it."

Surprise and concern spread over her face. "But they're all right," she said.

He was sobbing. Standing on the rim of an asphalt skillet, with Tess's leash wrapped around first his hand and now, as she circled him and Jill in consternation, his legs—he broke down.

"George?" said Jill. "Honey? Sweetheart, it's all right. Sandra and Dave and the kids. They know one of those people who was killed, someone who goes to their church, but it's not *them,* they've taken shelter at a YMCA on the edge of town."

"It's been so hard," George said, getting his chin under control. "It's just been awful."

Jill's body was wrapped against him. He pressed his face into the sunglasses on top of her head, smelled the oil of her unwashed hair, the funky armpit smell she always got during her period. Her shirt was soaked with sweat, but beneath it the sturdiness of her back received the convulsions of his sobs and grounded them, stilled them.

"I wanted it so much," he said. "The baby. Even if we ever get another one—I wanted *this* one."

"Yes."

They clung to each other.

He pulled back, trembling and weak. "I've been so *alone,"* said George. "I'm so lonely. I miss my job."

Jill nodded and kept patting him. "You must. I'm sorry. Oh, George. Damn it, Tess, hold still." She bent to unweave the leash, and her purse slipped to the ground. She stood up, put the purse strap back on her shoulder, and said, "We need to get going. They want me on a consult in the morning."

George nodded and took the car keys from his pocket. He wiped his eyes with the heel of his hand and started toward the car. But Jill didn't move. She put her arms again around George and laid her head on his chest. "It'll get better," she said. "You'll see." He was the one who shook her loose and said, "Come on."

By the time they got to Starkville, the hurricane was a system of squalls, and by the time they got to Memphis, it was giving needed rain to the fields and gardens of Georgia. They reached home a little after midnight. The house was warm and quiet. It smelled of waffle crumbs and dog hair and the banana they had left in the fruit bowl—of home. And the next morning, when they woke up to pursue their chosen lives, the sky was blue and clear, as if nothing untoward had happened.

TREASURE

Alecia McKenzie

It's funny what finding gold does to people. My father had been digging a hole to plant soursop seeds when he unearthed the small, rotting wooden box.

"But see ya! Is wha dis? Treasure, come look."

I went to look as he pried open the box with the blade of his machete. We stared together at the coins inside. They glinted in the sun—almost mockingly, I would think later.

My father lifted them one by one and lay them reverently on the pile of earth he had dug up. There were fifteen of them. He sent me inside to get a pot, and I ran to fetch Mama's old burnt Dutch pot. When I returned he quickly placed the coins in it and slammed the lid on. He carried the pot to his bedroom and closed the door.

That was a week ago, and my father hasn't left the house since then.

I cursed the soursop seeds. He shouldn't have been trying to plant them in our sandy soil anyway. Nothing grows here. But my father has always had dreams of sprawling trees that would shade us from the pitiless sun. Over the years he has tried to grow oranges, naseberries, and even breadfruit. Our back yard, though, remains stubbornly barren.

We live in Port Stanley, in a house that shifts in the sand every year. My mother used to call the house "the leaning shack of Mister Jack." That's my father's name. Jack Morgan. He always said that he could feel it in his bones that he was descended from buccaneer Henry Morgan. And now he has the gold to prove it.

Port Stanley used to be one of the wickedest places on earth, with pirates sailing gaily in from all over the world with their loot. All the textbooks will tell you this. But a violent quake in the late sixteen hundreds turned things upside down, and another shudder in 1907 sealed our fate. Nobody lives here if they can afford to go elsewhere.

My father was born in this house and has never earned enough to make the move to the capital, as so many of his neighbors did. Yet he sailed nearly every day to the city, towards the high government buildings along the waterfront. For years he operated the rusting old ferry that plied between Port Stanley and downtown. When it finally fell apart, the government gave up and refused to replace it.

There was grand talk of building a bridge, but that plan soon evaporated into silence. If people wanted to get to the city, they could travel by bus down the long, thin strip of land that curved around the harbor. Or they could save up for a motorbike or car.

When my father lost his job, he took up gardening, with never any fruit to show for his labor. My mother took the bus to the city to work in others' yards. The sun turned their skin to mahogany as they toiled under its blaze on opposite sides of the harbor.

When my mother died, only a month after first crying from the terrible pains in her belly and after the doctors told her there was nothing they could do, all the people she had worked for took up a collection so that I could continue going to school. Relatives that I didn't know we had sent letters with folded pound notes from England. I watched Papa weep as he opened them.

Throughout my childhood, I always felt Port Stanley was like a circus attraction. People came to stare at our half-buried buildings and to shiver briefly at the mischief that earthquakes could do. Then they hurried back across the water. Sometimes foreign archaeologists rushed in to dig for a few weeks and to cart off bags of who knows what. We heard that whatever they found all went into the government's pockets. The politicians didn't believe in finders keepers. At election time, they paid flying visits to Port Stanley, promising renovation and land-restoration, and reminding us that any significant "discovery" would assist in national development.

A big group of movie people turned up once as well, bringing excitement and spotlights piercing the night and police cars speeding around. For three full days, we had uninterrupted electricity and wondered how much the stars had paid the Public Service.

Mostly though we were left to ourselves, waiting for another earthquake to come and complete the job

As I grew up, rumors did circulate of ordinary people finding a few coins here and there and managing to sell them for good American dollars. But my father had always laughed in scorn at the stories.

"Pure foolishness," he'd said to me. "I don't want you filling up yu head with all that kinda rubbish, you hear me, Treasure? The only money poor people ever get is from working their backside off."

"Yes, Papa," I said.

But he has forgotten his own words.

For seven nights now, he has been sleeping with the heavy Dutch pot hugged tight to his chest, and he takes it with him when he goes into the shower or the shithouse.

The possibility that someone will hear about his fortune and that the government will descend on us and snatch it all away is making him tremble. He never had much, my father. Only Mama and then me, and even that's not sure. He and I don't look alike. I grew up to loud whispers of "sailor-pickney," and I knew that people were laughing behind my father's back. But his favorite quote was always: "who laughs last, laughs best."

He kept me with him after Mama died. Me, with my red-red hair and sea-blue eyes.

"Treasure," he said to me after Mama's funeral, "is just you and me down here now. But she up there looking out for us. She and Henry Morgan. Don't you worry."

And I asked a question that had sat quiet in my head for years.

"Papa, why you and Mama name me 'Treasure'?"

He answered right away. "Because you is better than gold. That's what I said when yu mother had you: pickney better than gold."

Now, though, he has found real treasure. Something that could truly be his. And I'm waiting for him to see me again. He will. I know.

SECTION V

THE HARMONICA

Tsai Suh-Fen

Translated by Nicholas Koss

One

When they were small, their house was in Hangchow. It was one of those traditional houses built around a courtyard and the three married sons occupied all the three quarters of the house. The front of the open courtyard had a banyan that was green year-long and whose sturdy trunk took the arms of two big men to encircle. The branches brimmed with little, flat leaves. When the sun trickled through the leaves, the ground was studded with bright circles of light. And when there was a breeze, the circles of light twinkled as if they were bright stars. Under this sparkling light, the fragrance of the earth seemed to rush upward. Their mother loved to play the harmonica under that banyan, and the music liltingly floated through the house.

The mother was the daughter of a distinguished Peking family, After she completed high school, she married into the Wang family and gave birth to Sha-min when she was eighteen. Two other sons followed immediately. When Sha-min was ten, her husband went away to fight the aggression of the Japanese. At that time, Sha-min's second uncle was working in a bank at Shanghai and resided there with his concubine. His wife was left home to look after their land. The household was run by his first uncle and the fields were taken care of by long-term help. So Sha-min's mother had much time for herself.

She loved to wear make-up and seemed to glow all the time. She often had her long black hair loosely pulled back. A few silken strands dangled by her ears and darkly fluttered and glistened in the wind. Such charming elegance was always enhanced by her light blue, silk *Ch'i-pao.*[1]

When Sha-min became older, she would, with a poutish smile, shyly say to him through her thin lips, "Your Papa always said I was his blue

---

[1] A traditional Chinese garment for women with a high-collar and fitted waist.

heavens!"

By then, it was already two or three years since there was any news of Sha-min's father. She couldn't help speaking to him of the love between his father and her. Sha-min realized how very much she was longing for his father. On a number of nights, he heard his mother faintly crying in the next door. He would get out of bed and quietly open the door to her room. It was all dark, except for the slightly glimmering moonlight coming in through the window and shining on his mother's bent and soft shoulders as if it were lightly dancing. She would be lying on her stomach in bed with her head buried in the pillow to cover her sobs. In the morning when he would take his brothers to say good morning to her, he could ascertain from her swollen eyes that she had indeed been crying during the night even though she would as usual see them off to school with a smile.

Sha-min's mother had a lovely, leisurely spirited look to her face, but there was a sorrowful resentment in her eyes, as if within she harbored a deceased spirit. Whenever Sha-min encountered those eyes, he felt that she was bestowing that look on him and it prohibited him from being happy, as if he were bearing a burden of a thousand pounds. Whenever he saw that his mother was looking at his two brothers in that same way, he surmised that she thought their father would never return.

The first summer Sha-min came home after going to Shanghai for high school, one afternoon when the sun was blazingly bright, his mother had a photographer from the local photo shop come. She dressed the three brothers in their very best. She sat on a stool under the banyan with the youngest on her lap. Sha-min and the other son each stood to one side of her. The sunlight and the shade made it seem as if they were sitting amid the Milky Way with its starry whiteness and brilliant radiance. His mother said that the picture was being taken to send to his father in the world of the spirits.

The photo was developed. It was a little, square, black and white photo, showing his mother's petite but full figure in her silk, sky-blue *ch'i-pao*. Her smile was bright and fearless like spring; her look soft and innocent. Her pointy nose stood defiant on her full face. She looked as if she had so much happiness that she didn't know how to judge it. Sha-min did not think that his father would never come back because there was such a smile on the face of the young woman in the picture.

"Has father really died?" Sha-min asked her.

His mother was in the formal parlor offering incense. She was reverently placing three sticks of incense in the incense burner. White streams of incense were ascending like thin strands of silk thread, representing the generation of the family. With arched eyebrows, she blandly said, "There's been no news for four years. He must no longer be with us."

She then stroked his head and, with a faint smile appearing on her face, calmly said, "Don't worry, Sha-min. Papa died for his country. He doesn't have any regrets."

Afterwards, she turned around and took the book *Marvelous Tales of the Tang Dynasty* from under her arm and spread it out on the tea table and started reading it with rapt concentration. Her head was bent over the book and she did not look up again, as if that was her real world. Sha-min stood behind her, knowing how difficult it was for her to have said this. Looking at her back, his thoughts wandered far away. Probably his mother was reading the story of Hung-fu-nu now or "The Tale of Li Wa." His mother was motionless as she read. He felt he too was reading a tale of the marvelous, but it was a tale about his mother.

His mother always had a warm, gentle smile for her sons, but that was just her outer appearance. Her look rather often covered up a deeper, unknown darkness. Sha-min felt that she must have cried much during the night.

The evening she had burnt the picture for his father, she had first played her harmonica beneath the banyan. There was a little, light bluish shadow thrown against the blackness of the moonless night. Only the melodious wailing of the harmonica spread throughout the yard. That familiar, mournful "Long long ago" seemed to be bidding someone farewell. He had heard it innumerable times but each time it seemed to be the first. A story was being told on that dark and silent evening. His mother played slowly. The rhythms were *andante*. The notes were drawn out longer and longer and longer, extending the night's desolation. Was this the story of this mother and father?

She called the three brothers to kneel on the soft ground where the incense burner had already been placed. As usual, she was all in blue, which made him feel at ease. It was extremely hot and humid that evening, with a light breeze. The summer cicadas seemed to be singing themselves to death. His mother, with her eyes closed, knelt there holding incense. The light from the courtyard corridor was on her back. The expression on her face was not entirely clear. The plainly dressed relatives from her first and second brothers-in-law's families were lined up respectfully along the courtyard corridor to accompany them in this ritual. All at once Sha-min felt confused. Did they also believe his father had been killed in battle? If his father was still alive and well, wasn't this wishing him to be dead? His father was a military office. If he had died, someone would have come to report it. How can we be doing this without knowing for sure? But then he had not come back these four years to see his wife and sons. Perhaps the fighting had taken him further into the interior. Maybe he is in Chunking now and is prevented from returning by the mountains. Sending a letter would be difficult, too. But these thoughts were a bit too wishful. It's naturally always the worst rather than the best. His mother should not be blamed for thinking that his father had given his life for his country.

The light from the lamps was hitting the back of his mother, making her seem foggy like an overexposed picture. She seemed to be engulfed in fog. There was no road behind her and only darkness ahead. Two dots of light frolicked on her light blue shoulders. Her soft sobbing could be heard. Then the light on her shoulders jumped furiously. His mother's shaking hands offered up the photo. She struck a match and one corner burst into flames. The red flames reflected on the face of his mother as if burning the last glory of her life to ashes. With this fire, he saw fully the tear marks filling both sides of his mother's face. She had not been crying just for a short time. The tears had swollen her face until it was unrecognizable. Such were the scars of life. It was as if a blaze of red light had been thrown on a chalk-white wall. His two brothers had already been frightened into crying. His mother madly held on to the photo, not feeling the pain from the fire at her fingertips. Sha-min forcefully hit the back of the hands of his mother and knocked down the burning photo. He grasped his mother's head with both of his hands. In the darkness, his mother called out the name of his father and then slumped on to his shoulders to cry her heart out, not looking up for a long long time. The relatives rushed around her to offer consolation. Sha-min held on tightly to his mother's choking and shaking body, wanting her to remove her mask of a smile and unabatedly cry for her lost husband.

His mother was sick for a month after this, the first few days of which she neither ate nor drank. It was as if that it was through this offering she confirmed to herself that her husband had really died, and started to mourn and was beginning to know the hardships of life.

Sha-min was by his mother's sick bed each day. The room reeked of the smell of medicine. Wherever he sat, he could smell the aroma. He was kind of happy that his mother was sick because it made him feel she was normal. He was not comfortable to see his youthful mother face the death of her beloved with a smile.

Later, when his mother realized that his summer vacation was coming to an end and that he would have to go back to school, her illness naturally went away. He didn't know for sure if it had really gone away, but at least she was again dressing up and looking well in the presence of her son.

Just before he was to leave, his mother called him before her and straightened his clothes. She seemed to have something of great length to tell him. Her eyes were twinkling.

His mother said quietly, "Sha-min, I think you have grown up, so that's why I have said what I did today. I hope you can understand. Your Papa has not returned for all these years, so I think he has passed away. I prefer to think that he has had an honorable death. We only were husband and wife for ten years. Can you remember that? He left when you were ten years old.

His mother took a photo out from the cabinet at the head of the bed and gave it to him. It was the picture of them under the banyan. He didn't know how many copies she had had developed. His mother sat on the edge of the bed, with her hands on her knees, sitting upright all in blue. He sat in the chair in front of her.

His mother animatedly said, "'If alive, he'll come back; if dead, I'll be with him forever.' He gave me ten years, which was a full life. There's no difference between life and death. He still lives in my heart. Alive or dead, we will be together." She laughed but the edges of her mouth betrayed a pale fragility, "I should not have allowed you and your brothers to have seen me this way these days. You do not have a father. I am the only example for you. I shouldn't be down and sick like this."

Sha-min interrupted and said, "Ma, seeing you suffer and bear it only with your strong will, how can I go off to study and be at peace?"

His mother lightly grasped his hand and said, "Not be at peace? If I trust you . . . how can you not be at peace?"

It seemed as if there was another meaning to what she was saying. She then added, "Do you know why I have given this photo to you? Do you think I don't know? One day you will leave me just like your father did. Considering the way you've been looking these few days, I would not think that you are going to continue your study. Is this so? You want to go and fight. You still think you have some chance to find your Papa."

He was astounded when he heard this, for his mother had seen through his intentions.

She continued, "You are still young. I certainly am not willing for you to go and join this war. But there is no way that I can stop your generation with its youthful, enthusiastic patriotism. I know that many youngsters of your age—not quite grown yet no longer small—have already gone to fight. With hearts like that there will be strength. Once you go, we will not easily see each other again. If you have this photo with you, you will not be alone. For my sake and that of your brothers, you must agree when you see this photo, you have to remember to take care of yourself; in the face of trouble, be determined and stay alive. If you understand what I'm saying you will know that since Papa has not come back, you must."

Sha-min fell to his knees before his mother. He buried his head in her knees and the tears ran down profusely, dampening her blue, silk *ch'I-pao.*

His sobbing intentionally lowered had the sound of the feeble autumn cicada. Such a youthful coming of age! Why should he have such tears? The soft hands of his mother on his head brought forth a feeling of warmth. He knew that even if he did not return, his mother would not blame him. He could leave in peace and go to the interior when there might actually be news of his father. He must do something for his mother. He could not allow the husband she had loved for a decade to mysteriously disappear without a trace. No complaints were on his mother's lips but there had to be sadness in her heart. He would return, he would come back after the war was won. His manhood would be a waste if he didn't take up arms at a time like this. His father would be on the battlefield awaiting him. He must personally present this photo to his father, this photo with his gentle, loving wife.

Two

The roads in China are endless, winding through mountain after mountain. The waterways—the lakes, the rivers, the marshes—are endless, too, never to be all traveled. Sha-min, in following the army, learned of the size of China. Its vastness made him dread that the next day would have an even longer road to go. And each next day as they made their way through the mountains and wilderness at any time a batch of repulsive Japanese soldiers could suddenly appear. Sha-min and his fellow soldiers were fearlessly fighting the Japanese on Chinese soil.

His hatred for the Japanese army came from the horrors he had seen around him. When he and his fellow soldiers were on patrol, he saw with his very eyes the Japanese army plunder villages and rape the women. Sha-min and the others stayed out of sight but the blood in their vessels was flowing with rage. They wanted to fire their guns. But since the Japanese army always set up camp in the village, they were afraid to enrage them. Their own camp would be in the next village, only a half hour away. If it weren't for their being so poorly armed and outnumbered by the Japanese, they would have attacked right away. Later, Wang Ming, one of their little group of six soldiers, could no longer control his rage; he put the bayonet on his rifle and rushed at those Japanese soldiers. Even though he had a clean blade going in and a bloodied one coming out, since it was one against many, he only wounded one soldier and then was subdued by more than ten Japanese. Before Wang Ming had charged forth, he had decided he would fight to his death. He had shouted back to Sha-min and the others, "When you get back tell Commander Lin to figure out a way to destroy them."

That night Sha-min had no choice but to hide in a grove of small trees. And he saw an atrocity beyond all human decency. Those Japanese soldiers rapidly dug a hole in the sandy marsh and buried the bound Wang Ming in it, but the sand did not cover his head, which stood out from the ground. A short, fat soldier then pulled out an iron nail from his pocket and picked up a large rock from the ground. He took aim at the head and at the savage order, smashed the nail downward with the rock. When he pulled the nail out under the glimmering moonlight, a stream of blood burst forth from Wang Ming's head like popcorn, spreading through the night air and splashing onto the sand. Drop by drop the fresh blood was sprinkled on Chinese soil, each drop marking Wang Ming's love and hate. He shed his blood out of love for his countrymen and out of hatred for the Japanese army. This was Sha-min's first encounter with death on the battlefield. And after this, he no longer feared death.

Moving on with the troops, whether it was a victory or a defeat, Sha-min always lost some of his comrades. He and his companions had become accustomed to use their bloodstained hands to dig a simple, earthen grave for those who had fallen in battle. The dead often had broken arms or were missing a leg. Some had lost half of their body. It even happened that only a bloodied head remained. But for them all, they sought to give the peace of a burial. Sha-min sometimes found they had a photo with them: of a young woman, or a family, or parents. It was so often the case that it had a numbing, disturbing effect. There was a story for each person and how many stories had their endings blown up by the war? And how many stories were rewritten by the war? He was no longer determined that he must find his father. He already felt that he was reunited with his father and that they were working together. It was as if his father was at his side all the time and he no longer had to search throughout land and sea for him.

Later, he finally learned that he would never see his father again. He heard from an officer that his father had shot himself after a defeat in battle. With the picture taken under the banyan in his hand, he cried for an entire evening looking up at the moon. Even the drying of the wind couldn't stop the flow of tears. He thought of the death of Wang Ming, and he honored the method his father used for ending his life. But he then suddenly felt that he had lost all his strength. A strange feeling of loneliness came upon him—the photo become a source of his being alone. He could not forget the evening when the photo was burned. He was seventeen then, young but serious. His company was full of sixteen and seventeen year-olds like that who went all over with the troops. Sometimes they were even foggy about the direction of home. Only when they saw the moon did they have the consolation that their home was under the same moon. With their family so far away, all they could do was to tell their troubles to the moon. The moonlight had seen them grow up.

After the war ended in victory, Sha-min at first thought he could go home to see his mother. Who would have thought that his company would not be demobilized. Having fought the Japs, they now had to fight the Commies. He never got back home. He did, however, exchange a couple of letters with his mother when he was left in Chungking after the war. Just before he left for Taiwan, he made the time hurriedly to send a telegram to his mother. He could not get home, but he wanted his mother to know that he was still alive. At last he remembered the parting words of his mother, "If you understand what I'm saying you will know that since Papa has not come back, you must."

He took out the photo and looked at it, holding it arched in his palm. The shiny paper had a layer of waxy yellow brought on by the passage of time. The images gradually were becoming indistinct, but the evening when the photo had been burnt was becoming more fresh in his mind. During the ravages of war, he had lost everything he carried with him, except for this photo which he valued as much as a gem. On the back was his mother's elegant writing, "My dear son, please take good care of yourself for my sake. Your mother. Hangchow. August 1942." Who would have thought that their separation would have lasted more than forty years.

Sha-min had thought that he would never see his mother again. How incredible that after over forty years the missing link was once more restored. He was told that his mother was still alive and quite well. Three years ago, through his cousin in Hong Kong, he was able to get in touch with his mother. He tried every possible means to arrange the reunion with his mother. Thanks to his cousin and his cousin's wife—they promised to bring him the mother he had been longing to see so much for all those years.

Sha-min had learned from his cousin that his youngest brother had died from scarlet fever two years after he had left Hangchow. His mother had never mentioned this in her letters, just as he had never brought up what he knew about his father's death. As for his other brother, he had been sent to Harbin for an extended period of time and was only off and on with his mother.

As he lovingly looked at the photo, he was not sure how many times he had done this. He even suspected that the reason for the images to have become indistinct was from his holding the photo in his hands so often. The shiny paper contained his tearful longings of over forty years, one layer on top of another. The image of his mother had almost disappeared. He couldn't remember how many times when he was young he had dreamed of meeting her again. He figured out that she should be seventy-six already. That she had survived the great disasters of our time, isn't that from her faith in her son that "If alive, he will come back"? The photo had yellowed, his mother under the banyan seemed younger than he was now. The only impressions he had of his mother were from the photo.

The moon over forty years ago was the same as the one tonight, with a wet, yellow halo around it darkening into deep indigo. The situation of men is like those encircling clouds. They leave but then come back. They are bright and then they are dark. They darkly cover even the littlest of lights. Such are the ever-changing realities of life. He did not sleep that night. He had long forgotten that period of struggle and the tear marks that had filled his mother's face on that desolate summer night. Tomorrow, his mother would come to see him.

Three

It wasn't easy to put in time until dawn and then have to wait for noon. Sha-min anxiously took his wife and daughter to the airport and arrived half an hour early. In the waiting room, he said to his wife, "In the future you're going to have a lot more work, Yu-chin."

His wife gently responded, "How can you still be that way with me? My parents have been long dead so I've not had a chance to be a good daughter. Now with your mother coming we can both be good children. How can you even mention more work?"

Sha-min didn't say a word but only held her tightly in appreciation.

Even though he had long known that the passing of time would have aged his mother, he felt that he could still recognize her from her special traits shown on the photo. He naively took his mother to be as he had preserved her in his memory and willingly exaggerated the brilliance of that photo. When his cousins brought his mother to him, he was so startled that he nearly lost consciousness. It was as if he had bumped into an ordinary stranger in the street. Only when his wife nudged him did he wake up and open his eyes to take a good look at that elderly woman.

She was much smaller than he had remembered and wore pants and a coarse, black traditional jacket that buttoned down the front. She had on cloth shoes. She was shriveled, thin, and bent over. Her silvery hair was shabbily pulled back and her eyebrows were very thin and colorless. The upper part of her face seemed like a curtain hanging over the lower part. Her small eyes twinkled like golden thread. What was really a pity was that her thin lips now looked like orange peels dried in the wind. The full round face in the photo had become a little pointed. Her chin was now sharp. Wave-like wrinkles hung from her cheeks in layers of dry skin. As he walked up to her, the closer he came, the more he felt the desolation of past events. Upon reaching her, he couldn't help but to fall to his knees. The blue figure of old had turned black. He burst out, "Mama!"

The hoarse voice typical of an elderly person floated over his head, nervously and unsure saying, "Sha-min? Sha-min? Are you Sha-min?"

That sound had been separated from him for a half of a century by the waters of the Taiwan Straits. Looking up at her, those years were shrunk into a timeless gaze.

The old woman was still uncertain and bending her humped back, asked "Are you really Sha-min? Eh! My son . . . "

His mother's wrinkled hands touched him, urging him to get up. He focused his eyes on her and took a good look. He was happy to see that his mother still had that determined, pointy nose he had remembered. This make him recall when he had asked her if his father was really dead, and she had replied with a bland expression on her face, "There's been no news for four years. He must no longer be with us."

That evening when he thought his mother would still be up, he wanted to go and talk with her about things that he couldn't bring up when everyone was talking to her. He had the yellowed photo with him. When he entered her room, from the light in the living room, he saw that she was sitting on the edge of her bed with no lights turned on.

"Mama," he called to her in a choked voice as he turned on one of the wall lights.

"Yes."

He pulled over a chair in front of her. It was a familiar setting, as if it had happened before but he couldn't for the moment recall when. Maybe it had never happened, maybe it was just in his dreams.

He tried to force out what he wanted to say while his hand was reaching into his pocket to pull out the photo, but suddenly he stopped. What if his mother had forgotten all about that night? He changed his position on the chair and said, "It's so late, Mother, and you still haven't gone to bed. I bet you are still not comfortable here."

"Not at all," she said but it seemed that there was something else on her lips she wanted to say. But she said nothing more, as if they were strangers. Her response must be her way to protect herself. Sha-min figured it must be that she rarely had the chance to speak freely about real things. When she met somebody, she had to be on the defensive at first.

He then asked, "Does my brother often write to you from Harbin?" As he heard what he himself was saying, he thought it to be a little formal and was annoyed with himself.

His mother looked at him and while moving a bit on the bed said, "He does. Last spring he came back, too." She moved again, and hoarsely said, "There's been no letters. He's not been back for a very long time."

What he heard sounded foolish and contradictory. Was this customary for her or had her memory at this age become unreliable? Whatever the case, he was even more reluctant to bring the photo out.

Now his mother asked him, "Sha-min . . . are you fifty-eight now?"

He stiffened. He did not expect her to have such a good memory. She must have been thinking of him day and night so she could remember so clearly his age. At times, he himself forgot how old he was. He didn't dare to respond to her as he would to an old friend, "I'm indeed getting old," which would have made her think of her own age. Both were indeed getting up in age, living in their golden years, awaiting the end, which in its own way brought a longing for the past and revealed the heartlessness of the passage of time.

So he only nodded in response to her question. His age brought them closer, reducing the strangeness between them. His mother's black shoulders had a red glow. The figure in light blue was now as distant as if it were a dream. Awakening, there was only darkness. Her shoulders, once so lovely and soft, had now become so thin that they could hardly hold up her black jacket.

His mother said nothing more. Her eyelids were drooping. Her tiny eyes seemed now almost closed. She obviously was not planning to say anything more. She seemed tired but was still sitting on the edge of her bed. Sha-min spread out a sheet for her and brought over a pillow. Helping her to lay back to sleep, he said, "You're tired, Mother. Have a good night's sleep. We're together now. You can be at peace and do whatever you want."

His mother did as he had wanted. Lying in the bed, she opened her eyes and took a long look at him. Sha-min carefully pulled up the blanket for her. When he was at the door, he heard his mother's rough voice saying behind him, "Little Min, please shut the door for me." He paused for a second, wondered, then walked quickly out, shutting the door behind him.

For the next few days, his mother sat spiritlessly on the sofa falling asleep as if she had not sleep well during the night. Sha-min was perplexed and wondered if she was not used to sleeping on a mattress. But she had never said anything about this. Maybe that was why she had sat at the edge of her bed that first night. He changed the mattress for a traditional plank bed and even found a harder pillow for her. Those days, the entire family was polite to her, as if she was a stranger. His mother did not say much. A person who is seventy-six can't be counted on to say much because sometimes they don't know where to start from. Her entire life had been one sad experience after another so when she tried to put everything together again, it was still fragmented. What should she mention first out of the thousands of broken pieces?

Days of strangeness will pass by. Even those who don't have much between them, if they are together long enough, will have times of joy and anger, laughter and tears. And it will be all the more the case for them if they are mother and son.

His wife was the first to say something to him, "Sha-min, it seems Hsiao-ching is having trouble getting used to having Grandma around."

One day, he saw this for himself. Hsiao-ching had thoughtfully invited some classmates to supper, happily wanting to introduce her grandmother to them. Yu-chin prepared a fine meal with succulent dishes filling up the table. But there was no way that Grandma could be called out of her room. Her door was locked tightly, and there was no answer if they called to her. After her classmates disappointedly went home, Grandma finally appeared at her door. That little, black figure said to Hsiao-ching, "I've never seen such waste, calling over all those people to gulp down this food."

She next said to Yu-chin, "How much money do you have dying to be spent? Must you really waste money like this? Later they will want to come often to our house."

The mother and daughter were left speechless. At last Yu-chin spoke with a forced smile and apologized. From that day on, Hsiao-ching did not go out of her way to be nice to Grandma.

Sha-min said to his wife, "It will be better after a while. You'd better teach that little girl not to get angry with her Grandma."

But things did not get better after a while. The sphere of the interference of his mother grew larger. They had a pet Pekinese name Circles. Before they went to work each day, they would put a piece of lean meat in its bowl to keep it from going hungry during the day. His mother, however, said that meat was for people and that animals shouldn't have such advantages. So he changed the time for feeding the dog. Early each morning he would take Circles outside to have its freshly-cooked piece of meat and then he would go to work. In the beginning Circles was not cooperative, but after going hungry for a few days, it became accustomed to storing up early in the morning for the day's activities.

Another time his mother mentioned to Yu-chin that she should not use the washing machine to do the clothes, because of the cost of electricity. Yu-chin very much felt put upon because since she worked during the day, she had to do housework at night and hardly had the energy to wash a lot of clothes by hand. Moreover, she had been using the washing machine for more than ten years, so she was of course unwilling to comply. But his mother's request was a sacred command and she must abide by it. Because of his mother's advanced age, she was unwilling to do anything to make her unhappy.

Nonetheless, she was not beyond complaining. She said to Sha-min, "How can your mother be like this? How is it possible?"

Sha-min had nothing to say in her defense.

His wife couldn't be blamed for being unaccustomed to this; it was even hard for him to adapt. Hsiao-ching, spoiled as she was, spent the entire day at school and only rarely came home for supper. The mother he remembered was not a person whom others avoided. When they were little, he and his brothers were never far from his mother's smiling face. She had never said an angry word to them. On the other hand, perhaps time had sweetened his memories. His mother might have even beat him, although he was sure it hadn't happened. Time marches on quickly. He was out in front with it. But his mother and her generation walked much more slowly. He and his mother had drawn far apart in their lives and it had almost become as if there was nothing between them. They couldn't go back to the pace of over forty years ago.

He said to Yu-chin, "Give her a little time. We need some time, too."

Four

He never did bring up the photo again, and just locked the cold loneliness of over forty years in a cabinet.

During the day, Hsiao-ching was at school. When she didn't have class, she was rarely at home, afraid of being alone with her grandmother, who seemed to be from another place and time. She feared hearing that heavy voice, wandering what colorless places and times it had been through. At college, she spent her time with a group of girls who dressed prettily and were busy running around campus. She joined them in their busyness and in this way found variety in her life. There were aerobic dancing, foreign language classes, and music lessons. With all these activities, she had a good reason to get home later than her parents. From the outside, it seemed she was living a rich life, not in the least wasting her youth. Sha-min and Yu-chin had their work to keep them busy. Only his mother and Circles were left at home. Now Circles had company, or should it be said that his mother had Circles as company.

Their home was an ordinary apartment in Hsintien. They lived at the top on the fourth floor. Because of this, they had to put steel bars on the doors and windows, which were painted white and even had inlaid flowers. It was natural for his mother to lock the door tightly. But these stainless-steel doors and windows also locked her in. She had just changed the space in which she lived. The only difference was that now her little space was comfortably luxurious. But she had lived to an age when she did not take material prosperity as anything special.

One day, Sha-min called from work the water heater company and said their heater had broken down the previous night. He wanted some one to go and repair it. An elderly woman would be there waiting for the repairman. After giving them his order, he at first wanted to call his mother to let her know but then thought it wasn't necessary as she didn't like the sound of the telephone and couldn't hear clearly on the phone.

That evening Sha-min and his wife were around the table having supper with his mother. Hsia-ching had just returned home. She was dressed in light blue, patterned jeans and her pink, hand-dyed shirt was not tucked in. a bulging, white backpack hung low on her back. Her flat, white, round face was the image of her mother's, with very dark eyes and long eyebrows. It was really very cute. Beneath her nose was a determined mouth that loved to pout girlishly. Her appearance suggested the willful authority of youth. As soon as she entered, she bent over to take off her very fashionable, patterned sneakers.

Yu-chin said to her, "You're back early this evening, Hsiao-ching. Have you had supper?"

"Yes," said Hsiao-ching as she entered the room.

Ever since her grandmother had moved in, Hsiao-ching regularly was not home for supper. This time she said, "Our teacher invited us out! There was no way I could refuse."

"What was the reason for the invitation?"

She couldn't think of a reason, so she fabricated by coolly saying, "There doesn't have to be a reason for a teacher to invite students out. And not everyone gets invited, you know."

He father didn't continue questioning and she calmly went into her room.

When her grandmother saw her go in, she said to Sha-min, "she's avoiding me. It's obvious she's spending her money to eat out." Scooping up a mouthful of rice, she rested her eyes on the fancy dishes of food on the table which they couldn't possibly finish. She said, "If the elders are wasteful, so will be the youngsters."

Yu-chin turned red as obviously his mother was suggesting that she didn't know how to run a kitchen as well as that she was not raising her daughter in the proper way. Because she was exhausted from the work that day, she was getting a little impatient. But she couldn't explode because after all she was an educated person. Furthermore, she didn't want her husband to lose face. Sha-min didn't make any expression. He was willing to let his mother talk however she wanted. He only gave a look at his wife to pacify her.

A sharp shout came from Hsiao-ching who was already in the bathroom, "Pa, how come you didn't call someone to repair the water heater? I can still smell the gas leaking." Right after shouting, she appeared wearing her bright yellow shower cap, leaving behind the dangers of a gas-filled room.

Sha-min suspiciously looked at his mother and asked, "Ma, didn't someone come to repair the water heater today?"

His mother tilted her head, thought for a second, and then slowly said, "Someone rang the doorbell."

"And then?"

His mother then emphatically pronounced the following, "I did not permit him in."

"Why didn't you let him in?" Sha-min asked with a frown, but then quickly relaxed his eyebrows.

His mother wriggled her shriveled, coarse lips and forced herself to look at him, as if she didn't want to, he felt. She said, "Could you have guaranteed that he wouldn't have taken anything of value?"

"The man at the appliance shop is a very good friend."

"A friend? It's a friend you have to be careful about," his mother stated with finality.

Yu-chin suddenly stood up. She didn't know why it was, but she was especially angry today. She couldn't put up with what Grandma had just said.

With unusual rancor, she yelled, "Why care about washing? We won't rot if we don't wash. This way we can save on water and electricity." She didn't know what she was talking about.

Hsiao-ching thought her mother was attacking her and she felt wronged. Her face became red in anger and she sharply shouted, "Who wants to be dirty like you? Why be so angry?"

Yu-chin was not to be stopped, "You're pretty. You're clean. Where do you think you came from?"

Hsiao-ching was left speechless standing by the wall, looking down at the tiled floor. Sha-min couldn't allow them to carry on like this. If this had happened in the past, he would enter the fray by hitting the table and starting to swear. But of course he couldn't do this now. Now his mother was present and there was no latitude for him to get angry. If his wife didn't have any restraint, at least he did. He checked his anger and said to Hsiao-ching, "Don't pick a fight with your mother." Then he said to his wife, "If we heat some water on the gas burner, everything will be alright. Why get so excited?"

Yu-chin sat down and continued eating what was left of her rice. Hsiao-ching started to heat a pan of water on the burner.

His mother didn't seem to have any opinion about the scene. After eating, she went to her room and locked the door.

Yu-chin threw her head on the table and cried. Sha-min moved over and patted her on the shoulders, comforting her by saying, "Forget about it. You've been working too hard and it's put you in a bad mood."

Yu-chin said, "I'm sorry. It wasn't intentional. It's really . . . " she didn't continue. Sha-min knowingly nodded and patted her shoulders.

A little later, Sha-min wanted to go see his mother. He knocked on her door, but she didn't pay any attention. Inside there was a low, scratchy sound of a radio. It sounded like a program of Peking Opera. Light was coming out from below the door. All along his mother never had a light on in her room, even at night. He didn't know why she had one on tonight. Obviously she hadn't gone to sleep yet and she seemed to be doing something. Still not being reassured, he knocked again on her door. The light suddenly disappeared. His mother's voice came through the scenic etching on the wooden door, "I'm going to sleep!" it sounded very crisp; going around the mountains and waters, it washed away the mountain mist and flew out from the door as a clear stream.

Five

Two weeks later on Sunday, they received an airmail package that had been sent from America by their son Hsiao-hang. Inside were four boxes of chocolate and a neatly wrapped harmonica. Sha-min was surprised to see this and opened the letter stuck between the boxes. A picture fell out. It was Hsiao-hang standing under a banyan tree on campus. He must have been very pleased with the picture. The letter read:

Dear Mother and Father,

Has Grandma been there for some time? How much I long to see my honorable Grandmother, that marvelous person you have said so much about. I imagine that she wants to see me, too, so I've sent a new picture of myself taken just for her. I especially selected a place under a banyan. Doesn't our old home in Hangchow have a dark green one?

I remember that you had said Grandma likes to play the harmonica, so I especially mail-ordered one to give to her to show my love and admiration. I hope that I can have my degree next year so that I can go back and hear her with my own ears play "Long Long Ago."

Of the four boxes of candy, one is for Grandma. It will melt in her mouth so will be easy to eat. Don't let my little sister steal it.

Are you all alright? I wish you all the best.

Your son,

Hsiao-hang

Sha-min reread the letter again and again and had it memorized. His face was beaming, and it lasted for a long time. His son wasn't that little and yet still wrote as a child. He didn't know that old people didn't dare eat chocolate. What was touching, however, was that he still remembered what his father had told him and his sister about the past. His sister wasn't as attentive. Sha-min held the harmonica in his hand, stroking it. It felt cold. He tried to play a few melodies. The bleak past circled through the cold sound of the harmonica, slowly spreading to the corners of the room.

It was almost dusk. The declining sun showered a bright red on the porch that lingered like mist around the row of potted plants. The flowers were all clothed in the red of the sunset. On the pavement scorched by the blistering sun someone on the floor below tossed out some water. The sky became darker, as if being covered by the shadow of a cloud. A breeze blew a few scrapes of white paper that landed on road. They seemed like the hemp hat of a person in mourning. The recitations of the breezes were the funeral cries along the road.

His mother was sitting in a rattan chair on the porch, wearing a bluish-green outfit Yu-chin had recently bought for her. The wind lightly stirred the strands of hair hanging by her cheeks. Sha-min sat to her left and read her the letter from Hsiao-hang.

His mother held the picture of Hsiao-hang and looked at it intently. A long while after he had finished reading the letter to her, she opened her mouth, "How old is Hsiao-hang?"

"Twenty-five."

Still looking at the picture, his mother said, "He looks very much like you did when you were young." She then added, "The feelings expressed in the letter are like yours, too."

He started to suspect that his mother kept a copy of the photo that he had preserved for over forty years. But he didn't dare ask her, fearing that his wishful thinking would be destroyed by her answer.

He pulled out the harmonica from his pocket and reaching over her slanted shoulders put it before her eyes, "Do you want to play it, Ma?"

"How could I? I've forgotten how to." His mother raised her hand to scratch behind her head and then placed it on her bluish-green pants. She was lost in her thoughts, staring into the distance. The setting sun glowed in her face highlighting her loose wrinkles, which were like rows of rivers flowing from her cheeks down to her neck and from there to her jacket, enveloping her body.

He placed the harmonica on his lips. It still had a cool feeling that seemed to awaken him. Unconsciously he started playing the tune he had long forgotten, "Long Long Ago." He drew out the easy melody. Bitterness and desolation filled the entire porch becoming entwined with the sunset, unable to be sorted out. He was telling a story . . . from long, long ago. Yes, from long, long ago . . .

His mother was apparently touched. Her tears sparkled in the sunset and fell from those small eyes surrounded by wrinkles. What was it that made a seventy-six-year-old cry? Shouldn't the ancient melody have been played through the harmonica? Did he disappoint her too much? Maybe, maybe his mother too was telling a story from long, long ago. He was sure, then he wasn't sure. His fingers that were holding the harmonica touched his cheeks. They were moist. The amber sunset was glowing. It was long, long ago . . .

He decided that he wanted to talk to his mother about that photo. Perhaps that night when he had seen the light beneath her door she had been carefully looking at that photo, admiring his heroic youthfulness. But what was before her now was an old man who was fat and had a head of graying hair.

The melody from the harmonica did not stop, it wad drawn out longer and longer. The unskillfulness. The desolation. So long, so long ago.

Geraniums

Billie Travalini

"All human nature vigorously resists grace because
grace changes us and the change is painful."
Flannery O'Connor, *The Habit of Being*

It was the summer the highway over the Oconee River was completed, Billy Bob Baker's still blew up, and Ruby Peale, curator of the Alexander H. Stephens Wax Museum, found the one thing she was missing her whole life.

Residents in the small town of Stephensville, Georgia, were warned not to park on Main Street so tourists who might want to take a break from their travels would feel welcome. Despite the temperature pushing ninety, no one minded the extra walking. But when three weeks had passed and no tourists showed up, some folks got to mumbling. Ruby was the first to go public.

"We need a sign," she said. "Then they'll come."

Ruby was almost sorry she said it when Mayor Grimes announced that the only way Stephensville could get a sign was for everyone to pitch in and pay for it. Ruby explained how she was an idea person, not a money person, and giving both was what she called "double dipping." Mayor Grimes said he didn't know what double dipping was, but he knew what money was, so he collected a lot of it and ordered a billboard. The billboard read, "Stephensville, Exit 7, Home of the Alexander H. Stephens Wax Museum," and had a picture of the former Vice-President of the Confederacy looking down on everybody.

On clear days folks would walk past the end of Main Street and keep walking until they caught a glimpse of the billboard above the highway. With right hands raised in salute, their eyes would brighten with thoughts of better days to come.

But weeks passed and not one tourist pulled off the highway to buy soda pop or gasoline or visit the museum with its four statues of Alexander H. Stephens, each in a different pose and with a different Civil War scene painted on the wall behind it. In front of each statue was a railing and a black button visitors could push to learn about the war and hear a woman in a high-pitch voice sing "Dixie." At the end of the railing, on easels in a place of honor, were genuine reproductions of two photographs taken by Matthew Brady himself. One showed the bird-thin Confederate Vice-President with his hands clasped in his lap and a firm look in his eyes. The other, taken after the war, was of an invalid and his faithful servant, Stephens, standing over him. Both shared the same name and wore fine clothes, only the servant was black and Mr. Stephens was pale as a bed sheet. On a third, larger easel was Stephens' famous Cornerstone speech in which he declared, "The Confederate government was founded upon the great truth that the negro is not equal to the white man; that slavery—subordination to the superior race—is his natural and normal condition."

Most of the younger generation preferred laughing and singing along with the woman with the high-pitch voice to looking at wax statues and reading.

"Racist," some school children remarked, and kept laughing.

"No respect," Ruby mumbled, as she steered them toward the gift shop where each morning she dusted and straightened rows of postcards and fold-up fans and coloring books with pictures of all four wax statues and war scenes.

If no visitors came at noon she would lock up and go next door to Hamilton's Café to use the restroom, order lunch, and talk to the regulars. Tammie Parker, who owned the town's only beauty shop and was a soloist at the First and Last Holy Child of God Emmanuel Baptist Church, always greeted Ruby as soon as she entered.

"More highway traffic every day," she would report and give the source of her update. "The paper . . . "

"Hogwash," Ruby interrupted. "Paper said Dewey won."

Tammie wanted to respond, but she knew Ruby would find some flaw in her argument to sound off about, so she reached for a menu and listened to Ruby talk about the importance of impartial and tedious documentation.

"Crazy Sadie . . . " That's all Tammy had to say to get Ruby off whatever she was talking about.

"Evil," Ruby said, as if that summed it all up.

"Amen," Tammie sang, in a voice more suited for a choir than ordinary conversation.

"And you?" Ruby said, directing her eyes at Earl Simms.

Earl, Stephensville's mailman, knew Ruby wasn't looking for an answer, so he shrugged his shoulders, ordered the ham and grits, and Tammy seconded it.

"Make that three." Betty Mae, Earl's wife, walked in with her voice raised almost as high as the hem on her skirt. "Any news, Ruby?" she added.

"Ask him."

Betty Mae looked at Earl as if somebody had suddenly switched his brain to the off position, then she looked at Ruby. "What's he know?"

"He delivers Crazy Sadie's mail. I reckon he has to know something."

Betty Mae kneed her husband good and hard. "You know something you ain't telling?"

Earl scooted his chair toward Ruby and said, "What was that for?"

"How dare you embarrasses me in public."

"You doing a right good job of that yourself."

Betty Mae caught hold of Earl's ear and began twisting.

"Calm down," Earl said, and undid her hand from his ear. "I never should have told you about seeing Crazy Sadie behind the still the day Billy Bob's leg flew through the night air like a burned out star looking for a place to land."

"Landed all right," Betty Mae said, and reached for Earl again, but he was too quick for her. "Another few inches it would've hit our sign, God have mercy."

"But it didn't."

"Almost did." Betty Mae passed Ruby a smile as she spoke.

Ruby nodded grudgingly. As the town's curator, she felt that it was it *her* job to know about Stephensville, and sharing that job just didn't set right with her.

"I need to get back to the museum," she said, and paid for her lunch and ran outside. "Busybodies," she mumbled, reminding herself to be extra vigilant.

Ruby lived at the bottom of Beeper Hill and Crazy Sadie at the top. In between them was what was left of Billy Bob's still and acres of trees and bushes so convoluting that rabbits had to hop extra high just to see where they were going. Sometimes the only way Ruby knew she had neighbors was when Earl delivered the wrong mail. On these occasions Ruby would steam open the envelopes to check if the name and address on the inside agreed with the name and address on the outside. Then she would press her thumb along the seal to make sure it didn't give her away.

After Earl was done eating and done delivering mail, he headed for Alexander's Bar, where he grinned his way back to childhood and a whole lot of other things he was looking for but couldn't quite name.

"Howdy." Honey smiled and poured a glass of whiskey.

"Howdy," he said.

"I said, "*Howdy.*"

"I heard you." Earl stopped when he saw Honey's eyes roll up into her head and her pencil-thin eyebrows roll down to meet them. He groaned, and took another drink.

Honey put a cigarette in her mouth and leaned over the bar for a light. Earl set her cigarette on fire and she took a deep breath and blew the smoke out slowly.

"Any news about . . . " She stopped short to focus on a stranger who had just walked in. "Get you something, handsome?" she said, and dropped her cigarette on the floor and killed it.

The stranger put two dollars on the bar. "Schaefer on tap."

Honey paused to wipe up an imaginary spill. "See our sign?" By her tone, the stranger knew that she was expecting a certain answer, so he gave it to her.

All he said was "yes," but that was enough to make Honey believe the solar system was suddenly in perfect alignment with the universe and Stephensville was destined for greatness.

"Ruby was right," she beamed. "Give 'em a sign and they'll come . . . just like in the Bible."

"Wasn't that Kevin Cosner?" Earl mumbled into his glass.

"He was quoting Jesus," Ruby said, shaking her head.

Earl paid his tab, and left.

The following day Betty Mae showed up at the museum at lunchtime and looked around real good.

"Honey says they're coming," she announced.

Ruby grabbed her purse and pushed Betty Mae to the door. "This job ain't as easy as it looks," she said, following Betty Mae outside and locking the door.

Betty Mae rolled her eyes but didn't say anything.

As they were approaching the café Ruby spotted Mayor Grimes coming toward them. Ruby walked as fast as she could but her words still got to the mayor before her feet did.

"Heard from Crazy Sadie?" she heard herself yell.

The mayor waited for her feet to catch up with her words before he answered.

"Talk to your friend," he said, and nodded at Betty Mae. "She's the expert."

Ruby squared her eyes at Betty Mae and snorted, "There is only room for one expert in this town."

Mayor Grimes raised his shoulders and let them drop with a sigh. "Good day ladies," he said, and tipped his hat and went on his way.

Ruby turned to Betty Mae. "If I remember correctly," she said, "*I am curator of the Alexander H. Stephens Wax Museum.*"

The following Friday Ruby sat on her porch staring at the road. A light breeze stirred the air and filled her nostrils with the sweet smell of whiskey.

She pinched her nostrils closed and quoted scripture to purify herself.

He shall know the truth and the truth shall set him free. This is what Ruby was saying when Betty Mae showed up with two Nehi orange sodas and a Kodak Instamatic camera. Ruby was more disappointed than surprised to see her, but she held onto her feelings like a general who doesn't want the enemy to know his plan. Ruby and Betty Mae were halfway through their soda when Ruby spotted a shiny black car stirring up dirt as it made its way past them doing about fifty.

Betty Mae sprung to her feet and snapped a picture. "I walk faster."

"Stay here," Ruby said, and put the camera in her skirt pocket. "You'll be the first to see the pictures."

Betty Mae protested but Ruby wouldn't budge.

"Stay here," Ruby repeated, and headed up the hill.

In a field halfway up the hill, on the backside of the burned-out still, she spotted geraniums with faces as round and wide as her own head. "Well, I'll be," she said, as small twigs crackled under foot. She stepped back and took a deep breath before moving forward. She was almost there. A little ways more she saw Crazy Sadie's house. On one side, long pine branches were clinging to loose shingles that a good sneeze could've shook off.

She slipped under the largest branch and put one foot in between two rows of geraniums and the other foot on the grass. Between her and the window was a four-foot statue of St. Francis of Assisi. She squatted and looked St. Francis in the eye. "Don't move," she mumbled, pressed her elbow into St. Francis' head, and leaned forward. The window was as choked with dirt as an old plow-horse, but when it came to seeing the truth, there wasn't anyone better at it than Ruby Pearle. Her eyes opened up that old house.

Standing next to Crazy Sadie was a man wearing a white shirt and tie and he was holding a leather folder of some sort. At first, Ruby thought he might be the stranger from the bar, but he was younger and had hair. She put her ear to the window.

"Open it." The stranger did as Sadie asked. Inside was a signed photograph of Abraham Lincoln to a Lieutenant John Stephens, and a handwritten note. The stranger studied each carefully, before he read the note aloud.

To the Hon. Alexander H. Stephens:
According to our agreement, your nephew, Lieutenant John Stephens, goes to you, bearing this note. Please, in return, to select and send to me, that officer of the same rank, imprisoned at Richmond, whose physical condition

most urgently requires his release.
Abraham Lincoln

"Your great, great granddaddy never gave his Uncle Alexander the note until after Mr. Lincoln was killed, and he almost wept reading it. You see they were friends. They respected each other; even the war didn't change that."

"No, schooling did."

"Folks believe what they want to believe."

"The stranger stared at the photograph and reread the note.

He paused to study the leather folder. "I see some initials."

"Should see three. AHS."

"How long you had all this?"

"Been in the family as long as I can remember."

The stranger slid the photograph and the note in the folder, and shook his head.

"And, not a mark on any of it."

"It's yours now. It's time."

"Aunt Sadie, you know how I feel about family, but . . . " He paused, this time as if he was thinking something over, and then he got to the point. " I saw uncle's picture on the highway; and, well, I think that was my sign to donate all this for the whole town to enjoy."

Ruby saw Sadie shake her head. "Whatever you want," she said, finally. "But, I don't want any fuss. Send them to Ruby Pearl at the museum . . . anonymously. I mean it. No fuss."

In the back of Ruby's head, she was seeing the photograph, note, and case in a lighted display case where the troublesome slave speech had once sat.

"Praise God," she whispered and kissed St. Francis on the lips before heading down Beeper Hill. Suddenly, she remembered Betty Mae's camera. She raised it to her face. Through the viewfinder she could see Sadie and the stranger. Ruby poised to take a picture but she never did. She opened the camera and exposed the film to the sun. Above the trees Stephensville's sign stood watch over the town.

In her mind's eye, Ruby saw dozens of motorists getting off Exit 7 to visit the museum to see a signed photograph of Abraham Lincoln and a note he wrote to Alexander H. Stephens himself.

"Ruby . . . Ruby Pearle." It was Earl's voice. In her excitement, Ruby had forgotten all about him delivering the mail. She took a deep breath and put a smile on her face. Then, with impartial and tedious documentation, she began to do what she did best. She added a little color here and there until her story about Crazy Sadie's visitor from The International Society of Pelargonium Growers sounded perfect.

Humble, Arkansas

Jay Jennings

The ball sang from his hand. Projected like a voice, it fought the resistance of air against its seam, stitched and red and raised like a healing wound, and jumped and wavered on its way to the catcher's mitt. A violent and beautiful act. So rarely hit, when he was young. His mother sang too, at the piano in the living room as she played. I'd sung with her there after dinners. His hands were hers, the long fingers easily spanning more than an octave, made for music but put to other more acceptable and domestic uses in the provinciality of that small Southern town: guiding cloth through a machine, the needle plunging and puncturing, repeatedly, too fast to see, dangerous but in the service of binding.

As the doctor in Humble, I knew both their hands well. First, Mary's, when she was distracted once and the plunging needle found her finger, driving straight through the nail, glancing off the bone. The machine's motor stalled in a whine. Her husband, Roy, broke the needle off from its brace, wrapped her hand in the muslin curtain she was stitching and drove her to my office. I gently raised the folds of the blood-stained covering and saw the pierced finger lying in its shroud, like some medieval religious relic, both beautiful and horrific. Of course it was only horrific to them, but as a doctor, your necessary objectivity can open a door to terrible beauty as well. Since you're trained not to think about the pain but the problem, aesthetic appreciation can fill the place of empathy.

Removing the needle was not an easy task, and though the pain must have been intense, she never parted her lips during its withdrawal.

Her son, Bert, had his share of boyish cuts requiring my needle and thread. Confident of his athletic ability from a young age, he'd once tried in a game of chase to hurdle a barbed-wire fence. His trailing knee caught a prong, which opened a three-inch gash. Again, in a pickup game of basketball in the gym of First Baptist, he'd made a layup and his elbow came down on a protruding counter connecting the gym and the kitchen, usually covered with a pad but not for this unofficial game. Twelve stitches he'd needed, but not in his pitching arm, his left. And worst, finding a Japanese soldier's sword from World War II deep in a cluttered closet in the garage of their house, he'd unsheathed it and run his thumb along its blade to test the sharpness. When the flesh opened and the blood sought the air, surprisingly, even to himself, he didn't stop, but abstractedly continued cutting into the thick flesh at the base of the thumb, flirting with the veins of his wrist. He was fourteen then. That was his left hand and ended his baseball season, during which the superiority of his skill was already beginning to show. He seemed relieved when I gave him the word that he'd play no more that year. At home he used his bandaged hand to turn the pages of his mother's music as she sang.

No one seems to have asked him why he had done it, except me. He'd told everyone else that the sword had slipped from his hand, but the angle of the lacerations on the thumb's ball and base weren't consistent with that story. He shrugged when I asked, seemingly puzzled himself about his motivations. But he added, "Please don't tell, Dr. Moore." I nodded that I would not.

No one pursued it further, since a boy is going to get into things and could hardly be expected to leave aside a sword from halfway around the world, especially one that had possibly severed the head of an American soldier. Discovering it there in the back of the closet in the garage, leaning in the corner anachronistically with a fishing rod and a canoe paddle, Bert could hardly be blamed for constructing a hormone-fueled boy's story in which his father, part of a lone platoon in hand-to-hand with the dirty Japs, watches a screaming ninja lop off the head of his buddy and, overcome by grief and anger, leaps to avenge his death, snatching the sword from its startled owner's hand and in a swift baseball swing slicing the Nip in two at the waist with his own instrument. What son, upon finding something so exotically out of character with his taciturn father, a mere roofer in a small town in Arkansas, would not turn the man into some heroic figure. Or so I imagine.

I knew different about the provenance of the sword. Roy had actually bought it at a pawn shop near the air base in Laredo, Texas, in 1944. We'd been stationed together there. During the war, he'd typed for an officer, like a secretary. He'd wanted badly to fly, to see action over the Pacific, but his office skills were valued by the commander. He chafed at his deskbound post. His best friend had been killed in a training crash. His cousin had been blinded in Belgium when he opened the hatch of his tank to have a look around at the same time a mortar struck. At Humble High, Roy had taken a typing class at the insistence of his mother, who thought he should acquire some practical skills, and it had been the most practical one; it had saved his life, by keeping him at the typewriter keys and out of a cockpit.

He'd played for the base fast-pitch softball team and been a star. He'd thrown a no-hitter in the South Texas interbase championship of 1944. The competition was heated. Though many able-bodied men were on ships in the Pacific or on the fields of Europe, plenty of great athletes remained on bases. Major-leaguers and college stars serving their hitch. And any number of high-school heroes. (I was not one of them, my flat feet and bookishness marking me for other pursuits.) They had specialties of one sort or another that kept them at home while their buddies were dying abroad. Mechanics, radio operators, accountants. I'd done pre-med before being mustered, so I helped the camp doctor. Held his clipboard while he examined the boys. Colds, blisters, headaches, the occasional broken bone from a training mishap. We heard of the horrors of the front but were about as far away from it as you could get there on the Texas-Mexico border. Playing our base games and upbraiding malingerers. It was a not unpleasant way to spend the war.

I was a couple of years older than Roy. His family lived in the hollow, on the road to the sawmill, where his father worked. Mine was the bank president. I lived in the Hill section of town where the historic Victorian houses of the old planters and plantation owners stood at the top of curving walkways, great magnolia trees with their broad, waxy leaves in the lawns. From the widow's walks that many of them had, including ours, you could see the rapids of the Pike River gleaming white in the Southern Arkansas sun.

One Saturday afternoon at the base in July of '44, when it was too hot to do anything but keep still, Roy came by my bunk, where I was reading Zola's *The Country Doctor.* I was making my way through doctor books and had polished off Chekhov already, but was not yet familiar with Celine.

"You want to fly down to Rio for a cerveza, doc?" he asked me.

"Sure," I said.

"Flying down to Rio" meant going to Nuevo Laredo, a counterintuitive name, since you'd think the newer Laredo would be on the north side of the river rather than in the old country. But it also had another connotation, one which Zola would have appreciated. It was a given, especially on a Saturday, that after the cerveza would come the puta. We took the bus across the new, modern International Bridge, which seemed hyperbolic at this time of year over the mostly dry bed of the Rio Grande. At an outdoor café in the main square of the town, we cooled our hands on a couple of sweating bottles. We turned away a gordo whore who assured us she could take us both to places gringos had never been.

"I've never been to hell, but I don't particularly want to go there either," Roy said to me after she left.

Even under the shade of the awning, our khaki shirts soon grew moons of sweat under the arms. Another beer appeared, gleaming, golden.

"*Yo soy Luz,*" a voice behind us said and we turned our heads to see what was on offer. She was standing between us, not with the cocked hip of the other whores but straight with her hands at her sides, her very posture a rebuke of her profession. She was small. When we turned we didn't have to look up at her. Her straight black hair bore none of the rosette pins the others used to affect sophistication. Her teeth tumbled together like a pile of the ivory dominoes the locals slapped on the tin tables of the café.

"You speak English?" Roy asked.

"If you want I should."

We all flinched a little at another metallic report of a domino slap, the table's ring echoing off the stucco walls of the square, followed by shouts of victory and groans from the defeated. I thought of how dominos were best-known for a purpose other than the game they were intended for. You stood them on end, precariously, painstakingly, and tipped one to start the chain, all falling. A kids' game, before the dots on them made sense, and money changed hands over them.

"How old are you?" Roy asked Luz.

"*Tiene veintiuno años,*" she answered.

Roy laughed at the absurdity and looked at me. "She's of age." He raised his eyebrows and nodded toward me in a question he didn't have to ask.

"No," I said. "You go ahead."

"Your friend need a friend?" she asked him, then turned to look at me. She remained stiff between us, not mussing our brilliantined hair as the others did in the parody of seduction.

"No. *Gracias,*" I said.

Soon, after they left, one of the teenage boys who'd been raising dust in a game of soccer came over to retrieve an errant ball, which had rolled at my feet. I leaned over to pick it up, and as I handed the ball back to him, he dropped a small, dirty card in my lap. Shortly after, I found the address printed on the card, the only words on it.

Roy and I met up back at the same café and had another beer. We didn't mention what we'd done, but instead talked about the Cardinals. The baseball loyalties of the state of Arkansas lay with St. Louis. It was the closest major-league franchise to the state, and the minor league team was in Little Rock, but most important, in our youth, the Dean brothers, Dizzy and Daffy, from tiny Lucas, had all the boys in the state hoping they'd one day wear that uniform with the birds perched on either end of the bat. That the Gashouse Gang could be led by two brothers from a town that made Humble look like Paris and that someone from our backward state could be a world champion of anything was a source of hope for us all. By July of 1944, the Deans had retired, but we hitched ourselves to Stan Musial, Marty Marion and the rest of the Redbirds who succeeded them. And in that town square in another country, as the dusky boys kicked a makeshift ball in the dirt and their fathers clanged dominoes on the table, we talked of the American game, envisioning its green diamonds and straight lines and reciting its talismanic numbers as easily as Bible verses.

"Stan went three for four yesterday," said Roy, reading from the box score in the paper. "He's now up to .337."

" . . . and Marion?" I asked, not because I cared so much, but because I liked to hear Roy talk about it, the only thing he was voluble about.

A lock of his black hair fell forward as he looked down at the paper and he smoothed it back with the flat of his hand.

"Marion went 0 for 3 with a walk, scored a run. Batting ahead of Musial, you'll score a lot of runs. They're already up ten games on the Pirates. I don't see anybody catching 'em." He tipped back his beer to finish it, the muscles in his neck as perfect as those in the anatomy books (or the art history books, for that matter) I'd studied at Yale.

"I saw Musial play once," said Roy. "Three years ago, his rookie year. My pap drove us down to Shreveport, where the Cardinals were making their way north after spring training, playing exhibition games. You could get up real close in this dinky stadium. When he was in the on-deck circle, I went down to the rail. I wasn't but six feet from him, I swear. His swing, even in practice, was the sweetest thing you ever saw. He looked like he didn't hear anything or see anything else, but just his body moving through air. He created this little space for himself with his swing that was only his space, that nobody else could enter. It was like, it was like . . . " he looked up beyond the ochre façade of the church across the square to the eternity of Mexican sky, "it was like . . . seeing some god's blessing the way he swung that bat, the way Jesus, you know, might have cast the nets into the sea. Some perfect motion." He paused and brought his eyes back to earth. "How often do we get to see that? Before you lift the hatch of a tank and a shell blows up in your face?" He brought the bottle to his mouth again and tipped it back almost violently but there was nothing left in it. Empty of weight against expectation, it fooled his hand and he brought it down too hard on the tin table. The domino players looked over.

"Let's go," he said and stood up and carelessly tossed a pocketful of worthless pesos on the table so they rolled and vibrated in different pitches even after we'd walked away.

We left the square and wandered the side streets. We passed the place where I'd been with the boy, the upstairs window of the room now filled with the hamhock forearms, square, creviced chest, and ebony-haired, flat-faced head of a woman. The boy's mother? Did she know what he was up to? Did my pesos help to put food on the table? This line of thought allowed me to assuage some of my guilt.

On the corner the familiar tripartite balls of a pawnbroker hung like moons of another planet. We paused and looked in the window at the guitars, horns, tambourines, phonographs, pocket watches and firearms. Lying in the case at the very front, as if a smile on the face of the display, was the curved glinting silver of a sword, resting on its wooden scabbard. Its handle was inlaid with a flower pattern, in ivory I guessed, the delicate pink of a cherry blossom tree in bloom. Its hilt, on the handle side, bore the tarnish of use, likely from the sweat of its owner's grip.

Lookit that," said Roy. "You think that's a real Jap sword?"

"Seems to be, not that I would know."

"Let's go in and ask about it."

The jingle of the bell on the door alerted the counterman. He came out from behind a curtain that led to a back room. His teeth and his shirt were both a bleached white, contrasting with the swarthy face.

"Welcome, señor U.S.A." he said. "Good customer from base. Many come. You have items for money?"

"No," said Roy. "I'm interested in that sword in the window."

"Very fine item. Not be disappointed," the man said in his pawnbroker's litany and walked behind the counter to the window to retrieve it.

He placed it gently on the glass.

"Soldier like you brought in. Back from Japan. Enemy sword. Impress the ladies. Tell them you kill Jap and take from him." He winked at Roy.

Roy picked it up by the handle and pointed it up. It was a thing of beauty, thick layers of metal compressed into a graceful curve and honed to imperial sharpness. He gently touched the blade edge with his free hand.

"That's sharper than a Bowie knife," he said. "Feel."

He turned it blade up for me. I tapped my forefinger lightly on the edge.

"You could do surgery with that," I said.

"Or some serious amputation," he said.

Roy placed it back on the counter. The handle's design interested me more, the flower's pink delicacy. What was the thinking behind such adornment?

"How much?" said Roy.

"What you think it worth?" said the counterman.

"I'll give you twenty dollars for it."

"Ancient beautiful weapon."

"Twenty-five and that's it. You aint gonna unload this thing for more than that. Not in this godforsaken place."

The counterman shrugged and reached out his hand to Roy to shake. Roy then removed a money clip from his front pocket and peeled off a twenty and a five. The counterman slid the sword into the wooden scabbard and handed it to Roy.

"Very fine item," he said. "Not be disappointed."

Commanding officers during the war years competed for high caliber ballplayers on their base sports teams as fiercely as any major league owner. With so many professionals on active duty, some of the military teams rivaled those in the National and American leagues. The Great Lakes Naval Base team even defeated the Chicago Cubs in an exhibition and racked up a record of 72-7 during the summer of 1943. Players like Musial and Ted Williams served their hitches, and though they also flew heroic combat missions, they kept their athletic skills honed on the fields at home too. COs often made "trades" to reassign players to their command. So interbase games between the best teams had the air of big events.

It was in this rarefied athletic atmosphere that Waco came to Laredo for a game. Our base didn't have a full-fledged baseball team but we did play fast-pitch softball. Waco was stocked with stars and had agreed to play softball instead since we'd be at a distinct disadvantage in skill playing small ball.

A crowd of 2,500 raucous servicemen, most no more than boys like us, filed into the stadium at Laredo City Park on that surprisingly temperate late summer Saturday in August. We slapped and pushed and tripped each other, giddy to be off the base. We whistled at the señoritas who came to the park and we hoped the kids they swung there were nieces and nephews and not their own.

When our mates took the field, we stood and cheered like banshees. Roy calmly walked to the mound, seemingly shutting out everything around him. I'd seen the intensity of this focus, the unwavering concentration that could bring both frightening self-involvement and a saving selflessness. On the shooting range, no one could match his barrel-sighting stillness. If the task was to rescue a fallen fellow in a training exercise, his unblinking execution spread confidence in his platoon. And even as he typed, someone approaching the office might have to knock three times before he'd stop the clattering of keys and answered.

Now on the mound, the small-town stadium humming with energy, he took his warm-up pitches, the swift sweep of his arm from front to back through the 360 degrees a blurred, speeded clock-hand, the ball flying out at the six o'clock position by his thigh to land in the catcher's mitt as if it were pulled back there by an elastic cord.

Roy wore his shirt cut above the biceps in the style made popular by the Cardinals' Frankie Frisch. He thought the exposure of almost the entire arm, the corded muscle's piston of pitching, proved both intimidating and distracting to a batter, and a pitcher needed every advantage. The umpire ordered play to begin, and the sling and pop of the pitch and catch ended.

Roy's whirling delivery crossed up the Waco players. They were used to seeing a ball come overhand, and even though the softball was much bigger, its approach from the low angle, rising into the strike zone, threw off their timing. In the field, the unfamiliar size and weight of the ball led to fielding errors. After five innings, we were leading 3-2, and they were growing more and more frustrated. The flasks had come out in the stands and the alcohol loosened the lips of our fellows, yelling themselves red-faced.

Amid this Roy remained an island of calm on the mound, the still hub of spinning spokes. With each rotation of his arm and missed swing of the Waco players, the anticipation of an upset grew. In the bottom of the fifth, Martinez, a generally shunned Dominican known for fighting on the base, tattooed a two-run home run to right to give us a 5-2 lead. The dugout emptied to meet him at home plate, except for Roy, who remained on the bench with his right arm through one sleeve of a jacket, and the rafters of the little stadium shook with the sound of our celebrating. A few bottles flew from the crowd, and the CO called for order over the PA. We were giddy with the spoils of apparent victory over long odds.

The lead held into the top of the ninth as a breeze blew in from the north. A rumble of thunder in the distance augured a coming storm. Roy would face the heart of the Waco order, the three, four and five hitters, all of whom had spent time in the minors. In these late months of the war, in the late bloom of our youth, in the late innings of a summer game, we saw hope in Roy's bare arm. We felt we might soon return home, to our towns and our girls, spitting the metallic taste of war out of our mouths. I would go back to school and dissect nameless cadavers to learn the raw material of which we are made with the ultimate aim of healing. A wind caught some of the dirt of the bare infield and collected it in a miniature wave that swept from first to third. The players shielded their eyes. The wind died and the dirt settled. We all stood.

Roy's arm whipped the ball to the catcher, and the batter swung and missed, twisting himself like a balsa-plane rubberband. We roared when he repeated the motion twice more and returned to the dugout. The cleanup hitter was a big-boned slugger, the first three buttons of his shirt undone, the bat as light in his hands as a conductor's baton.

We brought our army-issue brogans down on the concrete bleacher floor in a rhythmic three-step stomp that shook the stadium. Some rattled the folding seats with their hands in the same rhythm. We were a raucous symphony of noise.

The cleanup hitter pointed his bat at Roy for a still five seconds and then let it swing back, catching it with his right hand as a trapeze artist might catch a partner. The bat nervously twitched next to his head. Roy's first pitch came in low. Past the center field fence in the distance, dirty clouds moved slowly toward us. How far away they were was impossible to tell in the expanse of a flat Texas landscape. Whether they might miss the field altogether was unpredictable. Another ball went low, and we nervously looked at each other in the stands. Was Roy losing strength, his ball failing to rise? The batter stepped out of the box with his left foot, keeping his right anchored. He seemed to have more confidence when he stepped back in.

Roy wound and fired. The batter turned on the pitch and sent a hard grounder to Reinhardt at third, who bobbled the ball, which popped out of his glove as he brought it up to throw. It hung directly in front of his face for a seemingly gravity-defying time, making from my vantage point a surrealist painting of a man with a ball for a head. He finally snatched it from the air and threw to first, just ahead of the lumbering slugger. Two out.

In the playground past right field, the mothers or aunts, with sweeping hand motions, began to herd the children from the swings and slides as the clouds moved closer. The momentum of their play left phantoms continuing their games, swaying the swingsets' long chains ending in the U of the rubber seats and keeping the carousel spinning riderless. A sudden crack of thunder sent them running for their cars and startled us in the stands into jostling hilarity at our own jumpiness.

The next batter, the scrappy second baseman, stepped in quickly. He didn't want the rain, if and when it came, ending the game without a fight. And Roy wanted to complete the job he'd begun. With this right hand, he tugged at what remained of his right sleeve and took in and expelled a deep breath, the ball lodged in his glove. He met it there with his right hand and began the whipsaw motion. The batter swung, missing the rising ball by what looked like a foot. An artificial dark began to move over the field with the clouds. The moistening air carried a smell of honeysuckle, which climbed the fences of the park.

Roy set himself and hurled the next pitch. The batter got under it and popped it back, but it fell into the dirt behind home plate before the catcher could scramble to it. Strike two.

One or two drops began to strike the dusty infield, big drops that made an audible slap and raised a puff as they hit. Roy looked up, almost angrily,

I thought, willing the sky to hold off until he finished. He looked in toward home plate and wound up and fired the pitch from his seemingly spring-loaded arm. The batter, having learned from the previous two pitches, started his swing higher and connected, but he chopped down on the ball and it bounced in front of the mound once right into Roy's waiting glove. He caught it, pounded it once into his glove and threw overhand, the first time all day, to first, to end the game.

As the players on the field converged on Roy, the rain came harder, darkening the infield with wet splotches. We rushed from the stands to join the celebration, the railing a spillway of khaki as we hopped over it onto the field. A thunderclap shuddered the air and sheets of water began to fall. We quickly abandoned the field and headed for the waiting school buses, our dirt-colored uniforms soaked dark as the ground we left behind. I found Roy and, as we moved en masse to the parking lot, grabbed his right hand with my right and his bare right elbow with my left hand. I held it there for a moment, the forearm muscles twitching from the exertion of the day. Then I looked into his cobalt eyes. He winked at me and we trotted to the bus.

Water once dripping as now from our arms.

A summer Sunday in 1939 after church. Roy, his brother Kenneth, and I were milling around outside First Methodist while our mothers and other members of the altar guild tended to the sanctuary, folding altar cloths, removing numbers from the hymnal boards. Our fathers were chatting with Rev. Flemming and some of the other parishioners. We'd removed our ties, a once-a-week novelty, as soon as we were out the door and we flicked them at each other halfheartedly, more out of the memory of what we'd done for many Sundays when younger than because we liked the game today. Kenneth was my age, seventeen, and we knew each other from the high school but generally spoke only after church. He ran with a different crowd, one that got suspended that year for throwing dice against the playground wall during lunch break. As my parents never ceased to remind me, I was their representative in the community; no matter where I was, my conduct reflected on the family, so I avoided disgracing them with such actions.

I was itching for a cigarette, and when I put two fingers to my lips in question, we all wandered around the side of the church, where Kenneth produced a pack from deep in his baggy trousers' pocket. Lanky and bony, his mouth a knife slit, Kenneth moved with a kind of mechanical angularity. Though two years younger, Roy was as tall and more fully muscled, his face more open, even his casual leaning against the white clapboard wall hinting at a graceful comfort with his body. I was shorter and pudgier than both of the Askew boys, and Kenneth had to bend down considerable to light my cigarette for me.

"Didn't know you smoked, Moore," Kenneth said.

"Just took it up recently. After swim season." I was an unspectacular but effective breaststroker on the high school team.

"Hell to pay if your folks catch you, right Ned?" enjoined Roy, knowing my parents were pillars of the community.

"Frankly, my dear, I don't give a damn," I Gabled. *Gone with the Wind* had been playing at our movie house, The Palace, for weeks. They both laughed. Kenneth took off his beaten fedora and wiped his forehead with a handkerchief.

"I could use a swim today," Roy said. "You want to go up to the bauxite pits?"

"I'm beat," said Kenneth. He was working for the summer at the saw mill and his hands, even with the protective gloves the company provided, were speckled with thin gouges of red from the splinters.

"What about you, Moore? You up for a swim? If you can't go, I can't, since I'm still a year away from driving."

"Why not . . . " I said.

"Come by at one."

I got use of the car whenever I wanted it because I was good, just not as good as my parents suspected. The 1937 Pontiac De Luxe was not an ostentatious car, a family kind of car, but its like rarely went down into the part of town where the Askews lived. There was nothing wrong with their house or their neighborhood but there was an accepted dividing line between high and low in Humble, one that church could bridge on Sundays but which was more difficult to span the rest of the week. Most of the cars there at the curb in the Hollow were several model years older than those in the Hill section or the vehicles were trucks that betrayed the manual labor of the owner: a blacksmith's flatbed laden with iron bars and anvils, an electrician's truck dangling multicolored cables and clamps.

When I pulled up in front of the modest house on Cedar (all the streets in this part of town were named for native trees), the car drew a few stares from the kids playing in the yards. Roy loped out to meet me before I could honk. His black hair, slicked back, shone like the polished fender of the Pontiac.

"Let's roll," he said, as the heavy door swung shut behind him of its own weight.

As we sped up Highway 67 Roy picked a cigarette from a pack stashed in his breast pocket and tamped it down on the dashboard. He offered me one, but I shook my head. I was not a confident driver and liked to keep my hands at ten and two. He then scraped a wooden match across the dashboard, leaving a mark before lighting his smoke and flicking the match out the window. I reached over and tried to rub away the sulfur line he'd made.

"Sorry," he said.

Bauxite mining gouged huge pits in the land which filled with water when it rained. Steam shovels scooped the silty soil into their jaws and dumped it in open cars on a little railway that transported them into the plant for refining into aluminum. Everybody told you how dangerous the bauxite pits were, and that's why you went. I'd never been before but had heard stories of the disorienting qualities of the water there.

We cruised through the sleepy company town, unimaginatively or promotionally named Bauxite, to the edge of the property of Arkansas Mining and Refining Co. We walked along the chain-link fence until we found the gap our friends had told us about and we squeezed through, pausing for possible guard dogs, more perhaps out of our impression from prison movies than because of any real suspicion. The property was too vast for such a patrol, and who was going to steal a raw, unrefined mineral anyway? No dogs appeared, and we hunched along, pausing every so often to make sure the coast was clear.

Shortly, we reached the edge of a huge crater, a sheer thirty-foot cliff at our feet above an expanse of water as big as a lake. Rust-colored mounds the size of houses surrounded us as if we were on the surface of Mars. The water below, reflecting the relentless Sunday sun on a windless day, was an inviting though unnatural blue. Birds wheeling overhead appeared mirrored on the surface of the water, as real in their reflections as they were in the sky. Looking strangely down at the sky, I felt a surge of vertigo and began to sway.

Roy threw out his right arm across my chest to keep me from falling forward, as my father would have if we were in the car making a sudden stop. Though the force was not great, I stumbled back and fell flat on my ass.

"You're supposed to dive in, not fall in, dumbass," said Roy, not unaffectionately. He turned back around to finish his cigarette, and where I sat, I kicked off my shoes and removed my socks (which I placed carefully in the shoes), pulled my shirt and t-shirt over my head, and unbuckled my belt, letting my trousers fall as a I stood up, so only my jockey shorts remained. Then, without thinking too much, overcoming a common fault of mine, I took three steps and jumped. I saw myself on the glassy water plummeting toward myself. I plunged in with my arms pinwheeling, as they had been all the way down, to keep me from rotating onto my back or stomach. I was proud of my daring but embarrassed by my lack of grace.

When I rose again to the surface, I shook my hair out of my face and looked up at the cliff. It appeared Roy had shed all his clothes, even his undershorts, which I took to mean he was going to dive in head first instead of jump, since the force of entry in a dive would have ripped them from him anyway. I swam to a lower bank to get out of his way and to watch. He stepped back several yards and launched himself forward out from the cliff in a swan dive, arms extended in a horizontal crucifixion floating free against the sky. Above him a hawk or some other bird of prey circled. He rotated subtly as gravity took hold, bringing his hands together and entering the water arrowlike, with a small splash.

The danger, I'd heard, wasn't in jumping from the cliff but in the character of the water itself. The pits were deep enough for diving from any height, but even just a few feet under the surface, the water was so opaque from the reflective properties of the bauxite, you could barely see anything. After Roy's dive, I watched the water smooth over, wondering where he would arise. He was playing some game, I thought, perhaps popping up right next to me and scaring me. In another few seconds, I began to worry, as is my nature. A cloud came into focus on the water's surface, and the hawk—or whatever it was—circled the cloud. Roy did not reappear.

I dived into the water where Roy had gone in, suspecting the worst: perhaps spinning at the end of the dive, which took him deep, and lost in the opacity of the water, he'd become disoriented. I frogmanned farther into the spot, and within seconds, I saw him swimming in a panicked way toward what he imagined was the surface, but was actually in the opposite direction. Suddenly, he stopped, or I never would have caught him, and I grabbed his foot. He struggled and kicked for a moment but I held on until he realized who had him. I then manacled his right wrist with my hand. By that time I'd lost my bearings, too, in the glimmery dark. No light betrayed the surface, so I employed a trick I'd heard to make swimming there safer. I opened my mouth and let out an air bubble. I was surprised to see it travel, not past my nose and forehead in the direction I'd assumed was the surface, but the other way past my chest and feet. Still holding Roy's arm, I turned and followed the bubble's path.

We broke the surface, both nearly bursting for air, and paddled exhausted for the lowest point of the shore. Like the ancient amphibious creatures in our biology textbooks emerging from the primordial muck, we dragged ourselves onto the soft soil bank and collapsed on our backs, our chests heaving, the struggle of our breath the only thing breaking the silence of an industrial day of rest.

I turned my head to look at where Roy lay panting, an arm over his eyes against the sun. His body was hairless, except for the dark patch at the root of his cock. Something stirred in mine, twitching against my soaked briefs, which were warming and steaming slightly in the sun's condensing heat. It was a feeling I didn't want to acknowledge, so I spoke.

"You're supposed to swim to the surface, not the bottom, dumbass," I said.

He grabbed a handful of dirt and hurled it at me. "Now I suppose it'll be all over school that you saved my life."

I could tell he was sincerely worried by the idea.

"I won't tell," I said, with the moral certainty that only a seventeen-year-old can muster. "This is just between us."

"Hey!" a voice from the cliff called out to us. Silhouetted against the sky was the outline of a state trooper, his distinctive hat a halo around his head and his arms on his hips.

I rolled over and stood up and offered my right hand to Roy as both a pledge and a pulley. He clasped it and rose and we both ascended to face our punishment.

High hilarity and celebration, mixed with the smell of damp, starchy cloth and remoistened hair tonic, filled the team bus, which I had slipped onto. Roy was the center of the festivities, as the players recounted crucial moments on the game, many of which featured him. Martinez now took shots to the shoulder in comradeship rather than fisticuffs. The nonplayers brought out their flasks, and we passed them around and emptied them of the little that remained. A festive Saturday night and perhaps another trip to the cantinas of Nuevo Laredo were ahead, but not for me, as I had duty.

By the time we reached the base, the storm had passed over (we drove through it in the opposite direction). We debouched at the gate and scattered to our various quarters and assignments. We stepped lightly in the triumph of our youth. I showered and shined my shoes and headed over to the mess for a bite before reporting to the sick ward.

On my way, I noticed that over by one of the fences, around a big weeping willow tree, there was some kind of disturbance going on, shielded from my view by a crowd of khaki. I almost ignored it since I was hungry and figured I'd both hear about it later and perhaps be tending the cuts of the participants at the base hospital. I wondered if it was Martinez, back in fighting form so soon after his glory. But something strange was going on. The thin, curving branches of the willow, which cascaded up and then down like a fountain, were twitching above the heads of the line of soldiers, who were strangely silent. There was no cheering as there usually was during a fistfight.

I walked over and pushed through the crowd, my status as a pseudo-doctor allowing me some authority to do so. When I finally reached the front, I could see a man, partially obscured by the drooping branches of the tree. His breathing was loud, heaving, and he was simply standing there, with the crowd giving him lots of room. Just then, he whirled, and in the fading light I saw a glint of metal slice through the branches, which fell to reveal Roy, still in his softball uniform and holding in two hands the Japanese sword. He spun into motion again, swinging at the branches, which scattered around his feet. Loose leaves helicoptered to the ground more slowly. He swung again, carving another blank space in the willow's curtain.

A jeep pulled up with a skid, and an MP, his concave cheeks dotted with acne, pushed past me. He unsnapped his holster and put his hand on his gun.

"Roy," I called out. He turned and looked at me, dropping the sword to his side but still holding onto it with both hands. Others had called his name, but perhaps my voice, being long familiar, being of the tenor and pitch of his home, found him through whatever hazy anguish he was feeling. "Stop. Give it to me. Then we'll make everything all right."

He seemed to hear me. He looked me in the eye. Then he looked at the sword and dropped his left hand from its handle. I took a step. He extended the handle toward me, but as he did, he seemed to notice that the point was directed at his stomach in the position of what we'd all come to know in the years since Pearl Harbor as the prelude to hara-kiri. He tested the point for a moment just below the number sixteen of his uniform. "Roy," I said. "Don't be a dumbass."

He looked up at the branches of the ruined tree, and his eyes and mouth collapsed toward each other, drawn as if by a string, in a rictus of some pain, but the point of the sword remained unthrust. He tossed the sword toward me and it clanged on the dirt. I went closer to him and embraced him.

He pulled a telegram from the back pocket of his wool baseball uniform pants. "They got him, Ned," he said. "They got Kenneth."

FALLING

Egoyan Zheng

Translated by Laura Jane Wey

My cousin and her husband have come by to drink to everyone at our table.

This is my older cousin's wedding banquet. The entire banquet hall is chaotic, like the passenger cabin of an aircraft just before takeoff. Probably because I was late, I got ushered to this table as soon as I arrived, and so I find myself sitting among "friends and relatives" whom I don't even know. Of the twelve people at the table, I only recognize my younger cousin. (It's odd; why is the bride's younger sister stuck at a table like this?) When I noticed her, my first instinct was to greet her. But she immediately turned her head to the side.

Here we are, sitting awkwardly at the same table. During the entire course of the banquet we have been trying hard to avoid each other's eyes. We are constantly looking in different directions like two broken weathervanes, and when our eyes meet by accident, we try to keep them unfocused, pretending not to have seen each other.

Until now, when my older cousin arrives for the toast.

Now my cousin, clad in bridal white, has come to drink a toast to us. Her face is covered in a layer of makeup thick as whitewash. Her movements seem rather stiff and unnatural, but perhaps that is because her formal attire is constraining. On the other hand, she does not appear to be at all shy about showing off her social adeptness (even though she knows very well that her smoothness is surpassed by the awkward estrangement between us). She makes a special point of raising her glass to me, saying with a smile, "Don't be shy, my dear cousin. It will be your turn next year. You know, we're all here today only because we missed that flight . . . "

Missed that flight? What does she mean?

Snap. (Snow-blindness.)

That was when I was eight years old.

As a special celebration for my grandmother's sixtieth birthday, the entire clan arranged to go on a carefully coordinated big trip together. Almost everyone on my dad's side of the family (my father, his two older brothers, his younger brother, and his sister) set aside what they had to do to take part in it. We purchased a total of twenty-two tickets on a night flight to Japan; however, just before our departure, news came that Grandma had suffered a stroke. All of us hurried to the hospital to see Grandma, and, upon arrival, we saw in the TV news up in her room that there had been an air disaster. The plane we were supposed to have been on had crashed into the sea midway, and there were no survivors among the two hundred and thirty-seven passengers and the crew. Grandma's sudden illness had, by a strange twist of fate, saved my entire extended family. Nobody knew whether to be glad or sad at the time . . .

So that was how it came about that my older cousin and I even lived to be old enough to marry and have wedding banquets.

When we were little, I was actually pretty close to my two cousins, one of them older and the other one younger than me.

That was back when I was in elementary school. These cousins were the daughters of my oldest uncle. All of us were close in age, and we went to the same elementary school. In fact, my older cousin and I were born in the same year. Since classes were done pretty early, our parents would still be at work when we got out, so we always went first to Grandma's, which wasn't far from the school, and there we would do our homework, watch cartoons, play with paper dolls, and do whatever else it was that little girls did. Between six and seven in the evening, when my parents and my uncle and aunt got off from work, they would come to Grandma's to pick us up on their way home. And during summer and winter vacation time, the same arrangement would be extended to half or even whole days.

That was how well we knew each other. In those days, just before we parted company around dinnertime, we would discuss, chummily and enthusiastically, our play themes for the following day, and divide up among ourselves the responsibility of bringing various items that we needed. (Oh, if we're going to play hopscotch or rubber band jumping in the back alley outside the red doors, we'll need rubber bands strung together into a rope, and some chalk. If we want to make believe that we're cooking up a wedding banquet for our courting dolls, then we have to remember the pots and pans, the bowls and chopsticks, and the dolls' beautiful paper costumes. And if we plan to play doctor, then we must collect syringes and medicine bottles and leftover tissue paper to wrap pills in . . .)

(In that quiet apartment where the afternoons were cool and dark, all by ourselves we played our little girls' games. Grandma took her usual naps in the inner room. There was a breeze, and a dim blue light the color of veins silently traversed the four blue-white walls. Oh, this is Barbie. And this is Angie. Barbie and Angie's day. They went to the market. They went on a date with their boyfriends. They went out to afternoon tea . . .)

(Puppet dolls. Paper dolls. All with their beautiful, vacant eyes wide open. They wore evening dresses as gorgeous and intricate as silk paper embossed with gold. Touched by the dim blue light, the faint patterns on their sumptuous gowns flickered against the gloomy objects standing still in the background. In that cool, dark, cellar-like apartment, their bodies stiffly swaying from side to side, they floated silently over the cold floor tiles. In my memory, everything within my vision was like an occult painting suspended before a track camera, rippling with turbulent underwater shadows as the camera slowly glided forward . . .)

Snap. (Flashbulb. The flashbulb on the camera goes off again.)

I raise my head and look all around me. The guests continue to tackle the sumptuous dishes with gusto, entirely unperturbed. A couple I do not know (they are probably friends or relatives of the bridegroom's) frantically attempt to quiet down the sudden wailing of their toddler. Nobody else seems to have noticed the intrusive flashbulbs that have lighted up everything in the background so starkly just now.

This is of course understandable. Before the first course was served, when all the guests at the banquet were attentively watching the PowerPoint presentation specially prepared by my cousin and her husband for the occasion, the lights had gone into a bout of spasmodic flashing, as though a fuse had blown. Everyone must have become oblivious to flashing lights after that.

Those bright white flashes between photo slides. (Just a second. Weren't the lights dimmed for the PowerPoint presentation? Could it be possible that the leaping flashes that had caused me to squint and blink, my vision out of focus like a dying person's, were mere hallucinations on my part?) Sometimes we saw images of the two lovebirds on a trip together. (An unknown beach. Both of them in tank tops, shorts and straw hats. The ocean behind them was bathed in the glow of the setting sun, and, true to some age-old fantasy, the picture was filled with shimmering, diffused golden light.) Sometimes we saw funny pictures from their daily lives. (Ladies and Gentlemen. Now the bridegroom returns home from work. The bride immediately falls upon her knees in front of the cupboard and reverently fetches him his slippers. All these are signs of the sweet-as-honey, set-in-three-seconds-for-permanent-hold marital bliss in store for them . . .) (Just then, a shrill male voice in the audience piped up maliciously, "Hubby dear, you're home? Let me run the bath for you . . . " and everyone bursts into laughter.) Some of the pictures seemed rather artificial and contrived, depicting exotic, romantic settings, or passionate kisses between the Princess and her Prince (the kind that takes place on the center strip at some busy intersection, or in a skinny parkette under the shadow of the rapid transit train, with the bodies of the subjects absurdly contorted) . . .

Snap. (Snowblindness. Flashes of snowblindness.)

Later, everything changed. My cousins and I grew apart. They moved to the other end of town, and, a couple years later, we went to different middle schools. We couldn't play together all the time, like we did before. After a while we began to hear, off and on, about my older cousin falling behind in school and ending up in a second-tier class. (All these things we must have learned roundabout from various other gossipy relatives, for if we were to ask my aunt directly, she would adroitly change the subject with a smile.) With time, I graduated from middle school and donned the black and white uniform of a certain renowned girls' high school downtown, and so began my busy life as a daily commuter on city buses. Meanwhile, my older cousin entered a private vocational school with a very bad reputation, where she became something of a punk. She was allegedly spotted hanging out in Ximending with a bunch of youths who looked like drag racers, yelling and screaming as they chased and beat a lone young guy late at night . . .

Snap. (The screen goes blank. The image is drowned out by the light.)

After that came my older cousin's attempted suicide.

I remember when I went to visit her in her hospital room. That was during a disastrous romance with another man, before she met her husband.

I heard that the man was middle-aged and already had a wife and kids. The story was as corny as any penny romance novel (I envision my cousin as a formulaic, roughly constructed character in a novel, like a badly made shadow play puppet with head and arms inverted, churned out one after another from a plastic injection molding machine in some automated assembly line); my cousin fell in love with him. This was probably the crucial turning point that brought her life as a juvenile delinquent to an end. She quit her punk habits, tossed aside the faded, ragged, bell-cut jeans as dirty as the sneakers that were in fashion then, and began to wear dresses and flowing skirts. She grew her hair long, and exchanged her outlandishly oversized, jingling earrings for delicate girly necklaces. Her voice became soft and her speech affected . . .

From there on it turned into a soap opera. My cousin, learning that the man had a wife and kids, began harassing him to get a divorce. Once she ran into him outside a department store with his wife and younger daughter, and made a scene right in front of the doors, among the throngs of shoppers. I heard that my cousin even prostrated herself before the wife, passionately begging her to give up the man . . .

Some time after that, my cousin cut her wrist at home.

It was quite bad. Her blood stained the entire bathtub red. Fortunately someone found her in time and rushed her to the hospital, which saved her life.

I remember making a special trip to the hospital to visit her. She was asleep when I arrived. Her left wrist was thickly bandaged (from then on, she always wore a watch or some other jewelry such as a bracelet to hide the scar). Her face was white as a sheet of paper. There was something aggressive about that pallor; for a moment I almost thought that the pallid color, like a drop of white paint in water, would continue to spread, until it entirely swallowed up what was left of the lines demarcating her features. I thought I was seeing a completely blank, featureless face, a face slowly sinking into the boundless shadows of the hospital room.

But just then, the TV screen in the room caught my attention.

A once popular slapstick game show called "Dare to Win" was on. It was filmed out of doors in a water park, and showed teams representing various companies and organizations competing against each other by taking on all kinds of "challenges." Since the point of the program was to make fun of people's ridiculous positions when they tumbled into the water, I would ordinarily have found it difficult to refrain from laughing if by chance I saw the variety of absurd postures in which they fell splashing in. But that day at the hospital, I remember, I intently watched the show for twenty minutes, seeing members of each team repeating their graceless, sprawling falls over and over again; (they lost their grip on the rope; they dropped off the edge of the colorful floating cubes; they rolled down the plastic-covered incline; they were shot down with water jets by the hosts . . .) For some reason, I did not find any of it funny.

I couldn't laugh at all.

Later, I discovered that it was because there was no sound. I didn't know whether the speakers on the TV were broken, or if there was concern about disturbing the patients, (or maybe someone simply forgot to turn up the volume?); anyway, the picture was completely soundless. The entire string of images consisted of the hosts opening and closing their big mouths, their faces and limbs in exaggerated motion as though they were puppets; yet the entire performance was silent, like a dumb show. Moreover, the silly canned sound effects (those electronic chords, the ding-ding-dongs and doink-doinks) that usually accompanied the droll images of people stumbling and falling were now absent. The movements that had seemed hysterically funny on former occasions now appeared as tragic and dismal as a gymnastic routine that ended in failure again and again . . .

Just then, I noticed that my cousin had woken up all of a sudden. Her eyes opened, and she sat up, moving slowly and jerkily as though she were a cogwheel-operated device. She seemed entirely unaware of my presence. I saw her vacant eyes turn until they came to rest on the TV screen on which the silent exhibition of the countless ways of falling continued. Her face was entirely devoid of expression. Her features appeared as though they had been whimsically and sloppily sketched out with a careless bit of charcoal, like simplified geometric patterns rather than the lines of a human face. I saw the iris-blue light from the screen dancing upon her face in the dark hospital room.

I continued to look at her for quite some time. Horrified by my cousin's heavily outlined face, which looked like some still-life oil painting, expressionless yet flickering in the changing light, I forgot to say anything. But just then, in that dark hospital room quiet as a dream (there was even someone seriously ill sound asleep in the neighboring bed), my cousin, for some unknown reason, abruptly burst into raucous laughter . . .

(Ha ha ha ha ha ha . . .)

Snap snap. Snap. (Snow-blindness. Piercing white light like snow-blindness.)

"Don't be shy, my dear cousin. It will be your turn next year. You know, we're all here today only because we missed that flight . . . " my cousin is saying.

Missed that flight? What does she mean?

(But what about Grandma? What happened to Grandma after that?)

(Grandma? Isn't she still lying on that cold, damp bed in the hospital?)

(Like a vine that has ceased to grow. Her body completely wasted, her branch-like arms and legs withered and yellow. Her breath comes in gusts, like the white fog of early fall, quietly spreading in the stagnant, dark blue air.)

I suddenly notice that my cousin's left wrist, as she raises her glass, is completely unadorned with any of her customary jewelry. This exposes the large patch of twisted, gruesome, crustacean skin around her wrist, the scar from when she tried to commit suicide . . .

As I stare at my cousin's hand, her other hand involuntarily shoots out to hide that jagged, centipede-like, blood-colored mark clinging upon her wrist. But now, I notice to my astonishment that her two white arms, crossed to hide each other, are spontaneously breaking out in a rash of purple death-spots, like bramble bushes in bloom, or a broken jar of paint splattering everywhere . . .

Everyone present seems to have frozen still in mid motion. The hands momentarily lifted in speech, in movement, in consumption of food, in exhortations and polite declinations to drink, all hang unnaturally, stiffly in mid-air, like the hands of plastic mannequins in a boutique. Their bodies are completely naked. I see my uncle's oily, wax-colored potbelly sticking out. I see my aunt's gray, wrinkled neck and her sagging, withered breasts. I see my youthful mother, her stiff body bare, playfully making as if to fill my father's plate. I see my cousin, her fine, lovely white waist and black pubic hair exposed, sweetly hanging upon the arm of her equally naked husband, her empty wineglass tipped at a strange angle. Their elaborate clothing and jewelry are completely gone. And the lusterless skin on their bodies, like my cousin's dead, rotting hand, are rapidly becoming specked, at random, with purple death spots large and small, like the lotuses that had sprung up in the Buddha's steps at his birth.

They are all staring at me.

I'm having a sudden flashback to when I was eight, a snapshot of that happy trip the entire extended family was about to embark on. It was a rare family excursion, organized, I think, in celebration of my grandmother's sixtieth birthday. We purchased a total of twenty-two tickets on a night flight to Japan, and only missed that flight destined for death and destruction because my grandma suddenly fell ill. (Did we really miss it though? Did we really? . . .) An unaccountable fatiguing of the metal caused that Boeing 747 to slowly disintegrate at the altitude of twenty-eight thousand feet. I can almost see, as in a frame-by-frame analysis, the sealed cabin, cavernous as the belly of a whale, shattering into bits like a fallen porcelain vase in that cold, rarefied air. All the passengers, suddenly depressurized, die in the instant when the fuselage cracks open. Their bodies, their very blood vessels, burst apart. The jet stream rips away all their clothing. I can see the expression on their faces, frozen in the moment before destruction. I can see them, two hundred and thirty-seven dark and shadowy forms instantaneously deprived of life, falling through the clouds high up in the sky like shooting stars displaced from their constellations. During that seemingly interminable fall from twenty-eight thousand feet, as they hurtle through the fast-flowing air in the vast, empty night with their bare limbs spread like wings, they give one the illusion that they are flying . . .

That they are flying . . .

And shattering into smithereens in the instant when they hit the sea surface.

The Meaning of Missing

Evelyn Conlon

I think of the feeling around a person being missing as being a narrow thing. It has to be, in order to get into so many places. I told my husband this once and he laughed at me.

"Well if you can think of heartbreak as a thin piercing agony," I began again.

He said that the turnips needed thinning, and that he was away out to the garden. He didn't like talking about heartbreak, because he had once caused it to me by going off with his old girlfriend for three months. It obviously didn't work out because he turned up on my doorstep on Thursday, the sixth of June, twenty years ago. At ten past eight. Evening. He wasn't contrite, just chastened. He has been here since, but he never talks about that time. I don't mind too much because I never admitted that I had cried crossing every bridge in Dublin, the only way to get to know a city I was told by someone, who was clearly trying to get me away from her doorstep. Nor did I admit to what I'd done as soon as the crying had dried up and all the bridges had been crossed. I didn't have to, and he couldn't really ask me or hold me accountable.

Thinning turnips, hah! You'd think we had an acre out the back, and that he was going to have to tie old hot water bottles around his knees, because the length of time on the ground was going to be so hard on them. We have one drill of turnips, a half of cabbage and a half of broad beans. Although it's not strictly an economical use of the space, I insist on the broad beans, because of the feel of the inside of them. Only two drills. They could have waited. Of course he didn't like me talking about missing, either. It's about my sister.

"She's not missing," my husband insisted, "you've just not heard from her."

I often replay my conversations with him as if he is standing right beside me. I bet I'll be able to do that if he dies before me.

"For a year!"

"Yes, for a year. But you know how time goes when you're away."

I don't actually. I've never been away for a year. Nor for three months.

When my sister said that she was going to Australia there was a moment's silence between us, during which time a little lump came out of my heart and thumped into my stomach. We were having our second glass of Heineken. In deference to the scared part of our youth, when we were afraid to be too adventurous, she always drank Heineken when out with me. She didn't want to hold the predictability of my life up to the light. I know that she had gone through ten different favorite drinks since those days, none of them Heineken.

"Australia!" I squealed.

I coughed my voice down.

"Australia?" I said, a second time, in a more harmonious tone. Strange how the same word can mean two different things when the pitch is changed. *Béarla as Chinese.* I must have hit the right note, curious but not panicked, because she smiled and said yes. Not only was she going, she had everything ready, tickets bought, visa got. She may even have started packing for all I know. It was the secret preparation that rankled most. How could she have done those things without telling me? If we were going to Waterford for a winter break I'd tell her weeks in advance.

The day she left was beautifully frosty. She stayed with us the night before, and after I had gone to bed I could hear her and my husband surfing for hours on a swell of mumbling and laughing. Apparently she was too excited to go to sleep, and he decided to get in on the act, not often having an excited woman to lead him into the small hours. The morning Radio News said that if there was an earthquake in the Canaries, Ireland might only have two hours to prepare for a tsunami. Brilliant, another thing to worry about. And us just after buying a house in Skerries. At the airport, my emotions spluttered, faded, then surged again, like a fire of Polish coal going out. The effort involved in not crying stiffened my face, and yet it twitched, as if palsy had overcome every square inch from my forehead to my chin. But I was determined. I would keep my dignity, even if the effort was going to paralyze me. It would be an essential thing to have, this dignity, now that I was not going to have a sister. My husband touched my shoulder as we got back into the car, because he can do that sometimes, the right thing.

In the months that followed I mourned her in places that I had never noticed before, and in moods that I had not known existed.

First there is presence and then it has to grow into absence. There are all sorts of ways for it to do that, gently, unnoticeably, becoming a quiet rounded cloud that compliments the sun with its dashing about, making harmless shadows. Or the other way, darkly with thunder.

"It's not as if you saw her all the time," my husband said, unhelpfully.

"I did," I said back.

"What are you talking about, you only met every few months."

"But she was there."

She wrote well, often referring to the minutiae of her journey over. But no matter how often she talked about cramped legs or the heat in Singapore, and despite the fact that I'd seen her off at the airport myself, I still imagined her queuing for a ship at Southampton, sailing the seas for a month, having dinner in pre-arranged sittings at the sound of a bell, because that's the way I would have done it.

And then she stopped writing, fell out of touch, off the world. My letters went unanswered, her telephone was cut off. I'm afraid, that because my pride was so riled, the trail was completely cold by the time I took her real missing seriously. And still my husband insisted that there was nothing wrong with her, just absentmindedness.

I was in bed sick the day she rang. I love the trimmings of being sick, mainly the television at the bottom of the bed, although after two days I was getting a little TV'd out. I had just seen John Stalker, a former chief of English Police, advertising garden awnings. I was puzzled as to why they gave his full title. Did the police thing have anything to do with awnings? Was there a pun there, hidden from me? I didn't like being confused by advertisements. If I'd had a remote control device I could have switched the volume down occasionally and lip read the modern world. Then Countdown came on. Making up the words made me feel useful. I had seen the mathematician wearing that dress before. It was during the conundrum that the phone rang; it wasn't a crucial conundrum, because one of the fellows was streets ahead of the other, even I had beaten him hands down, and I had a temperature of one hundred degrees and rising.

"Hello?"

And there was her voice, brazen as all hell got up. I straightened myself against the headboard and thought, "It's the temperature." I straightened myself more and my heart thumped very hard. It sounded like someone rapping a door. I thought it would cut off my breathing.

"Hi," she said.

“Hello,” I said, as best as I could manage.

“Oh my God, it’s been soooo long.”

The sentence sounded ridiculous.

“And I’m really sorry about that. But I’ll make up for it. I’m on my way back for a couple of months. I’ll be arriving on Saturday morning.”

Back. Not home. Well Saturday didn’t suit me, and even if it had done so up until this moment, it suddenly wasn’t going to. I was speechless, truly. But my mind was working overtime dealing with silent words tumbling about. I could almost hear them cranking up, scurrying around looking for their place in the open. What would be the best way to get revenge?

She must have finally noticed because she asked, “Are you there?”

“Oh yes,” I said.

Short as that, “Oh yes.”

I don’t think I said more than ten words before limping to a satisfactorily oblique fade out.

“See you. Then.”

I put the phone down, my hand shaking. How many people had I told about my worry? And would I have to tell them all that she was no longer missing? And had I also told them about my husband’s view? And was he now right? If a person turns up have they ever been missing? How could I possibly remember what conversations I had set up or slipped into casually, over the past year? I hoped that my sister would have a horrible flight, bumpy, stormy, crowded, delayed. But that’s as far as my bile could flower.

My husband went to the airport. He would, having no sense of the insult of missing. He fitted the journey in around the bits and pieces of a Saturday, not wanting me to see him set out, not wanting to leave the house under the glare of my disapproval.

By evening I had mellowed a little because I had to. It was seeing her, the shape of her, the stance of her at doorways, the expressions of her. My sister had never giggled, even in the years that are set aside for that. She had always been too wry. Getting ready for her life, no doubt. On the third evening, by the time the ice in my chest had begun to melt, the three of us went out to our local.

“What’s Wollongong like?” I asked.

“Just a normal Australian town,” my sister said, and shrugged loudly, if that is possible. And then she mercilessly changed the subject. I had thought it would have jacaranda trees in bloom all year, birds calling so busily that it would be the first thing a person would mention, sun flitting continuously on the sparkling windows of every house. A town rampant with light. I had thought it a place for rumination, with color bouncing unforgettably off the congregation of gum trees.

"Are you sure it's just a normal town. Have you been there?"

"Yes, totally normal. Of course I've been there."

I didn't believe her for one second.

"Why do you particularly want to know what Wollongong is like?"

"The name," my husband said, as if he was my ventriloquist. But something in my demeanor made him hesitate, and he looked at me as if he had made some mistake.

"It's just that I met someone from there," I said.

"When?" they both asked. Normally my sister and my husband have a murmuring familiarity between them, born presumptuously of their relationship with me. But they were both suddenly quiet, each afraid to admit that they did not know when I, I of the dried up life, would have met someone from Wollongong. Was it during her year or his three months? Damn, they would be thinking, now they each knew that the other didn't know. And me sitting there smiling away to myself. Smug, they would have been surmising. But it wasn't smug. I admit to a moment of glee but I was mostly thinking of Wollongong, and I swallowed the sliver of triumph because I am known for my capacity to forgive.

However, I didn't answer their question and went to the bar to buy my round, feeling like a racehorse, unexpectedly out in front, showing the rest of the field a clear set of hooves.

Paradeability

Bret Anthony Johnston

Serious clowns have their faces painted onto blown-out goose eggs. My son tells me this on the drive from Corpus Christi to Houston. The custom began in the sixteenth century, a method of remembering makeup patterns, but now it serves as copyright. The eggs are done up with acrylic paint and accented with felt and glitter, with tiny flowers and ribbon and clay, and they're preserved in the Department of Clown Registry in Buchanan, Virginia. He says a clown's makeup is called his slap, and whiteface clowns rank highest in the hierarchy. Then the augustes, with their red cheeks and ivory mouths. Then character clowns, then hobos. The first-known clown appeared in a pharaoh's court during Egypt's fifth dynasty; he was a pygmy. Clowns in Russia carry the same clout as pianists, as ballerinas.

It's a tepid Friday in March, and we're going to a clown convention at a Marriot by Hobby Airport. On Sunday he'll compete in a contest hosted by Clowns of America, International. Asher is thirteen. He's a hobo.

"Fear of clowns is called coulrophobia," he says. He's paging through one of his clown books in the glow of my truck's interior light. Outside, the dusk is particulate. We cross the Brazos River, rust tinted with sediment. A megachurch's illuminated cross, as tall as the mast of a great ship, rolls over the horizon. My son says, "The fear stems from how the heavy makeup conceals and exaggerates the wearer's face. Also, the bulbous nose."

"Do ballerinas carry a lot of clout in Russia?" I ask.

"It's like being a football player in Texas. Like being one of the Cowboys."

"Hot damn," I say because it sometimes gets a laugh. Not tonight. He's too wound up; he's been x-ing out days on his calendar for two months. "Are we talking Landry years or Johnson years?"

"Landry. No question."

That Asher knows his Dallas Cowboys history always calms me. I'm suddenly more comfortable in the truck's cab. My wedding band catches the light of the low moon, reminding me of thrown copper. I say, "A lot of wide receivers study ballet. It helps with spatial awareness."

"Besides Santa Claus," Asher says, "Ronald McDonald is the most recognized figure in the world."

At the hotel, two giant plywood clown faces command the lobby. From chin to crown, they're eight feet tall. Asher stands in front of them while I check in—he's so enthralled that I half expect him to kneel—and only moves when a long-haired woman asks him to snap pictures of her posing between the clowns. The desk clerk hands me breakfast coupons and keycards, Asher's welcome packet and lanyard. Our room's on the sixth floor. As we ascend in a glass elevator, Asher tells me the long-haired woman has been here a week and she estimates there are over a hundred clowns at the hotel. "Tough luck for coulrophobics," I say, and he smiles like I've passed an exam. It fills my every cell with breath. My mystifying son—the boy can send a tight, arcing spiral forty yards, but he'd rather hole up in his room with Red Skelton videos. After showering, he emerges from the bathroom wearing a shirt that says *Can't Sleep, Clowns Will Eat Me*, and orders room service. Throughout the night, the hotel trembles when the nearby planes take off. I wake up often, confused as to how we got where we are.

I work in oil and gas. I'm a geological technician, which means I spend my days pulling well information. I study maps generated by geologists and run numbers to track which wells are still producing and which need to be plugged and abandoned. I like knowing what's burning beneath our feet, the black oil and farther down, the clean effervescing gas. The knowledge makes me feel simultaneously large and small, and in that I find comfort. After I blew out my knee during a college scrimmage—I played third-string receiver for the Longhorns, I bleed burnt orange—I switched my major from Communications to Geology. I wanted, I think, to encase myself in rock, in hard things that last.

Geo techs don't make a lot of money; we leave that to engineers and land men. This trip to Houston is a stretch, and although I could've saved half a month's pay by booking a room in the motor court across the freeway, I didn't want to skimp on what Asher's taken to calling the most important weekend of his "career." I want him to feel fussed over. I want him to know I'm on his team. As the convention approached, I imagined moments we might share: father and son splitting their first can of Lone Star, talking about the birds and bees, or maybe passing the pigskin, analyzing the pitiful seasons the Cowboys have been suffering, the injuries and heartbreaks that now define a once-great team. (Before we left Corpus, I aired up our old football and dropped it into the truckbed, just in case.) I also thought it might be a chance for us to finally talk about his mother. Jill's been gone two years. She was forty, and the first time she visited the doctor, the tumors lit her X-rays like a distant constellation. Three months later, the images were blurred with metastasis. "Like a snowstorm," Jill said, sounding oddly pleased. She didn't make it to Thanksgiving. Asher and I avoided turkey that year and ordered pizza, then we went to a movie full of explosions and rooftop chases. "We'll make new traditions," I said. That Christmas he asked for his first makeup kit and a foam nose.

On Saturday morning, at the breakfast buffet, I realize my son will likely get thumped in his contest. He's just outmatched. Even with their painted faces, these clowns look severe and cagey. Purposeful, I think. Ornery. There are probably thirty of them in the restaurant, and another fifty mingling in the atrium. Their costumes are elaborate and expensive—billowy and silken and intensely colored. Pigment assaults me. They wear patent leather shoes as big as rural mailboxes. Two of them walk on stilts and can rest their elbows atop the plywood clown heads in the lobby. Some are bald. Others are neon geysers of hair—red and orange and purple, Afro-ed and spiky and twisted into thick braids. One clown wears goggles and flippers and a small inflated pool around her waist. They're all adults, I'd guess mostly in their sixties, and they've come from as far away as Quebec and Maine. Seriousness radiates from them like heat from asphalt. They have swagger and business cards.

I'm embarrassingly relieved Asher didn't come to breakfast. He's awake, but wanted to rehearse his routine alone in the room. His event is Paradeability. He'll be judged on the originality of his act and how many times he can complete it in sixty seconds while moving through a gauntlet of would-be parade spectators. We've practiced in our backyard with a stopwatch. We record the sessions with a video camera propped on our propane grill, then Asher studies the footage and makes adjustments. As I eat my omelet, I catch myself hoping they give out ribbons for participation, something he can at least hang on his wall.

A clown in the hotel atrium starts squeezing a bicycle horn while another skips in circles, tossing confetti. His limberness surprises me. In a high falsetto, they sing, "We're having a hoot, an absolute hoot!" It's easy to imagine Jill here, trailing Asher, snapping candid pictures of him with the clowns. At home, framed photos of him hang on almost every wall—Asher selling raffle tickets, Asher feeding a brown pelican on Padre Island, Asher sleeping. Photography wasn't her hobby; watching Asher was. She was rarely in front of the camera, something I realized too late. Her absence blitzes me everywhere. The way the sheet and pillows on her side of the bed stay undisturbed, regardless of how I toss in my sleep, is menacing. The junk mail that still comes addressed to her leaves me as cored out as a cantaloupe. Lately, on Sunday mornings, I've been hitting open houses in different neighborhoods in Corpus, trying to wrap my head around moving. I tell Asher I'm going to church. Maybe he believes me.

"Here's someone who knows *eggs*-actly what he likes for breakfast," a woman says. She's beside my booth, but a beat passes before I realize she's talking to me. She's in a pinstripe suit, wielding a clipboard and walkie-talkie.

"Do what?" I say.

"Professor Sparkles got me with that one earlier this morning, but when I say it, people just seem baffled," she says. She extends her hand. "I'm Dayna. With a *y*."

"I'm—"

"Asher's daddy," she says.

I shake her hand, puzzled, wondering what kind of information is on that clipboard. Then I remember her: the woman from last night, the one Asher visited with while I registered. Her hair is up this morning, and she looks like a pretty librarian, drab amongst all the color. I say, "Are you a clown parent, too?"

"I wish," she says. "Mine's a cheerleader. She'd walk five miles to avoid a clown."

"I suspect that may be an epidemic among cheerleaders."

"Asher's a cutie. What kind of clown is he?"

"Hobo," I say.

"I would've guessed auguste."

"He likes thrift stores," I say.

"An original, I love it. Come to enough of these and you see the same getups every year."

"This is our first. I'm afraid we're out of our league."

"Horse feathers," Dayna says. "You're *eggs*-actly where you're supposed to be."

I smile and take a sip of cold coffee. "Professor Sparkles would give you high marks for that one."

"Let's hope not. Last time a clown left marks on me, my husband almost put both of us through a window."

Behind Dayna two clowns are covering a conference room door with pink balloons. Because I can't think of how to respond, I say, "That's not so good."

"Fourth floor, the Hilton in Nashville. Three years ago."

"I didn't know clowns were so prone to scandal."

"Neither did I," she says. "Isn't it fun?"

His name is Po' Boy the Hoboy. He keeps a notebook with ideas for costumes and gags, and on the cover, in pillowy letters, he's written, "Pretty

Much the Only Property of Po' Boy the Hoboy." He subscribes to a quarterly called *Clown Alley.* He's saving for a unicycle. Every couple of weeks we make thrift store rounds, hoping to scare up plaid trousers and polka-dot bowties. Once, he found a dented bowler hat at the Salvation Army and cradled it like a wounded animal the whole drive home. He spends hours in the bathroom applying and reapplying his slap. I'm positive he's never kissed a girl.

Not that he'd make a bad catch. He has his mother's blue eyes and dark hair. A good jaw and nice posture, sturdy shoulders. Before he cottoned to clowning, I had him pegged as a quarterback, maybe scholarship material. He used to love watching the Cowboys and casting for redfish in Baffin Bay. His grades are good, but not so good that he eats lunch alone; any chance he gets, he incorporates clowns into school projects. He has friends, kids who call too late at night, who invite him to the beach. Last year he flirted with cigarettes for a month; his clothes smelled of sour smoke when I did the wash, but just when I gathered the nerve to confront him, the odor evaporated. Occasionally he'll get detention for cutting up or skipping algebra, and I admit those infractions probably leave me feeling the way other parents do when their kids make honor roll. I'll manufacture some annoyed concern and tell him to mow the yard as punishment, but really it's in those moments when I feel most like a father, when my blood duty is clearly defined, when I halfway believe I can do right by my inscrutable son.

After breakfast, I find him in front of the mirror in our room, adjusting his red foam nose. He's painted on a charcoal beard, and his cheeks and eyes are chalky. His eyebrows are thick rectangles, like the black strips football players use to block the sun. He wears his bowler and baggy pants, a necktie as wide as a flounder and two-tone bowling shoes. I suspect the shoes are stolen. They appeared two weeks ago, after he went to a bowling birthday party.

"Looking mighty fine," I say. I've brought up pastries and chocolate milk that I show him in the mirror.

"I had my bowtie on, but I looked butler-ish."

"Good call," I say. "It's a sea of bowties down there. Originality matters."

Asher studies his reflection. He's remote again, the giddiness from last night buried under his slap. I wouldn't mind starting to chip away at his hopes for tomorrow's contest, but I can't figure out how, so I just sit on my bed and watch him. He fiddles with his tie, loosening and tightening, then moves toward the pastries. He shakes the milk carton and debates between a muffin and Danish. His mother used to do this. She never knew what she'd order until the last moment, and then it was even odds whether she'd flag the waiter and reverse her decision. He opts for the Danish.

"I didn't see any other hobos this morning," I say, though I'm not sure that's true.

He chews, takes a swig of milk. In the too-big clothes, he appears younger than he is. He says, "The hardcore clowns will come tomorrow for the contests. Today's novice-y. There's a talk on balloon sculpting. Workshops on improv and face-painting."

"Hot damn," I say. "Should I bring the video camera?"

"I think you'd need a conference badge."

"I bet there's an auguste who'd look the other way for a few jars of face cream."

Asher puts his Danish on the dresser. He slips into his blazer. There are mismatched patches sewn randomly on the coat; I stitched them using a needle and thread from Jill's nightstand. He says, "I just don't want you to be bored."

I'm about to say that whatever we do will be fine, I only want to spend the day by his side, but then I realize he's brushing me off. My mouth goes thick. I'm awash in a blunted, disconnected feeling, like I'm nothing more than a family friend watching someone else's kid for the weekend. I resist an urge to ask where he got his bowling shoes.

"Sure thing," I say. "I need to review some maps anyway, run some petroleum numbers."

He fishes a pair of fingerless gloves from his pocket and tugs them on. He says, "Are you going to church tomorrow?"

Maybe there's an edge of suspicion in his tone, maybe not. Either way, my guard goes up. At last week's open house, the realtor glanced at my wedding ring and suggested arranging a time to show my wife the property. I gave her a false name and the phone number for La Cocina, a Mexican place where Asher and I get takeout. Now I say, "I'd planned on skipping. I feel a bout of heresy coming on."

He steps back from the mirror, assessing his costume. My heart goes panicky. I'm afraid he's about to call me out on church or ban me from watching him compete tomorrow, but instead he says, "Then we should practice in the morning."

"I was thinking," I say, "if you'd rather just watch tomorrow, maybe get ideas for next year, I'd be game. We can make this an annual trip."

"It's in Chicago next year."

"One of America's finest cities," I say, though I've never been. "We'll make a vacation of it."

"Sweet," he says. "If I win tomorrow, next year's fees are waived. They want you to defend your title."

"The most important thing is to enjoy yourself," I say, sounding hokey and lame.

He crosses back to the dresser, takes another drink of milk. I think he's about to reach for his Danish again, but he goes for the muffin. He tears off a piece with his fingers and places it in his mouth like a dip of snuff. He chews slowly, careful not to disturb his makeup.

Before Asher goes downstairs, I take pictures of him on our balcony. He acts put upon, but he enjoys posing. We make plans to eat dinner together—it's clear he agrees to this out of pity, but I'm elated nonetheless—and then he's gone. In his wake, the room is littered with makeup sponges and a silence so complete I have to turn on the television. I surf the channels, flipping past adult pay-per-view, public access preachers, and movies with actors I don't recognize. I exhaust the stations a second time, then a third, and I feel unmoored and sullen. I try to review the maps for the new prospect my office is vying for, an oil play down near Laredo, but my thoughts keep veering. I worry that losing the contest will undo Asher. I worry that for all the ways I know I'm letting him down—my inability to buy the toothpaste and fabric softener he likes, the grief I occasionally allow him to glimpse, my lies about church, our eating too much takeout—there are still deeper, more insidious failures that will only rise to the surface after doing irreparable damage. It's disorienting, such melancholy. I can't remember a day when I haven't thought that, with his mother gone, I've forgotten how to be a father. Not a day when I haven't thought, I used to be good at this. I leave a note—addressed to Po' Boy rather than Asher—saying I'll be in the hotel bar.

The bar is closed, though, and the lobby is mostly deserted. A family is checking out while a housekeeper, a Mexican woman with multiple earrings, polishes the granite planters by the elevator. Behind closed conference room doors, I hear the murmur of people speaking into podium microphones. "Obviously," a man says, "miming wouldn't work there. You have to use your noodle." The plywood clown faces have been commandeered as message centers. There are pamphlets for a San Antonio clown camp tacked to a cheek, a sign-up sheet for ride-share on a nose, and pieces of personal correspondence all over—folded notes addressed to Spangles the Clown, Purple Peggy, Sir Smile-A-Lot. A table next to the door covered in pink balloons serves as a Lost and Found. So far, the only thing that's been lost is a yellow feather boa. The door is propped open with a box holding a disco ball. No lights are burning in the room, so the surfaces are dim, given to deep shadow. Most everything is draped in sheets.

Then a switch is flipped and fluorescent light opens the space. It's the vendors' area. A man in denim shorts and rainbow suspenders emerges from the back, whipping sheets from the tables. He says, "When you see something you can't live without, just holler."

The vendors' area is an L-shaped corridor; it might normally be a hallway leading to the laundry room or kitchen. Inside, I feel the inexplicable need to move stealthily. There are displays of leather shoes—jester-toed and oblong, sequined and high-heeled—and a few tables boasting nothing but makeup. There's a walk-in booth with frilly costumes on hangers and an elaborate wig arrangement—thirty Styrofoam heads, tiered according to style. Tables are devoted to magic tricks, juggling props, and party favors. The suspendered man leafs through a convention program in an airbrushing booth. He's surrounded by wispy clown portraits and stacks of white T-shirts emblazoned with his handiwork. At the far end of the corridor is an open space with a rack of unicycles and large three-wheeled bikes. I pick up a chrome unicycle, as if gauging its weight, though I have no idea how to assess such a strange machine. I lift it to my shoulder like a rifle and sight down the frame, foolishly making sure it's straight.

"Careful," the man says, "she's loaded."

I lower the tire to the ground, bounce it a couple of times to check the pressure. "How much?"

"That's Zany Laney's booth. She'll be back after the balloon talk."

I wheel the unicycle back to the rack.

"What type of clown are you?" he asks, bored.

Without thinking, I say, "Hobo."

"Hobos are destitute. Where's he getting the scratch for a unicycle?"

"I'm mixing it up. Come to enough of these and you see the same things over and over."

The man shrugs, puts his program under his chair, then goes to straighten the pallets of airbrushed shirts on his table. He says, "I like hobos. Emmett Kelly, Otto Griebling. It's the only truly American clown."

"You ever get folks asking you to airbrush their faces on goose eggs?"

"Son," he says, "I've been asked to airbrush faces on things that haunt my dreams."

"How long does it take?"

"To haunt my dreams?"

"To airbrush a face on something."

"Depends on the face. Depends on the something."

I like the suspendered man, his irascibility. I like how he's unfolding the shirts and then gingerly refolding them so his artwork is more visible. He's the size of a nose tackle. I say, "I'm not actually a clown."

"And thus the mystery of the unicycling hobo is solved."

"My son is, though. I'd like to get his face painted on something."

"Regrettably, I believe the gift shop is fresh out of goose eggs."

"How long will you be here?" I ask.

"Until the Lord our God rises again or Happy Hour, whichever comes first."

In the lobby, there are huddles of clowns deciding which workshops to attend. Someone, somewhere, puffs at a kazoo. Dayna is sitting with an auguste, an unhinged-looking woman in her seventies, and speaking into her walkie-talkie. I don't see Asher. Another hobo has materialized, though, a hunched man shuffling around with a sign that reads *Can You Spare a Laugh?* I watch him, searching out anything that might prove useful for Asher, but the hobo just mopes by, wearing a hangdog expression and tuxedo pants cut off at the calves. One clown waves him away, but another grants him a belly laugh; it's showy and territorial. The hobo bows. Then he catches sight of a clown with a tinselly wig pushing a whiteface in a wheelchair, and he's all energy as he maneuvers in front of them. They stop, and he brandishes his sign with a cocked head, pleading. The man in the wheelchair nods. He hunts around for something in his lap. I think he's misread the sign and is looking for change, but then he produces a device, one of those mechanical larynx numbers, and presses it to his throat. I don't hear anything at first, but soon there are low peals of disembodied laughter vibrating toward me like a flock of harsh, metallic birds. I retreat into the parking lot, the sad noise still buzzing in my ears when I reach my truck.

***

Hobo clowns likely came out of the Great Depression, though it's possible their roots stretch back to vaudeville. Asher wrote a report for his history class. They're forlorn and downtrodden, ever the brunt of jokes. They're always on the receiving end of pies to the face, kicks to the keester. That Asher reinvented himself as the only clown without hope or mirth bothers me. I assume it's because of his mother, but maybe not. I'm afraid to ask.

And yet when he returns to the room on Saturday evening, he's jazzed up and garrulous. I'm immediately optimistic about dinner. Maybe we'll split that beer. Maybe I'll find words to inoculate him against tomorrow's disappointment. He hangs his blazer on the desk chair and tells me, breathlessly, about the compliments he's gotten on his costume, about learning to twist balloons into airplanes and dinosaurs. Better still, a workshop instructor said he had such a knack for painting faces that he could get work at birthday parties. The instructor suggested setting up a website, running classified ads in the paper, acquiring a tax ID number.

He's in front of the mirror again. I think he's wiping off his makeup, but soon realize he's touching it up. I say, "Will Po' Boy be joining us for dinner?"

"Change of plans," he says. "The Calliope Ball is tonight. It's unmissable."

"You have to eat, Ash."

"There's a buffet. Mexican, I think. We can eat down there."

"We? What happened to that airtight clown security?"

"I scored you a badge from Mrs. Barrett," he says. "She didn't want you feeling left out."

"Mrs. Barrett?"

In the mirror, I can see him clipping on a bow tie, sliding the stem of a plastic sunflower through a hole in his lapel. Outside, a jet is descending and the noise rattles the windows.

"Ash?" I say.

"You met her at breakfast."

"Dayna?"

"She's the director of the conference. She said you seemed lonesome."

The lobby is transformed by darkness and oldies music. The disco ball I saw earlier now hangs from a tapestry of Christmas lights, spinning and refracting color. Asher hands me my badge and says he'll meet me in the room later, then, before I can protest, he squeezes into the crowd and disappears. Clowns sidle past each other with plates of enchiladas raised above their heads. I smell chili powder and corn tortillas. The suspendered man is sipping a beer by the glass elevator, chatting with two clowns in tutus. When he sees me, he cocks his arm and pantomimes throwing a pass. Seconds later, I act like I've caught it, right in the numbers.

I climb the stairs to the second floor balcony and peer down. Asher is already talking shop with the shuffling hobo and a female auguste. They're interested in whatever he's saying, nodding and letting him go on, and I hate that I didn't bring the camera. Jill would have. She would have stood beside me, snapping pictures and watching the mass of clowns move below us like a cloud of phosphorescent marsh gas. I try to imagine which costumes she'd like. It's a habit. When I take Asher to the mall, I guess which necklaces she'd want from jewelry store windows. Driving to my open houses, I keep an eye out for gardens she'd appreciate, and inside the rooms, I envision how she'd arrange our furniture, where she'd hang the photos of Asher. Now, I wonder if she'd like the cowboy with the checkerboard Stetson and matching boots. The woman in the yellow jumper and platinum wig? The scarecrow with a black balloon raven perched on his shoulder? I feel no affinity for any of them. They all look grave and infirm to me, an endangered species, a well that will soon be dry and abandoned.

A female clown, a whiteface in a pink jester costume, walks onto the balcony. She wears a ruffled collar and a three-point hat. I assume she's looking for someone in the group below, but she steps closer and says, "Sulking alone wasn't quite what I intended when I gave Asher your badge."

"Dayna?"

"Call me Ginger," she says. "Ginger the Jester."

"I didn't know you were a clown," I say.

"I'm good with secrets."

The glass elevator, packed tight with whitefaces, passes the balcony and stops in the lobby. Asher is still with the hobo and auguste, and soon he's being introduced to someone in a skunk costume. He doffs his bowler. The skunk curtsies. I feel conspicuous with Dayna beside me. Maybe Asher wouldn't recognize her dressed as a jester, or maybe keeping tabs on his old man is the furthest thing from his mind, but I worry. Before Jill died, she'd joke about my romantic future. "One year's too soon," she'd say, "but if you're not ringing some gal's bell by year three, I will, from on high, assume you've switched teams." I did an intentionally poor job of masking how much I despised such talk, but later, when she'd lost so much weight and asked me to promise that I'd eventually move on—"For me," she said, weeping, "for Ash"—I conceded only to spare us the rest of the conversation. I can't remember the last time I stood this close to a woman. Dayna's perfume smells of daylilies. Her gloves are satin. My blood is teeming with a miserable, traitorous vitality.

Dayna has been talking. She says, "That's what my daughter calls it, The John Wayne Gacy Convention."

"Asher wanted to do a school project on him, but I banned it. I got the silent treatment for a week," I say. I'd forgotten about that uncomfortable phase last year, when Asher was preoccupied with Gacy and seemed to always be spouting dark trivia. Gacy was a whiteface named Pogo. He painted sharp corners on his mouth, whereas traditional, non-mass-murdering clowns use round borders to keep from scaring children.

In the lobby, Asher is waving to a group in the glass elevator. They wave back as they ascend, the glimmer of the disco ball reflecting on the windowed wall. "Chantilly Lace" starts up. My heart feels dizzy in my chest.

"Kids are the pits," Dayna says, dancing a little with her bottom half. Behind her, the elevator opens and clowns slowly exit, like their joints hurt. Dayna says, "My daughter was spatting with another cheerleader, something about a boy, and she mixed Nair into the girl's shampoo. Can you say, Suspension? Can you say, Permanent Record? Can you say—"

"How good?" I interrupt.

"I'm sorry?"

"You said you were good with secrets. How good?"

"Oh," she says, a lovely lilt in her tone, her hips still keeping time with the music. "Really good. Unfathomably good. Better than—"

"Room 618," I say.

"Wow," she says. "Okay. Wow."

"Take the stairs," I say, making for the elevator.

When I go to my open houses on Sunday mornings, I worry Asher thinks I'm meeting a woman. I expect to return home and find him waiting, his eyes narrow with betrayal. Asher at the kitchen table, glowering. Asher pacing the house and brooding over the questions he'll hurl at me like stones: Who is she? Do you love her? What would Mom think? But he's always asleep when I get back, the door to his room unopened since the night before. The house is disappointingly quiet, indicting in its stillness, so I wash the week's dishes to bide time until my son emerges. Sometimes I intentionally clang pots and pans together, then apologize for waking him. Had I not started telling him I was going to church, he wouldn't even know I'd been gone.

At the showings, I ask about school districts and property taxes, mortgage liens and mineral rights. Such questions, I think, paint me as a serious buyer, but I'm also hoping for some combination of answers that will spur me to action. Early on, I expected to be easily swayed. The smell of new paint and freshly laid carpet, the gleam of marble counters and the pulsing sound of sprinkler systems in lush lawns—I thought they would prove irresistible and I'd want to make an offer on every property. But the houses punish me with loneliness, and I feel negligent and untethered, guilty for having left Asher at home. I can't actually imagine putting our house on the market or packing up our rooms. Once, the notion of surrendering my keys to another family brought me to tears. I was scrubbing bowls in the sink after visiting a three-bedroom ranch on Riley Drive, and Asher came out of his room and caught me.

"Dad, I think you're crying," he said, as if alerting me to a nosebleed. He wore his *Clowns Will Eat Me* shirt, his dark hair was mashed from the hard sleep of youth, and he seemed mortified to find me in such a state.

"The service this morning," I said. "It was beautiful."

On Sunday, the lobby has been transformed again for the Paradeability event. It's roped off in a zigzag course. One of the giant plywood faces marks the start point, the other stands at the finish line, and the route is lined with clowns and bleary-eyed family members slurping coffee. There are twice as many clowns as yesterday; if I look in one direction too long, the clashing colors make me lightheaded. I position myself halfway through the course and actually feel as though I'm at a parade. Asher waits in queue with the other competitors, pacing. I worry he'll vomit or faint. He didn't return to the room until after one this morning, and although Dayna was long gone, it's possible he spied her leaving. When we practiced his routine before breakfast, he was off his game, sluggish and tentative, and his lassitude felt like an indictment.

Before each competitor enters the circuit, an announcer rallies the crowd. He calls us ladies and germs, fillies and foals, boys and girls. If the clown is new to the competition, he says, "Ladies and Germs, our next contestant is a First of May." But the event is sleepy, tedious. My knees ache. I have to keep turning the video camera back on because it times out between competitors. Some clowns juggle through the course—rings, bowling pins, rubber chickens. Others just mosey along cracking jokes. There's a hobo who sneezes into a paper sack every few steps and sends a plume of powder into the air, then he offers the contents of the bag to the crowd and mocks offense when we decline. The woman wearing flippers and the inflatable pool acts like she's swimming by, and every so often she spits a high arch of water into the audience. How she refills her mouth is a mystery. A whiteface in a silver astronaut costume stomps along, occasionally lifting her bubble helmet to shout, *Moonwalk!* There's a clown on stilts who moves in slow motion, reciting poetry with an Irish accent. Passing me, he says, "I, through the terrible novelty of light, stalk on, stalk on."

Then the announcer says, "Boys and girls, how's about another First of May?"

There's a smattering of applause, a long, bending whistle.

"Well then, ladies and germs, set my head on fire and put it out with a hammer, here's Po' Boy the Hoboy!"

For his routine, Asher wears a pair of boxing gloves and has a small cardboard box tied to his ankle with a yard-long cut of twine. Once the clock starts, he says, "You want a piece of me? I'm the best kickboxer you'll ever see!" Then he kicks the cardboard box ahead of him, and starts bobbing and weaving and punching his way forward until he catches up to it again. Repeat, repeat, repeat. When he's throwing his jabs, he exhales through his red foam nose, sharp like a real pugilist. That was my idea. Granting the twine doesn't get tangled around his shoe, he can usually run through the routine six times in a minute.

And despite his lousy practice earlier, in the contest he's a crackerjack. I'm caught off guard by how his voice carries, the snap of his jab, the accuracy of his kick. The box lands directly in his path every time. When he passes, spectators whoop and cheer and sound horns. I feel like I'm in the bleachers at a bowl game and the audience wave is approaching. People maneuver for a better view; they lean and jostle and nod venerably. I record everything. I feel an almost unbearable pride, and my stomach roils with guilt for having ever doubted him. On his fourth stop, he's close enough that I have to unzoom the camera lens. "You want a piece of me?" he says to an auguste. She raises her hands in surrender. Everyone laughs.

Then, when he kicks the box, the twine breaks. The box is borne aloft, cartwheeling through the air, until, after what seems like minutes, it lands in the crowd. There's a collective gasping—"Holy smokes," someone says—and confusion as to whether this is part of Po' Boy's routine, a premeditated flourish at the end. Had he noticed the audience's credulity, Asher might've been able to call an audible. But he freezes. There's a wretched silence, and I want to run to him, to gather my son in my arms and spirit him away. By the time the box is being passed back toward him, he's composed enough to start throwing jabs again and proceed forward. I expect him to stop when he reaches the finish line, maybe to find me in the crowd so I can reassure or console him, but he bolts from the course. Everyone applauds, more confused than ever, while Asher heads for the exit. I stop recording just before he opens the door and disappears into the radiant sun. Then I go to our room.

Some mornings I wake up forgetting Jill is gone, and for a perfect crushing moment, a moment that is both too long and too brief, I think to reach for her in bed. Then I remember, and the old life recedes, like a tide being drawn back into the ocean. For the rest of the day, I feel halved. Other mornings, I'm positive I've lost Asher. Once, the fear was so consuming I snuck into his room and watched the blanket—a clown print—rise and fall with his breath; it was all I could do not to lie down beside him. Or I'll come home after work, calling his name as I close the front door, and if he doesn't answer right away, my heart will stutter. How often have I braced myself against finding a note, written in the same bubbly hand as Po' Boy's notebook, saying he's decided to light out on his own? I worry my son will run off with the circus the way parents of promiscuous daughters worry about abortions and elopements. I can't believe I'm enough to keep him here.

When I find Asher in the parking lot, he's on the tailgate of our truck, smoking a cigarette. In his costume and slap, and with the smoke ribboning into his eyes, he looks old and grizzled, convincingly penniless.

"Heads up," I call from across the parking lot and wing our football toward him. I've had it in our room since yesterday and went to retrieve it after he fled the lobby. My pass is wobbly, shamefully so, but with his cigarette clamped between his lips, Asher scrambles and catches it.

"What's this?" he says, turning the ball over in his hands.

"It's you," I say.

It only took the suspendered man half an hour to cover the football with Po' Boy's image—charcoal beard, thick eyebrows, alabaster complexion, and crimson nose. He worked from the screen of our camera, using a picture I'd snapped of Asher that morning. The ball looked so fine, so astoundingly lifelike, I'd thought to hold onto it for a birthday or Christmas present—I never know what to buy—but I knew I wouldn't be able to wait. When I showed it to Dayna last night, she said, "You're a good father."

"My wife died," I said.

"Oh, Sugar," she said, "I know that."

Maybe Asher told her. Maybe, given the hours she's spent surrounded by elaborate masks, my unpainted face seemed impossibly readable to her. I don't know. I broke into a humiliated sweat, sacked by guilt and relief, and willed Dayna to leave. Soon she kissed my scalp and slipped from the room without a word.

In the parking lot, Asher toes out his cigarette with his bowling shoe and blows a stream of smoke over his shoulder. The air smells acrid, poisoned. He studies the ball like a man deciding on a bottle of wine. He says, "This is pretty sweet, Dad."

"The gift shop was out of goose eggs," I say. Maybe he smiles a furtive smile, I can't tell. A silver jet rumbles into the sky behind him.

"The twine broke," he says.

"There should've been a flag on the play."

"It's never happened before."

"You handled it like a pro," I say. "Next time we'll use a nylon cord."

He spins the ball in the air, catches it. He says, "I don't smoke a lot. I just bummed that cigarette from a housekeeper coming off her break. I'm sorry."

I avert my eyes, arrange a pensive expression on my face. He expects me to be angry, and I know I should be. I should ground him. I should ask if he's taken a good gander at that crippled clown with the mechanical larynx. I'm aware of this just as I'm aware of the oil and gas coursing miles beneath our feet. This is prime fathering time here, the moment when I should impart solid, inviolable wisdom that will serve as his north star and guide him into a healthy future. But right now every truth seems porous, every judgment skewed. I feel something give inside my chest, as surely as when my knee buckled in the scrimmage and I knew my world was forever altered.

When I look at Asher—the dour mask, the clothes that once belonged to someone else, the weary secrets buried beneath his obsession—I see only the smallest traces of the boy Jill and I raised together. Instead, I see myself. It gives me a feeling of vertigo, this recognition, like I'm staring at a mirror that I've always taken for a window.

Asher is looking at his football again. I think he likes it, but I'm careful not to betray how much this pleases me. Cars and trucks are swooshing by on the freeway. A plane is about to touch down.

Asher says, "I really am sorry about smok—"

"Come to church with me," I interrupt.

"Right now?"

"Next week," I say. "I think a little fellowship might be in order."

He nods, contrite. He thinks I mean to scold him, and I'll let that ride to keep him honest, but punishment never enters my mind. The prospect of our finding a church together is invigorating, and I feel as though we're on the verge of something essential and new. We'll get dressed up. We'll file into a holy building and take our places among men in bowties and old women with powdered cheeks and bright lips, believers seeking shelter. We'll sing and pray, confess our sins and mourn our dead. We'll kneel before ancient altars, behold the glory of ritual and sacrifice. We'll weep and be saved. We'll go every Sunday. After services, Asher and I will hit a thrift store, or we'll swing by an open house and try to divine the years ahead. We'll talk about girls and college and his mother. We'll talk until our voices grow hoarse. When we return home, I'll slap a couple of steaks on the grill and we'll scroll through TV channels, looking for a game. If the Cowboys are playing, the stands will be packed with fragile men wearing wild wigs and oversized jerseys and war paint on their faces. Asher and I will root for all of them, the heartsick fans and their doomed, beleaguered team. We'll hold our breath when the quarterback lets fly with a Hail Mary. We'll hope for a miracle as the receiver stumbles toward the end zone. His arms will be extended and his legs weak and his palms open to the sky, and from where we sit, from our house, he'll look like a man trying to outrun everything behind him, like a man begging, at last, for mercy.

TWELVE STEPS

Mary Morrissey

After a month in Faithful, Arkansas, Ted Gavin met Paula Spears in the only bar in town where he could get away from work. Skipper's was the sort of place his students would never frequent. There were no happy-hour specials, no imported beers, and no bloated big screen tuned to sports. The only soundtrack was the low murmur of conversation and the thwock and rumble of billiard balls from the tables out back. The other patrons were aging, down-at-heel, occasionally raucous and seriously intent on quiet oblivion. They approached drinking with a steady diligence, as if it were a vocation. Joy and inebriation were intermittent by-products of the process but for a lot of the time, it was work, something to be got through. As he settled in at the bar, Ted noticed the lone woman perched precariously on the next stool and said hello. It was an old impulse—from home—though he was careful to say it as neutrally as possible, so it could be ignored or taken for an unattributed grunt if unwelcome.

"Howdy," she said cheerfully, and that's how it started.

Ted was relieved to have met Paula, to have met anyone. Even he realized that drinking alone in a place like Skipper's would have been too despairing, too lonely, too effing sad.

***

They met at Skipper's every Thursday—as if by chance. It had never become a fixed arrangement. Neither of them owned a mobile phone. They were pals, drinking partners, mates—he did not have the exact word for what Paula was to him. Female friend? Too cold and tame. Fuck-buddy? Hardly. He had never slept with Paula, never felt even the merest twinge of lust, and for Ted that was a blessing. (He had a history of miscalculation with women—with a few drinks he could come over all gamey but he couldn't sustain the bravado.) Sex had never come into the equation with Paula; for starters, she must have a decade on him. She was a small, wiry woman with stick-thin legs and rough-hewn dirty blonde hair. Her face was the only fleshy part of her—smooth, moon-like, with unaccountably merry eyes. Everything else about her was essential, necessary. Ted couldn't have described what she wore—some non-descript uniform of faded denim and pallid cotton. He could not even say she dressed carelessly—that would seem too deliberate, too much of a statement. Paula's clothes seemed immaterial, even to her. She didn't excite strong feelings in him; in her company, Ted found himself slowing, mellowing. They pondered on trivia—why are suitcases in movies always empty, where does the Mid-West end?

"The Mid-West doesn't end," she used to say, "it just goes on and on."

Ted had only the vaguest idea where Paula lived and he had never invited her back to his dim hangar-like flat. He had never invited anyone there. He was housed in a student block right by the railway tracks. Three nights a week, at 3 a.m., a goods train would roll by, thunderous but slow. The trains were so long—once he counted sixty-two cars—that it could take a half-hour for them to pass by which time their ponderous trundling would have lodged deep inside his brain. Afterwards, he couldn't sleep in the surging silence. Silence didn't bother him, but this busy emptiness did. It had become part of his routine never to be home on the nights the trains rolled.

He and Paula would sit companionably and drink until Paula's money ran out. Usually before his. She worked on a checkout in a supermarket. But what either of them did, didn't seem to matter much. That was a relief for Ted. Usually, when he mentioned he was a writer, it aroused the kind of curiosity he couldn't bear given the state of his novel—sprawling, amorphous, impossible to explain away in a quick sentence. He would start—it's about a woman in recovery from a disastrous marriage, as if you could recover from a disastrous marriage, who escapes by solitary drinking, well, not just drinking . . . All his explanations ran into qualifying clauses. What he didn't say was that it was about his mother, with the names changed to protect the guilty.

***

Of course, they shared stories. It's what people do over drinks in a bar with no laid-on entertainment. Paula's was unremarkable in its soap opera misery, its air of doomed statistic. Her first marriage, a teen wedding—shotgun, of course—was to Donny who did a flit when the baby was six months old. He picked up his coat one evening, she said, and just walked. It was a detail so deliberate that Ted immediately made a mental note of it. He imagined the coat—a lumberjack's large check, lime-dusted at the cuffs (Donny was a brick-layer) and saw a sandy-haired youth, jibby around the mouth, hooking a thick finger through the collar loop, maybe swinging it over his shoulder as he sauntered out to his car. Sauntered was how he'd do it, Ted decided. Or maybe he hadn't even planned it beforehand so his casualness was genuine. A single tumbleweed would brush by the steel toe of his boot as he opened the car door. No, it would be a truck, wouldn't it? Ted shook himself; these writerly riffs were too self-indulgent by far.

Paula moved in with her sister who was shacked up with Larry Spears. And, well, Larry was unemployed and Paula and baby Mikey were around the apartment all day while Jen was out at the plant and, well . . . Paula inhaled so deeply on her cigarette, her cheeks sucked into cadaverous hollows . . . well, things happened.

"He had two of us pregnant at the same time," she said. "I was further along. So I made him pick. And I won! The big door prize." Her laugh turned into a tubercular hacking.

Marriage number two lasted five years by which time Paula had had Debra, several miscarriages and had taken to drinking to dull the pain of bruised cheekbones and black eyes inflicted by Larry Spears. She stayed—for the kids—and to prove herself right.

"I'd lost my sister over this guy," she said, stubbing out the offending cigarette and making a sour face.

When she finally came to her senses and left Larry, she was so far gone on alcohol she couldn't look after the kids. That was six years ago.

"The funny thing is I didn't drink at all until I met him," Paula said.

Well, if you can't beat them, join them, Ted thought.

"I never beat them if that's what you're thinking . . . just couldn't handle them and the drink . . . " she said hotly and downed her vodka in one go.

Except for such flashes of feeling, she told Ted her sorry tale matter-of-factly, dry-eyed. It had the tone of a well-rehearsed and strangely impersonal monologue, the sort of thing he imagined you'd hear at an AA meeting. Everything about her seemed to have already passed into a kind of dirty realism, Ted thought. But although her life sounded fictional, he never doubted that Paula was telling the truth.

His own story, in comparison, sounded almost well-adjusted.

"Well," he began, "I'm Irish, as if you hadn't guessed. " He gestured to his flame-colored hair. "And the accent."

He had won a green card lottery in the Nineties; his sister Joan had entered his name. Before getting legal he'd worked on construction sites in New York for years.

"I was the joker, the storyteller, the Paddy with the gift of the gab. The fellas on the buildings with me were always telling me to write it down. So I did."

He didn't tell Paula that he'd kept the writing a secret. (She was getting the official version.) The scribbling wasn't something that would have gone down well with the same blokes whom he worked with by day and went drinking with by night. For all their loud exhortation, they'd have thought a writer in their company suspect. But the idea they had so casually planted, was surprisingly tenacious. Ted's writing ambitions grew in the dark he had consigned them to. Sometimes he thought it a curse—this "idea" of writing—but the urge was the strongest he'd felt in years. Strong enough to make him apply for and get through a writing program in Syracuse and get him this, his first teaching job.

"That's how I ended up in Faithful," he told Paula.

***

There had been a girl in Syracuse. Sandy. Rangy, intense, she looked like a throwback to the Seventies (before Ted's time but he recalled her type from films his sisters watched—*The Graduate, Play Misty for Me*) with a treacly mane of hair which she swung about like an extra arm—as much a part of her emphatic expression as her voice. She was like his very own cheerleader, as if he were a personal project. She enthused about the raw energy of his prose, his untutored way with words, his Irish syntax. But still he doubted her. Was she trying to butter him up? Had she fixed on him only for the curiosity of his accent, the whiff of the working class from him, the otherness of his experience? He remembered a trip they had taken towards the end, when, in his mind, their destinies had irretrievably forked. The trip had been Sandy's idea; she had a car. A mystery tour, she said.

"You're going to love it," she said as they drove towards the coast.

She brought him to Breezy Point, a bizarre gated community of Irish-Americans who had clustered together on the far tip of the Rockaway Peninsula.

"It'll be like going home," Sandy had said in her relentlessly confident way. Immediately he felt his truculence rising. Why did people presume you were homesick, he wondered, and that all you wanted was to go home. And if home wasn't on offer, that you'd be charmed by a miniature version of it, transplanted to Queens and set behind gates? They arrived at a checkpoint. Yes, a checkpoint with a mechanical arm and a lockhard with a cap!

"Not to worry, with your accent, I'm sure we'll pass," Sandy said gaily. She was right. The bloke in the uniform waved them through. Oblivious to his irritation, Sandy pointed out the store names—Deirdre Maeve's, the supermarket, the pub called The Blarney Stone. Ted seethed; she had brought him to theme park hell. The shore was the only place that seemed authentic. It could have been somewhere on the coast of Donegal. At home, he had always loved the sensation of being on the edge of land, of being able to look out and see nothing ahead but the tantalizing horizon. But now he was on the other side and he knew what he was looking back on. When he and Sandy stepped out on to the beach, they were almost blown away. The wind whipped the words out of their mouths. Sand swirled about them as they trod down a narrow passageway in the dunes between a high fence strung with netting. Notices were pinned on the wire.

"Plovers nesting. Please do not disturb the birds."

It was while they were considering this they were attacked. The birds seemed to come from nowhere. Flocks of them, clamoring and hostile, swooping low and aiming straight for their faces. Ted could hear their beaks clacking rustily at his ears as they squawked and screeched and constantly regrouped. This was no murmuration of starlings like you might see at home, where the sky would be sooted with waltzing swathes of birds putting on an aerial show. No, these birds were killer squadrons. The racket was terrible, louder even than the howling gale.

"Duck," he roared at Sandy as the plovers drilled towards them.

"Mother birds," Sandy shouted back informatively. Instead of keeping low, she stood and waved her arms about.

"Shush there, now, we're not going to touch your babies," she began shouting at the top of her lungs. "We wouldn't harm a hair on their little heads, would we, Ted?"

Feathers, he wanted to say, they have feathers on their heads. He did not want to be implicated in this coochy-coo baby talk.

Sandy smooched up her lips and made clucking sounds herself.

"Oh mommies . . . " she went on pursing her lips and pouting like a child, "there, there, don't fret," as the demented birds nosedived about her, pecking at the tails of her hair whipped into a frenzy by the wind. Even as she shielded her face, she continued her high-octane crooning. The tendernesses screamed at these decibels made Ted want to turn on her, just as the birds were doing. In the midst of the screeching flurry, he could hear only how loud and insistent Sandy's love would become. He threw his coat over her (her hair in a rage around her head seemed to particularly aggravate the birds) and manfully steered her back towards the car.

"Jesus," he said once they were safely inside. "That was like something out of Hitchcock."

But far from being upset, Sandy seemed exhilarated by the encounter, her face speckled with sea spray, her hair damply aflame.

"That was motherhood," she said. "Fierce motherhood."

"Time for a drink," he said and they repaired to The Blarney Stone.

Nothing personal he told Sandy when they broke up. It was straight after they'd graduated. She was going back to Cleveland, he to a summer on the buildings in New York. Why, she kept on asking him, tenderly but persistently. How could he say it? It was the way you talked to those effing birds.

***

When he had arrived in Faithful, Ted had been invited to several faculty dinners. He was always on his best behavior. He just didn't feel he could let his hair down among people who watered their wine or drank Dr Pepper. Delia Myerson, the chair of the department, was a middle-aged medievalist who threw vegetarian dinners for her staff with a missionary zeal. She was new to the job.

"You'd imagine given her speciality she should be serving huge sides of ham and great big drumsticks," Ted said to Miles Sandoval, one of the faculty poets. They were out on Delia's deck where the smokers were banished.

"She's desperate to be liked," said Miles. "Tries too hard."

Miles steered Ted to the edge of the decking.

"You've got to find a circle here," he said confidentially. "Something outside the university, preferably. Else you'll be stuck with this lot all the time." They both surveyed the scene—the littered remains of a dinner party, a heated discussion of the masculinism of Ernest Hemingway.

"Like what?"

"Well, there's the church," Miles started.

"I don't think so—can't see a lapsed Catholic making it as a born-again Baptist, can you?"

"There's always hunting . . . "

Ted didn't want to admit that he'd never seen a gun, let alone picked one up to shoot small furry animals.

"Or the gentlemen's clubs," Miles went on, using the euphemism Faithful employed for its strip joints.

"I'm not that sad, Miles, thanks."

"What about a writing group? Great way of getting chicks." Thrice-married Miles inhaled his considerable paunch and ran a large paw through his luxuriant mane of bottle-black hair.

"God, no. Sounds like a busman's holiday."

"Really, Ted, they're so grateful to have a guy in these groups they'll offer all sorts of favors. I love those serious artistic types. So intense."

Oily fucker, Ted thought.

“Two workshops and an Irish lit class a week is intense enough for me, thanks.”

“Or find some of your compatriots. There’s an Irish dame . . . “ he paused, frowning. “Say,” he roared sliding back the glass doors that led into the dining room. “What’s the name of that Irish gal who works for Hillbilly Realty?”

My god, Ted thought, is this for real? Property and irony lying down together.

“Hetty, you mean,” Delia called back. “Hetty Gardner.”

Delia rose from the table and came out on to the deck.

“Yes,” she agreed. “You Irish should stick together.”

Delia gave him Hetty’s card at the end of the evening. Realtor, it read, with the Hillbilly logo. He imagined Delia thinking with an efficient and good-natured sigh of relief—well, that’s Ted Gavin sorted. But he knew the last thing he would do was to ring Hetty Gardner. Moving in these circles he already felt like an impostor. He could scarcely believe himself that only five years ago he was a hod carrier, working away on scraps of short stories. The same stories that had been published by a university press with a tiny print run. But this Hetty Gardner wouldn’t necessarily be impressed by the slim volume entitled “Diaspora,” sparsely and grudgingly reviewed (“A tough new voice from the land of the Celtic mists,” said one. “But where are the women?” another complained.) He told himself he might look her up when he had the novel finished. He was used to putting things off; wasn’t his whole life in hock to this effing book? How else to explain his monk-like existence in Faithful, the long solitary hours spent in his dreary flat, poring over the derelict manuscript when he could have been out chasing women like Miles Sandoval? Time enough for that, he kept on telling himself, when the book was done. If he felt momentarily tempted to contact Hetty Gardner, he soon argued himself out of it. She probably wouldn’t be his type; her name alone made him think she was Anglo and a Prod. Anyway, she was probably here to get away from tribal associations. What other reason would there be for fetching up in Faithful, Arkansas?

***

His was shame. The baby of the family, sent to college while his sisters Brenda and Joan worked in a hairdressing salon to supplement his fees. Ted, who had gone to the US on a J1 visa in the final year of his arts degree and had never gone home.

“Is this what we educated you for?” his mother wrote. It was the strangest sensation receiving a letter from his mother—the first time ever.

"Your sisters scrubbing their fingers to the bone, so that you could hightail off to America? (Amerikay, he could hear her say it, like in some poor-mouth emigrant song) To work on the buildings?"

He couldn't tell her that the reason he wouldn't go home was her. That he couldn't face the claustrophobic disappointment that was their two-up, two-down house in Main Street, Mellick. Couldn't face another day with his mother sitting in the good room with the blinds drawn nursing miniatures in tea cups and melting into grandiose tears. Couldn't bear his sisters, all hair lacquer and nail polish, dancing attendance on her, trying to make up for the shortcomings of the man of the house. And latterly that meant Ted, not his unlamented father.

His poor Da, straight from Irish father central casting. A pigeon fancier, the only time he was at peace with the world was when he was whispering to his cooing birds locked in barracks in the backyard. Otherwise, he was an emotional caveman. He was given to volcanic rages in which he would slice and joust with anything at close quarters. Dinners were upended if the portions weren't large enough; furniture broken and knick-knacks smashed if he were thwarted. What saved his father from caricature was that he didn't drink—he wore a pioneer pin—but that made his moods even more unpredictable. Nowadays some underlying mental condition would probably be diagnosed—bipolar disorder, schizophrenia—but what difference did it make having a name for it, Ted thought. His father had made their lives a misery. But at least he'd had the grace exit early, keeling over in the midst of one of his choleric rages when Ted was twelve. For Ted's mother, though, that was his father's greatest crime. That he'd had the cheek to die, leaving her with three dependent children. His sisters were promptly apprenticed out, while his mother's life became a pooled and rancid stillness, a *grand mal* of resentful loss. The only thing that animated her was her punishing ambition for Ted.

"You're going to be a doctor," she would say, "or an engineer . . . that'll show him." As if Ted's whole purpose in life was to spite the memory of his father.

It was his mother who took to drinking—messily. Alcohol made her cravenly sentimental and affectionate, queasily so. She'd take Ted's hand and caress it, fingering the lines of his palm like a foolish astrologer.

"Oh Ted, Ted," she would say, "what would I do without you?"

Sometimes he wondered whom she was seeing when she planted a sloppy kiss on his fourteen-year-old lips.

"I never touched a drop until I was thirty," his mother used to say, "it was your father drove me to it."

Ted knew what was coming next.

"Do you know that when I got married to your father, my boss offered us a case of whiskey for the reception and I was disappointed."

His mother had been a barmaid in The Thirsty Scholar.

"I had no value for it. I'd have preferred a canteen of cutlery."

This was what Ted wanted to retrieve in his novel, the girl his mother had been, the one who would have chosen a case of knives.

***

Ted thought of himself as a social drinker—well, he liked to have other people to drink with. Days would go by and he wouldn't even think of alcohol, but once he stepped into Skipper's on a Thursday evening, it was the beginning of a roll that would finish up as a dull ache and a thick head on Monday morning. (Luckily he didn't teach on Mondays.) He didn't have blackouts, he didn't have bruises and scrapes he wasn't quite sure how he'd acquired, he'd never arrived at school drunk. He cleaned up well, and, usually he had prepared his classes. Usually. One Tuesday in February he was faced with a giant hangover and a workshop devoted—as he'd decreed the week previously—to the study of character. Snow had started to fall that morning in lazy swirls; by the time workshop was over it would be slick underfoot. Bypassing into the future was a favorite trick of his when he wasn't in the mood for teaching. He turned to face the students sitting in boardroom formation waiting for him to start. Paula was on his mind. She hadn't shown up at Skipper's on Thursday; she'd obviously had a better offer. He had camped out at the bar for the rest of the night expecting her to arrive at any moment and feeling both anxious and peeved that she had left him in the lurch. He brooded on her absence over the weekend, drinking steadily as he did. It was still rankling with him as he stood before his workshop. Three hours of unprepared class time yawned ahead of him. He improvised.

"Take a woman," he began.

Someone snickered.

"Late-thirties, victim of a violent marriage, who finally leaves her husband and then has her kids taken away from her because she drinks too much. A woman who lives in the vain hope she can get them back . . . "

Was it vain? He felt the first stab of misgiving.

"Delusional, in other words." That was Valerie Kleber. A professed Christian (her email tag was JCdiedforme), she was a severe beauty, with long black glossy hair, serious glasses and the kind of mouth, which was pert now and later, Ted suspected would grow thin and judgmental. Her father was some class of a minister.

"Let's not reach for labels, Valerie," he said, riled at her diagnostic certainties. "This is a study of character, not a case history."

There was a sharp rustling of papers and searching for pens.

"What does she do?" Valerie asked.

"Does it matter?" He was playing for time. Already, he felt seedlings of betrayal sprouting.

"What's her name?" Taylor Payne demanded.

"Let's call her Paula," he said. How pathetic was he that he couldn't even think up an alias for her? "She works in a store, on the register."

"This sounds like a total cliché." That was Taylor again shaking his shoulder-length blond locks, emanating a glassy boredom. A poet by aspiration, forced to dirty his hands with fiction. When he wrote in class a smirk played on his features as if he were contemptuously amused by his own trifles.

"Some clichés are true," Ted said.

"You mean this is a real person?" Sonia Matheson was either incredulous or sceptical; Ted couldn't work out the difference. He thought of her as large, sweet-natured and dim, but sometimes there was a gleam in her fat eye that could have been sarcasm.

"What I want you to do is to get inside the biography, so to speak. Find something authentic in the seemingly banal. See beyond the cliché."

"But is she real?" Sonia persisted.

"Let's go," Ted directed, anxious for the soothing silence that is fifteen students scribbling furiously, one eye on the clock, and would be a blessed balm for his hangover. The next best thing to the hair of the dog. But the class sat there, pens poised, waiting for something else, something more from him. At the corner of his eye, snow danced.

"Is she?" Sonia asked again.

"Okay," he relented. "She's a character in my novel."

Jesus!

Ted had a few golden rules, one of which was never to be confessional with his students. *Talk about their work, never your own.* So why had he just blurted that out? Because he thought it would divert attention from the truth, that he was using his best friend as writing fodder. It was Paula's biography that had been creeping into his novel, or as he had taken to calling it euphemistically, his work-in-progress. He'd spent the last couple of months not writing but taking notes. Little nuggets Paula had given him—the way Larry's voice would go all soft before he struck her, how for months she had spied on him emerging naked from the shower and felt the scalding burn of desire, how once she'd sucked him off with the baby watching. Ted listened avidly. Paula's experiences were so far removed from his mother's that they would give his book the burning frisson of fiction. And that was okay, he told himself. Divorced from their origins, even the most intimate details could be used, once you disguised them enough. To the toll of her confessions, he had added his own observations about Paula. His protagonist had developed her hairstyle, her furious way of smoking, her vulnerable optimism. Was that why he didn't fancy Paula? Because she was more value to him as raw material? No wonder he hadn't been troubled by inconvenient lust; he'd been trying to get inside Paula's head, not her knickers. She was the only one who could give the kiss of life to his forty thousand words of false beginnings.

Ted rose and walked to the window of the classroom. He pressed his forehead against the glass, glad of the cool clammy clasp of it on his temples. Outside the snow was having a tantrum. Angry trees made semaphore warnings. He felt like a character in a bad workshop story—overloaded with epiphany. *Jesus!*

***

"This Paula," Valerie said, cocking her head quizzically.

He wasn't in the mood. Two hours of student versions of Paulas—foxy lap dancer, bisexual trucker, Baptist preacher's wife—had exhausted him more than his thudding head. He felt dispirited—and chastened for using Paula as a quick fix for his class.

"This Paula," Valerie repeated. She looked like a scrubbed virgin but he had seen her at student parties—the girl had a sassy mouth and a taste for dirty martinis. But it was her sexual frankness which intimidated Ted. Though he would never admit it, he was afraid of her voraciousness. Afraid of her.

"Yes, what about her?"

"She's not just a character, is she? She's a real person."

Ted raised his hands in surrender.

"People are more than their biographies, Valerie. That's what today's exercise was all about."

"She needs help, you realize that, don't you?"

Valerie laid a polished fingertip on Ted's arm.

"She needs an intervention."

"A what?"

"You know," she said with a sweet fanged smile. "She needs to stop drinking, she needs a twelve-step program. She needs to be confronted. You know, tough love."

Ted was in no mood for tough love.

"Let's just stick to fiction, Valerie, there's a good girl."

"Don't patronize me," she snapped.

"Look, Valerie, there's a difference between writing and real life—the sooner you realize the difference between the two, the better."

She changed tack.

"Are you trying to tell me something, Ted? I can call you Ted, can't I?" He got a whiff of musky scent as she flicked her hair back over her shoulder.

"Look Valerie, if you want to talk about your writing, I'm happy to accommodate you. Otherwise . . . "

"You don't like my work, that's it, really, isn't it?"

He was tempted to be honest with her—it's not your work I don't like, it's you.

"Your character study of Paula was flashy, Valerie, amusing in its way, but there was no depth in it, no pain, no real pain. You failed to imagine her fully."

She grimaced sourly.

"It wasn't a character study, it was caricature. Whereas *my* Paula . . . "

"Your Paula?" she queried. "Who's confusing fiction and reality now?"

And she turned on her sharp heels and left.

***

An hour later, Ted was in Skipper's. He usually didn't go in on Tuesdays but he was parched and after the encounter with Valerie he felt in need of a stiff drink. He sat at the bar, slung his change on the counter.

"The usual?" Skipper, holding a glass aloft, asked.

The beauty of Skipper's was its monosyllabic omerta.

"Howdy!"

He looked up to see Paula just arriving. What was she doing here? He associated her with Thursdays and the well-oiled trajectory of the weekend. Somehow, he thought she only came in when he was here. Maybe she had a Ted for every night of the week? Get a grip, he told himself. You sound like a bloody jealous husband.

"Paula!" he said aiming for hearty, sounding feeble. He felt a twinge of irritation at her for not showing up last week. "There you are!"

Then he felt a piercing stab of guilt as he remembered what his students had been doing for the past couple of hours.

"What brings you in here on a Tuesday night?"

"I drink here every night, Ted."

It was his turn to feel betrayed.

"What happened last Thursday then?"

"Who are you?" she snapped. "My parole officer?"

"Steady on, Paula," he said. "What'll you have?"

Paula granted him a forgiving smile.

What an unlikely couple we are, Ted thought.

"Got a letter today," Paula was saying, "from Debra."

Debra was Paula's eight-year-old daughter; she was fostered out. She wrote dutiful letters to her mother every so often on notepaper dotted with pink hearts. Usually they were catalogues of her little doings—school, sleep-overs, her sister Amy (Paula always bristled at the mention of Amy; foster sister, she would spit) and finished with a flourish of smiley faces and florid endearments. *Lots and lots of love, Debra. Big kisses, Debra. I love you, Mommy.* Paula always latched on to these.

"See," she would say, "she hasn't forgotten me."

"Great," Ted said.

He was annoyed suddenly with Paula's awful faith that everything would work out.

"What the hell's bugging you?" she said.

"Nothing, nothing. Bad day, that's all."

"Tell me about it!" Paula started one of her long litanies. "Brian, you know the day manager, comes in today, he's in a foul mood. And I'm stacking, see, in detergents and he says Paula—hey Paula, you gone deaf or something? I've been calling you to the register for the last five minutes. We got a line stretching out to the parking lot. Get your fat ass up there! Little shit! He's not much older than my Mikey. I could put him across my knee and spank him . . . "

"Did you?"

"Did I what?"

"Did you ever hit Mikey?"

Mikey was her son by Donny, the brick-layer. Being older and more troublesome he was still in care and had refused to have any contact with her. Ted was thinking of when he was a boy. How he'd longed for his mother to strike him. He wanted the badge of a bruise, some physical proof of damage. His father's rages were aimed at things, not people—small portions of food, lost pigeons, recalcitrant plumbing. Lately Ted had begun to feel sorry for his father, the bull in the china shop beset by inarticulate rages. Sometimes he, too, just wanted to break things. He took a gulp of beer.

"What the hell is this?" Paula's eyes blazed.

"Nothing," Ted said miserably. "Want another?"

***

On the following Thursday he didn't go to Skipper's. He walked as far as the door but something stopped him. He had the sensation that there was someone right behind him, someone about to tap him on his shoulder. But when he looked back there was no one on Gibson Street, but the overhead traffic light turning from red to green. Another weekend in Faithful. He bought a slab of beer in the liquor store and went home to a TV dinner. The weekend felt all askew without the anchor of Thursday with Paula. His self-imposed exile didn't last. Damn it, he missed her, and his guilt about using her as biography fodder for his students had abated. Several days without drink had cleared his mind and cured him of the watchful paranoia he had fallen prey to. So it was with a light step that he pushed the swing doors open into Skipper's after a week's absence. His heart lifted at the sight of Paula perched at the bar swathed in cigarette smoke. It felt like a homecoming as she hallooed to him and tapped the stool beside her in that welcoming gesture that made him feel unquestioningly accepted.

"Hi Ted," she said.

He settled into his familiar seat—whoosh of torn leatherette—and gave her a comradely squeeze around the shoulders.

"Guess what?" she said. "I've had a letter from Mikey's case worker. Wanna see?"

"Sure," he said. He was determined not to yield to skepticism. He wanted to wind back to a time when his motives towards Paula were pure. If they had ever been. Paula rummaged in the large canvas sack that served as her handbag.

"Here it is," she said fishing out a crumpled looking piece of paper. "Dear Mrs Spears," she began, "Your son Mikey has been the subject of a special case conference . . . " she began haltingly. Paula was quick with her own words, but she stumbled over bureaucratic prose, Ted noticed. He found his attention wandering despite his best intentions. There was a scuffle at the door. Well, there often was at Skipper's—usually someone being thrown out. Ted turned towards the source of commotion. Three faces detached themselves from the blur of the crowd, for there was a crowd. And Ted recognized every single one of them. Eight of his graduate students from workshop, led by a determined, leather-jacketed Valerie. She marched up to the counter and clamped her hand on Paula's shoulder.

"Are you Paula?" she demanded.

"What the hell?" Paula started.

Ted swung down off the stool.

"Now look here, Valerie. I don't know what you're doing here. But leave Paula out of this," he muttered to her.

"So," Valerie said, side-stepping him, "there really is a Paula."

"What's it to you, lady?"

"Um," Valerie mused, "Ted here was rather unkind in his characterization of you."

Paula recoiled as the rangy Valerie looked her up and down. Beside her vividness, Ted thought, Paula looked like cardboard. Pale, depleted.

"We're here to save you, Paula."

"Save me, from what?"

"From yourself." She jerked her head towards Ted standing with his hands hanging. "And from him."

"Look, lady, I don't know what religion you're selling but I'm not buying."

"What we have here is a standard co-dependency situation. He needs you to drink so he can. You're enabling each other."

"Who the hell is this, Ted?"

"She's one of my students. Take no notice."

"You're never going to get your kids back, Paula. You've got to face that fact. Look at yourself! Why did you lose them in the first place? Because." Valerie paused here and advanced, wagging a crimson nailed finger. "Because your first loyalty is to this." She picked up Paula's vodka and slammed it down on the counter spilling its contents.

"Hey!" Paula said, affronted by the waste, and clambered down unsteadily from her stool to square up to Valerie. "What's it to you, anyway?"

Then she fixed on Ted. "How does she know all this about me?"

"Because dear old Ted's been getting off on your story."

"Ted?"

"Only last week we were all doing a character study of you which he tried to pass off as a person in his novel. This from the guy who's allergic to the confessional in *our* writing!"

"Valerie, that's enough!"

"You're not in the classroom now, Ted."

Ted turned to Paula beseechingly but Valerie persisted.

"What you need, Paula, is to get away from people who are sucking the life-blood out of you." She shot a steely glance at Ted.

"What the fuck!" Paula exhaled. "Is this, is this your idea of a joke?"

She was pacing up and down now, but there was nowhere to run to—no back entrance and Valerie's army stood four square blocking the front door. Skipper's regulars gaped dully.

"You need a real friend," Valerie went on, "the kind of friend who will be totally straight with you. With no bullshit."

Paula stared at Ted.

"You been writing about me, Ted?"

"It wasn't like that, Paula, honest."

"You been spilling my secrets?"

He shook his head vehemently.

"You sad mother-fucker!" she spat.

"Anger is good," Valerie said with triumphant reassurance.

"Know why I drank with you? Because I felt sorry for you. Living alone with the ghost of a fucking book, how sad is that"

"Paula, please . . . " Ted started.

"And all this time you've been sniffing around me like some perv going through my undies."

There was a ripple of gnarled laughter from the curious crowd of onlookers. Valerie placed her talons on Paula's shoulder.

"C'mon Paula," she declared, "let's get you sober, girl!"

She linked Paula's arm regally and to the applause of bar's patrons (even the billiard games had halted) the two women pushed their way towards the exit, surrounded by a phalanx of Ted's students.

He slumped back on to his stool. He signaled to Skipper for a double whiskey. The rest of the bar returned grumpily to their drinks, feeling let down in the wash of anti-climax. Ted drank greedily from the golden glass.

"Have I just lost a regular?" Skipper asked.

"She'll be back," Ted said. "Can you see Paula on a twelve-step program? I don't think so!"

***

That was three months ago. He had tried to track her down, desperately at first. He found out where she worked—Melvin's Superstore on Sycamore—but she wasn't there. Brian, the day manager, who looked about twelve, said she'd simply disappeared.

"Heard she went to one of those Christian rehab places, out Conway direction," he added as the pair of them stood in the dog food aisle.

"You don't have an address, do you?" Ted could hear the jilted panic in his voice.

Brian shrugged. "Sorry, dude. "

***

He's avoiding Skipper's these days. One public scene in a town this size is quite enough, thank you. But it comforts him to imagine Paula still there, sitting at the bar happily, blamelessly sozzled, easing into blissful unwind. Climbing carefully down from the stool to go to the ladies room, rubberlimbed, wavering—or was that only how she looked to him because he was often in a similar state, dreamily drunk and blearily semi-detached? He's still showing up for workshop. Well, life goes on; that's the trouble with it. Valerie Kleber smirks at him with a bitter lemon twist, while the others treat him with mutinous contempt. Well, why wouldn't they? He'd been unmasked as a sad old fuck. Wasn't that Paula's verdict? He felt bereft. Paula hadn't just walked out of his life—she'd walked out of his novel too. Now both of them were gone. There was a bleak sense of relief in acknowledging the novel had defeated him, but the loss of Paula, that was another thing entirely. Her absence struck at the very quick of him. That's the lesson, he wanted to shout at Valerie, smug with victory, that's the difference between fiction and reality. Reality breathes and hurts and drinks too much; it lets you down, it leaves things unfinished, up in the air, high and dry. Whereas fiction, fiction is just still life. Still fucking life.

He goes to the fridge—big as a starkly illuminated spare room—and reaches for a beer. He releases the ring pull—it seethes—and he raises the can in a silent toast. To Paula. Saved and lost.

LEAVING TAIWAN ALCATRAZ

Ciao Li

Translated by Angela Ku-Yuan Tzeng

No One Took Me Home

It was the afternoon after the Dragon Boat Festival in 1961.

Here was right out of the fence of TGCH, FDO (Taiwan Garrison Command Headquarters, Freshmen Disciplinary Office) on Fire-burn Island,[1] five hundred feet west of the "Husband-Lookout" at the back of the island.

Shih-Bin Yu put the note wrapped over and over with kraft paper on the roof of the five-foot high "cave," then secured it with two brick-sized stones.

After that, his first glance was fixed at the FDO, which was located at the base of a foothill in front of his position. FDO was over three-hundred-thousand square-meters and faced the north. On second glance he looked around at the scene of the island, and then zoomed out to see the ocean's green and white rolling waves. He knew that a shade of a bluish mountain at the far northwest end where the sea and the sky met marked where he'd been born, somewhere between New Port and East Port on the Island of Taiwan. Passing through the visible sea and sky, entering the realm of dream, his memories surfaced of a quiet little town on the countryside covered by falling snow, his hometown—a corner of Pu County in the Province of Shandong.

I was going home—I could go home now. All I needed was one more procedure. Yes, it was this "one procedure" that delayed my release from the prison. I could not leave the Fire-burn Island, could not go back to Taiwan, not to mention Pu County far far away in Shandong Province.

Shih-Bin Yu was sentenced seven years in prison because he was thought to be involved in the "Communist Rebelling Case of Espionage: Chuo-Min Jhou and others" in March of 1951. The key persons, Chuo-Min Jhou, Yao-Fu Ci and Ci-Yue Ci and six others were sentenced from ten year to life. Yu was not on the list. Afterwards, they found that the name "Shih-Bin Yu" appeared in a letter written by Syu-Chun Liou: he was then "involved" by some mysterious connection. In fact, he didn't even know Syu-Chun Liou, and the Shih-Bin Yu in the letter wasn't him either. Unfortunately, both Liou and the Yu in the letter were from Shandong Province, as was this other Shih-Bin Yu.

Yu had a bookstand in Taipei. He had a young kid who was not with him due to the chaotic era of war. His constantly ill wife was therefore utterly depressed, like a guttering candle nearly extinguished by the wind.

He was arrested preposterously in April 1951, involved circumstantially, and tortured inhumanly. After many near-death episodes he feel into a trance; he only knew he was sentenced for seven years after he regained consciousness sometime afterward. He "heard" that his crime was violating Article six of the "Betrayers Punishment Act." It was written in his indictment: deluded by traitors, he broadcasted false information through his bookstand to impede public order or to shake the people's faith. . . . According to the law, he should be sentenced with life or at least more than seven years. However, considering the alternative, he got the lightest sentence allowed.

After the sentence was confirmed, he was moved from the Detention Center to Taipei Jail (actually they were both part of Taipei jail, only in different sections), and moved again to Fire-burn Island only three month later. After he finished serving his sentence in March 1958 he was supposed to receive some "reinforcement education" and be released.

But he was kept in FDO. The reason was that his family never turned up to do the procedure, because his long-ill wife died soon after he was moved to Fire-burn Island. The jail didn't even bother to notify him. He learned this indirectly from Hsu, one of his fellows from the same province.

One year later, the jail administrator officially informed him the he needed to complete the releasing procedure, since his "enhancement education" was over and his thoughts had been "corrected;" so no need to worry about him anymore.

According to current regulation regarding releasing criminals who rebelled *in flagrante delicto*, the inmate had to find an immediate family member to take custody of him or her. This someone could be the prisoner's parents, spouse, children or children-in-law, brothers and their spouses whose household was currently registered on the Island of Taiwan and had to have a decent job. This someone also needed to come to the jail and sign the prisoner out, then take him home, otherwise he could not actually leave the jail.

In other words, Shih-Bin Yu was destined not to leave the jail. Unless the son left in Mainland China "defected for freedom" to Taiwan, then registered, then started a decent job, and also proved that they were father and son.

This story gradually spread among the Shangdong clansmen in Taipei. They appealed to the officials, and were willing to bail him in the name of his clansmen. Not only was the appeal denied, but the key persons were also brought in to question several times. Up to this point, everybody was silenced by the Yu case—nobody dared to talk about it anymore.

Practice to Go Back Home on Foot

Yu thought in silence, tried to set up a plan, but he never complained and never cursed about it. He hid this thought deep in his heart, only hoping to find some way out. But everything was in vain, absolutely hopeless.

He was a quiet guy before he came here with a full head of short white hair, a tall and extremely thin person. Now, he spoke less than before, often making no sound at all for several days. The jailors didn't care to discipline him anymore. They let him wander freely around FDO, more than thirty thousand square meters of land. In the end, even the wall and the gate were no longer restrictive for him. He only needed to return to the jail before curfew on his own. He became part of the legend of FDO on the Fire-burn Island.

However, he seldom left FDO and walked out of the wall. Since he could not leave Fire-burn Island, FDO and its more than thirty thousand square-meters was more than enough for him to walk.

After several more months had gone by, he suddenly appeared in another "character": he put on the green Chinese Tunic Suit which he had treasured for eight or nine years with his hair and beard both tidied and cleaned neatly, and on his feet he wore a pair of black leather shoes which were as aged as the Chinese Tunic Suit, with one bag in each hand. Using the wall of FDO as the boundary, he started his "patrol," walking one circle after another inside the enclosure.

He didn't rest at noon and often forgot to eat; he just kept walking and walking until 4:50 p.m., the time for dinner.

"What are you doing?" his fellow inmates could not help being curious.

"ME[2] is practicing, strengthening my feet—otherwise, hey, my hometown is so far away, without practice, there is no way I can make it. You think!"

His fellow inmates were astonished into silence. Shortly after this, someone couldn't help but whisper: "They won't let you go! Don't fool around! Go take a break!"

"Who said so? Who said they won't let me go? Could they lock ME up? When my feet are strong enough, when my practice is finished, from mountain to mountain, ME will walk back home. Of course, at this moment, my body is a constrained; but my mind is not. Didn't Sun Yat Sen say, 'To do is easier than to know.' Mind is to know, body is to do. One day, when my mind—my will reaches its peak, my body will be a constraint no more. ME can go home then."

Obviously this guy was a little insane. He became thinner and even looked taller. He always wore the Chinese Tunic Suit; he wouldn't take it off even in the evenings. He said he couldn't be delayed by changing clothes. He must be ready to act at any time. He always said: "ME time has been delayed already. No more delay . . . "

In the evening, this person who didn't really talk, started to talk to himself in a half-wake-half-sleep state, probably sleep-talking? He was too noisy, so that his fellow inmates couldn't sleep. The other inmates woke him up and started to talk to him gently; if he was clear-headed, they would explain the "reality" to him.

Then, he became completely silent again and looked really lost; tears started to pour out and splashed down. It was strange from such a thin and dry person, almost sixty years old now. Where did all these tear come from?

Then, of course, he returned to "the normal status" the next day, carrying his baggage, dressed up for his exercising trip.

"Still here, Shih-Bin Yu?" His fellow inmates teased him.

"Soon, ME will be gone very soon." He sincerely answered as he was walking.

"Soon? What for? Where exactly are you going back?"

"Going back to Taiwan, and to my hometown in Pu County, Shandong Province, you know..."

"You cannot go back! Even if he did go back, you cannot remember anything! It has been so long. Just stay and do your "strengthening feet thing" here!"

"No! Here is not ME home, ME has to go home—please don't trouble yourself to see me off!"

"Don't be a fool, just take this as your home. Life is so short, why bother? It doesn't matter where your hometown is, we could be content wherever we are—it all makes no difference, some day or another, we will all return into the earth peacefully, that's it!" This fellow inmate tried to convince and comfort him honestly and sincerely.

But he wouldn't listen. When his mind was wandering away, as well as when he was sober, he indulged in "practicing" home-going action; he was going home, nothing could change that. However, after arguing with others or with himself, he was full of tears and sobbed. Maybe those were the only moments when he was really clear-headed.

The awkward behavior gradually drew the attention of the high levels of FDO. They decided to lock him up, not allowing any chance for his "striding." Yet, right before the order was to be carried out, this tall and thin "odd figure," suited up with all of his "equipment" and barged into the Headquarters office.

"Aha! ME found it at last, I am back finally." He hailed cheerfully. Even his voice was different. This had never happened before.

"What are you saying, Old Yu!" Obviously, Sergeant Yo in the office had no clue about what he said.

"Well, well! After such a long journey, I am home at last!" He took a good look at Yo and said, "Pal, why are you here! This is ME home!"

"? . . ."

"ME said, Siou-Fong! Come out please Siou-Fong! ME is back!"

"Siou-Fong? Who is Siou-Fong? Shih-Bin Yu, you truly are..."

"Shut your mouth! Who are you to interfere in my business. Siou-Fong is my wife—You! You get out of here!"

It's truly a pity, he was indeed insane now.

It was said that FDO had called a meeting for him. The resolution was to ask the superior to have a "special program" to transport him back to Taiwan for further processing or therapy. An alternative was to release him when he returned to Taiwan, setting him free to take care of himself.

It was said that the superior rejected these proposals. The reason was that for his own sake he should not be left alone; for security's sake, he was to remain in FDO, until he was fully recovered.

ME Truly Mad?

Therefore, he was put in a "Special Room." The so-called Special Room was actually a confinement room for punishing inmates who violated regulations. They cleaned it well, moved his luggage in, and upgraded the lock.

Thus, Shih-Bin Yu not only couldn't leave the jail, but was also being locked up again. Even the regular two-times-a-day exercising was not possible now.

After being locked up, he was no more as silent as he used to be, and became a talkative old guy. The problem was that he had no one to talk to. However, maybe this was not a problem, since he didn't seem to need listeners. He lived in a compressed time and space. Either that or he was not restricted in any time or space or any other criteria of existence. He was free. All that long-lost memory was back. He could easily sing the songs from his childhood without any mistakes, as well as those "War of Resistance" songs[3], especially the "Song of Exile." He sang this song several times every day and every night, so much that half of his fellow inmates could sing some of it. Maybe that disaster described in this song shared some situation and deep sorrow with what he was experiencing now.

Like a moth by the fire,
Like a firefly in the night,
We were having a hard time—
A hard time.
No fear of the wind and the tide,
Chins up, we walked forward with pride,
Wiped off the tears on the cheeks,
Took off the embroidered outfits,
We didn't live in the greenhouse.
To the windy sand storm
Filled the sky—
The candles were dying,
The wine had dried.
Facing each other, we were quiet—
Quiet.
The sheep were all tied up.
To whom should they cry?
A long night,
Such a long night.
We talked tonight
On parted ways when the day turned bright
After long goodbyes.
There were still long goodbyes
Until we met next
With mountains in between.
In dream, we entwined,
Without wings, we couldn't fly—
Couldn't fly.
Looking into the distant cloud and sky
Tears on the clothes.
You, my old pal were in my mind.
I encouraged you for your spirit,
I wished you for more smiles,
I was imprinted in your heart,
and you were in mine.
No harm could be done
even when we were forced to divide.

Yes, "With mountains in between. In dream, we entwined," with barrier built with mountains and cloud, not because of the war, nor natural disaster, but for an unexplainable cause, for no reason at all. Shih-Bin Yu had changed from a silent person to a person who laughed and sang all day long. About one and a half months after that, his "Talkative Disorder" was suddenly gone—he became a silent person again; he often kept quiet for ten days or even half a month. Nonetheless, without any sound, his larynx vibrated quite often, sometimes even his lips trembled too. It seemed that he was still talkative in some way. Perhaps he just won't talk with someone he could see, but rather talked to himself, or some invisible soul, a fellow inmate who could understand him.

Due to no obvious security concern, and sympathy of his innocence, they decided to set him free—let him walk freely again in FDO. To show their compassion, the chief of FDO, a major general, summoned him into the office.

"Well, how is everything, health, daily life, everything?" the Chief asked gently.

He smiled, nodding shyly.

"Any problem? Need anything? We will assist you as much as we can."

He raised his head, glanced at the chief, and kept smiling.

"Wait here and don't worry—wait, umm, there would be one day . . . " the Chief ran out of words.

He nodded, and smiled.

"It is not that we won't let you go. In fact, you are set free, only there is no one to take you home, right? This is the law. There is nothing anybody can do about it. We would need to amend the law, you know, and this takes time. It is not up to my department to amend the law. Therefore . . . "

His eyes jolted, but he still smiled lightly.

"At any rate . . . " the Chief said and waved his hands to ask him to leave.

In short, since then, everybody got used to ignore the existence of "speechless Shih-Bin Yu." Like a ghost, like grass by the wall at the corner of the house, and like shapeless wind swirling around, he wandered, strayed, and moved about FDO. Nobody knew since when he stopped carrying his luggage day and night. He often just put his hands in his pockets, sometimes he lowered his head, and sometimes looked upwards pointlessly at the blue sky. That's why he got trapped on the ground or even fell into a mud pond from time to time. Even so, he was always sentimental about everything he saw, regardless of how others thought.

By March 1961, he was obsessed with the hill just outside the west wall of FDO. This was where they stored fuel. His fellow inmates often went up the mountain to chop trees for the kitchen's firewood.

On the left hand side of the hill, near the left border of FDO, there was a terrace about twenty feet high. Fellow inmates called it "Husband-Outlook."

It was said that the name came from a very rough but moving story made up by an inmate writer: a fiancée of an inmate with a very long sentence requested a visit. At first, the jail didn't approve, so the inmate wanted to make her give up the hope. He then refused to meet with her, only sending out mail to sincerely ask her to find some other guy.

As a matter of fact, the reason the fiancée requested the visit was to call off their engagement.

Now, upon receiving the long earnest letter from her fiancé asking her to find another guy for her own happiness, she was ashamed of herself. The more she thought about it, the more she felt upset about herself. Therefore, she climbed up this "back hill." She reached the terrace, looking down from above, with tears all over her face. What was love, what was happiness? What was she pursuing? She cried and fell on the hill.

That very night, the storm came. By the third day, inmates found her lying on the terrace, barely breathing. They carried her down for emergency treatment. Unfortunately it was in vain. Nobody knew her name, where she lived, or anything else about her. They then buried her carelessly under the terrace. Since then, a shape of a woman often appeared on the terrace in the moonlight. Sometimes, she sighed, sometimes she cried . . .

There was not much to do for these inmates, so they continued passing this story on. And the terrace was called "Husband-Outlook" for some time now.

Shih-Bin Yu was now "no threat to security," so there was almost no restriction at all on what he did. Except for the time of three meals and sleep, he often remained and wandered around "Husband-Lookout." In the warm and clear summer days, he even stayed overnight there, immersed in his own fantasy. Nobody could talk him out of it; everybody accepted this and let him be.

After that, a big shot political prisoner like Yang Kui built a hut here for a group of comrades to chat or discuss. Yu didn't contact or talk to anyone. After people left, he would stay in the hut to sleep or just to be lost in his own thoughts. Since he was "harmless," Yang and others let him come and go as he wished.

ME Would Go Home By My Own Way

One sunny afternoon, Shih-Bin Yu crossed the "Husband-Lookout" to the end of the terrace. The end of the terrace was oval-shaped, then the hill dropped down to form a hollow of thirty to fifty feet deep. On the right front, the shallowest of the hollow, the slope began. This was a north-facing spot, with one side of the standing wall which could be dug into, forming a little "cave." This scene looked somehow familiar to Yu.

Shih-Bin Yu stared at this spot with muddle-headed obsession. Thoughts suddenly surged through his mind as some very vague yet clear idea surfaced.

In this late autumn time, the bushes and the forest of huge trees all appeared the color of red ocher under the sun. He felt like he was in a dream.

He had made a decision. A very important decision, the last choice in this life.

He thought he had found the place connecting all his dreams and soul. After all, the land was all connected. At a place where he had such strong déjà vu, he would establish a place for himself, then the trouble in the reality out there meant nothing. Nobody could imprison him; he was going back; only people wouldn't imagine he could go home in such an unusual way.

He then started to carry out this "peculiar home-coming" plan step by step.

First of all, he chose a spot at the edge of the terrace where the slope was somewhat steep but not too much—a spot lined up with the flagstaff right in front of the main office. The ramp was only five meter deep. He dug here to make a cave half inside the ramp and half standing out. When he was done working, he would cover the "construction site" with grass and vines.

He spent three weeks building the structure of this little residence: about three feet wide, five feet deep, and went inside the ramp for about two feet down. The second step was to build the roof. He used tree stems to make a trellis, piled a layer of big and small stones on it, and used mud to concrete all these stones. The "roof" was then finished.

The little cave faced north. A door of three or four feet was right at the opening of the ramp, facing the flagstaff in front of the main office from a distance.

The work was done. Because it was all carried out secretly, and because he was a "wanderer" in FDO, nobody was interested in anything he was doing.

Up to this point, he realized that there was no "will" that led him to do anything. It was rather like there was a track and he existed in a trance during which he got on the track naturally. Everything on this track didn't work by the forms of language, words, sounds, or any kind of symbols. It worked by a shapeless, formless and totally unfamiliar way which he had never encountered before, but he understood it as soon as he was on this track. This gave him confidence in two things: he was going back, and no one could stop him. He was led by this "message," and carried out the home-coming plan step by step.

"Is it anger? Is it resentment?" a voice asked from a corner of his mind.

Umm, there was a deep and dull pain, a thick chill, but that was not anger or resentment. Or we should say it was beyond concepts like "anger" or "resentment," which had some limitation in their meaning.

He thought it over and over, checked everything cautiously, and felt everything was ready.

After he thought everything out, he wrote a serious letter. This letter must be seen, but could not be seen too early or too late. It would ruin everything if too early; the hand writing could be blurred if too late. He put the letter into a kraft envelope, wrapped by two layers of tarpaulin, and put the whole thing into another kraft envelope one size bigger than the first one.

The time had come. He brought some food and wine up to the terrace.

It was the Dragon Boat Festival yesterday, the temperature was not low; the sun felt very warm.

The "newly Inaugurated" cave raised from the ground about five feet tall. It looked really nice: some weeds had already sprouted on the roof with fresh greenness. Life! So beautiful and so fast. He felt he really liked this.

First, he used a brick-sized stone to press the "kraft package" on a flat spot of the roof; the location was quite eye-catching.

He put out bean curd, dried small fish, fermented egg, and fried peanuts; a half bottle of rice wine was still wrapped by old newspaper. What a sumptuous meal, he was going to really enjoy it. He forgot he cup, but drinking from the bottle in big gulps wasn't bad at all.

He wished to take his time to enjoy it, but somehow he couldn't help but speed up; as if time was up, there was an "order" deep in his mind to push him: Hurry! Go now! Otherwise, something unexpected might happen: he might be interrupted, there might be some change. . . .

Where did this thought come from? He had gone so far, he was not afraid of anything now. This was nonsense, a joke, and bullshit too. He didn't need to argue with anyone. He used the handkerchief and old newspaper beneath the food and wine to pack all of his leftovers neatly, and threw the package down to the bottom of the slope.

With no further ado, no more looking around, he squeezed himself sideways into the cave steadily and slowly. The "door" was kind of wide, but the poles supporting the roof had separated and narrowed the space.

It was complete dark in the north-facing cave, no sunlight at all. This darkness was rather enchanting, he felt everything was as he expected, all under his control.

He didn't want to push the poles down just yet. Now that there was no light at all indoors, but beneath him there was the shallow slope, the bushes, the woods in the color of red ocher, and the FDO's three-hundred-thousand square-meters of land. It was all in his sight. Even though his vision was not that good, his eyes filled with some kind of water that made the scene clear and wave in front of him vividly.

Ha! Now, all of those were separated from him by an invisible boundary. In other words, everything in front of him had nothing to do with him whatsoever. Any ugly, evil injustice couldn't hurt him anymore.

He shot a last glance at that world before he pulled the poles down.

How would people in this world see this somehow absurd behavior? A long-term prisoner, serving all of his term but couldn't leave the jail for there was no one to bail him out and take him home. If he couldn't save himself or find some way out, he would be kept here until death. And the so called "self-saving" was not a sensible way in this world. All sensible means were monopolized by the injustice-doers in this world. This despairing old man dug himself a hole in this strange land, to bury himself.

Only the Land Would Not Refuse ME

Only the land would not refuse him, the land took him in. The land had no opinion against anybody; men cannot disgrace or tarnish the land, and all lands are connected, therefore the land in this strange domain accepted him.

The letter pressed on the "roof" read:

ME is gone. The great government wouldn't allow me to go. ME buried myself, there was nothing they could do about it now.

ME had no family or relative in Taiwan, no one could prove my identity. I couldn't leave the jail because there was no one to take me? Fine, I now buried myself; I am out now. What could you say about it!

Nobody did this to ME, ME dug and built the grave myself. ME used poles to hold the frame of the door. After ME entered, ME would push the poles down let the rock and dirt cave in to seal the entrance. ME self-buried and committed suicide. The villains can't use this to frame anybody.

ME is gone. My soul will fly back home. Pu County in Sangdong Province Shih-Bin Yu, Autumn of Shin-Chou Year.[4] These are my final words.

All was done, the wishes were sent. He hesitated no more. Use all the strength he had left in this legs, he pushed down the four supporting poles. All the rock and dirt fell down from above, caved in from both sides, and sealed the cave. Shih-Bin Yu was buried, by himself.

On the third day, a group of fellow inmates found it when they went up the hill for the firewood, including the multi-wrapped testament. Among them, even the calmest old political prison, "Old Yang Kei," cried quietly.

Everybody thought and imagined silently, what exactly had gone through Shih-Bin Yu's mind? If we were to put the process of self-burial into words, how could we connect all the spots of light in his mind? No writer could imitate this by "transference."

People might want to carefully, sincerely put themselves in his shoes:

How dreadful was this "posture" to the death!

The way of searching, the process to make up his mind; what was he thinking at the time of death?

During the process of gradually, firmly building the "cave" step by step, the mind . . .

When the "cave" was completed, the image of him writing the testament . . .

How did he walk into the "cave"? How was his last glance toward the world? . . .

He entered the "cave," removed the poles—the boundary of the two worlds, the last chance he had, also the decisive move to absolute refusal of the world. Had he hesitated?

In fact, he had carried through this refusal act, entering the other world.

To the outer world, he gave up his life. It appeared so up to this point. But right at that moment, it didn't seem so anymore. Surely, the unjust world deprived him of the right of existence that he ought to be entitled to. He was all passive. However, from this moment, he was all initiative. He owned his life absolutely. He used his own hands to control his own fate. He refused this unjust world at last!

Was the space for his self-burial too limited? No, the "cave" was connected with the earth, he lied down on the back on this sweet-smelling ground, embraced by the mother land. Think of this, the letter in the inmate Yang's hand dropped and lightly landed on the ground. His tears dried, and he smiled.

His fellow inmates whispered to one another. A young and reckless inmate Lin who was serving a life-sentence, stepped on the already collapsed "cave" and shouted madly toward the FDO, yelling:

"Down With The . . . "

1. Fire-burn Island: A small volcanic island in the Pacific Ocean about thirty-three kilometers off the eastern coast of Taiwan. It was called "Fire-burn Island" during

the Japanese regime and has been called Green Island since 1948. This island is isolated from Taiwan, therefore it is primarily noted as the prison for political prisoners during the martial law period of Taiwan's KMT ruling (1947—1987).

2. In Shandong's dialect, "I" is pronounced as "aan." This is a very distinctive feature to recognize someone's Shangdong origin. In this story, "ME" is used when Shih-Bin Yu used to "aan," to distance himself from his origin.
3. The resistance in China against Japan during WWII (1937—1945).
4. In Chinese sexagenary cycle (aka Stem-and-Branches) sixty terms were used for recording days or years. Ten terms of stems and twelve terms of branches were used to form a total of sixty terms. In this cycling system, Shin-Chou is the thirty-eighth term. It refers to 1961 in this story.

SCENERY[1]

Fang Fang

Translated by Ling Jian'e and Guo-ou Zhuang

Behind the scenery of this immense
Existence, through abysmal blackness, I
Distinctly see the wonder of new worlds.
- Charles Baudelaire[2]

Brother Seven[3] says only when you hold everything in the world as dirt cheap, including the world itself, can you then feel you have really lived and make your round in this world with satisfaction.

Brother Seven says life is like the tree leaves that come and go all too soon. The buds in spring grow only to become the fallen leaves in the autumn. Since all lives end in the same way, why should we care whether we have robbed others to make our own leaves greener and fatter.

Brother Seven says those who claim to have a clean name often live for their own reputation. They may have done no harm to others, nor have they made much contribution to society and humanity. In contrast, those who are despised for having made their fortune by any means may benefit others by donating a large sum of money to build a hospital or a school. Between these two types of people, can you really tell which is superior and which is not?

Brother Seven would rave like a mad dog like this as soon as he steps in, as if to take merciless revenge against his deprived right to speak as a boy at home.

Father and Mother could not bear it and would run out of the house right away, crying that they've got a toothache. The railroad that connects Beijing and Guangzhou was only inches away from our eaves. Every seven minutes a train would pass by, bringing howling wind and crushing noises.

Out here, Father and Mother can hear with pleasure every single syllable uttered by Brother Seven being crushed into pieces by the giant wheels.

If Father goes by his old habit, he would have cut off the tongue of Brother Seven the first time he does so. But he dares not now. Brother Seven is now quite a character. Father has to hold back all his pride to get used to this big potato.

Brother Seven is now very tall and very fat. His face often glows with some reddish and greasy light. His belly bulges a little, just right. It is hard to imagine it is the same skeleton from the past that holds his fleshy body. I doubt if the operation he had when he was twenty was not to remove his appendix but to have his bones changed instead. This has to be true for there is no other explanation for the fact that he keeps growing bigger and bigger ever since. With his suit and tie on, Brother Seven looks like a businessman from Hong Kong. But when he wears a pair of frameless glasses, he looks like a professor or some expert. Whenever Brother Seven walks around in the street, he always invites admiring gazes from girls who simply can't help themselves. Brother Seven never speaks like a mad dog outside the house, instead he presents himself elegantly by talking about ideas that are supposed to have occurred only to those who have meditated for decades.

Brother Seven once stayed at Qing Chuan [Fine River] Hotel. Father wouldn't believe him at first. The hotel is the tall and white building that he sees everyday when he hangs around on the riverside. It is so tall that Father believes only high-ranking people like Chairman Mao or Premier Zhou can stay there. Having lived in Hankou for these many years, Father has never seen anything taller than that. Mother reminds him that both Chairman Mao and Premier Zhou had passed away before the hotel was built. Father replies right away that General Secretary Hu and Premier Zhao can stay there. It was 1984 when Father said so.

Trying to prove that he has indeed stayed in that hotel, Brother Seven says the Chinese character for Qing [晴 fine] on the sign in the building appears like the Chinese character for An [暗 dark].

Naturally Father and Mother can't imagine they can get a chance to check that out. But it is proved true after Brothers Five and Six went there, each bringing one thousand RMB with them. They did so after they heard about the news that a self-employed businessmen had stayed in Qing Chuan Hotel. They came back the next day assuring their Father that Brother Seven had indeed stayed in that hotel for the character 晴 inside the hotel does look like 暗.

Brother Seven says I always go there by taxi and each time a bell boy in red uniform would come to open the taxi door and bow to me saying, "Welcome."

This can't be proved for Brothers Five and Six went there by bus and had to walk a long way after they left the bridge. Yet by now Father and Mother have totally believed in Brother Seven and need no more proof.

Next time Father hangs around the riverside and runs into familiar faces, he can't help saying, "Qing Chuan Hotel is no big deal. My seventh boy stayed there many times. "

"Really? The boy that used to sleep under the bed?" they would exclaim.

With all love and pride on his face Father would say, "Yes, yes, he has indeed slept himself under the bed into somebody."

The irony is that Father used to suspect that Brother Seven is not his own. He had no idea of his conception until Mother's belly began to show. He calculated the dates and then he grabbed Mother and slapped her twice on the face. He said he was up in Anqing on a cargo ship to visit an old friend who was dying and who wished to see him for the last time. He was away for fifteen days and Mother must have become pregnant with Brother Seven during that period. Father knew well that Mother had been flirting around all her life. How could she ever stand being alone when he was not at home for half a month? Father thought Bai Liquan, the next door neighbor, was most likely to have fathered Brother Seven. Bai was a skinny man with his eyeballs forever roving around and his lips forever moving up and down to butter up women. What mattered most was the fact that Father once saw Bai flirting with Mother. The more Father thought it over, the more certain he became. As a result, Father would not even take a look at Brother Seven in his first month. When Mother stayed in bed to recover from the labor he gulped alcohol and chewed fried beans noisily at the door, as usual.

It was Big Brother who was waiting on Mother. He was seventeen then, and solemnly he looked after his baby brother that was as soft as a worm. Half a year later, Father took his first look at Brother Seven. He looked very carefully, and then threw him onto the bed as if throwing away a bundle. Brother Seven was so skinny that he didn't look like our tall and masculine Father at all. Father took Mother's hair in his hand by force and demanded to know who on earth fathered Brother Seven. Mother fought back with screams and curses, calling him all sorts of names like wild hog, barking dog, and blind devil. Mother also shouted that Father should have the guts to pick a fight with her when the real purpose of his long trip to Aiqing was to meet his one-time lover at her deathbed. Father and Mother both cried so loud that even the noises from the train passing by every seven minutes could not drown them out. All of the neighbors came to watch them fighting. It was dinner time and they all stood around the door with bowls in their hands, making funny comments while chewing their rice. The moment Mother spit on Father, they commented that Mother's gesture was not as pretty as before. The moment Father threw bowls to the floor, some of them commented it would sound better to crash the thermos, while others added if there had been a thermos in the house, Father would not have just crushed some bowls. It is a fact known to all that Father is quite a man in this place called Henan Shacks.[4]

1. This selection is from the first chapter of the story. The story comprises of fourteen chapters of irregular length in total.
2. The English version of the quote is by James McGowan. See "The Voice" in Charles Baudelaire, *The Flowers of Evil* (Oxford University Press, 1998), p. 313.
3. The narrator of the story is the eighth son in the poor family who had died from some cramps on the sixteenth day around 1961. This is revealed in the beginning of the second chapter, together with the fact that the dead baby happened to be born on his father's birthday and for this he was precious to the father and was buried right under the family window.
4. Henan Shacks are where the first generation of migrant workers from Henan, like the narrator's grandfather, settled down when they first arrived in Wuhan. The name itself rings of poverty to the local people.

A Common Tale

Velma Pollard

My conscience was bothering because since my parents dead I stop visiting their old friends so I take the country bus to Grove Park and walk over to Lime Hill to look for Maas Isaac. Him and Papa used to knock domino on a Saturday and Pinnie had send to tell me him was poorly.

Well, let me tell you if nobody was there to tell me I wouldn't recognize the man at all. Big fat round face Maas Isaac was as thin as a rake and you could see the outline of jaw teeth against his cheek.

"Maas Ize how you do?" I said "Vangie, Maas Albert big daughter Vangie."

"Oh Vangie my child how you do? You know the old man not seeing. But a think I would make our your voice."

"Yours still the same Maas Ize," I lied. "How you feel?"

"Girl I am as weak as a yam vine. Can hardly hold up. Is just through a sitting you don't notice. I glad you come. Albert would glad to know you still remember the old man. I soon see you father, soon gone to boneyard."

"Don't say that, Maas Ize," I said, watching death staring at me from his hollow eyes.

Miss Girlie was hanging about him with an anxious look which alternated with a plastic smile reserved for the likes of me.

"A so glad to see you (plastic smile). These days Maas Ize like to talk to people from the old time. I don't know what to do (anxious eyes) with him though; won't keep down a thing. Nothing will pass his lips, nothing solid, spit out everything. Him just drawing down drawing down and the doctors dem can't find out what cause him to lose the appetite. They say all his organ functions are OK. Still, I try him every day but no luck. As you are here let me try him with piece of this cake. Since is you bring it him might eat it."

She broke a piece of the carrot cake I had brought and I stood transfixed at the proceedings. She was feeding little bits into his mouth on a fork, but as each piece reached his lips it fell away in a rush as if he was spitting it out. But that couldn't be, because his face was motionless.

I kept staring at him. I was speechless. And then my own mouth fell open and I started to hope Miss Girlie wouldn't catch my eyes for I was sure they were popping out. Clear as day I could see Miss Margaret bending over him and using a thumb and first finger to bounce off each other, like she playing marble flicking away each piece of cake from his mouth. I remember how Teacher Bennett had seen me in my dark glasses and said how the midwife had said he would able to see Duppy and he only proved it then. Well I didn't know before that I could see Duppy.

"Miss Girlie a going inside go sit down," I said.

I flopped down on the sofa, not in the rocking chair that Miss Margaret used to occupy those last days. I leaned back and closed my eyes. Cold sweat was washing me. No wonder the doctors couldn't find out what was wrong with Maas Ize.

I must have fallen asleep there eventually, because when I catch myself it was lamplight. Lucky thing I wasn't going home same day. I was going to sleep over by Pinnie so it didn't really matter.

I woke up thinking about Miss Margaret. My mind went back to the days when Miss Girlie wasn't Miss Girlie but just Girlie washing and ironing and cooking the occasional meal in Miss Margaret kitchen, for Miss Mag was a lady very particular about her food.

Now Miss Mag was out there boxing food out Maas Isaac mouth.

You know I don't think she mind that him take young girl. For she could all glad that somebody looking after him. She was such a kind-hearted lady. I think it is that she mind how him didn't have the decency to go out the road and find somebody. Him just take Girlie. Near at hand and needy. Maybe she was wondering if him was going there from before she dead.

I could hear the sound of plates being washed in the kitchen. All those cups Girlie used to chip with her careless hands now belong to Miss Girlie self. What a life! If you don't die you will see everything.

I try to tell myself is a good thing him do, for all women are created equal and should get equal chance with food and house and man. But it wasn't working. I wasn't rejoicing for her. I was grieving for Miss Margaret although I know she was beyond grief, and that she obviously work out her own revenge

"Miss Vongie will you have a cup of tea?"

Miss Girlie's voice broke my reverie

"You have lime leaf?" I asked.

"Yes man."

"Well lime leaf tea," I said, remembering how lime leaf supposed to drive spirits away.

Stories of Sri Lanka

Minoli Salgado

The Breach

It had taken just two days for Sumana to master the art of flattening her body against the wall of the bund so that she was thin as could be, just a fine leaf of bone. Above and behind lay the danger. The sky sawn open by planes dropping huge exploding eggs, bullets lashed into screams, shells breaking the earth. The scramble and press of bodies. In front only the earth wall offered the possibility of protection.

Sumana thinned herself against it and kept her breath slow as another blast shook the ground and thrust more people upon her. A collective wave of panic added to her own fear. She absorbed it into the silence of an open mouth, her arms trembling down the length of her as if the earth itself had grown cold.

Cries erupted from further down the bund marking the place where a shell had hit.

"Mother," a man groaned. "Mother." And Sumana knew he would die.

For the dying always cried *mother* when about to be released, as if in sudden anticipation of the life yet to come. They never cried out for god, for water or help, for things that might offer a return to the world, but for mother: the first refuge and the last. And two days and nights before, her own mother had done the same.

"Here," her mother said, drawing something from the fold of her sari. "Here, eat."

And Sumana had broken the unleavened bread and placed a piece in her mouth. She did not recognize the contact, the dry wood of her mouth against the cardboard of bread, and had chewed until the saliva came. It was the only food she had eaten that day. They'd finished the small packet of biscuits distributed on a day of bounty when aid supplies got through. Ever since then aid supplies were confiscated by the men with guns.

"We are fighting for you," they said, carrying away the bottles of water, food packets and rolls of gauze delivered by the Red Cross. "We need the food to fight for you."

And Sumana had looked up to see the edge of her world marked by their guns.

"Tonight," her mother said, "we will leave this place. We will leave for the other side where there are quiet camps. Till then, stay inside, and stay against the wall."

It had been still for many hours. Her mother consulted the sky. Someone stirred.

"You should've gone earlier." A woman lay slouched with a boy on her lap. She was old, or had turned old. The wrinkles on her skin rippled into the whiteness of her hair.

"Why didn't you go?"

"I will wait. I can't walk. The fighting will stop. There are only so many bullets the sky can contain."

"We can leave together. I will help."

"No. But you can take him if you like."

She motioned to the boy who looked at them with moons in his eyes.

Her mother lifted the child. He scrambled up and disappeared over the top as a flare opened up the sky, catching her mother in its bright star. A gust of gunfire threw her mother back so she fell warm and bleeding, pressing Sumana against the earth.

Sumana opened her mouth for words and heard her mother's fall into it. *Mother.*

Two days later, after her mother's body had been removed, Sumana stayed close, pressed against the earth, opening her mouth for the words that would never come.

Invisible Island

It had begun with the touching of rocks. He stroked a tall granite boulder and saw a temple emerge. The square columns grew to support a panoply of gods that people came to worship from miles around. Their prayers consecrated the land and from the ground rose a past that might have been true. In time it was agreed this was an ancient, sacred land.

He touched the straight trees that grew about the village. The trees were thin palms that bore hard fruit. When he touched them they became fountains of honey that poured into vats brought forth by those without food.

He touched brown cows branded by ownership and made them holy white bulls. He touched his mother, his father, his brother and his betrothed, and watched them transformed into resplendent royalty.

And last he touched himself and saw his skin break into thorns. He became a magnificent mythical beast the like of which had never been seen.

"The land is mine," he said, and none dared to disagree. For was not this wonder all down to him?

"And it is your land too," he roared, "if you follow me."

There were questions, of course, from those unsure of what they saw.

"I still see rough rocks at the temple."

"There is no honey in these vats."

And the questions grew and gathered like a flock of hungry crows.

"Who is he?"

"Where is he leading us?"

"He looks ugly to me."

The man touched his doubters and made them disappear.

For those looking from a distance only hymns could be heard. The gods and new leader were being hailed as one.

It was now a land of wonder, with order in the streets. Everything the man touched was glorious to behold. All windows became mirrors that threw large reflections back: the wealthy saw that they were beautiful, the poor saw that they were loved. No one, it was decreed, could touch windows but him.

A map was required to show the boundaries of the land. The map cut the country from the rest of the world. His followers realized that they could cut through the earth in line with the map and thus release their land from the laws of gravity.

"We will dig underneath so our land moves across the sea. No one can touch us then. We will be truly free."

And so his people dug deep till they reached the place where all land is one. It took two thousand years to separate the island from the earth's magnetic core. When they finished, the country was so light it might lift into clouds.

The beautiful island was now buffeted by winds. The proud temples and homes stood on the thinnest ground. A change in tide or temperature required reinforcements of all kinds. Homes were dismantled to buttress the base, sails tied to school flagpoles, temples broken into stumps.

One day a storm broke and pushed the island towards rocks.

The ancient people were tired, weakened by the long effort to keep their island afloat.

"We need help," they cried, "we are about to collide into cliffs."

"We should call a passing ship to pull us on a new course."

The ruler emerged from his lair, shedding thorns in the wind. He was old and ready for his son to inherit his land.

"Throw yourselves forward," he called out, "Protect the sacred land that will most surely protect you. Your freedom is dependent on the freedom of this land."

The storm continued unabated. The island came up hard against the rocks. Some people rushed forward and were crushed between the rock face and remnants of their homes. Others were carried into air by a blast of sand and wind. The man saw his wife and son disappear in the storm.

He was alone as the earth gave way beneath him and he fell into the sea. Everything was unsteady apart from the high rocks. He reached through the storm and said a prayer to the gods. He was propelled forward so his hand touched solid ground. He stroked a tall granite boulder and saw a temple emerge. It had begun with the touching of rocks.

The End and Continuance

The Laws of Chance

Bharati Mukherjee

I am writing this in a shingled cottage on a leafy three-block lane in the village of Southampton, New York. My writing desk is a Chinese antique I bought on e-Bay as soon as I realized I needed to keep a journal. Ben and his partner Hugh, who live across from me, hauled it up my narrow staircase to the smaller of the two guest bedrooms. Ben's the real estate agent who sold this cottage to Rahul and me. We had a different agent, Traci Hollings, when I first glimpsed the cottage. Rahul had been in touch with Tracie by email about listings for a couple of weeks before he had time to take a day off to look at properties. Rahul was in investment banking at the time, and it was that time when Wall Street bankers in custom-made Italian suits were envied rather than detested. Rahul's end of year bonus had been more than decent, and he had more faith in real estate than in stocks. Because he could spare only one afternoon to buy a Hamptons property, we took the jitney in from Manhattan, prepared to make a bid on one of the seven she had lined up, and be back in our Manhattan loft by evening. What he talked of as "investment property," I thought of as a refuge, where there would be just the two of us, a bride and her groom playing house, feeding each other candlelit morsels in an eat-in kitchen, relaxing in rockers and gazing up at stars from windy porches, a place for that sort of in-love tenderness rather than dutiful conjugal sex. We were no longer newly marrieds, but because of Rahul's relentless professional ambition, our honeymoon was still on hold.

Traci was driving us to the fifth on her to-show list, when we passed the cottage. All I could see of it through a scruffy hedge were green-shuttered windows and brilliant purple domes of mature azalea bushes flanking a front porch. A For Sale sign from a realty company other than Traci's was stuck on the strip of grass between road and hedge.

Traci eased the SUV to a stop a couple of yards beyond the For Sale sign when I asked her to, but didn't turn off the engine. I sensed her sizing us up: we were the wrong kind of moneyed immigrants, clueless about the Hamptons, a waste of her time. She waved a manicured hand at the flaking frame houses with sagging stoops on large, untended lots on the block.

Mostly teardowns, she sniffed. The neighborhood was "unstable." Once the old-timer residents passed away, their heirs would sell to developers who would subdivide the lots. Also, how did we feel about buying so close to train tracks? We were aware, weren't we, that the train station was where the treed lane made a T with a noisy artery. "I took this shortcut only because we're running late for the next appointment." She glanced pointedly at her wafer-thin, gold watch. The wide watchband, I noticed, was made of genuine crocodile skin. "As I said," Traci continued. "Thanks to a nasty divorce, this one's a steal. Otherwise it'd never be on the market. The husband's anxious to dump it. For buyers and realtors nasty divorces are pure gold."

"Twenty-four carat gold or just eighteen carat?" Rahul joked, signaling her to drive on to our appointment. Traci didn't get the joke. She had no way of knowing that we Bengalis are purists when it comes to "pure gold," which to us means twenty-four carat, and that we are condescending towards Bombayites who are satisfied with twenty-two carat, and that we are downright scornful of Americans who don't know better than eighteen carat.

We viewed the former happy home of the now-acrimoniously divorcing sellers, then two more houses in the two million dollar range that Rahul had specified in his emails. All the properties, with their staged interiors, landscaped gardens, patios paved with tumbled travertine tiles, commodious hot tubs and tarp-covered Gunite pools, were grander than any home I'd ever fantasized owning. I tried to calculate what two million U.S. dollars came to in Indian rupees, but gave up. Like Rahul, I had grown up in a rented flat in a once-genteel part of Kolkata. But unlike Rahul, I was a diffident consumer. He had earned the right to a lavish lifestyle, he believed, because he was making and shrewdly multiplying his savings; he wasn't a lazy heir dissipating a family fortune. Even though Rahul had established a joint account for us the day after we were married, I wasn't comfortable spending money on anything other than groceries. Our savings and assets weren't really *ours*, I felt; I had happened on a financially astute man, a gregarious, good-looking Bengali bachelor, with a ladies'-man reputation I should add, at a time when he was looking to settle down with a Bengali, kayastha-caste virgin. When Rahul proposed marriage, I felt I'd won a lottery.

As Traci dropped us off at the Omni for our jitney back to Manhattan, Rahul let her know in a way that bordered on rudeness that he was underwhelmed by the tour she had put together, and that he was willing to raise his ceiling by a couple of hundred grand. On the ride back, however, he lectured me on how the cottage on an iffy street within the village of

Southampton for under a million dollars and low property taxes was a smarter investment than the pricey houses with better addresses we'd wasted our day on. That night he emailed Ben Moretti, the agent listed on the For Sale sign for the cottage.

The next weekend Ben Moretti took us through the cozy, two-storey structure and its modest grounds. Ben described the neighborhood as "transitional," but he made "transitional" sound desirable. He had sold a TLC on a parallel lane to a fortyish stockbroker with high alimony and child support payments, a teardown caddy-corner from the Long Island Rail Road [LIRR] station to two aromatherapist sisters, and he himself had just put in a bid for the older house directly across from the cottage. Rahul quizzed Ben on heating and cooling costs, financing options, summer rental potential. I left the two of them talking figures at the kitchen table, and settled into a deck chair on the front porch to savor the blinding radiance of azalea bushes in full bloom. Our azaleas. Our house. Our hide-out. In Rahul's Soho loft that I'd moved into after he married me, I felt more a housekeeper than wife.

My immediate dream of an intimate weekend in the modest cottage within walking distance of Main Street and easy bicycling distance from the beach remained just that. As soon as the sale went through, Rahul hired a local contractor recommended by Ben, and had a showy master bedroom suite built above the kitchen, the back and side yards landscaped, a new privet hedge planted, a heated pool put in. The contractor was a large blond affable man, whose ancestors had settled in Southampton Village in 1670. The contractor let us know that fact about him in order to inspire confidence that he was well-connected and so there would be no problems getting building permits and passing inspection. He had a hand-picked crew of Ecuadorans, ready to start. Not the unskilled Mexican day-laborers, who loitered on North Sea Road and ran after every passing vehicle in the hope of jobs. Rahul was inspired, but did some comparative checking of costs and workmanship before hiring the man. We had chanced on this cottage in a neighborhood Traci the first realtor had intended to avoid. Once Rahul had calculated cost of mortgage payment, renovation and property tax versus potential post-renovation rental income, he had approached it as a lucrative investment property. The renovations were completed almost on deadline. The delay was caused by two tragic workplace accidents. One of the Ecuadorans had tumbled off the roof of the pool-house and broken his back; another had mishandled equipment and nearly severed his right hand. The contractor had personally escorted the maimed employees back to Ecuador for medical care. He'd apologized to us in his affable way, "My men are skilled, but accidents happen, what can I say?" In spite of these ghastly accidents, by mid-April Rahul had the cottage rented out for the Memorial Day to Labor Day summer season. I would have preferred that we, not tenants, enjoy hot, lazy weekends in our Southampton home, but from the start of our married life I had had to accept that Rahul made decisions on his own for the both of us. The occasional winter and frequent spring weekends we did spend in Southampton were as hosts (he relaxed, I harassed) to swarms of his relatives visiting from Kolkata or his South Asian business associates. It's only been a month that I've been living in it full-time.

My subletting the Soho loft and moving into the cottage was Hugh's advice. Hugh is one of three owners of Haughty Haute, a home design boutique I can't afford to shop in on Jobs Lane. Most of the furniture in this room, the white wrought iron daybed for instance, the candy-striped loveseat, the white wicker bookcase, are from Ben's and Hugh's basement, as are the tastefully worn Aubusson rug, the pink, fringed Victorian shade on the floor lamp I scavenged from the town dump, the pile of cushions that pick up the rug's faded colors just so, the watercolors with nautical themes, and, the three-foot-long ceramic mermaid sunning on a ceramic rock. The sleek, silver MacBook Air that sits incompatibly on the ornate rosewood desk, too, is on loan from them. They aren't just good neighbors. Since Rahul drowned, they've morphed into dedicated caregivers.

Hugh wants me to stay put in the cottage until I am healed. Think of it as a retreat, he says. You'll know when you are ready to move on with your life, he says. Ben the pragmatic one tells me that even in these days of mortgage meltdown, I'll do all right if I sell. Extend the deck off the kitchen, Ben advises, spruce up the pool house, put up a pergola (he and Hugh went for a gazebo as well as a pergola), and voila! He knows local architects and contractors; he'll make sure I'm not taken advantage of. Both Hugh and Ben are trying to come up with therapeutic projects for me. Grief stagnates: they don't say it to my face, but that's what they're thinking. I need to progress from what Hugh's yoga instructor calls "the foothills of loss" to "the peak of serene solitude." The instructor has his own holistic fitness show on cable TV. Hugh has brought over a how-to DVD, but I haven't watched it yet. First I have to figure out what I'm grieving. I'm thirty-seven; widowed by a freak accident; childless. My life is on PAUSE.

The journal project gives my days comforting focus. I know the project's goals: assess the past; imagine the future; suppress the present. I've set myself rules. I must be at my desk by 9:10 a.m., switch off my cell phone, skim news events on the Internet, read and answer my email, light an incense stick in front of the shrine that holds a silver statue of Goddess Kali and a framed photograph of Rahul. I stay at the screen until two o'clock every day, weekends as well as weekdays. The UPS driver can ring the doorbell, the answering machine can record an urgent message, the refrigerator may be empty except for mold-speckled fruits and cheeses: between 9:10 a.m. and 2:00 p.m. I permit myself no procrastination. If I concentrate hard enough, journal entries will birth themselves on the screen. The fingers on the keyboard are the midwife's. I believe that. I really do.

While I wait for new life to emerge, I experiment with fonts, margins and line spacing. Does form inhibit content? As a schoolgirl in Kolkata I wrote my weekly essays for Mother Paul in careful longhand in a lined notebook with my grandfather's Parker '51 fountain pen. Some feelings are too nuanced, some discoveries too intimate, to feed into a word-processor.

This morning, as most mornings and afternoons, I find myself distracted by the angled view of North Sea Road that the only window in this room offers. Migrant workers, mostly stocky young men with morose faces under hooded sweatshirts, line its sidewalks. Fast food wrappers sprout like blooms on hedges; empty pop bottles and coffee cups roll like skittles in short driveways. Rahul didn't care that the cottage looks out on a year-round seafood store and a cantina instead of on dune and ocean. His mantra: Get a toe-hold; then trade up. Think investment, not nest. Attachment ends in disappointment. His only "home" was the rented ground floor flat on Rash Behari Avenue, Kolkata, where he'd been born, where his father had died, and where his mother was still living.

We grew up twenty minutes' bus ride apart in South Kolkata, but met by accident for the first time three and a half years ago in the Bloomfield, New Jersey, home of my father's first cousin. My uncle and aunt had invited a young Bengali-American doctor they knew for dinner hoping that something would come of this doctor meeting me, and they had included the doctor's room-mate, so that their matchmaking intention would be apparent but not embarrassing. In another month my tourist visa was to expire, and they had promised my father when they sent a pre-paid Air India ticket for me that they would find him a suitable Bengali-American son-in-law during my six-month stay with them. My father is a proud man on very limited income. He accepted the ticket on my behalf only after my uncle added that I would be doing *him* and his wife and married daughter a favor. The daughter, an oncologist married to a dermatologist, was about to give birth to twins and would be grateful for help with baby care. Unlike my father, I didn't think accepting a rich relative's charity was at all humiliating. A thirty-four-year-old unmarried woman with a Bachelor of Arts degree (Third Class) from Calcutta University, aging by the hour: what did I have to lose?

What little I knew of my New Jersey relatives before arriving in their home was from family gossip and brief letters, enclosing photographs and dutiful inquiries about our health, that my aunt wrote in Bangla to my mother every few months. The photographs disclosed a fuller biography than the letters. We understood that my aunt had become so Americanized that in winter she wore pants, parka, boots, cleared snow off the driveway with a huge shovel, and drove my uncle to his office in her very own Lexus. My uncle, too, had de-Indianized to the extent that he could pose without shame for the camera, wearing a bright red apron like a woman, and cooking thick slabs of meat on an outdoor grill. My father would never be caught in the kitchen, not even to boil water for tea.

According to family lore (details of which changed but never the outline), in the mid-1970s this uncle, a civil engineer, had resigned from pensionable government employment in a *mofussil* town in West Bengal and migrated to Trenton, New Jersey, on a tourist visa on the promise of a job by an engineering college classmate already settled there. That job had fallen through, but my uncle had worked full-time in the former classmate's brother-in-law's construction company in Trenton, lived five to a room with fellow Indian immigrants, saved obsessively, invested smartly, and within five years had acquired an immigrant's green card, brought over his wife, toddler daughter and all four of his younger brothers and their wives. When I shared my uncle's success story with Rahul soon after we were married, he snickered. "That first wave of Indians here, they were pathetic."

He was wrong to be so contemptuous of my uncle who, unlike his cousin my timid father, had taken such a big risk and dealt with the consequences. I should have corrected Rahul, should have described how loving and generous they were to me, and how I repaid them with diligence (my only currency in America) in the nursery and the kitchen, but I hadn't felt secure enough yet to contradict him. As Rahul might have put it, by accepting his marriage proposal I had traded up. Oh, I'd had my teenaged fantasies all right, but on a smaller, more local scale. My father would miraculously convince a good-hearted surgeon or solicitor to marry me without dowry. I would own, not rent, a flat, or maybe a whole house in Alipur. A chauffeur would drive me in air-conditioned comfort to the city's brand new mall for a whole day of self-indulgent shopping.

The doctor, with whom my uncle was matchmaking me, came down with the flu that morning, and knowing that my aunt must have gone to great lengths cooking the dinner for a potential bridegroom, he insisted that at least Rahul, his room-mate, show up, apologize to my uncle, and flatter my aunt's hospitality. Rahul charmed us all, and proposed after we had gone on four dates, the first two chaperoned by my New Jersey relatives, the next two in Rahul's Soho loft.

Rahul was practiced in the art of wooing. He sent elaborate flower arrangements in odd-shaped vases to my aunt, fruit baskets to my uncle, Belgian chocolates for my cousin and me. On the first date he arrived on our doorstep with enormous plush animals for the twins, and Chanel perfume for me. On the second of our chaperoned dates in Bloomfield, he brought an out-of-print copy of a Bengali poet-freedom-fighter's book of poems for the house, and a gold Rolex for me. But it was with tales of his devotion to his parents that he wooed and won me. On the two dates in his loft, after take-out meals from neighborhood restaurants, in mellow light, and with Nora Jones on Bose speakers, he laid out his life for me to examine. Whatever he had achieved—his ambition to be a "somebody," his dogged drive to make money, his decision to dive into the hedge fund business instead of going into traditional professions, such as medicine and engineering favored by the earlier wave of Indian immigrants—he owed to his father. His parents had done without, so that they could give him, their only child, the best: eggs and fish every day, vitamins, digestives and brain-enhancing tonics, visits to expensive preventive care specialists. His father had borrowed from a moneylender and bought him imported hardcover books on finance for exorbitant sums; he had even stolen copies of business magazines from the American Center library. From the moment, as a school boy, Rahul had discovered the word "plutocrat" in a newspaper clipping on an Indian entrepreneurial family for a class assignment, he had resolved to become one before he turned fifty. "Dream big, plan smart, live large," had been his father's mantra. What Rahul hadn't planned on was dying at age forty-one. He hadn't planned on dying, period.

When my New Jersey uncle learned that I was going to marry Rahul, he gave Rahul top marks for efficiency and expediency. My aunt hugged me and kept repeating that I was exceptionally lucky to have hooked such a go-getter "boy" who also happened to be of the right caste. I agreed. I didn't meet the doctor she had originally targeted as my bridegroom, a shy man with dimpled cheeks and oversized ears, until my wedding reception in New Jersey.

I have no plans, only the duty as Rahul's widow, to return to Kolkata and care physically for his aged, bed-ridden mother. He has left me comfortably off, very comfortably off, but with an unspoken understanding that I will live with his mother under one roof and financially support his large and needy extended family. His mother and his widow: two wary strangers bound together by Rahul's expectations and his money.

What am I to do?

Hugh asks instead, "What do you *want* to do?"

Ben's suggestion: Take the small decisions and graduate to the big one about staying on or going back. Get the house painted as a first step to selling it. The walls must sparkle when he shows it. He knows just the right house-painter for me. That man will bring in his team of migrants and get the spackling and painting done fast, and cheap.

My laptop screen is dark; I am patient.

Hugh, his rescue Chihuaha, and I stroll aimlessly on Main Street. "Sell the loft," but the way he says it, I hear a question, not advice. "Get a dog. You need a dog. Everybody needs a dog. We'll go to the shelter together the week after Labor Day. You'd be amazed how many people lose or abandon their pure breeds. A dog loves unconditionally. And this is a cozy small town when the summer people leave."

A balding young father walks his flaxen-haired daughter of three or four and a large chocolate Lab just ahead of us. "Now, when we get to the corner . . ."

"I want you to take me to Mummy's house," the child screams.

Hugh's Chihuaha, off-leash, darts towards the Lab, which is also off-leash. The young father smiles tolerantly at his hysterical daughter. "We'll let Dexter decide which way we turn when we get to the corner."

Dexter seems so reliable a name for a dog. Maybe only dogs can offer unconditional love.

"I want to go to Mummy's house," the child shrieks, pulling away from the father. "Now! Right now!" The father is staring at Dexter; Dexter is batting the hyper Chihuaha, circling him with a large, benevolent paw. The child runs to the curb. "I want us to turn left and get in the car! I want Mummy! I *hate* you, Daddy!"

"I'm trying to teach you the concept of randomness," the father is saying as we catch up with Hugh's Chihuhua. "We'll follow Dexter. Let's see where Dexter takes us. What you have, Blakelee, is a plan . . . "but I pretend I've overheard nothing, pluck Hugh's dog off the sidewalk and stride on, with Hugh following.

And in my panic to get away from this serene, philosophical father, I stumble hard into a Latino day-laborer swaggering out of the Thrift Store run to benefit the Southampton Hospital. The day-laborer is wearing an expensive navy blazer, complete with a yacht club's crest on the breast pocket and anchors on its shiny brass buttons, an in near-mint condition garment donated by a Doon Lane or Gin Lane multimillionaire. I remember my confident contractor's excuse for his delay in meeting his contractual deadline for renovating our cottage: accidents happen. In other words, *Don't blame me. Don't feel sorry for my workers. I pay them well enough.*

The Latino man is upset with me. He brushes imaginary dog hairs off his blazer. I mumble my apologies, eyes down. It's then that I notice that instead of boating shoes on sockless feet, the pre-used blazer's new owner has on a day-laborer's sensible thick socks and paint-splattered work boots.

"Mummy! Come and get me, Mummy!" Now I'm running, not striding. I'm running away from the child's commands. I don't want to be taken to my mother's flat. I don't want to take myself to Rahul's mother's flat. I want to tell Hugh that my life should not be in turmoil, that Rahul had no business to go on a business trip to Mexico with Keiko from his office, try para-sailing on a dare; he had no right to drown accidentally. I want to tell him I have accepted life's randomness but I have not learned the *lesson* of randomness that this divorced or estranged father is trying to teach his daughter, Blakelee. I don't know how to trust my next move in life to a Dexter as this serene father with the screeching daughter does. I shouldn't get myself a dog, because I don't know how to love or be loved. I want to tell Ben to go ahead, hire the house-painter he has worked with before. I want the cottage invaded by the migrant workers I spy on, the muscular men with desperate faces at the street corner, I want them to wreck and rebuild my home, but to do it slowly, very slowly, so that the absurdity of their hope for better times and the reality of hacked-off arms and broken spines has time to birth on my borrowed MacBook Air screen in redemptive, illuminated fonts.

***

I didn't go back to Kolkata. I sold the loft in Tribeca, and the cottage in Southampton, and took out a mortgage on an Upper West Side Manhattan brownstone in need of extreme rather than tender loving care.

CONTRIBUTORS

CLARK BLAISE's short-story collections include *A North American Education* (1973), *Tribal Justice* (1974), *Man and His World* (1992), and his collected stories in the volumes *Southern Stories* (2000), *Pittsburgh Stories* (2001), *Montreal Stories* (2003), and *World Body* (2006). In addition, he has published novels like *Lunar Attractions* (1979), which won the Books in Canada First Novel Award, *Lusts* (1983), and *If I Were Me* (1997). His non-fiction includes autobiographical works like *Days and Nights in Calcutta* (1977), co-authored by his wife, novelist Bharati Mukherjee. They also collaborated on *The Sorrow and the Terror* (1987), about the 1985 Air India bombing. *Resident Alien* (1986) combines fiction and autobiographical essays, and *I Had a Father* (1993) is subtitled *A Post-Modern Autobiography*. Blaise published a biography of Sir Sandford Fleming, *Time Lord: Sir Sandford Fleming and the Creation of Standard Time* (2000). He is also the author of *The Border As Fiction* (1990), the book whose title inspired the name and theme of the 2010 short story conference.

MARION BLOEM was born in the Netherlands in 1952, eighteen months after her parents (Dutch-Indonesian) emigrated from Indonesia to the Netherlands. After high school Bloem studied clinical psychology at the State University of Utrecht. During her studies there, she published her first books for children. Soon she started to write, produce and direct films. Her first novel came out the same year (1983) as her first feature-length documentary. Both were very successful. Known as a novelist and filmmaker, Marion Bloem has also received widespread appreciation as a visual artist, since her first major exhibition in 1987. Her paintings, objects and prints are exhibited regularly in the Netherlands and abroad.

LICIA CANTON is the author of *Almond Wine and Fertility* (2008)—short stories for women and their men—soon-to-be published in Italian. She is also a literary critic and translator, and the editor-in-chief of *Accenti*—the Canadian magazine for lovers of all things Italian. Her stories and essays have appeared in anthologies and journals. As editor she has published several collections of creative and critical writing—*The Dynamics of Cultural Exchange, Adjacencies: Minority Writing in Canada, Writing Beyond History, Reflections on Culture and Writing Our Way Home*—as well as two volumes on the internment of Italian Canadians.

BELINDA CHANG (who writes under the pseudonym Chang Yuan) was born in Tainan, Taiwan. She graduated from National Taiwan University, and earned her Master's degree in Performance Studies at New York University. After working as a reporter for *World Journal* (the largest Chinese newspaper in North America) for many years, she and her family moved to China. She now lives in Shanghai. Her stories appear regularly in literary magazines and newspapers in China, Taiwan, Hong Kong, and North America. Her publications include a novel, *The City of the Plague* (2003); a collection of essays, *Be the Neighbor of Eileen Chang* (2008); and five collections of short stories: *Women in the Locker Room* (1997), *Night of the Flood* (2000), *Two Ships in the Night* (2005), *Crossing the Boundary* (2009), and *It Takes Two to Tango* (2011). A new novel, *Old Flames*, is scheduled to be printed in 2012.

S. K. CHANG's literary activities include the writing of twenty eight novels, a collection of short stories and critical essays. His novels were translated into English, German, Japanese, and made into a musical play, movie and TV series. He is credited as the "Father of Science Fiction" in Taiwan, but his mainstream short stories and novels also receive critical acclamation. Most people in Taiwan know Dr. Chang as a novelist. In 2003 Columbia University Press published the English translation of Dr. Chang's three major sci-fi novels as a single volume entitled *The City Trilogy.*

KELLY CHERRY has published twenty books of fiction, poetry, and nonfiction, eight chapbooks, and translations of two classical plays. Her most recent titles are *The Woman Who* (2010), a collection of short stories, *The Retreats of Thought: Poems* (2009) and *Girl in a Library: On Women Writers & the Writing Life* (2009). Her short fiction has been represented in *Best American*

Short Stories, Prize Stories: The O. Henry Awards, New Stories from the South, and *The Pushcart Prize* and she received the Dictionary of Literary Biography Award for the best volume of short stories published in 1999. Other awards include the Hanes Poetry Prize for a body of work in that form, a USIS Speaker Award, and fellowships from the Rockefeller Foundation and NEA. In 2010 she was a Director's Visitor at the Institute for Advanced Study in Princeton. She is Eudora Welty Professor Emerita of English and Evjue-Bascom Professor Emerita in the Humanities at the University of Wisconsin-Madison and currently serves as the Poet Laureate of the Commonwealth of Virginia.

NUALA NÍ CHONCHÚIR was born in Dublin, Ireland, in 1970 and now lives in County Galway. Her dèbut novel *You* (New Island, 2010) was called "a heart-warmer" by *The Irish Times* and "a gem" by *The Irish Examiner.* Her third short story collection *Nude* (Salt, 2009) was shortlisted for the UK's Edge Hill Prize. Her second short story collection *To The World of Men, Welcome* has just been re-issued by Arlen House in an expanded paperback edition. *The Juno Charm,* her third full poetry collection was published by Salmon Poetry in November 2011.

CIAO LI was born in 1934 as Neng-Ci Li in Maio-Li County, Taiwan. He spent his entire childhood in this remote Hakka village very close to the mountain area where the Atayal tribe lives. His first short story was published in 1962. He has won many important literary prizes including the Taiwan Literary Prize (1968), Wu San Lian Award for Arts (1981) and National Award for the Arts (2006). Ciao Li's work includes short stories (180), novels (twenty) and many literary essays and cultural essays. In all of his literary work, he has always emphasized deep-level analysis of personality, conflicts between time, origins, cultures and perspectives. With this, he tries to tear apart all the phenomena he observed and imagined in search of the core of human nature. He is especially recognized for his diverse experimentation and craftsmanship in writing. His novel *The Trilogy of Wintry Night* was published in 1979, 1980, and 1981, and has since been translated into English (Columbia University Press, 2002). Through this trilogy's heroine in this roman-fleuve Den-Mei Yeh, he sophisticatedly presented the major events of Taiwan history from 1890 to 1945.

ALICE CLARK is an Associate Professor of Literature at the University of Nantes. Her work on Shakespeare and Nerval: *Le Théâtre romantique en crise, Shakespeare et Nerval* (Harmattan, 2005), was short-listed for a research prize by the SAES and the AFEA. She is the author of a collection of poems in French and English, *Imaginaires* (University of Nantes, 1997), and numerous critical articles in French literary reviews. She has also co-authored a book on the Anglo-Saxon short story, *La nouvelle anglo-saxonne, une étude psychanalytique* (Hachette, 1998). Alice Clark's short story collection, *A Darker Shade of Light,* received Technikart Manuscript's first prize award at le Salon du Livre (March 2011).

EVELYN CONLON was a winner of the European Schools Day essay competition in 1969 and had her first stories published at the age of seventeen in *New Irish Writing* (The Irish Press). Her first collection of short stories was published in 1987 and this has been followed to date by two more collections and three novels. She has compiled and edited three other books, and is an occasional reviewer on radio and television. She is a conscientious researcher and has lectured on this and many other aspects of a writing life. Her last novel entailed visiting Death Row in the US, and doing widespread interviews with people on both sides of the capital punishment debate.

HOPE COULTER is the author of two published novels, *The Errand of the Eye* (August House, 1988) and *Dry Bones* (August House, 1990); one children's book, *Uncle Chuck's Truck* (Bradbury Press, 1993); and several short stories and poems published in literary magazines, including *Spoon River Poetry Review, New Delta Review, Slant,* and *Rattle.* Her poem "Last Joke" in Spoon River Poetry Review was nominated for a Pushcart Prize in 2008. Other honors include Arkansas's Porter Fund for Literary Excellence, the Short Story Award of *Louisiana Life* magazine, and a residency at the Dairy Hollow Writers' Colony. A native of New Orleans, she grew up in Alexandria, Louisiana, and received her A.B. from Harvard University and her M.F.A. in creative writing from Queens University. She lives in Little Rock and teaches creative writing at Hendrix College.

SUSAN ROCHETTE CRAWLEY was born on December 14, 1952, in Sandusky, Ohio and was raised in a government subsidized tract home in Bellevue, Ohio along with her parents and siblings. She graduated in 1975 from Kent State University,

Kent Ohio, with a degree cum laude in English. She worked in a GM parts plant in her hometown and a Buick/Oldsmobile body plant in Framingham, Massachusetts to support her addiction to higher education. She graduated from Boston College in 1982 with a Master Degree in English and in 1994 with a Ph.D. from the University of Wisconsin-Madison. She is on leave from her current employer, The University of Northern Iowa, where she is an Associate Professor of English Language and Literatures. She has two devoted Russian Blues, Garbo and Spring Breeze. She writes, paints, draws, designs beadwork patterns and volunteers at the North Point Light Station in Milwaukee, WI.

CYRIL DABYDEEN was born in Canje, Guyana in 1945, and worked as a teacher prior to leaving Guyana. Dabydeen came to Canada in 1970 to pursue post-secondary studies and completed a B.A. at Lakehead University and both an M.A. and M.P.A. at Queen's University. His M.A. thesis was on the poetry of Sylvia Plath. Dabydeen is a prolific author of poetry and prose and his work has been included in numerous anthologies published in Canada, the U.S.A., the U.K., India and New Zealand. Dabydeen served as Poet Laureate of Ottawa from 1985–spring 1987. He worked for many years in the areas of human rights and race relations and later taught English at Algonquin College in Ottawa. He now teaches creative writing at the University of Ottawa and lives in the nation's capital.

WANG FANG, who writes under the pseudonym **FANG FANG**, was born in 1955 in Nanjing. She began writing and publishing poetry in her early twenties. In 1982, she published her first short story, "On the Big Caravan," and since has published several novels, collections of novellas and short stories. In 1987, Fang Fang published the novella *Landscape* and won the National Literary Award for Novellas. This story was regarded as opening an era for Neo-realism in Chinese Modern Literature, and has been translated into English and French. She has recently published stories about wars. Her latest novel, *Wuchang Wall* (2011), originates in the history of Wuchang, a city known for the great revolution in 1911 that helped to found China.

HAO YU-HSIANG, Ph.D. of Chinese Literature at National Taiwan University, is currently Professor of the Institute of Taiwanese Literature, National Chung Cheng University. As one of the most representative writers and critics in Taiwan, Dr. Hao has been regularly awarded for her achievements in creative writing. The literary prizes she has won are The Yearly Best Book of China Times Book Review, The Emerging Novelist of Unitas, and the Literary Awards of China Times, Central Daily News, and Taipei City, as well as GIO Fine Screenplay Award. Her publications include, among others, the short stories "Nether Story," "That Summer, The Most Peaceful Sea," "Annie the First Love," "Inner Challenge," "Washing"; collections of prose, *Sadness Taken Away by the Spring, A Blinking Dream: My Travelogue of China, A Secret Travel in Closet*; a screenplay, *A Case of Squirrels' Suicide*; and research works, *The Time of Fictionalization—On Contemporary Taiwanese Literature, The Fin de Siecle of Eros—On the Novels of Contemporary Taiwanese Female Writers*, and *Nuo: A Study of Chinese Ritual Theatre*. She also edits *the Tutorial of Contemporary Taiwanese Literature: A Fiction Reader.*

TANIA HERSHMAN's first book, *The White Road and Other Stories*, was commended by the judges of the 2009 Orange Award for New Writers, and included in New Scientist's Best Books of 2008. Tania's second collection, *My Mother Was An Upright Piano: Fictions*, will be published in May 2012 by Tangent Books in the UK. Tania is Grand Prize Winner of the 2009 Binnacle Ultra-Short Contest, and European winner of the 2008 Commonwealth Broadcasting Association's Short Story Competition. Her stories are published or forthcoming in, among others, *Nature, Metazen, Necessary Fiction, SPECS, Contrary Magazine, Smokelong Quarterly*, the *London Magazine and Electric Velocipede*, and a week of her flash fiction was broadcast on BBC Radio 4. Tania is currently writer-in-residence in Bristol University's Science Faculty and has been awarded an Arts Council England grant to work on a collection of biology-inspired short fiction. She is founder and editor of *The Short Review*, an online journal shining the spotlight on short story collections and their authors.

DARCIE FRIESEN HOSSACK is a graduate of the Humber School for Writers in Ontario, Canada, where she studied under Giller Prize finalist Sandra Birdsell. Her first book of short fictions, *Mennonites Don't Dance*, was published by Thistledown Press in September 2010. Acclaimed in the Canadian press, shortlisted for the Commonwealth Prize in the First Books Category, the book was also a runner up for the Danuta Gleed Award. Darcie grew up in the city of Swift Current, Saskatchewan, though was as much at home on her grandparents' farm in the Mennonite village of Schoenfeld. She eventually moved to Kelowna, British Columbia and married her high school sweetheart, international award-winning chef, Dean Hossack. Being Mennonite, with its accompanying experiences of farm and food, shaped the author's faith and love of land (even though she's never successfully grown anything in dirt), and led to a syndicated food column.

JAY JENNINGS is a fiction writer, journalist and humorist, whose stories have appeared in many national literary journals, magazines, and newspapers, including the *New York Times*, the *Wall Street Journal*, *Sport Literate*, *Elysian Fields Quarterly*, the *Lowbrow Reader*, the *Oxford American*, and *Travel & Leisure*. He is a regular contributor to the *New York Times Book Review*. He is a two-time MacDowell Colony fellow in fiction and a winner of a fiction grant from the Arkansas Arts Council for a novel-in-progress. His nonfiction book *Carry the Rock: Race, Football and the Soul of an American City* was published by Rodale in 2010 and named an Okra Pick by the Southern Independent Booksellers Alliance. He began his writing career as a reporter at *Sports Illustrated*, where he covered college football and basketball, followed by four years as the features editor at *Tennis* magazine. While at the latter, he edited an acclaimed anthology of short stories and poetry called *Tennis and the Meaning of Life: A Literary Anthology of the Game* (Breakaway Books, 1999), which the *New Yorker* called "a delight—and perhaps a surprise—to those who know and care about literature." His work has been recognized by *The Best American Sports Writing* annual and has appeared in the humor anthology *Mirth of a Nation: The Best Contemporary Humor*. He was born and raised in Little Rock, Arkansas, where he now lives.

SANDRA JENSEN was born in South Africa in 1961. She travelled extensively as a child, living in Greece, England and Ireland. After her BA in Classical Studies at Bristol, England, she lived in London for some years, studying mime and dance. She then traveled throughout South East Asia and later settled in Canada where she first began to focus on her writing, in addition to juggling a number of different careers including Jeet Kune Do instructor and internet consultant and project manager for the Canadian Imperial Bank of Commerce. She returned to Ireland in 2008, where she is currently based. Sandra's short stories have been published in *Word Riot*, *Sou'Wester*, *Per Contra*, *The Fiddlehead*, *Carousel*, *AGNI*, *The Irish Times* and others. She has received honorable mentions in a number of competitions including Glimmer Train. Recently she won Red Room's Scandalously Short Story Contest and was shortlisted for the Bridport Prize. Her short story manuscript, *A Sort of Walking Miracle*, was shortlisted for The Scott Prize (Salt Publishing).

BRET ANTHONY JOHNSTON is the author of *Corpus Christi: Stories* (Random House). His work appears in *The Paris Review* and *Tin House*, and in numerous anthologies, including *New Stories from the South: The Year's Best 2003, 2004, and 2005.* He is currently completing a novel and editing an anthology, both forthcoming from Random House. Johnston has been featured in *The Paris Review* and *Open City*, as well as many anthologies, including *New Stories from the South: The Year's Best, 2003 and 2004*; *Prize Stories: The O. Henry Prize Stories 2002*; and *Scribner's Best of the Fiction Workshops 1999.* He is a graduate of the Iowa Writers' Workshop, where he received a Teaching-Writing Fellowship. He teaches in the Bennington Writing Seminars, and at Harvard University, where he is the Director of Creative Writing.

VIJAY LAKSHMI was born and educated in India. She is Associate Professor of English at the Community College of Philadelphia, where she has taught since 1991. She did post-doctoral work at Yale, and has been writer-in-residence in Can Serrat, Spain. Her short-story publications include the collection *Pomegranate Dreams and Other Stories* (2002, 2004) and stories in such journals as *Amelia, Wasafiri, Paris Transcontinental, Short Story,* and *Journal of Indian Writing in English.* Lakshmi is also the author of *Virginia Woolf as Literary Critic: A Revaluation* (1977), and of about twenty scholarly articles.

CLAIRE LARRIÈRE has long been steeped in the short story as a genre as well as a source of personal inspiration. She started the International Conferences on the Short Story with the first one at the Sorbonne (Paris 1988). She created and was chief editor of *Paris Transcontinental*, a magazine of contemporary short stories in English from all over the world (1990-1997). A collection of her stories, in French, *Terre, terre . . . et le reste,* was published in 2002. Her latest novel, also in French, *Les crémières*, appeared in 2009, both at *Les éditions d'écarts.* Claire Larrière lives at Montlhéry, a Paris suburb, and in Brittany.

ALISON MACLEOD is a novelist and short story writer. Her most recent book, *Fifteen Modern Tales of Attraction* (Penguin), was "highly recommended" by *Time Out* and deemed by *The Guardian* to be "as inventive as it is original." In 2008, she won the U.K.'s Society of Authors' Award for Short Fiction. In 2011, she was shortlisted for the BBC National Short Story Award for her story "The Heart of Denis Noble." Her work, including her last novel, *The Wave Theory of Angels* (Penguin), has won major Writer's Awards from the Arts Council England and the Canada Council for the Arts. Her next novel, set in Brighton where she lives, will be published by Penguin early in 2013, and she is currently completing her next story collection. She is Professor of Contemporary Fiction at the University of Chichester (UK), and Director of Thresholds International Short Story Forum.

MOLLY MCCLOSKEY was born in Philadelphia and grew up in Oregon. She moved to Ireland in 1989. Having spent ten years on the west coast of Ireland, she now resides in Dublin. She is the author of a novel, *Protection*, and two short story collections—*Solomon's Seal* and *The Beautiful Changes*. Her short stories have won a number of prizes, including Ireland's RTE/Francis MacManus Award. Her first work of non-fiction—a memoir about her brother's schizophrenia and its effects on him and on the family—was published by Penguin in the UK and Ireland, and will be published in the US by Overlook Press in 2012. As a journalist, essayist and reviewer, McCloskey is a regular contributor to the *Irish Times* and the *Dublin Review*. Her work has also appeared in the *Guardian*, *ELLE*, *Five Dials* and elsewhere, and has been broadcasted on RTE and BBC Radio.

ALECIA MCKENZIE was born in Kingston, Jamaica. She grew up there, and has also lived in the United States, Europe and Asia. She and her family are currently based in France. Alecia's first book, *Satellite City,* won the regional Commonwealth Writers Prize for Best First Book. Her other works include *Stories from Yard, When the Rain Stopped in Natland* (a novella for young readers) and *Doctor's Orders*. Her latest book is *Sweetheart*, a novel (Peepal Tree Press, 2011). As an artist, Alecia has participated in exhibitions in Alabama, New York, Brussels, London, and Singapore. In the past two years, she has held several exhibitions in Paris, including one to commemorate the thirtieth anniversary of Bob Marley's death. She believes that writing and painting come from the same source.

MICHAEL MIROLLA's publications include the recently-released novel *Berlin* (a finalist for the 2009 Indie Book and National Best Books Awards), and two short story collections—*The Formal Logic of Emotion* and *Hothouse Loves & Other Tales.* A collection of poetry, *Light And Time,* was recently published with an English-Italian bilingual collection of poetry *Interstellar Distances/Distanze Interstellari.* His short story, "A Theory of Discontinuous Existence," was selected for The Journey Prize Anthology, while another short story, "The Sand Flea," was nominated for the Pushcart Prize. His short fiction and poetry have been published in numerous journals in Canada, the U.S. and Britain, including several anthologies such as *Event's Peace & War Anthology, Telling Differences: New English Fiction from Quebec, Tesseracts 2: Canadian Science Fiction,* the *Collection of Italian-Canadian Fiction, New Wave of Speculative Fiction Book 1,* and *The Best of Foliate Oak.*

PAULA MARTIN MORELL has an MFA from the University of New Orleans Creative Writing Workshop. She is the creator and Executive Producer of NPR's "Tales from the South," where she gleefully helps Southern writers bring their own true stories to life. She is also the founder and editor of Temenos Publishing, a small literary press publishing between two and four titles a year. Paula has been teaching creative writing for over twenty years, and her short stories, poetry, and her work has appeared in journals such as *Short Story Journal, Southern Hum, Outsider Ink, New Works Review,* and *The Double Dealer Redux.* Her novel-in-stories *broken water* was published in 2006, and her writing workshop *Invoking the Gifts* is being used in recovery centers nationwide. She is a mother of three incredible homeschooled kids and teaches Creative Writing for Pulaski Technical College in North Little Rock. She and her husband Jason own Starving Artist Cafe' in the Argenta Arts District, where "Tales from the South" takes place.

MARY MORRISSY was born in Dublin in 1957. She has published a collection of short stories, *A Lazy Eye,* and two novels inspired by real events: *Mother of Pearl,* the story of a baby kidnapped in 1950s Dublin, and *The Pretender,* a fictional biography of the woman who claimed to be the Anastasia, the daughter of the last Romanov Tsar. A third novel, *The Rising of Bella Casey,* based on the life of playwright Sean O'Casey, is under consideration. She reviews fiction for *The Irish Times* and is currently working on her second collection of short stories. In 1984, she won a Hennessy Award for short fiction, and a Lannan Literary Foundation Award in 1995. Her novel, *Mother of Pearl,* was shortlisted for the Whitbread Award and *The Pretender* was nominated for the Dublin Impac Award.

BHARATI MUKHERJEE was born in Calcutta (now Kolkata) in 1940. She received her B.A. from the University of Calcutta in 1959, an M.A. in English and Ancient Indian Culture from the University of Baroda in 1961, an M.F.A. from the Iowa Writers' Workshop in 1963, and her Ph.D. in English and Comparative Literature in 1969. She moved to Canada in 1968 with her husband, Clark Blaise, where they lived in Montreal and Toronto. They then returned to the United States in 1980. She wrote about the move and her reasons for it in "An Invisible Woman," which was published in the magazine *Saturday Night* (1981). She teaches at the University of California at Berkeley. Her short-story collections are *Darkness* (1985) and *The Middleman and Other Stories* (1988). Her novels include *The Tiger's Daughter* (1971), *Wife* (1975), *Jasmine* (1989), *The Holder of the World* (1993), *Leave it to Me* (1997), *Desirable Daughters* (2002), and *The Tree Bride* (2004). Mukherjee and Blaise co-authored the non-fiction works *Days and Nights in Calcutta* (1977) and *The Sorrow and the Terror: The Haunting Legacy of the Air India Tragedy* (1987).

SYLVIA PETTER grew up in Australia. After her BA in French and German at UNSW, Sydney, she moved to Vienna where she studied translation before relocating to Geneva via Helsinki. During her thirty years in the Geneva area where she worked for the UN in the area of telecommunications, she began to write fiction. Her stories have been published widely online and in print. Her first collection of stories, *The Past Present,* was published in 2001 in the UK; her second collection, *Back Burning,* was published in 2007 in Australia as IP Picks 2007 Best Fiction. She completed her PhD in Creative Writing at UNSW in 2009. She currently resides in Vienna where she writes and participates in local writing-related events while working part-time in the area of educational research at the University of Vienna.

VELMA POLLARD was born in Jamaica in 1937. She studied at the University College of the West Indies, and received an M.A. in Education from McGill University and an M.A. in the teaching of English from Columbia University. She taught in high schools and universities in Jamaica, Trinidad, Guyana and the USA. She is currently a retired Senior Lecturer in Language

Education and Dean of the Faculty of Education of the University of the West Indies, Mona. Pollard's short stories have appeared in various periodicals and anthologies, and her collections are *Karl and Other Stories* (1994) and *Considering Woman* (1989). *Karl and other Stories* won the Casa de las Americas in 1992. She has also published the novel *Homestretch* (1994). Some of her poetry collections are *Crown Point and Other Poems* (1988), *Shame Trees Don't Grow Here* (1992), *The Best Philosophers I Know Can't Read or Write* (2001), and *Leaving Traces* (2008). *Dread Talk: the Language of the Rastafari* was published in 1994.

KATHARINE CRAWFORD ROBEY writes short stories and picture books for children. "The Secret War," set during WWII is based on the war experiences of her father. Katharine Crawford Robey's first picture book, *Hare and the Big Green Lawn*, was published by Rising Moon/Northland Publishing in 2006. It won the National Wildlife Federation's book-of-the-month award in May, 2007 and is reviewed in the magazine for children, *Your Big Backyard.* Katharine's second picture book, *Where's the Party?* was published by Charlesbridge in July, 2011. Kirkus reviews calls it "an irresistible invitation." Katharine has lived in Atlanta, Georgia for over thirty years. She is married to Ronald G. Robey. They have two grown children, Kate and John Warren. Katharine received a B.A. from the University of Wisconsin-Madison, and a J.D. from the University of Kentucky. She is currently working on a young adult novel, *Fishing Upside Down.*

MINOLI SALGADO is a short story writer and poet of Sri Lankan descent whose work has been published in journals in the UK and North America and regularly featured in the International Conference on the Short Story. She also teaches English at the University of Sussex in the MA programs in Creative and Critical Writing and Colonial and Postcolonial Cultures. Her academic publications include *Writing Sri Lanka: Literature, Resistance and the Politics of Place* (Routledge, 2007)—the first monograph to situate Sri Lankan English literature within current postcolonial theories and debates—and critical essays in the *Cambridge Companion to Salman Rushdie* (Cambridge U. Press, 2007) and *Diaspora and Multiculturalism* (Rodopi, 2003). Minoli Salgado has been an associate editor of *Wasafiri* since 2004.

SARA SHUMAKER—when not tending her young son, the gardens, and a wild flock of hens—writes short stories and creative non-fiction, because she absolutely cannot stop herself from doing so. She formerly taught for the English, Writing, and Honors departments at the University of Central Arkansas and was managing editor for *The Journal of Caribbean Literatures*. One of her recent stories is published in UNLV's journal *Word River*.

KATIE SINGER has an MFA from Fairleigh Dickinson University and is a lecturer in the department of Literature, Language, Writing & Philosophy at Fairleigh Dickinson University in Madison, New Jersey. Her writing consists of short stories, poems and essays; she has published in various literary journals and newspapers including most recently *The Paterson Literary Review* and *Delaware Valley Poets Anthology*. Her most recent international literary experience took place at the International Conference on the Short Story held in Cork, Ireland June 2008. There she presented a paper entitled; "Labels in Learning and Literature" and gave a reading of her short story, "Oranges."

TSAI SUH-FEN's first novel *Children of Salt Fields*, acclaimed as an important work for the role played by hard-working women in the ever-changing society, received the Unit News Literature Prize. Suh-Fen has since received numerous other literary and radio program production awards. Suh-Fen's published short stories include *One of Six Plays* (1988), *Leaving Aloneness* (1991), *Taipei Station* (2000), and *Suh-Fen Tsai's Short Stories Collection* (2002). Her popular novels include *Children of Salt Fields* (1994), *Letters from Sisters* (1996), *Olive Tree* (1998), and *Candlelight Banquet* (2009). In addition, she edited *Best Short Stories of 2005* (2006), and *Top 30 Fiction Writers of Taiwan in 30 Years* (2007). Suh-Fen currently works as the *Literature and Life* section head of the daily newspaper *Liberty Times*. She is also the CEO of the Lin Rong San Culture and Welfare Foundation, which established an important literature prize of Taiwan. Prior to her current jobs, Suh-Fen worked as a chief-editor of a classical Chinese literature magazine *Chinese Literature World*.

BILLIE TRAVALINI's poetry and fiction have appeared in *Another Chicago Magazine*, the *Delaware Poetry Review*, *Review Revue*, *Out and About*, *Writers on Writing: Short Story Writers and Their Art*, among others. She is editor of the upcoming *Then and Now: An Anthology of Poetry and Prose, The Best of M.O.T. Poetry at the Gibby,* and the National League of American Pen Women's upcoming anthology of women poet laureates. She is on the editorial board of *The Journal of Caribbean Literatures;* edited *Teaching Troubled Youth: A Practical Pedagogical Approach;* co-edited with Fleda Brown *The Mason-Dixon Line: An Anthology of Contemporary Delaware Writers,* and wrote, edited, and photographed *Wilmington Senior Center: Fifty Years of Community.* Her memoir, *Bloodsisters,* was a finalist for the Bakeless Publication Prize and the James Jones Prize and won the Lewis and Clark Discovery Prize.

TZENG CHING-WEN has published more than two hundred short stories, three novels, three books of children's stories and three books of essays. Tzeng thinks literary work reflects life, arts, and thoughts. His work depicts life and thought of people in Taiwan. He writes about their bitterness and salvation through suffering. His works have been translated into several languages including English, Japanese, German, and Spanish. *Three-legged Horse* was published by Columbia University Press in 1999. This book was appreciated by book reviews from several countries, including *New York Times,* and was also awarded with Kiriyama Pacific Rim Book Award (renamed as Kiriyama Prize) in San Francisco. It was chosen from more than one hundred fiction books published and recommended in that year. In the prize announcement, it states that the book was awarded for its "stressing in both particular in its senses of place and universal in its themes."

KATHERINE VAZ is the author of the critically acclaimed novel *Saudade* (St. Martin's Press, 1994), the first contemporary novel about Portuguese-Americans from a major New York publisher. Her second novel, *Mariana,* has been printed in six languages (English, German, Italian, Spanish, Portuguese, and Greek) and is a bestseller, in its fourth printing plus a new mass-market edition, in Portugal. Rizzoli Publishers (Italy) selected it as one of their top three books of 1998, and the U.S. Library of Congress picked it as one of the Top 30 International Books of 1998. Film rights were optioned by Anne Harrison, former Director of Development for Martin Scorsese. Her collection *Fado & Other Stories* won the 1997 Drue Heinz Literature Prize, and her chapter on Baptism appeared in *Signatures of Grace* (Dutton, 2000). Her second collection, *Our Lady of the Artichokes and Other Portuguese-American Stories,* received the 2007 Prairie Schooner Book Prize in Fiction and will be published in 2008. Her short fiction has appeared in numerous literary magazines, including *Glimmer Train, BOMB Magazine, The Iowa Review, The Gettysburg Review, The Sun, Tin House, The Antioch Review, Triquarterly, The Malahat Review, the Provincetown Arts Journal,* and *Other Voices,* and she does occasional book reviews for *The Boston Globe.* Her children's stories have been included in the anthologies *A Wolf at the Door* (Simon & Schuster, 2000), *The Green Man* (Viking, 2002), *Swan Sister* (Simon & Schuster, 2003), and *The Faery Reel* (Viking, 2004).

WILLIAM WALL was born in Cork in 1955, and graduated from University College Cork in Philosophy and English. Wall has published short stories in various periodicals in Ireland and elsewhere, and they have been reprinted in such anthologies as *Faber Best New Irish Short Stories* and *Phoenix Irish Short Stories.* "What Slim Boy, O Pyrrha" won the Sean O'Faoláin Award, and "Surrender" was shortlisted for the Raymond Carver Award. He published the collection *No Paradiso* in 2006. His novels include *Alice Falling* (2000), *Minding Children* (2001), *The Map of Tenderness* (2003), and *This Is The Country* (2005), which was longlisted for the Man Booker Prize and shortlisted for The Irish Book Awards and the Young Mind Prize. His poetry collections are *Ghost Estate* (2011), *Mathematics and Other Poems* (1997) and *Fahrenheit Says Nothing to Me* (2004). He has won a number of poetry awards, including The Patrick Kavanagh Award. He lives in Cork City.

SU WEI-CHEN has won a series of literary awards, which include the Gold medal for Literature and arts from the Army of Taiwan, award for Novel from *United Daily News,* award for novel from *Chinese Daily,* the Judge's award from *Chinese Times,* and an award for contribution to literature from *Tainan City.* David Wang remarked that "her rise in the literary circle in early 1980s makes her an important representative of contemporary women writing in China and Taiwan." Her novel *The Silent Island* which won the top prize from *Chinese Times* in 1994 was "a brilliant example of her aesthetic of fiction." In 2006, she published *The Team of Times,* a work that represented her thoughts on love, time, and life. Her other works include collections of her critical essays, *Eileen Chang in Hong Kong* (2002), *Generations of Chang school writers in Taiwan* (2006), prose collection *Travel Alone* (1999), and collection of short stories *Aged Beauty, Leaving Tong Fang,* etc. *The Silent Island* was on the top ten list of novels of 2006 by *Asian Weekly. Letters of Eileen Chang* was named one of the top ten good books for 2007 recommended by Popular Press and *Xing Zhou Daily* in Malaysia.

ALLAN WEISS's first short story appeared in 1974, and since then he has published stories in such venues as *Fiddlehead, Windsor Review, Prairie Fire, On Spec, Short Story, Wascana Review,* and the anthologies *Arrowdreams* and *Tesseracts 4, 7,* and *9.* His story cycle *Living Room* was published in 2001. In addition to his fiction, Weiss has published scholarly articles, a newspaper column, book reviews, and interviews. Among his nonfiction publications are *A Comprehensive Bibliography of English-Canadian Short Stories, 1950-1983,* the proceedings of the 1997 and 2003 ACCSFFs, and articles in *Canadian Literature, Studies in Canadian Literature, Science-Fiction Studies,* and *Short Story.* He has given numerous conference papers on Canadian literature, science fiction and fantasy, and the short story; he has participated in every one of the short story conferences in this series.

XU XI is the author of nine books of fiction & essays, and editor of three anthologies of Hong Kong literature in English. A Chinese-Indonesian native of Hong Kong, the city was home until her mid-twenties, after which she led a peripatetic existence around Europe, America and Asia. She was inhabiting the flight path connecting New York, Hong Kong and New Zealand, but is now more or less squatting atop a Hong Kong rooftop again for a spell, with dental benefits, amazingly, since a foolish consistency is not her idea of how to conduct a life. There are a few awards, including an O. Henry prize story, the shortlist for the inaugural MAN Asian Literary Award, the Cohen Award from Ploughshares for best story, a NYFA fiction fellowship, the South China Morning Post story contest winner, among others.

EGOYAN ZHENG (real name 鄭千慈 Zheng Qianci) was born in 1977, Tainan, Taiwan. He studied medicine at Taipei Medical University and obtained an MA in Chinese Literature from Tamkang University. Previously artist-in-residence at National Cheng Kung University and writer-in-residence at Yuan Ze University. The recipient of several literary awards, his works have been selected for anthologies such as *Taiwanese Stories* 《台灣說故事》(2009) and *A Tale of Three Cities: Taipei* 《三城記：台北卷》. His first novel *Man in the Urn* 《甕中人》(2003) has become part of the contemporary canon. He was nominated for the Man Asian Literary Prize in 2007, and was named one of Taiwan's ten most promising Taiwanese people. In 2008, he was nominated for the Frank O'Connor International Short Story Award. His novel *The Dream Devourer* 《噬夢人》 (2010) has topped books.com.tw's Chinese literature list for the past two years, and came in first in Unitas' book picks for the year. It was also shortlisted for various awards. In 2011 he published a collection of poetry entitled *Your Light Shines Through My Eyes*《你是穿入我瞳孔的光》

ACKNOWLEDGMENTS

Thanks go to the North Little Rock Visitors' Bureau and its staff, and the Argenta Arts Foundation, for their support in hosting the 12th International Conference on the Short Story in English, and for their contributions to the vision of this anthology. The tireless efforts of Hazel Hernandez, Karen Trevino, Barbara Brockway, Donna Hardcastle, and John Gaudin are instrumental in this text coming to fruition.

In addition, the support, input, guidance, and professionalism of Paula Morell in the design, format and publication of this text are immeasurable. Her company, Temenos Publishing, took on this task at a most inconvenient time and has helped to create this final product that we can all be proud of.

Lastly, this text would not have been completed were it not for the incredible patience, editorial skills, and attention to detail by Aaron Penn, my graduate assistant, who has worked non-stop on this manuscript in helping to pull its various and many parts into a unified whole. His work as the Assistant Editor of the *Journal of Caribbean Literatures (JCLs)* was put on hold for the duration of this project in order to complete it in time for publication. I am forever indebted to him for his tireless efforts.

Maurice A. Lee, Editor

PUBLISHER'S NOTE

The stories in this collection which were written in other languages first and then translated into English have posed a significant challenge for the editor and the publisher. In all cases, we were concerned about the readers and their ability to both understand and accept paragraph structures and sentences which, although written in English, were not in patterns of which they were familiar. There was a real temptation to restructure them in some cases, to rewrite entire sentences, and to restructure paragraphs. The need to be true to the author's intent, while at the same time being sensitive to the reader's "ear" or what we thought was at times more "readable" was paramount in our decisions about either leaving text as-is or changing it. In most cases, we stuck with the author's intent, which, at times, may make some text more difficult to read. Nevertheless, we also felt that if this were to be a true representative of a global collection of short stories, this minor inconvenience was worth it to maintain integrity. In this regard, and with these stipulations, we hereby submit this collection of stories for your enjoyment.

CPSIA information can be obtained at www.ICGtesting.com
Printed in the USA
LVOW120232070612

284997LV00004B/1/P

9 780984 619955